A QUIVER FULL OF ARROWS
AND
SONS OF FORTUNE

Jeffrey Archer's writing career has spanned almost thirty years. His bestselling novels, which range from *Not a Penny More, Not a Penny Less* to *Kane and Abel* and *The Eleventh Commandment*, have sold over 120 million copies throughout the world.

In August 2001, he was sentenced to four years in prison for perjury. During that time he wrote three highly praised and bestselling works of non-fiction entitled *Prison Diaries*. He was released in July 2003.

He is married with two children and lives in London and Granchester.

ALSO BY JEFFREY ARCHER

JEFFREY ARCHER

A QUIVER FULL OF ARROWS

AND

SONS OF FORTUNE

PAN BOOKS

A Quiver Full of Arrows first published 1980 by Hodder and Stoughton Ltd.
First published in paperback 1981 by Coronet.
First published by Pan Books 2003.
Sons of Fortune first published 2002 by Macmillan.
First published in paperback 2003 by Pan Books.

This omnibus first published 2008 by Pan Books
an imprint of Pan Macmillan, a division of Macmillan Publishers Limited
Pan Macmillan, 20 New Wharf Road, London N1 9RR
Basingstoke and Oxford
Associated companies throughout the world
www.panmacmillan.com

ISBN 978-0-330-45778-1

3 5 7 9 8 6 4 2

A CIP catalogue record for this book is available from
the British Library.

Printed and bound in the UK by
CPI Mackays, Chatham ME5 8TD

A QUIVER FULL
OF ARROWS

To Robin and Carolyn

AUTHOR'S NOTE

Of these twelve short stories, eleven are based on known incidents (some embellished with considerable licence). Only one is totally the result of my own imagination.

In the case of 'The Century' I took my theme from three different cricket matches. Lovers of *Wisden* will have to do some considerable delving to uncover them.

'The Luncheon' was inspired by W. Somerset Maugham.

J.A.

CONTENTS

THE CHINESE STATUE

THE LITTLE CHINESE STATUE was the next item to come under the auctioneer's hammer. Lot 103 caused those quiet murmurings that always precede the sale of a masterpiece. The auctioneer's assistant held up the delicate piece of ivory for the packed audience to admire while the auctioneer glanced around the room to be sure he knew where the serious bidders were seated. I studied my catalogue and read the detailed description of the piece, and what was known of its history.

The statue had been purchased in Ha Li Chuan in 1871 and was referred to as what Sotheby's quaintly described as 'the property of a gentleman', usually meaning that some member of the aristocracy did not wish to admit that he was having to sell off one of the family heirlooms. I wondered if that was the case on this occasion and decided to do some research to discover what had caused the little Chinese statue to find its way into the auction rooms on that Thursday morning over one hundred years later.

'Lot No. 103,' declared the auctioneer. 'What am I bid for this magnificent example of . . .?'

*

Sir Alexander Heathcote, as well as being a gentleman, was an exact man. He was exactly six-foot-three and a quarter inches tall, rose at seven o'clock every morning, joined his wife at breakfast to eat one boiled egg cooked for precisely four minutes, two pieces of toast with one spoonful of Cooper's marmalade, and drink one cup of China tea. He would then take a hackney carriage from his home in Cadogan Gardens at exactly eight-twenty and arrive at the Foreign Office at promptly eight-fifty-nine, returning home again on the stroke of six o'clock.

Sir Alexander had been exact from an early age, as became the only son of a general. But unlike his father, he chose to serve his Queen in the diplomatic service, another exacting calling. He progressed from a shared desk at the Foreign Office in Whitehall to third secretary in Calcutta, to second secretary in Vienna, to first secretary in Rome, to Deputy Ambassador in Washington, and finally to minister in Peking. He was delighted when Mr Gladstone invited him to represent the government in China as he had for some considerable time taken more than an amateur interest in the art of the Ming dynasty. This crowning appointment in his distinguished career would afford him what until then he would have considered impossible, an opportunity to observe in their natural habitat some of the great statues, paintings and drawings which he had previously been able to admire only in books.

When Sir Alexander arrived in Peking, after a

journey by sea and land that took his party nearly two months, he presented his seals patent to the Empress Tzu-Hsi and a personal letter for her private reading from Queen Victoria. The Empress, dressed from head to toe in white and gold, received her new Ambassador in the throne room of the Imperial Palace. She read the letter from the British monarch while Sir Alexander remained standing to attention. Her Imperial Highness revealed nothing of its contents to the new minister, only wishing him a successful term of office in his appointment. She then moved her lips slightly up at the corners which Sir Alexander judged correctly to mean that the audience had come to an end. As he was conducted back through the great halls of the Imperial Palace by a Mandarin in the long court dress of black and gold, Sir Alexander walked as slowly as possible, taking in the magnificent collection of ivory and jade statues which were scattered casually around the building much in the way Cellini and Michelangelo today lie stacked against each other in Florence.

As his ministerial appointment was for only three years, Sir Alexander took no leave, but preferred to use his time to put the Embassy behind him and travel on horseback into the outlying districts to learn more about the country and its people. On these trips he was always accompanied by a Mandarin from the palace staff who acted as interpreter and guide.

On one such journey, passing through the muddy streets of a small village with but a few houses called

Ha Li Chuan, a distance of some fifty miles from Peking, Sir Alexander chanced upon an old craftsman's working place. Leaving his servants, the minister dismounted from his horse and entered the ramshackle wooden workshop to admire the delicate pieces of ivory and jade that crammed the shelves from floor to ceiling. Although modern, the pieces were superbly executed by an experienced craftsman, and the minister entered the little hut with the thought of acquiring a small memento of his journey. Once in the shop he could hardly move in any direction for fear of knocking something over. The building had not been designed for a six-foot-three and a quarter visitor. Sir Alexander stood still and enthralled, taking in the fine scented jasmine smell that hung in the air.

An old craftsman bustled forward in a long, blue coolie robe and flat black hat to greet him; a jet black plaited pigtail fell down his back. He bowed very low and then looked up at the giant from England. The minister returned the bow while the Mandarin explained who Sir Alexander was and his desire to be allowed to look at the work of the craftsman. The old man was nodding his agreement even before the Mandarin had come to the end of his request. For over an hour the minister sighed and chuckled as he studied many of the pieces with admiration and finally returned to the old man to praise his skill. The craftsman bowed once again, and his shy smile revealed no teeth but only genuine pleasure at Sir

Alexander's compliments. Pointing a finger to the back of the shop, he beckoned the two important visitors to follow him. They did so and entered a veritable Aladdin's Cave, with row upon row of beautiful miniature emperors and classical figures. The minister could have happily settled down in the orgy of ivory for at least a week. Sir Alexander and the craftsman chatted away to each other through the interpreter, and the minister's love and knowledge of the Ming dynasty was soon revealed. The little crafts-man's face lit up with this discovery and he turned to the Mandarin and in a hushed voice made a request. The Mandarin nodded his agreement and translated.

'I have, Your Excellency, a piece of Ming myself that you might care to see. A statue that has been in my family for over seven generations.'

'I should be honoured,' said the minister.

'It is I who would be honoured, Your Excellency,' said the little man who thereupon scampered out of the back door, nearly falling over a stray dog, and on to an old peasant house a few yards behind the workshop. The minister and the Mandarin remained in the back room, for Sir Alexander knew the old man would never have considered inviting an honou-red guest into his humble home until they had known each other for many years, and only then after he had been invited to Sir Alexander's home first. A few minutes passed before the little blue figure came trotting back, pigtail bouncing up and down on his shoulders. He was now clinging on to something that from the very way he held it close to his chest had to be a treasure. The craftsman passed the piece over for the minister to study. Sir Alexander's mouth opened wide and he could not hide his excitement. The little statue, no more than six inches in height, was of the Emperor Kung and as fine an example of Ming as the minister had seen. Sir Alexander felt confident that the maker was the great Pen Q who had been patronised by the Emperor, so that the date must have been around the turn of the fifteenth century. The statue's only blemish was that the ivory base on which such pieces usually rest was missing, and a small stick protruded from the bottom of the imperial robes; but in the eyes of Sir Alexander nothing could detract from its overall beauty. Although the craftsman's lips did not move, his eyes glowed with the pleasure his guest evinced as he studied the ivory Emperor.

'You think the statue is good?' asked the craftsman through the interpreter.

'It's magnificent,' the minister replied. 'Quite magnificent.'

'My own work is not worthy to stand by its side,' added the craftsman humbly.

'No, no,' said the minister, though in truth the little craftsman knew the great man was only being kind, for Sir Alexander was holding the ivory statue in a way that already showed the same love as the old man had for the piece.

The minister smiled down at the craftsman as he

handed back the Emperor Kung and then he uttered perhaps the only undiplomatic words he had ever spoken in thirty-five years of serving his Queen and country.

'How I wish the piece was mine.'

Sir Alexander regretted voicing his thoughts immediately he heard the Mandarin translate them, because he knew only too well the old Chinese tradition that if an honoured guest requests something the giver will grow in the eyes of his fellow men by parting with it.

A sad look came over the face of the little old craftsman as he handed back the figurine to the minister.

'No, no. I was only joking,' said Sir Alexander, quickly trying to return the piece to its owner.

'You would dishonour my humble home if you did not take the Emperor, Your Excellency,' the old man said anxiously and the Mandarin gravely nodded his agreement.

The minister remained silent for some time. 'I have dishonoured my own home, sir,' he replied, and looked towards the Mandarin who remained inscrutable.

The little craftsman bowed. 'I must fix a base on the statue,' he said, 'or you will not be able to put the piece on view.'

He went to a corner of the room and opened a wooden packing chest that must have housed a hundred bases for his own statues. Rummaging around he picked out a base decorated with small, dark figures that the minister did not care for but which nevertheless made a perfect fit; the old man assured Sir Alexander that although he did not know the base's history, the piece bore the mark of a good craftsman.

The embarrassed minister took the gift and tried hopelessly to thank the little old man. The craftsman once again bowed low as Sir Alexander and the expressionless Mandarin left the little workshop.

As the party travelled back to Peking, the Mandarin observed the terrible state the minister was in, and uncharacteristically spoke first:

'Your Excellency is no doubt aware,' he said, 'of the old Chinese custom that when a stranger has been generous, you must return the kindness within the calendar year.'

Sir Alexander smiled his thanks and thought carefully about the Mandarin's words. Once back in his official residence, he went immediately to the Embassy's extensive library to see if he could discover a realistic value for the little masterpiece. After much diligent research, he came across a drawing of a Ming statue that was almost an exact copy of the one now in his possession and with the help of the Mandarin he was able to assess its true worth, a figure that came to almost three years' emolument for a servant of the Crown. The minister discussed the problem with Lady Heathcote and she left her husband in no doubt as to the course of action he must take.

The following week the minister despatched a

letter by private messenger to his bankers, Coutts & Co in the Strand, London, requesting that they send a large part of his savings to reach him in Peking as quickly as possible. When the funds arrived nine weeks later the minister again approached the Mandarin, who listened to his questions and gave him the details he had asked for seven days later.

The Mandarin had discovered that the little craftsman, Yung Lee, came from the old and trusted family of Yung Shau who had for some five hundred years been craftsmen. Sir Alexander also learned that many of Yung Lee's ancestors had examples of their work in the palaces of the Manchu princes. Yung Lee himself was growing old and wished to retire to the hills above the village where his ancestors had always died. His son was ready to take over the workshop from him and continue the family tradition. The minister thanked the Mandarin for his diligence and had only one more request of him. The Mandarin listened sympathetically to the Ambassador from England and returned to the palace to seek advice.

A few days later the Empress granted Sir Alexander's request.

Almost a year to the day the minister, accompanied by the Mandarin, set out again from Peking for the village of Ha Li Chuan. When Sir Alexander arrived he immediately dismounted from his horse and entered the workshop that he remembered so well, the old man was seated at his bench, his flat hat slightly askew, a piece of uncarved ivory held lovingly between his fingers. He looked up from his work and shuffled towards the minister, not recognising his guest immediately until he could almost touch the foreign giant. Then he bowed low. The minister spoke through the Mandarin:

'I have returned, sir, within the calendar year to repay my debt.'

'There was no need, Your Excellency. My family is honoured that the little statue lives in a great Embassy and may one day be admired by the people of your own land.'

The minister could think of no words to form an adequate reply and simply requested that the old man should accompany him on a short journey.

The craftsman agreed without question and the three men set out on donkeys towards the north. They travelled for over two hours up a thin winding path into the hills behind the craftsman's workshop, and when they reached the village of Ma Tien they were met by another Mandarin, who bowed low to the minister and requested Sir Alexander and the craftsman to continue their journey with him on foot. They walked in silence to the far side of the village and only stopped when they had reached a hollow in the hill from which there was a magnificent view of the valley all the way down to Ha Li Chuan. In the hollow stood a newly completed small white house of the most perfect proportions. Two stone lion dogs, tongues hanging over their lips, guarded the front entrance. The little old craftsman who had not spoken since he had left his workshop remained mystified by the purpose of the journey until the minister turned to him and offered:

'A small, inadequate gift and my feeble attempt to repay you in kind.'

The craftsman fell to his knees and begged forgiveness of the Mandarin as he knew it was forbidden for an artisan to accept gifts from a foreigner. The Mandarin raised the frightened blue figure from the ground, explaining to his countryman that the Empress herself had sanctioned the minister's request. A smile of joy came over the face of the craftsman and he slowly walked up to the doorway of the beautiful little house unable to resist running his hand over the carved lion dogs. The three travellers then spent over an hour admiring the little house before returning in silent mutual happiness back to the workshop in Ha Li Chuan. The two men thus parted, honour satisfied, and Sir Alexander rode to his Embassy that night content that his actions had met with the approval of the Mandarin as well as Lady Heathcote.

The minister completed his tour of duty in Peking, and the Empress awarded him the Silver Star of China and a grateful Queen added the KCVO to his already long list of decorations. After a few weeks back at the Foreign Office clearing the China desk, Sir Alexander retired to his native Yorkshire, the only English county whose inhabitants still hope to be born and die in the same place – not unlike the Chinese.

Sir Alexander spent his final years in the home of his late father with his wife and the little Ming Emperor. The statue occupied the centre of the mantelpiece in the drawing room for all to see and admire.

Being an exact man, Sir Alexander wrote a long and detailed will in which he left precise instructions for the disposal of his estate, including what was to happen to the little statue after his death. He bequeathed the Emperor Kung to his first son requesting that he do the same, in order that the statue might always pass to the first son, or a daughter if the direct male line faltered. He also made a provision that the statue was never to be disposed of, unless the family's honour was at stake. Sir Alexander Heathcote died at the stroke of midnight on his seventieth year.

His first-born, Major James Heathcote, was serving his Queen in the Boer War at the time he came into possession of the Ming Emperor. The Major was a fighting man, commissioned with the Duke of Wellington's Regiment, and although he had little interest in culture even he could see the family heirloom was no ordinary treasure, so he loaned the statue to the regimental mess at Halifax in order that the Emperor could be displayed in the dining room for his brother officers to appreciate.

When James Heathcote became Colonel of the Dukes, the Emperor stood proudly on the table alongside the trophies won at Waterloo, Sebastopol in the

Crimea and Madrid. And there the Ming Statue remained until the colonel's retirement to his father's house in Yorkshire, when the Emperor returned once again to the drawing room mantelpiece. The colonel was not a man to disobey his late father, even in death, and he left clear instructions that the heirloom must always be passed on to the first-born of the Heathcotes unless the family honour was in jeopardy. Colonel James Heathcote MC did not die a soldier's death; he simply fell asleep one night by the fire, the *Yorkshire Post* on his lap.

The colonel's first-born, the Reverend Alexander Heathcote, was at the time presiding over a small flock in the parish of Much Hadham in Hertfordshire. After burying his father with military honours, he placed the little Ming Emperor on the mantelpiece of the vicarage. Few members of the Mothers' Union appreciated the masterpiece but one or two old ladies were heard to remark on its delicate carving. And it was not until the Reverend became the Right Reverend, and the little statue found its way into the Bishop's palace, that the Emperor attracted the admiration he deserved. Many of those who visited the palace and heard the story of how the Bishop's grandfather had acquired the Ming statue were fascinated to learn of the disparity between the magnificent statue and its base. It always made a good after-dinner story.

God takes even his own ambassadors, but He did not do so before allowing Bishop Heathcote to complete a will leaving the statue to his son, with his grandfather's exact instructions carefully repeated. The Bishop's son, Captain James Heathcote, was a serving officer in his grandfather's regiment, so the Ming statue returned to the mess table in Halifax. During the Emperor's absence, the regimental trophies had been augmented by those struck for Ypres, the Marne and Verdun. The regiment was once again at war with Germany, and young Captain James Heathcote was killed on the beaches of Dunkirk and died intestate. Thereafter English law, the known wishes of his great-grandfather and common sense prevailed, and the little Emperor came into the possession of the captain's two-year-old son.

Alex Heathcote was, alas, not of the mettle of his doughty ancestors and he grew up feeling no desire to serve anyone other than himself. When Captain James had been so tragically killed, Alexander's mother lavished everything on the boy that her meagre income would allow. It didn't help, and it was not entirely young Alex's fault that he grew up to be, in the words of his grandmother, a selfish, spoiled little brat.

When Alex left school, only a short time before he would have been expelled, he found he could never hold down a job for more than a few weeks. It always seemed necessary for him to spend a little more than he, and finally his mother, could cope with. The good lady, deciding she could take no more of this life, departed it, to join all the other Heathcotes, not in Yorkshire, but in heaven.

In the swinging sixties, when casinos opened in Britain, young Alex was convinced that he had found the ideal way of earning a living without actually having to do any work. He developed a system for playing roulette with which it was impossible to lose. He did lose, so he refined the system and promptly lost more; he refined the system once again which resulted in him having to borrow to cover his losses. Why not? If the worst came to the worst, he told himself, he could always dispose of the little Ming Emperor.

The worst did come to the worst, as each one of Alex's newly refined systems took him progressively into greater debt until the casinos began to press him for payment. When finally, one Monday morning, Alex received an unsolicited call from two gentlemen who seemed determined to collect some eight thousand pounds he owed their masters, and hinted at bodily harm if the matter was not dealt with within fourteen days, Alex caved in. After all, his great-great-grandfather's instructions had been exact: the Ming statue was to be sold if the family honour was ever at stake.

Alex took the little Emperor off the mantelpiece in his Cadogan Gardens flat and stared down at its delicate handiwork, at least having the grace to feel a little sad at the loss of the family heirloom. He then drove to Bond Street and delivered the masterpiece to Sotheby's, giving instructions that the Emperor should be put up for auction.

The head of the Oriental department, a pale, thin man, appeared at the front desk to discuss the masterpiece with Alex, looking not unlike the Ming statue he was holding so lovingly in his hands.

'It will take a few days to estimate the true value of the piece,' he purred, 'but I feel confident on a cursory glance that the statue is as fine an example of Pen Q as we have ever had under the hammer.'

'That's no problem,' replied Alex, 'as long as you can let me know what it's worth within fourteen days.'

'Oh, certainly,' replied the expert. 'I feel sure I could give you a floor price by Friday.'

'Couldn't be better,' said Alex.

During that week he contacted all his creditors and without exception they were prepared to wait and learn the appraisal of the expert. Alex duly returned to Bond Street on the Friday with a large smile on his face. He knew what his great-great-grandfather had paid for the piece and felt sure that the statue must be worth more than ten thousand pounds. A sum that would not only yield him enough to cover all his debts but leave him a little over to try out his new refined, refined system on the roulette table. As he climbed the steps of Sotheby's, Alex silently thanked his great-great-grandfather. He asked the girl on reception if he could speak to the head of the Oriental department.

She picked up an internal phone and the expert appeared a few moments later at the front desk with a sombre look on his face. Alex's heart sank as he listened to his words: 'A nice little piece, your Emperor, but unfortunately a fake, probably about two hundred, two hundred and fifty years old but only a copy of the original, I'm afraid. Copies were often made because . . .'

'How much is it worth?' interrupted an anxious Alex.

'Seven hundred pounds, eight hundred at the most.'

Enough to buy a gun and some bullets, thought Alex sardonically as he turned and started to walk away.

'I wonder, sir . . .' continued the expert.

'Yes, yes, sell the bloody thing,' said Alex, without bothering to look back.

'And what do you want me to do with the base?'

'The base?' repeated Alex, turning round to face the Orientalist.

'Yes, the base. It's quite magnificent, fifteenth century, undoubtedly a work of genius, I can't imagine how . . .'

'Lot No. 103,' announced the auctioneer. 'What am I bid for this magnificent example of . . .?'

The expert turned out to be right in his assessment. At the auction at Sotheby's that Thursday morning I obtained the little Emperor for seven hundred and twenty guineas. And the base? That was acquired by an American gentleman of not unknown parentage for twenty-two thousand guineas.

THE LUNCHEON

THE LUNCHEON

SHE WAVED AT ME across a crowded room of the St Regis Hotel in New York. I waved back realising I knew the face but I was unable to place it. She squeezed past waiters and guests and had reached me before I had a chance to ask anyone who she was. I racked that section of my brain which is meant to store people, but it transmitted no reply. I realised I would have to resort to the old party trick of carefully worded questions until her answers jogged my memory.

'How *are* you, darling?' she cried, and threw her arms around me, an opening that didn't help as we were at a Literary Guild cocktail party, and anyone will throw their arms around you on such occasions, even the directors of the Book-of-the-Month Club. From her accent she was clearly American and looked to be approaching forty, but thanks to the genius of modern make-up might even have overtaken it. She wore a long white cocktail dress and her blonde hair was done up in one of those buns that looks like a cottage loaf. The overall effect made her appear somewhat like a chess queen. Not that the cottage loaf helped because she might have had dark hair flowing to her shoulders when we last met. I do wish women would realise that when they change their hair style they often achieve exactly what they set out to do: look completely different to any unsuspecting male.

'I'm well, thank you,' I said to the white queen. 'And you?' I inquired as my opening gambit.

'I'm just fine, darling,' she replied, taking a glass of champagne from a passing waiter.

'And how's the family?' I asked, not sure if she even had one.

'They're all well,' she replied. No help there. 'And how is Louise?' she inquired.

'Blooming,' I said. So she knew my wife. But then not necessarily, I thought. Most American women are experts at remembering the names of men's wives. They have to be, when on the New York circuit they change so often it becomes a greater challenge than *The Times* crossword.

'Have you been to London lately?' I roared above the babble. A brave question, as she might never have been to Europe.

'Only once since we had lunch together.' She looked at me quizzically. 'You don't remember who I am, do you?' she asked as she devoured a cocktail sausage.

I smiled.

'Don't be silly, Susan,' I said. 'How could I ever forget?'

She smiled.

I confess that I remembered the white queen's name in the nick of time. Although I still had only vague recollections of the lady, I certainly would never forget the lunch.

I had just had my first book published and the critics on both sides of the Atlantic had been complimentary, even if the cheques from my publishers were less so. My agent had told me on several occasions that I shouldn't write if I wanted to make money. This created a dilemma because I couldn't see how to make money if I didn't write.

It was around this time that the lady, who was now facing me and chattering on oblivious to my silence, telephoned from New York to heap lavish praise on my novel. There is no writer who does not enjoy receiving such calls, although I confess to having been less than captivated by an eleven-year-old girl who called me collect from California to say she had found a spelling mistake on page forty-seven and warned me she would ring again if she discovered another. However, this particular lady might have ended her transatlantic congratulations with nothing more than goodbye if she had not dropped her own name. It was one of those names that can, on the spur of the moment, always book a table at a chic restaurant or a seat at the opera which mere mortals like myself would have found impossible to achieve given a month's notice. To be fair, it was her husband's name that had achieved the reputation, as one of the world's most distinguished film producers.

'When I'm next in London you must have lunch with me,' came crackling down the phone.

'No,' said I gallantly, 'you must have lunch with *me*.'

'How perfectly charming you English always are,' she said.

I have often wondered how much American women get away with when they say those few words to an Englishman. Nevertheless, the wife of an Oscar-winning producer does not phone one every day.

'I promise to call you when I'm next in London,' she said.

And indeed she did, for almost six months to the day she telephoned again, this time from the Connaught Hotel to declare how much she was looking forward to our meeting.

'Where would you like to have lunch?' I said, realising a second too late, when she replied with the name of one of the most exclusive restaurants in town, that I should have made sure it was I who chose the venue. I was glad she couldn't see my forlorn face as she added with unabashed liberation:

'Monday, one o'clock. Leave the booking to me – I'm known there.'

On the day in question I donned my one respectable suit, a new shirt which I had been saving for a special occasion since Christmas, and the only tie that looked as if it hadn't previously been used to hold up my trousers. I then strolled over to my bank and asked for a statement of my current account. The teller handed me a long piece of paper unworthy of its amount. I studied the figure as one who has to take a major financial decision. The bottom line stated in black lettering that I was in credit to the sum of thirty-seven pounds and sixty-three pence. I wrote out a cheque for thirty-seven pounds. I feel that a gentleman should always leave his account in credit, and I might add it was a belief that my bank manager shared with me. I then walked up to Mayfair for my luncheon date.

As I entered the restaurant I observed too many waiters and plush seats for my liking. You can't eat either, but you can be charged for them. At a corner table for two sat a woman who, although not young, was elegant. She wore a blouse of powder blue crêpe-de-chine, and her blonde hair was rolled away from her face in a style that reminded me of the war years, and had once again become fashionable. It was clearly my transatlantic admirer, and she greeted me in the same 'I've known you all my life' fashion as she was to do at the Literary Guild cocktail party years later. Although she had a drink in front of her I didn't order an apéritif, explaining that I never drank before lunch – and would like to have added, 'but as soon as your husband makes a film of my novel, I will.'

She launched immediately into the latest Hollywood gossip, not so much dropping names as reciting them, while I ate my way through the crisps from the bowl in front of me. A few minutes later a waiter materialised by the table and presented us with two large embossed leather menus, considerably better bound than my novel. The place positively reeked of unnecessary expense. I opened the menu and studied the first chapter with horror; it was eminently put-downable. I had no idea that simple food obtained from Covent Garden that morning could cost quite so much by merely being transported to Mayfair. I could have bought her the same dishes for a quarter of the price at my favourite bistro, a mere one hundred yards away, and to add to my discomfort I observed that it was one of those restaurants where the guest's menu made no mention of the prices. I settled down to study the long list of French dishes which only served to remind me that I hadn't eaten well for over a month, a state of affairs that was about to be prolonged by a further day. I remembered my bank balance and morosely reflected that I would probably have to wait until my agent sold the Icelandic rights of my novel before I could afford a square meal again.

'What would you like?' I said gallantly.

'I always enjoy a light lunch,' she volunteered. I sighed with premature relief, only to find that light did not necessarily mean 'inexpensive'.

She smiled sweetly up at the waiter, who looked as if *he* wouldn't be wondering where his next meal might be coming from, and ordered just a sliver of smoked salmon, followed by two tiny tender lamb cutlets. Then she hesitated, but only for a moment, before adding 'and a side salad'.

I studied the menu with some caution, running my finger down the prices, not the dishes.

'I also eat lightly at lunch,' I said mendaciously. 'The chef's salad will be quite enough for me.' The waiter was obviously affronted but left peaceably.

She chatted of Coppola and Preminger, of Al Pacino and Robert Redford, and of Greta Garbo as if she saw her all the time. She was kind enough to stop for a moment and ask what I was working on at present. I would have liked to have replied – on how I was going to explain to my wife that I only have sixty-three pence left in the bank; whereas I actually discussed my ideas for another novel. She seemed impressed, but still made no reference to her husband. Should I mention him? No. Mustn't sound pushy, or as though I needed the money.

The food arrived, or that is to say her smoked salmon did, and I sat silently watching her eat my bank account while I nibbled a roll. I looked up only to discover a wine waiter hovering by my side.

'Would you care for some wine?' said I, recklessly.

'No, I don't think so,' she said. I smiled a little too soon: 'Well, perhaps a little something white and dry.'

The wine waiter handed over a second leather-bound book, this time with golden grapes embossed on the cover. I searched down the pages for half bottles, explaining to my guest that I never drank at lunch. I chose the cheapest. The wine waiter reappeared a moment later with a large silver bucket full of ice in which the half bottle looked drowned, and, like me, completely out of its depth. A junior waiter cleared away the empty plate while another wheeled a large trolley to the side of our table and served the lamb cutlets and the chef's salad. At the same time a third waiter made up an exquisite side salad for my guest which ended up bigger than my complete order. I didn't feel I could ask her to swap.

To be fair, the chef's salad was superb – although I confess it was hard to appreciate such food fully while trying to work out a plot that would be convincing if I found the bill came to over thirty-seven pounds.

'How silly of me to ask for white wine with lamb,' she said, having nearly finished the half bottle. I ordered a half bottle of the house red without calling for the wine list.

She finished the white wine and then launched into the theatre, music and other authors. All those who were still alive she seemed to know and those who were dead she hadn't read. I might have enjoyed the performance if it hadn't been for the fear of wondering if I would be able to afford it when the curtain came down. When the waiter cleared away the empty dishes he asked my guest if she would care for anything else.

'No, thank you,' she said – I nearly applauded. 'Unless you have one of your famous apple surprises.'

'I fear the last one may have gone, madam, but I'll go and see.'

Don't hurry, I wanted to say, but instead I just smiled as the rope tightened around my neck. A few moments later the waiter strode back in triumph weaving between the tables holding the apple surprise, in the palm of his hand, high above his head. I prayed to Newton that the apple would obey his law. It didn't.

'The last one, madam.'

'Oh, what luck,' she declared.

'Oh, what luck,' I repeated, unable to face the menu and discover the price. I was now attempting some mental arithmetic as I realised it was going to be a close run thing.

'Anything else, madam?' the ingratiating waiter inquired.

I took a deep breath.

'Just coffee,' she said.

'And for you, sir?'

'No, no, not for me.' He left us. I couldn't think of an explanation for why I didn't drink coffee.

She then produced from the large Gucci bag by her side a copy of my novel, which I signed with a flourish, hoping the head waiter would see me and feel I was the sort of man who should be allowed to sign the bill as well, but he resolutely remained at the far end of the room while I wrote the words 'An unforgettable meeting' and appended my signature.

While the dear lady was drinking her coffee I

picked at another roll and called for the bill, not because I was in any particular hurry, but like a guilty defendant at the Old Bailey I preferred to wait no longer for the judge's sentence. A man in a smart green uniform, whom I had never seen before, appeared carrying a silver tray with a folded piece of paper on it looking not unlike my bank statement. I pushed back the edge of the bill slowly and read the figure: thirty-six pounds and forty pence. I casually put my hand into my inside pocket and withdrew my life's possessions and then placed the crisp new notes on the silver tray. They were whisked away. The man in the green uniform returned a few moments later with my sixty pence change, which I pocketed as it was the only way I was going to get a bus home. The waiter gave me a look that would have undoubtedly won him a character part in any film produced by the lady's distinguished husband.

My guest rose and walked across the restaurant, waving at, and occasionally kissing people that I had previously only seen in glossy magazines. When she reached the door she stopped to retrieve her coat, a mink. I helped her on with the fur, again failing to leave a tip. As we stood on the Curzon Street pavement, a dark blue Rolls-Royce drew up beside us and a liveried chauffeur leaped out and opened the rear door. She climbed in.

'Goodbye, darling,' she said, as the electric window slid down. 'Thank you for such a lovely lunch.'

'Goodbye,' I said, and summoning up my courage

added: 'I do hope when you are next in town I shall have the opportunity of meeting your distinguished husband.'

'Oh, darling, didn't you know?' she said as she looked out from the Rolls-Royce.

'Know what?'

'We were divorced ages ago.'

'Divorced?' said I.

'Oh, yes,' she said gaily, 'I haven't spoken to him for years.'

I just stood there looking helpless.

'Oh, don't worry yourself on my account,' she said. 'He's no loss. In any case I have recently married again' – another film producer, I prayed – 'In fact, I quite expected to bump into my husband today – you see, he owns the restaurant.'

Without another word the electric window purred up and the Rolls-Royce glided effortlessly out of sight leaving me to walk to the nearest bus stop.

As I stood surrounded by Literary Guild guests, staring at the white queen with the cottage loaf bun, I could still see her drifting away in that blue Rolls-Royce. I tried to concentrate on her words.

'I knew you wouldn't forget me, darling,' she was saying. 'After all, I did take you to lunch, didn't I?'

THE COUP

THE BLUE AND SILVER 707 jet, displaying a large 'P' on its tail plane, taxied to a halt at the north end of Lagos International Airport. A fleet of six black Mercedes drove up to the side of the aircraft and waited in a line resembling a land-bound crocodile. Six sweating, uniformed drivers leaped out and stood to attention. When the driver of the front car opened his rear door, Colonel Usman of the Federal Guard stepped out, and walked quickly to the bottom of the passenger steps which had been hurriedly pushed into place by four of the airport staff.

The front section cabin door swung back and the colonel stared up into the gap, to see, framed against the dark interior of the cabin, a slim, attractive hostess dressed in a blue suit with silver piping. On her jacket lapel was a large 'P'. She turned and nodded in the direction of the cabin. A few seconds later, an immaculately dressed tall man with thick black hair and deep brown eyes replaced her in the doorway. The man had an air of effortless style about him which self-made millionaires would have paid a considerable part of their fortune to possess. The colonel saluted as

Senhor Eduardo Francisco de Silveira, head of the Prentino empire gave a curt nod.

De Silveira emerged from the coolness of his air-conditioned 707 into the burning Nigerian sun without showing the slightest sign of discomfort. The colonel guided the tall, elegant Brazilian, who was accompanied only by his private secretary, to the front Mercedes while the rest of the Prentino staff filed down the back stairway of the aircraft and filled the other five cars. The driver, a corporal who had been detailed to be available night and day for the honoured guest, opened the rear door of the front car and saluted. Eduardo de Silveira showed no sign of acknowledgment. The corporal smiled nervously, revealing the largest set of white teeth the Brazilian had ever seen.

'Welcome to Lagos,' the corporal volunteered. 'Hope you make very big deal while you are in Nigeria.'

Eduardo did not comment as he settled back into his seat and stared out of the tinted window to watch some passengers of a British Airways 707 that had landed just before him form a long queue on the hot tarmac as they waited patiently to clear customs. The driver put the car into first gear and the black crocodile proceeded on its journey. Colonel Usman, who was now in the front seat beside the corporal, soon discovered that the Brazilian guest did not care for small talk, and the secretary who was seated by his employer's side never once opened his mouth. The colonel, used to doing things by example, remained silent, leaving de Silveira to consider his plan of campaign.

Eduardo Francisco de Silveira had been born in the small village of Rebeti, a hundred miles north of Rio de Janeiro, heir to one of the two most powerful family fortunes in Brazil. He had been educated privately in Switzerland before attending the University of California in Los Angeles. He went on to complete his education at the Harvard Business School. After Harvard he returned from America to work in Brazil where he started neither at the top nor the bottom of the firm but in the middle, managing his family's mining interests in Minas Gerais. He quickly worked his way to the top, even faster than his father had planned, but then the boy turned out to be not so much a chip as a chunk off the old block. At twenty-nine he married Maria, eldest daughter of his father's closest friend, and when twelve years later his father died Eduardo succeeded to the Prentino throne. There were seven sons in all: the second son, Alfredo, was now in charge of banking; João ran shipping; Carlos organised construction; Manoel arranged food and supplies; Jaime managed the family newspapers, and little Antonio, the last – and certainly the least – ran the family farms. All the brothers reported to Eduardo before making any major decision, for he was still chairman of the largest private company in Brazil, despite the boastful claims of his old family enemy, Manuel Rodrigues.

When General Castelo Branco's military regime overthrew the civilian government in 1964 the generals agreed that they could not kill off all the de Silveiras or the Rodrigues so they had better learn to live with the two rival families. The de Silveiras for their part had always had enough sense never to involve themselves in politics other than by making payments to every government official, military or civilian, according to his rank. This ensured that the Prentino empire grew alongside whatever faction came to power. One of the reasons Eduardo de Silveira had allocated three days in his crowded schedule for a visit to Lagos was that the Nigerian system of government seemed to resemble so closely that of Brazil, and at least on this project he had cut the ground from under Manuel Rodrigues' feet which would more than make up for losing the Rio airport tender to him. Eduardo smiled at the thought of Rodrigues not realising that he was in Nigeria to close a deal that could make him twice the size of his rival.

As the black Mercedes moved slowly through the teeming noisy streets paying no attention to traffic lights, red or green, Eduardo thought back to his first meeting with General Mohammed, the Nigerian Head of State, on the occasion of the President's official visit to Brazil. Speaking at the dinner given in General Mohammed's honour, President Ernesto Geisel declared a hope that the two countries would move towards closer co-operation in politics and commerce. Eduardo agreed with his unelected leader and was happy to leave the politics to the President if he allowed him to get on with the commerce. General Mohammed made his reply, on behalf of the guests, in an English accent that normally would only be associated with Oxford. The general talked at length of the project that was most dear to his heart, the building of a new Nigerian capital in Abuja, a city which he considered might even rival Brasilia. After the speeches were over, the general took de Silveira on one side and spoke in greater detail of the Abuja city project asking him if he might consider a private tender. Eduardo smiled and only wished that his enemy, Rodrigues, could hear the intimate conversation he was having with the Nigerian Head of State.

Eduardo studied carefully the outline proposal sent to him a week later, after the general had returned to Nigeria, and agreed to his first request by despatching a research team of seven men to fly to Lagos and complete a feasibility study on Abuja.

One month later, the team's detailed report was in de Silveira's hands. Eduardo came to the conclusion that the potential profitability of the project was worthy of a full proposal to the Nigerian government. He contacted General Mohammed personally to find that he was in full agreement and authorised the go-ahead. This time twenty-three men were despatched to Lagos and three months and one hundred and seventy pages later, Eduardo signed and sealed the proposal designated as, 'A New Capital for Nigeria'. He made only one alteration to the final document. The cover of the proposal was in blue and silver with the Prentino logo in the centre: Eduardo had that changed to green and white, the national colours of Nigeria, with the national emblem of an eagle astride two horses: he realised it was the little things that impressed generals and often tipped the scales. He sent ten copies of the feasibility study to Nigeria's Head of State with an invoice for one million dollars.

When General Mohammed had studied the proposal he invited Eduardo de Silveira to visit Nigeria as his guest, in order to discuss the next stage of the project. De Silveira telexed back, provisionally accepting the invitation, and pointing out politely but firmly that he had not yet received reimbursement for the one million dollars spent on the initial feasibility study. The money was telexed by return from the Central Bank of Nigeria and de Silveira managed to find four consecutive days in his diary for 'The New Federal Capital project': his schedule demanded that he arrived in Lagos on a Monday morning because he had to be in Paris at the latest by the Thursday night.

While these thoughts were going through Eduardo's mind, the Mercedes drew up outside Dodan Barracks. The iron gates swung open and a full armed guard gave the general salute, an honour normally afforded only to a visiting Head of State. The black Mercedes drove slowly through the gates and came to a halt outside the President's private residence. A brigadier waited on the steps to escort de Silveira through to the President.

The two men had lunch together in a small room that closely resembled a British officers' mess. The meal consisted of a steak that would not have been acceptable to any South American cowhand surrounded by vegetables that reminded Eduardo of his schooldays. Still, Eduardo had never yet met a soldier who understood that a good chef was every bit as important as a good batman. During the lunch they talked in overall terms about the problems of building a whole new city in the middle of an equatorial jungle.

The provisional estimate of the cost of the project had been one thousand million dollars but when de Silveira warned the President that the final outcome might well end up nearer three thousand million dollars the President's jaw dropped slightly. De Silveira had to admit that the project would be the most ambitious that Prentino International had ever tackled, but he was quick to point out to the President that the same would be true of any construction company in the world.

De Silveira, not a man to play his best card early, waited until the coffee to slip into the conversation that he had just been awarded, against heavy opposition (that had included Rodrigues), the contract to build an eight-lane highway through the Amazonian jungle, which would eventually link up with the Pan-American highway, a contract second in size only to the one they were now contemplating in Nigeria. The

President was impressed and inquired if the venture
would not prevent de Silveira involving himself in the
new capital project.

'I'll know the answer to that question in three
days' time,' replied the Brazilian, and undertook to
have a further discussion with the Head of State at
the end of his visit when he would let him know if he
was prepared to continue with the scheme.

After lunch Eduardo was driven to the Federal
Palace Hotel where the entire sixth floor had been
placed at his disposal. Several complaining guests who
had come to Nigeria to close deals involving mere
millions had been asked to vacate their rooms at short
notice to make way for de Silveira and his staff.
Eduardo knew nothing of these goings on, as there
was always a room available for him wherever he
arrived in the world.

The six Mercedes drew up outside the hotel and
the colonel guided his charge through the swing doors
and past reception. Eduardo had not checked himself
into a hotel for the past fourteen years except on those
occasions when he chose to register under an assumed
name, not wanting anyone to know the identity of the
woman he was with.

The chairman of Prentino International walked
down the centre of the hotel's main corridor and
stepped into a waiting lift. His legs went weak and he
suddenly felt sick. In the corner of the lift stood a
stubby, balding, overweight man, who was dressed in
a pair of old jeans and a tee-shirt, his mouth continu-

ally opening and closing as he chewed gum. The two men stood as far apart as possible, neither showing any sign of recognition. The lift stopped at the fifth floor and Manuel Rodrigues, chairman of Rodrigues International SA, stepped out, leaving behind him the man who had been his bitter rival for thirty years.

Eduardo held on to the rail in the lift to steady himself as he still felt dizzy. How he despised that uneducated self-made upstart whose family of four half-brothers, all by different fathers, claimed they now ran the largest construction company in Brazil. Both men were as interested in the other's failure as they were in their own success.

Eduardo was somewhat puzzled to know what Rodrigues could possibly be doing in Lagos as he felt certain that his rival had not come into contact with the Nigerian president. After all, Eduardo had never collected the rent on a small house in Rio that was occupied by the mistress of a very senior official in the government's protocol department. And the man's only task was to be certain that Rodrigues was never invited to any function attended by a visiting dignitary when in Brazil. The continual absence of Rodrigues from these state occasions ensured the absent-mindedness of Eduardo's rent collector in Rio.

Eduardo would never have admitted to anyone that Rodrigues' presence worried him, but he nevertheless resolved to find out immediately what had brought his old enemy to Nigeria. Once he reached his suite de Silveira instructed his private secretary to check what Manuel Rodrigues was up to. Eduardo was prepared to return to Brazil immediately if Rodrigues turned out to be involved in any way with the new capital project, while one young lady in Rio would suddenly find herself looking for alternative accommodation.

Within an hour, his private secretary returned with the information that his chairman had requested. Rodrigues, he had discovered, was in Nigeria to tender for the contract to construct a new port in Lagos and was apparently not involved in any way with the new capital, and in fact was still trying to arrange a meeting with the President.

'Which minister is in charge of the ports and when am I due to see him?' asked de Silveira.

The secretary delved into his appointments file. 'The Minister of Transport,' the secretary said. 'You have an appointment with him at nine o'clock on Thursday morning.' The Nigerian Civil Service had mapped out a four-day schedule of meetings for de Silveira that included every cabinet minister involved in the new city project. 'It's the last meeting before your final discussion with the President. You then fly on to Paris.'

'Excellent. Remind me of this conversation five minutes before I see the minister and again when I talk to the President.'

The secretary made a note in the file and left.

Eduardo sat alone in his suite, going over the reports on the new capital project submitted by his experts. Some of his team were already showing signs of nervousness. One particular anxiety that always came up with a large construction contract was the principal's ability to pay, and pay on time. Failure to do so was the quickest route to bankruptcy, but since the discovery of oil in Nigeria there seemed to be no shortage of income and certainly no shortage of people willing to spend that money on behalf of the government. These anxieties did not worry de Silveira as he always insisted on a substantial payment in advance; otherwise he wouldn't move himself or his vast staff one centimetre out of Brazil. However, the massive scope of this particular contract made the circumstances somewhat unusual. Eduardo realised that it would be most damaging to his international reputation if he started the assignment and then was seen not to complete it. He re-read the reports over a quiet dinner in his room and retired to bed early, having wasted an hour in vainly trying to place a call through to his wife.

De Silveira's first appointment the next morning was with the Governor of the Central Bank of Nigeria. Eduardo wore a newly-pressed suit, fresh shirt, and highly polished shoes: for four days no one would see him in the same clothes. At eight-forty-five there was a quiet knock on the door of his suite and the secretary opened it to find Colonel Usman standing to attention, waiting to escort Eduardo to the bank. As they were leaving the hotel Eduardo again saw Manuel Rodrigues, wearing the same pair of jeans, the same crumpled tee-shirt, and probably chewing the same gum as he stepped into a BMW in front of him. De Silveira only stopped scowling at the disappearing BMW when he remembered his Thursday morning appointment with the minister in charge of ports, followed by a meeting with the President.

The Governor of the Central Bank of Nigeria was in the habit of proposing how payment schedules would be met and completion orders would be guaranteed. He had never been told by anyone that if the payment was seven days overdue he could consider the contract null and void, and they could take it or leave it. The minister would have made some comment if Abuja had not been the President's pet project. That position established, de Silveira went on to check the bank's reserves, long-term deposits, overseas commitments, and estimated oil revenues for the next five years. He left the Governor in what could only be described as a jelly-like state. Glistening and wobbling. Eduardo's next appointment was an unavoidable courtesy call on the Brazilian Ambassador for lunch. He hated these functions as he believed embassies to be fit only for cocktail parties and discussion of out-of-date trivia, neither of which he cared for. The food in such establishments was invariably bad and the company worse. It turned out to be no different on this occasion and the only profit (Eduardo considered everything in terms of profit and loss) to be derived from the encounter was the information that Manuel Rodrigues was on a short list of three for the building of the new port in Lagos, and was expecting to have an audience with the President on Friday if he was awarded the contract. By Thursday morning that will be a short list of two and there will be no meeting with the President, de Silveira promised himself, and considered that was the most he was likely to gain from the lunch until the Ambassador added:

'Rodrigues seems most keen on you being awarded the new city contract at Abuja. He's singing your praises to every minister he meets. Funny,' the Ambassador continued, 'I always thought you two didn't see eye to eye.'

Eduardo made no reply as he tried to fathom out what trick Rodrigues could be up to by promoting his cause.

Eduardo spent the afternoon with the Minister of Finance and confirmed the provisional arrangements he had made with the Governor of the bank. The Minister of Finance had been forewarned by the Governor what he was to expect from an encounter with Eduardo de Silveira and that he was not to be taken aback by the Brazilian's curt demands. De Silveira, aware that this warning would have taken place, let the poor man bargain a little and even gave way on a few minor points that he would be able to tell the President about at the next meeting of the Supreme Military Council. Eduardo left the smiling minister believing that he had scored a point or two against the formidable South American.

That evening, Eduardo dined privately with his

senior advisers who themselves were already dealing with the ministers' officials. Each was now coming up with daily reports about the problems that would have to be faced if they worked in Nigeria. His chief engineer was quick to emphasise that skilled labour could not be hired at any price as the Germans had already cornered the market for their extensive road projects. The financial advisers also presented a gloomy report, of international companies waiting six months or more for their cheques to be cleared by the central bank. Eduardo made notes on the views they expressed but never ventured an opinion himself. His staff left him a little after eleven and he decided to take a stroll around the hotel grounds before retiring to bed. On his walk through the luxuriant tropical gardens he only just avoided a face-to-face confrontation with Manuel Rodrigues by darting behind a large Iroko plant. The little man passed by champing away at his gum, oblivious to Eduardo's baleful glare. Eduardo informed a chattering grey parrot of his most secret thoughts: by Thursday afternoon, Rodrigues, you will be on your way back to Brazil with a suitcase full of plans that can be filed under 'abortive projects'. The parrot cocked his head and screeched at him as if he had been let in on his secret. Eduardo allowed himself a smile and returned to his room.

Colonel Usman arrived on the dot of eight-forty-five again the next day and Eduardo spent the morning with the Minister of Supplies and Co-operatives – or lack of them, as he commented to his private secretary afterwards. The afternoon was spent with the Minister of Labour checking over the availability of unskilled workers and the total lack of skilled operatives. Eduardo was fast reaching the conclusion that, despite the professed optimism of the ministers concerned, this was going to be the toughest contract he had ever tackled. There was more to be lost than money if the whole international business world stood watching him fall flat on his face. In the evening his staff reported to him once again, having solved a few old problems and unearthed some new ones. Tentatively, they had come to the conclusion that if the present regime stayed in power, there need be no serious concern over payment, as the President had earmarked the new city as a priority project. They had even heard a rumour that the army would be willing to lend-lease part of the Service Corps if there turned out to be a shortage of skilled labour. Eduardo made a note to have this point confirmed in writing by the Head of State during their final meeting the next day. But the labour problem was not what was occupying Eduardo's thoughts as he put on his silk pyjamas that night. He was chuckling at the idea of Manuel Rodrigues' imminent and sudden departure for Brazil. Eduardo slept well.

He rose with renewed vigour the next morning, showered and put on a fresh suit. The four days were turning out to be well worth while and a single stone might yet kill two birds. By eight-forty-five, he was waiting impatiently for the previously punctual colonel. The colonel did not show up at eight-forty-five and had still not appeared when the clock on his mantelpiece struck nine. De Silveira sent his private secretary off to find out where he was while he paced angrily backwards and forwards through the hotel suite. His secretary returned a few minutes later in a panic with the information that the hotel was surrounded by armed guards. Eduardo did not panic. He had been through eight coups in his life from which he had learnt one golden rule: the new regime never kills visiting foreigners as it needs their money every bit as much as the last government. Eduardo picked up the telephone but no one answered him so he switched on the radio. A tape recording was playing:

'This is Radio Nigeria, this is Radio Nigeria. There has been a coup. General Mohammed has been overthrown and Lieutenant Colonel Dimka has assumed leadership of the new revolutionary government. Do not be afraid; remain at home and everything will be back to normal in a few hours. This is Radio Nigeria, this is Radio Nigeria. There has been a . . .'

Eduardo switched off the radio as two thoughts flashed through his mind. Coups always held up everything and caused chaos, so undoubtedly he had wasted the four days. But worse, would it now be possible for him even to get out of Nigeria and carry on his normal business with the rest of the world?

By lunchtime, the radio was playing martial music interspersed with the tape recorded message he now knew off by heart. Eduardo detailed all his staff to find out anything they could and to report back to him direct. They all returned with the same story; that it was impossible to get past the soldiers surrounding the hotel so no new information could be unearthed. Eduardo swore for the first time in months. To add to his inconvenience, the hotel manager rang through to say that regretfully Mr de Silveira would have to eat in the main dining room as there would be no room service until further notice. Eduardo went down to the dining room somewhat reluctantly only to discover that the head waiter showed no interest in who he was and placed him unceremoniously at a small table already occupied by three Italians. Manuel Rodrigues was seated only two tables away: Eduardo stiffened at the thought of the other man enjoying his discomfiture and then remembered it was that morning he was supposed to have seen the Minister of Ports. He ate his meal quickly despite being served slowly and when the Italians tried to make conversation with him he waved them away with his hand, feigning lack of understanding, despite the fact that he spoke their language fluently. As soon as he had finished the second course he returned to his room. His staff had only gossip to pass on and they had been unable to make contact with the Brazilian Embassy to lodge an official protest. 'A lot of good an official protest will do us,' said Eduardo, slumping down in his chair. 'Who do you send it to, the new regime or the old one?'

He sat alone in his room for the rest of the day, interrupted only by what he thought was the sound of gunfire in the distance. He read the New Federal Capital project proposal and his advisers' reports for a third time.

The next morning Eduardo, dressed in the same suit as he had worn on the day of his arrival, was greeted by his secretary with the news that the coup had been crushed; after fierce street fighting, he informed his unusually attentive chairman, the old regime had regained power but not without losses; among those killed in the uprising had been General Mohammed, the Head of State. The secretary's news was officially confirmed on Radio Nigeria later that morning. The ringleader of the abortive coup had been one Lieutenant Colonel Dimka: Dimka, along with one or two junior officers, had escaped, and the government had ordered a dusk to dawn curfew until the evil criminals were apprehended.

Pull off a coup and you're a national hero, fail and you're an evil criminal; in business it's the same difference between bankruptcy and making a fortune, considered Eduardo as he listened to the news report. He was beginning to form plans in his mind for an early departure from Nigeria when the newscaster made an announcement that chilled him to the very marrow.

'While Lieutenant Colonel Dimka and his accomplices remain on the run, airports throughout the country will be closed until further notice.'

When the newscaster had finished his report, martial music was played in memory of the late General Mohammed.

Eduardo went downstairs in a flaming temper. The hotel was still surrounded by armed guards. He stared at the fleet of six empty Mercedes which was parked only ten yards beyond the soldiers' rifles. He marched back into the foyer, irritated by the babble of different tongues coming at him from every direction. Eduardo looked around him: it was obvious that many people had been stranded in the hotel overnight and had ended up sleeping in the lounge or the bar. He checked the paperback rack in the lobby for something to read but there were only four copies left of a tourist guide to Lagos; everything had been sold. Authors who had not been read for years were now changing hands at a premium. Eduardo returned to his room which was fast assuming the character of a prison, and baulked at reading the New Federal Capital project for a fourth time. He tried again to make contact with the Brazilian Ambassador to discover if he could obtain special permission to leave the country as he had his own aircraft. No one answered the Embassy phone. He went down for an early lunch only to find the dining room was once again packed to capacity. Eduardo was placed at a table with some Germans who were worrying about a contract that had been signed by the government the previous week, before the abortive coup. They were wondering if it would still be honoured. Manuel

Rodrigues entered the room a few minutes later and was placed at the next table.

During the afternoon, de Silveira ruefully examined his schedule for the next seven days. He had been due in Paris that morning to see the Minister of the Interior, and from there should have flown on to London to confer with the chairman of the Steel Board. His calendar was fully booked for the next ninety-two days until his family holiday in May. 'I'm having this year's holiday in Nigeria,' he commented wryly to an assistant.

What annoyed Eduardo most about the coup was the lack of communication it afforded with the outside world. He wondered what was going on in Brazil and he hated not being able to telephone or telex Paris or London to explain his absence personally. He listened addictively to Radio Nigeria on the hour every hour for any new scrap of information. At five o'clock, he learned that the Supreme Military Council had elected a new President who would address the nation on television and radio at nine o'clock that night.

Eduardo de Silveira switched on the television at eight-forty-five; normally an assistant would have put it on for him at one minute to nine. He sat watching a Nigerian lady giving a talk on dressmaking, followed by the weather forecast man who supplied Eduardo with the revealing information that the temperature would continue to be hot for the next month. Eduardo's knee was twitching up and down nervously as he waited for the address by the new President. At nine o'clock, after the national anthem had been played, the new Head of State, General Obasanjo, appeared on the screen in full dress uniform. He spoke first of the tragic death and sad loss for the nation of the late President, and went on to say that his government would continue to work in the best interests of Nigeria. He looked ill at ease as he apologised to all foreign visitors who were inconvenienced by the attempted coup but went on to make it clear that the dusk to dawn curfew would continue until the rebel leaders were tracked down and brought to justice. He confirmed that all airports would remain closed until Lieutenant Colonel Dimka was in safe custody. The new President ended his statement by saying that all other forms of communication would be opened up again as soon as possible. The national anthem was played for a second time, while Eduardo thought of the millions of dollars that might be lost to him by his incarceration in that hotel room, while his private plane sat idly on the tarmac only a few miles away. One of his senior managers opened a book as to how long it would take for the authorities to capture Lieutenant Colonel Dimka; he did not tell de Silveira how short the odds were on a month.

Eduardo went down to the dining room in the suit he had worn the day before. A junior waiter placed him at a table with some Frenchmen who had been hoping to win a contract to drill bore holes in the Niger state. Again Eduardo waved a languid hand when they tried to include him in their conversation.

At that very moment he was meant to be with the French Minister of the Interior, not with some French hole-borers. He tried to concentrate on his watered-down soup, wondering how much longer it would be before it would be just water. The head waiter appeared by his side, gesturing to the one remaining seat at the table, in which he placed Manuel Rodrigues. Still neither man gave any sign of recognising the other. Eduardo debated with himself whether he should leave the table or carry on as if his oldest rival was still in Brazil. He decided the latter was more dignified. The Frenchmen began an argument among themselves as to when they would be able to get out of Lagos. One of them declared emphatically that he had heard on the highest authority that the government intended to track down every last one of those involved in the coup before they opened the airports and that might take up to a month.

'What?' said the two Brazilians together, in English.

'I can't stay here for a month,' said Eduardo.

'Neither can I,' said Manuel Rodrigues.

'You'll have to, at least until Dimka is captured,' said one of the Frenchmen, breaking into English. 'So you must both relax yourselves, yes?'

The two Brazilians continued their meal in silence. When Eduardo had finished he rose from the table and without looking directly at Rodrigues said goodnight in Portuguese. The old rival inclined his head in reply to the salutation.

The next day brought forth no new information. The hotel remained surrounded with soldiers and by the evening Eduardo had lost his temper with every member of staff with whom he had come into contact. He went down to dinner on his own and as he entered the dining room he saw Manuel Rodrigues sitting alone at a table in the corner. Rodrigues looked up, seemed to hesitate for a moment, and then beckoned to Eduardo. Eduardo himself hesitated before walking slowly towards Rodrigues and taking the seat opposite him. Rodrigues poured him a glass of wine. Eduardo, who rarely drank, drank it. Their conversation was stilted to begin with, but as both men consumed more wine so they each began to relax in the other's company. By the time coffee had arrived, Manuel was telling Eduardo what he could do with this god-forsaken country.

'You will not stay on, if you are awarded the ports contract?' inquired Eduardo.

'Not a hope,' said Rodrigues, who showed no surprise that de Silveira knew of his interest in the ports contract. 'I withdrew from the short list the day before the coup. I had intended to fly back to Brazil that Thursday morning.'

'Can you say why you withdrew?'

'Labour problems mainly, and then the congestion of the ports.'

'I am not sure I understand,' said Eduardo, under-standing full well but curious to learn if Rodrigues had picked up some tiny detail his own staff had missed.

Manuel Rodrigues paused to ingest the fact that the man he had viewed as his most dangerous enemy for over thirty years was now listening to his own inside information. He considered the situation for a moment while he sipped his coffee. Eduardo didn't speak.

'To begin with, there's a terrible shortage of skilled labour, and on top of that there's this mad quota system.'

'Quota system?' said Eduardo innocently.

'The percentage of people from the contractor's country which the government will allow to work in Nigeria.'

'Why should that be a problem?' said Eduardo, leaning forward.

'By law, you have to employ at a ratio of fifty nationals to one foreigner so I could only have brought over twenty-five of my top men to organise a fifty million dollar contract, and I'd have had to make do with Nigerians at every other level. The government are cutting their own throats with the wretched system; they can't expect unskilled men, black or white, to become experienced engineers overnight. It's all to do with their national pride. Someone must tell them they can't afford that sort of pride if they want to complete the job at a sensible price. That path is the surest route to bankruptcy. On top of that, the Germans have already rounded up all the best skilled labour for their road projects.'

'But surely,' said Eduardo, 'you charge according to the rules, however stupid, thus covering all eventualities, and as long as you're certain that payment is guaranteed . . .'

Manuel raised his hand to stop Eduardo's flow: 'That's another problem. You can't be certain. The government reneged on a major steel contract only last month. In so doing,' he explained, 'they had bankrupted a distinguished international company. So they are perfectly capable of trying the same trick with me. And if they don't pay up, who do you sue? The Supreme Military Council?'

'And the ports problem?'

'The port is totally congested. There are one hundred and seventy ships desperate to unload their cargo with a waiting time of anything up to six months. On top of that, there is a demurrage charge of five thousand dollars a day and only perishable foods are given any priority.'

'But there's always a way round that sort of problem,' said Eduardo, rubbing a thumb twice across the top of his fingers.

'Bribery? It doesn't work, Eduardo. How can you possibly jump the queue when all one hundred and seventy ships have already bribed the harbour master? And don't imagine that fixing the rent on a flat for one of his mistresses would help either,' said

Rodrigues grinning. 'With that man you will have to supply the mistress as well.'

Eduardo held his breath but said nothing.

'Come to think of it,' continued Rodrigues, 'if the situation becomes any worse, the harbour master will be the one man in the country who is richer than you.'

Eduardo laughed for the first time in three days.

'I tell you, Eduardo, we could make a bigger profit building a salt mine in Siberia.'

Eduardo laughed again and some of the Prentino and Rodrigues staff dining at other tables stared in disbelief at their masters.

'You were in for the big one, the new city of Abuja?' said Manuel.

'That's right,' admitted Eduardo.

'I have done everything in my power to make sure you were awarded that contract,' said the other quietly.

'What?' said Eduardo in disbelief. 'Why?'

'I thought Abuja would give the Prentino empire more headaches than even you could cope with, Eduardo, and that might possibly leave the field wide open for me at home. Think about it. Every time there's a cutback in Nigeria, what will be the first head to roll off the chopping block? "The unnecessary city" as the locals all call it.'

'The unnecessary city?' repeated Eduardo.

'Yes, and it doesn't help when you say you won't move without advance payment. You know as well as

I do, you will need one hundred of your best men here full time to organise such a massive enterprise. They'll need feeding, salaries, housing, perhaps even a school and a hospital. Once they are settled down here, you can't just pull them off the job every two weeks because the government is running late clearing the cheques. It's not practical and you know it.' Rodrigues poured Eduardo de Silveira another glass of wine.

'I had already taken that into consideration,' Eduardo said as he sipped the wine, 'but I thought that with the support of the Head of State—'

'The late Head of State.'

'I take your point, Manuel.'

'Maybe the next Head of State will also back you, but what about the one after that? Nigeria has had three coups in the past three years.'

Eduardo remained silent for a moment.

'Do you play backgammon?'

'Yes. Why do you ask?'

'I must make *some* money while I'm here.' Manuel laughed.

'Why don't you come to my room,' continued de Silveira. 'Though I must warn you I always manage to beat my staff.'

'Perhaps they always manage to lose,' said Manuel, as he rose and grabbed the half empty bottle of wine by its neck. Both men were laughing as they left the dining room.

After that, the two chairmen had lunch and dinner

together every day. Within a week, their staff were eating at the same tables. Eduardo could be seen in the dining room without a tie while Manuel wore a shirt for the first time in years. By the end of a fortnight, the two rivals had played each other at table tennis, backgammon and bridge with the stakes set at one hundred dollars a point. At the end of each day Eduardo always seemed to end up owing Manuel about a million dollars which Manuel happily traded for the best bottle of wine left in the hotel's cellar.

Although Lieutenant Colonel Dimka had been sighted by about forty thousand Nigerians in about as many different places, he still remained resolutely uncaptured. As the new President had insisted, airports remained closed but communications were opened which at least allowed Eduardo to telephone and telex Brazil. His brothers and wife were sending replies by the hour, imploring Eduardo to return home at any cost: decisions on major contracts throughout the world were being held up by his absence. But Eduardo's message back to Brazil was always the same: as long as Dimka is on the loose, the airports will remain closed.

It was on a Tuesday night during dinner that Eduardo took the trouble to explain to Manuel why Brazil had lost the World Cup. Manuel dismissed Eduardo's outrageous claims as ill-informed and prejudiced. It was the only subject on which they hadn't agreed in the past three weeks.

'I blame the whole fiasco on Zagalo,' said Eduardo.

'No, no, you cannot blame the manager,' said Manuel. 'The fault lies with our stupid selectors who know even less about football than you do. They should never have dropped Leao from goal and in any case we should have learned from the Argentinian defeat last year that our methods are now out of date. You must attack, attack, if you want to score goals.'

'Rubbish. We still have the surest defence in the world.'

'Which means the best result you can hope for is a 0–0 draw.'

'Never . . .' began Eduardo.

'Excuse me, sir.' Eduardo looked up to see his private secretary standing by his side looking anxiously down at him.

'Yes, what's the problem?'

'An urgent telex from Brazil, sir.'

Eduardo read the first paragraph and then asked Manuel if he would be kind enough to excuse him for a few minutes. The latter nodded politely. Eduardo left the table and as he marched through the dining room seventeen other guests left unfinished meals and followed him quickly to his suite on the top floor, where the rest of his staff were already assembled. He sat down in the corner of the room on his own. No one spoke as he read through the telex carefully, suddenly realising how many days he had been imprisoned in Lagos.

The telex was from his brother Carlos and the contents concerned the Pan-American road project, an eight-lane highway that would stretch from Brazil to Mexico. Prentinos had tendered for the section that ran through the middle of the Amazon jungle and had to have the bank guarantees signed and certified by midday tomorrow; Tuesday. But Eduardo had quite forgotten which Tuesday it was and the document he was committed to sign by the following day's deadline.

'What's the problem?' Eduardo asked his private secretary. 'The Banco do Brasil have already agreed with Alfredo to act as guarantors. What's stopping Carlos signing the agreement in my absence?'

'The Mexicans are now demanding that responsibility for the contract be shared because of the insurance problems. Lloyd's of London will not cover the entire risk if only one company is involved. The details are all on page seven of the telex.'

Eduardo flicked quickly through the pages. He read that his brothers had already tried to put pressure on Lloyd's, but to no avail. That's like trying to bribe a maiden aunt into taking part in a public orgy, thought Eduardo, and he would have told them as much if he had been back in Brazil. The Mexican Government was therefore insisting that the contract be shared with an international construction company acceptable to Lloyd's if the legal documents were to be signed by the midday deadline the following day.

'Stay put,' said Eduardo to his staff, and he returned to the dining room alone, trailing the long telex behind him. Rodrigues watched him as he scurried back to their table.

'You look like a man with a problem.'

'I am,' said Eduardo. 'Read that.'

Manuel's experienced eye ran down the telex, picking out the salient points. He had tendered for the Amazon road project himself and could still recall the details. At Eduardo's insistence, he re-read page seven.

'Mexican bandits,' he said as he returned the telex to Eduardo. 'Who do they think they are, telling Eduardo de Silveira how he must conduct his business. Telex them back immediately and inform them you're chairman of the greatest construction company in the world and they can roast in hell before you will agree to their pathetic terms. You know it's far too late for them to go out to tender again with every other section of the highway ready to begin work. They would lose millions. Call their bluff, Eduardo.'

'I think you may be right, Manuel, but any hold-up now can only waste my time and money, so I intend to agree to their demand and look for a partner.'

'You'll never find one at such short notice.'

'I will.'

'Who?'

Eduardo de Silveira hesitated only for a second. 'You, Manuel. I want to offer Rodrigues International SA fifty per cent of the Amazon road contract.'

Manuel Rodrigues looked up at Eduardo. It was the first time that he had not anticipated his old rival's next move. 'I suppose it might help cover the millions you owe me in table tennis debts.'

The two men laughed, then Rodrigues stood up and they shook hands gravely. De Silveira left the dining room on the run and wrote out a telex for his manager to transmit.

'Sign, accept terms, fifty per cent partner will be Rodrigues International Construction SA, Brazil.'

'If I telex that message, sir, you do realise that it's legally binding?'

'Send it,' said Eduardo.

Eduardo returned once again to the dining room where Manuel had ordered the finest bottle of champagne in the hotel. Just as they were calling for a second bottle, and singing a spirited version of 'Esta Chegando a Hora', Eduardo's private secretary appeared by his side again, this time with two telexes, one from the President of the Banco do Brasil and a second from his brother Carlos. Both wanted confirmation of the agreed partner for the Amazon road project. Eduardo uncorked the second bottle of champagne without looking up at his private secretary.

'Confirm Rodrigues International Construction to the President of the bank and my brother,' he said as he filled Manuel's empty glass. 'And don't bother me again tonight.'

'Yes, sir,' said the private secretary and left without another word.

Neither man could recall what time he climbed into bed that night but de Silveira was abruptly awakened from a deep sleep by his secretary early the next morning. Eduardo took a few minutes to digest the news. Lieutenant Colonel Dimka had been caught in Kano at three o'clock that morning, and all the airports were now open again. Eduardo picked up the phone and dialled three digits.

'Manuel, you've heard the news? . . . Good . . . Then you must fly back with me in my 707 or it may be days before you get out . . . One hour's time in the lobby . . . See you then.'

At eight-forty-five there was a quiet knock on the door and Eduardo's secretary opened it to find Colonel Usman standing to attention, just as he had done in the days before the coup. He held a note in his hand. Eduardo tore open the envelope to find an invitation to lunch that day with the new Head of State, General Obasanjo.

'Please convey my apologies to your President,' said Eduardo, 'and be kind enough to explain that I have pressing commitments to attend to in my own country.'

The colonel retired reluctantly. Eduardo dressed in the suit, shirt and tie he had worn on his first day in Nigeria and took the lift downstairs to the lobby where he joined Manuel who was once more wearing jeans and a tee-shirt. The two chairmen left the hotel and climbed into the back of the leading Mercedes and the motorcade of six began its journey to the airport. The colonel, who now sat in front with the driver, did not venture to speak to either of the distinguished Brazilians for the entire journey. The two men, he would be able to tell the new President later, seemed to be preoccupied with a discussion on an Amazon road project and how the responsibility should be divided between their two companies.

Customs were bypassed as neither man had anything they wanted to take out of the country other than themselves, and the fleet of cars came to a halt at the side of Eduardo's blue and silver 707. The staff of both companies climbed aboard the rear section of the aircraft, also engrossed in discussion on the Amazon road project.

A corporal jumped out of the lead car and opened the back door, to allow the two chairmen to walk straight up the steps and board the front section of the aircraft.

As Eduardo stepped out of the Mercedes, the Nigerian driver saluted smartly. 'Goodbye, sir,' he said, revealing the large set of white teeth once again.

Eduardo said nothing.

'I hope,' said the corporal politely, 'you made very big deal while you were in Nigeria.'

THE FIRST MIRACLE

TOMORROW IT WOULD BE 1 AD, but nobody had told him.

If anyone had, he wouldn't have understood because he thought that it was the forty-third year in the reign of the Emperor, and in any case, he had other things on his mind. His mother was still cross with him and he had to admit that he'd been naughty that day, even by the standards of a normal thirteen-year-old. He hadn't meant to drop the pitcher when she had sent him to the well for water. He tried to explain to his mother that it wasn't his fault that he had tripped over a stone; and that at least was true. What he hadn't told her was that he was chasing a stray dog at the time. And then there was that pomegranate; how was he meant to know that it was the last one, and that his father had taken a liking to them? The boy was now dreading his father's return and the possibility that he might be given another thrashing. He could still remember the last one when he hadn't been able to sit down for two days without feeling the pain, and the thin red scars didn't completely disappear for over three weeks.

He sat on the window ledge in a shaded corner of his room trying to think of some way he could redeem himself in his mother's eyes, now that she had thrown him out of the kitchen. Go outside and play, she had insisted, after he had spilt some cooking oil on his tunic. But that wasn't much fun as he was only allowed to play by himself. His father had forbidden him to mix with the local boys. How he hated this country; if only he were back home with his friends, there would be so much to do. Still, only another three weeks and he could . . . The door swung open and his mother came into the room. She was dressed in the thin black garments so favoured by locals: they kept her cool, she had explained to the boy's father. He had grunted his disapproval so she always changed back into imperial dress before he returned in the evening.

'Ah, there you are,' she said, addressing the crouched figure of her son.

'Yes, Mother.'

'Daydreaming as usual. Well, wake up because I need you to go into the village and fetch some food for me.'

'Yes, Mother, I'll go at once,' the boy said as he jumped off the window ledge.

'Well, at least wait until you've heard what I want.'

'Sorry, Mother.'

'Now listen, and listen carefully.' She started counting on her fingers as she spoke. 'I need a

74

chicken, some raisins, figs, dates and . . . ah yes, two pomegranates.'

The boy's face reddened at the mention of the pomegranates and he stared down at the stone floor, hoping she might have forgotten. His mother put her hand into the leather purse that hung from her waist and removed two small coins, but before she handed them over she made her son repeat the instructions.

'One chicken, raisins, figs, dates, and two pome-granates,' he recited, as he might the modern poet, Virgil.

'And be sure to see they give you the correct change,' she added. 'Never forget the locals are all thieves.'

'Yes, Mother . . .' For a moment the boy hesitated.

'If you remember everything and bring back the right amount of money, I might forget to tell your father about the broken pitcher and the pomegranate.'

The boy smiled, pocketed the two small silver coins in his tunic, and ran out of the house into the compound. The guard who stood on duty at the gate removed the great wedge of wood which allowed the massive door to swing open. The boy jumped through the hole in the gate and grinned back at the guard.

'Been in more trouble again today?' the guard shouted after him.

'No, not this time,' the boy replied. 'I'm about to be saved.'

He waved farewell to the guard and started to

walk briskly towards the village while humming a tune that reminded him of home. He kept to the centre of the dusty winding path that the locals had the nerve to call a road. He seemed to spend half his time removing little stones from his sandals. If his father had been posted here for any length of time he would have made some changes; then they would have had a real road, straight and wide enough to take a chariot. But not before his mother had sorted out the serving girls. Not one of them knew how to lay a table or even prepare food so that it was at least clean. For the first time in his life he had seen his mother in a kitchen, and he felt sure it would be the last, as they would all be returning home now that his father was coming to the end of his assignment.

The evening sun shone down on him as he walked; it was a very large red sun, the same red as his father's tunic. The heat it gave out made him sweat and long for something to drink. Perhaps there would be enough money left over to buy himself a pomegranate. He couldn't wait to take one home and show his friends how large they were in this barbaric land. Marcus, his best friend, would undoubtedly have seen one as big because his father had commanded a whole army in these parts, but the rest of the class would still be impressed.

The village to which his mother had sent him was only two miles from the compound and the dusty path ran alongside a hill overlooking a large valley. The road was already crowded with travellers who would be seeking shelter in the village. All of them had come down from the hills at the express orders of his father, whose authority had been vested in him by the Emperor himself. Once he was sixteen, he too would serve the Emperor. His friend Marcus wanted to be a soldier and conquer the rest of the world. But he was more interested in the law and teaching his country's customs to the heathens in strange lands.

Marcus had said, 'I'll conquer them and then you can govern them.'

A sensible division between brains and brawn he had told his friend, who didn't seem impressed and had ducked him in the nearest bath.

The boy quickened his pace as he knew he had to be back in the compound before the sun disappeared behind the hills. His father had told him many times that he must always be locked safely inside before sunset. He was aware that his father was not a popular man with the locals, and he had warned his son that he would always be safe while it was light as no one would dare to harm him while others could watch what was going on, but once it was dark anything could happen. One thing he knew for certain: when he grew up he wasn't going to be a tax collector or work in the census office.

When he reached the village he found the narrow twisting lanes that ran between the little white houses swarming with people who had come from all the neighbouring lands to obey his father's order and be registered for the census, in order that they might be taxed. The boy dismissed the plebs from his mind. (It was Marcus who had taught him to refer to all foreigners as plebs.) When he entered the market place he also dismissed Marcus from his mind and began to concentrate on the supplies his mother wanted. He mustn't make any mistakes this time or he would undoubtedly end up with that thrashing from his father. He ran nimbly between the stalls, checking the food carefully. Some of the local people stared at the fair-skinned boy with the curly brown hair and the straight, firm nose. He displayed no imperfections or disease like the majority of them. Others turned their eyes away from him; after all, he had come from the land of the natural rulers. These thoughts did not pass through his mind. All the boy noticed was that their native skins were parched and lined from too much sun. He knew that too much sun was bad for you: it made you old before your time, his tutor had warned him.

At the end stall, the boy watched an old woman haggling over an unusually plump live chicken and as he marched towards her she ran away in fright, leaving the fowl behind her. He stared at the stall-keeper and refused to bargain with the peasant. It was beneath his dignity. He pointed to the chicken and gave the man one denarius. The man bit the round silver coin and looked at the head of Augustus Caesar, ruler of half the world. (When his tutor had told him, during a history lesson, about the Emperor's achievements, he remembered thinking, I hope

Caesar doesn't conquer the whole world before I have a chance to join in.) The stallkeeper was still staring at the silver coin.

'Come on, come on, I haven't got all day,' said the boy sounding like his father.

The local did not reply because he couldn't understand what the boy was saying. All he knew for certain was that it would be unwise for him to annoy the invader. The stallkeeper held the chicken firmly by the neck and taking a knife from his belt cut its head off in one movement and passed the dead fowl over to the boy. He then handed back some of his local coins, which had stamped on them the image of a man the boy's father described as 'that useless Herod'. The boy kept his hand held out, palm open, and the local placed bronze talents into it until he had no more. The boy left him talentless and moved to another stall, this time pointing to bags containing raisins, figs and dates. The new stallkeeper made a measure of each for which he received five of the useless Herod coins. The man was about to protest about the barter but the boy stared at him fixedly in the eyes, the way he had seen his father do so often. The stallkeeper backed away and only bowed his head.

Now, what else did his mother want? He racked his brains. A chicken, raisins, dates, figs and . . . of course, two pomegranates. He searched among the fresh-fruit stalls and picked out three pomegranates, and breaking one open, began to eat it, spitting out the pips on the ground in front of him. He paid the stallkeeper with the two remaining bronze talents, feeling pleased that he had carried out his mother's wishes while still being able to return home with one of the silver denarii. Even his father would be impressed by that. He finished the pomegranate and, with his arms laden, headed slowly out of the market back towards the compound, trying to avoid the stray dogs that continually got under his feet. They barked and sometimes snapped at his ankles: they did not know who he was.

When the boy reached the edge of the village he noticed the sun was already disappearing behind the highest hill, so he quickened his pace, remembering his father's words about being home before dusk. As he walked down the stony path, those still on the way towards the village kept a respectful distance, leaving him a clear vision as far as the eye could see, which wasn't all that far as he was carrying so much in his arms. But one sight he did notice a little way ahead of him was a man with a beard – a dirty, lazy habit his father had told him – wearing the ragged dress that signified that he was of the tribe of Jacob, tugging a reluctant donkey which in turn was carrying a very fat woman. The woman was, as their custom demanded, covered from head to toe in black. The boy was about to order them out of his path when the man left the donkey on the side of the road and went into a house which from its sign, claimed to be an inn.

Such a building in his own land would never have

passed the scrutiny of the local councillors as a place fit for paying travellers to dwell in. But the boy realised that this particular week to find even a mat to lay one's head on might be considered a luxury. He watched the bearded man reappear through the door with a forlorn look on his tired face. There was clearly no room at the inn.

The boy could have told him that before he went in, and wondered what the man would do next, as it was the last dwelling house on the road. Not that he was really interested; they could both sleep in the hills for all he cared. It was about all they looked fit for. The man with the beard was telling the woman something and pointing behind the inn, and without another word he led the donkey off in the direction he had been indicating. The boy wondered what could possibly be at the back of the inn and, his curiosity roused, followed them. As he came to the corner of the building, he saw the man was coaxing the donkey through an open door of what looked like a barn. The boy followed the strange trio and watched them through the crack left by the open door. The barn was covered in dirty straw and full of chickens, sheep and oxen, and smelled to the boy like the sewers they built in the side streets back home. He began to feel sick. The man was clearing away some of the worst of the straw from the centre of the barn, trying to make a clean patch for them to rest on – a near hopeless task, thought the boy. When the man had done as best he could he lifted the fat woman down from the donkey and placed her gently in the straw. Then he left her and went over to a trough on the other side of the barn where one of the oxen was drinking. He cupped his fingers together, put them in the trough and filling his hands with water, returned to the fat woman.

The boy was beginning to get bored and was about to leave when the woman leaned forward to drink from the man's hands. The shawl fell from her head and he saw her face for the first time.

He stood transfixed, staring at her. He had never seen anything more beautiful. Unlike the common members of her tribe, the woman's skin was translucent in quality, and her eyes shone, but what most struck the boy was her manner and presence. Never had he felt so much in awe, even remembering his one visit to the Senate House to hear a declamation from Augustus Caesar.

For a moment he remained mesmerised, but then he knew what he must do. He walked through the open door towards the woman, fell on his knees before her and offered the chicken. She smiled and he gave her the pomegranates and she smiled again. He then dropped the rest of the food in front of her, but she remained silent. The man with the beard was returning with more water, and when he saw the young foreigner he fell on his knees spilling the water onto the straw and then covered his face. The boy stayed on his knees for some time before he rose, and walked slowly towards the barn door. When he reached the opening, he turned back and stared once more into the face of the beautiful woman. She still did not speak.

The young Roman hesitated only for a second, and then bowed his head.

It was already dusk when he ran back out on to the winding path to resume his journey home, but he was not afraid. Rather he felt he had done something good and therefore no harm could come to him. He looked up into the sky and saw directly above him the first star, shining so brightly in the east that he wondered why he could see no others. His father had told him that different stars were visible in different lands, so he dismissed the puzzle from his mind, replacing it with the anxiety of not being home before dark. The road in front of him was now empty so he was able to walk quickly towards the compound, and was not all that far from safety when he first heard the singing and shouting. He turned quickly to see where the danger was coming from, staring up into the hills above him. To begin with, he couldn't make sense of what he saw. Then his eyes focused in disbelief on one particular field in which the shepherds were leaping up and down, singing, shouting and clapping their hands. The boy noticed that all the sheep were safely penned in a corner of the field for the night, so they had nothing to fear. He had been told by Marcus that sometimes the shepherds in this land would make a lot of noise at night because they believed it kept away the evil spirits. How could anyone be that stupid, the boy wondered, when there was a flash of lightning across the sky and the field was suddenly ablaze with light. The shepherds fell to their knees, silent, staring up into the sky for several minutes as though they were listening intently to something. Then all was darkness again.

The boy started running towards the compound as fast as his legs could carry him; he wanted to be inside and hear the safety of the great gate close behind him and watch the centurion put the wooden wedge firmly back in its place. He would have run all the way had he not seen something in front of him that brought him to a sudden halt. His father had taught him never to show any fear when facing danger. The boy caught his breath in case it would make them think that he was frightened. He was frightened, but he marched proudly on, determined he would never be forced off the road. When they did meet face to face, he was amazed.

Before him stood three camels and astride the beasts three men, who stared down at him. The first was clad in gold and with one arm protected something hidden beneath his cloak. By his side hung a large sword, its sheath covered in all manner of rare stones, some of which the boy could not even name. The second was dressed in white and held a silver casket to his breast, while the third wore red and carried a large wooden box. The man robed in gold put up his hand and addressed the boy in a strange tongue which he had never heard uttered before, even by his tutor. The second man tried Hebrew but to no avail and the third yet another tongue without eliciting any response from the boy.

The boy folded his arms across his chest and told them who he was, where he was going, and asked where they might be bound. He hoped his piping voice did not reveal his fear. The one robed in gold replied first and questioned the boy in his own tongue.

'Where is he that is born King of the Jews? For we have seen his star in the east, and are come to worship him.'

'King Herod lives beyond the . . .'

'We speak not of King Herod,' said the second man, 'for he is but a king of men as we are.'

'We speak,' said the third, 'of the King of Kings and are come to offer him gifts of gold, frankincense and myrrh.'

'I know nothing of the King of Kings,' said the boy, now gaining in confidence. 'I recognise only Augustus Caesar, Emperor of the known world.'

The man robed in gold shook his head and, pointing to the sky, inquired of the boy: 'You observe that bright star in the east. What is the name of the village on which it shines?'

The boy looked up at the star, and indeed the village below was clearer to the eye than it had been in sunlight.

'But that's only Bethlehem,' said the boy, laughing. 'You will find no King of Kings there.'

'Even there we shall find him,' said the second king, 'for did not Herod's chief priest tell us:

> And thou Bethlehem, in the land of Judah,
> Art not least among the princes of Judah,
> For out of thee shall come a Governor
> That shall rule my people Israel.'

'It cannot be,' said the boy now almost shouting at them. 'Augustus Caesar rules Israel and all the known world.'

But the three robed men did not heed his words and left him to ride on towards Bethlehem.

Mystified the boy set out on the last part of his journey home. Although the sky had become pitch black, whenever he turned his eyes towards Bethlehem the village was still clearly visible in the brilliant starlight. Once again he started running towards the compound, relieved to see its outline rising up in front of him. When he reached the great wooden gate, he banged loudly and repeatedly until a centurion, sword drawn, holding a flaming torch, came out to find out who it was that disturbed his watch. When he saw the boy, he frowned.

'Your father is very angry. He returned at sunset and is about to send out a search party for you.'

The boy darted past the centurion and ran all the way to his family's quarters, where he found his father addressing a sergeant of the guard. His mother was standing by his side, weeping.

The father turned when he saw his son and shouted: 'Where have you been?'

'To Bethlehem.'

'Yes, I know that, but whatever possessed you to return so late? Have I not told you countless times never to be out of the compound after dark? Come to my study at once.'

The boy looked helplessly towards his mother, who was still crying, but not out of relief, and turned to follow his father into the study. The guard sergeant winked at him as he passed by but the boy knew nothing could save him now. His father strode ahead of him into the study and sat on a leather stool by his table. His mother followed and stood silently by the door.

'Now tell me exactly where you have been and why you took so long to return, and be sure to tell me the truth.'

The boy stood in front of his father and told him everything that had come to pass. He started with how he had gone to the village and taken great care in choosing the food and in so doing had saved half the money his mother had given him. How on the way back he had seen a fat lady on a donkey unable to find a place at the inn and then he explained why he had given her the food. He went on to describe how the shepherds had shouted and beat their breasts until there was a great light in the sky at which they had all fallen silent on their knees, and then finally how he had met the three robed men who were searching for the King of Kings.

The father grew angry at his son's words.

'What a story you tell,' he shouted. 'Do tell me more. Did you find this King of Kings?'

'No, Sir. I did not,' he replied, as he watched his father rise and start pacing around the room.

'Perhaps there is a more simple explanation as to why your face and fingers are stained red with pomegranate juice,' he suggested.

'No, Father. I did buy an extra pomegranate but even after I had bought all the food, I still managed to save one silver denarius.'

The boy handed the coin over to his mother believing it would confirm his story. But the sight of the piece of silver only made his father more angry. He stopped pacing and stared down into the eyes of his son.

'You have spent the other denarius on yourself and now you have nothing to show for it?'

'That's not true, Father, I . . .'

'Then I will allow you one more chance to tell me the truth,' said his father as he sat back down. 'Fail me, boy, and I shall give you a thrashing that you will never forget for the rest of your life.'

'I have already told you the truth, Father.'

'Listen to me carefully, my son. We were born Romans, born to rule the world because our laws and customs are tried and trusted and have always been based firmly on absolute honesty. Romans never lie; it remains our strength and the weakness of our enemies. That is why we rule while others are ruled and as long as that is so the Roman Empire will never fall. Do you understand what I am saying, my boy?'

'Yes, Father, I understand.'

'Then you'll also understand why it is imperative to tell the truth.'

'But I have not lied, Father.'

'Then there is no hope for you,' said the man angrily. 'And you leave me only one way to deal with this matter.'

The boy's mother wanted to come to her son's aid, but knew any protest would be useless. The father rose from his chair and removed the leather belt from around his waist and folded it double, leaving the heavy brass studs on the outside. He then ordered his son to touch his toes. The young boy obeyed without hesitation and the father raised the leather strap above his head and brought it down on the child with all his strength. The boy never flinched or murmured, while his mother turned away from the sight, and wept. After the father had administered the twelfth stroke he ordered his son to go to his room. The boy left without a word and his mother followed and watched him climb the stairs. She then hurried away to the kitchen and gathered together some olive oil and ointments which she hoped would soothe the pain of her son's wounds. She carried the little jars up to his room, where she found him already in bed. She went over to his side and pulled the sheet back. He turned on to his chest while she prepared the oils. Then she removed his night tunic gently for fear of adding to his pain. Having done so, she stared down at his body in disbelief.

The boy's skin was unmarked.

She ran her fingers gently over her son's unblemished body and found it to be as smooth as if he had just bathed. She turned him over, but there was not a mark on him anywhere. Quickly she covered him with the sheet.

'Say nothing of this to your father, and remove the memory of it from your mind forever, because the very telling of it will only make him more angry.'

'Yes, Mother.'

The mother leaned over and blew out the candle by the side of the bed, gathered up the unused oils and tiptoed to the door. At the threshold, she turned in the dim light to look back at her son and said:

'Now I know you were telling the truth, Pontius.'

THE PERFECT
GENTLEMAN

I WOULD NEVER have met Edward Shrimpton if he hadn't needed a towel. He stood naked by my side staring down at a bench in front of him, muttering, 'I could have sworn I left the damn thing there.'

I had just come out of the sauna, swathed in towels, so I took one off my shoulder and passed it to him. He thanked me and put out his hand.

'Edward Shrimpton,' he said smiling. I took his hand and wondered what we must have looked like standing there in the gymnasium locker room of the Metropolitan Club in the early evening, two grown men shaking hands in the nude.

'I don't remember seeing you in the club before,' he added.

'No, I'm an overseas member.'

'Ah, from England. What brings you to New York?'

'I'm pursuing an American novelist whom my company would like to publish in England.'

'And are you having any success?'

'Yes, I think I'll close the deal this week – as long as the agent stops trying to convince me that his author is a cross between Tolstoy and Dickens and should be paid accordingly.'

'Neither was paid particularly well, if I remember correctly,' offered Edward Shrimpton as he energetically rubbed the towel up and down his back.

'A fact I pointed out to the agent at the time who only countered by reminding me that it was my House who had published Dickens originally.'

'I suggest,' said Edward Shrimpton, 'that you *remind* him that the end result turned out to be successful for all concerned.'

'I did, but I fear this agent is more interested in "up front" than posterity.'

'As a banker that's a sentiment of which I could hardly disprove as the one thing we have in common with publishers is that our clients are always trying to tell us a good tale.'

'Perhaps you should sit down and write one of them for me?' I said politely.

'Heaven forbid, you must be sick of being told that there's a book in every one of us so I hasten to assure you that there isn't one in me.'

I laughed, as I found it refreshing not to be informed by a new acquaintance that his memoirs, if only he could find the time to write them, would overnight be one of the world's best sellers.

'Perhaps there's a story in you, but you're just not aware of it,' I suggested.

'If that's the case, I'm afraid it's passed me by.'

Mr Shrimpton re-emerged from behind the row of

little tin cubicles and handed me back my towel. He was now fully dressed and stood, I would have guessed, a shade under six feet. He wore a Wall Street banker's pinstripe suit and, although he was nearly bald, he had a remarkable physique for a man who must have been well into his sixties. Only his thick white moustache gave away his true age, and would have been more in keeping with a retired English colonel than a New York banker.

'Are you going to be in New York long?' he inquired, as he took a small leather case from his inside pocket and removed a pair of half-moon spectacles and placed them on the end of his nose.

'Just for the week.'

'I don't suppose you're free for lunch tomorrow, by any chance?' he inquired, peering over the top of his glasses.

'Yes, I am. I certainly can't face another meal with that agent.'

'Good, good, then why don't you join me and I can follow the continuing drama of capturing the elusive American Author?'

'And perhaps I'll discover there is a story in you after all.'

'Not a hope,' he said, 'you would be backing a loser if you depend on that,' and once again he offered his hand. 'One o'clock, members' dining room suit you?'

'One o'clock, members' dining room,' I repeated.

As he left the locker room I walked over to the

mirror and straightened my tie. I was dining that night with Eric McKenzie, a publishing friend, who had originally proposed me for membership of the club. To be accurate, Eric McKenzie was a friend of my father rather than myself. They had met just before the war while on holiday in Portugal and when I was elected to the club, soon after my father's retirement, Eric took it upon himself to have dinner with me whenever I was in New York. One's parents' generation never see one as anything but a child who will always be in need of constant care and attention. As he was a contemporary of my father, Eric must have been nearly seventy and, although hard of hearing and slightly stooped, he was always amusing and good company, even if he did continually ask me if I was aware that his grandfather was Scottish.

As I strapped on my watch, I checked that he was due to arrive in a few minutes. I put on my jacket and strolled out into the hall to find that he was already there, waiting for me. Eric was killing time by reading the out-of-date club notices. Americans, I have observed, can always be relied upon to arrive early or late; never on time. I stood staring at the stooping man, whose hair but for a few strands had now turned silver. His three-piece suit had a button missing on the jacket which reminded me that his wife had died last year. After another thrust-out hand and exchange of welcomes, we took the lift to the second floor and walked to the dining room.

The members' dining room at the Metropolitan

differs little from any other men's club. It has a fair sprinkling of old leather chairs, old carpets, old portraits and old members. A waiter guided us to a corner table which overlooked Central Park. We ordered, and then settled back to discuss all the subjects I found I usually cover with an acquaintance I only have the chance to catch up with a couple of times a year – our families, children, mutual friends, work; baseball and cricket. By the time we had reached cricket we had also reached coffee, so we strolled down to the far end of the room and made ourselves comfortable in two well-worn leather chairs. When the coffee arrived I ordered two brandies and watched Eric unwrap a large Cuban cigar. Although they displayed a West Indian band on the outside, I knew they were Cuban because I had picked them up for him from a tobacconist in St James's, Piccadilly, which specialises in changing the labels for its American customers. I have often thought that they must be the only shop in the world that changes labels with the sole purpose of making a superior product appear inferior. I am certain my wine merchant does it the other way round.

While Eric was attempting to light the cigar, my eyes wandered to a board on the wall. To be more accurate it was a highly polished wooden plaque with oblique golden lettering painted on it, honouring those men who over the years had won the club's Backgammon Championship. I glanced idly down the list, not expecting to see anybody with whom I would be

familiar, when I was brought up by the name of
Edward Shrimpton. Once in the late thirties he had
been the runner-up.

'That's interesting,' I said.

'What is?' asked Eric, now wreathed in enough
smoke to have puffed himself out of Grand Central
Station.

'Edward Shrimpton was runner-up in the club's
Backgammon Championship in the late thirties. I'm
having lunch with him tomorrow.'

'I didn't realise you knew him.'

'I didn't until this afternoon,' I said, and then
explained how we had met.

Eric laughed and turned to stare up at the board.
Then he added, rather mysteriously: 'That's a night
I'm never likely to forget.'

'Why?' I asked.

Eric hesitated, and looked uncertain of himself
before continuing: 'Too much water has passed under
the bridge for anyone to care now.' He paused again,
as a hot piece of ash fell to the floor and added to the
burn marks that made their own private pattern in
the carpet. 'Just before the war Edward Shrimpton
was among the best half dozen backgammon players
in the world. In fact, it must have been around that
time he won the unofficial world championship in
Monte Carlo.'

'And he couldn't win the club championship?'

'Couldn't would be the wrong word, dear boy.

"Didn't" might be more accurate.' Eric lapsed into another preoccupied silence.

'Are you going to explain?' I asked, hoping he would continue, 'or am I to be left like a child who wants to know who killed Cock Robin?'

'All in good time, but first allow me to get this damn cigar started.'

I remained silent and four matches later he said, 'Before I begin, take a look at the man sitting over there in the corner with the young blonde.'

I turned and glanced back towards the dining room area, and saw a man attacking a porterhouse steak. He looked about the same age as Eric and wore a smart new suit that was unable to disguise that he had a weight problem: only his tailor could have smiled at him with any pleasure. He was seated opposite a slight, not unattractive strawberry blonde of half his age who could have trodden on a beetle and failed to crush it.

'What an unlikely pair. Who are they?'

'Harry Newman and his fourth wife. They're always the same. The wives I mean – blonde hair, blue eyes, ninety pounds, and dumb. I can never understand why any man gets divorced only to marry a carbon copy of the original.'

'Where does Edward Shrimpton fit into the jig-saw?' I asked, trying to guide Eric back on to the subject.

'Patience, patience,' said my host, as he relit his

cigar for the second time. 'At your age you've far more time to waste than I have.'

I laughed and picked up the cognac nearest to me and swirled the brandy around in my cupped hands.

'Harry Newman,' continued Eric, now almost hidden in smoke, 'was the fellow who beat Edward Shrimpton in the final of the club championship that year, although in truth he was never in the same class as Edward.'

'Do explain,' I said, as I looked up at the board to check that it was Newman's name that preceded Edward Shrimpton's.

'Well,' said Eric, 'after the semi-final, which Edward had won with consummate ease, we all assumed the final would only be a formality. Harry had always been a good player, but as I had been the one to lose to him in the semi-finals, I knew he couldn't hope to survive a contest with Edward Shrimpton. The club final is won by the first man to twenty-one points, and if I had been asked for an opinion at the time I would have reckoned the result would end up around 21–5 in Edward's favour. Damn cigar,' he said, and lit it for a third time. Once again I waited impatiently.

'The final is always held on a Saturday night, and poor Harry over there,' said Eric, pointing his cigar towards the far corner of the room while depositing some more ash on the floor, 'who all of us thought was doing rather well in the insurance business, had a bankruptcy notice served on him the Monday morning before the final – I might add through no fault of his own. His partner had cashed in his stock without Harry's knowledge, disappeared, and left him with all the bills to pick up. Everyone in the club was sympathetic.

'On the Thursday the press got hold of the story, and for good measure they added that Harry's wife had run off with the partner. Harry didn't show his head in the club all week, and some of us wondered if he would scratch from the final and let Edward win by default as the result was such a foregone conclusion anyway. But the Games Committee received no communication from Harry to suggest the contest was off so they proceeded as though nothing had happened. On the night of the final, I dined with Edward Shrimpton here in the club. He was in fine form. He ate very little and drank nothing but a glass of water. If you had asked me then I wouldn't have put a penny on Harry Newman even if the odds had been ten to one.

'We all dined upstairs on the third floor, as the Committee had cleared this room so that they could seat sixty in a square around the board. The final was due to start at nine o'clock. By twenty to nine there wasn't a seat left in the place, and members were already standing two deep behind the square: it wasn't every day we had the chance to see a world champion in action. By five to nine, Harry still hadn't turned up and some of the members were beginning to get a little restless. As nine o'clock chimed, the referee went

over to Edward and had a word with him. I saw
Edward shake his head in disagreement and walk
away. Just at the point when I thought the referee
would have to be firm and award the match to
Edward, Harry strolled in looking very dapper
adorned in a dinner jacket several sizes smaller than
the suit he is wearing tonight. Edward went straight
up to him, shook him warmly by the hand and
together they walked into the centre of the room.
Even with the throw of the first dice there was a
tension about that match. Members were waiting to
see how Harry would fare in the opening game.'

The intermittent cigar went out again. I leaned
over and struck a match for him.

'Thank you, dear boy. Now, where was I? Oh,
yes, the first game. Well, Edward only just won the
first game and I wondered if he wasn't concentrating
or if perhaps he had become a little too relaxed while
waiting for his opponent. In the second game the dice
ran well for Harry and he won fairly easily. From that
moment on it became a finely fought battle, and by
the time the score had reached 11–9 in Edward's
favour the tension in the room was quite electric. By
the ninth game I began watching more carefully and
noticed that Edward allowed himself to be drawn into
a back game, a small error in judgment that only a
seasoned player would have spotted. I wondered how
many more subtle errors had already passed that I
hadn't observed. Harry went on to win the ninth
making the score 18–17 in his favour. I watched even

more diligently as Edward did just enough to win the tenth game and, with a rash double, just enough to lose the eleventh, bring the score to 20 all, so that everything would depend on the final game. I swear that nobody had left the room that evening, and not one back remained against a chair; some members were even hanging on to the window ledges. The room was now full of drink and thick with cigar smoke, and yet when Harry picked up the dice cup for the last game you could hear the little squares of ivory rattle before they hit the board. The dice ran well for Harry in that final game and Edward only made one small error early on that I was able to pick up; but it was enough to give Harry game, match and championship. After the last throw of the dice everyone in that room, including Edward, gave the new champion a standing ovation.'

'Had many other members worked out what had really happened that night?'

'No, I don't think so,' said Eric. 'And certainly Harry Newman hadn't. The talk afterwards was that Harry had never played a better game in his life and what a worthy champion he was, all the more for the difficulties he laboured under.'

'Did Edward have anything to say?'

'Toughest match he'd been in since Monte Carlo and only hoped he would be given the chance to avenge the defeat next year.'

'But he wasn't,' I said, looking up again at the board. 'He never won the club championship.'

'That's right. After Roosevelt had insisted we help you guys out in England, the club didn't hold the competition again until 1946, and by then Edward had been to war and had lost all interest in the game.'

'And Harry?'

'Oh, Harry. Harry never looked back after that; must have made a dozen deals in the club that night. Within a year he was on top again and even found himself another cute little blonde.'

'What does Edward say about the result now, thirty years later?'

'Do you know that remains a mystery to this day. I have never heard him mention the game once in all that time.'

Eric's cigar had come to the end of its working life and he stubbed the remains out in an ashless ashtray. It obviously acted as a signal to remind him that it was time to go home. He rose a little unsteadily and I walked down with him to the front door.

'Goodbye my boy,' he said, 'do give Edward my best wishes when you have lunch with him tomorrow. And remember not to play him at backgammon. He'd still kill you.'

The next day I arrived in the front hall a few minutes before our appointed time, not sure if Edward Shrimpton would fall into the category of early or late Americans. As the clock struck one, he walked through the door: there has to be an exception to every rule. We agreed to go straight up to lunch since he had to be back in Wall Street for a two-thirty appointment. We stepped into the packed lift, and I pressed the No. 3 button. The doors closed like a tired concertina and the slowest lift in America made its way towards the second floor.

As we entered the dining room, I was amused to see Harry Newman was already there, attacking another steak, while the little blonde lady was nibbling a salad. He waved expansively at Edward Shrimpton, who returned the gesture with a friendly nod. We sat down at a table in the centre of the room and studied the menu. Steak and kidney pie was the dish of the day, which was probably the case in half the men's clubs in the world. Edward wrote down our orders in a neat and legible hand on the little white slip provided by the waiter.

Edward asked me about the author I was chasing and made some penetrating comments about her earlier work, to which I responded as best I could while trying to think of a plot to make him discuss the pre-war backgammon championship, which I considered would make a far better story than anything she had ever written. But he never talked about himself once during the meal, so I despaired. Finally, staring up at the plaque on the wall, I said clumsily:

'I see you were runner-up in the club backgammon championship just before the war. You must have been a fine player.'

'No, not really,' he replied. 'Not many people

bothered about the game in those days. There is a different attitude today with all the youngsters taking it so seriously.'

'What about the champion?' I said, pushing my luck.

'Harry Newman? – He was an outstanding player, and particularly good under pressure. He's the gentleman who greeted us when we came in. That's him sitting over there in the corner with his wife.'

I looked obediently towards Mr Newman's table but my host added nothing more so I gave up. We ordered coffee and that would have been the end of Edward's story if Harry Newman and his wife had not headed straight for us after they had finished their lunch. Edward was on his feet long before I was, despite my twenty-year advantage. Harry Newman looked even bigger standing up, and his little blonde wife looked more like the dessert than his spouse.

'Ed,' he boomed, 'how are you?'

'I'm well, thank you, Harry,' Edward replied. 'May I introduce my guest?'

'Nice to know you,' he said. 'Rusty, I've always wanted you to meet Ed Shrimpton because I've talked to you about him so often in the past.'

'Have you, Harry?' she squeaked.

'Of course. You remember, honey. Ed is up there on the backgammon honours board,' he said, pointing a stubby finger towards the plaque. 'With only one name in front of him and that's mine. And Ed was the world champion at the time. Isn't that right, Ed?'

'That's right, Harry.'

'So I suppose I really should have been the world champion that year, wouldn't you say?'

'I couldn't quarrel with that conclusion,' replied Edward.

'On the big day, Rusty, when it really mattered, and the pressure was on, I beat him fair and square.'

I stood in silent disbelief as Edward Shrimpton still volunteered no disagreement.

'We must play again for old times' sake, Ed,' the fat man continued. 'It would be fun to see if you could beat me now. Mind you, I'm a bit rusty nowadays, Rusty.' He laughed loudly at his own joke but his spouse's face remained blank. I wondered how long it would be before there was a fifth Mrs Newman.

'It's been great to see you again, Ed. Take care of yourself.'

'Thank you Harry,' said Edward.

We both sat down again as Newman and his wife left the dining room. Our coffee was now cold so we ordered a fresh pot. The room was almost empty and when I had poured two cups for us Edward leaned over to me conspiratorially and whispered: 'Now there's a hell of a story for a publisher like you,' he said. 'I mean the real truth about Harry Newman.'

My ears pricked up as I anticipated his version of the story of what had actually happened on the night of that pre-war backgammon championship over thirty years before.

'Really?' I said, innocently.

'Oh, yes,' said Edward. 'It was not as simple as you might think. Just before the war Harry was let down very badly by his business partner who not only stole his money, but for good measure his wife as well. The very week that he was at his lowest he won the club backgammon championship, put all his troubles behind him and, against the odds, made a brilliant come-back. You know, he's worth a fortune today. Now, wouldn't you agree that that would make one hell of a story?'

ONE-NIGHT STAND

THE TWO MEN had first met at the age of five when they were placed side by side at school, for no more compelling reason than that their names, Thompson and Townsend, came one after each other on the class register. They soon became best friends, a tie which at that age is more binding than any marriage. After passing their eleven-plus examination they proceeded to the local grammar school with no Timpsons, Tooleys or Tomlinsons to divide them and, having completed seven years in that academic institution, reached an age when one either has to go to work or to university. They opted for the latter on the grounds that work should be put off until the last possible moment. Happily, they both possessed enough brains and native wit to earn themselves places at Durham University to read English.

Undergraduate life turned out to be as sociable as primary school. They both enjoyed English, tennis, cricket, good food and girls. Luckily, in the last of these predilections they differed only on points of detail. Michael, who was six-foot-two, willowy with dark curly hair, preferred tall, bosomy blondes with blue eyes and long legs. Adrian, a stocky man of five-foot-ten, with straight, sandy hair always fell for small, slim, dark-haired, dark-eyed girls. So whenever Adrian came across a girl that Michael took an interest in or vice versa, whether she was an undergraduate or barmaid, the one would happily exaggerate their friend's virtues. Thus they spent three idyllic years in unison at Durham, gaining considerably more than a Bachelor of Arts degree. As neither of them had impressed the examiners enough to waste a further two years expounding their theories for a PhD they could no longer avoid the real world.

Twin Dick Whittingtons, they set off for London, where Michael joined the BBC as a trainee while Adrian was signed up by Benton & Bowles, the international advertising agency, as an accounts assistant. They acquired a small flat in the Earl's Court Road which they painted orange and brown, and proceeded to live the life of two young blades, for that is undoubtedly how they saw themselves.

Both men spent a further five years in this blissful bachelor state until they each fell for a girl who fulfilled their particular requirements. They were married within weeks of each other: Michael to a tall, blue-eyed blonde whom he met while playing tennis at the Hurlingham Club; Adrian to a slim, dark-eyed, dark-haired executive in charge of the Kellogg's Cornflakes account. Both officiated as the other's best man and each proceeded to sire three children at yearly intervals, and in that again they differed, but as before only on points of detail, Michael having two sons and a daughter, Adrian two daughters and a son. Each became godfather to the other's first-born son.

Marriage hardly separated them in anything as they continued to follow much of their old routine, playing cricket together at weekends in the summer and football in the winter, not to mention regular luncheons during the week.

After the celebration of his tenth wedding anniversary, Michael, now a senior producer with Thames Television, admitted rather coyly to Adrian that he had had his first affair: he had been unable to resist a tall, well-built blonde from the typing pool who was offering more than shorthand at seventy words a minute. Only a few weeks later, Adrian, now a senior account manager with Pearl and Dean, also went under, selecting a journalist from Fleet Street who was seeking some inside information on one of the companies he represented. She became a tax-deductible item. After that, the two men quickly fell back into their old routine. Any help they could give each other was provided unstintingly, creating no conflict of interests because of their different tastes. Their married lives were not suffering – or so they convinced each other – and at thirty-five, having come through the swinging sixties unscathed, they began to make the most of the seventies.

Early in that decade, Thames Television decided to send Michael off to America to edit an ABC film about living in New York, for consumption by British viewers. Adrian, who had always wanted to see the eastern seaboard, did not find it hard to arrange a trip at the same time as he claimed it was necessary for him to carry out some more than usually spurious research for an Anglo-American tobacco company. The two men enjoyed a lively week together in New York, the highlight of which was a party held by ABC on the final evening to view the edited edition of Michael's film on New York, *An Englishman's View of the Big Apple.*

When Michael and Adrian arrived at the ABC studios they found the party was already well under way, and both entered the room together, looking forward to a few drinks and an early night before their journey back to England the next day.

They spotted her at exactly the same moment.

She was of medium height and build, with soft green eyes and auburn hair – a striking combination of both men's fantasies. Without another thought each knew exactly where he desired to end up that particular night and, two minds with but a single idea, they advanced purposefully upon her.

'Hello, my name is Michael Thompson.'

'Hello,' she replied. 'I'm Debbie Kendall.'

'And I'm Adrian Townsend.'

She offered her hand and both tried to grab it. When the party had come to an end, they had, between them, discovered that Debbie Kendall was an ABC floor producer on the evening news spot. She was divorced and had two children who lived with her in New York. But neither of them was any nearer to impressing her, if only because each worked so hard to outdo the other; they both showed off abominably and even squabbled over fetching their new companion her food and drink. In the other's absence they found themselves running down their closest friend in a subtle but damning way.

'Adrian's a nice chap if it wasn't for his drinking,' said Michael.

'Super fellow Michael, such a lovely wife and you should see his three adorable children,' added Adrian.

They both escorted Debbie home and reluctantly left her on the doorstep of her 68th Street apartment. She kissed the two of them perfunctorily on the cheek, thanked them and said goodnight. They walked back to their hotel in silence.

When they reached their room on the nineteenth floor of the Plaza, it was Michael who spoke first.

'I'm sorry,' he said. 'I made a bloody fool of myself.'

'I was every bit as bad,' said Adrian, 'we shouldn't fight over a woman. We never have done in the past.'

'Agreed,' said Michael. 'So why not an honourable compromise?'

'What do you suggest?'

'As we both return to London tomorrow morning, let's agree whichever one of us comes back first . . .'

'Perfect,' said Adrian and they shook hands to seal the bargain, as if they were both back at school playing a cricket match, and had to decide on who should bat first. The deal made, they climbed into their respective beds, and slept soundly.

Once back in London both men did everything in their power to find an excuse for returning to New York. Neither contacted Debbie Kendall by phone or letter as it would have broken their gentleman's agreement, but when the weeks grew to be months both became despondent and it seemed that neither was going to be given the opportunity to return. Then Adrian was invited to Los Angeles to address a media conference. He remained unbearably smug about the whole trip, confident he would be able to drop into New York on the way back to London. It was Michael who discovered that British Airways were offering cheap tickets for wives who accompanied their husbands on a business trip: Adrian was therefore unable to return via New York. Michael breathed a sigh of relief which turned to triumph when he was selected to go to Washington and cover the president's Address to Congress. He suggested to the head of Outside Broadcasts that it would be wise to drop into New York on the way home and strengthen the contacts he had previously made with ABC. The head of Outside Broadcasts agreed, but told Michael he must be back the following day to cover the opening of Parliament.

Adrian phoned up Michael's wife and briefed her on cheap trips to the States when accompanying your husband. 'How kind of you to be so thoughtful Adrian but alas my school never allows time off during term, and in any case,' she added, 'I have a dreadful fear of flying.'

Michael was very understanding about his wife's phobia and went off to book a single ticket.

Michael flew into Washington on the following Monday and called Debbie Kendall from his hotel room, wondering if she would even remember the two vainglorious Englishmen she had briefly met some months before, and if she did whether she would also recall which one he was. He dialled nervously and listened to the ringing tone. Was she in, was she even in New York? At last a click and a soft voice said hello.

'Hello, Debbie, it's Michael Thompson.'

'Hello, Michael. What a nice surprise. Are you in New York?'

'No, Washington, but I'm thinking of flying up. You wouldn't be free for dinner on Thursday by any chance?'

'Let me just check my diary.'

Michael held his breath as he waited. It seemed like hours.

'Yes, that seems to be fine.'

'Fantastic. Shall I pick you up around eight?'

'Yes, thank you, Michael. I'll look forward to seeing you then.'

Heartened by this early success Michael immediately penned a telegram of commiseration to Adrian on his sad loss. Adrian didn't reply.

Michael took the shuttle up to New York on the Thursday afternoon as soon as he had finished editing the President's speech for the London office. After settling into another hotel room – this time insisting on a double bed just in case Debbie's children were at home – he had a long bath and a slow shave, cutting himself twice and slapping on a little too much aftershave. He rummaged around for his most telling tie, shirt and suit, and after he had finished dressing he studied himself in the mirror, carefully combing his freshly washed hair to make the long thin strands appear casual as well as cover the parts where his hair was beginning to recede. After a final check, he was able to convince himself that he looked less than his thirty-eight years. Michael then took the lift down to the ground floor, and stepping out of the Plaza on to a neon-lit Fifth Avenue he headed jauntily towards 68th Street. En route, he acquired a dozen roses from a little shop at the corner of 65th Street and Madison Avenue and, humming to himself, proceeded confidently. He arrived at the front door of Debbie Kendall's little brownstone at eight-five.

When Debbie opened the door, Michael thought she looked even more beautiful than he had remembered. She was wearing a long blue dress with a frilly white silk collar and cuffs that covered every part of her body from neck to ankles and yet she could not have been more desirable. She wore almost no makeup except a touch of lipstick that Michael already had plans to remove. Her green eyes sparkled.

'Say something,' she said smiling.

'You look quite stunning, Debbie,' was all he could think of as he handed her the roses.

'How sweet of you,' she replied and invited him in.

Michael followed her into the kitchen where she hammered the long stems and arranged the flowers in a porcelain vase. She then led him into the living room, where she placed the roses on an oval table beside a photograph of two small boys.

'Have we time for a drink?'

'Sure. I've booked a table at Elaine's for eight-thirty.'

'My favourite restaurant,' she said, with a smile that revealed a small dimple on her cheek. Without asking, Debbie poured two whiskies and handed one of them to Michael.

What a good memory she has, he thought, as he nervously kept picking up and putting down his glass, like a teenager on his first date. When Michael had eventually finished his drink, Debbie suggested that they should leave.

'Elaine wouldn't keep a table free for one minute, even if you were Henry Kissinger.'

Michael laughed, and helped her on with her coat. As she unlatched the door, he realised there was no baby-sitter or sound of children. They must be staying with their father, he thought. Once on the street, he hailed a cab and directed the driver to 87th and 2nd. Michael had never been to Elaine's before. The restaurant had been recommended by a friend from ABC who had assured him: 'That joint will give you more than half a chance.'

As they entered the crowded room and waited by the bar for the maître d', Michael could see it was the type of place that was frequented by the rich and famous and wondered if his pocket could stand the expense and, more importantly, whether such an outlay would turn out to be a worthwhile investment.

A waiter guided them to a small table at the back of the room, where they both had another whisky while they studied the menu. When the waiter returned to take their order, Debbie wanted no first course, just the veal piccate, so Michael ordered the same for himself. She refused the addition of garlic butter. Michael allowed his expectations to rise slightly.

'How's Adrian?' she asked.

'Oh, as well as can be expected,' Michael replied. 'He sends you his love, of course.' He emphasised the word love.

'How kind of him to remember me, and please return mine. What brings you to New York this time, Michael? Another film?'

'No. New York may well have become everybody's second city, but this time I only came to see you.'

'To see me?'

'Yes, I had a tape to edit while I was in Washington, but I always knew I could be through with that by lunch today so I hoped you would be free to spend an evening with me.'

'I'm flattered.'

'You shouldn't be.'

She smiled. The veal arrived.

'Looks good,' said Michael.

'Tastes good, too,' said Debbie. 'When do you fly home?'

'Tomorrow morning, eleven o'clock flight, I'm afraid.'

'Not left yourself time to do much in New York.'

'I only came up to see you,' Michael repeated. Debbie continued eating her veal. 'Why would any man want to divorce you, Debbie?'

'Oh, nothing very original, I'm afraid. He fell in love with a twenty-two year old blonde and left his thirty-two year old wife.'

'Silly man. He should have had an affair with the twenty-two year old blonde and remained faithful to his thirty-two year old wife.'

'Isn't that a contradiction in terms?'

'Oh, no, I don't think so. I've never thought it unnatural to desire someone else. After all, it's a long life to go through and be expected never to want another woman.'

'I'm not so sure I agree with you,' said Debbie thoughtfully. 'I would like to have remained faithful to one man.'

Oh hell, thought Michael, not a very auspicious philosophy.

'Do you miss him?' he tried again.

'Yes, sometimes. It's true what they say in the glossy menopause magazines, one can be very lonely when you suddenly find yourself on your own.'

That sounds more promising, thought Michael, and he heard himself saying: 'Yes, I can understand that, but someone like you shouldn't have to stay on your own for very long.'

Debbie made no reply.

Michael refilled her glass of wine nearly to the brim, hoping he could order a second bottle before she finished her veal.

'Are you trying to get me drunk, Michael?'

'If you think it will help,' he replied laughing.

Debbie didn't laugh. Michael tried again.

'Been to the theatre lately?'

'Yes, I went to *Evita* last week. I loved it' – wonder who took you, thought Michael – 'but my mother fell asleep in the middle of the second act. I think I shall have to go and see it on my own a second time.'

'I only wish I was staying long enough to take you.'

'That would be fun,' she said.

'Whereas I shall have to be satisfied with seeing the show in London.'

'With your wife.'

'Another bottle of wine please, waiter.'

'No more for me, Michael, really.'

'Well, you can help me out a little.' The waiter faded away. 'Do you get to England at all yourself?' asked Michael.

'No, I've only been once when Roger, my ex, took the whole family. I loved the country. It fulfilled every one of my hopes but I'm afraid we did what all Americans are expected to do. The Tower of London, Buckingham Palace, followed by Oxford and Stratford, before flying on to Paris.'

'A sad way to see England; there's so much more I could have shown you.'

'I suspect when the English come to America they don't see much outside of New York, Washington, Los Angeles, and perhaps San Francisco.'

'I agree,' said Michael, not wanting to disagree. The waiter cleared away their empty plates.

'Can I tempt you with a dessert, Debbie?'

'No, no, I'm trying to lose some weight.' Michael slipped a hand gently around her waist. 'You don't need to,' he said. 'You feel just perfect.'

She laughed. He smiled.

'Nevertheless, I'll stick to coffee, please.'

'A little brandy?'

'No, thank you, just coffee.'

'Black?'

'Black.'

'Coffee for two, please,' Michael said to the hovering waiter.

'I wish I had taken you somewhere a little quieter and less ostentatious,' he said, turning back to Debbie.

'Why?'

Michael took her hand. It felt cold. 'I would like to have said things to you that shouldn't be listened to by people on the next table.'

'I don't think anyone would be shocked by what they overheard at Elaine's, Michael.'

'Very well then. Do you believe in love at first sight?'

'No, but I think it's possible to be physically attracted to a person on first meeting them.'

'Well I must confess, I was to you.'

Again she made no reply.

The coffee arrived and Debbie released her hand to take a sip. Michael followed suit.

'There were one hundred and fifty women in that room the night we met, Debbie, and my eyes never left you once.'

'Even during the film?'

'I'd seen the damn thing a hundred times. I feared I might never see you again.'

'I'm touched.'

'Why should you be? It must be happening to you all the time.'

'Now and then,' she said. 'But I haven't taken anyone too seriously since my husband left me.'

'I'm sorry.'

'No need. It's just not that easy to get over someone you've lived with for ten years. I doubt if many divorcees are quite that willing to jump into bed with the first man who comes along as all the latest films suggest.'

Michael took her hand again, hoping fervently he did not fall into that category.

'It's been such a lovely evening. Why don't we stroll down to the Carlyle and listen to Bobby Short?' Michael's ABC friend had recommended the move if he felt he was still in with a chance.

'Yes, I'd enjoy that,' said Debbie.

Michael called for the bill – eighty-seven dollars. Had it been his wife sitting on the other side of the table he would have checked each item carefully, but not on this occasion. He just left five twenty dollar bills on a side plate and didn't wait for the change. As they stepped out on to 2nd Avenue, he took Debbie's hand and together they started walking downtown. On Madison Avenue they stopped in front of shop windows and he bought her a fur coat, a Cartier watch and a Balenciaga dress. Debbie thought it was lucky that all the stores were closed.

They arrived at the Carlyle just in time for the eleven o'clock show. A waiter, flashing a pen torch, guided them through the little dark room on the ground floor to a table in the corner. Michael ordered a bottle of champagne as Bobby Short struck up a chord and drawled out the words: 'Georgia, Georgia, oh, my sweet . . .' Michael, now unable to speak to Debbie above the noise of the band, satisfied himself with holding her hand and when the entertainer sang,

'This time we almost made the pieces fit, didn't we, gal?' he leaned over and kissed her on the cheek. She turned and smiled – was it faintly conspiratorial, or was he just wishful thinking? – and then she sipped her champagne. On the dot of twelve, Bobby Short shut the piano lid and said, 'Goodnight, my friends, the time has come for all you good people to go to bed – and some of you naughty ones too.' Michael laughed a little too loud but was pleased that Debbie laughed as well.

They strolled down Madison Avenue to 68th Street chatting about inconsequential affairs, while Michael's thoughts were of only one affair. When they arrived at her 68th Street apartment, she took out her latch key.

'Would you like a nightcap?' she asked without any suggestive intonation.

'No more drink, thank you, Debbie, but I would certainly appreciate a coffee.'

She led him into the living room.

'The flowers have lasted well,' she teased, and left him to make the coffee. Michael amused himself by flicking through an old copy of *Time* magazine, looking at the pictures, not taking in the words. She returned after a few minutes with a coffee pot and two small cups on a lacquered tray. She poured the coffee, black again, and then sat down next to Michael on the couch, drawing one leg underneath her while turning slightly towards him. Michael downed his coffee in two gulps, scalding his mouth slightly. Then, putting down his cup, he leaned over and kissed her on the mouth. She was still clutching on to her coffee cup. Her eyes opened briefly as she manoeuvred the cup on to a side table. After another long kiss she broke away from him.

'I ought to make an early start in the morning.'

'So should I,' said Michael, 'but I am more worried about not seeing you again for a long time.'

'What a nice thing to say,' Debbie replied.

'No, I just care,' he said, before kissing her again.

This time she responded; he slipped one hand on to her breast while the other one began to undo the row of little buttons down the back of her dress. She broke away again.

'Don't let's do anything we'll regret.'

'I know we won't regret it,' said Michael.

He then kissed her on the neck and shoulders, slipping her dress off as he moved deftly down her body to her breast, delighted to find she wasn't wearing a bra.

'Shall we go upstairs, Debbie? I'm too old to make love on the sofa.'

Without speaking, she rose and led him by the hand to her bedroom which smelled faintly and deliciously of the scent she herself was wearing.

She switched on a small bedside light and took off the rest of her clothes, letting them fall where she stood. Michael never once took his eyes off her body as he undressed clumsily on the other side of the bed. He slipped under the sheets and quickly joined her.

When they had finished making love, an experience he hadn't enjoyed as much for a long time, he lay there pondering on the fact that she had succumbed at all, especially on their first date.

They lay silently in each other's arms before making love for a second time, which was every bit as delightful as the first. Michael then fell into a deep sleep.

He woke first the next morning and stared across at the beautiful woman who lay by his side. The digital clock on the bedside table showed seven-o-three. He touched her forehead lightly with his lips and began to stroke her hair. She woke lazily and smiled up at him. Then they made morning love, slowly, gently, but every bit as pleasing as the night before. He didn't speak as she slipped out of bed and ran a bath for him before going to the kitchen to prepare breakfast. Michael relaxed in the hot bath crooning a Bobby Short number at the top of his voice. How he wished that Adrian could see him now. He dried himself and dressed before joining Debbie in the smart little kitchen where they shared breakfast together. Eggs, bacon, toast, English marmalade, and steaming black coffee. Debbie then had a bath and dressed while Michael read the *New York Times*. When she reappeared in the living room wearing a smart coral dress, he was sorry to be leaving so soon.

'We must leave now, or you'll miss your flight.'

Michael rose reluctantly and Debbie drove him back to his hotel, where he quickly threw his clothes into a suitcase, settled the bill for his unslept-in double bed and joined her back in the car. On the journey to the airport they chatted about the coming elections and pumpkin pie almost as if they had been married for years or were both avoiding admitting the previous night had ever happened.

Debbie dropped Michael in front of the Pan Am building and put the car in the parking lot before joining him at the check-in counter. They waited for his flight to be called.

'Pan American announces the departure of their Flight Number 006 to London Heathrow. Will all passengers please proceed with their boarding passes to Gate Number Nine?'

When they reached the 'passengers-only' barrier, Michael took Debbie briefly in his arms. 'Thank you for a memorable evening,' he said.

'No, it is I who must thank you, Michael,' she replied as she kissed him on the cheek.

'I must confess I hadn't thought it would end up quite like that,' he said.

'Why not?' she asked.

'Not easy to explain,' he replied, searching for words that would flatter and not embarrass. 'Let's say I was surprised that . . .'

'You were surprised that we ended up in bed together on our first night? You shouldn't be.'

'I shouldn't?'

'No, there's a simple enough explanation. My friends all told me when I got divorced to find myself a man and have a one-night stand. The idea sounded fun but I didn't like the thought of the men in New York thinking I was easy.' She touched him gently on the side of his face. 'So when I met you and Adrian, both safely living over three thousand miles away, I thought to myself "whichever one of you comes back first" . . .'

THE CENTURY

'LIFE IS A GAME', said A. T. Pierson, thus immortalising himself without actually having to do any real work. Though E. M. Forster showed more insight when he wrote 'Fate is the Umpire, and Hope is the Ball, which is why I will never score a century at Lord's.'

When I was a freshman at university, my room mate invited me to have dinner in a sporting club to which he belonged called Vincent's. Such institutions do not differ greatly around the Western world. They are always brimful of outrageously fit, healthy young animals, whose sole purpose in life seems to be to challenge the opposition of some neighbouring institution to ridiculous feats of physical strength. My host's main rivals, he told me with undergraduate fervour, came from a high-thinking, plain-living establishment which had dozed the unworldly centuries away in the flat, dull, fen country of England, cartographically described on the map as Cambridge. Now the ultimate ambition of men such as my host was simple enough: in whichever sport they aspired to beat the 'Tabs' the select few were rewarded with a Blue. As there is no other way of gaining this distinction at either Oxford or Cambridge, every place in the team is contested for with considerable zeal. A man may be selected and indeed play in every other match of the season for the university, even go on to represent his country, but if he does not play in the Oxford and Cambridge match, he cannot describe himself as a Blue.

My story concerns a delightful character I met that evening when I dined as a guest at Vincent's. The undergraduate to whom I refer was in his final year. He came from that part of the world that we still dared to describe in those days (without a great deal of thought) as the colonies. He was an Indian by birth, and the son of a man whose name in England was a household word, if not a legend, for he had captained Oxford and India at cricket, which meant that outside of the British Commonwealth he was about as well known as Babe Ruth is to the English. The young man's father had added to his fame by scoring a century at Lord's when captaining the university cricket side against Cambridge. In fact, when he went on to captain India against England he used to take pride in wearing his cream sweater with the wide dark blue band around the neck and waist. The son, experts predicted, would carry on in the family tradition. He was in much the same mould as his father, tall and rangy with jet-black hair, and as a cricketer, a fine right-handed batsman and a useful left-arm spin bowler. (Those of you who have never been able to comprehend the English language let alone the game of cricket might well be tempted to ask why not a fine right-arm batsman and a useful left-handed spin bowler. The English, however, always cover such silly questions with the words: Tradition, dear boy, tradition.)

The young Indian undergraduate, like his father, had come up to Oxford with considerably more interest in defeating Cambridge than the examiners. As a freshman, he had played against most of the English county sides, notching up a century against three of them, and on one occasion taking five wickets in an innings. A week before the big match against Cambridge, the skipper informed him that he had won his Blue and that the names of the chosen eleven would be officially announced in *The Times* the following day. The young man telegraphed his father in Calcutta with the news, and then went off for a celebratory dinner at Vincent's. He entered the Club's dining room in high spirits to the traditional round of applause afforded to a new Blue, and as he was about to take a seat he observed the boat crew, all nine of them, around a circular table at the far end of the room. He walked across to the captain of boats and remarked: 'I thought you chaps sat one behind each other.'

Within seconds, four thirteen-stone men were sitting on the new Blue while the cox poured a jug of cold water over his head.

'If you fail to score a century', said one oar, 'we'll use hot water next time.' When the four oars had returned to their table, the cricketer rose slowly, straightened his tie in mock indignation, and as he passed the crew's table, patted the five-foot one inch, 102-pound cox on the head and said, 'Even losing teams should have a mascot.'

This time they only laughed but it was in the very act of patting the cox on the head that he first noticed his thumb felt a little bruised and he commented on the fact to the wicket-keeper who had joined him for dinner. A large entrecôte steak arrived and he found as he picked up his knife that he was unable to grip the handle properly. He tried to put the inconvenience out of his mind, assuming all would be well by the following morning, but the next day he woke in considerable pain and found to his dismay that the thumb was not only black but also badly swollen. After reporting the news to his captain he took the first available train to London for a consultation with a Harley Street specialist. As the carriage rattled through Berkshire, he read in *The Times* that he had been awarded his Blue.

The specialist studied the offending thumb for some considerable time and expressed his doubt that the young man would be able to hold a ball, let alone a bat, for at least a fortnight. The prognosis turned out to be accurate and our hero sat disconsolate in the stand at Lord's, watching Oxford lose the match and the twelfth man gain his Blue. His father, who had flown over from Calcutta especially for the encounter, offered his condolences, pointing out that he still had two years left in which to gain the honour.

As his second Trinity term approached, even the young man forgot his disappointment and in the opening match of the season against Somerset scored a memorable century, full of cuts and drives that reminded *aficionados* of his father. The son had been made Secretary of cricket in the closed season as it was universally acknowledged that only bad luck and the boat crew had stopped him from reaping his just reward as a freshman. Once again, he played in every fixture before the needle match, but in the last four games against county teams he failed to score more than a dozen runs and did not take a single wicket, while his immediate rivals excelled themselves. He was going through a lean patch, and was the first to agree with his captain that with so much talent around that year he should not be risked against Cambridge. Once again he watched Oxford lose the Blues match and his opposite number the Cambridge Secretary, Robin Oakley, score a faultless century. A man well into his sixties sporting an MCC tie came up to the young Indian during the game, patted him on the shoulder, and remarked that he would never forget the day his father had scored a hundred against Cambridge: it didn't help.

When the cricketer returned for his final year, he was surprised and delighted to be selected by his fellow teammates to be captain, an honour never previously afforded to a man who had not been awarded the coveted Blue. His peers recognised his outstanding work as Secretary and knew if he could reproduce the form of his freshman year he would undoubtedly not only win a Blue but go on to represent his country.

The tradition at Oxford is that in a man's final year he does not play cricket until he has sat Schools, which leaves him enough time to play in the last three county matches before the Varsity match. But as the new captain had no interest in graduating, he bypassed tradition and played cricket from the opening day of the summer season. His touch never failed him for he batted magnificently and on those rare occasions when he did have an off-day with the bat, he bowled superbly. During the term he led Oxford to victory over three county sides, and his team looked well set for their revenge in the Varsity match.

As the day of the match drew nearer, the cricket correspondent of *The Times* wrote that anyone who had seen him bat this season felt sure that the young Indian would follow his father into the record books by scoring a century against Cambridge: but the correspondent did add that he might be vulnerable against the early attack of Bill Potter, the Cambridge fast bowler.

Everyone wanted the Oxford captain to succeed,

for he was one of those rare and gifted men whose charm creates no enemies.

When he announced his Blues team to the press, he did not send a telegram to his father for fear that the news might bring bad luck, and for good measure he did not speak to any member of the boat crew for the entire week leading up to the match. The night before the final encounter he retired to bed at seven although he did not sleep.

On the first morning of the three-day match, the sun shone brightly in an almost cloudless sky and by eleven o'clock a fair sized crowd were already in their seats. The two captains in open necked white shirts, spotless white pressed trousers and freshly creamed white boots came out to study the pitch before they tossed. Robin Oakley of Cambridge won and elected to bat.

By lunch on the first day Cambridge had scored seventy-nine for three and in the early afternoon, when his fast bowlers were tired from their second spell and had not managed an early breakthrough, the captain put himself on. When he was straight, the ball didn't reach a full length, and when he bowled a full length, he was never straight; he quickly took himself off. His less established bowlers managed the necessary breakthrough and Cambridge were all out an hour after tea for 208.

The Oxford openers took the crease at ten to six;

forty minutes to see through before close of play on the first day. The captain sat padded up on the pavilion balcony, waiting to be called upon only if a wicket fell. His instructions had been clear: no heroics, bat out the forty minutes so that Oxford could start afresh the next morning with all ten wickets intact. With only one over left before the close of play, the young freshman opener had his middle stump removed by Bill Potter, the Cambridge fast bowler. Oxford were eleven for one. The captain came to the crease with only four balls left to face before the clock would show six-thirty. He took his usual guard, middle and leg, and prepared himself to face the fastest man in the Cambridge side. Potter's first delivery came rocketing down and was just short of a length, moving away outside the off stump. The ball nicked the corner of the bat – or was it pad? – and carried to first slip, who dived to his right and took the catch low down. Eleven Cambridge men screamed 'Howzat'. Was the captain going to be out – for a duck? Without waiting for the umpire's decision he turned and walked back to the pavilion, allowing no expression to appear on his face though he continually hit the side of his pad with his bat. As he climbed the steps he saw his father, sitting on his own in the members' enclosure. He walked on through the Long Room, to cries of 'Bad luck, old fellow' from men holding slopping pints of beer, and 'Better luck in the second innings' from large-bellied old Blues.

The next day, Oxford kept their heads down and

put together a total of 181 runs, leaving themselves only a twenty-seven run deficit. When Cambridge batted for a second time they pressed home their slight advantage and the captain's bowling figures ended up as eleven overs, no maidens, no wickets, forty-two runs. He took his team off the field at the end of play on the second day with Cambridge standing at 167 for seven, Robin Oakley the Cambridge captain having notched up a respectable sixty-three not out, and he looked well set for a century.

On the morning of the third day, the Oxford quickies removed the last three Cambridge wickets for nineteen runs in forty minutes and Robin Oakley ran out of partners, and left the field with eighty-nine not out. The Oxford captain was the first to commiserate with him. 'At least you notched a hundred last year,' he added.

'True,' replied Oakley, 'So perhaps it's your turn this year. But not if I've got anything to do with it!'

The Oxford captain smiled at the thought of scoring a century when his team only needed 214 runs at a little under a run a minute to win the match.

The two Oxford opening batsmen began their innings just before midday and remained together until the last over before lunch when the freshman was once again clean bowled by Cambridge's ace fast bowler, Bill Potter. The captain sat on the balcony nervously, padded up and ready. He looked down on the bald head of his father, who was chatting to a former captain of England. Both men had scored centuries in the Varsity match. The captain pulled on his gloves and walked slowly down the pavilion steps, trying to look casual; he had never felt more nervous in his life. As he passed his father, the older man turned his sun-burned face towards his only child and smiled. The crowd warmly applauded the captain all the way to the crease. He took guard, middle and leg again, and prepared to face the attack. The eager Potter who had despatched the captain so brusquely in the first innings came thundering down towards him hoping to be the cause of a pair. He delivered a magnificent first ball that swung in from his legs and beat the captain all ends up, hitting him with a thud on the front pad.

'Howzat?' screamed Potter and the entire Cambridge side as they leaped in the air.

The captain looked up apprehensively at the umpire who took his hands out of his pockets and moved a pebble from one palm to the other to remind him that another ball had been bowled. But he affected no interest in the appeal. A sigh of relief went up from the members in the pavilion. The captain managed to see through the rest of the over and returned to lunch nought not out, with his side twenty-four for one.

After lunch Potter returned to the attack. He rubbed the leather ball on his red-stained flannels and hurled himself forward, looking even fiercer than he had at start of play. He released his missile with every ounce of venom he possessed, but in so doing he tried a little too hard and the delivery was badly short. The captain leaned back and hooked the ball to the Tavern boundary for four, and from that moment he never looked as if anyone would prise him from the crease. He reached his fifty in seventy-one minutes, and at ten past four the Oxford team came into tea with the score at 171 for five and the skipper on eighty-two not out. The young man did not look at his father as he climbed the steps of the pavilion. He needed another eighteen runs before he could do that and by then his team would be safe. He ate and drank nothing at tea, and spoke to no one.

After twenty minutes a bell rang and the eleven Cambridge men returned to the field. A minute later, the captain and his partner walked back out to the crease, their open white shirts flapping in the breeze. Two hours left for the century and victory. The captain's partner only lasted another five balls and the captain himself seemed to have lost that natural flow he had possessed before tea, struggling into the nineties with ones and twos. The light was getting bad and it took him a full thirty minutes to reach ninety-nine, by which time he had lost another partner: 194 for seven. He remained on ninety-nine for twelve minutes, when Robin Oakley the Cambridge captain took the new ball and brought his ace speed man back into the attack.

Then there occurred one of the most amazing incidents I have ever witnessed in a cricket match. Robin Oakley set an attacking field for the new ball –

three slips, a gully, cover point, mid off, mid on, mid wicket and a short square leg, a truly vicious circle. He then tossed the ball to Potter who knew this would be his last chance to capture the Oxford captain's wicket and save the match; once he had scored the century he would surely knock off the rest of the runs in a matter of minutes. The sky was becoming bleak as a bank of dark clouds passed over the ground, but this was no time to leave the field for bad light. Potter shone the new ball once more on his white trousers and thundered up to hurl a delivery that the captain jabbed at and missed. One or two fielders raised their hands without appealing. Potter returned to his mark, shining the ball with even more relish and left a red blood-like stain down the side of his thigh. The second ball, a yorker, beat the captain completely and must have missed the off stump by about an inch; there was a general sigh around the ground. The third ball hit the captain on the middle of the pad and the eleven Cambridge men threw their arms in the air and screamed for leg before wicket but the umpire was not moved. The captain jabbed at the fourth ball and it carried tentatively to mid on, where Robin Oakley had placed himself a mere twenty yards in front of the bat, watching his adversary in disbelief as he set off for a run he could never hope to complete. His batting partner remained firmly in his crease, incredulous: one didn't run when the ball was hit to mid on unless it was the last delivery of the match.

The captain of Oxford, now stranded fifteen yards

from safety, turned and looked at the captain of Cambridge, who held the ball in his hand. Robin Oakley was about to toss the ball to the wicket-keeper who in turn was waiting to remove the bails and send the Oxford captain back to the pavilion, run out for ninety-nine, but Oakley hesitated and, for several seconds the two gladiators stared at each other and then the Cambridge captain placed the ball in his pocket. The Oxford captain walked slowly back to his crease while the crowd remained silent in disbelief. Robin Oakley tossed the ball to Potter who thundered down to deliver the fifth ball, which was short, and the Oxford captain effortlessly placed it through the covers for four runs. The crowd rose as one and old friends in the pavilion thumped the father's back.

He smiled for a second time.

Potter was now advancing with his final effort and, exhausted, he delivered another short ball which should have been despatched to the boundary with ease but the Oxford captain took one pace backwards and hit his own stumps. He was out, hit wicket, bowled Potter for 103. The crowd rose for a second time as he walked back to the pavilion and grown men who had been decorated in two wars had tears in their eyes. Seven minutes later, everyone left the field, drenched by a thunderstorm.

The match ended in a draw.

BROKEN ROUTINE

SEPTIMUS HORATIO CORNWALLIS did not live up to his name. With such a name he should have been a cabinet minister, an admiral, or at least a rural dean. In fact, Septimus Horatio Cornwallis was a claims adjuster at the head office of the Prudential Assurance Company Limited, 172 Holborn Bars, London EC1.

Septimus's names could be blamed on his father, who had a small knowledge of Nelson, on his mother who was superstitious, and on his great-great-great-grandfather who was alleged to have been a second cousin of the illustrious Governor-General of India. On leaving school Septimus, a thin, anaemic young man prematurely balding, joined the Prudential Assurance Company; his careers master having told him that it was an ideal opening for a young man with his qualifications. Some time later, when Septimus reflected on the advice, it worried him, because even he realised that he had no qualifications. Despite this set-back, Septimus rose slowly over the years from office boy to claims adjuster (not so much climbing the ladder as resting upon each rung for some considerable time), which afforded him the grandiose title of assistant deputy manager (claims department).

Septimus spent his day in a glass cubicle on the sixth floor, adjusting claims and recommending payments of anything up to one million pounds. He felt if he kept his nose clean (one of Septimus's favourite expressions), he would, after another twenty years, become a manager (claims department) and have walls around him that you couldn't see through and a carpet that wasn't laid in small squares of slightly differing shades of green. He might even become one of those signatures on the million pound cheques.

Septimus resided in Sevenoaks with his wife, Norma, and his two children, Winston and Elizabeth, who attended the local comprehensive school. They would have gone to the grammar school, he regularly informed his colleagues, but the Labour government had stopped all that.

Septimus operated his daily life by means of a set of invariant sub-routines, like a primitive microprocessor, while he supposed himself to be a great follower of tradition and discipline. For if he was nothing, he was at least a creature of habit. Had, for some inexplicable reason, the KGB wanted to assassinate Septimus, all they would have had to do was put him under surveillance for seven days and they would have known his every movement throughout the working year.

Septimus rose every morning at seven-fifteen and donned one of his two pin-head patterned dark suits.

He left his home at 47 Palmerston Drive at seven-fifty-five, having consumed his invariable breakfast of one soft-boiled egg, two pieces of toast, and two cups of tea. On arriving at platform one of Sevenoaks station he would purchase a copy of the *Daily Express* before boarding the eight-twenty-seven to Cannon Street. During the journey Septimus would read his newspaper and smoke two cigarettes, arriving at Cannon Street at nine-seven. He would then walk to the office, and be sitting at his desk in his glass cubicle on the sixth floor, confronting the first claim to be adjusted, by nine-thirty. He took his coffee break at eleven, allowing himself the luxury of two more cigarettes, when once again he would regale his colleagues with the imagined achievements of his children. At eleven-fifteen he returned to work.

At one o'clock he would leave the Great gothic cathedral (another of his expressions) for one hour, which he passed at a pub called the Havelock where he would drink a half-pint of Carlsberg lager with a dash of lime, and eat the dish of the day. After he finished his lunch, he would once again smoke two cigarettes. At one-fifty-five he returned to the insurance records until the fifteen minute tea break at four o'clock which was another ritual occasion for two more cigarettes. On the dot of five-thirty, Septimus would pick up his umbrella and reinforced steel briefcase with the initials S.H.C. in silver on the side and leave, double locking his glass cubicle. As he walked through the typing pool, he would announce with a mechanical jauntiness 'See you same time tomorrow, girls', hum a few bars from *The Sound of Music* in the descending lift, and then walk out into the torrent of office workers surging down High Holborn. He would stride purposefully towards Cannon Street station, umbrella tapping away on the pavement while he rubbed shoulders with bankers, shippers, oil men, and brokers, not discontent to think himself part of the great City of London.

Once he reached the station, Septimus would purchase a copy of the *Evening Standard* and a packet of ten Benson & Hedges cigarettes from Smith's bookstall, placing both on the top of his Prudential documents already in the briefcase. He would board the fourth carriage of the train on Platform Five at five-fifty, and secure his favoured window seat in a closed compartment facing the engine, next to the balding gentleman with the inevitable *Financial Times*, and opposite the smartly dressed secretary who read long romantic novels to somewhere beyond Sevenoaks. Before sitting down he would extract the *Evening Standard* and the new packet of Benson & Hedges from his briefcase, put them both on the armrest of his seat, and place the briefcase and his rolled umbrella on the rack above him. Once settled, he would open the packet of cigarettes and smoke the first of the two which were allocated for the journey while reading the *Evening Standard*. This would leave him eight to be smoked before catching the five-fifty the following evening.

As the train pulled into Sevenoaks station, he would mumble goodnight to his fellow passengers (the only word he ever spoke during the entire journey) and leave, making his way straight to the semi-detached at 47 Palmerston Drive, arriving at the front door a little before six-forty-five. Between six-forty-five and seven-thirty he would finish reading his paper or check over his children's homework with a tut-tut when he spotted a mistake, or a sigh when he couldn't fathom the new maths. At seven-thirty his 'good lady' (another of his favoured expressions) would place on the kitchen table in front of him the *Woman's Own* dish of the day or his favourite dinner of three fish fingers, peas and chips. He would then say 'If God had meant fish to have fingers, he would have given them hands,' laugh, and cover the oblong fish with tomato sauce, consuming the meal to the accompaniment of his wife's recital of the day's events. At nine, he watched the real news on BBC 1 (he never watched ITV) and at ten-thirty he retired to bed.

This routine was adhered to year in year out with breaks only for holidays, for which Septimus naturally also had a routine. Alternate Christmases were spent with Norma's parents in Watford and the ones in between with Septimus's sister and brother-in-law in Epsom, while in the summer, their high spot of the year, the family took a package holiday for two weeks in the Olympic Hotel, Corfu.

Septimus not only liked his life-style, but was distressed if for any reason his routine met with the slightest interference. This humdrum existence seemed certain to last him from womb to tomb, for Septimus was not the stuff on which authors base two hundred thousand word sagas. Nevertheless there was one occasion when Septimus's routine was not merely interfered with, but frankly, shattered.

One evening at five-twenty-seven, when Septimus was closing the file on the last claim for the day, his immediate superior, the Deputy Manager, called him in for a consultation. Owing to this gross lack of consideration, Septimus did not manage to get away from the office until a few minutes after six. Although everyone had left the typing pool, still he saluted the empty desks and silent typewriters with the invariable 'See you same time tomorrow, girls,' and hummed a few bars of 'Edelweiss' to the descending lift. As he stepped out of the Great Gothic Cathedral it started to rain. Septimus reluctantly undid his neatly rolled umbrella, and putting it up dashed through the puddles, hoping that he would be in time to catch the six-thirty-two. On arrival at Cannon Street, he queued for his paper and cigarettes and put them in his briefcase before rushing on to platform five. To add to his annoyance, the loudspeaker was announcing with perfunctory apology that three trains had already been taken off that evening because of a go slow.

Septimus eventually fought his way through the dripping, bustling crowds to the sixth carriage of a train that was not scheduled on any timetable. He discovered that it was filled with people he had never seen before and, worse, almost every seat was already occupied. In fact, the only place he could find to sit was in the middle of the train with his back to the engine. He threw his briefcase and creased umbrella onto the rack above him and reluctantly squeezed himself into the seat, before looking around the carriage. There was not a familiar face among the other six occupants. A woman with three children more than filled the seat opposite him, while an elderly man was sleeping soundly on his left. On the other side of him, leaning over and looking out of the window, was a young man of about twenty.

When Septimus first laid eyes on the boy he couldn't believe what he saw. The youth was clad in a black leather jacket and skin-tight jeans and was whistling to himself. His dark, creamed hair was combed up at the front and down at the sides, while the only two colours of the young man's outfit that matched were his jacket and fingernails. But worst of all to one of Septimus's sensitive nature was the slogan printed in boot studs on the back of his jacket. 'Heil Hitler' it declared unashamedly over a white-painted Nazi sign and, as if that were not enough, below the swastika in gold shone the words: 'Up Yours'. What was the country coming to? thought Septimus. They ought to bring back National Service for delinquents like that. Septimus himself had not been eligible for National Service on account of his flat feet.

Septimus decided to ignore the creature, and picking up the packet of Benson & Hedges on the armrest by his side, lit one and began to read the *Evening Standard*. He then replaced the packet of cigarettes on the armrest, as he always did, knowing he would smoke one more before reaching Sevenoaks. When the train eventually moved out of Cannon Street the darkly clad youth turned towards Septimus and, glaring at him, picked up the packet of cigarettes, took one, lit it, and started to puff away. Septimus could not believe what was happening. He was about to protest when he realised that none of his regulars was in the carriage to back him up. He considered the situation for a moment and decided that Discretion was the better part of Valour. (Yet another of the sayings of Septimus.)

When the train stopped at Petts Wood, Septimus put down the newspaper although he had scarcely read a word and as he nearly always did, took his second cigarette. He lit it, inhaled, and was about to retrieve the *Evening Standard* when the youth grabbed at the corner, and they ended up with half the paper each. This time Septimus did look around the carriage for support. The children opposite started giggling, while their mother consciously averted her eyes from what was taking place, obviously not wanting to become involved; the old man on Septimus's left was now snoring. Septimus was about to secure the packet of cigarettes by putting them in his pocket when the youth pounced on them, removed another and lit it,

inhaled deeply, and then blew the smoke quite delib-
erately across Septimus's face before placing the
cigarettes back on the armrest. Septimus's answering
glare expressed as much malevolence as he was able
to project through the grey haze. Grinding his teeth
in fury, he returned to the *Evening Standard*, only to
discover that he had ended up with situations vacant,
used cars and sports sections, subjects in which he had
absolutely no interest. His one compensation, however, was his certainty that sport was the only section
the oik really wanted. Septimus was now, in any case,
incapable of reading the paper, trembling as he was
with the outrages perpetrated by his neighbour.

His thoughts were now turning to revenge and
gradually a plan began to form in his mind with which
he was confident the youth would be left in no doubt
that virtue can sometimes be more than its own
reward. (A variation on a saying of Septimus.) He
smiled thinly and, breaking his routine, he took a
third cigarette and defiantly placed the packet back
on the armrest. The youth stubbed out his own
cigarette and, as if taking up the challenge, picked up
the packet, removed another one and lit it. Septimus
was by no means beaten; he puffed his way quickly
through the weed, stubbed it out, a quarter unsmoked,
took a fourth and lit it immediately. The race was
on for there were now only two cigarettes left. But
Septimus, despite a great deal of puffing and coughing, managed to finish his fourth cigarette ahead of
the youth. He leaned across the leather jacket and

stubbed his cigarette out in the window ashtray. The carriage was now filled with smoke, but the youth was still puffing as fast as he could. The children opposite were coughing and the woman was waving her arms around like a windmill. Septimus ignored her and kept his eye on the packet of cigarettes while pretending to read about Arsenal's chances in the FA cup.

Septimus then recalled Montgomery's maxim that surprise and timing in the final analysis are the weapons of victory. As the youth finished his fourth cigarette and was stubbing it out the train pulled slowly into Sevenoaks station. The youth's hand was raised, but Septimus was quicker. He had anticipated the enemy's next move, and now seized the cigarette packet. He took out the ninth cigarette and, placing it between his lips, lit it slowly and luxuriously, inhaling as deeply as he could before blowing the smoke out straight into the face of the enemy. The youth stared up at him in dismay. Septimus then removed the last cigarette from the packet and crumpled the tobacco into shreds between his first finger and thumb, allowing the little flakes to fall back into the empty packet. Then he closed the packet neatly, and with a flourish replaced the little gold box on the armrest. In the same movement he picked up from his vacant seat the sports section of the *Evening Standard*, tore the paper in half, in quarters, in eighths and finally in sixteenths, placing the little squares in a neat pile on the youth's lap.

The train came to a halt at Sevenoaks. A triumphant Septimus, having struck his blow for the silent majority, retrieved his umbrella and briefcase from the rack above him and turned to leave.

As he picked up his briefcase it knocked the armrest in front of him and the lid sprang open. Everyone in the carriage stared at its contents. For there, on top of his Prudential documents, was a neatly folded copy of the *Evening Standard* and an unopened packet of ten Benson & Hedges cigarettes.

HENRY'S HICCUP

WHEN THE GRAND PASHA's first son was born in 1900 (he had sired twelve daughters by six wives) he named the boy Henry after his favourite king of England. Henry entered this world with more money than even the most blasé tax collector could imagine and therefore seemed destined to live a life of idle ease.

The Grand Pasha, who ruled over ten thousand families, was of the opinion that in time there would be only five kings left in the world – the kings of spades, hearts, diamonds, clubs, and England. With this conviction in mind, he decided that Henry should be educated by the British. The boy was therefore despatched from his native Cairo at the age of eight to embark upon a formal education, young enough to retain only vague recollections of the noise, the heat, and the dirt of his birthplace. Henry started his new life at the Dragon School, which the Grand Pasha's advisers assured him was the finest preparatory school in the land. The boy left this establishment four years later, having developed a passionate love for the polo field and a thorough distaste for the classroom. He proceeded, with the minimum academic qualifications, to Eton, which the Pasha's advisers assured him was the best school in Europe. He was gratified to learn the school had been founded by his favourite king. Henry spent five years at Eton, where he added squash, golf and tennis to his loves, and applied mathematics, jazz and cross-country running to his dislikes.

On leaving school, he once again failed to make more than a passing impression on the examiners. Nevertheless, he was found a place at Balliol College, Oxford, which the Pasha's advisers assured him was the greatest university in the world. Three years at Balliol added two more loves to his life: horses and women, and three more ineradicable aversions: politics, philosophy and economics.

At the end of his time in *statu pupillari*, he totally failed to impress the examiners and went down without a degree. His father, who considered young Henry's two goals against Cambridge in the Varsity polo match a wholly satisfactory result of his university career, despatched the boy on a journey round the world to complete his education. Henry enjoyed the experience, learning more on the race course at Longchamps and in the back streets of Benghazi than he ever had acquired from his formal upbringing in England.

The Grand Pasha would have been proud of the tall, sophisticated and handsome young man who returned to England a year later showing only the slightest trace of a foreign accent, if he hadn't died before his beloved son reached Southampton. Henry, although broken-hearted, was certainly not broke, as his father had left him some twenty million in known assets, including a racing stud at Suffolk, a 100-foot yacht in Nice, and a palace in Cairo. But by far the most important of his father's bequests was the finest manservant in London, one Godfrey Barker. Barker could arrange or rearrange anything, at a moment's notice.

Henry, for the lack of something better to do, settled himself into his father's old suite at the Ritz, not troubling to read the situations vacant column in the London *Times*. Rather he embarked on a life of single-minded dedication to the pursuit of pleasure, the only career for which Eton, Oxford and inherited wealth had adequately equipped him. To do Henry justice, he had, despite a more than generous helping of charm and good looks, enough common sense to choose carefully those permitted to spend the unforgiving minute with him. He selected only old friends from school and university who, although they were without exception not as well breeched as he, weren't the sort of fellows who came begging for the loan of a fiver to cover a gambling debt.

Whenever Henry was asked what was the first love of his life, he was always hard pressed to choose between horses and women, and as he found it possible to spend the day with the one and the night with the other without causing any jealousy or recrimination, he never overtaxed himself with resolving the problem. Most of his horses were fine stallions, fast, sleek, velvet-skinned, with dark eyes and firm limbs; this would have adequately described most of his women, except that they were fillies. Henry fell in and out of love with every girl in the chorus line of the London Palladium, and when the affairs had come to an end, Barker saw to it that they always received some suitable memento to ensure no scandal ensued. Henry also won every classic race on the English turf before he was thirty-five and Barker always seemed to know the right year to back his master.

Henry's life quickly fell into a routine, never dull. One month was spent in Cairo going through the motions of attending to his business, three months in the south of France with the occasional excursion to Biarritz, and for the remaining eight months he resided at the Ritz. For the four months he was out of London his magnificent suite overlooking St James's Park remained unoccupied. History does not record whether Henry left the rooms empty because he disliked the thought of unknown persons splashing in the sunken marble bath or because he simply couldn't be bothered with the fuss of signing in and out of the hotel twice a year. The Ritz management never commented on the matter to his father; why should they with the son? This programme fully accounted for Henry's year except for the odd trip to Paris when some home counties girl came a little too close to the altar. Although almost every girl who met Henry wanted to marry him, a good many would have done so even if he had been penniless. However, Henry saw absolutely no reason to be faithful to one woman. 'I have a hundred horses and a hundred male friends,' he would explain when asked. 'Why, should I confine myself to one female?' There seemed no immediate answer to Henry's logic.

The story of Henry would have ended there had he continued life as destiny seemed content to allow, but even the Henrys of this world have the occasional hiccup.

As the years passed Henry grew into the habit of never planning ahead as experience – and his able manservant, Barker – had always led him to believe that with vast wealth you could acquire anything you desired at the last minute, and cover any contingencies that arose later. However, even Barker couldn't formulate a contingency plan in response to Mr Chamberlain's statement of 3 September, 1939, that the British people were at war with Germany. Henry felt it inconsiderate of Chamberlain to have declared war so soon after Wimbledon and the Oaks, and even more inconsiderate of the Home Office to advise him a few months later that Barker must stop serving the Grand Pasha and, until further notice, serve His Majesty the King instead.

What could poor Henry do? Now in his fortieth year he was not used to living anywhere other than

the Ritz, and the Germans who had caused Wimbledon to be cancelled were also occupying the George
V in Paris and the Negresco in Nice. As the weeks
passed and daily an invasion seemed more certain
Henry came to the distasteful conclusion that he
would have to return to a neutral Cairo until the
British had won the war. It never crossed Henry's
mind, even for one moment, that the British might
lose. After all, they had won the First World War and
therefore they must win the Second. 'History repeats
itself' was about the only piece of wisdom he recalled
clearly from three years of tutorials at Oxford.

Henry summoned the manager of the Ritz and
told him that his suite was to be left unoccupied until
he returned. He paid one year in advance, which he
felt was more than enough time to take care of
upstarts like Herr Hitler, and set off for Cairo. The
manager was heard to remark later that the Grand
Pasha's departure for Egypt was most ironic; he was,
after all, more British than the British.

Henry spent a year at his palace in Cairo and then
found he could bear his fellow countrymen no longer,
so he removed himself to New York only just before
it would have been possible for him to come face to
face with Rommel. Once in New York, Henry bivou-
acked in the Pierre Hotel on Fifth Avenue, selected
an American manservant called Eugene, and waited
for Mr Churchill to finish the war. As if to prove his
continuing support for the British, on the first of
January every year he forwarded a cheque to the Ritz

to cover the cost of his rooms for the next twelve months.

Henry celebrated V-J Day in Times Square with a million Americans and immediately made plans for his return to Britain. He was surprised and disappointed when the British Embassy in Washington informed him that it might be some time before he was allowed to return to the land he loved, and despite continual pressure and all the influence he could bring to bear, he was unable to board a ship for Southampton until July 1946. From the first-class deck he waved goodbye to America and Eugene, and looked forward to England and Barker.

Once he had stepped off the ship on to English soil he headed straight for the Ritz to find his rooms exactly as he had left them. As far as Henry could see, nothing had changed except that his manservant (now the batman to a general) could not be released from the armed forces for at least another six months. Henry was determined to play his part in the war effort by surviving without him for the ensuing period, and remembering Barker's words: 'Everyone knows who you are. Nothing will change,' he felt confident all would be well. Indeed on the *bonheur-du-jour* in his room at the Ritz was an invitation to dine with Lord and Lady Lympsham in their Chelsea Square home the following night. It looked as if Barker's prediction was turning out to be right: everything would be just the same. Henry penned an affirmative reply to the invitation, happy with the thought that he was going to pick up his life in England exactly where he had left off.

The following evening Henry arrived on the Chelsea Square doorstep a few minutes after eight o'clock. The Lympshams, an elderly couple who had not qualified for the war in any way, gave every appearance of not even realising that it had taken place or that Henry had been absent from the London social scene. Their table, despite rationing, was as fine as Henry remembered and, more important, one of the guests present was quite unlike anyone he could ever remember. Her name, Henry learned from his host, was Victoria Campbell, and she turned out to be the daughter of another guest, General Sir Ralph Colquhoun. Lady Lympsham confided to Henry over the quails' eggs that the sad young thing had lost her husband when the allies advanced on Berlin, only a few days before the Germans had surrendered. For the first time Henry felt guilty about not having played some part in the war.

All through dinner, he could not take his eyes from young Victoria whose classical beauty was only equalled by her well-informed and lively conversation. He feared he might be staring too obviously at the slim, dark-haired girl with the high cheek bones; it was like admiring a beautiful sculpture and wanting to touch it. Her bewitching smile elicited an answering smile from all who received it. Henry did everything in his power to be the receiver and was rewarded on several occasions, aware that, for the first time in his life, he was becoming totally infatuated – and was delighted to be.

The ensuing courtship was an unusual one for Henry, in that he made no attempt to persuade Victoria to compliance. He was sympathetic and attentive, and when she had come out of mourning he approached her father and asked if he might request his daughter's hand in marriage. Henry was overjoyed when first the General agreed and later Victoria accepted. After an announcement in *The Times* they celebrated the engagement with a small dinner party at the Ritz, attended by one hundred and twenty close friends who might have been forgiven for coming to a conclusion that Attlee was exaggerating about his austerity programme. After the last guest had left Henry walked Victoria back to her father's home in Belgrave Mews, while discussing the wedding arrangements and his plans for the honeymoon.

'Everything must be perfect for you, my angel,' he said, as once again he admired the way her long, dark hair curled at the shoulders. 'We shall be married in St Margaret's, Westminster, and after a reception at the Ritz we will be driven to Victoria Station where you will be met by Fred, the senior porter. Fred will allow no one else to carry my bags to the last carriage of the Golden Arrow. One should always have the last carriage, my darling,' explained Henry, 'so that one cannot be disturbed by other travellers.'

Victoria was impressed by Henry's mastery of the

arrangements, especially remembering the absence of his manservant, Barker.

Henry warmed to his theme. 'Once we have boarded the Golden Arrow, you will be served with China tea and some wafer-thin smoked salmon sandwiches which we can enjoy while relaxing on our journey to Dover. When we arrive at the Channel port, you will be met by Albert whom Fred will have alerted. Albert will remove the bags from our carriage, but not before everyone else has left the train. He will then escort us to the ship, where we will take sherry with the captain while our bags are being placed in cabin number three. Like my father, I always have cabin number three; it is not only the largest and most comfortable stateroom on board, but the cabin is situated in the centre of the ship, which makes it possible to enjoy a comfortable crossing even should one have the misfortune to encounter bad weather. And when we have docked in Calais you will find Pierre waiting for us. He will have organised everything for the front carriage of the Flèche d'Or.'

'Such a programme must take a considerable amount of detailed planning,' suggested Victoria, her hazel eyes sparkling as she listened to her future husband's description of the promised tour.

'More tradition than organisation I would say, my dear,' replied Henry, smiling, as they strolled hand in hand across Hyde Park. 'Although, I confess, in the past Barker has kept his eye on things should any untoward emergency arise. In any case I have *always* had the front carriage of the Flèche d'Or because it assures one of being off the train and away before anyone realises that you have actually arrived in the French capital. Other than Raymond, of course.'

'Raymond?'

'Yes, Raymond, a servant *par excellence*, who adored my father, he will have organised a bottle of Veuve Cliquot '37 and a little Russian caviar for the journey. He will also have ensured that there is a couch in the railway carriage should you need to rest, my dear.'

'You seem to have thought of everything, Henry darling,' she said, as they entered Belgrave Mews.

'I hope you will think so, Victoria; for when you arrive in Paris which I have not had the opportunity to visit for so many years, there will be a Rolls-Royce standing by the side of the carriage, door open, and you will step out of the Flèche d'Or into the car and Maurice will drive us to the George V, arguably the finest hotel in Europe. Louis, the manager, will be on the steps of the hotel to greet you and he will conduct us to the bridal suite with its stunning view of the city. A maid will unpack for you while you retire to bathe and rest from the tiresome journey. When you are fully recovered we shall dine at Maxim's, where you will be guided to the corner table furthest from the orchestra by Marcel, the finest head waiter in the world. As you are seated, the musicians will strike up 'A Room with A View' my favourite tune, and we will then be served with the most magnificent langouste you have ever tasted, of that I can assure you.'

Henry and Victoria arrived at the front door of the general's small house in Belgrave Mews. He took her hand before continuing.

'After you have dined, my dear, we shall stroll into the Madeleine where I shall buy a dozen red roses from Paulette, the most beautiful flower girl in Paris. She is almost as lovely as you.' Henry sighed and concluded: 'Then we shall return to the George V and spend our first night together.'

Victoria's hazel eyes showed delighted anticipation. 'I only wish it could be tomorrow,' she said.

Henry kissed her gallantly on the cheek and said: 'It will be worth waiting for, my dear, I can assure you it will be a day neither of us will ever forget.'

'I'm sure of that,' Victoria replied as he released her hand.

On the morning of his wedding Henry leaped out of bed and drew back the curtains with a flourish, only to be greeted by a steady drizzle.

'The rain will clear by eleven o'clock,' he said out loud with immense confidence, and hummed as he shaved slowly and with care.

The weather had not improved by mid-morning. On the contrary, heavy rain was falling by the time Victoria entered the church. Henry's disappointment evaporated the instant he saw his beautiful bride; all he could think of was taking her to Paris. The ceremony over, the Grand Pasha and his wife stood outside the church, a golden couple, smiling for the press photographers as the loyal guests scattered damp rice over them. As soon as they decently could, they set off for the reception at the Ritz. Between them they managed to chat to every guest present, and they would have been away in better time had Victoria been a little quicker changing and the general's toast to the happy couple been considerably shorter. The guests crowded on to the steps of the Ritz, overflowing on to the pavement in Piccadilly to wave good-bye to the departing honeymooners, and were only sheltered from the downpour by a capacious red awning.

The general's Rolls took the Grand Pasha and his wife to the station, where the chauffeur unloaded the bags. Henry instructed him to return to the Ritz as he had everything under control. The chauffeur touched his cap and said: 'I hope you and madam have a wonderful trip, sir,' and left them. Henry stood on the station, looking for Fred. There was no sign of him, so he hailed a passing porter.

'Where is Fred?' inquired Henry.

'Fred who?' came the reply.

'How in heaven's name should I know?' said Henry.

'Then how in hell's name should I know?' retorted the porter.

Victoria shivered. English railway stations are not designed for the latest fashion in silk coats.

'Kindly take my bags to the end carriage of the train,' said Henry.

The porter looked down at the fourteen bags. 'All right,' he said reluctantly.

Henry and Victoria stood patiently in the cold as the porter loaded the bags on to his trolley and trundled them off along the platform.

'Don't worry, my dear,' said Henry. 'A cup of Lapsang Souchong tea and some smoked salmon sandwiches and you'll feel a new girl.'

'I'm just fine,' said Victoria, smiling, though not quite as bewitchingly as normal, as she put her arm through her husband's. They strolled along together to the end carriage.

'Can I check your tickets, sir?' said the conductor, blocking the entrance to the last carriage.

'My what?' said Henry, his accent sounding unusually pronounced.

'Your tic . . . kets,' said the conductor, conscious he was addressing a foreigner.

'In the past I have always made the arrangements on the train, my good man.'

'Not nowadays you don't, sir. You'll have to go to the booking office and buy your tickets like everyone else, and you'd better be quick about it because the train is due to leave in a few minutes.'

Henry stared at the conductor in disbelief. 'I assume my wife may rest on the train while I go and purchase the tickets?' he asked.

'No, I'm sorry, sir. No one is allowed to board the train unless they are in possession of a valid ticket.'

'Remain here, my dear,' said Henry, 'and I will

deal with this little problem immediately. Kindly direct me to the ticket office, porter.'

'End of platform four, governor,' said the conductor, slamming the train door annoyed at being described as a porter.

That wasn't quite what Henry had meant by 'direct me'. Nevertheless, he left his bride with the fourteen bags and somewhat reluctantly headed back towards the ticket office at the end of platform four, where he went to the front of a long line.

'There's a queue, you know, mate,' someone shouted.

Henry didn't know. 'I'm in a frightful hurry,' he said.

'And so am I,' came back the reply, 'so get to the back.'

Henry had been told that the British were good at standing in queues, but as he had never had to join one before that moment, he was quite unable to confirm or deny the rumour. He reluctantly walked to the back of a queue. It took some time before Henry reached the front.

'I would like to take the last carriage to Dover.'

'You would like what . . .?'

'The last carriage,' repeated Henry a little more loudly.

'I am sorry, sir, but every first-class seat is sold.'

'I don't want a seat,' said Henry. 'I require the carriage.'

'There are no carriages available nowadays, sir,

and as I said, all the seats in first class are sold. I can still fix you up in third class.'

'I don't mind what it costs,' said Henry. 'I must travel first class.'

'I don't have a first-class seat, sir. It wouldn't matter if you could afford the whole train.'

'I can,' said Henry.

'I still don't have a seat left in first class,' said the clerk unhelpfully.

Henry would have persisted, but several people in the queue behind him were pointing out that there were only two minutes before the train was due to leave and that they wanted to catch it even if he didn't.

'Two seats then,' said Henry, unable to make himself utter the words 'third class'.

Two green tickets marked Dover were handed through the little grille. Henry took them and started to walk away.

'That will be seventeen and sixpence please, sir.'

'Oh, yes, of course,' said Henry apologetically. He fumbled in his pocket and unfolded one of the three large white five-pound notes he always carried on him.

'Don't you have anything smaller?'

'No, I do not,' said Henry, who found the idea of carrying money vulgar enough without it having to be in small denominations.

The clerk handed back four pounds and a half-crown. Henry did not pick up the half-crown.

'Thank you, sir,' said the startled man. It was more than his Saturday bonus.

Henry put the tickets in his pocket and quickly returned to Victoria, who was smiling defiantly against the cold wind; it was not quite the smile that had originally captivated him. Their porter had long ago disappeared and Henry couldn't see another in sight. The conductor took his tickets and clipped them.

'All aboard,' he shouted, waved a green flag and blew his whistle.

Henry quickly threw all fourteen bags through the open door and pushed Victoria on to the moving train before leaping on himself. Once he had caught his breath he walked down the corridor, staring into the third class carriages. He had never seen one before. The seats were nothing more than thin worn-out cushions, and as he looked into one half-full carriage a young couple jumped in and took the last two adjacent seats. Henry searched frantically for a free carriage but he was unable even to find one with two seats together. Victoria took a single seat in a packed compartment without complaint, while Henry sat forlornly on one of the suitcases in the corridor.

'It will be different once we're in Dover,' he said, without his usual self-confidence.

'I am sure it will, Henry,' she replied, smiling kindly at him.

The two-hour journey seemed interminable. Passengers of all shapes and sizes squeezed past him in the corridor, treading on his Lobbs hand-made leather shoes, with the words:

'Sorry, sir.'

'Sorry, guv.'

'Sorry, mate.'

Henry put the blame firmly on the shoulders of Clement Attlee and his ridiculous campaign for social equality, and waited for the train to reach Dover Priory Station. The moment the engine pulled in Henry leaped out of the carriage first, not last, and called for Albert at the top of his voice. Nothing happened, except a stampede of people rushed past him on their way to the ship. Eventually Henry spotted a porter and rushed over to him only to find he was already loading up his trolley with someone else's luggage. Henry sprinted to a second man and then on to a third and waved a pound note at a fourth, who came immediately and unloaded the fourteen bags.

'Where to, guv?' asked the porter amicably.

'The ship,' said Henry, and returned to claim his bride. He helped Victoria down from the train and they both ran through the rain until, breathless, they reached the gangplank of the ship.

'Tickets, sir,' said a young officer in a dark blue uniform at the bottom of the gangplank.

'I always have cabin number three,' said Henry between breaths.

'Of course, sir,' said the young man and looked at his clip board. Henry smiled confidently at Victoria.

'Mr and Mrs William West.'

'I beg your pardon?' said Henry.

'You must be Mr William West.'

'I am certainly not. I am the Grand Pasha of Cairo.'

'Well, I'm sorry, sir, cabin number three is booked in the name of a Mr William West and family.'

'I have never been treated by Captain Rogers in this cavalier fashion before,' said Henry, his accent now even more pronounced. 'Send for him immediately.'

'Captain Rogers was killed in the war, sir. Captain Jenkins is now in command of this ship and he never leaves the bridge thirty minutes before sailing.'

Henry's exasperation was turning to panic. 'Do you have a free cabin?'

The young officer looked down his list. 'No, sir, I'm afraid not. The last one was taken a few minutes ago.'

'May I have two tickets?' asked Henry.

'Yes, sir,' said the young officer. 'But you'll have to buy them from the booking office on the quayside.'

Henry decided that any further argument would be only time-consuming so he turned on his heel without another word, leaving his wife with the laden porter. He strode to the booking office.

'Two first-class tickets to Calais,' he said firmly.

The man behind the little glass pane gave Henry a tired look. 'It's all one class nowadays, sir, unless you have a cabin.'

He proffered two tickets. 'That will be one pound exactly.'

Henry handed over a pound note, took his tickets, and hurried back to the young officer.

The porter was off-loading their suitcases on to the quayside.

'Can't you take them on board,' cried Henry, 'and put them in the hold?'

'No, sir, not now. Only the passengers are allowed on board after the ten-minute signal.'

Victoria carried two of the smaller suitcases while Henry humped the twelve remaining ones in relays up the gangplank. He finally sat down on the deck exhausted. Every seat seemed already to be occupied. Henry couldn't make up his mind if he was cold from the rain or hot from his exertions. Victoria's smile was fixed firmly in place as she took Henry's hand.

'Don't worry about a thing, darling,' she said. 'Just relax and enjoy the crossing; it will be such fun being out on deck together.'

The ship moved sedately out of the calm of the bay into the Dover Straits. Later that night Captain Jenkins told his wife that the twenty-five mile journey had been among the most unpleasant crossings he had ever experienced. He added that he had nearly turned back when his second officer, a veteran of two wars, was violently sick. Henry and Victoria spent most of the trip hanging over the rails getting rid of everything they had consumed at their reception. Two people had never been more happy to see land in their life than Henry and Victoria were at the first sight of the Normandy coastline. They staggered off the ship, taking the suitcases one at a time.

'Perhaps France will be different,' Henry said lamely, and after a perfunctory search for Pierre he went straight to the booking office and obtained two third-class seats on the Flèche d'Or. They were at least able to sit next to each other this time, but in a carriage already occupied by six other passengers as well as a dog and a hen. The six of them left Henry in no doubt that they enjoyed the modern habit of smoking in public and the ancient custom of taking garlic in their food. He would have been sick again at any other time but there was nothing left in his stomach. Henry considered walking up and down the train searching for Raymond but feared it could only result in him losing his seat next to Victoria. He gave up trying to hold any conversation with her above the noise of the dog, the hen and the Gallic babble, and satisfied himself by looking out of the window, watching the French countryside and, for the first time in his life, noting the name of every station through which they passed.

Once they arrived at the Gare du Nord Henry made no attempt to look for Maurice and simply headed straight for the nearest taxi rank. By the time he had transferred all fourteen cases he was well down the queue. He and Victoria stood there for just over an hour, moving the cases forward inch by inch until it was their turn.

'*Monsieur?*'

'Do you speak English?'

'*Un peu, un peu.*'

'Hotel George V.'

'*Oui, mais je ne peux pas mettre toutes les valises dans le coffre.*'

So Henry and Victoria sat huddled in the back of the taxi, bruised, tired, soaked and starving, surrounded by leather suitcases, only to be bumped up and down over the cobbled stones all the way to the George V.

The hotel doorman rushed to help them as Henry offered the taxi driver a pound note.

'No take English money, monsieur.'

Henry couldn't believe his ears. The doorman happily paid the taxi driver in francs and quickly pocketed the pound note. Henry was too tired even to comment. He helped Victoria up the marble steps and went over to the reception desk.

'The Grand Pasha of Cairo and his wife. The bridal suite, please.'

'*Oui, monsieur.*'

Henry smiled at Victoria.

'You 'ave your booking confirmation with you?'

'No,' said Henry, 'I have never needed to confirm my booking with you in the past. Before the war I . . .'

'I am sorry, sir, but the 'otel is fully booked at the moment. A conference.'

'Even the bridal suite?' asked Victoria.

'Yes, madam, the chairman and his lady, you understand.' He nearly winked.

Henry certainly did not understand. There had always been a room for him at the George V whenever he had wanted one in the past. Desperate, he unfolded the second of his five-pound notes and slipped it across the counter.

'Ah,' said the booking clerk, 'I see we still have one room unoccupied, but I fear it is not very large.'

Henry waved a listless hand.

The booking clerk banged the bell on the counter in front of him with the palm of his hand, and a porter appeared immediately and escorted them to the promised room. The booking clerk had been telling the truth. Henry could only have described what they found themselves standing in as a box room. The reason that the curtains were perpetually drawn was that the view over the chimneys of Paris was singularly unprepossessing, but that was not to be the final blow, as Henry realised, staring in disbelief at the sight of the two narrow single beds. Victoria started unpacking without a word while Henry sat despondently on the end of one of them. After Victoria had sat soaking in a bath that was the perfect size for a six-year-old, she lay down exhausted on the other bed. Neither spoke for nearly an hour.

'Come on, darling,' said Henry finally. 'Let's go and have dinner.'

Victoria rose loyally but reluctantly and dressed for

dinner while Henry sat in the bath, knees on nose, trying to wash himself before changing into evening dress. This time he phoned the front desk and ordered a taxi as well as booking a table at Maxim's.

The taxi driver did accept his pound note on this occasion, but as Henry and his bride entered the great restaurant he recognised no one and no one recognised him. A waiter led them to a small table hemmed in between two other couples just below the band. As he walked into the dining room the musicians struck up 'Alexander's Rag Time Band'.

They both ordered from the extensive menu and the langouste turned out to be excellent, every bit as good as Henry had promised of Maxim's, but by then neither of them had the stomach to eat a full meal and the greater part of both their dishes was left on the plate.

Henry found it hard to convince the new head waiter that the lobster had been superb and that they had purposely come to Maxim's not to eat it. Over coffee, he took Victoria's hand and tried to apologise.

'Let us end this farce,' he said, 'by completing my plan and going to the Madeleine and presenting you with the promised flowers. Paulette will not be in the square to greet you but there will surely be someone who can sell us roses.'

Henry called for the bill and unfolded the third five-pound note (Maxim's are always happy to accept other people's currency and certainly didn't bother him with any change) and they left, walking hand in hand towards the Madeleine. For once Henry turned out to be right, for Paulette was nowhere to be seen. An old lady with a shawl over her head and a wart on the side of her nose stood in her place on the corner of the square, surrounded by the most beautiful flowers.

Henry selected a dozen of the longest stemmed red roses and then placed them in the arms of his bride. The old lady smiled at Victoria.

Victoria returned her smile.

'*Dix francs, monsieur,*' said the old lady to Henry.

Henry fumbled in his pocket, only to discover he had spent all his money. He looked despairingly at the old lady who raised her hands, smiled at him, and said:

'Don't worry, Henry, have them on me. For old time's sake.'

A MATTER OF
PRINCIPLE

SIR HAMISH GRAHAM had many of the qualities and most of the failings that result from being born to a middle-class Scottish family. He was well educated, hard working and honest, while at the same time being narrow-minded, uncompromising and proud. Never on any occasion had he allowed hard liquor to pass his lips and he mistrusted all men who had not been born north of Hadrian's Wall, and many of those who had.

After spending his formative years at Fettes School, to which he had won a minor scholarship, and at Edinburgh University, where he obtained a second-class honours degree in engineering, he was chosen from a field of twelve to be a trainee with the inter-national construction company, TarMac (named after its founder, J. L. McAdam, who discovered that tar when mixed with stones was the best constituent for making roads). The new trainee, through diligent work and uncompromising tactics, became the firm's young-est and most disliked project manager. By the age of thirty Graham had been appointed deputy man-aging director of TarMac and was already beginning to realise that he could not hope to progress much farther while he was in someone else's employ. He therefore started to consider forming his own company. When two years later the chairman of TarMac, Sir Alfred Hickman, offered Graham the opportunity to replace the retiring managing director, he resigned immediately. After all, if Sir Alfred felt he had the ability to run TarMac he must also be competent enough to start his own company.

The next day, young Hamish Graham made an appointment to see the local manager of the Bank of Scotland who was responsible for the TarMac account, and with whom he had dealt for the past ten years. Graham explained to the manager his plans for the future, submitting a full written proposal, and requesting that his overdraft facility might be extended from fifty pounds to ten thousand. Three weeks later Graham learned that his application had been viewed favourably. He remained in his lodgings in Edinburgh, while renting an office in the north of the city (or, to be more accurate, a room at ten shillings a week). He purchased a typewriter, hired a secretary and ordered some unembossed headed letter-paper. After a further month of diligent interviewing, he employed two engineers, both graduates of Aberdeen University, and five out-of-work labourers from Glasgow.

During those first few weeks on his own Graham tendered for several small road contracts in the central lowlands of Scotland, the first seven of which he failed to secure. Preparing a tender is always tricky and often expensive, so by the end of his first six months in business Graham was beginning to wonder if his sudden departure from TarMac had not been foolhardy. For the first time in his life he experienced self-doubt, but that was soon removed by the Ayrshire County Council, who accepted his tender to construct a minor road which was to join a projected school with the main highway. The road was only five hundred yards in length but the assignment took Graham's little team seven months to complete and when all the bills had been paid and all expenses taken into account Graham Construction made a net loss of £143.10s.6d.

Still, in the profit column was a small reputation which had been invisibly earned, and caused the Ayrshire Council to invite him to build the school at the end of their new road. This contract made Graham Construction a profit of £420 and added still further to its reputation. From that moment Graham Construction went from strength to strength, and as early as his third year in business he was able to declare a small pre-tax profit, and this grew steadily over the next five years. When Graham Construction was floated on the London Stock Exchange the demand for the shares was over-subscribed ten times and the newly quoted company was soon considered a blue-chip institution, a considerable achievement for Graham to have pulled off in his own lifetime. But then the City likes men who grow slowly and can be relied on not to involve themselves in unnecessary risks.

In the sixties Graham Construction built motorways, hospitals, factories, and even a power station, but the achievement the chairman took most pride in was Edinburgh's newly completed art gallery, which was the only contract that showed a deficit in the annual general report. The invisible earnings column however recorded the award of knight bachelor for the chairman.

Sir Hamish decided that the time had come for Graham Construction to expand into new fields, and looked, as generations of Scots had before him, towards the natural market of the British Empire. He built in Australia and Canada with his own finances, and in India and Africa with a subsidy from the British government. In 1963 he was named 'Businessman of the Year' by *The Times* and three years later 'Chairman of the Year' by *The Economist*. Sir Hamish never once altered his methods to keep pace with the changing times, and if anything grew more stubborn in the belief that his ideas of doing business were correct whatever anyone else thought; and he had a long credit column to prove he was right.

In the early seventies, when the slump hit the construction business, Graham Construction suffered the same cut in budgets and lost contracts as any of its major competitors. Sir Hamish reacted in a predictable way, by tightening his belt and paring his estimates while at the same time refusing one jot to compromise his business principles. The company therefore grew leaner and many of his more enterprising young executives left Graham Construction for firms which still believed in taking on the occasional risky contract.

Only when the slope of the profits graph started taking on the look of a downhill slalom did Sir Hamish become worried. One night, while brooding over the company's profit-and-loss account for the previous three years, and realising that he was losing contracts even in his native Scotland, Sir Hamish reluctantly came to the conclusion that he must tender for less established work, and perhaps even consider the odd gamble.

His brightest young executive, David Heath, a stocky, middle-aged bachelor, whom he did not entirely trust – after all, the man had been educated south of the border and worse, some extraordinary place in the United States called the Wharton Business School – wanted Sir Hamish to put a toe into Mexican waters. Mexico, as Heath was not slow to point out, had discovered vast reserves of oil off their eastern coast and had overnight become rich with American dollars. The construction business in Mexico was suddenly proving most lucrative and contracts were coming up for tender with figures as high as thirty to forty million dollars attached to them. Heath urged Sir Hamish to go after one such contract that had recently been announced in a full-page advertisement in *The Economist*. The Mexican Government were issuing tender documents for a proposed ring road around their capital, Mexico City. In an article in the business section of the *Observer*, detailed arguments were put forward as to why established British companies should try to fulfil the ring road tender. Heath had offered shrewd advice on overseas contracts in the past that Sir Hamish had subsequently let slip through his fingers.

The next morning, Sir Hamish sat at his desk listening attentively to David Heath, who felt that as Graham Construction had already built the Glasgow and Edinburgh ring roads any application they made to the Mexican Government had to be taken seriously. To Heath's surprise, Sir Hamish agreed with his project manager and allowed a team of six men to travel to Mexico to obtain the tender documents and research the project.

The research team was led by David Heath, and consisted of three other engineers, a geologist and an accountant. When the team arrived in Mexico they obtained the tender documents from the Minister of Works and settled down to study them minutely. Having pinpointed the major problems they walked around Mexico City with their ears open and their mouths shut and made a list of the problems they were clearly going to encounter: the impossibility of unloading anything at Vera Cruz and then transporting the cargo to Mexico City without half of the original assignment being stolen, the lack of communications between ministries, and worst of all the attitude of the Mexicans to work. But David Heath's most positive contribution to the list was the discovery that each minister had his own outside man, and that man had better be well disposed to Graham Construction if the firm were to be even considered for the short list. Heath immediately sought out the Minister of Works' man, one Victor Perez, and took him to an extravagant lunch at the *Fonda el Refugio* where both of them nearly ended up drunk, although Heath remained sober enough to agree all of the necessary terms, conditional upon Sir Hamish's approval. Having taken every possible precaution, Heath agreed on a tender figure with Perez which was to include the minister's percentage. Once he had completed the report for his chairman, he flew back to England with his team.

On the evening of David Heath's return, Sir Hamish retired to bed early to study his project manager's conclusions. He read the report through the night as others might read a spy story, and was left in no doubt that this was the opportunity he had been looking for to overcome the temporary setbacks Graham Construction was now suffering. Although Sir Hamish would be up against Costains, Sunleys, and John Brown, as well as many international companies, he still felt confident that any application he made must have a 'fair chance'. On arrival at his office the next morning Sir Hamish sent for David Heath, who was delighted by the chairman's initial response to his report.

Sir Hamish started speaking as soon as his burly project manager entered the room, not even inviting him to take a seat.

'You must contact our Embassy in Mexico City immediately and inform them of our intentions,' pronounced Sir Hamish. 'I may speak to the Ambassador myself,' he said, intending that to be the concluding remark of the interview.

'Useless,' said David Heath.

'I beg your pardon?'

'I don't wish to appear rude, sir, but it doesn't work like that any more. Britain is no longer a great power dispensing largesse to all far flung and grateful recipients.'

'More's the pity,' said Sir Hamish.

The project manager continued as though he had not heard the remark.

'The Mexicans now have vast wealth of their own and the United States, Japan, France and Germany keep massive embassies in Mexico City with highly professional trade delegations trying to influence every ministry.'

'But surely history counts for something,' said Sir Hamish. 'Wouldn't they rather deal with an established British company than some upstarts from—?'

'Perhaps, sir, but in the end all that really matters

is which minister is in charge of what contract and who is his outside representative.'

Sir Hamish looked puzzled. 'Your meaning is obscure to me, Mr Heath.'

'Allow me to explain, sir. Under the present system in Mexico, each ministry has an allocation of money to spend on projects agreed to by the government. Every Secretary of State is acutely aware that his tenure of office may be very short, so he picks out a major contract for himself from the many available. It's the one way to ensure a pension for life if the government is changed overnight or the minister simply loses his job.'

'Don't bandy words with me, Mr Heath. What you are suggesting is that I should bribe a government official. I have never been involved in that sort of thing in thirty years of business.'

'And I wouldn't want you to start now,' replied Heath. 'The Mexican is far too experienced in business etiquette for anything as clumsy as that to be suggested, but while the law requires that you appoint a Mexican agent, it must make sense to try and sign up the minister's man, who in the end is the one person who can ensure that you will be awarded the contract. The system seems to work well, and as long as a minister deals only with reputable international firms and doesn't become greedy, no one complains. Fail to observe either of those two golden rules and the whole house of cards collapses. The minister ends up in Le Cumberri for thirty years and the company concerned has all its assets expropriated and is banned from any future business dealings in Mexico.'

'I really cannot become involved in such shenanigans,' said Sir Hamish. 'I still have my shareholders to consider.'

'*You* don't have to become involved,' Heath rejoined. 'After we have tendered for the contract you wait and see if the company has been shortlisted and then, if we have, you wait again to find out if the minister's man approaches us. I know the man, so if he does make contact we have a deal. After all, Graham Construction is a respectable international company.'

'Precisely, and that's why it's against my principles,' said Sir Hamish with hauteur.

'I do hope, Sir Hamish, it's also against your principles to allow the Germans and the Americans to steal the contract from under our noses.'

Sir Hamish glared back at his project manager but remained silent.

'And I feel I must add, sir,' said David Heath moving restlessly from foot to foot, 'that the pickings in Scotland haven't exactly yielded a harvest lately.'

'All right, all right, go ahead,' said Sir Hamish reluctantly. 'Put in a tender figure for the Mexico City ring road and be warned if I find bribery is involved, on your head be it,' he added, banging his closed fist on the table.

'What tender figure have you settled on, sir?' asked

the project manager. 'I believe, as I stressed in my report that we should keep the amount under forty million dollars.'

'Agreed,' said Sir Hamish who paused for a moment and smiled to himself before saying: 'Make it $39,121,110.'

'Why that particular figure, sir?'

'Sentimental reasons,' said Sir Hamish, without further explanation.

David Heath left, pleased that he had convinced his boss to go ahead but he feared it might in the end prove harder to overcome Sir Hamish's principles than the entire Mexican government. Nevertheless he filled in the bottom line of the tender as instructed and then had the document signed by three directors including his chairman, as required by Mexican law. He sent the tender by special messenger to be delivered at the Ministry of Buildings in Paseo de la Reforma: when tendering for a contract for over thirty-nine million dollars, one does not send the document by first-class post.

Several weeks passed before the Mexican Embassy in London contacted Sir Hamish, requesting that he travel to Mexico City for a meeting with Manuel Unichurtu, the minister concerned with the city's ring road project. Sir Hamish remained sceptical, but David Heath was jubilant, because he had already learned through another source that Graham Construction was the only tender being seriously considered at that moment, although there were one or two outstanding items still to be agreed on. David Heath knew exactly what that meant.

A week later Sir Hamish, travelling first class, and David Heath, travelling economy, flew out of Heathrow bound for Mexico International airport. On arrival they took an hour to clear customs and another thirty minutes to find a taxi to take them to the city, and then only after the driver had bargained with them for an outrageous fare. They covered the fifteen-mile journey from the airport to their hotel in just over an hour and Sir Hamish was able to observe at first hand why the Mexicans were so desperate to build a ring road. Even with the windows down the ten-year-old car was like an oven that had been left on high all night, but during the journey Sir Hamish never once loosened his collar or tie. The two men checked into their rooms, phoned the minister's secretary to inform her of their arrival, and then waited.

For two days, nothing happened.

David Heath assured his chairman that such a hold up was not an unusual course of events in Mexico as the minister was undoubtedly in meetings most of the day, and after all wasn't '*mañana*' the one Spanish word every foreigner understood?

On the afternoon of the third day, only just before Sir Hamish was threatening to return home, David Heath received a call from the minister's man, who accepted an invitation to join them both for dinner in Sir Hamish's suite that evening.

Sir Hamish put on evening dress for the occasion,

despite David Heath's counselling against the idea. He even had a bottle of *Fina La Ina* sherry sent up in case the minister's man required some refreshment. The dinner table was set and the hosts were ready for seven-thirty. The minister's man did not appear at seven-thirty, or seven-forty-five, or eight o'clock or eight-fifteen, or eight-thirty. At eight-forty-nine there was a loud rap on the door, and Sir Hamish muttered an inaudible reproach as David Heath went to open it and find his contact standing there.

'Good evening, Mr Heath, I'm sorry to be late. Held up with the minister, you understand.'

'Yes, of course,' said David Heath. 'How good of you to come, Señor Perez. May I introduce my chairman, Sir Hamish Graham?'

'How do you do, Sir Hamish? Victor Perez at your service.'

Sir Hamish was dumbfounded. He simply stood and stared at the little middle-aged Mexican who had arrived for dinner dressed in a grubby white tee-shirt and Western jeans. Perez looked as if he hadn't shaved for three days and reminded Sir Hamish of those bandits he had seen in B-movies when he was a schoolboy. He wore a heavy gold bracelet around his wrist that could have come from Cartier's and a tiger's tooth on a platinum chain around his neck that looked as if it had come from Woolworth's. Perez grinned from ear to ear, pleased with the effect he was causing.

'Good evening,' replied Sir Hamish stiffly, taking a step backwards. 'Would you care for a sherry?'

'No, thank you, Sir Hamish. I've grown into the habit of liking your whisky, on the rocks with a little soda.'

'I'm sorry, I only have . . .'

'Don't worry, sir, I have some in my room,' said David Heath, and rushed away to retrieve a bottle of Johnnie Walker he had hidden under the shirts in his top drawer. Despite this Scottish aid, the conversation before dinner among the three men was somewhat stilted, but David Heath had not come five thousand miles for an inferior hotel meal with Victor Perez, and Victor Perez in any other circumstances would not have crossed the road to meet Sir Hamish Graham even if he'd built it. Their conversation ranged from the recent visit to Mexico of Her Majesty The Queen – as Sir Hamish referred to her – to the proposed return trip of President Portillo to Britain. Dinner might have gone more smoothly if Mr Perez hadn't eaten most of the food with his hands and then proceeded to clean his fingers on the side of his jeans. The more Sir Hamish stared at him in disbelief the more the little Mexican would grin from ear to ear. After dinner David Heath thought the time had come to steer the conversation towards the real purpose of the meeting, but not before Sir Hamish had reluctantly had to call for a bottle of brandy and a box of cigars.

'We are looking for an agent to represent the Graham Construction Company in Mexico, Mr Perez, and you have been highly recommended,' said

Sir Hamish, sounding unconvinced by his own statement.

'Do call me Victor.'

Sir Hamish bowed silently and shuddered. There was no way this man was going to be allowed to call him Hamish.

'I'd be pleased to represent you, Hamish,' continued Perez, 'provided that you find my terms acceptable.'

'Perhaps you could enlighten us as to what those – hm, terms – might be,' said Sir Hamish stiffly.

'Certainly,' said the little Mexican cheerfully. 'I require ten per cent of the agreed tender figure, five per cent to be paid on the day you are awarded the contract and five per cent whenever you present your completion certificates. Not a penny to be paid until you have received your fee, all my payments deposited in an account at Credit Suisse in Geneva within seven days of the National Bank of Mexico clearing your cheque.'

David Heath drew in his breath sharply and stared down at the stone floor.

'But under those terms you would make nearly four million dollars,' protested Sir Hamish, now red in the face. 'That's over half our projected profit.'

'That, as I believe you say in England, Hamish, is your problem, you fixed the tender price,' said Perez, 'not me. In any case, there's still enough in the deal for both of us to make a handsome profit which is surely fair as we bring half the equation to the table.'

Sir Hamish was speechless as he fiddled with his bow tie. David Heath examined his fingernails attentively.

'Think the whole thing over, Hamish,' said Victor Perez, sounding unperturbed, 'and let me know your decision by midday tomorrow. The outcome makes little difference to me.' The Mexican rose, shook hands with Sir Hamish and left. David Heath, sweating slightly, accompanied him down in the lift. In the foyer he clasped hands damply with the Mexican.

'Good night, Victor. I'm sure everything will be all right – by midday tomorrow.'

'I hope so,' replied the Mexican, 'for your sake.' He strolled out of the foyer whistling.

Sir Hamish, a glass of water in his hand, was still seated at the dinner table when his project manager returned.

'I do not believe it is possible that that – that that man can represent the Secretary of State, represent a government minister.'

'I am assured that he does,' replied David Heath.

'But to part with nearly four million dollars to such an individual . . .'

'I agree with you, sir, but that is the way business is conducted out here.'

'I can't believe it,' said Sir Hamish. 'I *won't* believe it. I want you to make an appointment for me to see the minister first thing tomorrow morning.'

'He won't like that, sir. It might expose his position, and put him right out in the open in a way that could only embarrass him.'

'I don't give a damn about embarrassing him. We are discussing a bribe, do I have to spell it out for you, Heath? A bribe of nearly four million dollars. Have you no principles, man?'

'Yes, sir, but I would still advise you against seeing the Secretary of State. He won't want any of your conversation with Mr Perez on the record.'

'I have run this company my way for nearly thirty years, Mr Heath, and I shall be the judge of what I want on the record.'

'Yes, of course, sir.'

'I will see the Secretary of State first thing in the morning. Kindly arrange a meeting.'

'If you insist, sir,' said David Heath resignedly.

'I insist.'

The project manager departed to his own room and a sleepless night. Early the next morning he delivered a handwritten, personal and private letter to the minister, who sent a car round immediately for the Scottish industrialist.

Sir Hamish was driven slowly through the noisy, exuberant, bustling crowds of the city in the minister's black Ford Galaxy with flag flying. People made way for the car respectfully. The chauffeur came to a halt outside the Ministry of Buildings and Public Works in Paseo de la Reforma and guided Sir Hamish through the long, white corridors to a waiting room. A few minutes later an assistant showed Sir Hamish through to the Secretary of State and took a seat by his side. The minister, a severe looking man who appeared to be well into his seventies, was dressed in an immaculate white suit, white shirt and blue tie. He rose, leaned over the vast expanse of green leather and offered his hand.

'Do have a seat, Sir Hamish.'

'Thank you,' the chairman said, feeling more at home as he took in the minister's office; on the ceiling a large propellor-like fan revolved slowly round making little difference to the stuffiness of the room, while hanging on the wall behind the minister was a signed picture of President José Lopez Portillo in full morning dress and below the photo a plaque displaying a coat of arms.

'I see you were educated at Cambridge.'

'That is correct, Sir Hamish, I was at Corpus Christi for three years.'

'Then you know my country well, sir.'

'I do have many happy memories of my stays in England, Sir Hamish; in fact, I still visit London as often as my leave allows.'

'You must take a trip to Edinburgh some time.'

'I have already done so, Sir Hamish. I attended the Festival on two occasions and now know why your city is described as the Athens of the North.'

'You are well informed, Minister.'

'Thank you, Sir Hamish. Now I must ask how I can help you. Your assistant's note was rather vague.'

'First let me say, Minister, that my company is honoured to be considered for the city ring road project and I hope that our experience of thirty years in construction, twenty of them in the third world' – he nearly said the undeveloped countries, an expression his project manager had warned him against – 'is the reason you, as Minister in charge, found us the natural choice for this contract.'

'That, and your reputation for finishing a job on time at the stipulated price,' replied the Secretary of State. 'Only twice in your history have you returned to the principal asking for changes in the payment schedule. Once in Uganda when you were held up by Amin's pathetic demands, and the other project, if I remember rightly, was in Bolivia, an airport, when you were unavoidably delayed for six months because of an earthquake. In both cases, you completed the contract at the new price stipulated and my principal advisers think you must have lost money on both occasions.' The Secretary of State mopped his brow with a silk handkerchief before continuing. 'I would not wish you to think my government takes these decisions of selection lightly.'

Sir Hamish was astounded by the Secretary of State's command of his brief, the more so as no prompting notes lay on the leather-topped desk in front of him. He suddenly felt guilty at the little he knew about the Secretary of State's background or history.

'Of course not, Minister. I am flattered by your

personal concern, which makes me all the more determined to broach an embarrassing subject that has . . .'

'Before you say anything else, Sir Hamish, may I ask you some questions?'

'Of course, Minister.'

'Do you still find the tender price of $39,121,110 acceptable in *all* the circumstances?'

'Yes, Minister.'

'That amount still leaves you enough to do a worthwhile job while making a profit for your company?'

'Yes, Minister, but . . .'

'Excellent, then I think all you have to decide is whether you want to sign the contract by midday today.' The minister emphasised the word midday as clearly as he could.

Sir Hamish, who had never understood the expression 'a nod is as good as a wink', charged foolishly on.

'There is, nevertheless, one aspect of the contract I feel that I should discuss with you privately.'

'Are you sure that would be wise, Sir Hamish?'

Sir Hamish hesitated, but only for a moment, before proceeding. Had David Heath heard the conversation that had taken place so far, he would have stood up, shaken hands with the Secretary of State, removed the top of his fountain pen and headed towards the contract – but not his employer.

'Yes, Minister, I feel I must,' said Sir Hamish firmly.

'Will you kindly leave us, Miss Vieites?' said the Secretary of State.

The assistant closed her shorthand book, rose and left the room. Sir Hamish waited for the door to close before he began again.

'Yesterday I had a visit from a countryman of yours, a Mr Victor Perez, who resides here in Mexico City and claims—'

'An excellent man,' said the Minister very quietly.

Still Sir Hamish charged on. 'Yes, I daresay he is, Minister, but he asked to be allowed to represent Graham Construction as our agent and I wondered—'

'A common practice in Mexico, no more than is required by the law,' said the Minister, swinging his chair round and staring out of the window.

'Yes, I appreciate that is the custom,' said Sir Hamish now talking to the minister's back, 'but if I am to part with ten per cent of the government's money I must be convinced that such a decision meets with your personal approval.' Sir Hamish thought he had worded that rather well.

'Um,' said the Secretary of State, measuring his words, 'Victor Perez is a good man and has always been loyal to the Mexican cause. Perhaps he leaves an unfortunate impression sometimes; not out of what you would call the 'top drawer', Sir Hamish, but then we have no class barriers in Mexico.' The Minister swung back to face Sir Hamish.

The Scottish industrialist flushed. 'Of course not, Minister, but that, if you will forgive me, is hardly the point. Mr Perez is asking me to hand over nearly four million dollars, which is over half of my estimated profit on the project without allowing for any contingencies or mishaps that might occur later.'

'You chose the tender figure, Sir Hamish. I confess I was amused by the fact you added your date of birth to the thirty-nine million.'

Sir Hamish's mouth opened wide.

'I would have thought,' continued the minister, 'given your record over the past three years and the present situation in Britain, you were not in a position to be fussy.'

The minister gazed impassively at Sir Hamish's startled face. Both started to speak at the same time. Sir Hamish swallowed his words.

'Allow me to tell you a little story about Victor Perez. When the war was at its fiercest' (the old Secretary of State was referring to the Mexican Revolution, in the same way that an American thinks of Vietnam or a Briton of Germany when they hear the word 'war'), 'Victor's father was one of the young men under my command who died on the battlefield at Celaya only a few days before victory was ours. He left a son born on the day of independence who never knew his father. I have the honour, Sir Hamish, to be godfather to that child. We christened him Victor.'

'I can understand that you have a responsibility to an old comrade but I still feel four million is—'

'Do you? Then let me continue. Just before Victor's father died I visited him in a field hospital and he asked only that I should take care of his wife. She died in childbirth. I therefore considered my responsibility passed on to their only child.'

Sir Hamish remained silent for a moment. 'I appreciate your attitude, Minister, but ten per cent of one of your largest contracts?'

'One day,' continued the Secretary of State, as if he had not heard Sir Hamish's comment, 'Victor's father was fighting in the front line at Zacatecas and looking out across a minefield he saw a young lieutenant, lying face down in the mud with his leg nearly blown off. With no thought for his own safety, he crawled through that minefield until he reached the lieutenant and then he dragged him yard by yard back to the camp. It took him over three hours. He then carried the lieutenant to a truck and drove him to the nearest field hospital, undoubtedly saving his leg, and probably his life. So you see the government have good cause to allow Perez's son the privilege of representing them from time to time.'

'I agree with you, Minister,' said Sir Hamish quietly. 'Quite admirable.' The Secretary of State smiled for the first time. 'But I still confess I cannot understand why you allow him such a large percentage.'

The minister frowned. 'I am afraid, Sir Hamish, if you cannot understand that, you can never hope to understand the principles we Mexicans live by.'

The Secretary of State rose from behind his desk, limped to the door and showed Sir Hamish out.

THE HUNGARIAN
PROFESSOR

COINCIDENCES, writers are told (usually by the critics) must be avoided, although in truth the real world is full of incidents that in themselves are unbelievable. Everyone has had an experience that if they wrote about it would appear to others as pure fiction.

The same week that the headlines in the world newspapers read 'Russia invades Afghanistan, America to withdraw from Moscow Olympics' there also appeared a short obituary in *The Times* for the distinguished Professor of English at the University of Budapest. 'A man who was born and died in his native Budapest and whose reputation remains assured by his brilliant translation of the works of Shakespeare into his native Hungarian. Although some linguists consider his *Coriolanus* immature they universally acknowledge his *Hamlet* to be a translation of genius.'

Nearly a decade after the Hungarian Revolution I had the chance to participate in a student athletics meeting in Budapest. The competition was scheduled to last for a full week so I felt there would be an opportunity to find out a little about the country. The team flew in to Ferihegy Airport on the Sunday night and we were taken immediately to the Hotel Ifushag. (I learned later that the word meant youth in Hungarian.) Having settled in, most of the team went to bed early as their opening round heats were the following day.

Breakfast the next morning comprised of milk, toast and an egg, served in three acts with long intervals between each. Those of us who were running that afternoon skipped lunch for fear that a matinee performance might cause us to miss our events completely.

Two hours before the start of the meeting, we were taken by bus to the Nép stadium and disembarked outside the dressing rooms (I always feel they should be called undressing rooms). We changed into track suits and sat around on benches anxiously waiting to be called. After what seemed to be an interminable time but was in fact only a few minutes, an official appeared and led us out on to the track. As it was the opening day of competition, the stadium was packed. When I had finished my usual warm-up of jogging, sprinting and some light callisthenics, the loudspeaker announced the start of the 100 m race in three languages. I stripped off my track suit and ran over to the start. When called, I pressed my spikes against the blocks and waited nervously for the starter's pistol. Felkészülni, Kész – bang. Ten seconds later the race was over and the only virtue in coming last was that it left me six free days to investigate the Hungarian capital.

Walking around Budapest reminded me of my childhood days in Bristol just after the war, but with one noticeable difference. As well as the bombed-out buildings, there was row upon row of bullet holes in some of the walls. The revolution, although eight years past, was still much in evidence, perhaps because the nationals did not want anyone to forget. The people on the streets had lined faces, stripped of all emotion, and they shuffled rather than walked, leaving the impression of a nation of old men. If you inquired innocently why, they told you there was nothing to hurry for, or to be happy about, although they always seemed to be thoughtful with each other.

On the third day of the games, I returned to the Nép stadium to support a friend of mine who was competing in the semi-finals of the 400m hurdles which was the first event that afternoon. Having a competitor's pass, I could sit virtually anywhere in the half-empty arena. I chose to watch the race from just above the final bend, giving me a good view of the home straight. I sat down on the wooden bench without paying much attention to the people on either side of me. The race began and as my friend hit the bend crossing the seventh hurdle with only three hurdles to cover before the finishing line, I stood and cheered him heartily all the way down the home straight. He managed to come in third, ensuring himself a place in the final the next day. I sat down again and wrote out the detailed result in my programme. I was about to leave, as there were no British competitors in the hammer or the pole vault, when a voice behind me said:

'You are English?'

'Yes,' I replied, turning in the direction from which the question had been put.

An elderly gentleman looked up at me. He wore a three-piece suit that must have been out of date when his father owned it, and even lacked the possible virtue that some day the style might come back into fashion. The leather patches on the elbows left me in no doubt that my questioner was a bachelor for they could only have been sewn on by a man – either that or one had to conclude he had elbows in odd places. The length of his trousers revealed that his father had been two inches taller than he. As for the man himself, he had a few strands of white hair, a walrus moustache, and ruddy cheeks. His tired blue eyes were perpetually half-closed like the shutter of a camera that has just been released. His forehead was so lined that he might have been any age between fifty and seventy. The overall impression was of a cross between a tram inspector and an out-of-work violinist.

I sat down for a second time.

'I hope you didn't mind my asking?' he added.

'Of course not,' I said.

'It's just that I have so little opportunity to converse with an Englishman. So when I spot one I always grasp the nettle. Is that the right colloquial expression?'

'Yes,' I said, trying to think how many Hungarian words I knew. Yes, No, Good morning, Goodbye, I am lost, Help.

'You are in the student games?'

'Were, not are,' I said. 'I departed somewhat rapidly on Monday.'

'Because you were not rapid enough, perhaps?'

I laughed, again admiring his command of my first language.

'Why is your English so excellent?' I inquired.

'I'm afraid it's a little neglected,' the old man replied. 'But they still allow me to teach the subject at the University. I must confess to you that I have absolutely no interest in sport, but these occasions always afford me the opportunity to capture someone like yourself and oil the rusty machine, even if only for a few minutes.' He gave me a tired smile but his eyes were now alight.

'What part of England do you hail from?' For the first time his pronounciation faltered as 'hail' came out as 'heel'.

'Somerset,' I told him.

'Ah,' he said, 'perhaps the most beautiful county in England.' I smiled; as most foreigners never seem to travel much beyond Stratford-on-Avon or Oxford. 'To drive across the Mendips,' he continued, 'through perpetually green hilly countryside and to stop at Cheddar to see Cough's caves, at Wells to be amused by the black swans ringing the bell on the Cathedral wall, or at Bath to admire the lifestyle of classical Rome, and then perhaps to go over the county border and on to Devon ... Is Devon even more beautiful than Somerset, in your opinion?'

'Never,' said I.

'Perhaps you are a little prejudiced,' he laughed. 'Now let me see if I can recall:

> Of the western counties there are seven
> But the most glorious is surely that of Devon.

Perhaps Blackmore, like you, was prejudiced and could think only of his beloved Exmoor, the village of Tiverton and Drake's Plymouth.'

'Which is *your* favourite county?' I asked.

'The North Riding of Yorkshire has always been underrated, in my opinion,' replied the old man. 'When people talk of Yorkshire, I suspect Leeds, Sheffield and Barnsley spring to mind. Coal mining and heavy industry. Visitors should travel and see the dales there; they will find them as different as chalk and cheese. Lincolnshire is too flat and so much of the Midlands must now be spoilt by sprawling towns. The Birminghams of this world hold no appeal for me. But in the end I come down in favour of Worcestershire and Warwickshire, quaint old English villages nestling in the Cotswolds and crowned by Stratford-upon-Avon. How I wish I could have been in England in 1959 while my countrymen were recovering from the scars of revolution. Olivier performing Coriolanus, another man who did not want to show his scars.'

'I saw the performance,' I said. 'I went with a school party.'

'Lucky boy. I translated the play into Hungarian at the age of nineteen. Reading over my work again last year made me aware I must repeat the exercise before I die.'

'You have translated other Shakespeare plays?'

'All but three, I have been leaving *Hamlet* to last, and then I shall return to *Coriolanus* and start again. As you are a student, am I permitted to ask which university you attend?'

'Oxford.'

'And your College?'

'Brasenose.'

'Ah. BNC. How wonderful to be a few yards away from the Bodleian, the greatest library in the world. If I had been born in England I should have wanted to spend my days at All Souls, that is just opposite BNC, is it not?'

'That's right.'

The professor stopped talking while we watched the next race, the first semi-final of the 1,500 metres. The winner was Anfras Patovich, a Hungarian, and the partisan crowd went wild with delight.

'That's what I call support,' I said.

'Like Manchester United when they have scored the winning goal in the Cup Final. But my fellow countrymen do not cheer because the Hungarian was first,' said the old man.

'No?' I said, somewhat surprised.

'Oh, no, they cheer because he beat the Russian.'

'I hadn't even noticed,' I said.

'There is no reason why you should, but their presence is always in the forefront of our minds and we are rarely given the opportunity to see them beaten in public.'

I tried to steer him back to a happier subject. 'And before you had been elected to All Souls, which college would you have wanted to attend?'

'As an undergraduate, you mean?'

'Yes.'

'Undoubtedly Magdalen is the most beautiful college. It has the distinct advantage of being situated on the River Cherwell; and in any case I confess a weakness for perpendicular architecture and a love of Oscar Wilde.' The conversation was interrupted by the sound of a pistol and we watched the second semi-final of the 1,500 metres which was won by Orentas of the USSR and the crowd showed its disapproval more obviously this time, clapping in such a way that left hands passed by right without coming into contact. I found myself joining in on the side of the Hungarians. The scene made the old man lapse into a sad silence. The last race of the day was won by Tim Johnston of England and I stood and cheered unashamedly. The Hungarian crowd clapped politely.

I turned to say goodbye to the professor, who had not spoken for some time.

'How long are you staying in Budapest?' he asked.
'The rest of the week. I return to England on Sunday.'

'Could you spare the time to join an old man for dinner one night?'

'I should be delighted.'

'How considerate of you,' he said, and he wrote out his full name and address in capital letters on the back of my programme and returned it to me. 'Why don't we say tomorrow at seven? And if you have any old newspapers or magazines do bring them with you,' he said looking a little sheepish. 'And I shall quite understand if you have to change your plans.'

I spent the next morning looking over St Matthias Church and the ancient fortress, two of the buildings that showed no evidence of the revolution. I then took a short trip down the Danube before spending the afternoon supporting the swimmers at the Olympic pool. At six I left the pool and went back to my hotel. I changed into my team blazer and grey slacks, hoping I looked smart enough for my distinguished host. I locked my door, and started towards the lift and then remembered. I returned to my room to pick up the pile of newspapers and magazines I had collected from the rest of the team.

Finding the professor's home was not as easy as

I had expected. After meandering around cobbled streets and waving the professor's address at several passers-by, I was finally directed to an old apartment block. I ran up the three flights of the wooden staircase in a few leaps and bounds, wondering how long the climb took the professor every day. I stopped at the door that displayed his number and knocked.

The old man answered immediately as if he had been standing there, waiting by the door. I noticed that he was wearing the same suit he had had on the previous day.

'I am sorry to be late,' I said.

'No matter, my own students also find me hard to find the first time,' he said, grasping my hand. He paused. 'Bad to use the same word twice in the same sentence. "Locate" would have been better, wouldn't it?'

He trotted on ahead of me, not waiting for my reply, a man obviously used to living on his own. He led me down a small, dark corridor into his drawing room. I was shocked by its size. Three sides were covered with indifferent prints and watercolours, depicting English scenes, while the fourth wall was dominated by a large bookcase. I could spot Shakespeare, Dickens, Austen, Trollope, Hardy, Evelyn Waugh and Graham Greene. On the table was a faded copy of the *New Statesman* and I looked round to see if we were on our own, but there seemed to be no sign of a wife or child either in person or picture, and indeed the table was only set for two.

The old man turned and stared with childish delight at my pile of newspapers and magazines.

'*Punch*, *Time* and the *Observer*, a veritable feast,' he declared gathering them into his arms before placing them lovingly on his bed in the corner of the room.

The professor then opened a bottle of Szürkebarát and left me to look at the pictures while he prepared the meal. He slipped away into an alcove which was so small that I had not realised the room contained a kitchenette. He continued to bombard me with questions about England, many of which I was quite unable to answer.

A few minutes later he stepped back into the room, requesting me to take a seat. 'Do be seated,' he said, on reflection. 'I do not wish you to remove the seat. I wish you to sit on it.' He put a plate in front of me which had on it a leg of something that might have been a chicken, a piece of salami and a tomato. I felt sad, not because the food was inadequate, but because he believed it to be plentiful.

After dinner, which despite my efforts to eat slowly and hold him in conversation, did not take up much time, the old man made some coffee which tasted bitter and then filled a pipe before we continued our discussion. We talked of Shakespeare and his views on A. L. Rowse and then he turned to politics.

'Is it true,' the professor asked, 'that England will soon have a Labour government?'

'The opinion polls seem to indicate as much,' I said.

'I suppose the British feel that Sir Alec Douglas-Home is not swinging enough for the sixties,' said the professor, now puffing vigorously away at his pipe. He paused and looked up at me through the smoke. 'I did not offer you a pipe as I assumed after your premature exit in the first round of the competition you would not be smoking.' I smiled. 'But Sir Alec,' he continued, 'is a man with long experience in politics and it's no bad thing for a country to be governed by an experienced gentleman.'

I would have laughed out loud had the same opinion been expressed by my own tutor.

'And what of the Labour leader?' I said, forebearing to mention his name.

'Moulded in the white heat of a technological revolution,' he replied. 'I am not so certain. I liked Gaitskell, an intelligent and shrewd man. An untimely death. Attlee, like Sir Alec, was a gentleman. But as for Mr Wilson, I suspect that history will test his mettle – a pun which I had not intended – in that white heat and only then will we discover the truth.'

I could think of no reply.

'I was considering last night after we parted,' the old man continued, 'the effect that Suez must have had on a nation which only ten years before had won a world war. The Americans should have backed you. Now we read in retrospect, always the historian's privilege, that at the time Prime Minister Eden was tired and ill. The truth was he didn't get the support from his closest allies when he most needed it.'

'Perhaps we should have supported you in 1956.'

'No, no, it was too late then for the West to shoulder Hungary's problems. Churchill understood that in 1945. He wanted to advance beyond Berlin and to free all the nations that bordered Russia. But the West had had a belly full of war by then and left Stalin to take advantage of that apathy. When Churchill coined the phrase "the Iron Curtain", he foresaw exactly what was going to happen in the East. Amazing to think that when that great man said, "if the British Empire should last a thousand years", it was in fact destined to survive for only twenty-five. How I wish he had still been around the corridors of power in 1956.'

'Did the revolution greatly affect your life?'

'I do not complain. It is a privilege to be the Professor of English in a great university. They do not interfere with me in my department and Shakespeare is not yet considered subversive literature.' He paused and took a luxuriant puff at his pipe. 'And what will you do, young man, when you leave the University – as you have shown us that you cannot hope to make a living as a runner?'

'I want to be a writer.'

'Then travel, travel, travel,' he said. 'You cannot hope to learn everything from books. You must see the world for yourself if you ever hope to paint a picture for others.'

I looked up at the old clock on his mantelpiece only to realise how quickly the time had passed.

'I must leave you, I'm afraid; they expect us all to be back in the hotel by ten.'

'Of course,' he said smiling at the English Public School mentality. 'I will accompany you to Kossuth Square and then you will be able to see your hotel on the hill.'

As we left the flat, I noticed that he didn't bother to lock the door. Life had left him little to lose. He led me quickly through the myriad of narrow roads that I had found so impossible to navigate earlier in the evening, chatting about this building and that, an endless fund of knowledge about his own country as well as mine. When we reached Kossuth Square he took my hand and held on to it, reluctant to let go, as lonely people often will.

'Thank you for allowing an old man to indulge himself by chattering on about his favourite subject.'

'Thank you for your hospitality,' I said, 'and when you are next in Somerset you must come to Lympsham and meet my family.'

'Lympsham? I cannot place it,' he said, looking worried.

'I'm not surprised. The village only has a population of twenty-two.'

'Enough for two cricket teams,' remarked the professor. 'A game, I confess, with which I have never come to grips.'

'Don't worry,' I said, 'neither have half the English.'

'Ah, but I should like to. What is a gully, a no-ball, a night watchman? The terms have always intrigued me.'

'Then remember to get in touch when you're next in England and I'll take you to Lord's and see if I can teach you something.'

'How kind,' he said, and then he hesitated before adding: 'But I don't think we shall meet again.'

'Why not?' I asked.

'Well, you see, I have never been outside Hungary in my whole life. When I was young I couldn't afford to and now I don't imagine that those in authority would allow me to see your beloved England.'

He released my hand, turned and shuffled back into the shadows of the side streets of Budapest.

I read his obituary in *The Times* once again as well as the headlines about Afghanistan and its effect on the Moscow Olympics.

He was right. We never met again.

OLD LOVE

GIOLOVE

SOME PEOPLE, it is said, fall in love at first sight but that was not what happened to William Hatchard and Philippa Jameson. They hated each other from the moment they met. This mutual loathing commenced at the first tutorial of their freshmen terms. Both had come up in the early thirties with major scholarships to read English language and literature, William to Merton, Philippa to Somerville. Each had been reliably assured by their schoolteachers that they would be the star pupil of their year.

Their tutor, Simon Jakes of New College, was both bemused and amused by the ferocious competition that so quickly developed between his two brightest pupils, and he used their enmity skilfully to bring out the best in both of them without ever allowing either to indulge in outright abuse. Philippa, an attractive, slim red-head with a rather high-pitched voice, was the same height as William so she conducted as many of her arguments as possible standing in newly acquired high-heeled shoes, while William, whose deep voice had an air of authority, would always try to expound his opinions from a sitting position. The more intense their rivalry became the harder the one tried to outdo the other. By the end of their first year they were far ahead of their contemporaries while remaining neck and neck with each other. Simon Jakes told the Merton Professor of Anglo-Saxon Studies that he had never had a brighter pair up in the same year and that it wouldn't be long before they were holding their own with him.

During the long vacation both worked to a gruelling timetable, always imagining the other would be doing a little more. They stripped bare Blake, Wordsworth, Coleridge, Shelley, Byron, and only went to bed with Keats. When they returned for the second year, they found that absence had made the heart grow even more hostile; and when they were both awarded alpha plus for their essays on Beowulf, it didn't help. Simon Jakes remarked at New College high table one night that if Philippa Jameson had been born a boy some of his tutorials would undoubtedly have ended in blows.

'Why don't you separate them?' asked the Dean, sleepily.

'What, and double my work-load?' said Jakes. 'They teach each other most of the time: I merely act as referee.'

Occasionally the adversaries would seek his adjudication as to who was ahead of whom, and so confident was each of being the favoured pupil that one would always ask in the other's hearing. Jakes was far too canny to be drawn; instead he would remind them that the examiners would be the final arbiters. So they began their own subterfuge by referring to each other, just in earshot, as 'that silly woman', and 'that arrogant man'. By the end of their second year they were almost unable to remain in the same room together.

In the long vacation William took a passing interest in Al Jolson and a girl called Ruby while Philippa flirted with the Charleston and a young naval lieutenant from Dartmouth. But when term started in earnest these interludes were never admitted and soon forgotten.

At the beginning of their third year they both, on Simon Jakes' advice, entered for the Charles Oldham Shakespeare prize along with every other student in the year who was considered likely to gain a First. The Charles Oldham was awarded for an essay on a set aspect of Shakespeare's work, and Philippa and William both realised that this would be the only time in their academic lives that they would be tested against each other in closed competition. Surreptitiously, they worked their separate ways through the entire Shakespearian canon, from *Henry VI* to *Henry VIII*, and kept Jakes well over his appointed tutorial hours, demanding more and more refined discussion of more and more obscure points.

The chosen theme for the prize essay that year was 'Satire in Shakespeare'. *Troilus and Cressida* clearly called for the most attention but both found there were nuances in virtually every one of the bard's thirty-seven plays. 'Not to mention a gross of sonnets,' wrote Philippa home to her father in a rare moment of self-doubt. As the year drew to a close it became obvious to all concerned that either William or Philippa had to win the prize while the other would undoubtedly come second. Nevertheless no one was willing to venture an opinion as to who the victor would be. The New College porter, an expert in these matters, opening his usual book for the Charles Old-ham, made them both evens, ten to one the rest of the field.

Before the prize essay submission date was due, they both had to sit their final degree examinations. Philippa and William confronted the examination papers every morning and afternoon for two weeks with an appetite that bordered on the vulgar. It came as no surprise to anyone that they both achieved first class degrees in the final honours school. Rumour spread around the university that the two rivals had been awarded alphas in every one of their nine papers.

'I would be willing to believe that is the case,' Philippa told William. 'But I feel I must point out to you that there is a considerable difference between an alpha plus and an alpha minus.'

'I couldn't agree with you *more*,' said William. 'And when you discover who has won the Charles Oldham, you will know who was awarded *less*.'

With only three weeks left before the prize essay had to be handed in they both worked twelve hours a day, falling asleep over open text books, dreaming that the other was still beavering away. When the appointed hour came they met in the marble-floored entrance hall of the Examination Schools, sombre in subfusc.

'Good morning, William, I do hope your efforts will manage to secure a place in the first six.'

'Thank you, Philippa. If they don't I shall look for the names C. S. Lewis, Nichol Smith, Nevill Coghill, Edmund Blunden, R. W. Chambers and H. W. Garrard ahead of me. There's certainly no one else in the field to worry about.'

'I am only pleased,' said Philippa, as if she had not heard his reply, 'that you were not seated next to me when I wrote my essay, thus ensuring for the first time in three years that you weren't able to crib from my notes.'

'The only item I have ever cribbed from you, Philippa, was the Oxford to London timetable, and that I discovered later to be out-of-date, which was in keeping with the rest of your efforts.'

They both handed in their twenty-five thousand word essays to the collector's office in the Examination Schools and left without a further word, returning to their respective colleges impatiently to await the result.

William tried to relax the weekend after submitting his essay, and for the first time in three years he played some tennis, against a girl from St Anne's, failing to win a game, let alone a set. He nearly sank when he went swimming, and actually did so when punting. He was only relieved that Philippa had not been witness to any of his feeble physical efforts.

On Monday night after a resplendent dinner with the Master of Merton, he decided to take a walk along the banks of the Cherwell to clear his head before going to bed. The May evening was still light as he made his way down through the narrow confines of Merton Wall, across the meadows to the banks of the Cherwell. As he strolled along the winding path, he thought he spied his rival ahead of him under a tree reading. He considered turning back but decided she might already have spotted him, so he kept on walking.

He had not seen Philippa for three days although she had rarely been out of his thoughts: once he had won the Charles Oldham, the silly woman would have to climb down from that high horse of hers. He smiled at the thought and decided to walk nonchalantly past her. As he drew nearer, he lifted his eyes from the path in front of him to steal a quick glance in her direction, and could feel himself reddening in anticipation of her inevitable well-timed insult. Nothing happened so he looked more carefully, only to discover on closer inspection that she was not reading: her head was bowed in her hands and she appeared to be sobbing quietly. He slowed his progress to observe, not the formidable rival who had for three years dogged his every step, but a forlorn and lonely creature who looked somewhat helpless.

William's first reaction was to think that the winner of the prize essay competition had been leaked to her and that he had indeed achieved his victory. On reflection, he realised that could not be the case: the examiners would only have received the essays that morning and as all the assessors read each submission the results could not possibly be forthcoming until at least the end of the week. Philippa did not look up when he reached her side – he was even unsure whether she was aware of his presence. As he stopped to gaze at his adversary William could not help noticing how her long red hair curled just as it touched the shoulder. He sat down beside her but still she did not stir.

'What's the matter?' he asked. 'Is there anything I can do?'

She raised her head, revealing a face flushed from crying.

'No, nothing William, except leave me alone. You deprive me of solitude without affording me company.'

William was pleased that he immediately recognised the little literary allusion. 'What's the matter, Madame de Sévigné?' he asked, more out of curiosity than concern, torn between sympathy and catching her with her guard down.

It seemed a long time before she replied.

'My father died this morning,' she said finally, as if speaking to herself.

It struck William as strange that after three years

of seeing Philippa almost every day he knew nothing about her home life.

'And your mother?' he said.

'She died when I was three. I don't even remember her. My father is—' She paused. 'Was a parish priest and brought me up, sacrificing everything he had to get me to Oxford, even the family silver. I wanted so much to win the Charles Oldham for him.'

William put his arm tentatively on Philippa's shoulder.

'Don't be absurd. When you win the prize, they'll pronounce you the star pupil of the decade. After all, you will have had to beat me to achieve the distinction.'

She tried to laugh. 'Of course I wanted to beat you, William, but only for my father.'

'How did he die?'

'Cancer, only he never let me know. He asked me not to go home before the summer term as he felt the break might interfere with my finals and the Charles Oldham. While all the time he must have been keeping me away because he knew if I saw the state he was in that would have been the end of my completing any serious work.'

'Where do you live?' asked William, again surprised that he did not know.

'Brockenhurst. In Hampshire. I'm going back there tomorrow morning. The funeral's on Wednesday.'

'May I take you?' asked William.

Philippa looked up and was aware of a softness in her adversary's eyes that she had not seen before. 'That would be kind, William.'

'Come on then, you silly woman,' he said. 'I'll walk you back to your college.'

'Last time you called me "silly woman" you meant it.'

William found it natural that they should hold hands as they walked along the river bank. Neither spoke until they reached Somerville.

'What time shall I pick you up?' he asked, not letting go of her hand.

'I didn't know you had a car.'

'My father presented me with an old MG when I was awarded a first. I have been longing to find some excuse to show the damn thing off to you. It has a press button start, you know.'

'Obviously he didn't want to risk waiting to give you the car on the Charles Oldham results.' William laughed more heartily than the little dig merited.

'Sorry,' she said. 'Put it down to habit. I shall look forward to seeing if you drive as appallingly as you write, in which case the journey may never come to any conclusion. I'll be ready for you at ten.'

On the journey down to Hampshire, Philippa talked about her father's work as a parish priest and inquired after William's family. They stopped for lunch at a pub in Winchester. Rabbit stew and mashed potatoes.

'The first meal we've had together,' said William.

No sardonic reply came flying back; Philippa simply smiled.

After lunch they travelled on to the village of Brockenhurst. William brought his car to an uncertain halt on the gravel outside the vicarage. An elderly maid, dressed in black, answered the door, surprised to see Miss Philippa with a man. Philippa introduced Annie to William and asked her to make up the spare room.

'I'm so glad you've found yourself such a nice young man,' remarked Annie later. 'Have you known him long?'

Philippa smiled. 'No, we met for the first time yesterday.'

Philippa cooked William dinner, which they ate by a fire he had made up in the front room. Although hardly a word passed between them for three hours, neither was bored. Philippa began to notice the way William's untidy fair hair fell over his forehead and thought how distinguished he would look in old age.

The next morning, she walked into the church on William's arm and stood bravely through the funeral. When the service was over William took her back to the vicarage, crowded with the many friends the parson had made.

'You mustn't think ill of us,' said Mr Crump, the vicar's warden, to Philippa. 'You were everything to your father and we were all under strict instructions not to let you know about his illness in case it should interfere with the Charles Oldham. That is the name of the prize, isn't it?'

'Yes,' said Philippa. 'But that all seems so unimportant now.'

'She will win the prize in her father's memory,' said William.

Philippa turned and looked at him, realising for the first time that he actually wanted her to win the Charles Oldham.

They stayed that night at the vicarage and drove back to Oxford on the Thursday. On the Friday morning at ten o'clock William returned to Philippa's college and asked the porter if he could speak to Miss Jameson.

'Would you be kind enough to wait in the Horse-box, sir,' said the porter as he showed William into a little room at the back of the lodge and then scurried off to find Miss Jameson. They returned together a few minutes later.

'What on earth are you doing here?'

'Come to take you to Stratford.'

'But I haven't even had time to unpack the things I brought back from Brockenhurst.'

'Just do as you are told for once; I'll give you fifteen minutes.'

'Of course,' she said. 'Who am I to disobey the next winner of the Charles Oldham? I shall even allow you to come up to my room for one minute and help me unpack.'

The porter's eyebrows nudged the edge of his cap but he remained silent, in deference to Miss Jameson's recent bereavement. Again it surprised William to think that he had never been to Philippa's room during their three years. He had climbed the walls of all the women's colleges to be with a variety of girls of varying stupidity but never with Philippa. He sat down on the end of the bed.

'Not there, you thoughtless creature. The maid has only just made it. Men are all the same, you never sit in chairs.'

'I shall one day,' said William. 'The chair of English Language and Literature.'

'Not as long as I'm at this university, you won't,' she said, as she disappeared into the bathroom.

'Good intentions are one thing but talent is quite another,' he shouted at her retreating back, privately pleased that her competitive streak seemed to he returning.

Fifteen minutes later she came out of the bathroom in a yellow flowered dress with a neat white collar and matching cuffs. William thought she might even be wearing a touch of make-up.

'It will do our reputations no good to be seen together,' she said.

'I've thought about that,' said William. 'If asked, I shall say you're my charity.'

'Your charity?'

'Yes, this year I'm supporting distressed orphans.'

Philippa signed out of college until midnight and

the two scholars travelled down to Stratford, stopping off at Broadway for lunch. In the afternoon they rowed on the River Avon. William warned Philippa of his last disastrous outing in a punt. She admitted that she had already heard of the exhibition he had made of himself, but they arrived safely back at the shore: perhaps because Philippa took over the rowing. They went to see John Gielgud playing Romeo and dined at the Dirty Duck. Philippa was even quite rude to William during the meal.

They started their journey home just after eleven and Philippa fell into a half sleep as they could hardly hear each other above the noise of the car engine. It must have been about twenty-five miles outside of Oxford that the MG came to a halt.

'I thought,' said William, 'that when the petrol gauge showed empty there was at least another gallon left in the tank.'

'You're obviously wrong, and not for the first time, and because of such foresight you'll have to walk to the nearest garage all by yourself – you needn't imagine that I'm going to keep you company. I intend to stay put, right here in the warmth.'

'But there isn't a garage between here and Oxford,' protested William.

'Then you'll have to carry me. I am far too fragile to walk.'

'I wouldn't be able to manage fifty yards after that sumptuous dinner and all that wine.'

'It is no small mystery to me, William, how you

could have managed a first-class honours degree in English when you can't even read a petrol gauge.'

'There's only one thing for it,' said William. 'We'll have to wait for the first bus in the morning.'

Philippa clambered into the back seat and did not speak to him again before falling asleep. William donned his hat, scarf and gloves, crossed his arms for warmth, and touched the tangled red mane of Philippa's hair as she slept. He then took off his coat and placed it so that it covered her.

Philippa woke first, a little after six, and groaned as she tried to stretch her aching limbs. She then shook William awake to ask him why his father hadn't been considerate enough to buy him a car with a comfortable back seat.

'But this is the niftiest thing going,' said William, gingerly kneading his neck muscles before putting his coat back on.

'But it isn't going, and won't without petrol,' she replied getting out of the car to stretch her legs.

'But I only let it run out for one reason,' said William following her to the front of the car.

Philippa waited for a feeble punch line and was not disappointed.

'My father told me if I spent the night with a barmaid then I should simply order an extra pint of beer, but if I spent the night with the vicar's daughter, I would have to marry her.'

Philippa laughed. William, tired, unshaven, and

encumbered by his heavy coat, struggled to get down on one knee.

'What are you doing, William?'

'What do you think I'm doing, you silly woman. I am going to ask you to marry me.'

'An invitation I am happy to decline, William. If I accepted such a proposal I might end up spending the rest of my life stranded on the road between Oxford and Stratford.'

'Will you marry me if I win the Charles Oldham?'

'As there is absolutely no fear of that happening I can safely say, yes. Now do get off your knee, William, before someone mistakes you for a straying stork.'

The first bus arrived at five-past-seven that Saturday morning and took Philippa and William back to Oxford. Philippa went to her rooms for a long hot bath while William filled a petrol can and returned to his deserted MG. Having completed the task, he drove straight to Somerville and once again asked if he could see Miss Jameson. She came down a few minutes later.

'What you again?' she said. 'Am I not in enough trouble already?'

'Why so?'

'Because I was out after midnight, unaccompanied.'

'You were accompanied.'

'Yes, and that's what's worrying them.'

'Did you tell them we spent the night together?'

'No, I did not. I don't mind our contemporaries thinking I'm promiscuous, but I have strong objections to their believing that I have no taste. Now kindly go away, as I am contemplating the horror of your winning the Charles Oldham and my having to spend the rest of my life with you.'

'You know I'm bound to win, so why don't you come live with me now?'

'I realise that it has become fashionable to sleep with just anyone nowadays, William, but if this is to be my last weekend of freedom I intend to savour it, especially as I may have to consider committing suicide.'

'I love you.'

'For the last time, William, go away. And if you haven't won the Charles Oldham don't ever show your face in Somerville again.'

William left, desperate to know the result of the prize essay competition. Had he realised how much Philippa wanted him to win he might have slept that night.

On Monday morning they both arrived early in the Examination Schools and stood waiting impatiently without speaking to each other, jostled by the other undergraduates of their year who had also been entered for the prize. On the stroke of ten the chairman of the examiners, in full academic dress, walking at tortoise-like pace, arrived in the great hall and with a considerable pretence at indifference pinned a notice to the board. All the undergraduates who had entered for the prize rushed forward except for William and Philippa who stood alone, aware that it was now too late to influence a result they were both dreading.

A girl shot out from the mêlée around the notice board and ran over to Philippa.

'Well done, Phil. You've won.'

Tears came to Philippa's eyes as she turned towards William.

'May I add my congratulations,' he said quickly, 'you obviously deserved the prize.'

'I wanted to say something to you on Saturday.'

'You did, you said if I lost I must never show my face in Somerville again.'

'No, I wanted to say: I do love nothing in the world so well as you; is not that strange?'

He looked at her silently for a long moment. It was impossible to improve upon Beatrice's reply.

'As strange as the thing I know not,' he said softly.

A college friend slapped him on the shoulder, took his hand and shook it vigorously. *Proxime accessit* was obviously impressive in some people's eyes, if not in William's.

'Well done, William.'

'Second place is not worthy of praise,' said William disdainfully.

'But you won, Billy boy.'

Philippa and William stared at each other.

'What do you mean?' said William.

'Exactly what I said. You've won the Charles Oldham.'

Philippa and William ran to the board and studied the notice.

CHARLES OLDHAM MEMORIAL PRIZE
The examiners felt unable on this occasion to
award the prize to one person and have therefore
decided that it should be shared by

They gazed at the notice board in silence for some moments. Finally, Philippa bit her lip and said in a small voice:

'Well, you didn't do too badly, considering the competition. I'm prepared to honour my undertaking but by this light I take thee for pity.'

William needed no prompting. 'I would not deny you, but by this good day I yield upon great persuasion, for I was told you were in a consumption.'

And to the delight of their peers and the amazement of the retreating don, they embraced under the notice board.

Rumour had it that from that moment on they were never apart for more than a few hours.

The marriage took place a month later in Philippa's family church at Brockenhurst. 'Well, when you think about it,' said William's room-mate, 'who else could she have married?' The contentious couple started their honeymoon in Athens arguing about the relative significance of Doric and Ionic architecture of which neither knew any more than they had covertly conned from a half-crown tourist guide. They sailed on to Istanbul, where William prostrated himself at the front of every mosque he could find while Philippa stood on her own at the back fuming at the Turks' treatment of women.

'The Turks are a shrewd race,' declared William, 'so quick to appreciate real worth.'

'Then why don't you embrace the Muslim religion, William, and I need only be in your presence once a year.'

'The misfortune of birth, a misplaced loyalty and the signing of an unfortunate contract dictate that I spend the rest of my life with you.'

Back at Oxford, with junior research fellowships at their respective colleges, they settled down to serious creative work. William embarked upon a massive study of word usage in Marlowe and, in his spare moments, taught himself statistics to assist his findings. Philippa chose as her subject the influence of the Reformation on seventeenth-century English writers and was soon drawn beyond literature into art and music. She bought herself a spinet and took to playing Dowland and Gibbons in the evening.

'For Christ's sake,' said William, exasperated by the tinny sound, 'you won't deduce their religious convictions from their key signatures.'

'More informative than ifs and ands, my dear,' she said, imperturbably, 'and at night so much more relaxing than pots and pans.'

Three years later, with well-received D. Phils, they

moved on, inexorably in tandem, to college teaching fellowships. As the long shadow of fascism fell across Europe, they read, wrote, criticised and coached by quiet firesides in unchanging quadrangles.

'A rather dull Schools year for me,' said William, 'but I still managed five firsts from a field of eleven.'

'An even duller one for me,' said Philippa, 'but somehow I squeezed three firsts out of six, and you won't have to invoke the binomial theorem, William, to work out that it's an arithmetical victory for me.'

'The chairman of the examiners tells me,' said William, 'that a greater part of what your pupils say is no more than a recitation from memory.'

'He told me,' she retorted, 'that yours have to make it up as they go along.'

When they dined together in college the guest list was always quickly filled, and as soon as grace had been said, the sharpness of their dialogue would flash across the candelabra.

'I hear a rumour, Philippa, that the college doesn't feel able to renew your fellowship at the end of the year.'

'I fear you speak the truth, William,' she replied. 'They decided they couldn't renew mine at the same time as offering me yours.'

'Do you think they will ever make you a Fellow of the British Academy, William?'

'I must say, with some considerable disappointment, never.'

'I am sorry to hear that; why not?'

'Because when they did invite me, I informed the President that I would prefer to wait to be elected at the same time as my wife.'

Some non-university guests sitting in high table for the first time took their verbal battles seriously; others could only be envious of such love.

One Fellow uncharitably suggested they rehearsed their lines before coming to dinner for fear it might be thought they were getting on well together. During their early years as young dons, they became acknowledged as the leaders in their respective fields. Like magnets, they attracted the brightest undergraduates while apparently remaining poles apart themselves.

'Dr Hatchard will be delivering half these lectures,' Philippa announced at the start of the Michaelmas Term of their joint lecture course on Arthurian legend. 'But I can assure you it will not be the better half. You would be wise always to check which Dr Hatchard is lecturing.'

When Philippa was invited to give a series of lectures at Yale, William took a sabbatical so that he could be with her.

On the ship crossing the Atlantic, Philippa said, 'Let's at least be thankful the journey is by sea, my dear, so we can't run out of petrol.'

'Rather let us thank God,' replied William, 'that the ship has an engine because you would even take the wind out of Cunard's sails.'

The only sadness in their lives was that Philippa could bear William no children, but if anything it drew the two closer together. Philippa lavished quasi-maternal affection on her tutorial pupils and allowed herself only the wry comment that she was spared the probability of producing a child with William's looks and William's brains.

At the outbreak of war William's expertise with handling words made a move into cipher-breaking inevitable. He was recruited by an anonymous gentleman who visited them at home with a briefcase chained to his wrist. Philippa listened shamelessly at the keyhole while they discussed the problems they had come up against and burst into the room and demanded to be recruited as well.

'Do you realise that I can complete *The Times* crossword puzzle in half the time my husband can?'

The anonymous man was only thankful that he wasn't chained to Philippa. He drafted them both to the Admiralty section to deal with enciphered wireless messages to and from German submarines.

The German signal manual was a four-letter code book and each message was reciphered, the substitution table changing daily. William taught Philippa how to evaluate letter frequencies and she applied her new knowledge to modern German texts, coming up with a frequency analysis that was soon used by every code-breaking department in the Commonwealth.

Even so breaking the ciphers and building up the master signal book was a colossal task which took them the best part of two years.

'I never knew your ifs and ands could be so informative,' she said admiringly of her own work.

When the allies invaded Europe husband and wife could together often break ciphers with no more than half a dozen lines of encoded text to go on.

'They're an illiterate lot,' grumbled William. 'They don't encipher their umlauts. They deserve to be mis-understood.'

'How can you give an opinion when you never dot your i's William?'

'Because I consider the dot is redundant and I hope to be responsible for removing it from the English language.'

'Is that to be your major contribution to scholar-ship, William? If so, I am bound to ask how anyone reading the work of most of our undergraduates' essays would be able to tell the difference between an l and an i.'

'A feeble argument, my dear, that if it had any conviction would demand that you put a dot on top of an n so as to be sure it wasn't mistaken for an h.'

'Keep working away at your theories, William, because I intend to spend my energy removing more than the dot and the l from Hitler.'

In May 1945 they dined privately with the Prime Minister and Mrs Churchill at Number Ten Downing Street.

'What did the Prime Minister mean when he said

to me he could never understand what you were up to?' asked Philippa in the taxi to Paddington Station.

'The same as when he said to me he knew exactly what you were capable of, I suppose,' said William.

When the Merton Professor of English retired in the early nineteen-fifties the whole university waited to see which Doctor Hatchard would be appointed to the chair.

'If Council invite you to take the chair,' said William, putting his hand through his greying hair, 'it will be because they are going to make me Vice-Chancellor.'

'The only way you could ever be invited to hold a position so far beyond your ability would be nepotism, which would mean I was already Vice-Chancellor.'

The General Board, after several hours' discussion of the problem, offered two chairs and appointed William and Philippa full professors on the same day.

When the Vice-Chancellor was asked why precedent had been broken he replied: 'Simple; if I hadn't given them both a chair, one of them would have been after my job.'

That night, after a celebration dinner when they were walking home together along the banks of the Isis across Christ Church Meadows, in the midst of a particularly heated argument about the quality of the last volume of Proust's monumental works, a policeman, noticing the affray, ran over to them and asked:

'Is everything all right, madam?'

'No, it is not,' William interjected, 'this woman has been attacking me for over thirty years and to date the police have done deplorably little to protect me.'

In the late fifties Harold Macmillan invited Philippa to join the board of the IBA.

'I suppose you'll become what's known as a telly don,' said William, 'and as the average mental age of those who watch the box is seven you should feel quite at home.'

'Agreed,' said Philippa. 'Twenty years of living with you has made me fully qualified to deal with infants.'

The chairman of the BBC wrote to William a few weeks later inviting him to join the Board of Governors.

'Are you to replace "Hancock's Half Hour" or "Dick Barton, Special Agent"?' Philippa inquired.

'I am to give a series of twelve lectures.'

'On what subject, pray?'

'Genius.'

Philippa flicked through the *Radio Times*. 'I see that *Genius* is to be viewed at two o'clock on a Sunday morning, which is understandable, as it's when you are at your most brilliant.'

When William was awarded an honorary doctorate at Princeton, Philippa attended the ceremony and sat proudly in the front row.

'I tried to secure a place at the back,' she

explained, 'but it was filled with sleeping students who had obviously never heard of you.'

'If that's the case, Philippa, I am only surprised you didn't mistake them for one of your tutorial lectures.'

As the years passed, many anecdotes, only some of which were apocryphal, passed into the Oxford fabric. Everyone in the English school knew the stories about the 'fighting Hatchards'. How they spent their first night together. How they jointly won the Charles Oldham. How Phil would complete *The Times* crossword before Bill had finished shaving. How they were both appointed to professorial chairs on the same day, and worked longer hours than any of their contemporaries as if they still had something to prove, if only to each other. It seemed almost required by the laws of symmetry that they should always be judged equals. Until it was announced in the New Year's Honours that Philippa had been made a Dame of the British Empire.

'At least our dear Queen has worked out which one of us is truly worthy of recognition,' she said over the college dessert.

'Our dear Queen,' said William, selecting the Madeira, 'knows only too well how little competition there is in the women's colleges: sometimes one must encourage weaker candidates in the hope that it might inspire some real talent lower down.'

After that, whenever they attended a public function together, Philippa would have the MC announce them as Professor William and Dame Philippa Hatchard. She looked forward to many happy years of starting every official occasion one up on her husband, but her triumph lasted for only six months as William received a knighthood in the Queen's Birthday Honours. Philippa feigned surprise at the dear Queen's uncharacteristic lapse of judgment and forthwith insisted on their being introduced in public as Sir William and Dame Philippa Hatchard.

'Understandable,' said William. 'The Queen had to make you a Dame first in order that no one should mistake you for a lady. When I married you, Philippa, you were a young fellow, and now I find I'm living with an old Dame.'

'It's no wonder,' said Philippa, 'that your poor pupils can't make up their minds whether you're homosexual or you simply have a mother fixation. Be thankful that I did not accept Girton's invitation: then you would have been married to a mistress.'

'I always have been, you silly woman.'

As the years passed, they never let up their pretended belief in the other's mental feebleness. Philippa's books, 'works of considerable distinction' she insisted, were published by Oxford University Press while William's 'works of monumental significance' he declared were printed at the presses of Cambridge University.

The tally of newly appointed professors of English

they had taught as undergraduates soon reached double figures.

'If you will count polytechnics, I shall have to throw in Maguire's readership in Kenya,' said William.

'You did not teach the Professor of English at Nairobi,' said Philippa. 'I did. You taught the Head of State, which may well account for why the university is so highly thought of while the country is in such disarray.'

In the early sixties they conducted a battle of letters in the TLS on the works of Philip Sidney without ever discussing the subject in each other's presence. In the end the editor said the correspondence must stop and adjudicated a draw.

They both declared him an idiot.

If there was one act that annoyed William in old age about Philippa, it was her continued determination each morning to complete *The Times* crossword before he arrived at the breakfast table. For a time, William ordered two copies of the paper until Philippa filled them both in while explaining to him it was a waste of money.

One particular morning in June at the end of their final academic year before retirement, William came down to breakfast to find only one space in the crossword left for him to complete. He studied the clue: 'Skelton reported that this landed in the soup.' He immediately filled in the eight little boxes.

Philippa looked over his shoulder. 'There's no such word, you arrogant man,' she said firmly. 'You made it up to annoy me.' She placed in front of him a very hard-boiled egg.

'Of course there is, you silly woman; look whym-wham up in the dictionary.'

Philippa checked in the *Oxford Shorter* among the cookery books in the kitchen, and trumpeted her delight that it was nowhere to be found.

'My dear Dame Philippa,' said William, as if he were addressing a particularly stupid pupil, 'you surely cannot imagine because you are old and your hair has become very white that you are a sage. You must understand that the *Shorter Oxford Dictionary* was cobbled together for simpletons whose command of the English language stretches to no more than one hundred thousand words. When I go to college this morning I shall confirm the existence of the word in the *OED* on my desk. Need I remind you that the *OED* is a serious work which, with over five hundred thousand words, was designed for scholars like myself?'

'Rubbish,' said Philippa. 'When I am proved right, you will repeat this story word for word, including your offensive non-word, at Somerville's Gaudy Feast.'

'And you, my dear, will read the *Collected Works of John Skelton* and eat humble pie as your first course.'

'We'll ask old Onions along to adjudicate.'

'Agreed.'

'Agreed.'

With that, Sir William picked up his paper, kissed his wife on the cheek and said with an exaggerated sigh, 'It's at times like this that I wish I'd lost the Charles Oldham.'

'You did, my dear. It was in the days when it wasn't fashionable to admit a woman had won anything.'

'You won me.'

'Yes, you arrogant man, but I was led to believe you were one of those prizes one could return at the end of the year. And now I find I shall have to keep you, even in retirement.'

'Let us leave it to the *Oxford English Dictionary*, my dear, to decide the issue the Charles Oldham examiners were unable to determine,' and with that he departed for his college.

'There's no such word,' Philippa muttered as he closed the front door.

Heart attacks are known to be rarer among women than men. When Dame Philippa suffered hers in the kitchen that morning she collapsed on the floor calling hoarsely for William, but he was already out of earshot. It was the cleaning woman who found Dame Philippa on the kitchen floor and ran to fetch someone in authority. The Bursar's first reaction was that she was probably pretending that Sir William had hit her with a frying pan but nevertheless she hurried over to the Hatchards' house in Little Jericho just in case. The Bursar checked Dame Philippa's pulse and called for the college doctor and then the Principal. Both arrived within minutes.

The Principal and the Bursar stood waiting by the side of their illustrious academic colleague but they already knew what the doctor was going to say.

'She's dead,' he confirmed. 'It must have been very sudden and with the minimum of pain.' He checked his watch; the time was nine-forty-seven. He covered his patient with a blanket and called for an ambulance. He had taken care of Dame Philippa for over thirty years and he had told her so often to slow down that he might as well have made a gramophone record of it for all the notice she took.

'Who will tell Sir William?' asked the Principal. The three of them looked at each other.

'I will,' said the doctor.

It's a short walk from Little Jericho to Radcliffe Square. It was a long walk from Little Jericho to Radcliffe Square for the doctor that day. He never relished telling anyone of the death of a spouse but this one was going to be the unhappiest of his career.

When he knocked on the professor's door, Sir William bade him enter. The great man was sitting at his desk poring over the *Oxford Dictionary*, humming to himself.

'I told her, but she wouldn't listen, the silly woman,' he was saying to himself and then he turned and saw the doctor standing silently in the doorway.

'Doctor, you must be my guest at Somerville's Gaudy next Thursday week where Dame Philippa will he eating humble pie. It will be nothing less than game, set, match and championship for me. A vindication of thirty years' scholarship.'

The doctor did not smile, nor did he stir. Sir William walked over to him and gazed at his old friend intently. No words were necessary. The doctor said only, 'I'm more sorry than I am able to express,' and he left Sir William to his private grief.

Sir William's colleagues all knew within the hour. College lunch that day was spent in a silence broken only by the Senior Tutor inquiring of the Master if some food should be taken up to the Merton professor.

'I think not,' said the Master. Nothing more was said.

Professors, Fellows and students alike crossed the front quadrangle in silence and when they gathered for dinner that evening still no one felt like conversation. At the end of the meal the Senior Tutor suggested once again that something should be taken up to Sir William. This time the Master nodded his agreement and a light meal was prepared by the college chef. The Master and the Senior Tutor climbed the worn stone steps to Sir William's room and while one held the tray the other gently knocked on the door. There was no reply, so the Master, used to William's ways, pushed the door ajar and looked in.

The old man lay motionless on the wooden floor in a pool of blood, a small pistol by his side. The two men walked in and stared down. In his right hand, *William* was holding the *Collected Works of John Skelton*. The book was open at 'The Tunnyng of Elynour Rummyng', and the word 'whym wham' was underlined.

a 1529, Skelton, *E. Rummyng* 75

After the Sarasyns gyse,
Woth a whym wham,
Knyt with a trym tram,
Upon her brayne pan.

Sir William, in his neat hand, had written a note in the margin: 'Forgive me, but I had to let her know.'

'Know what, I wonder?' said the Master softly to himself as he attempted to remove the book from Sir William's hand, but the fingers were already stiff and cold around it.

Legend has it that they were never apart for more than a few hours.

THE END

SONS OF FORTUNE

TO ALISON

CONTENTS

BOOK ONE

GENESIS

1

SUSAN PLONKED THE ice cream firmly on Michael Cartwright's head. It was the first occasion the two of them had met, or that was what Michael's best man claimed when Susan and Michael were married twenty-one years later.

Both of them were three years old at the time, and when Michael burst into tears, Susan's mother rushed over to find out what the problem was. All Susan was willing to say on the subject, and she repeated it several times, was, 'Well, he asked for it, didn't he?' Susan ended up with a spanking. Not the ideal start for any romance.

The next recorded meeting, according to the best man, was when they both arrived at their elementary school. Susan declared with a knowing air that Michael was a cry-baby, and what's more, a sneak. Michael told the other boys that he would share his Graham Crackers with anyone who was willing to pull Susan Illingworth's pigtails. Few boys tried a second time.

At the end of their first year, Susan and Michael were jointly awarded the class prize. Their teacher considered it the best course of action if she hoped to prevent another ice-cream incident. Susan told her friends that Michael's mother did his homework for him, to which Michael responded that at least it was in his own handwriting.

The rivalry continued unabated through junior and senior high until they departed for different universities,

3

Michael to Connecticut State and Susan to Georgetown. For the next four years, they both worked hard at avoiding each other. In fact the next occasion their paths crossed was, ironically, at Susan's home, when her parents threw a surprise graduation party for their daughter. The biggest surprise was not that Michael accepted the invitation, but that he turned up.

Susan didn't recognize her old rival immediately, partly because he had grown four inches and was, for the first time, taller than her. It wasn't until she offered him a glass of wine and Michael remarked, 'At least this time you didn't pour it all over me,' that she realized who the tall handsome man was.

'God, I behaved dreadfully, didn't I,' said Susan, wanting him to deny it.

'Yes, you did,' he said, 'but then I expect I deserved it.'

'You did,' she said, biting her tongue.

They chatted like old friends, and Susan was surprised at how disappointed she felt when a classmate from Georgetown joined them and started flirting with Michael. They didn't speak to each other again that evening.

Michael phoned the following day and invited her to see Spencer Tracy and Katharine Hepburn in *Adam's Rib*. Susan had already seen the movie, but still heard herself accepting, and couldn't believe how long she spent trying on different dresses before he arrived for that first date.

Susan enjoyed the film, even though it was her second time, and wondered if Michael would put an arm around her shoulder when Spencer Tracy kissed Katharine Hepburn. He didn't. But when they left the movie house, he took her hand as they crossed the road, and didn't let it go until they reached the coffee shop. That was when they had their first row, well, disagreement. Michael admitted that he was going to vote for Thomas Dewey in November, while Susan made it clear that she wanted Harry Truman to remain in the White House. The waiter placed an ice cream in front of Susan. She stared down at it.

'Don't even think about it,' Michael said.

Susan wasn't surprised when he called the following day, although she had been sitting by the phone for over an hour pretending to be reading.

Michael had admitted to his mother over breakfast that morning it had been love at first sight.

'But you've known Susan for years,' remarked his mother.

'No I haven't, Mom,' he replied, 'I met her for the first time yesterday.'

Both sets of parents were delighted, but not surprised, when they became engaged a year later, after all, they'd hardly spent a day apart since Susan's graduation party. Both had landed jobs within days of leaving college, Michael as a trainee with the Hartford Life Insurance Company and Susan as a history teacher at Jefferson High, so they decided to get married during the summer vacation.

What they hadn't planned was that Susan would become pregnant while they were on their honeymoon. Michael couldn't hide his delight at the thought of being a father, and when Dr Greenwood told them in the sixth month that it was going to be twins he was doubly delighted.

'Well at least that will solve one problem,' was his first reaction.

'Namely?' asked Susan.

'One can be a Republican, and the other a Democrat.'

'Not if I have anything to do with it,' said Susan, rubbing her stomach.

Susan continued teaching until her eighth month, which happily coincided with the Easter vacation. She arrived at the hospital on the twenty-eighth day of the ninth month carrying a small suitcase. Michael left work early and joined her a few minutes later, with the news that he had been promoted to account executive.

'What does that mean?' asked Susan.

'It's a fancy title for an insurance salesman,' Michael told her. 'But it does include a small pay raise, which can only help now we're going to have two more mouths to feed.'

Once Susan was settled in her room, Dr Greenwood suggested to Michael that he wait outside during the delivery, as with twins there just might be complications.

Michael paced up and down the long corridor. Whenever he reached the portrait of Josiah Preston hanging on the far wall, he turned and retraced his steps. On the first few of these route marches, Michael didn't stop to read the long biography printed below the portrait of the hospital's founder. By the time the doctor emerged through the double doors, Michael knew the man's entire life history by heart.

The green-clad figure walked slowly towards him before removing his mask. Michael tried to fathom the expression on his face. In his profession it was an advantage to be able to decipher expressions and second-guess thoughts, because when it came to selling life insurance you needed to anticipate any anxieties a potential client might have. However, when it came to this life insurance policy, the doctor gave nothing away. When they came face to face, he smiled and said, 'Congratulations, Mr Cartwright, you have two healthy sons.'

Susan had delivered two boys, Nathaniel at 4.37 and Peter at 4.43 that afternoon. For the next hour, the parents took turns cuddling them, until Dr Greenwood suggested that perhaps mother and babies should be allowed to rest. 'Having to feed two children will prove exhausting enough. I shall put them both in the special care nursery overnight,' he added. 'Nothing to worry about, because it's something we always do with twins.'

Michael accompanied his two sons to the nursery, where once again he was asked to wait in the corridor. The proud father pressed his nose up against the pane of glass that divided the corridor from the row of cribs, gazing at the boys as they lay sleeping, wanting to tell everyone who passed, 'they're both mine'. He smiled at the nurse who was standing by their side, keeping a watchful eye over the latest arrivals. She was placing name tags around their tiny wrists.

Michael couldn't remember how long he remained there before eventually returning to his wife's bedside. When he opened the door, he was pleased to find that Susan was fast asleep. He kissed her gently on the forehead. 'I'll see you in the morning my darling, just before I go to work,' he said, ignoring the fact that she couldn't hear a word. Michael left her, walked down the corridor and stepped into the elevator to find Dr Greenwood had exchanged his green scrubs for a sports jacket and grey flannels.

'I wish they were all that easy,' he told the proud father as the elevator stopped on the ground floor. 'Still, I'll drop by this evening, Mr Cartwright, to check on your wife and see how the twins are doing. Not that I anticipate any problems.'

'Thank you, doctor,' said Michael. 'Thank you.'

Dr Greenwood smiled, and would have left the hospital and driven home had he not spotted an elegant lady coming through the swing doors. He walked quickly across to join Ruth Davenport.

Michael Cartwright glanced back to see the doctor

holding open the elevator doors for two women, one heavily pregnant. An anxious look had replaced Dr Greenwood's warm smile. Michael only hoped that the doctor's latest charge would have as uncomplicated a birth as Susan had managed. He strolled across to his car, trying to think about what needed to be done next, still unable to remove the broad grin from his face.

The first thing he must do was phone his parents . . . grandparents.

2

RUTH DAVENPORT HAD already accepted that this would be her last chance. Dr Greenwood, for professional reasons, would not have put it quite so bluntly, although after two miscarriages in as many years, he could not advise his patient to risk becoming pregnant again.

Robert Davenport, on the other hand, was not bound by the same professional etiquette and when he learned that his wife was expecting for a third time, he had been characteristically blunt. He simply issued an ultimatum: 'this time you will take it easy', a euphemism for don't do anything that might harm the birth of our son. Robert Davenport assumed his first born would be a boy. He also knew that it would be difficult, if not impossible, for his wife to 'take it easy'. She was, after all, the daughter of Josiah Preston, and it was often said that if Ruth had been a boy, she, and not her husband, would have ended up as president of Preston Pharmaceuticals. But Ruth had to settle for the consolation prize when she succeeded her father as chairman of St Patrick's Hospital Trust, a cause with which the Preston family had been associated for four generations.

Although some of the older fraternity at St Patrick's needed to be convinced that Ruth Davenport was of the same mettle as her father, it was only weeks before they acknowledged that not only had she inherited the old man's energy and drive, but he had also passed on to her his considerable knowledge and wisdom, so often lavished on an only child.

Ruth hadn't married until the age of thirty-three. It certainly wasn't for lack of suitors, many of whom went out of their way to claim undying devotion to the heir of the Preston millions. Josiah Preston hadn't needed to explain the meaning of fortune hunters to his daughter, because the truth was that she simply hadn't fallen in love with any of them. In fact, Ruth was beginning to doubt if she would ever fall in love. Until she met Robert.

Robert Davenport had joined Preston Pharmaceuticals from Roche via Johns Hopkins and Harvard Business School, on what Ruth's father described as the 'fast track'. In Ruth's recollection, it was the nearest the old man had come to using a modern expression. Robert had been made a vice-president by the age of twenty-seven, and at thirty-three was appointed the youngest deputy chairman in the company's history, breaking a record that had been set by Josiah himself. This time Ruth did fall in love, with a man who was neither overwhelmed nor overawed by the Preston name or the Preston millions. In fact when Ruth suggested that perhaps she should become Mrs Preston-Davenport, Robert had simply enquired, 'When do I get to meet this Preston-Davenport fellow who hopes to prevent me from becoming your husband?'

Ruth announced she was pregnant only weeks after their wedding, and the miscarriage was almost the only blemish in an otherwise charmed existence. However, even this quickly began to look like a passing cloud in an otherwise clear blue sky, when she became pregnant again eleven months later.

Ruth had been chairing a board meeting of the Hospital Trust when the contractions began, so she only needed to take the elevator up two floors to allow Dr Greenwood to carry out the necessary check-up. However, not even his expertise, his staff's dedication or the latest medical equipment could save the premature child. Kenneth Greenwood couldn't help recalling how, as a young doctor, he had faced a similar problem when he had delivered Ruth, and for a week the hospital staff didn't believe the baby girl would survive. And now the family were going through the same trauma thirty-five years later.

Dr Greenwood decided to have a private word with Mr Davenport, suggesting that perhaps the time had come for them to consider adoption. Robert reluctantly agreed, and said he would raise the subject with his wife just as soon as he felt she was strong enough.

Another year passed before Ruth agreed to visit an adoption society and with one of those coincidences that fate decides, and novelists are not allowed to consider, she became pregnant on the day she was due to visit a local children's home. This time Robert was determined to ensure that human error would not be the reason for their child failing to enter this world.

Ruth took her husband's advice, and resigned as chairman of the Hospital Trust. She even agreed that a full-time nurse should be employed – in Robert's words – to keep a watchful eye on her. Mr Davenport interviewed several applicants for the post and short-listed those whom he considered held the necessary qualifications. But his final choice would be based solely on whether he was convinced the applicant was strong-willed enough to make sure that Ruth kept to her agreement to 'take it easy', and to insist she didn't lapse into any old habits of wanting to organize everything she came across.

After a third round of interviews, Robert settled on a Miss Heather Nichol, who was a senior nurse on the maternity wing of St Patrick's. He liked her no-nonsense approach and the fact that she was neither married nor graced with the kind of looks that would ensure that situation was likely to change in the foreseeable future. However, what finally tipped the balance was that Miss Nichol had already delivered over a thousand children into the world.

Robert was delighted by how quickly Miss Nichol settled into the household, and as each month slipped by, even he started to feel confident that they wouldn't be facing the same problem a third time. When Ruth passed first five, six, and then seven months without incident, Robert even raised the subject of possible Christian names: Fletcher Andrew if it was a boy, Victoria Grace if it was a girl. Ruth expressed only one preference: that were it a boy he should be known as Andrew, but all she hoped for was to be delivered of a healthy child.

Robert was in New York attending a medical conference, when Miss Nichol called him out of a seminar to report that his wife's contractions had begun. He assured her he would return by train immediately and then take a cab straight to St Patrick's.

Dr Greenwood was leaving the building, having successfully delivered the Cartwright twins, when he spotted Ruth Davenport coming through the swing doors accompanied by Miss Nichol. He turned round and caught up with the two ladies before the elevator doors closed.

Once he had settled his patient into a private room, Dr Greenwood quickly assembled the finest obstetrics team the hospital could muster. Had Mrs Davenport been a normal patient, he and Miss Nichol could have delivered the child without having to call on any extra assistance. However, following an examination, he realized that Ruth would require a Caesarean section if the child was to be delivered safely. He looked towards the ceiling and sent up a silent prayer, acutely aware that this was going to be her last chance.

The delivery took just over forty minutes. At the first glimpse of the baby's head, Miss Nichol let out a sigh of relief, but it wasn't until the doctor cut the umbilical cord that she added 'Alleluia'. Ruth, who was still under a general anaesthetic, was unable to see the relieved smile on Dr Greenwood's face. He quickly left the theatre to tell the expectant father, 'It's a boy.'

While Ruth slept peacefully it was left to Miss Nichol to take Fletcher Andrew off to the special care unit, where he would share his first few hours with several other progeny. Once she had tucked up the child in his little crib, she left the nurse to watch over him before returning to Ruth's room. Miss Nichol settled herself into a comfortable chair in the corner and tried to stay awake.

Just as night was contemplating day, Miss Nichol woke with a start. She heard the words, 'Can I see my son?'

'Of course you can, Mrs Davenport,' replied Miss Nichol rising quickly from her chair. 'I'll just go and fetch little Andrew.' As she closed the door behind her, she added, 'I'll be back in a few moments.'

Ruth pulled herself up, plumped up her pillow, switched on the bedside lamp and waited in eager anticipation.

As Miss Nichol walked along the corridor, she checked her watch. It was 4.31 a.m. She took the stairs down to the fifth floor and made her way to the nursery. Miss Nichol opened the door quietly so as not to wake any of the sleeping offspring. As she entered a room illuminated by a small fluorescent light glowing overhead, her eyes settled on the night nurse dozing in the corner. She didn't disturb the young woman as it was probably the only few moments of slumber that she would manage during her eight-hour shift.

Miss Nichol tiptoed between the two rows of cots, stopping only for a moment to glance at the twins in the double crib that had been placed next to Fletcher Andrew Davenport.

She stared down at a child who would want for nothing for the rest of his life. As she bent over to lift the little boy from his crib, she froze. After a thousand births, you are well qualified to recognize death. The pallor of the skin and the stillness of the eyes made it unnecessary for her to check the pulse.

It is often spur-of-the-moment decisions, sometimes made by others, that can change our whole lives.

3

WHEN DR GREENWOOD was woken in the middle of the night to be told that one of his new charges had died, he knew exactly which child it was. He also realized that he would have to return to the hospital immediately.

Kenneth Greenwood had always wanted to be a doctor. After only a few weeks at medical school, he had known in which field he would specialize. He thanked God every day for allowing him to carry out his vocation. But then from time to time, as if somehow the Almighty felt it was necessary to balance the scales, he had to tell a mother that she had lost her child. It was never easy, but having to tell Ruth Davenport for a third time . . .

There were so few cars on the road at five o'clock in the morning that Dr Greenwood was parked in his reserved spot at the hospital twenty minutes later. He pushed through the swing doors, strode past the reception desk and had stepped into the elevator before any of the staff could speak to him.

'Who's going to tell her?' asked the nurse who was waiting for him as the elevator doors opened on the fifth floor.

'I will,' said Dr Greenwood. 'I've been a friend of the family for years,' he added.

The nurse looked surprised. 'I suppose we must be thankful that the other baby survived,' she said, interrupting his thoughts.

Dr Greenwood stopped in his tracks. 'The other baby?' he repeated.

'Yes, Nathaniel's just fine, it was Peter who died.'

Dr Greenwood remained silent for a moment as he tried to take in this piece of information. 'And the Davenport boy?' he ventured.

'Doing well, as far as I know,' replied the nurse. 'Why do you ask?'

'I delivered him just before I went home,' he said, hoping the nurse hadn't spotted the hesitation in his voice.

Dr Greenwood walked slowly between the rows of cribs, passing offspring who were sleeping soundly and others who were yelling, as if to prove they had lungs. He stopped when he came to the double crib where he had left the twins only a few hours before. Nathaniel lay peacefully asleep while his brother was motionless. He glanced across to check the name on the headboard of the next crib, Davenport, Fletcher Andrew. That little boy was also sleeping soundly, his breathing quite regular.

'Of course I couldn't move the child until the doctor who had delivered . . .'

'You don't have to remind me of hospital procedure,' snapped Dr Greenwood uncharacteristically. 'What time did you come on duty?' he asked.

'Just after midnight,' she replied.

'And have you been in attendance since then?'

'Yes, sir.'

'Did anyone else enter the nursery during that time?'

'No, doctor,' the nurse replied. She decided not to mention that about an hour ago she thought she'd heard a door close, or at least not while he was in such a foul mood. Dr Greenwood stared down at the two cribs marked Cartwright, Nathaniel and Peter. He knew where his duty lay.

'Take the child to the morgue,' he said quietly. 'I'll write up a report immediately, but I won't inform the mother until the morning. No purpose will be served by waking her at this hour.'

'Yes, sir,' said the nurse meekly.

Dr Greenwood left the nursery, walked slowly down the corridor and stopped outside Mrs Cartwright's door. He opened it noiselessly, relieved to discover that his patient was fast asleep. After climbing the staircase up to the sixth floor, he carried out the same exercise when he reached Mrs Davenport's private room. Ruth was also sleeping. He glanced across the room to see Miss Nichol seated awkwardly in her chair. He could have sworn that she opened her eyes, but he decided not to disturb her. He pulled the door closed, walked to the far end of the corridor and slipped out on to the fire escape stairs that led to the parking lot. He didn't want to be seen leaving by those on duty at the front desk. He needed some time to think.

Dr Greenwood was back in his bed twenty minutes later, but he didn't sleep.

When his alarm went off at seven he was still awake. He knew exactly what his first course of action must be, although he feared the repercussions could reverberate for many years.

—◆—

Dr Greenwood took considerably longer to drive back to St Patrick's for a second time that morning, and it wasn't just because of the increased traffic. He dreaded having to tell Ruth Davenport that her child had died during the night, and only hoped it could be done without any accompanying scandal. He knew he would have to go straight to Ruth's room and explain what had happened, otherwise he would never be able to go through with it.

'Good morning, Dr Greenwood,' said the nurse on reception, but he didn't respond.

When he stepped out onto the sixth floor and began walking towards Mrs Davenport's room, he found his pace became slower and slower. He came to a halt in front of her door, hoping she would still be asleep. He eased it open, to be greeted with the sight of Robert Davenport sitting beside his wife. Ruth was holding a baby in her arms. Miss Nichol was nowhere to be seen.

Robert jumped up from his side of the bed.

'Kenneth,' he said, shaking him by the hand, 'we will be eternally in your debt.'

'You owe me nothing,' the doctor replied quietly.

'Of course we do,' said Robert, turning back to face his wife. 'Shall we let him know what we've decided, Ruth?'

'Why not, then we'll both have something to celebrate,' she said, kissing the boy's forehead.

'But I must first tell you . . .' began the doctor.

'No buts,' said Robert, 'because I want you to be the first to know that I've decided to ask the board of Preston's to finance the new maternity wing that you have always hoped would be completed before you retire.'

'But . . .' repeated Dr Greenwood.

'I thought we agreed on no buts. After all, the plans have been drawn up for years,' he said, looking down at his son, 'so I can't think of any reason why we shouldn't start on the building programme right away.' He turned to face the hospital's senior obstetrician. 'Unless of course you . . .?'

Dr Greenwood remained silent.

When Miss Nichol saw Dr Greenwood coming out of Mrs Davenport's private room, her heart sank. He was carrying the little boy in his arms and walking back towards the elevator that would take him to the special care nursery. As they passed each other in the corridor their eyes met, and although he didn't speak, she was in no doubt that he was aware of what she must have done.

Miss Nichol accepted that if she was going to make a run for it, it had to be now. Once she had taken the child back to the nursery, she'd lain awake in the corner of Mrs Davenport's room for the rest of the night, wondering if she would be found out. She had tried not to stir when Dr Greenwood had looked in. She had no idea what time it was because she didn't dare glance down at her watch. She had quite expected him to call her out of the room and tell her he knew the truth, but he had left just as silently as he had come, so she was none the wiser.

Heather Nichol went on walking towards the private room, while her eyes remained firmly fixed on the fire escape exit at the far end of the corridor. Once she had passed Mrs Davenport's door she tried not to quicken her pace. She had only a couple of yards to go when she heard a voice she immediately recognized say, 'Miss Nichol?' She froze on the spot, still staring towards the fire escape, as she considered her options. She swung round to face Mr Davenport. 'I think we need to have a private word,' he said.

Mr Davenport stepped into an alcove on the other side of the corridor, assuming she would follow. Miss Nichol thought her legs would give way long before she collapsed into the chair opposite him. She couldn't tell from the expression on his face if he also realized she was the guilty party. But then with Mr Davenport you never could. It wasn't in his nature to give anything away, and that was something he found difficult to change, even when it came to his private life. Miss Nichol couldn't look him in the eye, so she stared over his left shoulder and watched Dr Greenwood as the elevator doors closed.

'I suspect you know what I'm about to ask you,' he said.

'Yes, I do,' Miss Nichol admitted, wondering if anyone would ever employ her again, and even if she might end up in prison.

When Dr Greenwood reappeared ten minutes later, Miss Nichol knew exactly what was going to happen to her and where she would end up.

'When you've thought about it Miss Nichol, perhaps you could give me a call at my office, and if your answer is yes, then I'll need to have a word with my lawyers.'

'I've already thought about it,' said Miss Nichol. This time she did look Mr Davenport directly in the eye. 'The answer is yes,' she told him, 'I'd be delighted to continue working for the family as nanny.'

4

SUSAN HELD NAT in her arms unable to hide her distress. She was tired of friends and relations telling her to thank God that one of them had survived. Didn't they understand that Peter was dead, and she had lost a son? Michael hoped that his wife would begin to recover from the loss once she'd left hospital and returned home. But it wasn't to be. Susan still talked endlessly of her other son, and kept a photograph of the two boys by her bedside.

Miss Nichol studied the photograph when it was published in the *Hartford Courant*. She was relieved to find that although both boys had inherited their father's square jaw, Andrew had curly fair hair, while Nat's was straight and already turning dark. But it was Josiah Preston who saved the day, by frequently remarking that his grandson had inherited his nose and pronounced forehead in the great tradition of the Prestons. Miss Nichol constantly repeated these observations to fawning relatives and sycophantic employees, prefaced with the words, 'Mr Preston often remarks . . .'

Within two weeks of returning home, Ruth had been reappointed as Chairman of the Hospital Trust, and immediately set about honouring her husband's pledge to build a new maternity wing for St Patrick's.

Miss Nichol meanwhile took on any job, however menial, that allowed Ruth to resume her outside activities while she took charge of Andrew. She became the boy's nanny, mentor, guardian and governess. But not a day went by without her dreading that the truth might eventually come out.

Miss Nichol's first real anxiety arose when Mrs Cartwright phoned to say that she was holding a birthday party for her son, and as Andrew had been born on the same day, would she like him to be included.

'How kind of you to ask,' Miss Nichol replied, without missing a beat, 'but Andrew is having his own birthday party, and I'm only sorry that Nat won't be able to join us.'

'Well, please pass on my best wishes to Mrs Davenport, and tell her how much we appreciate being invited to the opening of the new maternity wing next month.' An invitation Miss Nichol could not cancel. When Susan put the phone down, her only thought was how did Miss Nichol know her son's name.

Within moments of Mrs Davenport arriving home that evening, Miss Nichol suggested that she should organize a party for Andrew's first birthday. Ruth thought it was a splendid idea, and was only too happy to leave all the arrangements, including the guest list, in nanny's hands. Organizing a birthday party where you can control who should or should not be invited is one thing, but trying to make sure that her employer and Mrs Cartwright did not meet up at the opening of the Preston Maternity Wing was quite another.

In fact, it was Dr Greenwood who introduced the two women while giving his guided tour of the new facility. He couldn't believe that no one would notice that the two little boys looked so alike. Miss Nichol turned away when he glanced in her direction. She quickly placed a bonnet over Andrew's head which made him look more like a girl, and before Ruth could comment, said, 'It's turning quite cold and I wouldn't want Andrew to catch a chill.'

'Will you be staying in Hartford once you've retired, Dr Greenwood?' Mrs Cartwright asked.

'No, my wife and I plan to retire to our family home in Ohio,' the doctor replied, 'but I'm sure we'll return to Hartford from time to time.'

Miss Nichol would have let out a sigh of relief had the doctor not stared pointedly at her. However, with Dr Greenwood out of the way, Miss Nichol felt a little more confident that her secret would not be discovered.

Whenever Andrew was invited to join in any activity, become a member of any group, participate in any sport or just sign up for the summer pageant, Miss Nichol's first priority was to ensure that her charge didn't come into contact with any member of the Cartwright family. This she managed to achieve with considerable success throughout the child's formative years, without arousing the suspicions of either Mr or Mrs Davenport.

－◇－

It was two letters that arrived in the morning mail that persuaded Miss Nichol that she need no longer be apprehensive. The first was addressed to Andrew's father and confirmed that the boy had been admitted to Hotchkiss, Connecticut's oldest private school. The second, post-marked Ohio, was opened by Ruth.

'How sad,' she remarked as she turned the hand-written page. 'He was such a fine man.'

'Who?' asked Robert, looking up from his copy of the *New England Journal of Medicine*.

'Dr Greenwood. His wife has written to say that he passed away last Friday, aged seventy-four.'

'He was a fine man,' Robert repeated, 'perhaps you should attend the funeral.'

'Yes, of course I will,' said Ruth, 'and Heather might

23

like to accompany me,' she added. 'After all, she used to work for him.'

'Of course,' said Miss Nichol, hoping that she looked suitably distressed.

—◦—

Susan read the letter a second time, saddened by the news. She would always recall how personally Dr Greenwood had taken Peter's death, almost as if he felt somehow responsible. Perhaps she should go to the doctor's funeral. She was about to share the news of his death with Michael, when her husband suddenly leapt in the air and shouted, 'Well done, Nat.'

'What is it?' asked Susan, surprised by such uncharacteristic exuberance.

'Nat's won a scholarship to Taft,' said her husband, waving his letter in the air.

Susan didn't share the same enthusiasm as her husband for Nat being sent away at such an early age to board with children whose parents came from a different world. How could a child of fourteen begin to understand that they couldn't afford so many of the things that his school friends would take for granted. She had long felt that Nathaniel should follow in Michael's footsteps and go to Jefferson High. If it was good enough for her to teach at, why wasn't it good enough for their child to be taught at?

Nat had been sitting on his bed rereading his favourite book, when he heard his father's outburst. He'd reached the chapter where the whale was about to escape yet again. He reluctantly jumped off the bed and put his head round the door to find out what was causing the commotion. His parents were furiously debating – they never rowed, despite the much-reported incident with the ice cream – about which school he should attend. He caught his father in mid-sentence . . . 'chance of a lifetime,' he was saying. 'Nat will be able to mix with children who will end up as leaders in every field, and therefore influence the rest of his life.'

'Rather than go to Jefferson High and mix with children who he might end up leading and influence for the rest of *their* lives?'

'But he's won a scholarship, so we wouldn't have to pay a penny.'

'And we wouldn't have to pay a penny if he went to Jefferson.'

'But we must think of Nat's future. If he goes to Taft, he might well end up at Harvard or Yale . . .'

'But Jefferson has produced several pupils who have attended both Harvard and Yale.'

'If I had to take out an insurance policy on which of the two schools would be more likely . . .'

'It's a risk I'm willing to take.'

'Well, I'm not,' said Michael, 'and I spend every day of my life trying to eliminate risks like that.' Nat listened intently as his mother and father continued their debate, never once raising their voices or losing their temper.

'I'd rather my son graduate as an egalitarian than a patrician,' Susan retorted with passion.

'Why should they be incompatible?' asked Michael.

Nat disappeared back into his room without waiting to hear his mother's reply. She had taught him to immediately look up any word that he'd never heard before; after all, it was a Connecticut man who had compiled the greatest lexicography in the world. Having checked all three words in his Webster's dictionary, Nat decided that his mother was more egalitarian than his father, but that neither of them was a patrician. He wasn't sure if he wanted to be a patrician.

When Nat had finished the chapter, he emerged from

his room for a second time. The atmosphere seemed to be more settled, so he decided to go downstairs and join his parents.

'Perhaps we should let Nat decide,' said his mother.

'I already have,' said Nat, as he took a seat between them. 'After all, you've always taught me to listen to both sides of any argument before coming to a conclusion.'

Both parents were speechless as Nat nonchalantly unfolded the evening paper, suddenly aware that he must have overheard their conversation.

'And what decision have you come to?' his mother asked quietly.

'I would like to go to Taft rather than Jefferson High,' Nat replied without hesitation.

'And may we know what helped you come to that conclusion?' asked his father.

Nat, aware that he had a spellbound audience, didn't hurry his reply. '*Moby Dick*,' he finally announced, before turning to the sports page.

He waited to see which of his parents would be the first to repeat his words.

'*Moby Dick*?' they pronounced together.

'Yes,' he replied, 'after all, the good folks of Connecticut considered the great whale to be the *patrician* of the sea.'

5

'EVERY INCH A Hotchkiss man,' Miss Nichol said as she checked Andrew's appearance in the hall mirror. White shirt, blue blazer with tan corduroy trousers. Miss Nichol straightened the boy's blue and white striped tie, removing a speck of dust from his shirt. 'Every inch,' she repeated. I'm only five foot three, Andrew wanted to say as his father joined them in the hall. Andrew checked his watch, a present from his maternal grandfather – a man who still sacked people for being late.

'I've put your suitcases in the car,' his father said, touching his son on the shoulder. Andrew turned cold when he heard his father's words. The casual remark only reminded him that he really was leaving home. 'It's less than three months until Thanksgiving,' his father added. Three months is a quarter of a year – a not insignificant percentage of your life when you're only fourteen years old, Andrew wanted to remind him.

Andrew strode out of the front door and on to the gravel courtyard, determined not to look back at the house he loved, and would not see again for a quarter of a year. When he reached the car, he held the back door open for his mother. He then shook hands with Miss Nichol as if she were an old friend, and said that he looked forward to seeing her at Thanksgiving. He couldn't be sure, but he thought she had been crying. He looked away and waved to the housekeeper and cook, before he jumped into the car.

As they drove through the streets of Farmington, Andrew stared at the familiar buildings he had considered until that moment to be the centre of the whole world.

'Now make sure you write home every week,' his mother was saying. He ignored the redundant comment, not least because Miss Nichol had issued the same instruction at least twice a day for the past month.

'And if you need any extra cash, don't hesitate to give me a call,' his father added.

Someone else who hadn't read the rule-book. Andrew didn't remind his father that boys in their first year at Hotchkiss were only allowed ten dollars a term. It was spelled out on page seven, and had been underlined in red by Miss Nichol.

No one spoke again during the short journey to the station, each anxious in his own particular fashion. His father brought the car to a halt next to the station and stepped out. Andrew remained seated, reluctant to leave the safety of the car, until his mother opened the door on his side. Andrew quickly joined her, determined not to let anyone know how nervous he was. She tried to take his hand, but he quickly ran to the back of the car to help his father with the cases.

A blue cap arrived by their side, pushing a trolley. Once the cases were loaded, he led them on to the station platform and came to a halt at carriage eight. As the porter lifted the cases on to the train, Andrew turned to say goodbye to his father. He had insisted that only one parent accompany him on the train journey to Lakeville, and as his father was a Taft man, his mother seemed the obvious choice. He was already regretting his decision.

'Have a good journey,' his father said, shaking his son's outstretched hand. What silly things parents say at stations, Andrew thought; surely it was more important that he worked hard when he got there. 'And don't forget to write.'

Andrew boarded the train with his mother and as the engine pulled out of the station he didn't once look back at his father, hoping it would make him appear more grown up.

'Would you like some breakfast?' his mother asked as the porter placed his cases on the overhead rack.

'Yes, please,' replied Andrew, cheering up for the first time that morning.

Another uniformed man showed them to a table in the dining car. Andrew studied the menu and wondered if his mother would allow him to have the full breakfast.

'Have anything you like,' she said, as if reading his thoughts.

Andrew smiled when the waiter reappeared. 'Double hash browns, two eggs, sunny side up, bacon and toast.' He only left out the mushrooms because he didn't want the waiter to think that his mother never fed him.

'And you, ma'am?' enquired the waiter, turning his attention to the other side of the table.

'Just coffee and toast, thank you.'

'The boy's first day?' asked the waiter.

Mrs Davenport smiled and nodded.

How does he know? wondered Andrew.

Andrew munched nervously through his breakfast, not sure if he would be fed again that day. There had been no mention of meals in the handbook, and Grandpa had told him that when he was at Hotchkiss, they were only fed once a day. His mother kept telling him to put his knife and fork down while he was eating. 'Knives and forks are not airplanes and shouldn't remain in mid-air longer than is necessary,' she reminded him. He had no way of knowing that she was almost as nervous as he was.

Whenever another boy, dressed in the same smart uniform, passed by their table, Andrew looked out of the window, hoping they wouldn't notice him, because none of their uniforms were as new as his. His mother was on her third cup of coffee when the train pulled into the station.

'We've arrived,' she announced, unnecessarily.

Andrew sat staring at the sign for Lakeville as several boys leapt off the train, greeting each other with 'Hi there, how was your holiday?' and 'Good to see you again', followed by much shaking of hands. He finally glanced across at his mother, and wished she would disappear in a cloud of smoke. Mothers were just another announcement that it was his first day.

Two tall boys dressed in double-breasted blue blazers and grey slacks began shepherding the new boys on to a waiting bus. Andrew prayed that parents were banned from the bus, otherwise everyone would realize he was a new boy.

'Name?' said one of the young men in a blue blazer as Andrew stepped off the train.

'Davenport, sir,' said Andrew, staring up at him. Would he ever be that tall?

The young man smiled, almost a grin. 'You don't call me sir, I'm not a master, just a senior proctor.' Andrew's head dropped. The first words he'd uttered, and he'd made a fool of himself. 'Has your luggage been placed on the bus, Fletcher?'

Fletcher? thought Andrew. Of course, Fletcher Andrew Davenport; he didn't correct the tall young man for fear of making another mistake.

'Yes,' Andrew replied.

The god turned his attention to Andrew's mother. 'Thank you, Mrs Davenport,' he said, checking his list, 'I hope you have a pleasant journey back to Farmington. Fletcher will be just fine,' he added kindly.

Andrew thrust out his hand, determined to stop his mother cuddling him. If only mothers could read thoughts. He shuddered as she threw her arms around him. But then he couldn't begin to understand what she was going through. When his mother finally released him, Andrew quickly joined the flow of boys who were jumping on to the waiting bus. He spotted a boy, even smaller than himself, who was sitting on his own looking out of the window. He quickly sat down beside him.

'I'm Fletcher,' he said, reverting to the name bestowed on him by the god. 'What's yours?'

'James,' he replied, 'but my friends call me Jimmy.'

'Are you a new boy?' asked Fletcher.

'Yes,' said Jimmy quietly, still not looking round.

'Me too,' replied Fletcher.

Jimmy took out a handkerchief and pretended to blow his nose, before he finally turned to face his new companion.

'Where are you from?' he asked.

'Farmington.'

'Where's that?'

'Not far from West Hartford.'

'My dad works in Hartford,' said Jimmy, 'he's in the government. What does your dad do?'

'He sells drugs,' said Fletcher.

'Do you like football?' asked Jimmy.

'Yes,' said Fletcher, but only because he knew Hotchkiss had an unbeaten record for the past four years, something else Miss Nichol had underlined in the handbook.

The rest of the conversation consisted of a series of unrelated questions to which the other rarely knew the answer. It was a strange beginning for what was to become a life-long friendship.

6

'SPOTLESS,' SAID HIS father as he checked the boy's uniform in the hall mirror. Michael Cartwright straightened his son's blue tie, and removed a hair from his jacket. 'Spotless,' he repeated.

Five dollars for a pair of corduroys was all Nathaniel could think about, even if his father had said they were worth every cent.

'Hurry up, Susan, or we'll be late,' his father called, glancing up towards the landing. But Michael still found time to pack the case in the trunk and move the car out of the driveway before Susan finally appeared to wish her son luck on his first day. She gave Nathaniel a big hug, and he was only grateful that there wasn't another Taft man in sight to witness the event. He hoped that his mother had got over her disappointment that he hadn't chosen Jefferson High, because he was already having second thoughts. After all, if he'd gone to Jefferson High he could come home every night.

Nathaniel took the seat next to his father in the front of the car, and checked the clock on the dashboard. It was nearly seven o'clock. 'Let's get going, Dad,' he said, desperate not to be late on his first day and to be remembered for all the wrong reasons.

Once they reached the highway, his father moved across to the outside lane and put the speedometer up to sixty-five, five miles an hour over the limit, calculating that the odds of being pulled over at that time in the

morning were in his favour. Although Nathaniel had
visited Taft to be interviewed, it was still a terrifying
moment when his father drove their old Studebaker
through the vast iron gates and slowly up the mile-long
drive. He was relieved to see two or three other cars filing
in behind them, though he doubted if they were new
boys. His father followed a line of Cadillacs and Buicks
into a car park, not altogether sure where he should park;
after all, he was a new father. Nathaniel jumped out of
the car, even before his father had pulled on the hand
brake. But then he hesitated. Did he follow the stream
of boys heading towards Taft Hall, or were new boys
expected to go somewhere else?

His father didn't hesitate in joining the throng, and
only came to a halt when a tall, self-assured young man
carrying a clipboard looked down at Nathaniel and asked,
'Are you a new boy?'

Nathaniel didn't speak, so his father said, 'Yes.'

The young man's gaze was not averted. 'Name?' he
said.

'Cartwright, sir,' Nathaniel replied.

'Ah yes, a lower mid; you've been assigned to Mr
Haskins, so you must be clever. All the bright ones start off
with Mr Haskins.' Nathaniel lowered his head while his
father smiled. 'When you go into Taft Hall,' said the young
man, 'you can sit anywhere in the front three rows on the
left hand side. The moment you hear nine chimes on the
clock, you will stop talking and not speak again until the
principal and the rest of the staff have left the hall.'

'What do I do then?' asked Nathaniel, trying to hide
the fact that he was shaking.

'You will be briefed by your form master,' said the
young man who turned his attention to the new father.
'Nat will be just fine, Mr Cartwright. I hope you have a
good journey home, sir.'

That was the moment Nathaniel decided in the future he would always be known as Nat, even though he realized it wouldn't please his mother.

As he entered Taft Hall, Nat lowered his head and walked quickly down the long aisle, hoping no one would notice him. He spotted a place on the end of the second row, and slipped into it. He glanced at the boy seated on his left, whose head was cupped in his hands. Was he praying, or could he possibly be even more terrified than Nat. 'My name's Nat,' he ventured.

'Mine's Tom,' said the boy, not raising his head.

'What happens next?'

'I don't know, but I wish it would,' said Tom as the clock struck nine, and everyone fell silent.

A crocodile of masters proceeded down the aisle – no mistresses, Nat observed. His mother wouldn't approve. They walked up on to the stage, and took their places, leaving only two seats unoccupied. The faculty began to talk quietly amongst themselves, while those in the body of the hall remained silent.

'What are we waiting for?' whispered Nat, and a moment later his question was answered as everyone rose, including those seated on the stage. Nat didn't dare look round when he heard the footsteps of two men proceeding down the aisle. Moments later, the school chaplain, followed by the principal, passed him on their way up to the two vacant seats. Everyone remained standing as the chaplain stepped forward to conduct a short service, which included the Lord's Prayer, and ended with the assembly singing the Battle Hymn of the Republic.

The chaplain then returned to his seat, allowing the principal to take his place. Alexander Inglefield paused for a moment, before gazing down at the assembled gathering. He then raised his hands, palms down, and everyone resumed their seat. Three hundred and eighty pairs of eyes stared up at a man of six foot two with thick bushy eyebrows and a square jaw, who presented such a frightening figure that Nat hoped they would never meet.

The principal gripped the edges of his long black gown before addressing the gathering for fifteen minutes. He began by taking his charges through the long history of the school, extolling Taft's past academic and sporting achievements. He stared down at the new boys and reminded them of the school's motto, '*Non ut sibi ministretur sed ut ministret*'.

'What does that mean?' whispered Nat.

'Not to be served, but to serve,' muttered Tom.

The principal concluded by announcing that there were two things a Bearcat could never afford to miss – an exam, or a match against Hotchkiss – and, as if making clear his priorities, he promised a half-day's holiday if Taft beat Hotchkiss in the annual football game. This was immediately greeted by a rousing cheer from the whole assembly, although every boy beyond the third row knew that this had not been achieved for the past four years.

When the cheering had died down, the principal left the stage, followed by the chaplain and the rest of the staff. Once they had departed, the chattering began again as the upper-class men started to file out of the hall, while only those boys in the front three rows remained seated, because they didn't know where to go.

Ninety-five boys sat waiting to see what would happen next. They did not have long to wait, because an elderly master – well actually he was only fifty-one, but Nat thought he looked much older than his dad – came to a halt in front of them. He was a short, thick-set man, with a semicircle of grey hair around an otherwise bald pate. As he spoke, he clung on to the lapels of his tweed jacket, imitating the principal's pose.

'My name is Haskins,' he told them. 'I am master of

the lower middlers,' he added with a wry smile. 'We'll begin the day with orientation, which you will have completed by first break at ten thirty. At eleven you will attend your assigned classes. Your first lesson will be American history.' Nat frowned, as history had never been his favourite subject. 'Which will be followed by lunch. Don't look forward to that,' Mr Haskins said with the same wry smile. A few of the boys laughed. 'But then that's just another Taft tradition,' Mr Haskins assured them, 'which any of you who are following in your fathers' footsteps will have already been warned about.' One or two of the boys, including Tom, smiled.

Once they had begun what Mr Haskins described as the nickel and dime tour, Nat never left Tom's side. He seemed to have prior knowledge of everything Haskins was about to say. Nat quickly discovered that not only was Tom's father a former alumni, but so was his grandfather.

By the time the tour had ended and they had seen everything from the lake to the sanatorium, he and Tom were best friends. When they filed into the classroom twenty minutes later, they automatically sat next to each other.

As the clock chimed eleven, Mr Haskins marched into the room. A boy followed in his wake. He had a self-assurance about him, almost a swagger, that made every other boy look up. The master's eyes also followed the new pupil as he slipped into the one remaining desk.

'Name?'

'Ralph Elliot.'

'That will be the last time you will be late for my class while you're at Taft,' said Haskins. He paused. 'Do I make myself clear, Elliot?'

'You most certainly do.' The boy paused, before adding, 'Sir.'

Mr Haskins turned his gaze to the rest of the class.

'Our first lesson, as I warned you, will be on American history, which is appropriate, remembering that this school was founded by the brother of a former president.' With a portrait of William H. Taft in the main hall and a statue of his brother in the quadrangle, it would have been hard for even the least inquisitive pupil not to have worked that out.

'Who was the first president of the United States?' Mr Haskins asked. Every hand shot up. Mr Haskins nodded to a boy in the front row.

'George Washington, sir.'

'And the second?' asked Haskins. Fewer hands rose, and this time Tom was selected.

'John Adams, sir.'

'Correct, and the third?'

Only two hands remained up, Nat's and the boy who had arrived late. Haskins pointed to Nat.

'Thomas Jefferson, 1801 to 1809.'

Mr Haskins nodded, acknowledging that the boy also knew the correct dates, 'And the fourth?'

'James Madison, 1809 to 1817,' said Elliot.

'And the fifth, Cartwright?'

'James Monroe, 1817 to 1825.'

'And the sixth, Elliot?'

'John Quincy Adams, 1825 to 1829.'

'And the seventh, Cartwright?'

Nat racked his brains. 'I don't remember, sir.'

'You don't remember, Cartwright, or do you simply not know?' Haskins paused. 'There is a considerable difference,' he added. He turned his attention back to Elliot.

'William Henry Harrison, I think, sir.'

'No, he was the ninth president, Elliot, 1841, but as he died of pneumonia only a month after his inauguration, we won't be spending a lot of time on him,' added

Haskins. 'Make sure everyone can tell me the name of the seventh president by tomorrow morning. Now let's go back to the founding fathers. You may all take notes as I require you to produce a three-page essay on the subject by the time we next meet.'

Nat had filled three long sheets even before the lesson had ended, while Tom barely managed a page. As they left the classroom at the end of the lesson, Elliot brushed quickly past them.

'He already looks like a worthy adversary,' remarked Tom.

Nat didn't comment.

What he couldn't know was that he and Ralph Elliot would be adversaries for the rest of their lives.

7

THE ANNUAL FOOTBALL game between Hotchkiss and Taft was the sporting highlight of the semester. As both teams were undefeated that season, little else was discussed once the mid-terms were over, and for the jocks, long before mid-terms began.

Fletcher found himself caught up in the excitement, and in his weekly letter to his mother named every member of the team, although he realized that she wouldn't have a clue who any of them were.

The game was due to be played on the last Saturday in October and once the final whistle had been blown, all boarders would have the rest of the weekend off, plus an extra day should they win.

On the Monday before the game, Fletcher's class sat their first mid-terms, but not before the principal had declared at morning assembly that, 'Life consists of a series of tests and examinations, which is why we take them every term at Hotchkiss.'

On Tuesday evening Fletcher phoned his mother to tell her he thought he'd done well.

On Wednesday he told Jimmy he wasn't so sure.

By Thursday, he'd looked up everything he hadn't included, and wondered if he had even achieved a pass grade.

On Friday morning, class rankings were posted on the school notice board and the preps were headed by the name of Fletcher Davenport. He immediately ran to the nearest phone and rang his mother. Ruth couldn't hide her delight when she learned her son's news, but didn't tell him that she wasn't surprised. 'You must celebrate,' she said. Fletcher would have done so, but felt he couldn't when he saw who had come bottom of the class.

At the full school assembly on Saturday morning, prayers were offered by the chaplain 'for our undefeated football team, who played only for the glory of our Lord'. Our Lord was then vouchsafed the name of every player and asked if his Holy Spirit might be bestowed on each and every one of them. The principal was obviously in no doubt which team God would be supporting on Saturday afternoon.

At Hotchkiss, everything was decided on seniority, even a boy's place in the bleachers. During their first term preps were relegated to the far end of the field, so both boys sat in the right-hand corner of the stand every other Saturday, and watched their heroes extend the season's unbeaten run, a record they realized Taft also enjoyed.

As the Taft game fell on a homecoming weekend, Jimmy's parents invited Fletcher to join them for a tailgate picnic before the kick-off. Fletcher didn't tell any of the other boys in preps, because he felt it would only make them jealous. It was bad enough being top of the class, without being invited to watch the Taft game with an old boy who had seats on the centre line.

'What's your dad like?' asked Jimmy, after lights-out the night before the game.

'He's great,' said Fletcher, 'but I should warn you that he's a Taft man, and a Republican. And how about your dad? I've never met a senator before.'

'He's a politician to his fingertips, or at least that's how the press describe him,' said Jimmy. 'Not that I'm sure what it means.'

On the morning of the game no one was able to

concentrate during chemistry, despite Mr Bailey's enthusiasm for testing the effects of acid on zinc, not least because Jimmy had turned the gas off at the mains, so Mr Bailey couldn't even get the Bunsen burners lit.

At twelve o'clock a bell rang, releasing 380 screaming boys out into the courtyard. They resembled nothing less than a warring tribe, with their cries of, 'Hotchkiss, Hotchkiss, Hotchkiss will win, death to all Bearcats.'

Fletcher ran all the way to the assembly point to meet his parents, as cars and taxis came streaming in past the lake. Fletcher scanned every vehicle, searching for his father and mother.

'How are you, Andrew my darling?' were his mother's first words as she stepped out of the car.

'Fletcher, I'm Fletcher at Hotchkiss,' he whispered, hoping that none of the other boys had heard the word 'darling'. He shook hands with his father, before adding, 'We must leave for the field immediately, because we've been invited to join Senator and Mrs Gates for a tailgate lunch.'

Fletcher's father raised an eyebrow. 'If I remember correctly, Senator Gates is a Democrat,' he said with mock disdain.

'And a former Hotchkiss football captain,' said Fletcher. 'His son Jimmy and I are in the same class, and he's my best friend, so Mom had better sit next to the senator, and if you don't feel up to it, Dad, you can sit on the other side of the field with the Taft supporters.'

'No, I think I'll put up with the senator. It will be so rewarding to be seated next to him when Taft scores the winning touchdown.'

It was a clear autumnal day and the three of them strolled through a golden carpet of leaves all the way to the field. Ruth tried to take her son's hand, but Fletcher stood just far enough away to make it impossible. Long before they reached the field, they could hear the cheers erupting from the pre-game rally.

Fletcher spotted Jimmy standing behind an Oldsmobile wagon, its open tailgate covered in far more sumptuous food than anything he'd seen for the past two months. A tall elegant man stepped forward. 'Hello, I'm Harry Gates.' The senator thrust out his politician's hand to welcome Fletcher's parents.

Fletcher's father grasped the outstretched hand. 'Good afternoon, Senator, I'm Robert Davenport and this is my wife Ruth.'

'Call me Harry. This is Martha, my first wife.' Mrs Gates stepped forward to welcome them both. 'I call her my first wife – well, it keeps her on her toes.'

'Would you like a drink?' asked Martha, not laughing at a joke she had heard so many times before.

'It had better be quick,' said the senator, checking his watch, 'that is if we still hope to eat before the kick-off. Let me serve you, Ruth, and we'll let your husband fend for himself. I can smell a Republican at a hundred paces.'

'I'm afraid it's worse than that,' said Ruth.

'Don't tell me he's an old Bearcat because I'm thinking of making that a capital offence in this state.' Ruth nodded. 'Then Fletcher, you'd better come and talk to me because I intend to ignore your father.'

Fletcher was flattered by the invitation, and soon began grilling the senator on the workings of the Connecticut legislature.

'Andrew,' said Ruth.

'Fletcher, Mother.'

'Fletcher, don't you think the senator might like to talk about something other than politics?'

'No, that's fine by me, Ruth,' Harry assured her. 'The voters rarely ask such insightful questions, and I'm rather hoping it might rub off on Jimmy.'

After lunch had been cleared away the group walked quickly across to the bleachers, sitting down only moments before the game was due to begin. The seats were better than any prep could have dreamed of, but then Senator Gates hadn't missed the Taft match since his own graduation. Fletcher couldn't contain his excitement as the clock on the score board edged towards two. He stared across at the far stand, to be greeted with the enemy's cries of, 'Give me a T, give me an A, give me a . . .' and fell in love.

—◇—

Nat's eyes remained on the face above the letter A.

'Nat's the brightest boy in our class,' Tom told Nat's father. Michael smiled.

'Only just,' said Nat, a little defensively, 'don't forget I only beat Ralph Elliot by one grade.'

'I wonder if he's Max Elliot's son?' said Nat's father, almost to himself.

'Who's Max Elliot?'

'In my business he's what's known as an unacceptable risk.'

'Why?' asked Nat, but his father didn't expand on the bland statement, and was relieved when his son was distracted by the cheerleaders, who had blue and white pom-poms attached to their wrists and were performing their ritual war dance. Nat's eyes settled on the second girl on the left, who seemed to be smiling up at him, although he realized to her he could only be a speck at the back of the stand.

'You've grown, if I'm not mistaken,' said Nat's father, noting that his son's trousers were already an inch short of his shoes. He only wondered how often he would have to buy him new clothes.

'Well, it can't be the school food that's responsible,'

suggested Tom, who was still the smallest boy in the class. Nat didn't reply. His eyes remained fixed on the group of cheerleaders.

'Which one of them have you fallen for?' enquired Tom, punching his friend on the arm.

'What?'

'You heard me the first time.'

Nat turned away so that his father couldn't overhear his reply. 'Second one from the left, with the letter A on her sweater.'

'Diane Coulter,' said Tom, pleased to discover that he knew something his friend didn't.

'How do you know her name?'

'Because she's Dan Coulter's sister.'

'But he's the ugliest player on the team,' said Nat. 'He's got cauliflower ears and a broken nose.'

'And so would Diane if she'd played on the team every week for the past five years,' said Tom with a laugh.

'What else do you know about her?' Nat asked his friend conspiratorially.

'Oh, it's that serious is it?' said Tom. It was Nat's turn to punch his friend. 'Having to revert to physical violence, are we? Hardly part of the Taft code,' added Tom. 'Beat a man with the strength of your argument, not the strength of your arm; Oliver Wendell Holmes, if I remember correctly.'

'Oh, do stop droning on,' said Nat, 'and just answer the question.'

'Don't know a lot more about her, to be honest. All I remember is that she goes to Westover and plays right wing on their hockey team.'

'What are you two whispering about?' asked Nat's father.

'Dan Coulter,' said Tom, without missing a beat, 'one

of our running backs – I was just telling Nat that he eats eight eggs for breakfast every morning.'

'How do you know that?' asked Nat's mother.

'Because one of them is always mine,' said Tom ruefully.

As his parents burst out laughing, Nat continued to gaze down at the A in TAFT. The first time he'd really noticed a girl. His concentration was distracted by a sudden roar, as everyone on his side of the stadium rose to greet the Taft team as they ran out onto the field. Moments later the Hotchkiss players appeared from the other side of the ground and just as enthusiastically their supporters leapt to their feet.

—◦—

Fletcher was also standing, but his eyes remained fixed on the cheerleader with an A on her sweater. He felt guilty that the first girl he'd ever fallen for was a Taft supporter.

'You don't seem to be concentrating on our team,' said the senator, leaning over and whispering in Fletcher's ear.

'Oh, yes I am, sir,' said Fletcher, immediately turning his attention back to the Hotchkiss players as they began to warm up.

The two team captains jogged across to join the umpire, who was waiting for them on the fifty-yard line. The Zebra flicked a silver coin into the air which flashed in the afternoon sun before landing in the mud. The Bearcats clapped each other on the back when they saw the profile of Washington.

'He should have called heads,' said Fletcher.

—◦—

Nat continued to stare as Diane climbed back into the bleachers. He wondered how he could possibly meet her. It wouldn't be easy. Dan Coulter was a god. How could a new boy possibly hope to scale Olympus?

'Good run,' hollered Tom.

'Who?' said Nat.

'Coulter, of course. He's just picked up first down.'

'Coulter?'

'Don't tell me you were still staring at his sister when the Kissies fumbled?'

'No, I wasn't.'

'Then you'll be able to tell me how many yards we gained,' Tom said, looking at his friend. 'I thought so, you weren't even watching.' He let out an exaggerated sigh, 'I do believe that the time has come to put you out of your misery.'

'What do you mean?'

'I shall have to arrange a meeting.'

'You can do that?'

'Sure, her father's a local auto dealer, and we always buy our cars from him, so you'll just have to come and stay with me during the holidays.'

Tom didn't hear if his friend accepted the invitation, because his reply was drowned by another roar from the Taft supporters as the Bearcats intercepted.

When the whistle blew at the end of the first quarter, Nat let out the biggest cheer, having forgotten that his team was trailing. He remained standing in the hope that the girl with the head of curly fair hair and the most captivating smile, might just notice him. But how could she, as she leapt energetically up and down, encouraging the Taft supporters to cheer even louder.

The whistle for the start of the second quarter came all too quickly, and when A disappeared back in the bleachers to be replaced by thirty muscle-bound heavies,

Nat reluctantly resumed his place and pretended to concentrate on the game.

—◦—

'Can I borrow your binoculars, sir?' Fletcher asked Jimmy's father at half time.

'Of course, my boy,' said the senator, passing them across. 'Let me have them back when the game restarts.' Fletcher missed the innuendo in his host's voice as he focused on the girl with an A on her sweater and wished she would turn round and face the opposition more often.

'Which one are you interested in?' whispered the senator.

'I was just checking on the Tafties, sir.'

'I don't think they've come back on to the field yet,' said the senator. Fletcher turned scarlet. 'T, A, F or T?' enquired Jimmy's father.

'A, sir,' admitted Fletcher.

The senator retrieved his binoculars, focused on the second girl from the left, and waited for her to turn round. 'I approve of your choice, young man, but what do you intend to do about it?'

'I don't know, sir,' said Fletcher helplessly. 'To be honest, I don't even know her name.'

'Diane Coulter,' said the senator.

'How do you know that?' asked Fletcher, wondering if senators knew everything.

'Research, my boy. Haven't they taught you that at Hotchkiss yet?' Fletcher looked bewildered. 'All you need to know is on page eleven of the programme,' added the senator, as he passed the open booklet across. Page eleven had been devoted to the cheerleaders supporting each school. 'Diane Coulter,' repeated Fletcher, staring at the photo. She was a year younger than Fletcher – women are still willing to admit their age at thirteen – and she

47

also played the violin in her school orchestra. How he wished he'd taken his mother's advice and learned to play the piano.

◄○►

After gaining painful yard upon painful yard, Taft finally crossed the line and took the lead. Dutifully Diane reappeared on the touchline to perform her energetic routine.

'You've got it bad,' said Tom, 'I guess I'm going to have to introduce you.'

'You really know her?' said Nat in disbelief.

'Sure do,' said Tom. 'We've been going to the same parties since the age of two.'

'I wonder if she has a boyfriend,' said Nat.

'How should I know? Why don't you come and spend a week with us during vacation, and then you can leave the rest to me.'

'You'd do that?'

'It'll cost you.'

'What do you have in mind?'

'Make sure you finish the holiday assignments before you turn up – then I won't have to bother double-checking all the facts.'

'It's a deal,' said Nat.

◄○►

The whistle blew for the third quarter, and after a series of brilliant passes, it was Hotchkiss's turn to make it over the end zone, putting them back into the lead, which they clung on to until the end of the quarter.

'Hello, Taft, hello, Taft, you're back where you belong,' sang the senator out of tune, while the teams took a timeout.

'There's still the final quarter to come,' Fletcher

48

reminded the senator as his host passed the glasses across to him.

'Have you decided which side you're supporting, young man, or have you been ensnared by the Tafties' Mata Hari?' Fletcher looked puzzled. He would have to check on who Mata Hari was just as soon as he got back to his room. 'She probably lives locally,' continued the senator, 'in which case it will take a member of my staff about two minutes to find out everything you need to know about her.'

'Even her address and telephone number?' asked Fletcher.

'Even whether she has a boyfriend,' replied the senator.

'Wouldn't you be abusing your position?' asked Fletcher.

'Damn right I would,' replied Senator Gates, 'but then any politician would do as much if he felt it might ensure two more votes at some future election.'

'But that doesn't solve the problem of meeting her while I'm stuck in Farmington.'

'That can also be solved if you'd come and spend a few days with us after Christmas, and then I'll make sure that she and her parents are invited to some function at the Capitol.'

'You'll do that for me?'

'Sure will, but at some time you'll have to learn about trade-offs if you're going to deal with a politician.'

'What's the trade-off?' asked Fletcher. 'I'll do anything.'

'Never admit to that, my boy, because it immediately puts you in the weaker bargaining position. However, all I want in return on this occasion is for you to make sure Jimmy somehow scrapes off the bottom of the class. That will be your part of the bargain.'

'It's a deal, senator,' said Fletcher, shaking hands.

'That's good to hear,' said the senator, 'because Jimmy seems only too willing to follow your lead.'

It was the first time anyone had suggested that Fletcher might be a leader. Until that moment it hadn't even crossed his mind. He thought about the senator's words, and failed to notice Taft's winning touchdown until Diane rushed up out of the bleachers and began a ritual that unfortunately resembled a victory ceremony. There would be no extra day off this year.

―◦―

On the other side of the stadium, Nat and Tom stood outside the locker rooms, along with a multitude of Taft supporters who, with one exception, were waiting to greet their heroes. Nat nudged his friend in the ribs as she came out. Tom stepped quickly forward. 'Hi, Diane,' he said and, not waiting for a reply, added, 'I want you to meet my friend Nat. Actually, the truth is he wanted to meet you.' Nat blushed, and not just because he thought Diane was even prettier than her photo. 'Nat lives in Cromwell,' added Tom helpfully, 'but he's coming to spend a few days with us after Christmas, so you can get to know him better then.'

Nat only felt confident of one thing: Tom's chosen career wasn't destined to be in the diplomatic corps.

8

NAT SAT AT his desk, trying to concentrate on the Great Depression. He managed about half a page, but he found his mind kept wandering. He went over the short meeting he'd had with Diane, again and again. This didn't take long because she'd hardly said a word before his father had joined them and suggested they ought to be leaving.

Nat had cut out her picture from the football programme, and carried it around with him wherever he went. He was beginning to wish he'd picked up at least three programmes, because the little photo was becoming so worn. He'd rung Tom at home the morning after the game on the pretence of discussing the Wall Street crash, and then casually threw in, 'Did Diane say anything about me after I'd left?'

'She thought you were very nice.'

'Nothing else?'

'What else could she say? You only had about two minutes together before your father dragged you off.'

'Did she like me?'

'She thought you were very nice, and if I remember correctly, she said something about James Dean.'

'No, she didn't – did she?'

'No, you're right – she didn't.'

'You're a rat.'

'True, but a rat with a telephone number.'

'You have her telephone number?' said Nat in disbelief.

'You catch on quickly.'

'What is it?'

'Have you completed that essay on the Great Depression?'

'Not quite, but I'll have it finished by the weekend, so hold on while I get a pencil.' Nat wrote the number down on the back of Diane's photograph. 'Do you think she'll be surprised if I give her a call?'

'I think she'll be surprised if you don't.'

—◇—

'Hi, I'm Nat Cartwright. I don't suppose you remember me.'

'No, I don't. Who are you?'

'I'm the one you met after the Hotchkiss game and thought looked like James Dean.'

Nat glanced in the mirror. He'd never thought about his looks before. Did he really look like James Dean?

It took another couple of days, and several more rehearsals before Nat had the courage to dial her number. Once he'd completed his essay on the Great Depression, he'd prepared a list of questions which varied according to who picked up the phone. If it was her father, he would say, 'Good morning, sir, my name is Nat Cartwright. May I please speak to your daughter,' if it was her mother he would say, 'Good morning, Mrs Coulter, my name is Nat Cartwright. May I please speak to your daughter.' If Diane answered the phone, he had prepared ten questions, in a logical order. He placed three sheets of paper on the table in front of him, took a deep breath, and carefully dialled the digits. He was greeted by a busy signal. Perhaps she was talking to another boy. Had she already held his hand, even kissed him? Was he her regular date? Fifteen minutes later he phoned again. Still busy. Had another suitor called in between? This time he only waited ten minutes before he tried again. The moment he heard the ringing tone he felt his heart thumping in his chest, and wanted to put the phone straight back down. He stared at his list of questions. The ringing stopped. Someone picked up the phone.

'Hello,' said a deep voice. He didn't need to be told it was Dan Coulter.

Nat dropped the phone on the floor. Surely gods don't answer phones, and in any case, he hadn't prepared any questions for Diane's brother. Hastily he picked the receiver up off the floor and placed it back on the phone.

Nat read through his essay before he dialled a fourth time. At last a girl's voice answered.

'Diane?'

'No, it's her sister Tricia,' said a voice that sounded older, 'Diane's out at the moment, but I'm expecting her back in about an hour. Who shall I say called?'

'Nat,' he replied, 'would you tell her I'll phone again in about an hour?'

'Sure,' said the older voice.

'Thank you,' said Nat and put the receiver down. He hadn't any questions or answers prepared for an older sister.

Nat must have looked at his watch sixty times during the next hour, but he still added another fifteen minutes before he redialled the number. He'd read in *Teen* magazine – if you like a girl, don't appear too keen, it puts them off. The phone was eventually picked up.

'Hello,' said a younger voice.

Nat glanced down at his script. 'Hello, can I speak to Diane?'

'Hi, Nat, it's Diane. Tricia told me you'd called, how are you?'

How are you wasn't in the script. 'I'm fine,' he eventually managed, 'how are you?'

'I'm fine too,' she replied, which was followed by

53

another long silence while Nat searched for an appropriate question.

'I'm coming over to Simsbury next week to spend a few days with Tom,' he read out in a monotone.

'That's great,' replied Diane, 'then let's hope we bump into each other.' There certainly wasn't anything in the script about bumping into each other. He tried to read all ten questions at once. 'Are you still there, Nat?' asked Diane.

'Yes. Any hope of seeing you while I'm in Simsbury?' Question number nine.

'Yes, of course,' said Diane, 'I'd like that very much.'

'Goodbye,' said Nat looking at answer number ten.

During the rest of the evening, Nat tried to recall the conversation in detail, and even wrote it down line by line. He underlined three times her words – yes, of course, I'd like that very much. As there were still four days before he was due to visit Tom, he wondered if he should call Diane again – just to confirm. He returned to *Teen* magazine to seek their advice, as they seemed to have anticipated all his previous problems. *Teen* gave no help on calling a second time, but did suggest for a first date he should dress casually, be relaxed, and whenever he got the chance talk about other girls he'd been out with. He'd never been out with another girl, and worse, he didn't have any casual clothes, other than a plaid shirt that he had hidden in a bottom drawer half an hour after he'd bought it. Nat checked to see how much money he'd saved from his paper round – seven dollars and twenty cents – and wondered if that was enough to purchase a new shirt and a casual pair of slacks. If only he had an older brother.

He put the finishing touches to his essay only hours before his father drove him across to Simsbury.

As they travelled north, Nat kept asking himself why

he hadn't rung Diane back and fixed a time and place to meet her. She might have gone away – decided to stay with a friend – a boy-friend. Would Tom's parents mind if he asked to use their phone the moment he arrived?

'Oh, my God,' said Nat as his father swung his car into a long drive and drove past a paddock full of horses. Nat's father would have chastised him for blaspheming, but was somewhat taken aback himself. The driveway must have stretched for over a mile before they turned into a gravelled courtyard to be greeted by the most magnificent white pillared colonial home surrounded by evergreens.

'Oh, my God,' said Nat a second time. This time his father did remonstrate with him.

'Sorry, Dad, but Tom never mentioned he lived in a palace.'

'Why should he?' replied his father. 'When it's all he's ever known. By the way, he's not your closest friend because of the size of his house, and if he had felt it was necessary to impress you, he would have mentioned it some time ago. Do you know what his father does, because one thing's for sure, he doesn't sell life insurance.'

'I think he's a banker.'

'Tom Russell, of course. Russell's Bank,' said his father as they pulled up in front of the house.

Tom was waiting on the top step to greet them. 'Good afternoon, sir, how are you?' he asked, as he opened the door on the driver's side.

'I'm well, thank you, Tom,' replied Michael Cartwright as his son climbed out of the car, clinging on to a small battered suitcase with the initials M. C. printed next to the lock.

'Would you care to join us for a drink, sir?'

'That's kind of you,' said Nat's father, 'but my wife will be expecting me back in time for supper, so I ought to be on my way.'

Nat waved as his father circled the courtyard and began his return journey to Cromwell.

Nat looked up at the house to see a butler standing on the top step. He offered to take the suitcase, but Nat clung on to it as he was escorted up a magnificent wide circular staircase to the second floor, where he was shown into a guest bedroom. In Nat's home they only had one spare bedroom, which would have passed as a broom closet in this house. Once the butler had left him, Tom said, 'When you've unpacked, come down and meet my mother. We'll be in the kitchen.'

Nat sat at the end of one of the twin beds, painfully aware that he would never be able to invite Tom to stay with him.

It took Nat about three minutes to unpack as all he had were two shirts, one spare pair of trousers and a tie. He spent some considerable time checking out the bathroom before finally bouncing up and down on the bed. It was so springy. He waited for a couple more minutes before he left the room to stroll back down the wide staircase, wondering if he would ever be able to find the kitchen. The butler was waiting on the bottom step and escorted him along the corridor. Nat stole a quick glance into each room he passed.

'Hi,' said Tom, 'your room OK?'

'Yes, it's great,' said Nat, aware that his friend was not being sarcastic.

'Mom, this is Nat. He's the cleverest boy in the class, damn him.'

'Please don't swear, Tom,' said Mrs Russell. 'Hello, Nat, how nice to meet you.'

'Good evening Mrs Russell, it's nice to meet you too. What a lovely home you have.'

'Thank you, Nat, and we were delighted that you were able to join us for a few days. Can I get you a Coke?'

'Yes, please.'

A uniformed maid went straight to the fridge, took out a Coke and added some ice.

'Thank you,' he repeated, as he watched the maid return to the sink and continue chopping potatoes. He thought of his mother back in Cromwell. She would also be chopping up potatoes, but only after a full day's teaching.

'Want me to show you around?' asked Tom.

'Sounds great,' said Nat, 'but can I first make a phone call?'

'You don't need to, Diane's already called.'

'She's already called?'

'Yeah, she phoned this morning, to ask what time you'd be arriving. She begged me not to tell you, so I think we can assume she's interested.'

'Then I'd better call her back immediately.'

'No, that's the last thing you should do,' said Tom.

'But I said I would.'

'Yes, I know you did, but I think we'll walk around the grounds first.'

◄○►

When Fletcher's mother dropped him off at Senator and Mrs Gates's home in East Hartford, it was Jimmy who answered the door.

'Now don't forget to always address Mr Gates as Senator or sir.'

'Yes, Mom.'

'And don't bother him with too many questions.'

'No, Mom.'

'Remember that a conversation conducted by two people should be fifty per cent talking and fifty per cent listening.'

'Yes, Mom.'

'Hello, Mrs Davenport, how are you?' asked Jimmy as he opened the door to greet them.

'I'm well, thank you, Jimmy, and you?'

'Just great. I'm afraid Mom and Dad are out at some function, but I could make you a cup of tea?'

'No thank you, I have to be back in time to chair a meeting of the Hospital Trust, but please remember to pass on my best wishes to your parents.'

Jimmy carried one of Fletcher's suitcases up to the spare room. 'I've put you next to me,' he said, 'which means we have to share the same bathroom.'

Fletcher put his other suitcase on the bed, before studying the pictures on the walls – prints of the Civil War, just in case a southerner should come to stay and might have forgotten who won. They reminded Jimmy to ask Fletcher if he'd finished his essay on Lincoln.

'Yes, but have you found out Diane's phone number?'

'I've gone one better. I've discovered which coffee shop she goes to most afternoons. So I thought we might just drop in casually, say around five, and should that fail, my father has invited her parents to a reception at the Capitol tomorrow evening.'

'But they might not come.'

'I've checked the guest list, and they've accepted.'

Fletcher suddenly remembered the trade-off he'd agreed with the senator. 'How far have you got with your homework?'

'Haven't even started,' admitted Jimmy.

'Jimmy, if you don't get a pass grade next term, you'll be put on probation and then I won't be able to help.'

'I know, but I'm also aware of the deal you struck with my father.'

'Then if I'm to keep it, we'll have to start work first thing tomorrow. We'll begin by doing two hours every morning.'

'Yes sir,' said Jimmy, snapping to attention. 'But before we worry about tomorrow, perhaps you should get changed,' he added.

Fletcher had packed half a dozen shirts and a couple of pairs of slacks, but still hadn't a clue what to wear on his first date. He was about to seek his friend's advice, when Jimmy said, 'Once you've unpacked why don't you come down and join us in the living room? The bathroom's at the end of the hall.'

Fletcher changed quickly into the shirt and slacks he'd bought the previous day at a local tailor his father had recommended. He checked himself in the long mirror. He had no idea how he looked, because he'd never taken any interest in clothes before. Act casual, look sharp, he'd heard a disc jockey telling his radio audience, but what did that mean? He'd worry about it later. As Fletcher walked downstairs, he could hear voices coming from the front room, one of which he didn't recognize.

'Mom, you remember Fletcher,' Jimmy said as his friend strolled into the room.

'Yes, of course I do. My husband never stops telling everyone about the fascinating conversation the two of you had at the Taft game.'

'That's kind of him to remember,' said Fletcher, not looking at her.

'And I know he's looking forward to seeing you again.'

'That's kind of him,' said Fletcher a second time.

'And this is my kid sister, Annie,' said Jimmy.

Annie blushed, and not only because she hated being described by Jimmy as his kid sister: his friend hadn't taken his eyes off her from the moment he'd walked into the room.

9

'GOOD EVENING, Mrs Coulter, how nice to meet you and your husband, and this must be your daughter Diane, if I remember correctly.' Mr and Mrs Coulter were impressed because they had never met the senator before, and not only had their son scored the winning touchdown against Hotchkiss, but they were also registered Republicans. 'Now, Diane,' continued the senator, 'I have someone I want you to meet.' Harry Gates's eyes swept the room, searching for Fletcher, who had been standing by his side only a moment before. 'Strange,' he said, 'but you mustn't leave without meeting him. Otherwise I won't have kept my end of the bargain,' he added without explanation.

'Where's Fletcher disappeared off to?' Harry Gates asked his son once the Coulters had joined the other guests.

'If you can spot Annie, you won't find Fletcher far behind; he hasn't left her side since he arrived in Hartford. In fact I'm thinking of buying him a dog leash and calling him Fletch.'

'Is that right?' said the senator. 'I hope he doesn't think that releases him from our deal.'

'No, he doesn't,' said Jimmy. 'In fact we studied *Romeo and Juliet* for two hours this morning, and guess who he sees himself as.'

The senator smiled. 'And which part do you imagine fits your character?' he asked.

'I think I'm Mercutio.'

'No,' said Harry Gates, 'you can only be Mercutio if he starts to chase Diane.'

'I don't understand.'

'Ask Fletcher. He'll explain it to you.'

—◦—

Tricia answered the door. She was dressed for a game of tennis.

'Is Diane home?' Nat asked.

'No, she's gone to some party at the Capitol with my parents. She should be back in about an hour. I'm Tricia, by the way. I spoke to you on the phone. I was just going to have a Coke. Want to join me?'

'Is your brother at home?'

'No, he's training down at the gym.'

'Yes, please.'

Tricia led Nat through to the kitchen and pointed towards a stool on the other side of the table. Nat sat down and didn't speak as Tricia pulled open the fridge door. As she bent over to remove two Cokes, her short skirt rose. Nat couldn't stop staring at her white tennis panties.

'What time are you expecting them back?' he asked as she added some ice cubes to his drink.

'No idea, so for the time being, you're stuck with me.'

Nat sipped his drink, not sure what to say, because he thought he and Diana had agreed to see *To Kill a Mockingbird*.

—◦—

'I don't know what you see in her,' said Jimmy.

'She's got everything you haven't,' said Fletcher smiling. 'She's bright, pretty, fun to be with and . . .'

'Are you sure we're talking about my sister?'

'Yes, which is why you're the one who has to wear glasses.'

'By the way, Diane Coulter has just turned up with her parents. Dad wants to know if you're still hoping to meet her.'

'Not particularly, she's gone from A to Z, so she's now a natural for you.'

'No thanks,' said Jimmy, 'I don't need your cast offs. By the way, I told Dad about *Romeo and Juliet*, and said I saw myself as Mercutio.'

'Only if I start to date Dan Coulter's sister, but I'm no longer interested in the daughter of that house.'

'I still don't understand.'

'I'll explain tomorrow morning,' said Fletcher, as Jimmy's sister reappeared carrying two Dr Peppers. Annie scowled at her brother, and he quickly disappeared.

For some time, neither of them spoke, until Annie said, 'Would you like me to show you the Senate Chamber?'

'Sure, that would be great,' said Fletcher. She turned and began walking towards the door, with Fletcher following a pace behind.

'Do you see what I see?' said Harry Gates, turning to his wife as Fletcher and his daughter disappeared out of the room.

'I certainly do,' replied Martha Gates, 'but I shouldn't get too worried about it, as I doubt if either of them is capable of seducing the other.'

'It didn't stop me trying at that age, as I feel sure you remember.'

'Typical politician. That's another story you've embellished over the years. Because if I remember correctly, it was me who seduced you.'

Nat was sipping his Coke when he felt a hand on his thigh. He blushed, but made no attempt to remove it. Tricia smiled across the table at him. 'You can put your hand on my leg if you want to.' Nat thought she might consider him rude if he didn't comply, so he reached under the table and placed a hand on her thigh. 'Good,' she said as she sipped her Coke, 'that's a little more friendly.' Nat didn't comment as her hand moved further up his newly pressed slacks. 'Just follow my lead,' she said. He moved his hand further up her thigh, but came to a halt when he reached the hem of her skirt. She didn't stop until she had reached his crotch.

'You've still got some way to go to catch up with me,' Tricia said, as she began to undo the top button of his slacks. 'Under the skirt, not over,' she added, without any trace of mockery. He slipped his hand under her skirt as she continued to unbutton his slacks. He hesitated again when his fingers reached her panties. He couldn't remember anything in *Teen* magazine about what he was expected to do next.

◄○►

'This is the Senate Chamber,' said Annie as they looked down from the gallery on to a semicircle of blue leather chairs.

'It's very impressive,' said Fletcher.

'Daddy says you'll end up here one day, or perhaps go even further.' Fletcher didn't reply, because he had no idea what exams you had to pass to become a politician. 'I heard him tell my mother he'd never met a more brilliant boy.'

'Well, you know what they say about politicians,' said Fletcher.

'Yes I do, but I can always tell when Daddy doesn't

mean it because he smiles at the same time, and this time he didn't smile.'

'Where does your father sit?' asked Fletcher, trying to change the subject.

'As majority leader he sits third along from the left in the front row,' she said, pointing down, 'but I'd better not tell you too much because I know he's looking forward to showing you around the Capitol himself.' He felt her hand touch his.

'Sorry,' he said, quickly removing his hand, thinking it had been a mistake.

'Don't be silly,' she said. She took his hand again, this time holding on to it.

'Don't you think we ought to go back and join the party?' asked Fletcher. 'Otherwise they might start to wonder where we are.'

'I suppose so,' said Annie, but she didn't move. 'Fletcher, have you ever kissed a girl?' she asked quietly.

'No I haven't,' he admitted, turning scarlet.

'Would you like to?'

'Yes, I would,' he said.

'Would you like to kiss me?'

He nodded and then turned and watched as Annie closed her eyes and pursed her lips. He checked to make sure that all the doors were closed, before he leant forward and kissed her gently on the mouth. Once he'd stopped, she opened her eyes.

'Do you know what a French kiss is?' she asked.

'No I don't,' said Fletcher.

'No, neither do I,' admitted Annie. 'If you find out, will you tell me?'

'Yes, I will,' said Fletcher.

BOOK TWO

EXODUS

10

'ARE YOU GOING to run for president?' asked Jimmy.

'Haven't decided yet,' Fletcher replied.

'Everyone assumes you will.'

'That's one of the problems.'

'My father wants you to.'

'But my mother doesn't,' said Fletcher.

'Why not?' asked Jimmy.

'She thinks I should spend my final year concentrating on getting a place at Yale.'

'But if you become student president, it will only assist your application. It's me who's going to find it a struggle.'

'I'm sure your father has several markers to call in,' said Fletcher with a grin.

'What does Annie think?' asked Jimmy, ignoring the comment.

'She's happy to go along with whatever I decide.'

'Then perhaps I should be the deciding factor.'

'What do you have in mind?'

'If you hope to win, you'll have to appoint me as your campaign manager.'

'That should certainly lengthen the odds,' said Fletcher. Jimmy picked up a cushion from the sofa and threw it at his friend. 'In fact, if you really want to guarantee my victory,' added Fletcher as he caught it, 'you should volunteer your services as campaign manager for my closest rival.'

Their sparring was interrupted when Jimmy's father

walked into the room. 'Fletcher, could you spare me a moment?'

'Of course, sir.'

'Perhaps we could have a chat in my study.' Fletcher quickly rose and followed the senator out of the room. He looked back at Jimmy, but his friend just shrugged his shoulders. He wondered if he had done something wrong.

'Have a seat,' said Harry Gates as he took his place behind the desk. He paused before he added, 'Fletcher, I need a favour.'

'Anything, sir. I'll never be able to repay you for all you've done for me.'

'You've more than honoured our agreement,' said the senator. 'For the past three years, Jimmy has somehow kept his place in the top stream, and he wouldn't have had a prayer without your continued vigilance.'

'That's kind of you to say so, but . . .'

'It's no more than the truth, but all I want for the boy now is to see that he has a fair shot at getting in to Yale.'

'But how can I help when I'm not even certain of a place myself?'

The senator ignored the comment. 'Pork barrel politics, my boy.'

'I'm not sure I understand, sir.'

'If you become student government president, as I'm confident you will, the first thing you'll have to do is appoint a vice-president.' Fletcher nodded. 'And that could just tip the balance for Jimmy when the admissions office at Yale decides who gets those last few places.'

'And it's just tipped the balance for me, sir.'

'Thank you, Fletcher, I appreciate that, but please don't let Jimmy know that we've had this conversation.'

—◇—

As soon as he woke the following morning, Fletcher went next door and sat on the end of Jimmy's bed. 'This had better be good,' said Jimmy, 'because I was dreaming about Daisy Hollingsworth.'

'Dream on,' said Fletcher, 'half the football team are in love with her.'

'So why did you wake me?'

'I've decided to run for president, and I don't need a campaign manager who lies in bed all morning.'

'Was it something my father said?'

'Indirectly.' He paused. 'So who do you think will be my main rival?'

'Steve Rodgers,' said Jimmy without hesitation.

'Why Steve?'

'He's a three-letter man, so they'll try to run him as the popular jock up against the austere academic. You know, Kennedy against Stevenson.'

'I had no idea you knew what the word austere meant.'

'No more jokes, Fletcher,' said Jimmy as he rolled off the bed. 'If you're going to beat Rodgers, you'll have to be prepared for anything and everything they throw at you. I think we ought to begin by having a breakfast meeting with Dad; he always has breakfast meetings before he starts a campaign.'

—◦—

'Will anyone bother to stand against you?' asked Diane Coulter.

'No one I can't beat.'

'What about Nat Cartwright?'

'Not while it's known that he's the principal's favourite, and if elected will simply carry out his wishes; at least that's what my supporters are telling everyone.'

'And don't let's forget the way he treated my sister.'

69

'I thought it was you who dumped him? I didn't even realize he knew Tricia.'

'He didn't, but that didn't stop him trying to make a move on her when he came round to the house to see me.'

'Does anyone else know about this?'

'Yes, my brother Dan. He caught him in the kitchen with his hand up her skirt. My sister complained bitterly that she just couldn't stop him.'

'Did she?' He paused. 'Do you think your brother would be willing to back me for president?'

'Yes, but there's not much he can do while he's at Princeton.'

'Oh yes there is,' said Elliot. 'To start with . . .'

'Who's my main rival?' asked Nat.

'Ralph Elliot, who else?' said Tom. 'He's been working on his campaign since the beginning of last term.'

'But that's against the rules.'

'I don't think Elliot has ever cared much about rules, and as he knows you're far more popular than he is, we can look forward to a dirty campaign.'

'But I'm not going down that road . . .'

'So we'll have to take the Kennedy route.'

'What do you have in mind?'

'You should open your campaign by challenging Elliot to a debate.'

'He'll never accept.'

'Then you win either way. If he does accept, you'll wipe the floor with him. If he doesn't, we can play the "he flunked it" card.'

'So how would you set up such a challenge?'

'Send him a letter, a copy of which I'll post on the bulletin board.'

'But you're not allowed to post notices without the principal's permission.'

'By the time they take it down, most people will have read it, and those that haven't will want to know what it said.'

'And by then I'll have been disqualified.'

'Not while the principal thinks Elliot might win.'

'I lost my first campaign,' said Senator Gates, when he heard Fletcher's news, 'so let's be sure that you don't make the same mistakes. For a start, who's your campaign manager?'

'Jimmy, of course.'

'Never "of course"; only select someone who you are convinced can do the job, even if you're not close friends.'

'I'm convinced he can do the job,' said Fletcher.

'Good. Now, Jimmy, you will be of no value to the candidate' – it was the first time Fletcher thought of himself as the candidate – 'unless you're always open and frank with Fletcher, however unpleasant it might be.' Jimmy nodded. 'Who's your main rival?'

'Steve Rodgers.'

'What do we know about him?'

'A nice enough guy, but not a lot between his ears,' said Jimmy.

'Except a good-looking face,' said Fletcher.

'And several touchdowns last season, if I remember correctly,' added the senator. 'So now we know who the enemy is, let's start working on our friends. First, you must pick an inner circle – six, eight at most. They only need two qualities, energy and loyalty – if they've got brains as well, that's a bonus. How long is the campaign?'

'Just over a week. School reassembles at nine o'clock on Monday, and the vote takes place on the Tuesday morning of the following week.'

'Don't think week,' said the senator, 'think hours, 192 of them, because every hour will count.'

Jimmy began making notes.

'So who's allowed to vote?' was the senator's next question.

'Every student.'

'Then make sure you spend as much time with the boys in the lower grades as with your contemporaries. They'll be flattered that you're taking so much interest in them. And, Jimmy, get your hands on an up-to-date list of the voters, so that you can be certain to make contact with every one of them before election day. And don't forget, new boys will vote for the last person who speaks to them.'

'There are 380 students,' said Jimmy, unfolding a large sheet of paper on the floor, 'I've marked the ones we already know in red, everyone I feel confident will support Fletcher in blue, new boys in yellow and left the rest blank.'

'And if you're in any doubt,' said the senator, 'leave them blank, and don't forget younger brothers.'

'Younger brothers?' said Fletcher.

'I've marked them in green,' said Jimmy. 'Every younger brother of one of our supporters who is in a lower grade will be appointed a rep. Their only job will be signing up support in their class and reporting back to their brothers.'

Fletcher looked on with admiration. 'I'm not sure it shouldn't be you who's running for president,' he said. 'You're a natural.'

'No, I'm a natural campaign manager,' said Jimmy, 'it's you who should be president.'

Although the senator agreed with his son's assessment, he didn't offer an opinion.

—◦—

It was six thirty on the first day of term when Nat and Tom stood alone in the parking lot. The first vehicle to come through the gates was the principal's.

'Good morning, Cartwright,' he barked, as he climbed out of his car, 'from your excess of enthusiasm at this early hour, am I to assume that you're running for president?'

'Yes, sir.'

'Excellent, and who is your main rival?'

'Ralph Elliot.'

The principal frowned. 'Then it will be a fiercely fought competition, because Elliot won't roll over easily.'

'True,' admitted Tom, as the principal disappeared towards his study, leaving the two of them to greet the second car. The occupant turned out to be a terrified new boy, who ran away when Nat approached him, and worse, the third car was full of Elliot supporters, who quickly fanned across the car park, obviously having already been through a dress rehearsal.

'Damn,' said Tom, 'our first team meeting isn't scheduled until the ten o'clock break. Elliot obviously briefed his team during the vacation.'

'Don't worry,' said Nat, 'just grab our people as they get out of their cars, and put them to work immediately.'

By the time the last car had disgorged its occupants, Nat had answered nearly a hundred questions and shaken hands with over three hundred boys, but only one fact became clear. Elliot was happy to promise them anything in exchange for their vote.

'Shouldn't we be letting everyone know what a sleaze-bag Elliot really is?'

'What do you have in mind?' Nat asked.

'How he cajoles new boys into parting with their allowances?'

'There's never been any proof.'

'Just endless complaints.'

'If there're that many, they'll know where to put their cross, won't they?' said Nat. 'In any case, that's not the sort of campaign I want to run,' he added. 'I'd prefer to assume the voters can make up their own minds which one of us can be trusted.'

'That's an original idea,' said Tom.

'Well, at least the principal is making it clear that he doesn't want Elliot to be president,' said Nat.

'I don't think we should tell anyone that,' said Tom. 'It may well swing a few more votes to Elliot.'

—◦—

'How do you think it's going?' asked Fletcher as they walked around the lake.

'Can't be sure,' Jimmy replied. 'A lot of the upper-mids are telling both camps that they'll be supporting their candidate, simply because they want to be seen backing the winner. Just be thankful that the vote isn't on Saturday evening,' Jimmy added.

'Why?' asked Fletcher.

'Because we play Kent on Saturday afternoon, and if Steve Rodgers scores the winning touchdown, we can kiss goodbye to any chance of you becoming president. It's just a pity it's a home game. If you'd been born a year earlier or a year later, it would have been an away match, and the impact would have been negligible. But as it is, every voter will be in the stadium watching the encounter, so pray we lose, or at least that Rodgers has a bad game.'

By two o'clock on Saturday, Fletcher was seated in

the stand, prepared for four quarters which would make up the longest hour of his life. But even he couldn't have predicted the outcome.

─◇─

'Damn, how did he manage to pull that off?' growled Nat.

'Bribery and corruption would be my bet,' said Tom. 'Elliot has always been a useful player, but never good enough to make the school team.'

'Do you think they'll risk putting him in the game?'

'Why not? St George's often field a weak side, so they could leave him out there for a few minutes once they're confident it won't affect the result. Then Elliot will spend the rest of the game running up and down the side lines, waving at the voters, while all we can do is stare down at him from the bleachers.'

'Then let's make sure all our workers are in position outside the stadium a few minutes before the game ends, and don't let anyone see our new hand-held placards until Saturday afternoon. That way Elliot won't have time to come up with his own.'

'You're learning fast,' said Tom.

'When Elliot's your opponent, you're not left with a lot of choice.'

─◇─

'I'm not sure how it will affect the vote,' said Jimmy, as the two of them ran towards the exit to join up with the rest of the team. 'At least Steve Rodgers can't shake hands with everyone as they leave the stadium.'

'I wonder how long he'll be in the hospital,' Fletcher said.

'Three days is all we need,' said Jimmy. Fletcher laughed.

Fletcher was delighted to find that his team were already well spread out by the time he joined them, and several boys came up to say they would be supporting him, although it still felt close. He never moved beyond the main exit as he continued to shake hands with any boy over the age of fourteen and under the age of nineteen, including, he suspected, a few supporters from the visiting team. Fletcher and Jimmy didn't leave until they were sure the stadium was empty of everyone except the groundsmen.

As they walked back to their rooms, Jimmy admitted that no one could have predicted a tie, or that Rodgers would have been on his way to the local hospital before the end of the first quarter.

'If the vote was tonight he'd win on sympathy. If no one sees him again before Tuesday at nine o'clock, you'll be the president.'

'Doesn't ability to do the job come into the equation?'

'Of course not, you fool,' said Jimmy. 'This is politics.'

-<o>-

When Nat arrived at the game, his placards were to be seen everywhere, and all that the Elliot supporters could do was cry foul play. Nat and Tom couldn't hide their smiles as they took their places in the bleachers. The smiles broadened when St George's scored early in the first quarter. Nat didn't want Taft to lose, but no coach was going to risk putting Elliot on the field while St George's remained in the lead. And that didn't change until the final quarter.

Nat shook hands with everyone as they left the stadium, but he knew that Taft's last-minute victory over St George's hadn't helped his cause, even if Elliot had only been able to run up and down the sideline until the last person had left the bleachers.

'Just be thankful he never got in the game,' said Tom.

◄○►

Fletcher was invited to read the lesson in chapel that Sunday morning, making it abundantly clear who the principal would have voted for. During lunch, he and Jimmy visited every dorm, to ask the boys how they felt about the food. 'A sure vote winner,' the senator had assured them, 'even if you can't do anything about it.' That evening, they climbed into bed exhausted. Jimmy set the alarm for five thirty. Fletcher groaned.

'A master stroke,' said Jimmy as they stood outside assembly the following morning waiting for the boys to go off to their classrooms.

'Brilliant,' admitted Fletcher.

'I'm afraid so,' said Jimmy. 'Not that I can complain, because I would have recommended that you do exactly the same thing, given the circumstances.'

The two of them stared across at Steve Rodgers, who was standing on crutches by the exit to the hall, allowing the boys to sign their autographs on his plastered leg.

'A master stroke,' repeated Jimmy. 'It brings a new meaning to the sympathy vote. Perhaps we should ask the question, do you want a cripple for president?'

'One of the greatest presidents in the history of this country was a cripple,' Fletcher reminded his campaign manager.

'Then there's only one thing for it,' said Jimmy, 'you'll have to spend the next twenty-four hours in a wheelchair.'

◄○►

Over the final weekend, Nat's workers tried to project an air of confidence, even though they realized it was too close to call. Neither candidate stopped smiling, until Monday evening, when the school bell struck six.

'Let's go back to my room,' said Tom, 'and tell stories of the death of kings.'

'Sad stories,' said Nat.

The team all crowded into Tom's little room and swapped anecdotes of the roles they had played in the campaign, and laughed at jokes that weren't funny, as they waited impatiently to learn the result.

A loud rap on the door interrupted their noisy exuberance. 'Come in,' called Tom.

They all stood up the moment they saw who it was standing in the doorway.

'Good evening, Mr Anderson,' said Nat.

'Good evening, Cartwright,' replied the dean of students formally. 'As the returning officer in the election for president of student government, I have to inform you that due to the closeness of the result, I will be calling for a recount. Assembly has therefore been postponed until eight o'clock.'

'Thank you, sir,' was all Nat could think of saying.

When eight o'clock had struck, every boy was seated in his place. They rose dutifully when the dean of students entered the hall. Nat tried to read any sign of the result from the expression on his face, but even the Japanese would have been proud of Mr Anderson's inscrutability.

The dean walked to the centre of the stage and invited the assembly to be seated. There was a hush, rarely experienced at a normal gathering.

'I must tell you,' began the dean, 'that this was the closest result in the school's seventy-five-year history.' Nat could feel the palms of his hands sweating, as he tried to remain calm. 'The voting for president of student council was Nat Cartwright, 178, Ralph Elliot, 181.'

Half the gathering leapt to their feet and cheered, while the other half remained seated and silent. Nat rose from his place, walked across to Elliot and offered his outstretched hand.

The new president ignored it.

—o—

Although everyone knew the result wouldn't be announced until nine o'clock, the assembly hall was packed long before the principal made his entrance.

Fletcher sat in the back row, with his head bowed, while Jimmy stared directly in front of him. 'I should have got up earlier every morning,' said Fletcher.

'I should have broken your leg,' Jimmy responded.

The principal, accompanied by the chaplain, marched down the aisle as if to show God was somehow involved in who became president of student government at Hotchkiss. The principal walked to the front of the stage and cleared his throat.

'The result of the election for student government president,' said Mr Fleming, 'is Fletcher Davenport 207 votes, Steve Rodgers 173 votes. I therefore declare Fletcher Davenport to be president.'

Fletcher immediately walked across and shook hands with Steve, who smiled warmly, looking almost relieved. Fletcher turned round to see Harry Gates standing by the door. The senator bowed respectfully to the new president.

'You never forget your first election victory,' was all he said.

They both ignored Jimmy, who was leaping up and down, unable to contain himself.

'I believe you know my vice-president, sir,' Fletcher replied.

11

NAT'S MOTHER SEEMED to be one of the few people who wasn't disappointed that her son hadn't been elected president. She felt it would give him more time to concentrate on his work. And if Susan Cartwright could have seen the hours Nathaniel was putting in, she would have stopped worrying. Even Tom found it difficult to prise Nat away from his books for more than a few minutes, unless it was to go on his daily five-mile run. And even when he broke the school cross-country record, Nat only allowed himself a couple of hours off to celebrate.

Christmas Eve, Christmas Day, New Year's Eve – it made no difference. Nat remained in his room, head buried in his books. His mother only hoped that when he left to spend a long weekend in Simsbury with Tom, he would take a real break. He did. Nat cut his work load down to two hours in the morning and another two in the afternoon. Tom was grateful that his friend kept him to the same routine, even if he declined the invitation to join him for his daily run. It amused Nat that he could complete the five miles without ever leaving Tom's estate.

'One of your many sweethearts?' asked Nat over breakfast the following morning as his friend tore open a letter.

'I only wish,' said Tom. 'No, it's from Mr Thompson asking if I want to be considered for a part in *Twelfth Night*.'

'And do you?' asked Nat.

'No. It's more your world than mine. I'm a producer by nature, not a performer.'

'I would have put my name down for a part if I was confident about my Yale application, but I haven't even completed my independent study.'

'I haven't even started mine,' admitted Tom.

'Which of the five subjects did you select?' asked Nat.

'Control of the lower Mississippi during the Civil War,' replied Tom. 'And you?'

'Clarence Darrow and his influence on the trade union movement.'

'Yeah, I considered Mr Darrow, but wasn't sure I could manage five thousand words on the subject. No doubt you've already written ten.'

'No, but I've almost finished a first draft, and should have a final copy ready by the time we return in January.'

'Yale's deadline isn't until February; you really ought to consider taking a part in the school play. At least read for the audition. After all, it doesn't have to be the lead.'

Nat thought about his friend's suggestion as he buttered himself a piece of toast. Tom was right, of course, but Nat felt it would be just another distraction if he was hoping to win a scholarship to Yale. He glanced out of the window across acres of land and wondered what it must be like to have parents who didn't have to worry about tuition payments, pocket money, and whether he could get a holiday job during the summer vacation.

⟨◦⟩

'Do you wish to read for any particular role, Nat?' asked Mr Thompson as he stared up at the six-foot-two boy with a mop of black hair, whose trousers always seemed to be a couple of inches too short.

'Antonio, possibly Orsino,' replied Nat.

81

'You're a natural Orsino,' said Mr Thompson, 'but I have your friend, Tom Russell, in mind for that part.'

'I'm hardly Malvolio,' said Nat with a laugh.

'No, Elliot would be my first choice for Malvolio,' said Thompson with a wry smile. Mr Thompson, like so many others at Taft, wished Nat had become the student government president. 'But sadly he's not available, whereas in truth, you are best suited for the role of Sebastian.'

Nat wanted to protest, although when he first read the script he had to admit he thought the part would be a challenge. However, its sheer length would demand hours of learning, not to mention time spent in rehearsals. Mr Thompson sensed Nat's reservations. 'I think the time has come for a little bribery, Nat.'

'Bribery, sir?'

'Yes, my boy. You see the admissions director at Yale is one of my oldest friends. We studied classics together at Princeton, and he always spends a weekend with me every year. I think I'll make it the weekend of the school play,' he paused, 'that is, if you feel able to play Sebastian.' Nat didn't respond. 'Ah, I see bribery is not enough for someone of your high moral standards, so I shall have to stoop to corruption.'

'Corruption, sir?' said Nat.

'Yes, Nat, corruption. You will have observed that there are three parts in the play for females – the fair Olivia, your twin Viola, and the feisty Maria, not to mention understudies and maidservants, and don't let's forget that they all fall in love with Sebastian.' Nat still didn't respond. 'And,' continued Mr Thompson, revealing his trump card, 'my opposite number at Miss Porter's has suggested that I should take a boy over on Saturday to read the male parts while we decide who should audition for the females.' He paused again. 'Ah, I see I have finally caught your attention.'

—◦—

'Do you believe it's possible to spend your whole life loving only one person?' Annie asked.

'If you're lucky enough to find the right person, why not?' responded Fletcher.

'I suspect that when you go to Yale in the fall you'll be surrounded by so many bright and beautiful women, I'll pale by comparison.'

'Not a chance,' said Fletcher. He sat down next to her on the sofa and put an arm round her shoulder. 'And in any case, they'll quickly discover that I'm in love with somebody else, and once you're at Vassar, they'll discover why.'

'But that won't be for another year,' said Annie, 'and by then . . .'

'Shh . . . haven't you noticed that every man who meets you is immediately jealous of me?'

'No, I haven't,' she replied honestly.

Fletcher turned to look at the girl he'd fallen in love with when she'd had a flat chest and braces on her teeth. But even then he couldn't resist that smile, her black hair, inherited from an Irish grandmother, and steel-blue eyes from the Swedish side of the family. But now, four years later, time had added a slim graceful figure and legs that made Fletcher grateful for the new fashion of mini-skirts.

Annie put a hand on Fletcher's thigh, 'Do you realize that half the girls in my form are no longer virgins?' she said.

'So Jimmy tells me,' said Fletcher.

'And he should know.' Annie paused, 'I'm seventeen next month, and you've never once suggested . . .'

83

'I've thought about it many times, of course I have,' said Fletcher as she moved her body so that his hand touched her breast, 'but when it happens, I want it to be right for both of us and for there never to be any regrets.'

Annie nestled her head in his shoulder. 'For me there wouldn't be any regrets,' she said, placing a hand on his leg.

He took her in his arms. 'When are you expecting your parents back?'

'Around midnight. They're attending another of those never-ending functions politicians seem to thrive on.'

Fletcher didn't move as Annie began to unbutton her blouse. When she reached the last button, she slipped it off and let it fall to the floor. 'Your turn I think,' she said. Fletcher quickly unbuttoned his shirt and cast it aside. Annie stood up and faced him, amused by the sudden power she seemed to have over him. She unzipped her skirt slowly in the way she had seen Julie Christie do in *Darling*. Like Miss Christie, she hadn't bothered with a petticoat. 'Your turn I think,' she said again.

Oh my God, thought Fletcher, I daren't take off my trousers. He slipped off his shoes and socks.

'That's cheating,' said Annie, who had removed her shoes even before Fletcher knew what she had in mind. He reluctantly pulled down his trousers, and she burst out laughing. Fletcher blushed as he looked down at his pants.

'It's good to know I can do that to you,' said Annie.

―◦―

'Would it be possible for you to concentrate on the words, Nat?' asked Mr Thompson, not attempting to disguise his sarcasm. 'Take it from *"But here the lady comes"*.'

Even dressed in her school uniform, Rebecca stood out from the rest of the girls Mr Thompson was auditioning. The tall, slim girl with fair hair cascading down her shoulders had an air of self-confidence that captivated Nat, and a smile that made him respond immediately. When she returned his smile, he turned away, embarrassed to have embarrassed her. All he knew about her was her name. *'What's in a name,'* he said.

'Wrong play Nat, try again.'

Rebecca Armitage waited as Nat stumbled through his words, *'But here the lady comes . . .'* Rebecca was surprised because when she'd stood at the back of the hall and heard him earlier, he had sounded so totally self-assured. She looked down at her script and read, *'Blame not this haste of mine. If you mean well, now go with me and with this holy man into the chantry by: there, before him, and underneath that consecrated roof, plight me the full assurance of your faith; that my most jealous and too doubtful soul may live at peace. He shall conceal it while you are willing it shall come to note, what time we will our celebration keep according to my birth. What do you say?'*

Nat said nothing.

'Nat, had you thought of joining in?' suggested Mr Thompson. 'So that Rebecca can at least deliver a few more lines? I admit that the adoring look is most effective, and for some might pass as acting, but this is not a mime we're performing. One or two of the audience might even have come to hear the familiar words of Mr Shakespeare.'

'Yes, sir; sorry, sir,' said Nat, returning to the script. *'I'll follow this good man, and go with you; and having sworn truth, ever will be true.'*

'Then lead the way, good father; and heavens so shine, that they may fairly note this act of mine.'

'Thank you, Miss Armitage, I don't think I need to hear any more.'

'But she was wonderful,' said Nat.

'Ah, you can deliver an entire line without pausing,'

said Mr Thompson. 'That's a relief to discover at this late stage, but then I had no idea you wanted to be the director as well as play the lead. However, Nat, I think I have already made up my mind who will play the fair Olivia.'

Nat watched Rebecca as she quickly left the stage. 'Then what about Viola?' he persisted.

'No, if I've understood the plot correctly, Nat, Viola is your twin sister, and unfortunately or fortunately Rebecca bears absolutely no resemblance to you.'

'Then Maria, she'd make a wonderful Maria.'

'I'm sure she would, but Rebecca is far too tall to play Maria.'

'Have you thought of playing Feste as a woman?' asked Nat.

'No, to be honest, Nat, I hadn't, partly because I don't have the time to rewrite the entire script.'

Nat didn't notice Rebecca slip behind a pillar, trying to hide her embarrassment as he blundered on. 'What about the maidservant in Olivia's household?'

'What about her?'

'Rebecca would make a wonderful maidservant.'

'I'm sure she would, but she can't play Olivia and be her maidservant at the same time. Someone in the audience might notice.' Nat opened his mouth but didn't speak. 'Ah, silence at last, but I feel confident that you will be rewriting the play overnight, in order to ensure that Olivia has several new scenes with Sebastian that Mr Shakespeare hadn't even considered.' Nat heard a giggle from behind the pillar. 'Anyone else you fancy for the maidservant, Nat, or can I carry on with casting the play?'

'Sorry, sir,' said Nat. 'Sorry.'

Mr Thompson leapt on to the stage, smiled at Nat and whispered, 'If you were considering playing hard to get, Nat, I'm bound to say I think you've blown it. You've made yourself more available than a whore in a Las Vegas casino. And I feel sure you'll be interested to learn that next year's play will be *The Taming of the Shrew*, which I feel might have been more appropriate. If only you'd been born a year later how different your life would have been. However, good luck with Miss Armitage.'

◄○►

'The boy must be expelled,' said Mr Fleming. 'No other punishment would be appropriate.'

'But, sir,' said Fletcher, 'Pearson is only fifteen, and he apologized to Mrs Appleyard immediately.'

'I would have expected nothing less,' said the chaplain, who until that moment had not offered an opinion.

'And in any case,' said the principal, rising from behind his desk, 'can you imagine the effect on school discipline if it became known that you could get away with swearing at a master's wife?'

'And because of the words, "bloody woman", the boy's entire future is to be determined?'

'That's the consequence of such ill manners,' said the principal, 'and at least, this way, one can be certain he'll learn from it.'

'But what will he learn?' asked Fletcher. 'That you can never afford to make a mistake in life, or that you must never swear?'

'Why are you defending the boy so vehemently?'

'In the first lecture I ever heard you deliver sir, you told us that not to stand up and be counted when an injustice had been done was the act of a coward.'

Mr Fleming glanced at the chaplain, who made no comment. He remembered the lecture well. After all, he delivered the same text to every new intake.

'May I be allowed to ask you an impertinent question?' asked Fletcher, turning to face the chaplain.

'Yes,' said Dr Wade a little defensively.

'Have you ever wanted to swear at Mrs Appleyard, because I have, several times.'

'But that's the point, Fletcher, you showed some self restraint. Pearson didn't, and therefore he must be punished.'

'If that punishment is to be expulsion, sir, then I must resign as president of the student government, because the Bible tells us that the thought is as evil as the deed.'

Both men stared at him in disbelief. 'But why, Fletcher? Surely you realize that if you were to resign it could even affect your chances of being offered a place at Yale?'

'The type of person who would allow that to influence him isn't worthy of a place at Yale.'

Both men were so stunned by this remark that neither spoke for some time. 'Isn't that a bit extreme, Fletcher?' the chaplain eventually managed.

'Not for the boy in question it isn't, Dr Wade, and I am not willing to stand and watch this student sacrificed on the altar of a woman who gets her kicks from goading pubescent boys.'

'And you would resign as president to prove your point?' asked the principal.

'Not to do it, sir, would be only one step away from what your generation condoned at the time of McCarthy.'

Another long silence followed, before the chaplain said quietly, 'Did the boy apologize in person to Mrs Appleyard?'

'Yes, sir,' said Fletcher, 'and he followed it up with a letter.'

'Then perhaps probation for the remainder of the term would be more appropriate,' suggested the principal, glancing at the chaplain.

'Along with the loss of all privileges, including week-end leaves, until further notice,' added Dr Wade.

'Does that seem to you a fair compromise, Fletcher?' asked the principal, raising an eyebrow. It was Fletcher's turn to remain silent. 'Compromise, Fletcher,' interjected the chaplain, 'is something you will have to learn to live with if you hope to become a successful politician.'

Fletcher didn't respond immediately. 'I accept your judgement, Dr Wade,' he eventually said, and, turning to the principal, added, 'and thank you for your indulgence, sir.'

'Thank you, Fletcher,' said Mr Fleming as the student president rose from his place and left the principal's study.

'Wisdom, courage and conviction are rare enough in a grown man,' said the principal quietly as the door closed, 'but in a child . . .'

—◇—

'Then what *is* your explanation, Mr Cartwright?' asked the dean of Yale's examination board.

'I don't have one, sir,' Nat admitted. 'It must be a coincidence.'

'It's quite a coincidence,' said the dean of academic affairs, 'that large sections of your paper on Clarence Darrow are word for word identical to those of another student in your class.'

'And what's his explanation?'

'As he submitted his independent study a week before yours, and it was hand-written, while yours was typed, we haven't felt it necessary to ask him for an explanation.'

'Would his name be Ralph Elliot, by any chance?' asked Nat.

No one on the board commented.

'How did he manage it?' asked Tom, when Nat returned to Taft later that evening.

'He must have copied it out word for word while I was over at Miss Porter's rehearsing for *Twelfth Night*.'

'But he still had to remove the thesis from your room.'

'That wouldn't have been difficult,' said Nat. 'If it wasn't on my desk, he would have found it filed under Yale.'

'But he still took a hell of a risk going into your room when you weren't there.'

'Not when you're the student president. Don't forget he has the run of the place – no one questions his coming or going. He would easily have had enough time to copy out the text and return the original to my room the same evening without anyone being any the wiser.'

'So what have the board decided?'

'Thanks to the principal going overboard on my behalf, Yale has agreed to defer my application for a year.'

'So Elliot gets away with it once again.'

'No, he does not,' said Nat firmly. 'The principal worked out what must have happened, because Yale have also withdrawn Elliot's place.'

'But that only delays the problem for a year,' said Tom.

'Happily not,' said Nat, smiling for the first time. 'Mr Thompson also decided to step in, and rang the admissions tutor, with the result that Yale have not offered Elliot the chance to reapply.'

'Good old Thomo,' said Tom. 'So what are you planning to do in your year out? Join the Peace Corps?'

'No, I'm going to spend the year at the University of Connecticut.'

'Why UConn?' asked Tom, 'when you could . . .'

'Because it was Rebecca's first choice.'

12

THE PRESIDENT OF YALE stared down at a thousand expectant freshmen. In a year's time, some of them would have found the going too tough and moved on to other universities, while others would have simply given up. Fletcher Davenport and Jimmy Gates sat in the body of the hall and listened intently to every word President Waterman had to say.

'Do not waste a moment of your time while you are at Yale, or you will regret for the rest of your life not having taken advantage of all this university has to offer. A fool leaves Yale with only a degree, a wise man with enough knowledge to face whatever life throws at him. Seize every opportunity that is offered to you. Do not be frightened of any new challenge, and should you fail, there is no reason to be ashamed. You will learn far more from your mistakes than from your triumphs. Do not be afraid of your destiny. Be afraid of nothing. Challenge every writ, and let it not be said of you, I walked a path but never left an imprint.'

The president of Yale resumed his place after nearly an hour on his feet, and received a prolonged standing ovation. Trent Waterman, who did not approve of such displays, rose and left the stage.

'I thought you weren't going to join in the standing ovation?' said Fletcher to his friend as they filed out of the hall. '"Just because everyone else has for the past ten years, doesn't mean I shall join in the ritual," if I remember your sentiments correctly.'

'I admit it, I was wrong,' said Jimmy. 'It was even more impressive than my father had assured me it would be.'

'I feel confident your endorsement will come as a relief to Mr Waterman,' said Fletcher, as Jimmy spotted a young woman laden with books walking a few paces ahead of them.

'Seize every opportunity,' he whispered in Fletcher's ear. Fletcher wondered whether to stop Jimmy making a complete fool of himself, or just let him find out the hard way.

'Hi, I'm Jimmy Gates. Would you like me to help you with your books?'

'What did you have in mind, Mr Gates? Carrying them, or reading them to me?' replied the woman who didn't break her stride.

'I was thinking of carrying them to begin with, and then why don't we see how it goes from there?'

'Mr Gates, I have two rules I never break: dating a freshman and dating someone with red hair.'

'Don't you think the time has come,' said Jimmy, 'to break them both at once? After all, the president did tell us to never be frightened of a new challenge.'

'Jimmy,' said Fletcher, 'I think . . .'

'Ah yes, this is my friend Fletcher Davenport, he's very clever, so he could help you with the reading part.'

'I don't think so, Jimmy.'

'And he's also very modest, as you can see.'

'Not a problem you suffer from, Mr Gates.'

'Certainly not,' said Jimmy. 'By the way, what's your name?'

'Joanna Palmer.'

'So you're obviously not a freshman, Joanna,' said Jimmy.

'No, I'm not.'

'Then you're the ideal person to help and succour me.'

'What do you have in mind?' asked Miss Palmer, as they climbed the steps to Sudler Hall.

'Why don't you invite me to supper this evening, and then you can tell me everything I should know about Yale,' ventured Jimmy just as they came to a halt outside the lecture hall. 'Hey,' he said, turning to Fletcher, 'isn't this where we're meant to be?'

'Yes it is, and I did try to warn you.'

'Warn me? About what?' asked Jimmy, as he opened the door for Miss Palmer and followed her into the room, hoping he could sit next to her. The undergraduates immediately stopped talking, which took Jimmy by surprise.

'I apologize for my friend, Miss Palmer,' whispered Fletcher, 'but I can assure you he has a heart of gold.'

'And the balls to go with it, it would seem,' Joanna replied. 'By the way, never let him know, but I was extremely flattered that he thought I might be a freshman.'

Joanna Palmer placed her books on the long desk and turned to face the packed lecture theatre. 'The French Revolution is the turning point of modern European history,' she began to a rapt audience. 'Although America had already removed a monarch,' she paused, 'without having to remove his head . . .' Her eyes swept the tiered benches as her pupils laughed, before coming to rest on Jimmy Gates. He winked.

━◆━

They held hands as they walked across the campus to their first lecture. They had become friends during the rehearsals of the play, inseparable in the week of the performance, and had both lost their virginity together during spring vacation. When Nat told his lover that he would not be going to Yale, but joining her at the University of Connecticut, Rebecca felt guilty about how happy the news made her.

Susan and Michael Cartwright liked Rebecca the moment they met her, and their disappointment over Nat not being offered an immediate place at Yale was softened by seeing their son so relaxed for the first time in his life.

The opening lecture in Buckley Hall was on the subject of American literature, and delivered by Professor Hayman. During the summer vacation, Nat and Rebecca had read all the authors on the assigned list – James, Steinbeck, Hemingway, Fitzgerald and Bellow – and then discussed in detail *Washington Square*, *The Grapes of Wrath*, *For Whom the Bell Tolls*, *The Great Gatsby*, and *Herzog*. So by the time they took their places in the lecture theatre that Tuesday morning, they both felt confident they were well prepared. Within moments of Professor Hayman delivering his opening salvo, they both realized that they had done little more than read the texts. They had not considered the different influences on the authors that birth, upbringing, education, religion and mere circumstance had brought to their work, nor given any thought to the fact that the gift of storytelling was not bestowed on any particular class, colour or creed.

'Take, for example, Scott Fitzgerald,' continued the professor, 'in his short story, "Bernice Bobs Her Hair" . . .'

Nat looked up from his notes and saw the back of his head. He felt sick. He stopped listening to Professor Hayman's views on Fitzgerald and continued to stare for some time before the student turned and began talking to his neighbour. Nat's worst fears were confirmed. Ralph Elliot was not only at the same university, but taking the same course. Almost as if conscious of being stared at, Elliot suddenly turned round. He didn't acknowledge Nat, as his attention settled on Rebecca. Nat glanced across at her, but she was too busy taking notes on Fitzgerald's drinking problems during his time in Hollywood to register Elliot's unsubtle interest.

Nat waited until Elliot had left the lecture theatre before he collected up his books and rose from his place.

'Who was that who kept turning round and staring at you?' asked Rebecca, as they strolled over to the dining hall.

'His name's Ralph Elliot,' said Nat. 'We were both at Taft, and I think he was staring at you, not me.'

'He's very good looking,' said Rebecca with a grin. He reminds me a little of Jay Gatsby. Is he the one Mr Thompson thought would make a good Malvolio?'

'A natural, I think were Thomo's exact words.'

Over lunch, Rebecca pressed Nat to tell her more about Elliot, but he said that there wasn't that much to tell, and continually tried to change the subject. If enjoying Rebecca's company also meant having to be at the same university as Ralph Elliot, it was something he'd learn to live with.

Elliot didn't attend the afternoon lecture on the Spanish influence over the colonies, and by the time Nat accompanied Rebecca back to her room that evening, he had almost forgotten the unwelcome presence of his old rival.

The women's dorms were on south campus, and Nat's freshman advisor had warned him that it was against the regulations for men to be found in residence after dark.

'Whoever fixed the regulations,' said Nat, as he lay

next to Rebecca on her single bed, 'must have thought that students could only make love in the dark.' Rebecca laughed as she pulled her sweater back on.

'Which means that during the spring semester you won't have to go back to your room until after nine o'clock,' she said.

'Perhaps the regulations will allow me to stay with you after the summer semester,' said Nat without explanation.

During his first term, Nat was relieved to discover that he rarely came into contact with Ralph Elliot. His rival showed no interest in cross-country running, acting or music, so it came as a surprise when Nat found him chatting to Rebecca outside the chapel on the last Sunday of term. Elliot quickly walked away the moment he saw Nat approaching them.

'What did he want?' asked Nat defensively.

'Just going over his ideas to improve the student council. He's running as the freshman representative, and wanted to know if you were thinking of putting your name forward.'

'No, I'm not,' said Nat firmly. 'I've had enough of elections.'

'I think that's a pity,' said Rebecca, squeezing Nat's hand, 'because I know a lot of our year hope you will run.'

'Not while he's in the field,' said Nat.

'Why do you hate him so much?' asked Rebecca. 'Is it just because he beat you in that silly school election?' Nat stared across at Elliot and watched him chatting to a group of students – the same insincere smile, and no doubt the same glib promises. 'Don't you think it's possible that he might have changed?' said Rebecca.

Nat didn't bother to reply.

–◦–

'Right,' said Jimmy, 'the first election you can run for, is as freshman representative on the Yale college council.'

'I thought I'd skip elections during my first year,' said Fletcher, 'and just concentrate on work.'

'You can't risk it,' declared Jimmy.

'And why not?' asked Fletcher.

'Because it's a statistical fact that whoever gets elected to the college council in his first year, is almost certain to end up as president three years later.'

'Perhaps I don't want to be president of the college council,' said Fletcher with a grin.

'Perhaps Marilyn Monroe didn't want to win an Oscar,' said Jimmy, as he produced a booklet from his briefcase.

'What's that?'

'The freshman face book – there's 1,021 of them.'

'I see you've once again begun the campaign without consulting the candidate.'

'I had to, because I can't afford to hang around waiting for you to make up your mind. I've done some research and discovered that you have little or no chance of even being considered for the college council unless you speak in the freshman's debate in the sixth week.'

'Why's that?' asked Fletcher.

'Because it's the only occasion when all the frosh come together in one room and are given the chance to listen to any prospective candidate.'

'So how do you get selected as a speaker?'

'Depends which side of the motion you want to support.'

'So what's the motion?'

'I'm glad to see you're finally warming to the challenge, because that's our next problem.' Jimmy removed a leaflet from an inside pocket. 'Resolved: America should withdraw from the Vietnam War.'

'I don't see any problem with that,' said Fletcher, 'I'd be quite happy to oppose such a motion.'

'That's the problem,' said Jimmy, 'because anyone who opposes is history, even if they look like Kennedy and speak like Churchill.'

'But if I present a good case, they might feel I was the right person to represent them on the council.'

'However persuasive you are, Fletcher, it would still be suicide, because almost everyone on campus is against the war. So why not leave that to some madman who never wanted to be elected in the first place?'

'That sounds like me,' said Fletcher, 'and in any case, perhaps I believe . . .'

'I don't care what you believe,' interrupted Jimmy. 'My only interest is getting you elected.'

'Jimmy, do you have any morals at all?'

'How could I?' Jimmy replied. 'My father's a politician and my mother sells real estate.'

'Despite your pragmatism, I still couldn't get myself to speak in favour of such a motion.'

'Then you're doomed to a life of endless study and holding hands with my sister.'

'Sounds pretty good to me,' said Fletcher, 'especially as you seem quite incapable of having a serious relationship with any woman for more than twenty-four hours.'

'That isn't Joanna Palmer's opinion,' said Jimmy.

Fletcher laughed, 'And what about your other friend, Audrey Hepburn? I haven't seen her on campus lately.'

'Neither have I,' said Jimmy, 'but it will only be a matter of time before I capture Miss Palmer's heart.'

'In your dreams, Jimmy.'

'You will in time, apologize, O ye of little faith, and I predict that it will be before your disastrous contribution to the freshman debate.'

'You won't change my mind, Jimmy, because if I take part in the debate, it will be to oppose the motion.'

'You do like to make life difficult for me, don't you, Fletcher. Well, one thing's for certain, the organizers will welcome your participation.'

'Why's that?' asked Fletcher.

'Because they haven't been able to find anyone half electable who is willing to put the case against withdrawal.'

—◦—

'Are you sure?' asked Nat quietly.

'Yes, I am,' replied Rebecca.

'Then we must get married as soon as possible,' said Nat.

'Why?' asked Rebecca. 'We live in the Sixties, the age of the Beatles, pot, and free love, so why shouldn't I have an abortion?'

'Is that what you want?' asked Nat in disbelief.

'I don't know what I want,' said Rebecca. 'I only found out this morning. I need some more time to think about it.'

Nat took her hand. 'I'd marry you today if you'd have me.'

'I know you would,' said Rebecca, squeezing his hand, 'but we have to face the fact that this decision will affect the rest of our lives. We shouldn't rush into it.'

'But I have a moral responsibility to you and our child.'

'And I have my future to consider,' said Rebecca.

'Perhaps we should tell our parents, and see how they react?'

'That's the last thing I want to do,' said Rebecca. 'Your mother will expect us to get married this afternoon, and my father will turn up on campus with a shotgun under his arm. No, I want you to promise you won't mention that I'm pregnant to anyone, especially our parents.'

'But why?' pressed Nat.

'Because there's another problem . . .'

'How's the speech coming on?'

'Just finished the third draft,' said Fletcher cheerfully, 'and you'll be happy to learn that it's likely to make me the most unpopular student on campus.'

'You do like making my task more difficult . . .'

'Impossible is my ultimate aim,' admitted Fletcher. 'By the way, who are we up against?'

'Some guy called Tom Russell.'

'What have you found out about him?'

'Went to Taft.'

'Which means that we have a head start,' said Fletcher with a grin.

'No, I'm afraid not,' said Jimmy. 'I met him at Mory's last night, and I can tell you he's bright and popular. I can't find anyone who doesn't like him.'

'Have we got anything going for us?'

'Yes, he admitted that he's not looking forward to the debate. He'd rather support another candidate, if the right one came forward. Sees himself as more of a campaign organizer than a leader.'

'Then perhaps we could ask Tom to join our team,' said Fletcher. 'I'm still looking for a campaign organizer.'

'Funnily enough, he offered *me* that job,' said Jimmy.

Fletcher stared at his friend. 'Did he really?'

'Yes,' replied Jimmy.

'Then I'll have to take him seriously, won't I?' Fletcher paused, 'Perhaps we should start by going over my speech tonight, then you can tell me if . . .'

'Not possible tonight,' said Jimmy. 'Joanna's invited me over to her place for supper.'

'Ah yes, that reminds me, I can't make it either. Jackie Kennedy has asked me to accompany her to the Met.'

'Now you mention it, Joanna did wonder if you and Annie would like to join us for a drink next Thursday. I told her that my sister was coming over to New Haven for the debate.'

'Are you serious?' said Fletcher.

'And if you do decide to join us, please tell Annie not to hang around for too long, because Joanna and I like to be tucked up in bed by ten.'

—◦—

When Nat found Rebecca's hand-written note slipped under his door, he ran all the way across campus, wondering what could possibly be that urgent.

When he walked into her room she turned away as he tried to kiss her, and without explanation locked the door. Nat sat by the window, while Rebecca perched herself on the end of the bed. 'Nat, I have to tell you something that I've been avoiding for the past few days.' Nat just nodded, as he could see that Rebecca was finding it difficult to get the words out. There followed what seemed to him to be an interminable silence.

'Nat, I know you'll hate me for this . . .'

'I'm incapable of hating you,' said Nat, now looking directly at her.

She met his gaze but then lowered her head. 'I'm not sure you're the father.'

Nat gripped the sides of his chair. 'How's that possible?' he eventually asked.

'That weekend you went over to Penn for the cross-country meet, I ended up at a party and I'm afraid I drank a little too much.' She paused again. 'Ralph Elliot joined us and I don't remember a great deal after that, except waking up in the morning, and finding him sleeping next to me.'

It was Nat's turn not to speak for some time. 'Have you told him that you're pregnant?'

'No,' said Rebecca. 'What's the point? He's hardly spoken to me since.'

'I'll kill the bastard,' said Nat, rising from his chair.

'I don't think that will help,' said Rebecca quietly.

'It doesn't change anything,' said Nat, walking across to take her in his arms, 'because I still want to marry you. In any case, the odds are far more likely that it's my child.'

'But you could never be sure,' said Rebecca.

'That's not a problem for me,' said Nat.

'But it's a problem for me,' said Rebecca, 'because there's something else I haven't told you . . .'

—◇—

The moment Fletcher entered the packed Woolsey Hall he regretted not heeding Jimmy's advice. He took his place on the bench opposite Tom Russell, who greeted him with a warm smile, as a thousand students began to chant, 'Hey, hey LBJ, how many kids have you killed today?'

Fletcher looked up at his opponent as he rose from his place to open the debate. Tom was welcomed by the assembled throng with acclamation even before he'd opened his mouth. To Fletcher's surprise he appeared to be just as nervous as he was, beads of sweat appearing on his forehead.

The crowd fell silent the moment Tom began to speak, but he had only delivered two words when it turned to boos. 'Lyndon Johnson,' he waited. 'Lyndon Johnson has told us that it is America's duty to defeat the

North Vietnamese and save the world from creeping communism. I say it's the president's duty not to sacrifice one American life on the altar of a doctrine that, given time, will defeat itself.'

Once again the throng erupted, this time into cheers, and it was nearly a minute before Tom could continue. In fact the remainder of his words were punctuated with so many interruptions of approval, that he'd barely delivered half his speech before he came to the end of his allotted time.

The cheers turned to boos the moment Fletcher rose from his place. He had already decided that this was the last public speech he would ever make. He waited for a silence that never came, and when someone shouted, 'Get on with it,' he delivered his first faltering words.

'The Greeks, the Romans and the British have all, in their time, taken on the mantle of world leadership,' Fletcher began.

'That's no reason why we should!' hollered someone from the back of the hall.

'And after the break-up of the British Empire following the Second World War,' continued Fletcher, 'that responsibility has been passed on to the United States. The greatest nation on the earth.' A smattering of applause broke out in the hall. 'We can of course sit back and admit that we are unworthy of that responsibility, or we can offer leadership to millions around the world, who admire our concept of freedom and wish to emulate our way of life. We could also walk away, allowing those same millions to suffer the yoke of communism as it engulfs the free world, or we could support them as they too try to embrace democracy. Only history will be left to record the decision we make, and history must not find us wanting.'

Jimmy was amazed that they had thus far listened

with only the occasional interruption, and surprised by the respectful applause Fletcher received when he resumed his place some twenty minutes later. At the end of the debate everyone in the hall recognized that Fletcher had won the argument, even if it was Tom who won the motion by over two hundred votes.

Jimmy somehow managed to look cheerful after the result had been read out to the cheering mob. 'It's nothing less than a miracle,' said Jimmy.

'Some miracle,' said Fletcher. 'Didn't you notice that we lost by two hundred and twenty-eight votes?'

'But I was expecting to be beaten by a landslide, so I consider two hundred and twenty-eight to be nothing less than a miracle. We've got five days to change the minds of a hundred and fourteen voters, because most frosh accept that you're the obvious choice to represent them on the student council,' said Jimmy as they walked out of Woolsey Hall, with several people whispering to Fletcher, 'Well done' and 'Good luck.'

'I thought Tom Russell spoke well,' said Fletcher, 'and more important, he represents their views.'

'No, he won't do any more than keep the seat warm for you.'

'Don't be too sure of that,' said Fletcher. 'Tom might quite like the idea of becoming president.'

'Not a chance with what I have planned for him.'

'Dare I ask what you have in mind?' said Fletcher.

'I had a member of our team present whenever he gave a speech. During the campaign he made forty-three pledges, most of which he will not be able to keep. After he's been reminded of that fact twenty times a day, I don't think his name will be appearing on the ballot paper for president.'

'Jimmy, have you ever read Machiavelli's *The Prince*?' asked Fletcher.

'No, should I?'

'No, don't bother, he has nothing to teach you. What are you doing for dinner tonight?' he added, as Annie came across to join them. She gave Fletcher a big hug. 'Well done,' she said, 'your speech was brilliant.'

'Too bad a couple of hundred others didn't agree with you,' said Fletcher.

'They did, but most of them had decided how they were going to vote long before they entered the hall.'

'That's exactly what I've been trying to tell him.' Jimmy turned to Fletcher. 'My kid sister's right, and what's more . . .'

'Jimmy, I'll be eighteen in a few weeks' time,' said Annie, scowling at her brother, 'just in case you haven't noticed.'

'I've noticed, and some of my friends even tell me that you're passably pretty, but I can't see it myself.'

Fletcher laughed. 'So are you going to join us at Dino's?'

'No, you've obviously forgotten that Joanna and I invited you both to dinner at her place.'

'I hadn't forgotten,' said Annie, 'and I can't wait to meet the woman who's tied my brother down for more than a week.'

'I haven't looked at another woman since the day I met her,' said Jimmy quietly.

—◆—

'But I still want to marry you,' said Nat, holding on to her.

'Even if you can't be sure who the father is?'

'That's all the more reason for us to get married, then you'll never doubt my commitment.'

'I've never doubted it for a moment,' said Rebecca, 'or that you're a good and decent man, but haven't you considered the possibility that I might not love you enough to want to spend the rest of my life with you?' Nat let go of her and looked into her eyes. 'I asked Ralph what he would do if it turned out to be his child, and he agreed with me that I should have an abortion.' Rebecca placed the palm of her hand on Nat's cheek. 'Not many of us are good enough to live with Sebastian, and I'm certainly no Olivia.' She took her hand away and quickly left the room without another word.

Nat lay on her bed unaware of the darkness setting in. He couldn't stop thinking about his love for Rebecca, and of his loathing for Elliot. He eventually fell asleep, and woke only when the telephone rang.

Nat listened to the familiar voice and congratulated his old friend when he heard the news.

13

WHEN NAT WENT to pick up his mail from the student union, he was pleased to find he had three letters: a bumper crop. One of them bore the unmistakable hand of his mother. The second was postmarked New Haven, so he assumed it had to be from Tom. The third was a buff envelope containing his monthly scholarship cheque, which he would bank immediately as his funds were running low.

He walked across to McConaughy and grabbed a bowl of cornflakes and a couple of slices of toast, avoiding the powdered scrambled eggs. He took a vacant seat in the far corner of the room, and tore open his mother's letter. He felt guilty that he hadn't written to her for at least two weeks. There were only a few days to go before the Christmas vacation, so he hoped she would understand if he didn't reply immediately. He'd had a long conversation with her on the phone the day after he had broken up with Rebecca. He hadn't mentioned her being pregnant or given a particular reason for them breaking up.

My dear Nathaniel – she never called him Nat. If anyone ever read a letter from his mother, Nat reckoned that they would quickly learn everything they needed to know about her. Neat, accurate, informative, caring but somehow leaving an impression of being late for her next appointment. She always ended with the words, *Must dash, love Mother*. The only piece of real news she had to impart was Dad's promotion to regional manager, which meant he would no longer have to spend endless hours on the road, but in future would be working in Hartford.

Dad is delighted about the promotion and the pay rise, which means we can just about afford a second car. However, he's already missing the personal contact with the customers.

Nat took another spoonful of cereal before he opened the letter from New Haven. Tom's missive was typed and contained the occasional spelling mistake, probably caused by the excitement of describing his election victory. In his usual disarming way, Tom reported that he had won only because his opponent had made a passionate speech defending America's involvement in the Vietnam War, which hadn't helped his cause when it came to the ballot. Nat liked the sound of Fletcher Davenport, and realized that he might well have run up against him had he gone to Yale. He bit into his toast as he continued to read Tom's letter: *I was sorry to hear about your break-up with Rebecca. Is it irreconcilable?* Nat looked up from the letter not sure of the answer to that question, although he realized his old friend wouldn't be at all surprised once he discovered Ralph Elliot was involved.

Nat buttered a second piece of toast and for a moment considered whether a reconciliation was still possible, but quickly returned to the real world. After all, he still planned to go on to Yale just as soon as he'd completed his first year.

Finally Nat turned his attention to the brown envelope and decided he would drop his monthly cheque off at the bank before his first lecture – unlike some of his fellow students, he couldn't afford to leave banking his meagre funds until the last moment. He slit open the envelope, and was surprised to find that there was no cheque enclosed, just a letter. He unfolded the single sheet of paper, and stared at the contents in disbelief.

SELECTIVE SERVICE SYSTEM

ORDER TO REPORT FOR

ARMED FORCES PHYSICAL EXAMINATION

To:

Nathaniel Cartwright
University of Connecticut
North Eagleville Road
Storrs, Connecticut

Local Board No 21
Selective Service System
205 Walter Street
Rockville, CT

December 14th, 1966

SELECTIVE SERVICE NO.

6 21 48 270

You are hereby directed to present yourself for
Armed Forces Physical Examination
to the Local Board named above by reporting at:

Routes 195 & 44 (Mansfield Corners), Storrs, Connecticut

(Place of reporting)

at   7.58   a. m.,   on the   5th   of   January   19 67

(Hour of reporting)   (Day)   (Month)   (Year)

Greg Rodgers

(Member or clerk at Local Board)

Nat placed the letter on the table in front of him, and considered its consequences. He accepted that the draft was a lottery, and his number had come up. Was it morally right to apply for an exemption simply because he was a student, or should he, as his old man had done in 1942, sign up and serve his country? His father had spent two years in Europe with the Eightieth Division before returning home with the Purple Heart. Over twenty-five years later he felt just as strongly that America should be playing a role in Vietnam. Did such sentiments apply only to those uneducated Americans who were given little choice?

Nat immediately phoned home, and was not surprised when his parents had one of their rare disagreements on the subject. His mother was in no doubt that he should complete his degree, and then reconsider his position; the war could be over by then. Hadn't President Johnson promised as much during the election campaign? His father, on the other hand, felt that though it might have been an unlucky break, it was nothing less than Nat's duty to answer the call. If everyone decided to burn their draft card, a state of anarchy would prevail, was his father's final word on the subject.

He next phoned Tom at Yale to find out if he'd received a draft notice.

'Yes I have,' said Tom.

'Did you burn it?' Nat asked.

'No, I didn't go that far, though I know several students who have.'

'Does that mean you're going to sign up?'

'No, I don't have your moral fibre, Nat. I'm going to take the legal route. My father's found a lawyer in Washington who specializes in exemption, and he's pretty confident he can get me deferred, at least until I've graduated.'

'What about that guy who ran against you for freshman rep and felt so strongly about America's responsibility to those "who wished to participate in democracy" – what decision has he come to?' asked Nat.

'I've no idea,' said Tom, 'but if his name comes up in the ballot, you'll probably meet up with him in the front line.'

—◇—

As each month passed, and no buff envelope appeared in his mail slot, Fletcher began to believe that he had been among the fortunate ones that hadn't made the ballot. However, he had already decided what his reply would be should the slim brown envelope appear.

When Jimmy was called up, he immediately consulted his father, who advised him to apply for an exemption while he was still an undergraduate, but to make it clear that he would be willing to reconsider his position in three years' time. He also reminded Jimmy that by then there might well be a new president, new legislation and a strong possibility that Americans would no longer be in Vietnam. Jimmy took his father's advice, and was outspoken when he discussed the moral issue with Fletcher.

'I have no intention of risking my life against a bunch of Vietcong, who will, in the end, succumb to capitalism, even if they fail in the short term to respond to military superiority.'

Annie agreed with her brother's views, and was relieved that Fletcher hadn't received a draft notice. She wasn't in any doubt how he would respond.

—◇—

On 5 January 1967 Nat reported to his local draft board.

After a rigorous medical examination, he was interviewed by a Major Willis. The major was impressed; Cartwright scored ninety-two per cent in his pre-induction

111

physical, having spent a morning with young men who came up with a hundred different reasons why he should find them medically unfit to serve. In the afternoon, Nat sat the General Classification Test, and scored ninety-seven per cent.

The following night, along with fifty other inductees, Nat boarded a bus destined for New Jersey. During the slow, interminable journey across the state lines, Nat toyed with little plastic trays of food that made up his boxed lunch, before falling into a fitful sleep.

The bus finally came to a halt at Fort Dix in the early hours of the morning. The would, and would not be, soldiers off-loaded to be greeted by the yells of troop handlers. They were quickly billeted in prefabricated huts, and then allowed to sleep for a couple of hours.

The following morning, Nat rose – he had no choice – at five, and after being given a 'buzz cut', was issued with fatigues. All fifty new recruits were then ordered to write a letter to their parents, while at the same time returning every item of civilian origin to their home of record.

During the day, Nat was interviewed by Specialist Fourth Class Jackson, who, having checked through his papers, had only one question, 'You do realize, Cart-wright, that you could have applied for exemption?'

'Yes, I do, sir.'

Specialist Jackson raised an eyebrow. 'And having taken advice, you made the decision not to?'

'I didn't need to take advice, sir.'

'Good, then just as soon as you've completed your basic training, Private Cartwright, I'm sure you'll want to apply for officer cadet school.' He paused. 'About two in fifty make it, so don't get your hopes up. By the way,' he added, 'you don't call me sir. Specialist 4th Class will be just fine.'

After years of cross-country running Nat considered himself in good shape, but he quickly discovered that the army had a totally different meaning for the word, not fully explained in Webster's. And as for the other word – basic – everything was basic: the food, the clothing, the heating, and especially the bed he was expected to sleep on. Nat could only assume that the army were importing their mattresses direct from North Vietnam, so that they could experience the same hardship as the enemy.

For the next eight weeks Nat rose every morning at five, took a cold shower – heat simply didn't exist in army parlance – was dressed, fed and had his clothes neatly folded on the end of the bed before standing to attention on the parade ground by six a.m. along with all the other members of Second Platoon Alpha Company.

The first person to address him each morning was Drill Sergeant Al Quamo, who always looked so smart that Nat assumed he must have risen at four to press his uniform. And if Nat attempted to speak to anyone else during the next fourteen hours, Quamo wanted to know who and why. The drill sergeant was the same height as Nat, and there the resemblance ended. Nat never stood still long enough to count the sergeant's medals. 'I'm your mother, your father, and your closest friend,' he bellowed at the top of his voice. 'Do you hear me?'

'Yes, sir,' shouted back thirty-six raw recruits from the Second Platoon. 'You're my mother, my father and my closest friend.'

Most of the platoon had applied for exemption and been turned down. Many of them considered Nat was crazy to volunteer, and it took several weeks before they changed their minds about the boy from Cromwell. Long before the course had ended, Nat had become the platoon counsellor, letter writer, advisor and confidant. He even taught a couple of the recruits to read. He didn't choose to tell his mother what they had taught him in return. Half-way through the course, Quamo made him up to squad leader.

At the end of the two-month stint, Nat came top in everything which involved spelling. He also surprised his fellow rookies by beating them all round the cross-country course and although he had never fired a weapon before basic training, he even out-shot the boys from Queens when it came to mastering the M60 machine gun and the M70 grenade launcher. They were more practised in smaller weapons.

It didn't take eight weeks for Quamo to change his mind about Nat's chances of making Officer Cadet School. Unlike most of the other 'sadsacks' who were destined for 'Nam, he found that Nat was a born leader.

'Mind you,' Quamo warned Nat, 'a butter bar second lieutenant is just as likely to have his ass blown off as a private soldier, because one thing's for certain, the VC can't tell the difference.' Sergeant Quamo turned out to be right, because only two soldiers were selected to go to Fort Benning. The other was a college boy from third platoon named Dick Tyler.

—◦—

For the first three weeks at Fort Benning, the main outdoor activity was alongside the black hats. The parachute instructors took their new recruits through their landing falls, first from a thirty-five-foot wall, and later from the dreaded three-hundred-foot tower. Of the two hundred soldiers who began the course, less than a hundred made it through to the next stage. Nat was among the final ten chosen to wear a white helmet during jump week. Fifteen jumps later, and it was his turn to have silver jump wings pinned to his chest.

When Nat returned home for a week's furlough, his

mother hardly recognized the child who had left her three months earlier. He had been replaced by a man, an inch taller and half a stone lighter, with a crew cut that made his father reminisce about his days in Italy.

After the short break, Nat returned to Fort Benning, pulled back on his glistening Corcoran jump boots, threw his barrack bag over his shoulder, and took the short walk from airborne to the other side of the road.

Here he began his training as an infantry officer. Although he rose just as early each morning, he now spent far more of his time in the classroom, studying military history, map reading, tactics and command strategy, along with seventy other would-be officers who were also preparing to be sent to Vietnam. The one statistic no one would talk about was that more than fifty per cent of them could expect to return in a body bag.

--◇--

'Joanna's going to have to face a disciplinary enquiry,' said Jimmy as he sat on the end of Fletcher's bed. 'Whereas it's me who should be suffering the wrath of the ethics committee,' he added.

Fletcher tried to calm his friend, but he had never seen him so incensed. 'Why can't they understand that it's not a crime to fall in love?'

'I think you'll find that they are more worried about the consequences of it happening the other way round,' said Fletcher.

'What do you mean?' asked Jimmy, looking up.

'Simply that the administration is genuinely concerned about male teachers taking advantage of young impressionable female undergraduates.'

'But can't they tell when it's genuine?' asked Jimmy. 'Anyone can see that I adore Joanna, and she feels the same way about me.'

'And they might even have turned a blind eye in your case if you both hadn't made it so public.'

'I would have thought you of all people would have respected Joanna for her refusal to be disingenuous on the subject,' said Jimmy.

'I do,' said Fletcher, 'but she's left the authorities with no option but to respond to that honesty, given the university regulations.'

'Then it's the regulations that need changing,' said Jimmy. 'Joanna believes as a teacher, you shouldn't have to hide your true feelings. She wants to make sure that the next generation never have to face the same predicament.'

'Jimmy, I'm not disagreeing with you, and knowing Joanna, she will have thought about those regulations carefully and also have a strong view on the relevance of rule 17b.'

'Of course she does, but Joanna isn't going to become engaged just to let the board off the hook.'

'That's some woman you asked if you could carry her books,' said Fletcher.

'Don't remind me,' Jimmy replied. 'You know that they're now cheering her at the beginning and end of every lecture she gives.'

'So when does the ethics committee convene to make its decision?'

'Next Wednesday at ten o'clock. It's going to be a media field day. I just wish my father wasn't coming up for re-election in the fall.'

'I wouldn't worry about your father,' said Fletcher. 'My bet is that he'll have already found a way of turning the problem to his advantage.'

◀◆▶

Nat had never expected to come into contact with his commanding officer, and wouldn't have done so if his mother hadn't parked her car in the colonel's reserved space. When Nat's father spotted the sign COMMANDANT, he suggested she should quickly reverse. Susan reversed a little too quickly, and collided with Colonel Tremlett's jeep just as he swung in.

'Oh, God,' said Nat as he leapt out of the car.

'I wouldn't go that far,' said Tremlett. 'Colonel will do just fine.'

Nat leapt to attention and saluted as his father surreptitiously checked the commandant's medals. 'We must have served together,' he said, staring at a red and green ribbon among the cluster on his chest. The colonel looked up from studying the dent in his fender. 'I was with the Eightieth in Italy,' Nat's father explained.

'I hope you manoeuvred those Shermans a damn sight better than you drive a car,' said the colonel as the two men shook hands. Michael didn't mention that it was his wife who was driving. Tremlett looked at Nat. 'Cartwright, isn't it?'

'Yes, sir,' said Nat, surprised that the commanding officer knew his name.

'Your son looks as though he's going to top his class when he graduates next week,' Tremlett said, turning his attention back to Nat's father. He paused, 'I may have an assignment in mind for him,' he added without explanation. 'Report to my office at eight tomorrow morning, Cartwright.' The colonel smiled at Nat's mother, and shook hands once again with his father, before turning back to Nat. 'And if I can see a dent in that fender when I leave tonight, Cartwright, you can forget your next furlough.' The colonel winked at Nat's mother as the boy sprang to attention and saluted again.

Nat spent the afternoon on his knees with a hammer and a pot of khaki paint.

The following morning, Nat arrived at the colonel's

office at seven forty-five, and was surprised to be ushered straight through to see the commandant. Tremlett pointed to a chair on the other side of his desk.

'So you've stood up and been counted, Nat,' were the colonel's first words as he glanced down at his file. 'What do you want to do next?'

Nat looked across at Colonel Tremlett, a man with five rows of ribbons on his chest. He'd seen action in Italy and Korea and had recently returned from a tour of duty in Vietnam. His nickname was the terrier, because he enjoyed getting so close to the enemy that he could bite their ankles. Nat responded to his question immediately. 'I expect to be among those posted to Vietnam, sir.'

'It's not necessary for you to serve in the Asian sector,' said his CO. 'You've proved your point, and there are several other postings I can recommend, ranging from Berlin to Washington DC, so that once you've completed your two years, you can return to university.'

'That rather defeats the object, doesn't it, sir?'

'But it's almost unknown to send an enlisted officer to 'Nam,' said the CO, 'especially one of your calibre.'

'Then perhaps the time has come for someone to break the mould. After all, that's what you keep reminding us leadership is all about.'

'What if I asked you to complete your service as my staff officer, then you could assist me here at the academy with the next intake of rookies?'

'So that they can all go off to Vietnam and get themselves killed?' Nat stared across the table at his CO. He immediately regretted over-stepping the mark.

'Do you know who the last person was who sat there and told me he was determined to go to 'Nam, and nothing I could say would change his mind?'

'No, sir.'

'My son, Daniel,' replied Tremlett, 'and on that

occasion I had no choice but to accept his decision.' The colonel paused, glancing at a photo on his desk that Nat couldn't see. 'He survived for eleven days.'

—◦—

'WOMAN LECTURER SEDUCES SENATOR'S SON', screamed the banner headline in the *New Haven Register*.

'That's a bloody insult,' said Jimmy.

'What do you mean?' asked Fletcher.

'I seduced her.'

When Fletcher stopped laughing, he continued to read the front page article:

> Joanna Palmer, a lecturer in European history at Yale, has had her contract terminated by the University Ethics Committee, after admitting that she was having an affair with James Gates, a freshman she has been teaching for the past six months. Mr Gates is the son of Senator Harry Gates. Last night, from their home in East Hartford . . .

Fletcher looked up. 'How has your father taken it?'

'Tells me he'll win by a landslide,' said Jimmy. 'All the women's rights groups are backing Joanna, and all the men think I'm the coolest thing since Dustin Hoffman's *Graduate*. Dad also believes that the committee will be left with no choice but to reverse their decision long before term ends.'

'And if they don't?' asked Fletcher. 'What chance is there of Joanna being offered another job?'

'That's the least of her problems,' Jimmy replied, 'because the phone hasn't stopped ringing since the committee announced their decision. Both Radcliffe, where she did her undergraduate degree, and Columbia, where she completed her PhD, have offered her jobs, and that was before the opinion poll on the *Today Show* reported that eighty-two per cent of their viewers thought she should be reinstated.'

'So what does she plan to do next?'

'Appeal, and my bet is that the committee won't be able to ignore public opinion.'

'But where does that leave you?'

'I still want to marry Joanna, but she won't hear of it until she knows the result of her arbitration. She refuses to become engaged in case it influences the committee in her favour. She's determined to win the case on its merits, not on public sentiment.'

'That's a remarkable woman you've got yourself involved with,' said Fletcher.

'I agree,' said Jimmy. 'And you only know the half of it.'

14

LT NAT CARTWRIGHT had been stencilled on the door of his little office at MACV headquarters even before he'd arrived in Saigon. It quickly became clear to Nat that he was to be desk-bound for his entire watch, not even allowed to discover where the front line was. On arrival, he did not join his regiment in the field, but was assigned to Combat Service Support. Colonel Tremlett's dispatches had obviously landed in Saigon long before he had.

Nat was described on the daily manifest as a quartermaster, which allowed those above him to pile up the paperwork, and those below him to take their time carrying out his orders. They all seemed to be involved in the plot, a plot that resulted in Nat spending every working hour filling in regulation forms for items as varied as baked beans and Chinook helicopters. Seven hundred and twenty-two tons of supplies were flown into the capital every week, and it was Nat's duty to see they reached the front line. In any one month, he handled over nine thousand items. Everything managed to get there except him. He even resorted to sleeping with the commanding officer's secretary, but quickly discovered that Mollie had no real influence over her boss, although he did find out about her considerable expertise in unarmed combat.

Nat began leaving the office later and later each evening, and even began to wonder if he was in a foreign country. When you have a Big Mac and Coke for lunch, a Kentucky Fried Chicken with a Budweiser for dinner, and return to the officers' quarters every evening to watch the *ABC News* and reruns of *77 Sunset Strip*, what proof is there that you ever left home?

Nat made several surreptitious attempts to join his regiment in the front line, but he came to realize that Colonel Tremlett's influence permeated everywhere; his applications would land back on his desk a month later, rubber-stamped: *Refused; re-apply in one month*.

Whenever Nat requested an interview to discuss the problem with a field officer, he never managed to see anyone above the rank of staff major. On each occasion, a different officer would spend half an hour trying to convince Nat that he was doing a valuable and worthwhile job in requisition. His combat file was the thinnest in Saigon.

Nat was beginning to realize that his stand on 'a matter principle' had served no purpose. In a month's time Tom would be starting his second year at Yale, and what did he have to show for his efforts other than a crew cut and an inside knowledge of how many paper clips the army required in Vietnam in any one month?

Nat was sitting in his office, preparing for the new intake of rookies due to report the following Monday, when all that changed.

Accommodation, clothing and travel documents had kept him occupied all day and well into the evening. *Urgent* was stamped on several of them, as the CO always wanted to be fully briefed on the background of any new intake before they landed in Saigon. Nat hadn't noticed how long the task had taken, and when he had completed the final form, he decided to drop them off in the adjutant's office before grabbing something to eat in the officers' mess.

As he strolled past the ops room, he experienced a surge of anger; all the training he had been put through at Fort Dix and Fort Benning had been a complete waste of time. Although it was nearly eight o'clock, there were still a dozen or so operatives, some of whom he recognized, manning the phones and updating a large operational map of North Vietnam.

On his way back from the adjutant's office, Nat dropped into the ops room to see if anyone was free to join him for dinner. He found himself listening to the troop movements of the Second Battalion, 503rd Parachute Infantry Regiment. He would have slipped back out and gone to the mess alone if it hadn't been his own regiment. The Second Battalion was facing a barrage of mortar fire from the Vietcong and was holed up on the wrong side of the Dyng river, defending itself from a further onslaught. The red phone on the desk in front of Nat began to ring insistently. Nat didn't move a muscle.

'Don't just stand there, lieutenant, pick it up and find out what they want,' demanded the operations officer. Nat quickly obeyed the order.

'Mayday, Mayday, this is Captain Tyler, do you read me?'

'I do, captain, this is Lieutenant Cartwright. How can I help, sir?'

'My platoon has been ambushed by Victor Charlie just above the Dyng River, grid reference SE42 NNE71. I need a flight of Hueys with full medical back-up. I have ninety-six men, eleven of them are already down, three dead, eight injured.'

A staff sergeant came off another phone. 'How do I reach emergency rescue?' asked Nat.

'Contact Blackbird base at the Eisenhower field. Pick up the white phone and give the officer of the watch the grid reference.'

Nat grabbed the white phone, and a sleepy voice answered.

'This is Lieutenant Cartwright. We have a Mayday call. Two platoons trapped on the north side of the Dyng river, grid reference SE42 NNE71; they've been ambushed and require immediate assistance.'

'Tell them we'll be off the ground and on our way in five minutes,' said a voice now fully alert.

'Can I join you?' asked Nat, cupping his hand over the mouthpiece, expecting the inevitable rejection.

'Are you authorized to fly in U.H.I.s?'

'Yes I am,' lied Nat.

'Any parachute experience?'

'Trained at Fort Benning,' said Nat, 'sixteen jumps at six hundred feet from S-123s, and in any case, it's my regiment out there.'

'Then if you can get here in time, Lieutenant, be my guest.'

Nat replaced the white phone and returned to the red one. 'They're on their way, captain,' was all he said.

Nat ran out of the ops room and into the parking lot. A duty corporal was dozing behind the wheel of a jeep. Nat leapt in beside him, banged the palm of his hand on the horn and said, 'Blackbird base in five minutes.'

'But that's about four miles away, sir,' said the driver.

'Then you'll have to get moving, won't you, Corporal,' shouted Nat.

The corporal switched on the engine, threw the jeep into gear, and accelerated out of the parking lot, lights full on, leaving the palm of one hand on the horn and the other on the steering wheel. 'Faster, faster,' repeated Nat, as those who were still on the streets of Saigon after curfew leapt out of their way along with several startled chickens. Three minutes later, Nat spotted a dozen Huey helicopters perched on the airfield up ahead. The blades on one of them were already rotating.

'Put your foot down,' Nat repeated.

'It's already touching the floor, sir,' replied the corporal as the gates of the airfield came into sight. Nat counted again: seven of the helicopters now had their blades whirring.

'Shit,' he said as the first one took off.

The jeep screeched to a halt at the gates to the compound, where an MP asked to see their identity cards.

'I have to be on one of those choppers in under a minute,' shouted Nat passing over his papers. 'Can't you speed it up?'

'Just doing my job, sir,' said the MP as he checked both men's papers.

Once both identity cards had been handed back, Nat pointed to the one helicopter whose blades were not yet rotating, and the corporal shot off towards it, skidding to a halt by an open door, just as its blades began to turn.

The pilot looked down and grinned, 'You only just made it, Lieutenant,' he said. 'Climb aboard.' The helicopter had lifted off even before Nat had been given a chance to click on his safety harness. 'You want to hear the bad news, or the bad news?' asked the pilot.

'Try me,' said Nat.

'The rule in any emergency is always the same. Last off the ground is the first to land on enemy territory.'

'And the bad news?'

─◇─

'Will you marry me?' asked Jimmy.

Joanna turned and looked at the man who had brought her more happiness in the past year than she could ever have imagined possible. 'If you still want to ask me the same question on the day you graduate, freshman, my reply will be yes, but today the answer is still no.'

'But why? What could have possibly changed in a year or two's time?'

'You'll be a little older, and hopefully even a little wiser,' replied Joanna with a smile. 'I'm twenty-five and you're not yet twenty.'

'What difference can that make if we want to spend the rest of our lives together?'

'Just that you might not feel that way when I'm fifty and you're forty-five.'

'You've got it all wrong,' said Jimmy. 'At fifty you'll be in your prime, and I'll be a debauched husk, so you'd better grab me while I've still got some energy left.'

Joanna laughed. 'Try not to forget, freshman, that what we've been through during the past few weeks may also be affecting your judgement.'

'I don't agree. I believe the experience can only have strengthened our relationship.'

'That's possible,' said Joanna, 'but in the long run, you should never make an irreversible decision on the back of good or bad news, because it's just possible that one of us will feel differently when this all blows over.'

'Do you feel differently?' asked Jimmy quietly.

'No, I don't,' said Joanna firmly, as she touched his cheek. 'But my parents have been married for nearly thirty years, and my grandparents lived to celebrate their golden wedding anniversary, so when I get married I want it to be for life.'

'All the more reason for us to get married as quickly as possible,' said Jimmy. 'After all, I'm going to have to live to the age of seventy if we hope to celebrate our golden wedding.'

Joanna laughed. 'I'll bet your friend Fletcher would agree with me.'

'You could be right, but you're not marrying Fletcher. In any case, my bet is that he and my sister will be together for at least fifty years.'

'Freshman, I couldn't love you any more if I wanted

126

to, but remember that I'll be at Columbia next fall, and you'll be still at Yale.'

'But you can still change your mind about taking that job at Columbia.'

'No, it was only public opinion that forced the board to reverse their decision. If you'd seen the look on their faces when they delivered their verdict, you'd have realized they couldn't wait to see the back of me. We've made our point, freshman, so I think it would be better for everyone if I moved on.'

'Not everyone,' said Jimmy quietly.

'Because once I'm no longer around to haunt them, they're going to find it far easier to amend the rules,' said Joanna, ignoring his comment. 'In twenty years' time, students will never believe such a ridiculous regulation even existed.'

'Then I'll have to get myself a commuter ticket to New York, because I'm not going to let you out of my sight.'

'I'll be at the station to meet you, freshman, but while I'm away, I hope you'll take out other women. Then, if you still feel the same way about me on the day you graduate, I'll be happy to say yes,' she added as the alarm went off.

'Hell,' said Jimmy, as he leapt out of bed, 'can I use the bathroom first, because I've a nine o'clock lecture, and I don't even know what the subject is.'

'Napoleon and his influence on the development of American law,' said Joanna.

'I thought you told us that American law was more influenced by the Romans and the English than any other nation?'

'Half a mark, freshman, but you'll still need to attend my nine o'clock lecture if you hope to find out why. By the way, do you think you could do two things for me?'

'Only two?' said Jimmy as he turned on the shower.

'Could you stop staring at me like a lost puppy whenever I give a lecture?'

Jimmy stuck his head back round the door, 'No,' he said, as he watched Joanna slip out of her nightie. 'What's the second?'

'Well, could you at least look interested in what I'm saying, and perhaps even take the occasional note?'

'Why should I bother to take notes when it's you who grades my papers?'

'Because you won't be pleased with the grade I've given your latest effort,' said Joanna, as she joined him in the shower.

'Oh, and I was hoping for an A for that particular masterpiece,' said Jimmy as he began soaping her breasts.

'Do you by any chance recall who you suggested was the biggest influence on Napoleon?'

'Josephine,' said Jimmy without hesitation.

'That might even have been the correct answer, but it isn't what you wrote in your essay.'

Jimmy stepped out of the shower and grabbed a towel. 'What did I write?' he asked, turning to face her.

'Joanna.'

—◦—

Within minutes, all twelve helicopters were flying in a V formation. Nat looked behind him at the two rear gunners, who were staring intently out into the black cloudless night. He slipped on a pair of earphones and listened to the flight lieutenant.

'Blackbird One to group, we'll be out of allied air space in four minutes, then I anticipate an ETA of twenty-one hundred hours.'

Nat found himself sitting bolt upright as he listened

to the young pilot. He glanced out of a side window at stars that would never be seen on the American continent. He could feel the adrenalin pumping through his body as they flew nearer to the enemy lines. At last he felt he was part of this damn man's war. His only surprise was that he sensed no fear. Perhaps that would come later.

'We're moving into enemy territory,' said the flight lieutenant as if he were crossing a busy road. 'Are you receiving me, ground leader?'

There was a crackling on the line before a voice said, 'I hear you, Blackbird One, what's your position?' Nat recognized the southern drawl of Captain Dick Tyler.

'We're approximately fifty miles south of you.'

'Copy that, expect you to rendezvous in fifteen minutes.'

'Roger. You won't see us until the last moment, because we're keeping all our external lights off.'

'Copy that,' came back the same drawl.

'Have you identified a possible landing spot?'

'There's a small piece of sheltered land on a ridge just below me,' replied Tyler, 'but it will only take one helicopter at a time, and because of the rain, not to mention the mud, landing could be a hell of a problem.'

'What's your current position?'

'I'm still at my same grid reference just north of the Dyng River.' Tyler paused. 'And I'm fairly sure that the VC have begun crossing the river.'

'How many men do you have with you?'

'Seventy-eight.' Nat knew that the full complement of two platoons was ninety-six. 'And how many bodies?' asked the flight lieutenant, as if he were asking how many eggs the captain wanted for breakfast.

'Eighteen.'

'OK, be ready to put six men and two bodies into each chopper, and make sure you're able to climb on board the moment you see me.'

'We'll be ready,' said the captain. 'What time do you have?'

'Twenty thirty-three,' said the flight lieutenant.

'Then at twenty forty-eight, I'll put up one red flare.'

'Twenty forty-eight, one red flare,' repeated the flight lieutenant, 'Roger and out.'

Nat was impressed by how calm the flight lieutenant appeared to be when he, his co-pilot and both rear gunners could be dead in twenty minutes. But as he had been reminded so often by Colonel Tremlett, more lives are saved by calm men than brave ones. No one spoke for the next fifteen minutes. It gave Nat time to think about the decision he'd made; would he also be dead in twenty minutes?

Nat then endured the longest fifteen minutes of his life, staring out across acres of dense jungle lit only by a half moon while radio silence was maintained. He looked back at the rear gunners as the chopper skimmed above the tree line. They were already clasping their guns, thumbs on the buttons, alert for any trouble. Nat was looking out of a side window when suddenly a red flare shot high into the sky. He couldn't help thinking that he would have been having coffee in the mess around now.

'This is Blackbird One to flight,' said the pilot, breaking radio silence. 'Don't switch on your under-belly lights until you're thirty seconds from rendezvous, and remember, I'm going in first.'

A green tracer of bullets shot in front of the cockpit, and the rear gunners immediately returned fire.

'The VC have identified us,' said the flight leader crisply. He dipped his helicopter to the right and Nat saw the enemy for the first time. The VC were advancing up the hill, only a few hundred yards away from where the chopper would try to land.

—◦—

Fletcher read the article in the *Washington Post*. It was an heroic episode that had caught the imagination of the American public in a war no one wanted to know about. A group of seventy-eight infantrymen, cornered in the North Vietnamese jungle, easily outnumbered by the Vietcong, had been rescued by a fleet of helicopters that had flown over dangerous terrain, unable to land while encountering enemy fire. Fletcher studied the detailed diagram on the opposite page. Flight Lieutenant Chuck Philips had been the first to swoop down and rescue half a dozen trapped men. He had hovered only a few feet above the ground while the rescue took place. He hadn't noticed that another officer, Lieutenant Cartwright, had leapt off the aircraft just as he dipped his nose and rose back up into the sky to allow the second helicopter to take his place.

Among the bodies on the third helicopter was that of the officer in command, Captain Dick Tyler. Lieutenant Cartwright had immediately assumed command, and taken over the counter-attack while at the same time coordinating the rescue of the remaining men. He was the last person to leave the battlefield and climb on board the remaining rescue helicopter. All twelve helicopters headed back to Saigon, but only eleven landed at Eisenhower airfield.

Brigadier General Hayward immediately dispatched a rescue party, and the same eleven pilots and their crews volunteered to go in search of the missing Huey, but despite making repeated sorties into enemy territory, they could find no sign of Blackbird Twelve. Hayward later described Nat Cartwright – an enlisted man, who had left the University of Connecticut in his freshman year to sign up – as an example to all Americans of someone who, in Lincoln's words, had given 'the last full measure of devotion'. 'Alive or dead, we'll find him,' vowed Hayward.

Fletcher scoured every paper for articles that mentioned Nat Cartwright after reading a profile that revealed he had been born on the same day, in the same town and in the same hospital.

<o>

Nat leapt off the first helicopter as it continued to hover a few feet above the ground. He assisted Captain Tyler as he sent back the first group to board the Huey while a wave of bullets and mortars shrieked across the nose cone.

'You take over here,' said Tyler, 'while I go back and organize my men. I'll send up half a dozen at a time.'

'Go,' shouted Nat as the first helicopter dipped to the left before ascending into the sky. As the second helicopter flew in, despite being under constant fire, Nat calmly organized the next group to take their place on board. He glanced down the hill to see Dick Tyler still leading his men in a rearguard action while at the same time giving orders for the next group to join Nat. When Nat turned back, the third chopper was dropping into place to hover above the small square of muddy ground. A staff sergeant and five soldiers ran up to the side of the helicopter and began to clamber on board.

'Shit,' said the staff sergeant looking back, 'the captain's hit.'

Nat turned to see Tyler lying face down in the mud, two soldiers lifting him up. They quickly carried his body towards the waiting helicopter.

'Take over here, sergeant,' said Nat, and then ran

down towards the ridge. He grabbed the captain's M60, took cover and began firing at the advancing enemy. Somehow he selected six more men to run up the hill and join the fourth helicopter. He was only on that ridge for about twenty minutes, as he continued to try and repel the waves of advancing VC, while his own support group became fewer and fewer because he kept sending them up the hill to the safety of the next helicopter.

The last six men on that ridge didn't retreat until they saw Blackbird Twelve swoop in. As Nat finally turned and began to run up the hill, the bullet ripped into his leg. He knew he should have felt pain, but it didn't stop him running as he had never run before. When he reached the open door of the aircraft, firing as he ran, he heard the staff sergeant say, 'For fuck's sake, sir, get your ass on board.'

As the staff sergeant yanked him up, the helicopter dipped its nose and lurched starboard, throwing Nat across the floor before swinging quickly away.

'Are you OK?' asked the skipper.

'I think so,' gasped Nat, finding himself lying across the body of a private soldier.

'Typical of the army, can't even be sure if they're still alive. With luck and a tail wind,' he added, 'we should be back in time for breakfast.'

Nat stared down at the body of the soldier, who had stood by his side only moments before. His family would now be able to attend his burial, rather than having to be informed that he had been left to an unceremonious death in an unceremonious land.

'Christ Almighty,' he heard the flight lieutenant say.

'Problem?' Nat managed.

'You could say that. We're losing fuel fast; the bastards must have hit my fuel tank.'

'I thought these things had two fuel tanks,' said Nat.

'What do you imagine I used on the way out, soldier?'

The pilot tapped the fuel gauge and then checked his milometer. A flashing red light showed he had less than thirty miles left before he would be forced to put down. He turned around to see Nat, still lying on top of the dead soldier as he clung to the floor. 'I'm going to have to look for somewhere to land.'

Nat stared out of an open door, but all he could see was acres of dense forest.

The pilot switched on all his lights, searching for a break in the trees, and then Nat felt the helicopter shudder. 'I'm going down,' said the pilot, sounding just as calm as he had done throughout the whole operation. 'I guess we'll have to postpone breakfast.'

'Over to your right,' shouted Nat as he spotted a clearing in the forest.

'I see it,' said the pilot as he tried to swing the helicopter towards the open space, but the three-ton juggernaut just wouldn't respond. 'We're going down, whether we like it or not.'

Nat thought of his mother and felt guilty that he hadn't replied to her latest letter, and then of his father, who he knew would be so proud of him, of Tom and his triumph of being elected to the Yale student council – would he in time become president? And of Rebecca, whom he still loved and feared he always would. As he clung to the floor, Nat suddenly felt very young; he was, after all, still only nineteen. He discovered some time later that the flight lieutenant, known as Blackbird Twelve, was only a year older.

As the helicopter blades stopped whirring and the aircraft plummeted towards the trees, the staff sergeant spoke, 'Just in case we don't meet again, sir, my name's Speck Foreman, it's been an honour to know you.'

They shook hands, as one does at the end of any game.

—◦—

Fletcher stared at the picture of Nat on the front page of the *New York Times* below the headline 'AN AMERICAN HERO'. A man who had signed up the moment he'd received the draft notice, although he could have cited three different reasons for claiming exemption. He'd been promoted to lieutenant and later, as a requisition officer, he'd taken command of an operation to rescue a stranded platoon on the wrong side of the Dyng River. No one seemed to be able to explain what a requisition officer was doing on a helicopter during a front-line operation.

Fletcher knew he would spend the rest of his life wondering what decision he would have made if that buff envelope had ended up in his mailbox, a question that could only be properly answered by those who had been put to the test. But even Jimmy conceded that Lieutenant Cartwright must have been a remarkable man. 'If this had happened a week before the vote,' he told Fletcher, 'you might even have beaten Tom Russell – it's all in the timing.'

'No, I wouldn't,' said Fletcher.

'Why not?' asked Jimmy.

'That's the weird thing,' Fletcher replied. 'He turns out to be Tom's closest friend.'

—◦—

A fleet of eleven helicopters had returned to search for the missing men, but all they could come up with a week later were the remains of an aircraft that must have exploded the moment it hit the trees. Three bodies had been identified, one of them Flight Lieutenant Carl

135

Mould's, but despite an extensive search of the area, no trace could be found of Lieutenant Cartwright or Staff Sergeant Speck Foreman.

Henry Kissinger, the national security advisor, asked the nation to both mourn and honour men who exemplified the courage of every fighting soldier at the front.

'He shouldn't have said mourn,' remarked Fletcher.

'Why not?' asked Jimmy.

'Because Cartwright's still alive.'

'What makes you so sure of that?'

'I don't know how I know,' Fletcher replied, 'but I promise you, he's still alive.'

—◇—

Nat couldn't recall hitting the trees, or being thrown from the helicopter. When he eventually woke, the blazing sun was burning down on his parched face. He lay there, wondering where he was, and then the memory of that dramatic hour came flooding back.

For a moment a man who wasn't even sure there was a God prayed. Then he raised his right arm. It moved like an arm should move, so he wiggled the fingers, all five of them. He lowered the arm and raised the left one. It too obeyed the telegraphed message from his brain, so he wiggled his fingers and, once again, all five of them responded. He lowered the arm and waited. He slowly raised his right leg and carried out the same exercise with the toes. He lowered the leg before raising the other one, and that's when he felt the pain.

He turned his head from side to side, and then placed the palms of his hands on the ground. He prayed again and pressed down on his hands to push himself giddily up. He waited for a few moments in the hope that the trees would stop spinning, and then tried to stand. Once he was on his feet he tentatively placed one foot in front of the other, as a child would do, and as he didn't fall over, he tried to move the other one in the same direction. Yes, yes, yes, thank you, yes, and then he felt the pain again, almost as if until that moment he had been anaesthetized.

He fell to his knees, and examined the calf of his left leg where the bullet had torn straight through. Ants were crawling in and out of the wound, oblivious to the fact that this human thought he was still alive. It took Nat some time to remove them one by one, before binding his leg with a sleeve of his shirt. He looked up to see the sun retreating towards the hills. He only had a short time to discover if any of his colleagues had survived.

He stood and turned a complete circle, only stopping when he spotted smoke coming from the forest. He began to limp towards it, vomiting when he stumbled across the charred body of the young pilot, whose name he didn't know, the jacket of his uniform hanging from a branch. Only the lieutenant's bars on his epaulette indicated who it had been. Nat would bury him later, but for now he had a race with the sun. It was then that he heard the groan.

'Where are you?' shouted Nat. The groan went up a decibel. Nat swung round to see the massive frame of Staff Sergeant Foreman lodged in the trees, only a few feet above the wreckage. As he reached the man, the groan rose yet another decibel. 'Can you hear me?' asked Nat. The man opened and closed his eyes as Nat lowered him on to the ground. He heard himself saying, 'Don't worry, I'll get you home,' like some schoolboy hero from the pages of a comic book. Nat removed the compass from the staff sergeant's belt, looked up at the sun, and then he spotted an object in the trees. He would have cheered if only he could have thought of some way of retrieving it. Nat dragged himself over to the base of the tree. He somehow jumped up and down on one foot as he grabbed at a branch and shook it, hoping to dislodge its load. He was about to give up when it shifted an inch. He tugged at the branch even more vigorously, and then it moved again and suddenly, without warning, came crashing down. It would have landed on Nat's head if he hadn't quickly fallen to one side. He couldn't jump.

Nat rested for a moment, before slowly lifting the staff sergeant up and gently placing him on the stretcher. He then sat on the ground and watched the sun disappear behind the highest tree, having completed its duty for the day in that particular land.

He had read somewhere about a mother who had kept her child alive after a car crash by talking to him all through the night. Nat talked to the staff sergeant all night.

⊷⊶

Fletcher read in sheer disbelief how, with the help of local peasants, Lieutenant Nat Cartwright had dragged that stretcher from village to village for two hundred and eleven miles, and seen the sun rise and fall seventeen times before he reached the outskirts of the city of Saigon, where both men were rushed to the nearest field hospital.

Staff Sergeant Speck Foreman died three days later, never discovering the name of the lieutenant who had rescued him and who was now fighting for his own life.

Fletcher followed every snippet of news he could find about Lieutenant Cartwright, never doubting he would live.

A week later they flew Nat to Camp Zama in Japan, where they operated on him to save his leg. The following month he was allowed to return home to the Walter Reed Army Medical Center in Washington DC to complete his recuperation.

The next time Fletcher saw Nat Cartwright was on the front page of the *New York Times*, shaking hands with President Nixon in the Rose Garden at the White House. He was receiving the Medal of Honour.

15

MICHAEL AND SUSAN Cartwright were 'bowled over' by their visit to the White House to witness their only son being decorated with the Medal of Honour in the Rose Garden. After the ceremony, President Nixon listened attentively to Nat's father as he explained the problems Americans would be facing if they all lived to the age of ninety and were not properly covered by life insurance. 'In the next century, Americans will spend as long in retirement as they do in work,' were the words LBJ repeated to his cabinet the following morning.

On their journey back to Cromwell, Nat's mother asked him what plans he had for the future.

'I can't be sure, because it's not in my hands,' he replied. 'I've received orders to report to Fort Benning on Monday, when I'll find out what Colonel Tremlett has in mind for me.'

'Another wasted year,' said his mother.

'Character building,' said his father, who was still glowing from his long chat with the president.

'I hardly think Nat's in need of much more of that,' was his mother's response.

Nat smiled as he glanced out of the window and took in the Connecticut landscape. While pulling a stretcher for seventeen days and seventeen nights with snatches of sleep and little food, he had wondered if he would ever see his homeland again. He thought about his mother's words, and had to agree with her. The idea of a wasted year of form-filling, making and returning salutes before training someone else to take his place angered him. The top brass had made it clear that they weren't going to let him return to Vietnam and thereby risk the life of one of America's few recognized heroes.

Over dinner that night, after his father had repeated the conversation he'd had with the president several times, he asked Nat to tell them more about 'Nam.

For over an hour, Nat described the city of Saigon, the countryside and its people, rarely referring to his job as a requisition officer. 'The Vietnamese are hard-working and friendly,' he told his parents, 'and they seem genuinely pleased that we're there, but no one, on either side, believes that we can stay for ever. I fear history will regard the whole episode as pointless, and once it's over it will be quickly erased from the national psyche.' He turned to his father. 'At least your war had a purpose.' His mother nodded her agreement, and Nat was surprised to see that his father didn't immediately offer a contrary view.

'Did you come away with any particular abiding memory?' asked his mother, hoping that her son might talk about his experience at the front.

'Yes, I did. The inequality of man.'

'But we're doing everything we can to assist the people of South Vietnam,' said his father.

'I'm not referring to the Vietnamese, father,' Nat replied, 'I'm talking about what Kennedy described as "my fellow Americans".'

'Fellow Americans?' his mother repeated.

'Yes, because my abiding memory will be our treatment of the poor minorities, in particular the blacks. They were on the battlefield in great numbers for no other reason than that they couldn't afford a smart lawyer who could show them how to avoid the draft.'

'But your closest friend . . .'

'I know,' said Nat, 'and I'm glad Tom didn't sign up, because he might well have suffered the same fate as Dick Tyler.'

'So do you regret your decision?' asked his mother quietly.

Nat took some time before he responded. 'No, but I often think of Speck Foreman, his wife and three children in Alabama, and wonder what purpose his death served.'

—◇—

Nat rose early the next morning to catch the first train bound for Fort Benning. When the engine pulled into Columbus station, he checked his watch. There was still another hour before his meeting with the colonel, so he decided to walk the two miles up to the academy. On the way, he was continually reminded that he was in a garrison town, by how regularly he had to return salutes from everyone below the rank of captain. Some even smiled in recognition when they spotted the Medal of Honour, as they might with a college football hero.

He was standing outside Colonel Tremlett's office a full fifteen minutes before his appointment.

'Good morning, Captain Cartwright. The colonel told me to take you straight through to his office the moment you arrived,' said an even younger ADC.

Nat marched into the colonel's office, stood to attention, and saluted. Tremlett came round from behind his desk, and threw his arms around Nat. The ADC was unable to hide his surprise, as he thought only the French greeted their fellow officers in that way. The colonel motioned Nat to a seat on the other side of his desk. After returning to his chair, Tremlett opened a thick file and began studying its contents. 'Do you have any idea what you want to do for the next year, Nat?'

'No, I don't, sir, but as I'm not being allowed to return to Vietnam, I'd be happy to take up your earlier offer, and remain at the academy to assist you with any new intake.'

'That job has already been taken,' said Tremlett, 'and I'm no longer sure if that's what's best for you in the long term.'

'Do you have something else in mind?' asked Nat.

'Now you mention it, I do,' admitted the colonel. 'Once I knew you were coming home, I called in the academy's top lawyers to advise me. Normally I despise lawyers – a breed who only fight their battles in a courtroom, but I have to admit on this occasion one of them has come up with a most ingenious scheme.' Nat didn't comment, as he was keen to learn what the colonel had in mind. 'Rules and regulations can be interpreted in so many ways. How else would lawyers keep their jobs?' asked the colonel. 'A year ago, you signed up for the draft without question, and having been commissioned, you were sent to Vietnam, where you proved me wrong, thank God.'

Nat wanted to say, get on with it colonel, but restrained himself.

'By the way Nat, I forgot to ask if you'd like a coffee.'

'No thank you, sir,' said Nat, trying not to sound impatient.

The colonel smiled, 'I think I'll have one.' He picked up his phone. 'Fix me up with a coffee, will you, Dan,' he said, 'and perhaps even some donuts.' He looked across at Nat. 'Are you sure you won't change your mind?'

'You're enjoying yourself, aren't you, sir?' said Nat with a smile.

'To be honest, I am,' said the colonel. 'You see, it's taken me several weeks to get Washington to fall in line with my proposal, so I hope you'll forgive me if I indulge myself for a few more minutes.'

Nat smiled wryly, and settled back in his chair.

'It appears that there are several avenues left open to you, and most of them in my view are a complete waste of time. You could, for example, apply for a discharge on the grounds of an injury sustained in action. If we went down that path you would end up with a small pension, and be out of here in about six months – after your spell as a requisition officer you don't need to be told how long the paperwork would take. You could, of course, as you suggested, complete your service here at the academy, but do I really want a cripple on my staff?' the colonel asked with a grin, as his ADC entered the room with a tray of piping hot coffee, and two cups. 'You could on the other hand take up some other posting, in a more friendly environment, like Honolulu, but I don't expect you need to go that far to find yourself a dancing girl. But whatever I have to offer,' he once again glanced down at Nat's file, 'you would still only end up clicking your heels for another year. So now I need to ask you a question, Nat. What had you planned to do, once you'd completed your two years?'

'Return to university, sir, and continue with my studies.'

'Exactly what I thought you'd say,' said the colonel, 'so that's exactly what you're going to do.'

'But the new term starts next week,' said Nat, 'and as you pointed out, the paperwork alone . . .'

'Unless you were to sign up for another six years, then you might find that the paperwork moves surprisingly quickly.'

'Sign up for another six years?' repeated Nat in disbelief. 'I was hoping to get out of the army, not stay in it.'

'And you will,' said the colonel, 'but only if you sign up for six years. You see, with your qualifications, Nat,' he added as he stood up and began to pace round the room, 'you can immediately apply for any course of higher education and what's more, the army will pay for it.'

'But I already have a scholarship,' Nat reminded his commanding officer.

'I'm well aware of that, it's all in here,' said the colonel, looking down at the open file in front of him. 'But the university doesn't offer you a captain's pay to go with it.'

'I would be paid to go to university?' said Nat.

'Yes, you would receive a full captain's pay, plus an added allowance for an overseas posting.'

'An overseas posting? But I'm not applying for a place at the University of Vietnam – I want to return to Connecticut, and then go on to Yale.'

'And so you will, because the regulations state that if, and only if, you have served abroad, in a war sector, and, I quote,' the colonel turned another page in his file, 'then an application for advanced education will be given the same status as your last posting. I've decided I now love lawyers,' said the colonel looking up, 'because, can you believe it, they've come up with something even better.' Tremlett sipped his coffee while Nat remained silent. 'Not only will you receive your full captain's salary as well as an overseas allowance,' the colonel continued, 'but because of your injury, at the end of six years, you will automatically be discharged, when you will qualify for a captain's pension.'

'How did they ever get that through Congress?' asked Nat.

'I don't suppose they worked out that anyone would qualify in all four categories at the same time,' replied the colonel.

'There has to be a downside,' said Nat.

'Yes, there is,' said the colonel gravely, 'because even Congress has to cover its backside.' Once again, Nat didn't bother to hold him up. 'First, you will have to return to Fort Benning every year for two weeks' intensive training to bring you up to scratch.'

'But I'd enjoy that,' said Nat.

'And at the end of the six years,' said the colonel, ignoring the interruption, 'you will remain on the active list until your forty-fifth birthday, so in the event of another war, you could be called up.'

'That's it?' said Nat in disbelief.

'That's it,' repeated the colonel.

'So what do I have to do next?'

'Sign all six documents that the lawyers have prepared, and we'll have you back at the University of Connecticut by this time next week. By the way, I've already spoken to the provost, and he tells me that they're looking forward to seeing you on Monday week. He asked me to inform you that the first lecture begins at nine o'clock. Sounds a bit late to me,' he added.

'You even knew how I would respond, didn't you?' said Nat.

'Well, I admit,' said Tremlett, 'that I did think you would consider it a better alternative to brewing my coffee for the next twelve months. By the way, are you sure you won't join me?' the colonel asked, as he poured himself a second cup.

<o>

'Will you take this woman to be your lawful wedded wife?' intoned the bishop of Connecticut.

'I will,' said Jimmy.

'Will you take this man to be your lawful wedded husband?'

'I will,' said Joanna.

'Will you take this woman to be your lawful wedded wife?' repeated the bishop.

'I will,' said Fletcher.

'Will you take this man to be your lawful wedded husband?'

'I will,' said Annie.

Double weddings were a rare event in Hartford, and the bishop admitted that it was the first he'd ever conducted.

Senator Gates stood at the head of a long receiving line, smiling at each new guest. He knew almost all of them. After all, both his children were being married on the same day.

'Who would have thought Jimmy would end up marrying the smartest girl in the class?' said Harry proudly.

'Why shouldn't he?' asked Martha. 'You did. And don't forget, thanks to Joanna, he also managed *cum laude*.'

'We'll cut the cake, just as soon as everyone is seated at their tables,' announced the maître d', 'and I'll need the brides and grooms in front, and the parents behind the cake when the photographs are taken.'

'You won't have to round up my husband,' said Martha Gates. 'If a flashbulb goes off, he'll be on the other side of the camera within moments – it's an occupational hazard.'

'How right she is,' admitted the senator. He turned his attention to Ruth Davenport, who was looking wistfully at her daughter-in-law.

'I sometimes wonder if they aren't both a little too young.'

'She's twenty,' said the senator, 'Martha and I were married when she was twenty.'

'But Annie still hasn't graduated.'

'Does it matter? They've been together for the past six years.' The senator turned to greet another guest.

'I sometimes wish . . .' began Ruth.

'What do you sometimes wish?' enquired Robert, who was standing on the other side of his wife.

Ruth turned so that the senator couldn't overhear her. 'No one could love Annie more than I do, but I sometimes wish they, well,' she hesitated, 'they had both dated more.'

'Fletcher met lots of other girls, he just didn't want to date them, and by the way,' said Robert, allowing his champagne glass to be refilled yet again, 'how often have I gone shopping with you, only to find you end up buying the dress you first looked at?'

'That didn't stop me considering several other men before I settled for you,' said Ruth.

'Yes, but that was different, because none of the others wanted you.'

'Robert Davenport, I would have you know . . .'

'Ruth, have you forgotten how many times I asked you to marry me before you finally accepted? I even tried to make you pregnant.'

'You never told me that,' said Ruth, turning to face her husband.

'You've obviously forgotten how long it was before you eventually had Fletcher.'

Ruth looked back at her daughter-in-law. 'Let's hope she doesn't have to face the same problem.'

'No reason why they should,' said Robert. 'It's not Fletcher who is going to have to give birth. And my bet is,' he continued, 'that Fletcher, like me, will never look at another woman for the rest of his life.'

'You've never looked at another woman since we've been married?' said Ruth after shaking hands with two more guests.

'No,' said Robert, before he took another gulp of champagne, 'I slept with several of them, but I never looked at them.'

'Robert, how much have you had to drink?'

'I haven't counted,' Robert admitted, as Jimmy broke away from the line.

'What are you two laughing about, Mr Davenport?'

'I was telling Ruth about my many conquests, but she refuses to believe me. So tell me, Jimmy, what are you hoping to do when you graduate?'

'I'll be joining Fletcher at law school. It's likely to be a tough ride, but with your son to get me through the day, and Joanna the night, I might just about manage it. You must be very proud of him,' said Jimmy.

'*Magna cum laude* and president of the college council,' said Robert. 'We sure are,' he added as he held out his empty glass to a passing waiter.

'You're drunk,' said Ruth, trying not to smile.

'You're right as always, my darling, but that won't stop me being inordinately proud of my only son.'

'But he would never have become president without Jimmy's contribution,' said Ruth firmly.

'It's very kind of you to say so, Mrs Davenport, but don't forget, Fletcher won by a landslide.'

'But only after you had convinced Tom . . . whatever his name was, that he should stand down and back Fletcher.'

'It may have helped, but it was Fletcher who instigated the changes that will affect a generation of Yalies,' said Jimmy as Annie came over to join them. 'Hi, kid sister.'

'When I'm chairman of General Motors, will you still address me in that tiresome manner?'

'Sure will,' said Jimmy, 'and what's more, I'll stop driving Caddies.'

Annie was just about to hit him, when the maître d' suggested that the time had come to cut the cake.

Ruth put an arm around her daughter-in-law. 'Take no notice of your brother,' she said, 'because once you've graduated, he'll have been put firmly in his place.'

'It's not my brother I need to prove anything to,' said Annie. 'It's always been your son who sets the pace.'

'Then you'll just have to beat him as well,' said Ruth.

'I'm not sure I want to,' said Annie. 'You know he's talking about going into politics once he's obtained his law degree.'

'That shouldn't stop you having your own career.'

'It won't, but I'm not too proud to make sacrifices if it will help him to achieve his ambitions.'

'But you've the right to a career of your own,' said Ruth.

'Why?' said Annie. 'Because it's suddenly become fashionable? Perhaps I'm not like Joanna,' she said glancing across at her sister-in-law. 'I know what I want, Ruth, and I'll do whatever is necessary to achieve it.'

'And what's that?' asked Ruth quietly.

'Support the man I love for the rest of my life, bring up his children, delight in his success, and with all the pressures of the seventies, that may prove a lot harder than gaining a *magna cum laude* from Vassar,' said Annie as she picked up the silver knife with an ivory handle. 'You know, I suspect there are going to be far fewer golden wedding anniversaries in the twenty-first century than there have been in the twentieth.'

'You're a lucky man, Fletcher,' said his mother as Annie placed the knife on the bottom layer of the cake.

'I knew that even before the braces had been removed from her teeth,' said Fletcher.

Annie passed the knife across to Joanna. 'Make a wish,' whispered Jimmy.

'I already have, freshman,' she replied, 'and what's more, it's been granted.'

'Ah, you mean the privilege of being married to me?'

'Good heavens no, it's far more significant than that.'

'What could possibly be more significant than that?'

'The fact that we're going to have a baby.'

Jimmy threw his arms around his wife. 'When did that happen?'

'I don't know the exact moment, but I stopped taking the pill once I was convinced you'd graduate.'

'That's wonderful. Come on, let's share the news with our guests.'

'You say a word, and I'll plant this knife in you instead of the cake. Mind you, I always knew it was a mistake to marry a freshman with red hair.'

'I bet the baby has red hair.'

'Don't be too sure, freshman, because if you mention it to anyone, I'll tell them I'm not certain who the father is.'

'Ladies and gentlemen,' said Jimmy, as his wife raised the knife, 'I have an announcement to make.' The room fell silent. 'Joanna and I are going to have a baby.' The silence continued for a moment, before the five hundred guests broke into spontaneous applause.

'You're dead, freshman,' said Joanna, as she plunged the knife into the cake.

'I knew that the moment I met you, Mrs Gates, but I think we should have at least three children before you finally kill me.'

'Well, senator, you're about to become a grandfather,' said Ruth. 'My congratulations. I can't wait to be a grandmother, although I suspect it will be some time before Annie has her first child.'

'She won't even consider it until she's graduated, would be my bet,' said Harry Gates, 'especially when they find out what I have planned for Fletcher.'

'Is it possible that Fletcher might not fall in with your plans?' suggested Ruth.

'Not as long as Jimmy and I continue to make him feel that it was always his idea in the first place.'

'Don't you think by now he might just have worked out what you're up to?'

'He's been able to do that since the day I met him at the Hotchkiss versus Taft game nearly a decade ago. I knew then he was capable of raising the bar far higher than I ever could.'

The senator placed an arm around Ruth. 'However, there's one problem I may need your help with.'

'And what's that?' asked Ruth.

'I don't think Fletcher has made up his mind yet if he's a Republican or a Democrat, and I know how strongly your husband . . .'

'Isn't it wonderful news about Joanna?' said Fletcher to his mother-in-law.

'Sure is,' said Martha, 'Harry's already counting the extra votes he'll pick up once he becomes a grand-father.'

'What makes him so confident of that?' asked Fletcher.

'Senior citizens are the fastest growing section of the electorate, so it must be worth at least a percentage point for the voters to see Harry wheeling a stroller everywhere.'

'And if Annie and I have a child, will that be worth another percentage point?'

'No, no,' said Martha, 'it's all in the timing. Just try to remember that Harry will be up for re-election again in two years' time.'

'Do you think we should plan the birth of our first child simply to coincide with the date of Harry's next election?'

'You'd be surprised how many politicians do,' replied Martha.

'Congratulations, Joanna,' said the senator, giving his daughter-in-law a hug.

'Will your son ever be able to keep a secret?' Joanna hissed as she extracted the knife from the cake.

'No, not if it will make his friends happy,' admitted the senator, 'but if he thought it would harm someone he loved, he would carry the secret to his grave.'

16

Professor Karl Abrahams entered the lecture theatre as the clock struck nine. The professor gave eight lectures a term, and it was rumoured that he had never missed one in thirty-seven years. Many of the other rumours about Karl Abrahams could not be substantiated, and so he would have dismissed them as hearsay and therefore inadmissible.

However, such rumours persisted, and thus became part of folklore. There was no doubting his sardonic wit should any student be foolish enough to take him on; that could be testified to on a weekly basis. Whether it was the case that three presidents had invited him to join the Supreme Court, only the three presidents knew. However it was recorded that, when questioned about this, Abrahams said he felt the best service he could give the nation was to instruct the next generation of lawyers and create as many decent, honest counsellors as possible, rather than clear up the mess made by so many bad ones.

The *Washington Post*, in an unauthorized profile, observed that Abrahams had taught two members of the present Supreme Court, twenty-two federal judges and several of the deans of leading law schools.

When Fletcher and Jimmy attended the first of Abrahams' eight lectures, they weren't under any illusion about how much work lay ahead of them. Fletcher was, however, under the illusion that during his final year as an undergraduate, he had put in sufficiently long hours, often ending up in bed after midnight. It took Professor Abrahams about a week to familiarize him with hours when he had normally slept.

Professor Abrahams continually reminded his first-year students that not all of them would attend his final address to the law graduates at the end of the course. Jimmy bowed his head. Fletcher began to spend so many hours researching that Annie rarely saw him before the library doors had been locked and bolted. Jimmy would sometimes leave a little earlier so that he could be with Joanna, but he rarely departed without several books under his arm. Fletcher told Annie that he'd never known her brother to work so hard.

'And it won't be any easier for him once the baby arrives,' Annie reminded her husband one evening after she had come to pick him up from the library.

'Joanna will have planned for the child to be born during the vacation so she can be back at work on the first day of term.'

'I don't want our first child to grow up like that,' said Annie. 'I intend to raise my children in our home as a full-time mother and with a father who will be back early enough in the evening to read to them.'

'Suits me,' said Fletcher. 'But if you change your mind and decide to become the chairman of General Motors, I'll be happy to change the diapers.'

⊷◦⊷

The first thing that surprised Nat when he returned to university was how immature his former classmates seemed to be. He had sufficient credits to allow him to move on to his sophomore year, but the students he had mixed with before signing up were still discussing the latest pop group or movie star, and he'd never even heard of the Doors. It wasn't until he attended his first lecture

155

that he became aware just how much the experience of Vietnam had changed his life.

Nat was also aware that his fellow students didn't treat him as if he was one of them, not least because a few of the professors also appeared somewhat in awe. Nat enjoyed the respect he was afforded, but quickly discovered there was another side to that coin. Over the Christmas vacation, he discussed the problem with Tom, who told him that he understood why some of them were a bit wary of him; after all, they believed he had killed at least a hundred Vietcong. 'At least a hundred?' repeated Nat.

'While others have read what our soldiers got up to with the Vietnamese women,' said Tom.

'I should have been so lucky; if it hadn't been for Mollie, I'd have remained celibate.'

'Well, don't disillusion them would be my advice,' said Tom, 'because my bet is that the men are envious and the women intrigued. The last thing you want them to discover is that you're a normal law-abiding citizen.'

'I sometimes wish they'd remember that I'm also only nineteen,' Nat replied.

'The trouble is,' said Tom, 'that Captain Cartwright, holder of the Medal of Honour, doesn't sound as if he's only nineteen, and I'm afraid the limp only reminds them.'

Nat took his friend's advice, and decided to dissipate his energy in the classroom, in the gym and on the cross-country course. The doctors had warned him that it could take at least a year before he would be able to run again – if ever. After their pessimistic prediction, Nat never spent less than an hour a day in the gym, climbing ropes, lifting weights and even playing the occasional game of paddle tennis. By the end of the first term back he was able to jog slowly round the course – even if it did take him an hour and twenty minutes to cover six miles. He looked up his old training schedule, and found that his record as a freshman remained on the books at thirty-four minutes, eighteen seconds. He promised himself that he would break that by the end of his sophomore year.

The next problem Nat faced was the response he got whenever he asked a woman out on a date. They either wanted to jump straight into bed with him or simply turned him down out of hand. Tom had warned him that his scalp in bed was probably a prize several undergraduates wanted to claim, and Nat quickly discovered that some he hadn't even met were already doing so.

'Reputation has its disadvantages,' complained Nat.

'I'll swap places with you if you like,' said Tom.

The one exception turned out to be Rebecca, who made it clear from the day Nat arrived back on campus that she wanted to be given a second chance. Nat was circumspect about rekindling that particular old flame, and concluded that if they were to rebuild any relationship, it would have to be done slowly. Rebecca, however, had other plans.

After their second date, she invited him back to her room for coffee, and started trying to undress him only moments after she'd closed the door. Nat broke away, and could only come up with the lame excuse that he was running a time trial the following day. She wasn't put off that easily, and when she reappeared a few minutes later carrying two cups of coffee, Rebecca had already changed into a silk robe that revealed she was wearing little if anything underneath. Nat suddenly realized that he no longer felt anything for her, and quickly drank his coffee, repeating that he needed an early night.

'Time trials never worried you in the past,' teased Rebecca.

'That was when I had two good legs,' replied Nat.

'Perhaps I'm no longer good enough for you,' said Rebecca, 'now that everybody thinks you're some kind of hero.'

'It's got nothing to do with that. It's just . . .'

'It's just that Ralph was right about you from the start.'

'What do you mean by that?' asked Nat sharply.

'You're simply not in his class.' She paused. 'In or out of bed.'

Nat was about to respond but decided it just wasn't worth it. He left without saying another word. Later that night he lay awake, realizing that Rebecca, like so many other things, was part of his past life.

One of Nat's more surprising discoveries on returning to the university was how many students pressed him to run against Elliot for the president of the student senate. But Nat made it clear that he had no interest in fighting an election while he still needed to make up for the time he'd lost.

When he returned home at the end of his sophomore year, Nat told his father that he was just as pleased that his cross-country time was now down to under an hour as to discover he was placed in the top six on the class list.

—◇—

During the summer Nat and Tom travelled to Europe. Nat found that one of the many advantages of a captain's salary was that it allowed him to accompany his closest friend without ever feeling he couldn't afford to pay his way.

Their first stop was London, where they watched the guards march down Whitehall. Nat was left in no doubt that they would have been a formidable force in Vietnam. In Paris, they strolled along the Champs Elysées and regretted having to turn to a phrase book every time they saw a beautiful woman. They then travelled on to Rome, where in tiny back street cafés they discovered for the first time how pasta really should taste, and swore they would never eat at McDonald's again.

But it wasn't until they reached Venice that Nat fell in love, and overnight became promiscuous, his taste ranging from nudes to virgins. It began with a one-day stand – Da Vinci, followed by Bellini, and then Luini. Such was the intensity of these affairs that Tom agreed they should spend a few more days in Italy and even add Florence to their itinerary. New lovers were quickly picked up on every street corner – Michelangelo, Caravaggio, Canaletto, Tintoretto. Almost anyone with an o at the end of their name qualified to join Nat's harem.

 —◦—

Professor Karl Abrahams stood in front of his desk for the fifth lecture of the term and stared up at the semicircle of tiered seats that rose above him.

He began his lecture, not a book, not a file, not even a note in front of him, as he took them through the landmark case of Carter v Amalgamated Steel.

'Mr Carter,' began the professor, 'lost an arm in an industrial accident in 1923, and was sacked without receiving a cent in compensation. He was unable to seek further employment, as no other steel company would consider offering work to a one-armed man, and when he was turned down for a job as door-keeper at a local hotel, he realized that he would never work again. There wasn't an Industry Compensation Act until 1927, so Mr Carter decided to take the rare and almost unheard of step at that time of suing his employers. He wasn't able to afford a lawyer – that hasn't changed over the years – however, a young law student who felt that Mr Carter had not received fair recompense volunteered to represent him in court. He won the case and Carter was awarded one hundred dollars in compensation – not a large amount for such a grievance you might well feel. However, together these two men were responsible for bringing about a change in the law. Let us hope that one of you might at some time in the future cause the law to be changed when faced with such an injustice. Subtext, the young lawyer's name was Theo Rampleiri. He only narrowly avoided being thrown out of law school for spending too much time on the Carter case. Later, much later, he was appointed to the Supreme Court.'

The professor frowned. 'Last year General Motors paid a Mr Cameron five million dollars for the loss of a leg. This was despite the fact that GM was able to prove that it was Mr Cameron's negligence that was the cause of the injury.' Abrahams took them through the case slowly, before adding, 'The law so often is, as Mr Charles Dickens would have us believe, an ass, and perhaps more important, indiscriminately imperfect. I have no brief for counsel who look only for a way around the law, especially when they know exactly what the Senate and Congress intended in the first place. There will be those amongst you who forget these words within days of joining some illustrious firm, whose only interest is to win at all costs. But there will be others, perhaps not so many, who will remember Lincoln's dictum, "let justice be done".' Fletcher looked up from his notes and stared down at his mentor. 'By the time we next meet, I expect you to have researched the five cases that followed Carter versus Amalgamated Steel, through to Demetri versus Demetri, all of which resulted in changes in the law. You may work in pairs, but not consult any other pair. I hope I make myself clear.' The clock struck eleven. 'Good morning, ladies and gentlemen.'

Fletcher and Jimmy shared the work load as they trawled through case after case, and by the end of the week, they had found three that were relevant. Joanna pulled from the recesses of her memory a fourth that had been heard in Ohio when she was a child. She refused to give them any more clues.

'What does love, honour and obey mean?' demanded Jimmy.

'I never agreed to obey you, freshman,' was all she said, 'and by the way, if Elizabeth wakes up during the night, it's your turn to change her diaper.'

'Sumner versus Sumner,' Jimmy told her triumphantly as he slipped into bed just after midnight.

'Not bad, freshman, but you still have to find the fifth by ten o'clock on Monday if you're hoping to get a smile out of Professor Abrahams.'

'I think we'd have to do a whole lot more than that to move the lips on that block of granite,' said Jimmy.

—◇—

As Nat climbed the hill, he spotted her running ahead of him. Nat assumed he would pass her on the downward slope. He checked his watch as he reached the half-way mark. Seventeen minutes and nine seconds. Nat felt confident that he would break his personal best, and be back on the team for the first meet of the season.

He felt full of energy as he surged over the brow of the hill and then he swore out loud. The stupid woman had taken the wrong path. She had to be a freshman. He began to shout at her back, but she didn't respond. He cursed again, changed direction and chased after her. As he came bounding down the slope, she suddenly turned and looked startled.

'You're going the wrong way,' shouted Nat, ready to turn and quickly retrace his steps, but even at twenty yards he wanted to take a closer look. He jogged quickly up to her, and kept running on the spot.

'Thank you,' she said, 'it's only my second time on the course, and I couldn't remember which path to take at the top of the hill.'

Nat smiled. 'You have to take the smaller path; the wider one leads you into the woods.'

'Thank you,' she repeated, and began running back up the hill without another word.

He chased after her, and once he had caught up jogged by her side until they reached the top. He waved goodbye once he was certain she had returned to the straight and narrow. 'See you later,' he said, but if she replied, Nat didn't hear her.

Nat checked his watch as he crossed the finishing line. Forty-three minutes, fifty-one seconds. He cursed again, wondering how much time he'd lost re-directing the wrong-path woman. He didn't mind. He began to warm down, and took longer over his stretching exercises than he normally would have done, as he waited for the young woman to return.

Suddenly she appeared at the top of the hill, running slowly down towards the finishing line. 'You made it,' Nat said with a smile as he jogged over to join her. She didn't return his smile. 'I'm Nat Cartwright,' he said.

'I know who you are,' she replied curtly.

'Have we met before?'

'No,' she said, 'I know you only by reputation.' She jogged off in the direction of the women's locker room without offering any further explanation.

―◦―

'Stand up those who managed to find all five cases.'

Fletcher and Jimmy rose triumphantly, an emotion that deflated when they discovered at least seventy per cent of the class were also on their feet. 'Four?' said the professor trying not to sound too disdainful. Most of those remaining rose, leaving around ten per cent still seated. Fletcher could only wonder how many of them would complete the course. 'Sit down,' he said. 'Let us begin with Maxwell River Gas versus Pennstone; what change in the law came about because of that particular case?' He pointed to a student in the third row.

'In 1932 it became the company's responsibility to ensure that all equipment complied with safety regulations, and all employees understood any emergency procedure.' The professor moved his finger on.

'Any written instructions had to be posted where every employee could read them.'

'When did that become redundant?'

The finger moved again, another voice, 'Reynolds versus McDermond Timber.'

'Correct.' The finger moved again. 'And why?'

'Reynolds lost three fingers when cutting a log, but his defence counsel was able to show he couldn't read, and had not been given any verbal instruction on how to operate the machine.'

'What was the basis of the new law?' The finger moved again.

'The Industry Act 1934, when it became an employer's responsibility to instruct all staff, verbally and in writing, how to use any equipment.'

'When did that need further amendments?' Someone else was selected.

'Rush versus the government.'

'Correct, but why did the government still win the case despite being in the wrong?'

Yet another selection. 'I don't know, sir.' The finger moved scornfully on, in search of someone who did.

'The government was able to defend its position when it was shown that Rush had signed an agreement stating . . .' The finger moved.

'. . . that he'd received full instructions as demanded by law.' The finger moved again.

'That he had also been in their employ beyond the statutory three-year period.' The finger continued moving . . .

'. . . but the government went on to prove they were not a company in the meaning of the word, as the bill had been badly drafted by the politicians.'

'Don't blame the politicians,' said Abrahams. 'Lawyers draft legislation, so they must take the responsibility. The politicians were not culpable on this occasion, so once the courts accepted that the government was not subject to its own legislation, who caused the law to be changed yet again?' He pointed the finger at another terrified face. 'Demetri versus Demetri,' came the reply.

'How did this differ from past laws?' The finger came to rest on Fletcher.

'It was the first time that one member of a family sued another for negligence while they were still married, as well as being fifty–fifty shareholders in the company concerned.'

'Why did that action fail?' he continued to stare at Fletcher.

'Because Mrs Demetri refused to give evidence against her husband.'

The finger moved on to Jimmy. 'Why did she refuse?' demanded Abrahams.

'Because she was stupid.'

'Why was she stupid?' demanded the professor again.

'Because her husband probably made love to her, or hit her, the night before or possibly even both, so she caved in.' A little laughter broke out.

'Were you present to witness the love-making, Mr Gates, or the attack on her?' asked Abrahams, to even more laughter.

'No, sir,' said Jimmy, 'but I'll bet it's what happened.'

'You may well be right, Mr Gates, but you would not have been able to prove what took place in the bedroom that night unless you could provide a reliable witness. Had you made such a rash statement in court, opposing counsel would have objected, the judge would have sustained his objection, and the jury would have dismissed you as a fool, Mr Gates. And more importantly, you would have let down your client. Don't ever rely what might have happened, however likely it appears, unless you can prove it. If you can't, remain silent.'

'But . . .' began Fletcher. Several students quickly bowed their heads, others held their breath, while the rest just stared at Fletcher in disbelief.

'Name?'

'Davenport, sir.'

'No doubt you feel able to explain what you mean by the word "but", Mr Davenport?'

'Mrs Demetri was advised by her counsel that if she won the case, as neither of them owned a majority holding, the company would have to cease trading. The Kendall Act 1941. She then placed her shares on the open market and they were picked up by her husband's greatest rival, a Mr Canelli, for $100,000. I cannot prove that Mr Canelli was, or wasn't, sleeping with Mrs Demetri, but I do know that the company went into liquidation a year later, when she repurchased her shares for ten cents each, at a cost of $7,300, and then immediately signed a new partnership deal with her husband.'

'Was Mr Canelli able to prove the Demetris were acting in collusion?' Fletcher thought carefully. Was Abrahams setting him a trap? 'Why do you hesitate?' demanded Abrahams.

'It wouldn't constitute proof, professor.'

'Nevertheless, what is it you wish to tell us?'

'Mrs Demetri produced a second child a year later, and the birth certificate indicated that Mr Demetri was the father.'

'You're right, that is not proof, so what charge was brought against her?'

'None; in fact, the new company went on to be very successful.'

'Then how did they cause the law to be changed?'

'The judge brought this case to the attention of the attorney general of that state.'

'Which state?'

'Ohio, and as a consequence, they passed the Marriage Partnership Act.'

'Year?'

'1949.'

'Changes of relevance?'

'Husbands and wives could no longer repurchase shares sold in a former company in which they had been partners, if that directly benefited them as individuals.'

'Thank you, Mr Davenport,' said the professor, as the clock struck eleven. 'Your "but" was well qualified.' A ripple of applause broke out. 'But not that well qualified,' added Abrahams, as he left the lecture theatre.

-◦-

Nat sat on the wall opposite the dining hall and waited patiently. After he had seen about five hundred young women leave the building, he decided the reason she was so slim was because she simply didn't eat. Then she suddenly came rushing through the swing doors. Nat had been given more than enough time to rehearse his lines, but still felt nervous when he caught up with her. 'Hi, I'm Nat.' She looked up, but didn't smile. 'We met the other day.' She still didn't respond.

'On the top of the hill.'

'Yes, I do remember,' she said.

'But you didn't tell me your name.'

'No, I didn't.'

'Have I done something to annoy you?'

'No.'

'Then can I ask what you meant by "your reputation"?'

'Mr Cartwright, you may be surprised to learn that there are some women on this campus who don't think you have the automatic right to claim their virginity simply because you've won the Medal of Honour.'

'I never thought I did.'

'But you must be aware that half the women on campus claim they've slept with you.'

'They may well claim it,' said Nat, 'but the truth is that only two of them can prove it.'

'But everyone knows how many girls chase after you.'

'And most of them can't keep up, as I'm sure you remember.' He laughed, but she didn't respond. 'So why can't I fall for someone just like anyone else?'

'But you're not just like anyone else,' she said quietly. 'You're a war hero on a captain's salary, and as such you expect everyone else to fall in line.'

'Who told you that?'

'Someone who's known you since your schooldays.'

'Ralph Elliot, no doubt?'

'Yes, the man you tried to cheat out of the Taft student government presidency . . .'

'I did *what*?' said Nat.

'. . . and then passed off his essay as yours when you applied for Yale,' she said ignoring his interruption.

'Is that what he told you?'

'Yes,' the young woman replied calmly.

'Then perhaps you should ask him why he isn't at Yale.'

'He explained that you transferred the blame on to

him so he lost his place as well.' Nat was about to explode again, when she added, 'And now you want to be president of the student senate, and your only strategy seems to be to sleep your way to victory.'

Nat tried to control his temper. 'First, I don't want to run for president, second I've only slept with three women in my life: a student I also knew when I was at school, a secretary in Vietnam, and a one-night stand I now regret. If you can find anyone else, please introduce me because I'd like to meet them.' She stopped and looked at Nat for the first time. 'Anyone else,' he repeated. 'Now can I at least know your name?'

'Su Ling,' she said quietly.

'Su Ling, if I promise never to try and seduce you until after I've asked for your hand in marriage, sought your father's permission, produced a ring, booked the church, and had the banns read, will you at least let me take you out to dinner?'

Su Ling laughed. 'I'll think about it,' she said. 'I'm sorry to rush, but I'm already late for my afternoon lecture.'

'But how do I find you?' asked Nat desperately.

'You managed to find the Vietcong, Captain Cartwright, surely it shouldn't be too difficult to find me?'

17

'ALL RISE. The state versus Mrs Anita Kirsten. His Honour Mr Justice Abernathy presiding.'

The judge took his place and looked towards the defence counsel's table. 'How do you plead, Mrs Kirsten?'

Fletcher rose from behind the defence table. 'My client pleads Not Guilty, your honour.'

The judge looked up, 'Are you representing the defendant?'

'Yes I am, your honour.'

Judge Abernathy glanced down at the charge sheet. 'I don't think I've come across you before, Mr Davenport?'

'No, your honour, it's my first appearance in your court.'

'Will you please approach the bench, Mr Davenport?'

'Yes, sir.' Fletcher stepped out from behind the little table and walked towards the judge, where the prosecution counsel joined them.

'Good morning, gentlemen,' said Mr Justice Abernathy. 'May I enquire what legal qualifications you have that are recognized in my court, Mr Davenport?'

'None, sir.'

'I see. Is your client aware of this?'

'Yes sir, she is.'

'But she still wants you to represent her, despite this being a capital charge?'

'Yes, sir.'

The judge turned to face the attorney general for

Connecticut. 'Do you have any objection to Mr Davenport representing Mrs Kirsten?'

'None whatsoever, your honour; in fact the state welcomes it.'

'I feel sure they do,' said the judge, 'but I must ask you, Mr Davenport, if you have any experience of the law at all.'

'Not a great deal, your honour,' Fletcher admitted. 'I'm a second year law student at Yale, and this will be my first case.' The judge and the attorney general smiled.

'May I ask who your director of studies is?' asked the judge.

'Professor Karl Abrahams.'

'Then I am proud to preside over your first case, Mr Davenport, because that is something you and I have in common. How about you, Mr Stamp?'

'No sir, I qualified in South Carolina.'

'Although it is most irregular, in the end it must be the defendant's decision, so let us proceed with the case in hand.' The attorney general and Fletcher returned to their places.

The judge looked down at Fletcher. 'Will you be applying for bail, Mr Davenport?'

Fletcher rose from his place. 'Yes, sir.'

'On what grounds?'

'That Mrs Kirsten has no previous record, and constitutes no danger to the public. She is the mother of two children, Alan aged seven, and Della aged five, who are currently living with their grandmother in Hartford.'

The judge turned his attention to the attorney general. 'Does the state have any objection to bail Mr Stamp?'

'We most certainly do, your honour. We oppose bail not only on the grounds that this is a capital charge, but because the murder itself was premeditated. We therefore contend that Mrs Kirsten constitutes a danger to society, and may also try to leave the state's jurisdiction.'

Fletcher shot up. 'I must object, your honour.'

'On what grounds, Mr Davenport?'

'This is indeed a capital charge, so leaving the state is hardly relevant, your honour, and in any case, Mrs Kirsten's home is in Hartford, where she earns her living working as a hospital cleaner at St Mary's, and her children are both at a local school.'

'Any further submission, Mr Davenport?'

'No, sir.'

'Bail refused,' said the judge, and brought his hammer down. 'This court is adjourned until Monday the seventeenth.'

'All rise.'

Mr Justice Abernathy winked at Fletcher as he left the court room.

–◇–

Thirty-four minutes and ten seconds. Nat couldn't hide his delight that he had not only broken his personal best, but had managed sixth place in the university trials, and was therefore certain to be picked for the opening meet against Boston University.

As Nat warmed down, and went through his usual stretching routine, Tom walked over to join him. 'Congratulations,' he said, 'and my bet is that by the end of the season, you'll have knocked another minute off your time.'

Nat stared at the sour red scar on the back of his leg as he pulled on his sweat-pants. 'Why don't we have dinner tonight,' continued Tom, 'and celebrate, because there's something I need to discuss with you before I go back to Yale.'

'Can't manage tonight,' said Nat as they began to stroll across to the locker rooms. 'I've got a date.'

'Anyone I know?'

'No,' said Nat, 'but as it's my first for months, I have to admit I'm quite nervous.'

'Captain Cartwright nervous? Whatever next?' mocked Tom.

'That's the problem,' admitted Nat. 'She thinks I'm a cross between Don Juan and Al Capone.'

'She sounds a good judge of character,' said Tom. 'So tell me all about her.'

'There's not that much to tell. We ran into each other on the top of a hill. She's bright, ferocious, quite beautiful, and thinks I'm a bastard.' Nat then recounted their conversation outside the refectory.

'Ralph Elliot obviously got his version in first,' said Tom.

'To hell with Elliot. Do you think I should wear a jacket and tie?'

'You haven't asked for that sort of advice since we were at Taft.'

'And in those days I needed to borrow your jacket and your tie, so what do you think?'

'Full dress uniform with medals.'

'Be serious.'

'Well, it would certainly confirm her opinion of you.'

'That's exactly what I'm trying to disabuse her of.'

'Well then, try looking at it from her point of view.'

'I'm listening.'

'What do you think she'll wear?'

'I have no idea, I've only seen her twice in my life, and on one of those occasions she was in her running shorts covered in mud.'

'God, that must have been sexy, but I don't suppose

she'll turn up in a tracksuit, so what about the other occasion?'

'Smart and understated.'

'Then follow her lead, which won't be easy, because there's nothing smart about you, and from what you say, she doesn't believe that you're capable of being understated.'

'Answer the question,' Nat said.

'I'd go for casual,' said Tom. 'Shirt, not T-shirt, slacks and a sweater. I could, of course, as your advisor on sartorial elegance, join you both for dinner.'

'I don't want you anywhere near the place, because you'll only fall in love with her.'

'You really care about this girl, don't you?' said Tom quietly.

'I think she's divine, but that doesn't stop her being very uncertain about me.'

'But she's agreed to have dinner with you, so she can't believe you're all bad.'

'Yes, but the terms of that agreement were somewhat unusual,' said Nat as he told Tom what he had proposed before she would agree to a date.

'As I said, you've got it bad, but that doesn't alter the fact that I need to see you. How about breakfast? Or will you also be having eggs and bacon with this mysterious oriental lady?'

'I'd be very surprised if she agreed to that,' said Nat wistfully. 'And disappointed.'

'How long do you expect the trial to last?' asked Annie.

'If we plead not guilty to murder, but guilty to manslaughter, it could be over in a morning, with perhaps a further court appearance for sentencing.'

'Is that possible?' asked Jimmy.

'Yes, the state is offering me a deal.'

'What sort of deal?' asked Annie.

'If I agree to a charge of manslaughter, Stamp will only call for three years, no more, which means with good behaviour and parole, Anita Kirsten could be out in eighteen months. Otherwise he intends to press for first degree and demand the death penalty.'

'They would never send a woman to the electric chair in this state for killing her husband.'

'I agree,' said Fletcher, 'but a tough jury might settle for ninety-nine years, and as the defendant is only twenty-five, I have to accept the fact that she might be better off agreeing to eighteen months; at least that way she could look forward to spending the rest of her life with her family.'

'True,' said Jimmy. 'But I ask myself, why is the attorney general willing to agree to three years if he feels he's got such a strong case? Don't forget this is a black woman, accused of murdering a white man, and at least two members of the jury will be black. If you play your cards right, it could be three, and then you can almost guarantee a hung jury.'

'Plus the fact that my client has a good reputation, holds down a responsible job, and has no previous convictions. That's bound to influence any jury, whatever colour.'

'I wouldn't be so sure of that,' said Annie. 'Your client poisoned her husband with an overdose of curare, which caused paralysis and then she sat on the staircase waiting for him to die.'

'But he'd been beating her up for years – and he also abused their children,' said Fletcher.

'Do you have any proof of that, counsellor?' asked Jimmy.

'Not a lot, but on the day she agreed to appoint me, I

took several photographs of the bruises on her body, and the burn on the palm of her hand will remain with her for the rest of her life.'

'How did she get that?' asked Annie.

'That bastard of a husband pressed her hand down on a burning stove, and only stopped when she fainted.'

'Sounds a lovely guy,' said Annie. 'So what's stopping you pleading manslaughter and pressing for extenuating circumstances?'

'Only the fear of losing, and Mrs Kirsten having to spend the rest of her life in jail.'

'Why did she ask you to be her defence counsel in the first place?' asked Jimmy.

'No one else stepped up to the plate,' replied Fletcher. 'And in any case, she found my fee irresistible.'

'But you're up against the state's attorney.'

'Which is a bit of a mystery, because I can't work out why he's bothering to represent the state in a case like this.'

'That's simply answered,' said Jimmy. 'Black woman kills white man in a state where only twenty per cent of the population is black, and over half of them don't bother to vote, and surprise, surprise, there's an election coming up in May.'

'How long has Stamp given you before you have to tell him your decision?' asked Annie.

'We're back in court next Monday.'

'Can you spare the time to be involved in a long trial?' she asked.

'No, but I mustn't make that an excuse for agreeing to any compromise.'

'So we'll be spending our holiday in court number three, will we?' asked Annie with a grin.

'It could even be court number four,' said Fletcher, putting an arm round his wife.

'Have you thought of asking Professor Abraham's advice on how she should plead?'

Jimmy and Fletcher stared at her in disbelief. 'He advises presidents and heads of state,' said Fletcher.

'And possibly the occasional governor,' added Jimmy.

'Then perhaps the time has come for him to start advising a second-year law student. After all, that's what he's paid for.'

'I wouldn't know where to start,' said Fletcher.

'How about picking up the phone and asking if he'll see you,' said Annie. 'My bet is that he'd be flattered.'

—◇—

Nat arrived at Mario's fifteen minutes early. He'd chosen the restaurant because it was unpretentious – tables with red and white checked cloths, a small arrangement of flowers, with black-and-white photos of Florence decorating the walls. Tom had also told him the pasta was homemade, cooked by the patron's wife and had brought back memories of their trip to Rome. He'd taken Tom's advice and selected a casual blue shirt, grey slacks and a navy sweater, no tie and no jacket – Tom had approved.

Nat introduced himself to Mario, who suggested a quiet table in the corner. After Nat had read the menu several times, he looked at his watch again, becoming ever more nervous. He must have checked a dozen times to be sure he had enough cash on him in case they didn't accept credit cards. Perhaps it would have been more sensible if he had walked round the block a couple of times.

The moment he saw her, he realized he'd blown it. Su Ling was wearing a smart, well-cut blue suit, cream blouse and navy shoes. Nat rose from his place and waved. She smiled – a smile he hadn't experienced until then, which made her look even more captivating. She walked over to join him.

'I apologize,' he said, rising from his place as he waited for her to be seated.

'What for?' she asked, looking puzzled.

'My clothes. I confess I spent a lot of time thinking about what I should wear, and still got it wrong.'

'Me too,' said Su Ling. 'I expected you to turn up in a uniform covered in medals,' she added as she slipped off her jacket and placed it over the back of her chair.

Nat burst out laughing, and they didn't seem to stop laughing for the next two hours, until Nat asked if she'd like some coffee. 'Yes, black please,' said Su Ling.

'I've told you about my family, now tell me about yours,' Nat said. 'Are you, like me, an only child?'

'Yes, my father was a master sergeant in Korea when he met my mother. They were only married for a few months before he was killed at the battle of Yudam-ni.'

Nat wanted to lean across and take her hand. 'I'm sorry,' he said.

'Thank you,' she said simply. 'Mom decided to emigrate to America so that we could meet up with my grandparents. But we were never able to trace them.' This time he did take her hand. 'I was too young to know what was going on, but my mother doesn't give up that easily. She took a job in Storrs Laundry, near the bookstore, and the owner allowed us to live above the shop.'

'I know that laundry,' said Nat. 'My father has his shirts done there – it's very efficient and . . .'

'. . . And has been ever since my mother took it over, but she's had to sacrifice everything to ensure that I had a good education.'

'Your mother sounds just like mine,' said Nat as Mario appeared by their side.

'Everything to your satisfaction, Mr Cartwright?'

'An excellent meal, thank you, Mario,' said Nat. 'All I need now is the check.'

'Certainly, Mr Cartwright, and may I say what an honour it has been to have you in the restaurant.'

'Thank you,' said Nat, trying to hide his embarrassment.

'How much did you tip him to say that?' asked Su Ling once Mario had slipped away.

'Ten dollars, and he's word-perfect every time.'

'But does it always pay off?' asked Su Ling.

'Oh yes, most of my dates start taking off their clothes even before we get back to the car.'

'So do you always bring them here?'

'No. If I think it's likely to be a one-night stand, I take them to McDonald's, followed by a motel – if it's serious, we go to the Altnaveigh Inn.'

'So which group are chosen for Mario's?' asked Su Ling.

'I can't answer that,' said Nat, 'because I've never taken anyone to Mario's before.'

'I'm flattered,' said Su Ling as he helped her on with her jacket. As they walked out of the restaurant, Su Ling took his hand. 'You're really quite shy, aren't you?'

'Yes, I suppose I am,' said Nat, as they continued walking towards the campus.

'Not at all like your arch rival, Ralph Elliot.' Nat didn't comment. 'He asked me for a date within minutes of meeting me.'

'To be fair,' said Nat, 'I would have too, but you walked away.'

'I thought I was running at the time,' she said. He turned and smiled. 'And even more interesting is how much action you actually saw in Vietnam to turn you into such a hero.' Nat was about to protest when she added, 'Answer, about half an hour.'

'How do you know that?' asked Nat.

'Because I did some research on you, Captain Cartwright, and to quote Steinbeck, "you're sailing under false colours". I learned that quote today,' she said, 'just in case you might think I'm well read. When you jumped on the helicopter, you weren't even carrying a gun. You were a requisition officer who shouldn't have been on that aircraft in the first place. In fact, it was bad enough that you jumped on the helicopter without permission, but you also jumped off it without permission. Mind you, if you hadn't, you might well have been court-martialled.'

'True,' said Nat, 'but don't tell anyone else, because it will stop me having my usual three girls a night.'

Su Ling placed a hand in front of her mouth and laughed. 'But I did read on, and your action after the helicopter crashed in the jungle was that of an extremely brave man. To have dragged that poor soldier on a stretcher with half your leg blown away must have taken immense courage, and then to discover he had later died can only have left an irremediable scar.' Nat didn't reply. 'I'm sorry,' she said as they reached south campus, 'that last remark was inconsiderate of me.'

'It was kind of you to search for the truth,' he said, looking down into her dark brown eyes. 'Not many have bothered to do that.'

18

'MEMBERS OF THE jury, in most murder trials it is the responsibility of the state, and rightly so, to prove that the defendant is guilty of homicide. That has not proved necessary in this case. Why? Because Mrs Kirsten signed a confession within an hour of her husband's brutal killing. And even now, eight months later, you will have noted that her legal representative has not at any time during this trial suggested that his client didn't commit the crime, or even challenged how she went about it.

'So let us turn to the facts in this case, because this was not what could be described as a crime of passion where a woman seeks to defend herself with the nearest weapon to hand. No, Mrs Kirsten was not interested in the nearest weapon to hand, because she spent several weeks planning this cold-blooded murder, well aware that her victim would have no chance of defending himself.

'How did Mrs Kirsten set about her task? Over a period of nearly three months, she collected several phials of curare from different drug dealers who reside in the shadows of Hartford. The defence tried to suggest that none of the dealers' evidence could be relied upon, which might have influenced you had Mrs Kirsten herself not confirmed from the witness stand that they were all telling the truth.

'Having collected the phials over several weeks, what does Mrs Kirsten do next? She waits until a Saturday night, when she knows her husband goes out drinking with his friends, and covertly pours the drug into six bottles of beer, and even replaces the tops. She then puts these bottles on the kitchen table, leaves the light on and goes to bed. She even places a bottle opener and a glass next to them. She does everything except pour out the drink herself.

'Ladies and gentlemen of the jury, this was a well planned and cleverly executed murder. However, if you can believe it possible, there was even worse to follow.

'When her husband arrives home that night, he does indeed fall into her trap. First he goes to the kitchen, probably to turn off the light, and, seeing the bottles on the table, Alex Kirsten is tempted into having a beer before going to bed. Even before he has put the second bottle to his lips, the drug has begun to take effect. When he calls for help his wife leaves the bedroom and walks slowly down to the hall, where she hears her husband crying out in pain. Does she phone for an ambulance? No, she does not. Does she even go to his assistance? No, she does not. She sits on the staircase and waits patiently until his agonized cries have stopped and she can be certain he's dead. And then, and only then, does she raise the alarm.

'How can we be so sure this is what actually took place? Not just because the neighbours were woken by her husband's haunting screams for help, but because when one of those neighbours came to the door to see if they could assist, in her panic Mrs Kirsten forgot to dispose of the contents of the other four bottles.' He paused for several seconds. 'When analysed, they contained enough curare to kill a football team.

'Members of the jury, the only defence Mr Davenport has suggested for this crime is that Mrs Kirsten's husband regularly beat her. If this was the case, why didn't she inform the police? If this was true, why didn't she go and live with her mother, who resides on the other side of the city? If we are to believe her story, why didn't she leave him? I'll tell you why. Because once her husband was out of the way, she would own the house they lived in and collect his pension from the company he worked for, making it possible for her to live in relative comfort for the rest of her life.

'In normal circumstances, the state would not hesitate to call for the death penalty for such a horrendous crime, but we do not feel it is appropriate on this occasion. It is nevertheless, your duty to send a clear message to any person who believes they can get away with murder. Such a crime may be lightly regarded in some other states, but we don't need one of those to be Connecticut. Do we want to be known as the state that condones murder?'

The attorney general lowered his voice almost to a whisper, and looked straight at the jury. 'When you indulge yourself in a moment of sympathy for Mrs Kirsten, and indeed you should, if only because you are caring human beings, place that on one side of the scales called justice. On the other side, place the facts – the cold-blooded murder of a forty-two-year-old man who would still be alive today if it were not for the premeditated crime cunningly executed by that evil woman.' He turned and pointed directly at the defendent. 'The state has no hesitation in asking you to find Mrs Kirsten guilty, and sentence her according to the law.' Mr Stamp returned to his place, the suggestion of a smile on his face.

'Mr Davenport,' said the judge, 'I intend to break for lunch. When we return, you may begin your summing up.'

—◇—

'You look very pleased with yourself,' said Tom as they settled down for breakfast in the kitchen.

'It was an unforgettable evening.'

'From that I assume consummation took place?'

'No, you cannot assume anything of the sort,' said Nat. 'But I can tell you that I held her hand.'

'You did what?'

'I held her hand,' Nat repeated.

'That won't do your reputation any good.'

'I'm rather hoping it will ruin my reputation,' said Nat as he poured some milk over his Wheaties. 'And how about you?' he asked.

'If you are referring to my sex life, it is currently non-existent, though not through lack of offers, one even persistent. But I'm just not interested.' Nat stared across at his friend and raised an eyebrow. 'Rebecca Thornton has made it all too obvious that she's available.'

'But I thought . . .'

'That she was back with Elliot?'

'Yes,'

'Possibly, but whenever I see her, she prefers to talk about you – in very flattering terms, I might add, though I'm told she tells a different story whenever she's with Elliot.'

'If that's the case,' said Nat, 'why do you think she's bothering to chase you?'

Tom pushed aside his empty bowl and began to concentrate on the two boiled eggs in front of him. He cracked the shell and looked at the yolk before he continued. 'If it's known that you're an only child and your father is worth millions, most women view you in a completely different light. So I never can be sure if it's me, or my money they're interested in. Just be thankful that you don't suffer from the same problem.'

'You'll know when it's the right person,' said Nat.

'Will I? I wonder. You're one of the few people who's never shown the slightest interest in my wealth, and you're almost the only person I know who always insists on paying his own way. You'd be surprised by how many people assume I'll pick up the tab just because I can afford it. I despise such people, which means that my circle of friends ends up being very small.'

'My latest friend is very small,' said Nat, hoping to snap Tom out of his morose mood, 'and I know you'll like her.'

'The "I held her hand" girl?'

'Yes, Su Ling – she's about five foot four, and now that thin is fashionable, she'll be the most sought-after woman on the campus.'

'Su Ling?' said Tom.

'You know her?' asked Nat.

'No, but my father tells me that she's taken over the new computer lab that his company funded, and the tutors have virtually stopped bothering to try and teach her.'

'She never mentioned anything about computers to me last night,' said Nat.

'Well, you'd better move quickly, because Dad also mentioned that MIT and Harvard are both trying to tempt her away from UConn, so be warned, there's a big brain on top of that little body.'

'And I've made a complete fool of myself again,' said Nat, 'because I even teased her about her English, when she's obviously mastered a new language that everyone wants to know about. By the way, is that why you wanted to see me?' asked Nat.

'No, I had no idea you were dating a genius.'

'I'm not,' said Nat, 'she's a gentle, thoughtful, beautiful woman, who considers holding hands is one step away from promiscuity.' He paused. 'So if it wasn't to discuss my sex life, why did you call this high-powered breakfast meeting in the first place?'

Tom gave up on the eggs and pushed them to one side. 'Before I return to Yale, I wanted to know if you're going to run for president.' He waited for the usual barrage of count me out, not interested, you've got the wrong person, but Nat didn't respond for some time.

'I discussed it with Su Ling last night,' he eventually said, 'and in her usual disarming way, she told me that it was not so much that they wanted me, as they didn't want Elliot. The lesser of two evils were her exact words, if I remember correctly.'

'I'm sure she's right,' said Tom, 'but that could change if you gave them a chance to get to know you. You've been pretty much of a recluse since you returned to college.'

'I've had a lot of catching up to do,' said Nat defensively.

'Well that's no longer the case, as your grade point average clearly shows,' said Tom, 'and now you've been selected to run for the university . . .'

'If you were at UConn, Tom, I wouldn't hesitate to run for president, but while you're at Yale . . .'

—◇—

Fletcher rose from his place to face the jury – ninety-nine years was written on every one of their faces. If he could have turned the clock back and accepted the offer of three years, he would have done so without hesitation. Now he had been left with only one throw of the dice to try and give Mrs Kirsten the rest of her life back. He touched his client's shoulder, and turned to seek a reassuring smile from Annie, who had felt so strongly that he should defend this woman. The smile disappeared the

185

moment he saw who was seated two rows behind her. Professor Karl Abrahams graced him with a nod. At least Jimmy would discover what it took to get a nod out of Homer.

'Members of the jury,' Fletcher began, a slight tremor in his voice. 'You have listened to the persuasive advocacy of the attorney general as he poured venom on my client, so perhaps the time has come to show where that venom should have been directed. But first may I spend a moment talking about you. The press have made great play of the fact that I did not object to every white juror who was selected; indeed there are ten of you on this jury. They went further, and suggested that had I achieved an all-black jury with a majority of women, then Mrs Kirsten would have been certain to walk free. But I didn't want that. I chose each one of you for a different reason.' The jury members looked puzzled.

'Even the attorney general couldn't work out why I didn't object to some of you,' added Fletcher turning to face Mr Stamp. 'I crossed my fingers, because neither did any of his vast team fathom why I selected you. So what is it that you all have in common?' The attorney general was now looking just as puzzled as the jurors. Fletcher swung round and pointed to Mrs Kirsten. 'Like the defendant, every one of you has been married for more than nine years.' Fletcher turned his attention back to the jury. 'No bachelors or spinsters who have never experienced married life, or what goes on between two people behind closed doors.' Fletcher spotted a woman in the second row who shuddered. He remembered Abrahams saying that in a jury of twelve, there is a strong possibility that one of them will have suffered the same experience as the defendant. He had just identified that juror.

'Which of you dreads the thought of your spouse returning home after midnight, drunk, with only violence in mind? For Mrs Kirsten, this was something she had come to expect six nights out of seven, for the past nine years. Look at this frail and fragile woman and ask yourself what chance she would have up against a man of six foot two who weighed two hundred and thirty pounds?'

He focused his attention on the woman juror who had shuddered. 'Which of you arrives home at night and expects their husband to grab the bread board, a cheese grater or even a steak knife for use not in the kitchen for preparing a meal, but in the bedroom to disfigure his wife? And what did Mrs Kirsten have to call on for her defence, this five foot four, one hundred and five pound woman? A pillow? A towel? A fly-swatter perhaps?' Fletcher paused. 'It's never crossed your mind, has it?' he added, facing the rest of the jurors. 'Why? Because your husbands and wives are not evil. Ladies and gentlemen, how can you begin to understand what this woman was being subjected to, day in and day out?

'But not satisfied with such degradation, one night this thug returns home drunk, goes upstairs, drags his wife out of bed by her hair, back down the stairs and into the kitchen; he is bored with simply beating her black and blue.' Fletcher began to walk in the direction of his client. 'He needs some other thrill to reach new heights of excitement, and what does Anita Kirsten see immediately she's dragged into the kitchen? The ring on the stove is already red hot, and waiting for its victim.' He swung back to face the jury. 'Can you imagine what must have been going through her mind when she first saw that ring of fire? He grabs her hand like a piece of raw steak, and slams it down on the stove for fifteen seconds.'

Fletcher picked up Mrs Kirsten's scarred hand and held it up so that the palm was clearly visible to the jury, looked at his watch and counted to fifteen, before he added, 'And then she fainted.

'Which of you can even imagine such horror, let alone be asked to endure it? So why did the attorney general demand ninety-nine years? Because, he told us, the killing was premeditated. It was, he assured us, most certainly not a crime of passion carried out by someone defending their life in a moment of rage.' Fletcher swung round to face the attorney general and said, 'Of course it was premeditated and of course she knew exactly what she was doing. If you were five foot four, being attacked by a man of six foot two, would you rely on a knife, a gun, or some blunt instrument that this thug could so easily turn against you?' Fletcher turned and walked slowly towards the jury. 'Which one of you would be that stupid? Which one of you, after what she had been through, *wouldn't* plan it? Think of that poor woman when you next have a row with your spouse. After a few angry words have been exchanged, will you resort to putting the stove on to 220 degrees to prove you've won the argument?' He looked at the seven men on the jury one by one. 'Does such a man deserve your sympathy?

'If this woman is guilty of murder, which one of you would not have done the same thing if you had been unfortunate enough to marry Alex Kirsten?' This time he turned his attention to the five women before he continued. '"But I didn't," I hear you cry. "I married a good and decent man." So now we can all agree on Mrs Kirsten's crime. She married an evil man.'

Fletcher leant on the rail of the jury box. 'I must beg the jury's indulgence for my youthful passion, for passion it is. I chose to take this case as I feared justice would not be done for Mrs Kirsten, and in my youth I hoped that twelve fair-minded citizens would see what I had seen and would be unable to condemn this woman to spend the rest of her life in jail.

'I must close my submission, by repeating to you the

words Mrs Kirsten said to me when we sat alone in her cell this morning. "Mr Davenport, although I am only twenty-five, I would rather spend the rest of my life in jail than have to spend another night under the same roof as that evil man."

'Thank God she does not have to return home to him tonight. It is in your power, as members of the jury, to send this woman home tonight to her loving children, with the hope that together they might rebuild their lives, because twelve decent people understood the difference between good and evil.' Fletcher lowered his voice to almost a whisper. 'When you go home to your husbands and wives this evening, tell them what you did today in the name of justice, for I am confident if you bring in a verdict of Not Guilty, your spouses will not turn the stove up to 220 degrees because they don't agree with you. Mrs Kirsten has already suffered a nine-year sentence. Do you really think she deserves another ninety?'

Fletcher returned to his seat, but did not turn round to look at Annie, for fear that Karl Abrahams would notice he was fighting back the tears.

19

'HI, MY NAME'S Nat Cartwright.'

'Not *the* Captain Cartwright?'

'Yes, the hero who killed all those Vietcong with his bare hands because he forgot to take any paper clips with him.'

'No,' said Su Ling in mock admiration. 'Not the one who flew a helicopter alone across enemy-infested jungle when he didn't have a pilot's licence?'

'And then killed so many of the enemy that they stopped counting them, while at the same time he rescued a whole platoon of stranded men.'

'And the people back home believed it, so he was decorated, given vast financial rewards and offered a hundred vestal virgins.'

'I only get four hundred dollars a month, and I've never met a vestal virgin.'

'Well you have now,' said Su Ling with a smile.

'Well, can you tell her that I have been chosen to run against Boston University.'

'No doubt you'd expect her to stand around in the rain and wait until you trail in near the back, like all your other adoring fans?'

'No, the truth is that I need my tracksuit cleaned, and I'm told her mother takes in washing.' Su Ling burst out laughing. 'Of course I'd like you to come to Boston,' said Nat taking her in his arms.

'I've already booked a place on the supporters' bus.'

'But Tom and I are driving up the night before, so why don't you come with us?'

'But where would I stay?'

'One of Tom's numerous aunts has a house in Boston, and has offered to put us all up for the night.' Su Ling hesitated. 'I'm told she has nine bedrooms, and even a separate wing, but if that's not enough, I could always spend the night in the back of the car.' Su Ling didn't reply as Mario appeared carrying two cappuccinos.

'This is my friend Mario,' said Su Ling, 'very good of you to keep my usual table' she added.

'Do you bring all your men here?'

'No, I tend to select a different restaurant each time, so that way no one finds out about my vestal reputation.'

'Like your reputation as a computer whiz?'

Su Ling blushed. 'How did you find out about that?'

'What do you mean, how did I find out? It seems everyone on campus knew except me. In fact my closest friend told me, and he's at Yale.'

'I was going to tell you, but you never asked the right question.'

'Su Ling, you can tell me things without having to be asked the right question.'

'Then I must ask if you've also heard that both Harvard and MIT have invited me to join their computer science departments.'

'Yes, but I don't know how you responded.'

'Tell me, captain,' she said, 'can I ask you something first?'

'You're trying to change the subject again, Su Ling.'

'Yes I am, Nat, because I need my question answered before I can reply to yours.'

'OK, so what's your question?'

Su Ling lowered her head as she always did when she

was slightly embarrassed. 'How can two such different people,' she hesitated, 'end up liking each other so much.'

'End up falling in love, I think is what you're trying to say. If I knew the answer to that question, little flower, I'd be a professor of philosophy, and not worrying about my end-of-term exam grades.'

'In my country,' said Su Ling, 'love is something you do not talk about until you have known each other for many years.'

'Then I promise not to discuss the matter again for many years – on one condition.'

'And what is that?'

'That you will agree to come to Boston with us on Friday.'

'Yes, if I can have Tom's aunt's telephone number.'

'Of course you can, but why?'

'My mother will need to speak to her.' Su Ling lifted her right foot, slipped it under the table and placed it on top of Nat's left foot.

'Now I feel sure that has a significant meaning in your country.'

'Yes, it does. It means I wish to walk with you, but not in a crowd.'

Nat placed his right foot on her left. 'And what does that mean?'

'That you agree to my request,' she hesitated. 'But I should not have done it first, otherwise I would be considered a loose woman.' Nat immediately removed his foot and then replaced it. 'Honour restored,' she said.

'Then after we have been on our uncrowded walk, what happens next?'

'You must wait for an invitation to take tea with my family.'

'How long will that take?'

'Normally a year would be considered appropriate.'

'Couldn't we speed up the process a little?' suggested Nat. 'How about next week?'

'All right, then you will be invited to tea on Sunday afternoon, because Sunday is the traditional day for a man to have a first meal with a woman under the watchful eye of family.'

'But we've already had several meals together.'

'I know, so you must come to tea before my mother finds out, otherwise I will be abandoned and disinherited.'

'Then I shall not accept your invitation to tea,' said Nat.

'Why not?'

'I'll just stand outside your house and grab you when your mother throws you out, and then I won't have to wait for another two years.' Nat placed both his feet on hers, and she withdrew them immediately. 'What did I do wrong?'

'Two feet means something completely different.'

'What?' asked Nat.

'I can't tell you, but as you were clever enough to find out the correct translation of Su Ling, I feel sure you will discover the meaning of two feet, and never do it again, unless . . .'

—◇—

On Friday afternoon, Tom drove Nat and Su Ling up to his aunt's home in the leafy suburbs of Boston. Miss Russell had obviously spoken to Su Ling's mother, because she'd put her in the bedroom on the main landing, next to hers, while Nat and Tom were relegated to the east wing.

After breakfast the following morning, Su Ling left to keep her appointment with the professor of statistics at Harvard, while Nat and Tom spent some time walking slowly round the cross-country course, something Nat always did whenever he would be running over unfamiliar territory. He checked out all the well-worn paths, and whenever he came to a stream, a gate or a sudden undulation, he practised crossing it several times.

On the way back across the meadow, Tom asked him what he would do if Su Ling agreed to a transfer to Harvard.

'I'll move at the same time and enrol at the business school.'

'You feel that strongly about her?'

'Yes, and I can't risk letting anyone else place both feet on hers.'

'What are you talking about?'

'I'll explain another time,' said Nat as he came to a halt by a stream. 'Where do you imagine they cross it?'

'No idea,' said Tom, 'but it looks too wide to jump.'

'Agreed, so I expect they aim for the large flat pebbles in the middle.'

'What do you do if you're not sure?' asked Tom.

'Follow closely behind one of their team, because they'll do the right thing automatically.'

'Where are you hoping to end up this early in the season?'

'I'd be satisfied with being a counter.'

'I don't understand, doesn't everybody count?'

'No, although there are eight runners on each team, only six count when the final score is calculated. If I come in twelfth or higher, I would be a counter.'

'So how is the counting done?'

'First across the line counts as one, second two, and so on. When the race is over, the first six in each team are added together, and the team with the lowest overall score is the winner. That way, seven and eight can only contribute if they stay ahead of any of the first six runners on the other team. Is that clear?'

'Yes, I think so,' said Tom, looking at his watch. 'I'd better get back, because I promised Aunt Abigail I'd have lunch with her. Are you coming?'

'No, I'm joining the rest of the team for a banana, a lettuce leaf and a glass of water. Could you pick up Su Ling and make sure that she's back in time to watch the race.'

'She won't need to be reminded,' said Tom.

When Tom strolled into the house, he found his aunt and Su Ling deep in conversation over a bowl of clam chowder. Tom sensed that his aunt had changed the subject the moment he'd entered the room. 'You'd better grab something to eat,' she said, 'if you're hoping to be back in time to see the start.'

After a second bowl of clam chowder, Tom accompanied Su Ling across to the course. He explained to her that Nat had selected a spot about half-way round, where they could see all the runners for at least a mile and then if they took a short cut, they would be back in time to watch the winner crossing the finishing line.

'Do you understand what a counter is?' Tom asked.

'Yes, Nat explained it to me – an ingenious system, which makes the abacus look positively modern. Would you like me to explain it to you?' she asked.

'Yes, I think I would,' said Tom.

By the time they reached the vantage point that Nat had selected, they didn't have long to wait before the first runner came into view over the brow of the hill. They watched Boston's captain shoot past them, and ten other runners had come and gone before Nat appeared. He gave a wave as he sped off down the hill.

'He's the last counter,' said Su Ling as they set off to take the short cut back to the finishing line.

'My bet is that he'll move up two or three places now he knows you're here to watch him,' said Tom.

'How flattering,' said Su Ling.

'Will you be taking up the Harvard offer?' asked Tom quietly.

'Did Nat ask you to find out?' she enquired.

'No,' said Tom, 'though he talks of little else.'

'I have said yes, but only on one condition.' Tom remained silent. Su Ling didn't tell Tom what the condition was, so he didn't ask.

They almost had to jog the last couple of hundred yards to make sure they were back in time to see the Boston captain raise his arms in triumph as he crossed the finishing line. Tom turned out to be right, because Nat ended up in ninth position, and fourth counter for his team. Both of them rushed over to congratulate him as if he were the winner. Nat lay on the ground exhausted, disappointed that he hadn't done better when he learned that Boston had won by 31 to 24.

After supper with Aunt Abigail, they started out on the long drive back to Storrs. Nat rested his head in Su Ling's lap and quickly fell asleep.

'I can't imagine what my mother would say about our first night together,' she whispered to Tom as he drove on through the night.

'Why don't you go the whole hog and tell her that it was a *ménage à trois*?'

―◇―

'Mother thought you were wonderful,' said Su Ling as they walked slowly back towards south campus after tea the following afternoon.

'What a woman,' said Nat. 'She can cook, run a home and is also a successful businesswoman.'

'And don't forget,' said Su Ling, 'that she was shunned in her own land for bearing a foreigner's child and wasn't even welcomed in this country when she first arrived, which is the reason I've been brought up so strictly. Like so many children of immigrants, I'm no cleverer than my mother, but by sacrificing everything to give me a first-class education, she has allowed me a better chance than she ever had. Perhaps you can now understand why I always try to respect her wishes.'

'Yes, I can,' said Nat, 'and now that I've met your mother, I'd like you to meet mine, because I am equally proud of her.' Su Ling laughed.

'Why do you laugh, little flower?' asked Nat.

'In my country, for a man to meet a woman's mother is to admit to a relationship. If the man then asks you to meet his mother, it means betrothal. If he then does not marry the girl, she will be a spinster for the rest of her life. However, I will take that risk, because Tom asked me to marry him yesterday when you were running away.'

Nat bent down, kissed her on the lips and then placed both his feet gently on top of hers. She smiled. 'I love you too,' she said.

20

'WHAT DO YOU make of it?' asked Jimmy.

'I've no idea,' said Fletcher, who glanced over at the attorney general's table, but none of the state's team gave any sign of looking either anxious or confident.

'You could always ask Professor Abrahams for his opinion,' said Annie.

'Why, is he still around?'

'I saw him roaming up and down the corridor only a few moments ago.'

Fletcher left the table, pushed open the little wooden gate dividing the court from the public and strode quickly out of the courtroom into the corridor. He glanced up and down the wide marble expanse, but didn't spot the professor until the crowds near the rotunda staircase parted to reveal a distinguished looking man seated in the corner, head down, writing notes on a legal pad. Court officials and members of the public rushed past him, unaware of his presence. Fletcher walked apprehensively across to join him and watched as the old man continued making notes. He didn't feel he could interrupt, so waited until the professor eventually looked up.

'Ah, Davenport,' he said, tapping the bench beside him. 'Take a seat. You have an enquiring look on your face, so how may I assist you?'

Fletcher sat beside him. 'I only wanted to ask your opinion on why the jury has been out for so long. Should I read anything into it?'

The professor checked his watch. 'Just over five hours,' he said. 'No, I wouldn't consider that long for a capital charge. Juries like to let you know that they've taken their responsibility seriously, unless of course it's cut and dried, and this case certainly wasn't.'

'Do you have any feel for what the outcome might be?' asked Fletcher anxiously.

'You can never second-guess a jury, Mr Davenport; twelve people chosen at random, with little in common, though I must say, with a couple of exceptions, they looked a fair-minded lot. So what's your next question?'

'I don't know, sir, what is my next question?'

'What should I do if the verdict goes against me?' He paused. 'An eventuality you must always prepare for.' Fletcher nodded. 'Answer? You immediately ask the judge for leave to appeal.' The professor tore off one of the sheets of yellow paper and handed it across to his pupil. 'I hope you will not consider it presumptuous of me, but I have jotted down a simple form of words for every eventuality.'

'Including guilty?' said Fletcher.

'No need to be that pessimistic yet. First we must consider the possibility of a hung jury. I observed in the centre of the back row a juror who never once looked at our client while she was on the witness stand. But I noticed that you also spotted the lady on the far end of the front row who lowered her eyes when you held up the scorched palm of Mrs Kirsten's right hand.'

'What do I do if it is a hung jury?'

'Nothing. The judge, although not the brightest legal mind currently sitting on the appellant bench, is meticulous and fair when it comes to points of law, so he will ask the jury if they are able to return a majority verdict.'

'Which in this state is ten to two.'

'As it is in forty-three other states,' the professor reminded him.

'But if they are unable to agree on a majority verdict?'

'The judge is left with no choice but to dismiss the jury and ask the attorney general if he wishes to call for a retrial, and before you ask, I can't second-guess how Mr Stamp will react to that eventuality.'

'You seem to have made a lot of notes,' Fletcher said, looking down at line after line of neatly written script.

'Yes, I intend to refer to this case next term when I give my lecture on the legal difference between manslaughter and homicide. It will be for my third-year students, so you should not be too embarrassed.'

'Should I have accepted the attorney general's deal of manslaughter, and settled for three years?'

'I suspect we will find out the answer to that question in the not-too-distant future.'

'Did I make a lot of mistakes?' asked Fletcher.

'A few,' said the professor turning the pages of his pad.

'What was the biggest one?'

'Your only glaring error, in my opinion, was not calling a doctor to describe in graphic detail – something doctors always enjoy doing – how the bruises on Mrs Kirsten's arms and legs might have been inflicted. Juries admire doctors. They assume that they are honest people, and in the main they are. But like every other group, if you ask them the right question – and it is after all the lawyers who select the questions – they are as prone to exaggeration as the rest of us.' Fletcher felt guilty that he had missed such an obvious gambit, and only wished he had taken Annie's advice and sought the professor's counsel earlier.

'Don't worry, the state still has one or two hurdles to

cross, because the judge is certain to grant us a stay of execution.'

'Us?' said Fletcher.

'Yes,' said the professor quietly, 'although I have not appeared in court for many years, and may well be a little rusty, I was hoping that you might allow me to assist you on this occasion.'

'You would serve as my co-counsel?' said Fletcher in disbelief.

'Yes, Davenport, I would,' said the professor, 'because you did convince me of one thing. Your client should not be spending the rest of her life in jail.'

'Jury's coming back,' shouted a voice that echoed down the corridor.

'Good luck, Davenport,' added the professor. 'And may I say before I hear the result, that for a second-year student, your defence was a remarkable tour de force.'

❖

Nat could sense how nervous Su Ling was the closer they got to Cromwell. 'Are you sure your mother will approve of the way I'm dressed?' she asked, pulling her skirt down even further.

Nat looked across to admire the simple yellow suit that Su Ling had selected, that just hinted how graceful her figure was. 'My mother will approve, and my father won't be able to take his eyes off you.'

Su Ling squeezed his leg. 'How will your father react when he finds out that I'm Korean?'

'I shall remind him of your Irish father,' said Nat. 'In any case, he's spent his whole life dealing with figures, so it will take him only a few minutes to realize how bright you are.'

'It's not too late to turn back,' said Su Ling. 'We could always visit them next Sunday.'

'It is too late,' said Nat. 'In any case, haven't you considered how nervous my parents might be? After all, I have already told them that I'm desperately in love with you.'

'Yes, but my mother adored you.'

'And mine will adore you.' Su Ling remained silent until Nat told her that they were approaching the outskirts of Cromwell.

'But I don't know what to say.'

'Su Ling, it's not an examination that you have to pass.'

'Yes it is, that's exactly what it is.'

'This is the town where I was born,' said Nat, trying to relax her as they drove down the main street. 'When I was a child, I thought it was a great metropolis. But to be fair, I also used to think Hartford was the capital of the world.'

'How long before we get there?' she asked.

Nat glanced out of the window. 'I'd say about ten minutes. But please don't expect anything too grand, we only live in a small house.'

'My mother and I live above the shop,' said Su Ling.

Nat laughed, 'And so did Harry Truman.'

'And look where that got him,' she replied.

Nat turned the car into Cedar Avenue. 'We're the third house on the right.'

'Could we drive around the block a few times?' said Su Ling, 'I need to think about what I'm going to say.'

'No,' said Nat firmly, 'try to remember how the professor of statistics at Harvard reacted when he first met you.'

'Yes, but I didn't want to marry his son.'

'I feel sure he would have agreed to that if he'd thought it might have convinced you to join his team.' Su Ling laughed for the first time in over an hour, just as

Nat brought the car to a halt outside the house. He went quickly round to Su Ling's side and opened the door for her. She stepped out and lost one of her shoes in the gutter.

'I'm sorry, I'm sorry,' she said as she slipped it back on. 'I'm sorry.'

Nat laughed and took her in his arms.

'No, no,' said Su Ling, 'your mother might see us.'

'I hope she does,' said Nat. He smiled and took her by the hand as they walked up the short driveway.

The door was opened long before they'd reached it, and Susan ran out to greet them. She immediately took Su Ling in her arms and said, 'Nat didn't exaggerate. You are quite beautiful.'

Fletcher walked slowly back down the corridor towards the courtroom, surprised to find that the professor remained by his side. When they reached the swing doors, the young counsellor assumed his mentor would return to his place a couple of rows behind Annie and Jimmy, but he continued walking towards the front of the courtroom and took the vacant seat next to Fletcher's. Annie and Jimmy could barely conceal their surprise. The court usher announced, 'All rise. His Honour Judge Abernathy presiding.'

Once he was seated, the judge looked towards the attorney general and acknowledged him, then turned his attention to the defence team, and for the second time during the trial, surprise registered on his face.

'I see you have acquired an assistant, Mr Davenport. Is his name to be entered on the register before I recall the jury?'

Fletcher turned to the professor, who rose from his place and said, 'That would be my wish, your honour.'

'Name?' asked the judge, as if he had never seen him before.

'Karl Abrahams, your honour.'

'Are you qualified to appear in my court?' asked the judge solemnly.

'I believe I am, sir,' said Abrahams, 'I first became a member of the Connecticut bar in 1937, though I have never had the privilege of appearing before your honour.'

'Thank you, Mr Abrahams. If the attorney general has no objection, I will enter your name on my register as Mr Davenport's co-counsel.'

The attorney general rose, gave the professor a slight bow, and said, 'It is a privilege to be in the same court as Mr Davenport's assistant.'

'Then I think we should waste no more time in recalling the jury,' said the judge.

Fletcher examined the faces of the seven men and five women as they filed back to their places. The professor had suggested that Fletcher check to see if any jury members looked directly at their client, which would possibly indicate a verdict of not guilty. He thought two or three of them did, but he couldn't be sure.

The foreman rose. 'Have you reached a verdict in this case?' the judge asked.

'No, your honour, we have been unable to do so,' the foreman replied.

Fletcher could feel the sweat on the palms of his hands even more intensely than when he had first stood to address the jury. The judge tried a second time. 'Are you able to return a majority verdict?'

'No, we are not your honour,' replied the foreman.

'Do you feel, given more time, you might eventually reach a majority verdict?'

'I don't think so, your honour. We have been equally divided for the past three hours.'

'Then I have no choice but to declare a mistrial, and dismiss the jury. On behalf of the state, I thank you for your service.' He turned his attention to the attorney general, and as he did so Mr Abrahams rose to his feet.

'I wonder, your honour, if I might seek your guidance on a small point of protocol.'

The judge looked puzzled, as did the attorney general. 'I can't wait to hear your small point of protocol, Mr Abrahams.'

'Allow me first to enquire of your honour, if I am correct in thinking that should there be a retrial, the defence team must be announced within fourteen days?'

'That would be the normal practice, Mr Abrahams.'

'Then may I assist the court by making it clear that should that situation arise, Mr Davenport and I will continue to represent the defendant.'

'I am obliged for your small point of protocol,' said the judge, no longer puzzled.

'So I must now ask you Mr Stamp,' said the judge, turning his attention back to the attorney general, 'if it is your intention to apply for a retrial of this case.'

The court's attention swung to the state's lawyers, all five of whom were in a huddle, holding an animated conversation. Judge Abernathy made no attempt to hurry them, and it was some time before Mr Stamp rose from his place. 'We do not believe, your honour, that it is in the state's best interest to reopen this case.'

Cheering broke out in the well of the court as the professor tore a sheet from his yellow pad and pushed it across to his pupil. Fletcher glanced down at it, rose from his place and read it, word for word. 'You honour, in the circumstances, I would ask for the immediate release of my client.' He looked down at the professor's next sentence and continued to read, 'And may I say how grateful I am for the gracious and professional manner in which

Mr Stamp and his team have conducted the case for the prosecution.'

The judge nodded, and Mr Stamp rose again. 'May I in turn congratulate the defence counsel and his assistant on their first case before your honour, and wish Mr Davenport every success in what I feel certain will be a promising career.'

Fletcher beamed at Annie, as Professor Abrahams rose from his place. 'Objection, your honour.'

Everyone turned to face the professor. 'I wouldn't have thought it was that certain,' he said. 'It is my belief that a lot of work still needs to be done before that promise will be realized.'

'Sustained,' said Judge Abernathy.

◄○►

'My mother taught me two languages up until the age of nine and by then I was just about ready to be mainstreamed into the Storrs' school system.'

'That's where I started my academic life,' said Susan.

'But I discovered from an early age that I was more at ease with numbers than words.' Michael Cartwright nodded his understanding. 'And I was most fortunate to have a maths teacher whose hobby was statistics, and who was also fascinated by the role the computer might play in the future.'

'We're beginning to rely a lot on them in the insurance business,' said Michael as he refilled his pipe.

'How big is your firm's computer, Mr Cartwright?' asked Su Ling.

'About the size of this room.'

'The next generation of students will work with computers no larger than the lids of their desks, and the generation after that will be able to hold them in the palm of their hand.'

'Do you really believe that's possible?' asked Susan, transfixed.

'The technology is moving at such a pace, and the demand will be so high, that the price must fall quickly. Once that happens, computers will become like the phone and the television were in the forties and fifties, as more people purchase them, the cheaper and smaller they will be.'

'But surely some computers will still need to be large?' suggested Michael. 'After all, my company has over forty thousand customers.'

'Not necessarily,' said Su Ling. 'The computer that sent the first man to the moon was larger than this house, but we will live to see a space capsule land on Mars controlled by a computer no larger than this kitchen table.'

'No larger than the kitchen table?' repeated Susan, trying to grasp the concept.

'In California, Silicon Valley has become the new hotbed of technology. Already IBM and Hewlett Packard are finding that their latest models can be out of date in a matter of months, and once the Japanese are fully up to speed, it might even be weeks.'

'Then how can firms like mine be expected to keep up?' asked Michael.

'You'll simply have to replace your computer just as often as you change your car, and in the not-too-distant future, you'll be able to carry in your inside pocket detailed information on every customer you represent.'

'But I repeat,' said Michael, 'our company currently has forty-two thousand clients.'

'It won't matter if you have four hundred thousand Mr Cartwright, a hand-held computer will still be able to do the same job.'

'But think of the consequences,' said Susan.

'They are very exciting, Mrs Cartwright,' said Su Ling. She paused and blushed, 'I apologize, I've been talking far too much.'

'No, no,' said Susan, 'it's fascinating, but I was hoping to ask you about Korea, a country I've always wanted to visit. If it's not a silly question, are you more like the Chinese or the Japanese?'

'Neither,' replied Su Ling. 'We are as different as a Russian is from an Italian. The Korean nation was originally a tribal one and probably first existed as early as the second century . . .'

◄◦►

'And to think I told them that you were shy,' Nat remarked as he slipped in beside her later that night.

'I'm very sorry,' said Su Ling. 'I broke your mother's golden rule.'

'Which one?' said Nat.

'That when two people meet, the conversation should be equally shared, three people, thirty-three per cent, four people, twenty-five per cent. I talked,' she paused, 'for about ninety per cent of the time. I feel ashamed, because I behaved so disgracefully, I don't know what came over me. I was just so nervous. I feel sure they already regret any suggestion of me as a daughter-in-law.'

Nat laughed. 'They adored you,' he said, 'my father was mesmerized by your knowledge of computers, and my mother fascinated by the customs of Korea, though you didn't mention what has to take place if a Korean girl takes tea with her suitor's parents.'

'That doesn't apply to a first generation American, like myself.'

'Who wears pink lipstick and mini skirts,' said Nat, holding up a tube of pink lipstick.

'I didn't know you used lipstick, Nat. Another habit you picked up in Vietnam?'

'Only on night ops, now turn over.'

'Turn over?'

'Yes,' said Nat firmly, 'I thought Korean women were meant to be subservient, so do as you're told and turn over.'

Su Ling turned over, and placed her face down on the pillow. 'What is your next order, Captain Cartwright?'

'To take off your nightdress, little flower.'

'Does this happen to all American girls on the second night?'

'Take off your nightdress.'

'Yes, captain.' She slowly pulled her white silk nightdress over the top of her head, and dropped it on the floor. 'What next,' she asked. 'Is it now that you beat me?'

'No, that doesn't happen until the third date, but I am going to ask you a question.' Nat took the pink lipstick and wrote four words on her olive skin, followed by a question mark.

'What have you written, Captain Cartwright?'

'Why don't you find out for yourself?'

Su Ling climbed off the bed and stared over her shoulder into the long mirror. It was some time before a smile spread across her face. She turned to find Nat lying spread-eagled on the bed, holding the lipstick high above his head. Su Ling walked slowly across, grabbed the lipstick, stared down at his broad shoulders for some time, before she wrote the words, YES I WILL.

21

'ANNIE'S PREGNANT.'

'That's wonderful news,' said Jimmy as they left the dining hall and strolled across the campus for their first lecture of the morning. 'How many months is she?'

'Only a couple, so now it will be your turn to give the advice.'

'What do you mean?'

'Don't forget, you're the one with all the experience. You're a father of a six-month-old baby daughter. To start with, how can I help Annie during the next seven months?'

'Just try to be supportive. Never forget to tell her that she looks wonderful even when she resembles a beached whale, and if she gets any crazy ideas, just play along with them.'

'Such as?' asked Fletcher.

'Joanna liked to eat half-pint tubs of double chocolate chip ice cream just before she went to bed each night, so I had a tub as well, and then if she woke up in the middle of the night she often asked for another one.'

'That must have been a real sacrifice,' said Fletcher.

'Yes it was, because it always had to be followed by a spoonful of cod liver oil.'

Fletcher laughed. 'Keep going,' he said as they approached the Andersen building.

'Annie will start going to pre-natal classes fairly soon, and the instructors usually recommend that husbands also attend so they can appreciate what their wives are going through.'

'I'd enjoy that,' said Fletcher, 'especially if I'm going to have to eat all that ice cream.' They climbed the steps and walked through the swing doors.

'With Annie, it may turn out to be onions or pickle,' said Jimmy.

'Then I may not be quite as enthusiastic.'

'And then there's the preparation for the birth. Who'll help Annie with this?'

'Mom asked if she wanted Miss Nichol, my old nanny to come out of retirement, but Annie wouldn't hear of it. She's determined to bring up this child without any outside assistance.'

'Joanna would have taken advantage of Miss Nichol without a second thought, because from what I remember of that lady, she would have happily agreed to paint the nursery as well as change the diapers.'

'We don't have a nursery,' said Fletcher, 'just a spare room.'

'Then as of today, that becomes the nursery, and Annie will expect you to repaint it, while she goes out and buys a whole new wardrobe.'

'She's got more than enough clothes already,' said Fletcher.

'No woman has more than enough clothes,' said Jimmy, 'and in a couple of months' time she won't be able to fit into any of them, and that's before she starts thinking about the baby's needs.'

'I'd better start looking for a job as a waiter or bartender right away,' said Fletcher, as they walked down the corridor.

'But surely your father will . . .'

'I don't intend to spend my whole life sponging off my old man.'

'If my father had that sort of money,' said Jimmy, 'I wouldn't do a day's work.'

'Yes, you would,' said Fletcher, 'otherwise Joanna would never have agreed to marry you.'

'I don't think you'll end up being a bartender Fletcher, because after your triumph in the Kirsten case you'll get the pick of the summer association jobs. And if there's one thing I know about my kid sister, she won't allow anything to get in the way of you coming out top of our year.' Jimmy paused. 'Why don't I have a word with my mother? She certainly helped Joanna with a lot of the chores without ever making it at all obvious.' He paused. 'But I'd expect something in return.'

'What do you have in mind?' asked Fletcher.

'Well, for a start, how about your father's money?' he said with a grin.

Fletcher laughed. 'You want my father's money in exchange for asking your mother to help her daughter with the birth of her grandchild? You know, Jimmy, I have a feeling you'd make a very successful divorce lawyer.'

◄○►

'I've decided to run for president,' he said without even announcing who it was on the other end of the line.

'That's good news,' said Tom, 'but how does Su Ling feel about it?'

'I wouldn't have taken the first step if she hadn't suggested it. And she also wants to play a role in the campaign. She's asked to be responsible for polling and anything to do with figures or statistics.'

'Then that's one of your problems solved,' said Tom. 'Have you appointed a campaign manager?'

'Yes, just after you returned to Yale, I settled on a guy

called Joe Stein. He's fought two campaigns in the past, and will also bring in the Jewish vote,' said Nat.

'There's a Jewish vote in Connecticut?' said Tom.

'In America, there's always a Jewish vote, and on this campus, there are four hundred and eighteen Jews, and I need the support of every one of them.'

'So what's your considered opinion on the future of the Golan Heights?' asked Tom.

'I don't even know where the Golan Heights are,' Nat replied.

'Well you'd better find out by this time tomorrow.'

'I wonder what Elliot's view is on the Golan Heights?'

'That they should always be part of Israel, and not one inch should ever be sacrificed to the Palestinians, would be my bet,' said Tom.

'So what will be his line with the Palestinians?'

'There are probably so few on campus, he won't have an opinion.'

'That would certainly make the decision easy for him.'

'The next thing you'll have to consider is your opening address, and where you're going to deliver it,' said Tom.

'I was thinking of Russell Hall.'

'But that only holds four hundred. Isn't there anything bigger?'

'Yes,' said Nat, 'the Assembly Rooms hold over a thousand, but Elliot made that mistake, because when he gave his opening speech, the place looked half empty. No, I'd rather book the hall and have people sitting on the ledges, hanging from the rafters, even standing on the steps outside unable to get in, which will leave a much better impression with the voters.'

'Then you'd better select a date and reserve the hall immediately, and at the same time get on with putting the rest of your team in place.'

'What else should I be worrying about?' asked Nat.

'The candidate's bread-and-butter speech, and don't forget to talk to every student you come across – you remember the routine, "Hi, my name is Nat Cartwright, and I'm running for president, and I hope I can rely on your support." Then listen to what they have to say, because if they believe you're interested in their views, you have a far better chance of their support.'

'Anything else?'

'Be ruthless in using Su Ling, and ask her to carry out the same routine with every female student, because she's bound to be one of the most admired women on campus after her decision to remain at the university. There aren't many people who turn down Harvard.'

'Don't remind me,' said Nat. 'Is that it, because you seem to have thought of just about everything?'

'Yes, I'll come back and help you for the last ten days of term, but I won't be officially part of your team.'

'Why not?'

'Because Elliot will tell everyone your campaign is being run by an outsider and worse, a millionaire banker's son from Yale. Try not to forget you would have won your last election if it hadn't been for Elliot's deceit, so be prepared for him to come up with something that might derail you.'

'Like what?'

'If I could work that out, I'd be Nixon's chief of staff.'

—◇—

'How do I look?' asked Annie, propped up on the front seat of the car, clutching her seatbelt.

'You look fantastic, honey,' said Fletcher, not even glancing across at her.

'No I don't, I look awful, and it's going to be such an important occasion.'

'It's probably only one of his get-togethers for a dozen or so students.'

'I doubt it,' said Annie. 'It was a hand-written invitation, and even I couldn't miss the words, "do try to make it, there's someone I want you to meet".'

'Well we're about to find out who that is,' said Fletcher as he parked his old Ford behind a limousine surrounded by a dozen Secret Service agents.

'Who can that possibly be?' whispered Annie as he helped her from the car.

'I've no idea, but . . .'

'How nice to see you, Fletcher,' said the professor, who was standing at the front door. 'Good of you to come,' he added. It would have been damn stupid of me not to, Fletcher wanted to reply. 'And you too, Mrs Davenport, of course I remember you well, because for a couple of weeks I sat just two rows behind you in court.'

Annie smiled. 'I was a little slimmer then.'

'But no more beautiful,' said Abrahams. 'May I ask when the baby is due?'

'In ten weeks, sir.'

'Please call me Karl,' said the professor. 'It makes me feel so much younger when an undergraduate from Vassar calls me by my first name. A privilege I might add, that I shall not be extending to your husband for at least another year.' He winked as he put an arm round Annie's shoulder. 'Come on in because there's someone I want you both to meet.'

Fletcher and Annie followed the professor into the living room, where they found a dozen guests already deep in conversation. It looked as if they were the last to arrive.

'Mr Vice-President, I should like to introduce Annie Davenport.'

'Good evening, Mr Vice-President.'

'Hi, Annie,' said Spiro Agnew thrusting out his hand, 'I'm told you've married a very bright guy.'

Karl whispered loudly, 'Try not to forget, Annie, that politicians have a tendency to exaggerate, because they are always hoping for your vote.'

'I know, Karl, my father is a politician.'

'Is that right?' said Agnew.

'No, left, sir,' she replied with a smile, 'he's the majority leader in the Connecticut state senate.'

'Are there no Republicans among us this evening?'

'And this, Mr Vice-President, is Annie's husband, Fletcher Davenport.'

'Hi, Fletcher, is your father also a Democrat?'

'No, sir, he's a card-carrying Republican.'

'Great, so at least we've got two votes wrapped up in your household.'

'No sir, my mother wouldn't allow you across the threshold.'

The vice-president burst out laughing. 'I don't know what that does for your reputation, Karl.'

'I shall continue to remain neutral, Spiro, as I have no politics. However, may I leave Annie with you, sir, as there's someone else I want Fletcher to meet.'

Fletcher was puzzled as he had assumed it was the vice-president to whom the professor must have been referring in his letter, but he dutifully followed his host to join a group of men standing by a blazing fire on the far side of the room.

'Bill, this is Fletcher Davenport, Fletcher, this is Bill Alexander of Alexander . . .'

'. . . Dupont and Bell,' completed Fletcher as he shook hands with the senior partner of one of New York's most prestigious law firms.

'I've been keen to make your acquaintance for some

time, Fletcher,' said Bill Alexander. 'You have managed something I failed to achieve in thirty years.'

'And what was that, sir?'

'Getting Karl to appear as second chair in one of my cases – how did you manage it?'

Both men waited to hear his reply. 'I didn't have a lot of choice, sir. He forced himself on me in a most unprofessional manner, but then you must realize he was desperate. No one has offered him any real work since 1938.' Both men laughed.

'But I'm bound to ask if he was worth his fee, which must have been handsome, remembering you kept that woman out of jail?'

'It certainly was,' said Abrahams, before his young guest could reply. He placed a hand on the bookshelf behind Bill Alexander and removed a hardback copy of *The Trials of Clarence Darrow*. Mr Alexander studied the book. 'I have one myself, of course,' said Alexander.

'And so did I,' said Abrahams. Fletcher looked disappointed. 'But not a signed first edition with a dust jacket in perfect condition. They are indeed a collector's item.'

Fletcher thought about his mother, and her invaluable advice; 'Try to choose something he'll treasure, it doesn't have to cost a lot of money.'

—◇—

Nat went round the circle of eight men and six women who made up his team, asking each of them to give a brief biography for the rest of the group. He then allocated their particular responsibilities in the run-up to the election. Nat could only admire Su Ling's commitment, because following Tom's off-stage advice, she had selected a remarkable cross-section of students, most of whom had obviously wanted Nat to stand for some time.

'OK, let's start with up-dates,' said Nat.

Joe Stein rose from his place. 'Because the candidate has made it clear that no single contribution can exceed one dollar, I have increased the number in the fund-raising team so we can approach as many of the students as possible. That group currently meets once a week, usually on a Monday. It would be helpful if the candidate was able to address them some time.'

'Would next Monday suit you?' asked Nat.

'Fine by me,' said Joe. 'To date, we've raised $307, most of which was collected after your speech at Russell Hall. Because the room was so packed many of them were convinced that they were backing the winner.'

'Thanks, Joe,' said Nat. 'Next: what's the opposition up to? Tim?'

'My name's Tim Ulrich, and my job is to cover the opposition's campaign, and make sure we know what they're up to the whole time. We have at least two people taking notes whenever Elliot opens his mouth. He's made so many promises during the past few days, that if he tried to keep them all, the university would be bankrupt by this time next year.'

'Now how about groups. Ray?'

'Groups fall into three categories, ethnic, religious and club, so I have three deputy leaders to cover each one. There is of course a considerable amount of over-lapping, for example, Italians and Catholics.'

'Sex?' suggested someone.

'No,' said Ray, 'we found sex to be universal, and therefore couldn't group it, but opera, food, fashion are examples of where the over-lapping came for Italians – but we're on top of it. Mario's even offering free coffee to those customers who promise to vote Cartwright.'

'Be careful. Elliot will pick that up as an election expense,' said Joe. 'Don't let's lose on a technicality.'

'Agreed,' said Nat. 'Sports?'

Jack Roberts, the basketball captain, didn't need to introduce himself. 'Track and field is well covered by Nat's personal involvement, especially after his victory in the final cross-country meet against Cornell. I'm covering the baseball team as well as basketball. Elliot already has football sewn up, but the surprise is women's lacrosse – that club has over three hundred members.'

'I've got a girlfriend on the second team,' said Tim.

'I thought you were homosexual?' said Chris. Some of them laughed.

'Who *is* covering the gay vote?' asked Nat.

No one spoke. 'If anyone admits to being openly gay, find a place for them on the team, and no more snide remarks.'

Chris nodded his agreement. 'Sorry, Nat.'

'Finally, polls and statistics, Su Ling.'

'My name is Su Ling. There are 9,628 students registered – 5,517 men, 4,111 women. A very amateur poll conducted on campus last Saturday morning showed Elliot had 611 votes and Nat 541, but don't forget Elliot's had a head start on us, because he's been campaigning for over a year, and his posters are already displayed everywhere. Ours will be up by Friday.'

'And torn down by Saturday.'

'Then we replace them immediately,' said Joe, 'without resorting to the same tactics. Sorry, Su Ling.'

'No, that's fine. Every member of the team must be sure to speak to at least twenty voters a day,' Su Ling said. 'With sixty days still to go, we must try to canvass every student several times before election day. Now this exercise should not be done casually,' she continued. 'On the wall behind you, you will find a board with the name of every student in alphabetical order. On the table below you will see seventeen crayons. I have allocated a colour for each member of the team. Every evening, you will place a tick by the voters that you have spoken to. This is just another way of finding out who are the talkers and who are the workers.'

'But you said there were seventeen crayons on the table,' said Joe, 'when there are only fourteen members of the team?'

'Correct, but there's also one black, one yellow and one red crayon. If the person has said they will be voting for Elliot, you cross him or her out in black, if you're unsure, give them a yellow tick, but if you're confident they will be voting for Nat, then use red. Each evening I'll enter any new data on my computer, and hand you all print-outs first thing the following morning. Any questions?' asked Su Ling.

'Will you marry me?' asked Chris.

Everyone burst out laughing. 'Yes, I will,' said Su Ling. She paused. 'And remember not to believe everything you're told, because Elliot has already asked me, and I said yes to him as well.'

'What about me?' said Nat.

Su Ling smiled. 'Don't forget, I gave you your answer in writing.'

◄◦►

'Goodnight, sir, and thank you for a memorable evening.'

'Goodnight, Fletcher. I'm glad you enjoyed yourself.'

'We certainly did,' said Annie. 'It was fascinating to meet the vice-president. I'll be able to tease my father for weeks,' she added, as Fletcher helped her into the car.

Before he had pulled the door closed on his side, Fletcher said, 'Annie, you were fantastic.'

'I was only trying to survive,' said Annie. 'I hadn't expected Karl to place me between the vice-president and

Mr Alexander during dinner. I even wondered if it was a mistake.'

'The professor doesn't make that sort of mistake,' said Fletcher. 'I suspect that Bill Alexander requested it.'

'But why would he do that?' asked Annie.

'Because he's the senior partner of an old-fashioned, traditional firm, so he'll figure that he can learn a great deal about me if he gets to know my wife; if you're invited to join Alexander Dupont and Bell, it's nothing short of marriage.'

'Then let's hope I didn't hold up a proposal.'

'Far from it. What you did was to make sure I reach the courting stage. Don't imagine that it was coincidental that Mrs Alexander came and sat next to you when coffee was being served in the drawing room.'

Annie gave out a slight moan, and Fletcher looked anxiously across. 'Oh, my God,' she said, 'the contractions have begun.'

'But you've still got another ten weeks,' said Fletcher. 'Just relax and I'll have you back home and tucked up in no time.'

Annie groaned again, a little louder. 'Don't bother with going home,' she said, 'get me to a hospital.'

Speeding across Westville, Fletcher checked the names on the street corners and tried to work out which would be the best route to Yale-New Haven Hospital, when he spotted a taxi stand on the far side of the road. He swung the car sharply across and pulled up alongside the front cab. He wound down the window, and shouted, 'My wife's gone into labour, which is the quickest route to Yale-New Haven?'

'Follow me,' shouted the cab driver and shot off in front of them.

Fletcher tried to keep up with the taxi as he nipped

in and out of the traffic, with a palm pressed down on the horn, while flashing his lights, as he took a route Fletcher didn't even know existed. Annie clutched her stomach, as the groans became louder and louder.

'Don't worry my darling, we're nearly there,' he said, as he jumped another red light to make sure he didn't lose contact with the cab.

When the two cars finally reached the hospital, Fletcher was surprised to see a doctor and nurse standing next to a gurney by an open door, obviously expecting them. As the cab driver jumped out, he gave the nurse a thumbs-up sign, and Fletcher guessed that he must have asked his dispatcher to call ahead; he hoped he had enough money on him to pay the fare, not to mention a large tip for the man's initiative.

Fletcher jumped out of the car, and ran round to help Annie, but the cab driver beat him to it. They took an elbow each and helped to lift her out of the car and gently on to the gurney. The nurse began to unbutton Annie's dress even before she was wheeled through the open door. Fletcher removed his wallet, turned to the taxi driver and said, 'Thank you, you couldn't have been more helpful. How much do I owe you?'

'Not a cent, it's on me,' the taxi driver replied.

'But . . .' began Fletcher

'If I told my wife I'd charged you, she'd kill me. Good luck,' he shouted and without another word walked back to his cab.

'Thank you,' Fletcher repeated before he dashed into the hospital. He quickly caught up with his wife and took her hand. 'It's going to be just fine, honey,' he assured her.

The orderly asked Annie a series of questions, all of which received a monosyllabic yes in reply. His enquiries complete, he rang through to theatre to alert Dr Redpath and the waiting team that they were less than a minute away. The slow, vast elevator lurched to a halt on the fifth floor. Annie was wheeled quickly down the corridor, Fletcher trotting by her side, clinging on to her outstretched hand. He could see two nurses in the distance holding open double doors so that the gurney would never lose its momentum.

Annie continued to hold on to Fletcher's hand as she was lifted on to the operating table. Three more people came bursting into the room, their faces hidden behind masks. The first checked the instruments laid out on the table, the second prepared an oxygen mask, while the third tried to ask Annie more questions, although she was now screaming with pain. Fletcher never let go of his wife's hand, until an older man came through the door. He pulled on a pair of surgical gloves and said, 'Are we all ready?' even before he'd had a chance to check the patient.

'Yes, Dr Redpath,' replied the nurse.

'Good,' he said and, turning to Fletcher, he added, 'I'm afraid I'll have to ask you to leave Mr Davenport. We'll call for you just as soon as the baby has been delivered.'

Fletcher kissed his wife on the forehead. 'I'm so proud of you,' he whispered.

22

NAT WOKE AT FIVE on the day of the election, only to discover that Su Ling was already in the shower. He checked the schedule on the bedside table. Full team meeting at seven, followed by an hour and a half outside the dining hall to meet and greet voters as they went in and out of breakfast.

'Come and join me,' shouted Su Ling, 'we haven't any time to waste.' She was right, because they arrived at the team meeting only moments before the clock on the bell tower struck seven times. Every other member of the team was already present, and Tom, who had come over from Yale for the day, was passing on the experience of his own recent election. Su Ling and Nat took the two empty seats each side of their unofficial chief of staff, who continued the briefing as if they weren't there.

'No one stops, even to draw breath, until one minute past six when the last vote will have been cast. Now I suggest that the candidate and Su Ling are outside the dining hall between seven thirty and eight thirty while the rest of you go into breakfast.'

'We're expected to go on eating that rubbish for an hour?' said Joe.

'No, I don't want you to eat anything, Joe, I need you moving from table to table, never two of you at the same table, and remember that Elliot's team will probably be carrying out exactly the same exercise, so don't waste any time asking for their vote. OK, let's go.'

Fourteen people ran out of the room and across the lawn, disappearing through the swing doors and into the dining hall, leaving Nat and Su Ling to hang around near the entrance.

'Hi, I'm Nat Cartwright, and I'm running for student president, and I hope you'll be able to support me in today's election.'

Two sleepy-eyed students said, 'Fine, man, you've already wrapped up the gay vote.'

'Hi, I'm Nat Cartwright, and I'm running for student president, and I hope you'll be able to support me . . .'

'Yes, I know who you are, but how can you possibly understand what it's like to survive on a student loan, when you earn an extra four hundred dollars a month?' came back the sharp reply.

'Hi, I'm Nat Cartwright, I'm running for student president and . . .'

'I won't be voting for either of you,' said another student, as he pushed through the swing doors.

'Hi, I'm Nat Cartwright, and I'm running for . . .'

'Sorry, just visiting from another campus, so I don't have a vote.'

'Hi, I'm Nat Cartwright and I'm . . .'

'Good luck, but I'm only voting for you because of your girlfriend, I think she's terrific.'

'Hi, I'm Nat Cartwright . . .'

'And I'm a member of Ralph Elliot's team, and we're going to kick your butt.'

'Hi, I'm Nat . . .'

Nine hours later, Nat could only wonder how many times he had delivered that line, and how many hands he'd shaken. All he knew for certain was that he had lost his voice and was sure his fingers would fall off. At one minute past six, he turned to Tom and said, 'Hi, I'm Nat Cartwright and . . .'

'Forget it,' said Tom with a laugh, 'I'm the president of Yale, and all I know is if it wasn't for Ralph Elliot you'd have my job.'

'What have you planned for me now,' asked Nat, 'because my schedule ends at six, so I don't have a clue what to do next.'

'Typical of every candidate,' said Tom, 'but I thought the three of us could have a relaxed dinner at Mario's.'

'What about the rest of the team?' asked Su Ling.

'Joe, Chris, Sue and Tim are acting as observers at the count over in the Commons, while the others are getting a well-earned rest. As the count begins at seven and should take at least a couple of hours, I've suggested that everybody be there by eight thirty.'

'Sounds good to me,' said Nat. 'I could eat a horse.'

Mario guided the three of them to their table in the corner, and kept addressing Nat as Mr President. As the three of them sipped their drinks and tried to relax, Mario reappeared with a large bowl of spaghetti which he covered in a bolognese sauce, before sprinkling parmesan cheese all over it. However many times Nat stuck his fork in the heap of pasta, it never seemed to diminish. Tom noticed that his friend was becoming more and more nervous and eating less and less.

'I wonder what Elliot is up to right now?' asked Su Ling.

'He'll be at McDonald's along with the rest of his wretched gang, eating burgers and fries and pretending to enjoy them,' said Tom as he sipped a glass of house wine.

'Well, at least there are no more dirty tricks he can play now,' said Nat.

'I wouldn't be so sure of that,' said Su Ling, just as Joe Stein came rushing through the door.

'What can Joe want?' asked Tom as he stood and

waved at him. Nat smiled as his chief of staff rushed over to their table, but Joe didn't return his smile.

'We've got a problem,' said Joe. 'You'd better come over to the Commons immediately.'

—◦—

Fletcher began pacing up and down the corridor, much in the same way as his father had done over twenty years before, an evening that had been described to him by Miss Nichol on many occasions. It was like the replaying of an old black-and-white movie, always with the same happy ending. Fletcher found he was never more than a few paces from the door of the operating room as he waited for someone – anyone – to come out.

At last the rubber doors swung open and a nurse rushed out, but she hurried quickly past Fletcher without saying a word. It was several more minutes before Dr Redpath finally emerged. He removed his face mask, but his lips weren't smiling. 'They're just settling your wife into her room,' he said. 'She's fine, exhausted, but fine. You should be able to see her in a few moments.'

'What about the baby?'

'Your son has been transferred to the special care nursery. Let me show you,' he said, touching Fletcher's elbow and guiding him along the corridor, stopping at a large plate-glass window. On the other side were three incubators. Two of them were already occupied. He watched as his son was placed gently in the third. A scrawny, helpless little thing, red and wrinkled. The nurse was inserting a rubber tube down his nose. She then attached a sensor to his chest and plugged the lead into a monitor. Her final task was to place a tiny band around the baby's left wrist, displaying the name Davenport. The screen began to flicker immediately, but even with his slight knowledge of medicine, Fletcher could see that his son's heartbeat was weak. He looked anxiously across at Dr Redpath.

'What are his chances?'

'He's ten weeks premature, but if we can get him through the night, he'll have a good chance of survival.'

'What are his chances?' Fletcher pressed.

'There are no rules, no percentages, no laid-down laws. Every child is unique, your son included,' the doctor added as a nurse joined them.

'You can see your wife now, Mr Davenport,' she said, 'if you'd like to come with me.'

Fletcher thanked Dr Redpath and followed the nurse down one flight of stairs to the floor below, where he was taken to his wife's bedside. Annie was propped up with several pillows behind her.

'How's our son?' were her opening words.

'He looks terrific, Mrs Davenport, and he's lucky to begin his life with such an amazing mother.'

'They won't let me see him,' said Annie quietly, 'and I so much want to hold him in my arms.'

'They've put him in an incubator for the time being,' Fletcher said gently, 'but he has a nurse with him the whole time.'

'It seems years ago that we were having dinner with Professor Abrahams.'

'Yes, it's been quite a night,' said Fletcher, 'and a double triumph for you. You wowed the senior partner of a firm I want to join, and then produced a son, all on the same evening. What next?'

'That all seems so unimportant now we have a child to take care of.' She paused. 'Harry Robert Davenport.'

'It has a nice ring about it,' said Fletcher, 'and both our fathers will be delighted.'

'What shall we call him,' asked Annie, 'Harry or Robert?'

'I know what I'm going to call him,' said Fletcher as the nurse returned to the room.

'I think you should try and get some sleep, Mrs Davenport, it's been an exhausting time for you.'

'I agree,' said Fletcher. He removed several pillows from behind his wife's head, as she lowered herself slowly down the bed. Annie smiled and rested her head on the remaining pillow as her husband kissed her. As Fletcher left, the nurse switched off the light.

Fletcher raced back up the stairs and along the corridor to check if his son's heartbeat was any stronger. He stared through the plate glass window at the monitor, willing it to flicker a little higher, and managed to convince himself that it had. Fletcher kept his nose pressed up against the window. 'Keep fighting, Harry,' he said, and then began counting the heartbeats per minute. Suddenly he felt exhausted. 'Hang in there, you're going to make it.'

He took a couple of paces backwards and collapsed into a chair on the other side of the corridor. Within minutes, he had fallen into a deep sleep.

Fletcher woke with a start when he felt a hand gently touch his shoulder. His tired eyes blinked open; he had no idea how long he'd been asleep. The first thing he saw was a nurse, her face solemn. Dr Redpath stood a pace behind her. He didn't need to be told that Harry Robert Davenport was no longer alive.

◄◦►

'So what's the problem?' asked Nat as they ran towards the Commons where the vote was being counted.

'We were leading comfortably until a few minutes ago,' said Joe, already out of breath from his trip there and back and unable to keep up with what Nat would have described as a jog. He slowed to a fast walk. 'And then suddenly two new ballot boxes appeared, stuffed with votes – and nearly ninety per cent of them in favour of Elliot,' he added as they reached the bottom step.

Nat and Tom didn't wait for Joe as they bounded up the steps and through the swing doors. The first person they saw was Ralph Elliot – a smug look on his face. Nat turned his attention to Tom, who was already being briefed by Sue and Chris. He quickly joined them.

'We were leading by just over four hundred votes,' said Chris, 'and we assumed it was all over, when two new boxes appeared out of nowhere.'

'What do you mean, out of nowhere?' asked Tom.

'Well, they were discovered under a table, but hadn't been included among those that were registered in the original count. In those two boxes,' Chris checked his clipboard, 'Elliot polled 319, to Nat's 48, and 322 to Nat's 41, which reversed the original outcome and put him in the lead by a handful of votes.'

'Give me a few examples of figures from some of the other boxes,' said Su Ling.

'They were all fairly consistent,' said Chris, returning to his list. 'The most extreme was 209 for Nat, against 176 for Elliot. In fact, Elliot only polled higher in one box, 201 to 196.'

'The votes in the last two boxes,' said Su Ling, 'are not statistically possible, when you compare them with the other ten that have already been counted. Someone must have literally stuffed those boxes with enough ballot papers to reverse the original decision.'

'But how could they have managed that?' asked Tom.

'It would be easy enough if you could get your hands on any unused ballots,' said Su Ling.

'And that wouldn't have been too difficult,' said Joe.

'How can you be so sure?' asked Nat.

'Because, when I voted in my dorm during the lunch

hour, there was only one teller on duty, and she was writing an essay. I could have removed a handful of ballots without her even noticing.'

'But that doesn't explain the sudden appearance of two missing boxes,' said Tom.

'You don't need a PhD to work out that one,' chipped in Chris, 'because once the poll has closed, all they had to do was hold back two of the boxes, and then stuff them with ballots.'

'But we have no way of proving that,' said Nat.

'The statistics prove it,' said Su Ling. 'They never lie, though I admit we don't have any first-hand proof.'

'So what are we going to do about it?' asked Joe, as he stared across at Elliot, the same self-satisfied look still in place.

'There's not much we can do except pass on our observations to Chester Davies. After all, he is the chief elections officer.'

'OK, Joe, why don't you do that, and we'll wait to see what he has to say.'

Joe left them to make his submission to the dean of students. They watched as the expression on the elderly academic's face became grimmer and grimmer. Once Joe had made his point, the dean immediately called for Elliot's chief of staff, who did nothing more than shrug his shoulders and point out that every ballot was valid.

Nat watched apprehensively as Mr Davies questioned both men, and saw Joe nod his agreement, before they broke away to join their respective teams.

'The dean is calling an immediate meeting of the elections committee in his office, and he will report back after they've discussed the matter, which should be in about thirty minutes.'

Su Ling took Nat's hand. 'Mr Davies is a good and just man,' she said, 'he'll come to the right conclusion.'

'He may well come to the right conclusion,' said Nat, 'but in the end he can only follow the election rules whatever his personal reservations.'

'I agree,' said a voice from behind them. Nat swung round to see Elliot grinning at him. 'They won't have to look in the rule book to discover that the person with the most votes is the winner,' Elliot added with disdain.

'Unless they come across something about one person, one vote,' said Nat.

'Are you accusing me of cheating?' Elliot snapped back, as a group of his supporters drifted over and stood behind him.

'Well, let's put it this way. If you win this election, you can apply for a job in Chicago as a teller in Cook County, because Mayor Daly has nothing to teach you.'

Elliot took a step forward and raised his fist just as the dean reentered the room, a single sheet of paper in his hand. He made his way back up onto the stage.

'You just escaped a hiding,' whispered Elliot.

'And I suspect you're just about to get one,' replied Nat, as they both turned to face the stage.

The chattering in the hall died down as Mr Davies adjusted the height of the microphone and faced those who had hung around to hear the result. He read slowly from a prepared script.

'In the election for president of the student senate, it has been brought to my attention that two ballot boxes were discovered some time after the count had been concluded. When they were opened, the outcome of those votes varied considerably from all the other boxes. Therefore as delegated officials, we were left with no choice but to refer to the rule book on elections. Search as we might, we were unable to find any mention of missing boxes, or what action to take should there be a disproportionate ratio of votes found in any one box.'

'Because no one has ever cheated in the past,' shouted Joe from the back of the hall.

'And no one did this time,' came back the immediate reply, 'you're just bad losers.'

'How many more boxes have you got hidden away just in case . . .?'

'We don't need any more.'

'Quiet,' said the dean. 'These outbursts do not reflect well on either side.' He waited for silence before he continued to read from his script. 'We are, however, mindful of our responsibility as officers, and have come to the conclusion that the result of the election must stand.' Elliot's supporters leapt in the air and cheered.

Elliot turned to Nat and said, 'I think you'll find it's you who just got the hiding.'

'It's not over yet,' said Nat, his eyes still fixed on Mr Davies.

It was some time before the dean could continue, as few present realized that he had not yet completed his statement.

'As there have been several irregularities in this election, one of which in our opinion remains unresolved, I have therefore decided that under rule 7B of the Student Senate Charter, the defeated candidate should be given the opportunity to appeal. Should he do so, the committee will be faced with three choices.' He opened the rule book and read: 'a) to confirm the original result, b) to reverse the original result, or c) to call for a new election, which would be held during the first week of the following term. We therefore propose to give Mr Cartwright twenty-four hours to appeal.'

'We won't need twenty-four hours,' called out Joe. 'We appeal.'

'I shall need that in writing from the candidate,' said the Dean.

Tom glanced across at Nat, who was looking down at Su Ling.

'Do you remember what we agreed if I didn't win?'

BOOK THREE

CHRONICLES

23

NAT TURNED AND watched Su Ling walk slowly towards him and recalled the day they had first met. He had chased her down a hill, and when she turned on that occasion, she'd taken his breath away.

'Do you have any idea how lucky you are?' whispered Tom.

'Could you please concentrate on your job. Now, where's the ring?'

'The ring, what ring?' Nat turned and stared at his best man. 'Hell, I knew there was something I was meant to bring with me,' Tom whispered frantically. 'Can you hold things up for a moment while I go back to the house and look for it?'

'Do you want me to strangle you?' said Nat, grinning.

'Yes please,' said Tom, gazing at Su Ling as she advanced towards them. 'Let her be my last memory of this world.'

Nat turned his attention to his bride, and she gave him that smile that he remembered when she'd stood at the entrance to the café on their first date. She stepped up and took her place beside him, head slightly bowed as they waited for the priest to begin the service. Nat thought about the decision they had made the day after the election, and knew he would never regret it. Why should he hold up Su Ling's career on the off-chance of winning the presidency? The idea of rerunning the ballot during the first week of the following term, and having to ask Su Ling to hang around for another year if he failed, left him in no doubt what he should do. The priest turned to the congregation. 'Dearly beloved . . .'

When Su Ling had explained to Professor Mullden that she was getting married, and her future husband was at the University of Connecticut, they immediately offered him the chance to complete his undergraduate degree at Harvard. They already knew of Nat's record in Vietnam and his success on the cross-country team, but it was his grades that tipped the balance. They remained puzzled as to why he hadn't taken up his place at Yale because it was clear to the admissions office that they would not be carrying Su Ling's husband.

'Do you take this woman to be your lawful wedded wife?'

Nat wanted to shout 'I do.' 'I do,' he said quietly.

'Do you take this man to be your lawful wedded husband?'

'I do,' said Su Ling, head bowed.

'You may kiss the bride,' said the priest.

'I think that means me,' said Tom, taking a pace forward. Nat took Su Ling in his arms and kissed her as he lifted his left leg sharply and kicked Tom in the shins.

'So that's what I get for all the sacrifices I've made over the years? Well, at least it's my turn now.' Nat swung round and took Tom in his arms and hugged him, while the congregation burst out laughing.

Tom was right, thought Nat. He hadn't even remonstrated with him when he refused to appeal to the elections committee, although Nat knew Tom believed he would have been victorious in a re-run contest. And the following morning Mr Russell had phoned and offered Nat the use of their home for the reception. How could he ever begin to repay them?

'Be warned,' said Tom, 'Dad will expect you to join

238

him at the bank as a trainee once you've graduated from Harvard Business School.'

'That may turn out to be the best offer I get,' said Nat.

The bride and groom turned to face their family and friends. Susan made no attempt to hide her tears, while Michael beamed with pride. Su Ling's mother stepped forward and took a photo of the two of them in their first moment as man and wife.

Nat didn't recall much about the reception, other than feeling that Mr and Mrs Russell couldn't have done any more had he been their own son. He moved from table to table, especially thanking those who had travelled a long distance. It was only when he heard the sound of silver against crystal that he checked to make sure his speech was still in his inside pocket.

Nat quickly slipped into his place at the top table just as Tom rose to speak. The best man opened by explaining why the reception was being held in his home. 'Don't forget that I proposed to Su Ling long before the bride-groom did, although inexplicably, on this occasion she was willing to settle for second best.' Nat smiled across at Tom's aunt Abigail from Boston, as the guests applauded.

Nat sometimes wondered if Tom's jokes about his love for Su Ling didn't betray an underlying truth about his real feelings. He looked up at his best man, recalling, because he was late – thank you, mother – how he had come to sit next to the tearful little boy at the end of the row on their first day at Taft. He thought how lucky he was to be blessed with such a friend, and hoped it would not be long before he was carrying out the same duty for him.

Tom received a warm reception when he sat down to make way for the bridegroom.

Nat began his speech by thanking Mr and Mrs Russell

for their generosity in allowing them the use of their beautiful home for the reception. He thanked his mother for her wisdom and his father for his looks, which brought applause and laughter. 'But most of all I thank Su Ling, for going down the wrong path, and my parents for an upbringing that made me follow her, to warn her that she was making a mistake.'

'She made a far bigger mistake chasing you back up the hill,' said Tom.

Nat waited for the laughter to die down, before he said, 'I fell in love with Su Ling the moment I saw her, a feeling that was clearly not reciprocated, but then, as I've already explained, I'm blessed with my father's looks. And so let me end by inviting you all to our golden wedding anniversary on July 11, 2024.' He paused. 'Only wimps and those who dare to die in between will be excused attendance.' He raised his glass. 'To my wife, Su Ling.'

When Su Ling disappeared upstairs to change, Tom finally asked Nat where they were going on honeymoon.

'Korea,' whispered Nat. 'We're planning to find the village where Su Ling was born, and see if we can trace any other members of her family. But don't tell Su Ling's mother – we want to surprise her when we return.'

Three hundred guests surged out to join them in the driveway, and applauded as the car carrying the bride and groom disappeared on its journey to the airport.

'I wonder where they're spending their honeymoon,' said Su Ling's mother.

'I have no idea,' Tom replied.

◄◦►

Fletcher held Annie in his arms. A month had passed since the funeral of Harry Robert, and she was still blaming herself.

'But that's just not fair,' said Fletcher. 'If anyone's to blame, it must be me. Look at the pressure Joanna was under when she gave birth, and it made absolutely no difference to her.' But Annie couldn't be consoled. The doctor told him the quickest way to solve the problem, and Fletcher happily acquiesced.

As each day passed, Annie grew a little stronger, but her first interest remained supporting her husband in his determination to be top of his year. 'You owe it to Karl Abrahams,' she reminded him. 'He's invested a lot in you, and there is only one way you can repay him.'

Annie inspired her husband to work night and day during his summer vacation before he returned for his final year. She became his assistant and researcher while remaining his lover and friend. And she only ignored his advice when he pressed her to consider going on to graduate school herself.

'No,' said Annie, 'I want to be your wife and God willing in time . . .'

---◇---

Once he'd returned to Yale, Fletcher accepted it would not be too long before he would have to start the meat run. Although several firms had already invited him for an interview, and one or two had even offered him jobs, Fletcher didn't want to work out of Dallas or Denver, Phoenix or Pittsburgh. But as the weeks passed, and he heard nothing from Alexander Dupont & Bell, his hopes began to fade and he concluded that if he still hoped to be invited to join one of the big firms it would require a full round of interviews.

Jimmy had already sent out over fifty letters and to date had only received three replies; not one of them had offered him a job. He would have settled for Dallas or Denver, Phoenix or Pittsburgh if it hadn't been for

Joanna. Annie and Fletcher agreed on the cities they would be happy to live in, and then she carried out some research on the leading firms in those states. Together they composed a letter which was duplicated fifty-four times, and then dispatched on the first day of term.

When Fletcher returned to college later that morning, he found a letter in his mailbox.

'That was quick,' said Annie, 'we only posted them an hour ago.'

Fletcher laughed until he saw the postmark on the letter. He tore it open. The simple black-embossed heading announced Alexander Dupont & Bell. Of course, the distinguished New York firm always began interviewing candidates during March, so why should it be any different for Fletcher Davenport?

Fletcher didn't stop working during those long winter months leading up to the interview, but he still had every reason to feel apprehensive when he finally set out on the journey to New York. As soon as he stepped off the train at Grand Central Station, Fletcher was intoxicated by the babble of a hundred tongues, and feet that moved more swiftly than he'd experienced in any other city. He spent the cab ride to 54th Street peering out of an open window, taking in a smell that no other city produces.

The cab drew up outside a seventy-two-floor glass skyscraper, and Fletcher knew straight away that he didn't want to work anywhere else. He hung around on the ground floor for a few minutes, not wishing to be stuck in a waiting room with several other candidates. When he finally stepped out of the elevator on the thirty-sixth floor, the receptionist ticked off his name. She then handed him a sheet of paper, which listed a schedule of interviews that would take the rest of the day.

His first meeting was with the senior partner, Bill Alexander, which Fletcher felt went well, although Alexander didn't exude the same warmth as he had at Karl Abrahams' party. However, he did ask after Annie, expressing the hope that she had fully recovered from the sad loss of Harry. It also became clear during the meeting that Fletcher was not the only person who was being interviewed – six upside down names appeared on a list facing Mr Alexander.

Fletcher then spent an hour with three other partners who specialized in his chosen field, criminal law. When the last interview ended, he was invited to join the rest of the board for lunch. It was the first time he came into contact with the other five applicants, and the lunch conversation left him in no doubt what he was up against. He could only wonder how many days the firm had put aside for interviews with other would-be applicants.

What he couldn't know was that Alexander Dupont & Bell had carried out a rigorous sifting process months before any of the candidates had been invited for interview, and he had made the final six, on recommendation and reputation. He also didn't realize that only one, perhaps two, would be offered a position with the firm. As with a good wine, there were even years when no one was selected, simply because it just wasn't a vintage crop.

More interviews followed in the afternoon, by which time Fletcher was convinced he wouldn't make it, and would soon have to begin the long trek round those firms who had replied to his letter and offered him an interview.

'They'll let me know by the end of the month if I've made it to the next round,' he told Annie, who was waiting for him at the station, 'but don't stop sending the letters, although I confess I no longer want to work anywhere but New York.'

Annie continued to question Fletcher on the way home, wanting to know every detail of what had taken place. She was touched that Bill Alexander had remembered her;

more so that he had even taken the trouble to find out the name of their son.

'Perhaps you should have told him,' said Annie as she brought the car to a halt outside their home.

'Told him what?' asked Fletcher

'That I'm pregnant again.'

—◇—

Nat loved the hustle and bustle of Seoul, a city determined to put all memories of war behind it. Skyscrapers loomed on every corner, as the old and new tried to live in harmony. Nat was impressed by the potential of such a well-educated, intelligent workforce who survived on wages a quarter of what would be acceptable back home. Su Ling couldn't help noticing the subservient role women still played in Korean society and silently thanked her mother for having the courage and foresight to set out for America.

Nat rented a car so that they could move from village to village as and when it suited them. Once they'd driven a few miles out of the capital, the first thing that struck them both was how quickly the way of life changed. By the time they had travelled a hundred miles, they had also travelled back a hundred years. The modern skyscrapers were quickly replaced by little wooden shacks, and the hustle and bustle by a slower, more considered pace.

Although Su Ling's mother had rarely talked about her upbringing in Korea, Su Ling knew the village where she had been born, and her family name. She also knew that two of her uncles had been killed in the war, so that when they arrived in Kaping with its population of 7,303 – according to the guide book – she wasn't all that hopeful of being able to find anyone who would remember her mother.

Su Ling Cartwright began her quest at the town hall,

where a register was kept of all the local citizens. It didn't help that, of the 7,000 inhabitants, over a thousand shared Su Ling's mother's maiden name of Peng. However, the lady at reception also exhibited that name on the plaque on her desk. She told Su Ling that her great-aunt, who was now over ninety, claimed to know every branch of the family, and if she would like to meet her, that could be arranged. Su Ling nodded her agreement, and was asked to return later that day.

She called back in the afternoon, to be told that Ku Sei Peng would be happy to take tea with her the following day. The receptionist apologized before politely explaining that Su Ling's American husband would not be welcome.

Su Ling returned to their little hotel the following night, bearing a piece of paper and a happy smile. 'We've travelled all this way out here, only to be told to go back to Seoul,' she said.

'How come?' asked Nat.

'It's simple. Ku Sei Peng remembers my mother leaving the village to seek work in the capital, but she never returned. But her younger sister, Kai Pai Peng, still lives in Seoul and Ku Sei has given me her last known address.'

'So it's back to the capital,' said Nat, who phoned down to reception to warn them they would be checking out immediately. They arrived back in Seoul just before midnight.

'I think it might be wise if I were to visit her on my own,' said Su Ling over breakfast the following morning, 'as she may not be willing to say a great deal once she discovers I'm married to an American.'

'Suits me,' said Nat. 'I was hoping to visit the market on the other side of the city as I'm searching for something in particular.'

'What?' asked Su Ling,

'Wait and see,' teased Nat.

Nat took a taxi to the Kiray district, and spent the day roaming around one of the biggest open markets in the world – row upon row of laden stalls crammed with everything from Rolex watches to cultured pearls, from Gucci bags to Chanel perfume, from Cartier bracelets to Tiffany hearts. He avoided the cries of 'Over here, American, please to look at my goods, much cheaper', as he could never be sure what, if anything, was the real thing.

By the time he arrived back at the hotel that evening, Nat was exhausted and laden down with six shopping bags, mostly full of presents for his wife. He took the elevator to the third floor, and as he pushed open the door to their room, he hoped to find that Su Ling had returned from visiting her great aunt. As he closed the door, he thought he heard sobbing. He stood still. The unmistakable sound was coming from the bedroom.

Nat dropped the bags on the floor, walked across the room and pushed open the bedroom door. Su Ling was curled up on the bed, like an unsprung coil, weeping. He slipped off his shoes and jacket and climbed on to the bed beside her and took her in his arms.

'What is it, little flower?' he said, caressing her gently.

She didn't reply. Nat held her close, aware that she would tell him in her own time.

When it grew dark and the neon streetlights began to flicker on, Nat drew the curtains. He then sat beside her and took her hand.

'I will always love you,' said Su Ling, not looking directly at him.

'And I'll always love you,' said Nat, taking her back into his arms.

'Do you remember the night of our marriage, we

agreed on no secrets, so I must now tell you what I discovered this afternoon.'

Nat had never seen a face so sad. 'Nothing you found out could make me love you less,' he said, trying to reassure her.

Su Ling pulled her husband towards her while lowering her head on to his chest, as if she didn't want their eyes to meet. 'I kept my appointment with my great aunt this morning,' she began. 'She remembered my mother well, and explained to me why she had left the village to join her in Seoul.' As she clung on to Nat, Su Ling repeated everything Kai Pai had told her. When she had finished her story, she eased away and looked up at her husband for the first time.

'Can you still love me now you know the truth?' she asked.

'I didn't believe it was possible to love you any more, and I can only imagine what courage it must have taken to share this news with me.' He paused. 'It will only strengthen a bond that now no one will ever be able to break.'

⟨o⟩

'I don't think it would be wise for me to go with you,' said Annie.

'But you're my lucky mascot, and . . .'

'. . . and Dr Redpath says it wouldn't be wise.' Fletcher reluctantly accepted that he would have to make the journey to New York alone. Annie was in her seventh month of pregnancy, and although there had been no complications, he never argued with the doctor.

Fletcher had been delighted to be invited back for a second interview with Alexander Dupont & Bell, and wondered how many of the other candidates had been short-listed. He had a feeling Karl Abrahams knew, though the professor wasn't sharing any confidences.

When the train pulled into Penn Station, Fletcher took a taxi to 54th Street, arriving outside the vast entrance hall twenty minutes early. He had been told that on one occasion a candidate had arrived three minutes late, so they didn't bother to interview him.

He took the elevator to the thirty-sixth floor and was directed by the receptionist to a spacious room that was almost as smart as the senior partner's office. Fletcher sat alone and wondered if that was a good sign, until a second candidate joined him a few minutes before nine. He smiled at Fletcher.

'Logan Fitzgerald,' he said, his hand outstretched. 'I heard you address the freshman debate at Yale. Your speech on Vietnam was brilliant, although I didn't agree with a word you said.'

'You were at Yale?'

'No, I was visiting my brother. I went to Princeton, and I guess we both know why we're here.'

'How many others are there, do you imagine?' asked Fletcher.

'Looking at the clock, I would suggest we're the last two. So all I can say is good luck.'

'I am sure you mean that sincerely,' said Fletcher with a grin.

The door opened and a woman who Fletcher remembered as Mr Alexander's secretary addressed them. 'Gentlemen, if you'll come this way,' she said.

'Thank you, Mrs Townsend,' said Fletcher, whose father had once told him never to forget a secretary's name – after all, they spend more time with the boss than his wife ever does. The two candidates followed her out of the room, and Fletcher wondered if Logan could possibly be as nervous as he was. On either side of the long carpeted corridor the names of the partners were lettered in gold beside each oak-panelled door they passed. William Alexander's was the last before the conference room.

Mrs Townsend knocked gently on the door, opened it and stood to one side as twenty-five men and three women rose from their places and began to applaud.

'Please be seated,' said Bill Alexander, once the applause had died down. 'May I be the first to congratulate you both on being offered the opportunity to join Alexander Dupont and Bell, but be warned, the next time you'll hear such approbation from your colleagues will be when you're invited to become a partner, and that won't be for at least seven years. During the morning you will have meetings with different members of the executive committee who between them should be able to answer any of your questions. Fletcher, you have been assigned to Matthew Cunliffe, who heads up our criminal office, while you, Logan, will report directly to Graham Simpson in mergers and acquisitions. At twelve thirty, you will both return and join the partners for lunch.'

The midday meal turned out to be a friendly affair after the gruelling process of interviews; the partners stopped behaving like Mr Hyde and reverted to being Dr Jekyll. Roles they played every day with clients and adversaries.

'They tell me that you are both going to be top of your respective classes,' said Bill Alexander, after the main course was served – there had been no first course or drink supplied, other than bottled water. 'And I can only hope so, because I haven't yet decided which offices to assign you to.'

'And should one of us flunk?' asked Fletcher nervously.

'Then you will spend your first year in the mail room,

delivering briefs to other law firms.' Mr Alexander paused. 'On foot.' No one laughed, and Fletcher couldn't be sure if he meant it. The senior partner was about to continue when there was a knock on the door and his secretary reappeared.

'There's a call for you on line three, Mr Alexander.'

'I said no interruptions, Mrs Townsend.'

'It's an emergency, sir.'

Bill Alexander picked up the boardroom phone, the scowl on his face turned to a smile as he listened intently. 'I'll let him know,' he said and put the phone down.

'Let me be the first to congratulate you, Fletcher,' said the senior partner. Fletcher was puzzled because he knew final grades wouldn't be published for at least another week. 'You're the proud father of a little girl. Mother and daughter are doing just fine. I knew the moment I met that girl she was just the kind of woman we appreciate at Alexander Dupont and Bell.'

24

'Lucy.'

'But what about Ruth or Martha?'

'We can give her all three names,' said Fletcher, 'which will make both our mothers happy, but we'll call her Lucy.' He smiled as he gently placed his daughter back in her crib.

'And have you thought about where we're going to live?' asked Annie. 'I don't want Lucy brought up in New York.'

'I agree,' said Fletcher, as he tickled his daughter under the chin, 'I've been talking to Matt Cunliffe and he told me he faced the same problem when he joined the firm.'

'So what does Matt recommend?'

'He suggested three or four small towns in New Jersey that are less than an hour away by train from Grand Central Station. So I thought we might drive up there next Friday and spend a long weekend seeing if there's any particular area we like.'

'I suppose we'll have to rent a place to begin with,' said Annie, 'until we've saved enough to buy something of our own.'

'It seems not, because the firm would prefer us to purchase our own property.'

'It's all very well for the firm to prefer something, but what if we simply can't afford it?'

'That doesn't seem to pose a problem either,' said

Fletcher, 'because Alexander Dupont and Bell will cover the cost with an interest-free loan.'

'That's very generous of them,' said Annie, 'but if I know Bill Alexander, there has to be an ulterior motive.'

'There sure is,' said Fletcher. 'It ties you into the firm, and Alexander Dupont and Bell are very proud of having the smallest turnover of employees of any legal practice in New York. It's becoming obvious to me that once they've gone to all the trouble of selecting you and training you in their ways, they then make damn sure they don't lose you to a rival firm.'

'Sounds to me like a shotgun marriage,' said Annie. She paused. 'Have you ever mentioned your political ambitions to Mr Alexander?'

'No, I wouldn't have passed first base if I had, and in any case, who knows how I'll feel in two or three years' time?'

'I know exactly how you'll feel,' said Annie, 'in two years, ten years, twenty years. You're happiest when you're running for something, and I'll never forget when Dad was re-elected to the Senate, you were the only person who was more excited about the result than he was.'

'Don't ever let Matt Cunliffe hear you say that,' said Fletcher with a smile, 'because you can be sure Bill Alexander would know about it ten minutes later, and the firm are just not interested in anyone who isn't fully committed. Remember their motto, *there are twenty-five billing hours in every day.*'

-◇-

When Su Ling woke, she could hear Nat on the phone in the next room. She wondered who he could possibly be talking to so early in the morning. She heard the phone click, and a moment later her husband returned to the bedroom.

'I want you up and packed, little flower, because we have to be out of here in under an hour.'

'What . . .?'

'In under an hour.'

Su Ling jumped out of bed and ran into the bathroom. 'Captain Cartwright, am I allowed to know where you are taking me?' she called above the sound of running water.

'All will be revealed once we're on the plane, Mrs Cartwright.'

'Which direction?' she asked the moment the taps had been turned off.

'I'll tell you when the plane has taken off, not before.'

'Are we going home?'

'No,' said Nat, without offering to elaborate.

Once she was dry, Su Ling concentrated on what to wear while Nat picked up the phone again.

'An hour doesn't give a girl a lot of time,' said Su Ling.

'That was the idea,' said Nat, who was asking the front desk if they could order him a cab.

'Damn,' said Su Ling as she looked at all the presents. 'There just isn't going to be enough room to cram them all in.'

Nat replaced the receiver, walked over to the cupboard and produced a suitcase she'd never seen before. 'Gucci?' she asked, surprised by Nat's unusual extravagance.

'I don't think so,' said Nat, 'not for ten dollars.'

Su Ling laughed as her husband picked up the phone once more. 'I need a porter and could the bill be ready by the time we come down, as we'll be checking out.' He paused, listened, and said, 'Ten minutes.'

He turned to see Su Ling buttoning up her blouse. He thought about her finally falling asleep the night before, and his decision to leave Korea as quickly as possible. Every moment spent in that city would only remind her . . .

At the airport Nat waited in the queue to collect the tickets, and thanked the woman behind the counter for dealing with his early morning request so promptly. Su Ling had gone off to order breakfast while he checked their bags in. Nat then took the escalator to the first floor restaurant, to find his wife seated in a corner, chatting to a waitress.

'I haven't ordered for you,' she said as Nat joined her, 'because I told the waitress that after a week of marriage I wasn't sure if you'd turn up.'

Nat looked up at the waitress. 'Yes, sir?' she said.

'Two eggs, sunny side up, bacon, hash browns and black coffee.'

The waitress studied her pad. 'Your wife has already ordered that for you.'

Nat turned and looked at Su Ling. 'Where are we going?' she asked.

'You'll find out once we're at the gate, and if you go on being a nuisance, not until we land.'

'But . . .' she began.

'I'll blindfold you if necessary,' said Nat as the waitress returned with a pot of steaming coffee. 'Now I need to ask you some serious questions,' Nat said, and saw that Su Ling immediately tensed. He pretended not to notice. He would have to remember not to tease her too much for the next few days as she so obviously still had one thing uppermost in her mind. 'I recall you telling my mother that when Japan came on-line with the computer revolution, the entire technological process would speed up.'

'We're going to Japan?'

'No, we're not,' said Nat, as his order was placed in front of him. 'Now concentrate, because I may have to rely on your expertise.'

'The whole industry is on the gallop right now,' said Su Ling, 'Canon, Sony, Fujitsu have already overtaken the Americans. Why? Are you thinking of looking into new IT companies? In which case, you should consider . . .'

'Yes and no,' said Nat as he turned his head and listened carefully to an announcement on the PA system. He checked the bill and covered it with his last few Korean notes, and then stood up.

'Going somewhere, are we, Captain Cartwright?' asked Su Ling.

'Well, I am,' said Nat, 'because that was my last call, and by the way, if you have other plans, I've got the tickets and the travellers' cheques.'

'Then I'm stuck with you, aren't I?' said Su Ling as she quickly drained her coffee and checked the departure board to see which gate was showing final calls. There were at least a dozen. 'Honolulu?' she said as she caught up with him.

'Why would I want to take you to Honolulu?' asked Nat.

'To lie on the beach and make love all day.'

'No, we're going somewhere where we can meet my former lovers by day, while we still make love all night.'

'Saigon?' said Su Ling, as another city flicked up on the departure board. 'Are we going to visit the scene of Captain Cartwright's past triumphs?'

'Wrong direction,' said Nat, as he continued walking towards the international departure gate. Once their passports and tickets had been checked, Nat didn't bother to stop at duty free, as he continued heading for the check-in desks.

'Bombay?' hazarded Su Ling as they passed gate number one.

'I don't think there are many of my old lovers to be found in India,' Nat assured her as they passed gates two, three and four.

Su Ling continued to study the posted names as they walked towards each gate. 'Singapore, Manila, Hong Kong?'

'No, no, and no,' he repeated as they passed gates eleven, twelve and thirteen.

Su Ling remained silent as they continued on – Bangkok, Zurich, Paris, London, before Nat came to a halt at gate twenty-one.

'Are you travelling to Rome and Venice with us, sir?' asked the lady behind the Pan Am desk.

'Yes,' said Nat. 'The tickets are booked in the name of Mr and Mrs Cartwright,' he said as he turned to face his wife.

'You know something, Mr Cartwright,' Su Ling said, 'you are a very special man.'

—◦—

Over the next four weekends Annie lost count of the number of potential homes the two of them viewed. A few were too large, some too small, while others were in a district they didn't want to live in, and when they were in a neighbourhood they liked, they simply couldn't afford the asking price, even with Alexander Dupont & Bell's assistance. Then one Sunday afternoon, they found exactly what they were looking for in Ridgewood, and within ten minutes of walking in the front door they had nodded to each other behind the agent's back. Annie immediately phoned her mother. 'It's absolutely ideal,' she enthused. 'It's in a quiet neighbourhood with more churches than bars, more schools than movie houses and it's even got a river meandering right through the centre of town.'

'And the price?' said Martha.

'A little more than we wanted to pay, but the realtor is expecting a call from my agent Martha Gates; if you can't get the price down, Mom, I don't know anyone who can.'

'Did you follow my instructions?' asked Martha.

'To the letter. I told the agent we were both school teachers, because you said they always hike the price for lawyers, bankers and doctors. He looked suitably disappointed.'

Fletcher and Annie spent the afternoon strolling round the town, praying that Martha could get them a sensible deal, because even the station was only a short drive from their front door.

After four long weeks finalizing the deal, Fletcher, Annie and Lucy Davenport spent their first night at their new home in Ridgewood, New Jersey on 1 October 1974. No sooner had they closed the front door than Fletcher announced, 'Do you think you can leave Lucy with your mother for a couple of weeks?'

'It doesn't worry me having her around while we're getting the house in shape,' said Annie.

'That wasn't what I had in mind,' said Fletcher. 'I just thought it was time we had a holiday, a sort of second honeymoon.'

'But . . .'

'No buts . . . we're going to do something you've always talked about – go to Scotland and trace our ancestors, the Davenports and the Gates.'

'When were you thinking of leaving?' asked Annie.

'Our plane takes off at eleven tomorrow morning.'

'Mr Davenport, you do like to give a girl a lot of notice, don't you?'

'What are you up to?' asked Su Ling as she leaned across to watch her husband checking over a column of figures on the financial pages of the *Asian Business News*.

'Studying currency movements over the past year,' Nat replied.

'Is that how Japan fits into the equation?' enquired Su Ling.

'Sure is,' said Nat, 'because the yen is the only major currency in the past ten years that has consistently risen in value against the dollar, and several economists are predicting that the trend will continue for the foreseeable future. They claim the yen is still massively undervalued. If the experts are correct, and you're right about Japan's expanding role in new technology, then I think I've identified a good investment in an uncertain world.'

'Is this to be the subject of your business school thesis?'

'No, however that's not a bad idea,' said Nat, 'I was thinking of making a small currency investment and if I prove to be right, I'll notch it up a few dollars each month.'

'A bit of a risk, isn't it?'

'If you hope to make a profit, there's bound to be a certain amount of risk involved. The secret is to eliminate the elements that add to that risk.' Su Ling didn't look convinced. 'I'll tell you what I have in mind,' said Nat. 'I'm currently earning $400 a month as a captain in the army. If I sell those dollars a year in advance for yen at today's rate, then convert them back in twelve months' time, and if the dollar–yen exchange rate continues as it has done for the past seven years, I should make an annual profit of around $400 to $500.'

'And if it goes the other way?' said Su Ling.

'But it hasn't for the past seven years.'

'But if it did?'

'I'd lose around $400, or a month's salary.'

'I'd rather have a guaranteed pay cheque each month.'

'You can never create capital on earned income,' said Nat. 'Most people live well beyond their means, and their only form of savings ends up as life insurance or bonds, both of which can be decimated by inflation. Ask my father.'

'But what do we need all this money for?' asked Su Ling.

'For my lovers,' said Nat.

'And where are all these lovers?'

'Most of them are in Italy, but there are a few others hanging around in the world's major capitals.'

'So that's why we're going to Venice?'

'And Florence, Milan and Rome. When I left them, many were in the nude, and one of the things I most liked about them is they don't age, other than to crack a little if they're exposed to too much sunlight.'

'Lucky women,' said Su Ling. 'And do you have a favourite?'

'No, I'm fairly promiscuous, though if I were forced to choose, I confess there is a lady in Florence who resides in a small palace, whom I adore, and am longing to meet up with again.'

'Is she a virgin, by any chance?' enquired Su Ling.

'You're bright,' said Nat.

'Goes by the name of Maria?'

'You've found me out, although there are a lot of Marias in Italy.'

'*The Adoration of the Magi*, Tintoretto.'

'No.'

'Bellini, *Mother and Child*?'

'No, they still reside at the Vatican.'

Su Ling went silent for a moment as the stewardess asked them to fasten their seatbelts. 'Caravaggio?'

'Very good. I left her in the Pitti Palace on the right-hand wall of the third floor gallery. She promised she would be faithful until I returned.'

'And there she will remain, because such a lover would cost you more than $400 a month, and if you're still hoping to go into politics, you won't even be able to afford the frame.'

'I won't be going into politics until I can afford the whole gallery,' Nat assured his wife.

—◇—

Annie began to appreciate why the British could be so dismissive about American tourists who somehow managed to cover London, Oxford, Blenheim and Stratford in three days. It didn't help when she observed coachloads of tourists descending on the Royal Shakespeare Theatre in Stratford, take their seats, and then leave during the interval, to be replaced by another coachload of her countrymen. Annie wouldn't have thought it possible, if she hadn't returned after the interval to find the two rows in front of her full of people with familiar accents whom she had never seen before. She wondered if those who attended the second act told those who watched the first act what had happened to Rosencrantz and Guildenstern or was that coachload already on its way back to London?

Annie felt less guilty after they'd spent a leisurely ten days in Scotland. They enjoyed being in Edinburgh for the Festival, where they could choose between Marlowe and Mozart, or Pinter and Orton. However for both of them, the highlight of the trip was the long drive up and down the two coastlines. The scenery was so breathtaking they thought there could be no more beautiful landscape on earth.

In Edinburgh, they tried to trace the Gates and the Davenport lineage, but all they ended up with was a large coloured chart of the clans, and a skirt made in the garish Davenport tartan, which Annie doubted she would ever wear again once they were back in the States.

Fletcher fell asleep within minutes of their plane taking off from Edinburgh for New York. When he woke, the sun that he'd seen dip on one side of the cabin, still hadn't risen on the other. As they began their descent into JFK – Annie couldn't get used to it not being called Idlewild – all Annie could think about was being reunited with Lucy, while Fletcher anxiously looked forward to his first day with Alexander Dupont & Bell.

◅○▻

When Nat and Su Ling returned from Rome, they were exhausted, but the change of plans could not have been more successful. Su Ling had relaxed more and more as each day passed; in fact during the second week, neither of them even mentioned Korea. They agreed on their flight home to tell Su Ling's mother that they had honey-mooned in Italy. Only Tom would be puzzled.

While Su Ling slept, Nat once again studied the currency market in the *International Herald Tribune* and London's *Financial Times*. The trend continued unabated, a dip, a slight recovery, followed by another dip, but the long term graph was only going one way for the yen, and in the opposite direction from the dollar. This was also true for the yen against the mark, the pound and the lira, and Nat decided to continue researching which of the exchange rates had the greatest disparity. Just as soon as they were back in Boston he would talk to Tom's father, and use the currency department at Russell's Bank rather than reveal his ideas to someone he didn't know.

Nat glanced across at his sleeping wife, grateful for her suggestion that he make exchange rates the subject of his final-year thesis at business school. His time at

Harvard would pass all too quickly, and he realized that he could not put off a decision that would affect both their futures. They had already discussed the three possible options: he could look for a job in Boston so that Su Ling could remain at Harvard, but as she had pointed out, that would limit his horizons. He could take up Mr Russell's offer and join Tom at a large bank in a small town, but that would seriously curtail his future prospects. Or he could apply for a job on Wall Street and find out if he could survive in the big league.

Su Ling wasn't in any doubt which of the three options he should pursue, and although they had some time to consider their future, she was already talking to her contacts at Columbia.

25

LOOKING BACK ON his final year at Harvard, Nat had had few regrets.

Only hours after touching down at Logan International, he'd phoned Tom's father to share his currency ideas. Mr Russell pointed out that the sums he wished to deal in were too small for any foreign exchange counter to handle. Nat was disappointed until Mr Russell suggested that the bank put up a thousand dollar loan, and asked that he and Tom might be allowed to invest a thousand dollars each. This became Nat's first currency fund.

When Joe Stein heard about the project, another thousand appeared on the same day. Within a month, the fund had grown to $10,000. Nat told Su Ling that he was more worried about losing the investors' money than his own. By the end of the term, the Cartwright Fund had grown to $14,000, and Nat had made a clear profit of $726.

'But you could still lose it all,' Su Ling reminded him.

'True, but now the fund is more substantial there's less chance of a severe loss. Even if the trend suddenly reverses, I could hedge my position by selling ahead, so keeping the losses to a minimum.'

'But doesn't this take a great deal of your time, when you should be writing your thesis?' Su Ling asked.

'It only takes about fifteen minutes a day,' said Nat. 'I check the Japanese market at six each morning and the closing prices in New York at six every night, and as long as there isn't a run against me for several days in a row, I have nothing to do except reinvest the capital each month.'

'It's obscene,' said Su Ling.

'But what's wrong with using my skill, knowledge and an ounce of enterprise?' Nat enquired.

'Because you earn more working fifteen minutes a day than I can hope to pick up in a year as a senior researcher at Columbia University – in fact, it may be more than my supervisor earns.'

'Your supervisor will still be in place this time next year, whatever happens to the market. That's free enterprise. The downside is that I can lose everything.'

Nat didn't tell his wife that the British economist Maynard Keynes had once remarked, *A shrewd man ought to be able to make a fortune before breakfast, so that he can do a proper job during the rest of the day*. He knew how strongly his wife felt about what she called easy money, so he only talked about his investments whenever *she* raised the subject. He certainly didn't let her know that Mr Russell felt the time had come to consider leverage.

Nat felt no guilt when it came to spending fifteen minutes a day managing his mini-fund, as he doubted if there was any student in his class studying more diligently. In fact the only real break he took from work was to run for an hour every afternoon, and the highlight of his year came when, wearing a Harvard vest, he crossed the finishing line in first place in the meet against UConn.

After several interviews in New York Nat received a plethora of offers from financial institutions, but there were only two he took seriously. In reputation and size there was nothing to choose between them, but once he'd met Arnie Freeman, who headed the currency desk at Morgan's, he was quite happy to sign up there and then. Arnie had a gift for making fourteen hours a day on Wall Street sound like fun.

Nat wondered what else could happen that year, until Su Ling asked how much profit the Cartwright Fund had accumulated.

'Around forty thousand dollars,' said Nat.

'And your share?'

'Twenty per cent. So what are you planning to spend it on?'

'Our first child,' she replied.

—◇—

Looking back on his first year with Alexander Dupont & Bell, Fletcher also had few regrets. He'd no idea what his responsibilities would be, but first-year associates were not known as 'pack horses' for nothing. He quickly found out that his principal responsibility was to make sure that whatever case Matt Cunliffe was working on, he never needed to look beyond his desk for any relevant documents or case histories. It had only taken Fletcher a matter of days to discover that any idea of non-stop appearances in glamorous court cases defending innocent women accused of murder was the stuff of television dramas. Most of his work was painstaking and meticulous and more often than not rewarded by plea bargaining before a trial date had even been set.

Fletcher also discovered that it wasn't until you became a partner that you started earning 'the big bucks' and got to go home in the daylight. Despite this, Matt did lighten his work-load by not insisting on a thirty-minute lunch break, which allowed him to play squash twice a week with Jimmy.

Although Fletcher took work home on the train, he tried whenever possible to spend an hour in the evening with his daughter. His father frequently reminded him that once those early years had passed, he wouldn't be able to rewind the reel marked 'important moments in Lucy's childhood'.

Lucy's first birthday party was the noisiest event outside a football stadium that Fletcher had ever attended. Annie had made so many friends in the neighbourhood that he found his home full of young children who seemed to all want to laugh or cry at the same time. Fletcher marvelled at how calmly Annie handled spilled ice cream, chocolate cake trodden into the carpet, a bottle of milk poured over her dress, without the familiar smile ever leaving her face. When the last brat had finally departed, Fletcher was exhausted, but all Annie said was, 'I think that went just fine.'

Fletcher continued to see a lot of Jimmy, who, thanks to his father – his own words – had landed a job with a small but well respected law practice on Lexington Avenue. His hours were almost as bad as Fletcher's, but the responsibility of fatherhood seemed to have given him a new incentive, which only increased when Joanna gave birth to a second child. Fletcher marvelled how successful their marriage was, remembering the age gap and academic disparity. But it seemed to make no difference, because the couple simply adored each other and were the envy of many of their contemporaries who had already filed for divorce. When Fletcher heard the news of Jimmy's second child, he hoped it wouldn't be long before Annie followed suit; he so envied Jimmy having a son. He often thought about Harry Robert.

Because of his workload, Fletcher made few new friends, with the exception of Logan Fitzgerald, who had joined the firm on the same day. They would often compare notes over lunch, and have a drink together before Fletcher caught his train home in the evening. Soon the tall, fair-haired Irishman was being invited back to Ridgewood to meet Annie's unmarried girlfriends. Although Fletcher accepted that Logan and he were rivals, it didn't appear to harm their friendship; in fact, if anything, it seemed to make the bond between them even stronger. Both had their minor triumphs and set-backs during the first year, and no one in the firm seemed willing to offer an opinion on which of them would become a partner first.

Over a drink one evening, Fletcher and Logan agreed they were now fully fledged members of the firm. In a few weeks' time a new brace of trainees would appear and they would progress from pack horses to yearlings. They had both studied with interest the CVs of all those who made the shortlist.

'What do you think of the applicants?' asked Fletcher, trying not to sound superior.

'Not bad,' said Logan, as he ordered Fletcher his usual light beer, 'with one exception – that guy from Stanford, I couldn't work out how he even got on the shortlist.'

'I'm told he's Bill Alexander's nephew.'

'Well, that's a good enough reason to put him on the short list, but not to offer him a job, so I don't expect we'll ever see him again. Come to think of it,' said Logan, 'I can't even remember his name.'

-<o>-

Nat was the youngest in a team of three at Morgan's. His immediate boss was Steven Ginsberg, who was twenty-eight, and his number two, Adrian Kenwright, had just celebrated his twenty-sixth birthday. Between them, they controlled a fund of over a million dollars.

As the currency markets open in Tokyo just as most civilized Americans are going to bed, and close in Los Angeles when the sun no longer shines on the American continent, one of the team had to be on call to cover every hour of the night or day. In fact the only occasion Steven allowed Nat to take an afternoon off was to watch Su Ling receiving her doctorate at Harvard, and even then he had to leave the celebration party so he could take an urgent phone call and explain why the Italian lira was going south.

'They could have a Communist government by this time next week,' said Nat, 'so start switching into Swiss francs,' he added. 'And get rid of any sterling we have on our books because the UK has a left-wing government, and will be the next to feel the strain.'

'And the deutschmark?'

'Hold on to the mark, because the currency will remain undervalued as long as the Berlin Wall is in place.'

Although the two senior members of the team had a great deal more financial experience than Nat, and were willing to work just as hard, they both acknowledged that because of his political antennae Nat could read a market more quickly than anyone else they had ever worked with – or against.

The day everyone sold the dollar and went into pounds, Nat immediately sold the pound on the forward market. For eight days it looked as if he might have lost the bank a fortune and his colleagues rushed past him quickly in the corridor without looking him in the eye. A month later, seven other banks were offering him a job and a considerable rise in salary. Nat received a bonus cheque for eight thousand dollars at the end of the year, and decided the time had come to go in search of a mistress.

He didn't tell Su Ling about the bonus, or the mistress, as she had recently received a pay rise of ninety dollars a month. As for the mistress, he'd had his eye on one particular lady he passed on the street corner every morning as he went to work. And she was still reposing there in the window when he returned to their flat in SoHo every evening. As each day passed, he gave the lady soaking in a bath more than a casual glance, and finally decided to ask her price.

'Six thousand five hundred dollars,' the gallery owner informed him, 'and if I may say so, sir, you have an excellent eye because not only is it a magnificent picture, but you will also have made a shrewd investment.' Nat was quickly coming to the conclusion that art dealers were nothing more than used car salesmen dressed in Brooks Brothers suits.

'Bonnard is greatly undervalued compared to his contemporaries Renoir, Monet and Matisse,' continued the dealer, 'and I predict his prices will soar in the near future.' Nat didn't care about Bonnard's prices, because he was a lover not a pimp.

–o–

His other lover called that afternoon to warn him that she was on her way to hospital. He asked Hong Kong to hold.

'Why?' Nat asked anxiously.

'Because I'm having your baby,' his wife replied.

'But it's not due for another month.'

'Nobody told the baby that,' said Su Ling.

'I'm on my way, little flower,' said Nat, dropping the other phone.

–o–

When Nat returned from the hospital that night, he called his mother to tell her she had a grandson.

'Wonderful news,' she said, 'but what are you going to call him?'

'Luke,' he replied.

'And what do you plan to give Su Ling to commemorate the occasion?'

He hesitated for a moment, and then said, 'A lady in a bath.'

It was another couple of days before he and the dealer finally agreed on five thousand seven hundred and fifty dollars, and the little Bonnard was transferred from the gallery in SoHo to the bedroom wall in their apartment.

'Do you fancy her?' asked Su Ling the day she and Luke returned from the hospital.

'No, although there would be more of her to cuddle than you. But then I prefer thin women.'

Su Ling stood and looked at her present for some time before she gave a pronouncement.

'It's quite magnificent. Thank you.'

Nat was delighted that his wife seemed to appreciate the painting as much as he did. He was only relieved that she didn't ask how much the lady had cost.

What had begun as a whim on a journey from Rome to Venice to Florence with Tom had quickly turned into an addiction that Nat couldn't kick. Every time he received a bonus he went in search of another picture. Nat might well have been dismissive of the used-car salesman, but his judgement turned out to be correct, because Nat continued to select impressionists who were still within reach of his pocket – Vuillard, Luce, Pissarro, Camoin and Sisley – only to find that they increased in value as fast as any of the financial investments he selected for his clients on Wall Street.

Su Ling enjoyed watching their collection grow. She took no interest in what Nat paid for his mistresses, and even less in their investment value. Perhaps this was because when, at the age of twenty-five, she was appointed as the youngest associate professor in Columbia's history, she was earning less in a year than Nat was making in a week.

He no longer needed to be reminded that it was obscene.

—◦—

Fletcher remembered the incident well.

Matt Cunliffe had asked him to take a document over to Higgs & Dunlop for signing. 'Normally I'd ask a paralegal to do this,' Matt explained, 'but it's taken Mr Alexander weeks to get the terms agreed, and he doesn't want any last-minute hitches that might just give them another excuse for not signing.'

Fletcher had expected to be back at the office in less than thirty minutes, because all he needed was to get four agreements signed and witnessed. However, when Fletcher reappeared two hours later and told his boss that the documents had neither been signed nor witnessed, Matt put down his pen and waited for an explanation.

When Fletcher had arrived at Higgs & Dunlop, he was left waiting in reception, and told that the partner whose signature he needed had not yet returned from lunch. This surprised Fletcher, as it was the partner in question, Mr Higgs, who had scheduled the meeting for one o'clock, and Fletcher had skipped his own lunch to be sure he wouldn't be late.

While Fletcher sat in the reception area, he read through the agreement and familiarized himself with its terms. After a takeover bid had been agreed, a partner's compensation package was challenged, and it had taken some considerable time before both partners had been able to agree on a final figure.

At 1.15 p.m. Fletcher glanced up at the receptionist, who looked apologetic and offered him a second coffee. Fletcher thanked her; after all it wasn't her fault that he was being kept waiting. But once he'd read through the document a second time, and had drunk three coffees, he decided Mr Higgs was either downright rude or plain inefficient.

Fletcher checked his watch again. It was 1.35 p.m. He

sighed and asked the receptionist if he could use the washroom. She hesitated for a moment, before producing a key from inside her desk. 'The executive washroom is one floor up,' she told him. 'It's only meant for partners and their most important clients, so if anyone asks, please tell them you're a client.'

The washroom was empty, and, not wishing to embarrass the receptionist, Fletcher locked himself into the end cubicle. He was just zipping up his trousers, when two people walked in, one of them sounding as if he had just arrived back from a long lunch, where water had not been the only drink imbibed.

First voice: 'Well I'm glad that's settled. There's nothing I enjoy more than getting the better of Alexander Dupont and Bell.'

Second voice: 'They've sent over some messenger boy with the agreement. I told Millie to leave him in reception and let him sweat a little.'

Fletcher removed a pen from an inside pocket and tugged gently on the toilet roll.

First voice, laughing: 'What did you finally settle for?'

Second voice: 'That's the good news, $1,325,000, which is a lot more than we anticipated.'

First voice: 'The client must be delighted.'

Second voice: 'That's who I was having lunch with. He ordered a bottle of Château Lafitte '52 – after all we'd told him to expect half a million, which he would have been quite happy to settle for – for obvious reasons.'

First voice, more laughter: 'Are we working on a contingency fee?'

Second voice: 'We sure are. We pick up fifty per cent of anything over half a million.'

First voice: 'So the firm has netted a cool $417,500. But what did you mean by "for obvious reasons"?'

A tap was turned on. 'Our biggest problem was the

client's bank – the company's currently $720,000 over-drawn, and if we don't cover the full sum by close of business on Friday, they're threatening non-payment, which would have meant we might not even have got . . .' – the tap was turned off – '. . . the original $500,000, and that after months of bargaining.'

Second voice: 'Pity about one thing.'

First voice: 'What's that?'

Second voice: 'That you can't tell those snobs over at Alexander Dupont and Bell that they don't know how to play poker.'

First voice: 'True, but I think I'll have a little sport with . . .' – a door opened – '. . . their messenger boy.' The door closed.

Fletcher rolled up the toilet paper and stuffed it in his pocket. He left the cubicle and quickly washed his hands before slipping out and taking the fire escape stairs to the floor below. Once back in reception, he handed over the executive washroom key.

'Thank you,' said the receptionist just as the phone rang. She smiled at Fletcher. 'That was good timing. If you'll take the elevator to the eleventh floor, Mr Higgs is available to see you now.'

'Thank you,' Fletcher said as he walked back out of the room, stepped into the elevator and pressed the button marked 'G'.

Matt Cunliffe was unravelling the toilet roll when the phone rang.

'Mr Higgs is on line one,' said his secretary.

'Tell him I'm not available.' Matt sat back in his chair and winked at Fletcher.

'He's asking when you will be available.'

'Not before close of business on Friday.'

26

FLETCHER COULDN'T REMEMBER an occasion when he'd disliked someone so much on first meeting, and even the circumstances didn't help.

The senior partner had asked Fletcher and Logan to join him for coffee in his office – an unusual event in itself. When they arrived, they were introduced to one of the new trainees.

'I want you both to meet Ralph Elliot,' were Bill Alexander's opening words.

Fletcher's first reaction was to wonder why he'd singled out Elliot from the two successful applicants. He quickly found out.

'I have decided this year to take on a trainee myself. I'm keen to keep in touch with what the new generation are thinking, and as Ralph's grades at Stanford were exceptional, he seemed to be the obvious choice.'

Fletcher recalled Logan's disbelief that Alexander's nephew had even made the shortlist, and they both came to the conclusion that Mr Alexander must have overruled any objections from the other partners.

'I hope both of you will make Ralph feel welcome.'

'Of course,' said Logan. 'Why don't you join us for lunch?'

'Yes, I feel sure I could fit that in,' replied Elliot, as if granting them a favour.

Over lunch, Elliot never missed an opportunity to remind them that he was the nephew of the senior partner, with the unspoken implication that if either Fletcher or Logan should cross him, he could slow their progress to a partnership. The threat only served to strengthen the bond between the two men.

'He's now telling anyone who will listen that he's going to be the first person to make partner in under seven years,' Fletcher told Logan over a drink a few days later.

'You know he's such a cunning bastard, it wouldn't surprise me if he pulled it off,' was Logan's only response.

'How do you think he became student president of UConn if he treated everyone the same way as he does us?'

'Perhaps no one dared to oppose him.'

'Is that how you managed it?' asked Logan.

'How did you know that?' asked Fletcher, as the bartender collected their glasses.

'I checked your CV the day I joined the firm. Don't tell me you didn't read mine?'

'Of course I did,' admitted Fletcher, raising his glass, 'I even know that you were the Princeton chess champion.' Both men laughed. 'I must run, or I'll miss my train,' said Fletcher, 'and Annie might begin to wonder if there's another woman in my life.'

'I envy you that,' said Logan quietly.

'What do you mean?'

'The strength of your marriage. It wouldn't cross Annie's mind even for a second that you could look at another woman.'

'I'm very fortunate,' said Fletcher. 'Maybe you'll be just as lucky one day. Meg on the reception desk can't take her eyes off you.'

'Which one is Meg?' asked Logan as Fletcher left him to pick up his coat.

Fletcher had only walked a few yards down Fifth

Avenue, when he spotted Ralph Elliot approaching. Fletcher slipped into a doorway, and waited for him to pass. Stepping back out into a raw cold wind that requires ear muffs even if you're only walking a single block, he reached into his pocket to retrieve his scarf, but it wasn't there. He cursed. He must have left it in the bar. He would have to collect it tomorrow, but then he cursed again when he remembered Annie had given it to him for Christmas. He turned round and began to retrace his steps.

Back in the bar, he asked the girl at the coat check if she'd seen a red woollen scarf.

'Yes,' she replied, 'it must have fallen out of your sleeve when you put your coat on. I found it on the floor.'

'Thank you,' said Fletcher as he turned to leave, not expecting to see Logan still standing at the bar. He froze when he saw the man he was talking to.

—◦—

Nat was fast asleep.

La Dévaluation Française – three simple words sent the tapes from a gentle murmur into a chattering panic. The phone by Nat's bed was ringing thirty seconds later, and he immediately gave Adrian the order, 'Get out of francs as fast as you can.' He listened and then replied, 'Dollars.'

Nat couldn't remember a day in the last ten years when he hadn't shaved. He didn't shave.

Su Ling was awake by the time he came out of the bathroom a few minutes later. 'Is there a problem?' she asked, rubbing her eyes.

'The French have devalued by seven per cent.'

'Is that good or bad?' she asked.

'Depends how many francs we're holding. I'll be able

to make an assessment just as soon as I can get to a screen.'

'You'll have one by the side of your bed in a few years' time, so you wouldn't even need to go into your office,' said Su Ling, letting her head fall back on the pillow when she saw 5.09 flick up on the bedside clock.

Nat picked up the phone; Adrian was still on the other end of the line. 'It's proving difficult to get out of francs; there are very few buyers other than the French government and they won't be able to go on propping up the currency for much longer.'

'Keep selling. Pick up yen, deutschmarks or Swiss francs, but nothing else. I'll be with you in fifteen minutes. Is Steven there?'

'No, he's on his way. It took me some time to find out whose bed he was in.'

Nat didn't laugh as he replaced the receiver. He leaned over and kissed his wife before running to the door.

'You're not wearing a tie,' said Su Ling.

'By tonight I might not be wearing a shirt,' Nat replied.

When they had moved from Boston to Manhattan, Su Ling had found an apartment only a cab ride away from Wall Street. As each bonus came in, she'd been able to furnish and decorate the four rooms, so that Nat soon felt able to bring his colleagues and even some clients back for dinner. Seven paintings – few that laymen would have recognized – now adorned the walls.

Su Ling fell back into a half sleep as her husband left. Nat broke with his usual routine as he leapt down the stairs in twos and threes, not bothering to wait for the elevator. On a normal day, he would have risen at six, and phoned the office from his study to ask for an update. He rarely had to make any major decisions over the phone, as most of their positions were locked in for several months. He would then shower, shave and be dressed by six thirty. He would read the *Wall Street Journal* while Su Ling prepared breakfast, and leave the apartment around seven, having looked in on Luke. Rain or shine, he would walk the five blocks to work, picking up a copy of the *New York Times* from a box on the corner of William and John. He immediately turned to the financial section and if the headline grabbed his attention, he would read it on the move, and still be at his desk by seven twenty. The *New York Times* wouldn't be informing its readers of the French devaluation until tomorrow morning, by which time, for most bankers, it would be history.

When Nat reached the street, he hailed the first available cab, removing a ten-dollar bill for a five block journey, and said, 'I need to be there yesterday.' The driver immediately changed gear and lanes, and they pulled up outside his office four minutes later. Nat ran into the building and headed for the first open elevator. It was packed with traders, all talking at the tops of their voices. Nat learnt nothing new, except that the simple announcement had been made by the French Ministry of Finance at ten o'clock, central European time. He cursed as the elevator stopped eight times on its slow progress to the eleventh floor.

Steven and Adrian were already at their desks in the trading room.

'Tell me the latest,' he shouted as he threw off his coat.

'Everyone's taking a bath,' said Steven. 'The French have officially devalued by seven per cent, but the markets are discounting it as too little too late.'

Nat checked his screen. 'And the other currencies?'

'The pound, lira and peseta are also going south. The dollar is climbing, the yen and the Swiss franc are holding steady, while the deutschmark is bobbing.'

Nat continued to stare at his screen, watching the figures flick up and down every few seconds. 'Try and buy some yen,' he said as he watched the pound drop another point.

Steven picked up a phone linked directly to the trading desk. Nat stared in his direction. They were losing valuable seconds as they waited for a trader.

'How much is the trade?' barked Steven.

'Ten million at 2068.'

Adrian looked away as Steven gave the order.

'And sell any pounds or lire we're still holding because they'll be the next to devalue,' said Nat.

'What about the rate?'

'To hell with the rate, just sell,' said Nat, 'and get into dollars. If it's a real storm, everyone will try to shelter in New York.' Nat was surprised how calm he felt amidst the barrage of shouting and cursing around him.

'We're out of lire,' said Adrian, 'and are being offered yen at 2027.'

'Grab them,' intoned Nat, his eyes not moving from the screen.

'We're out of the pound,' said Steven, 'at 2.37.'

'Good, transfer half our dollars back into yen.'

'I'm out of guilders,' shouted Adrian.

'Switch them all into Swiss francs.'

'Do you want to sell our deutschmark position?' asked Steven.

'No,' said Nat.

'Do you want to buy any?'

'No,' repeated Nat. 'They're sitting on the equator and don't seem to be moving in either direction.'

He'd finished making decisions in less than twenty

minutes, and then all he could do was stare at the screens and wait to see how much damage had been done. As most currencies continued their downward trend Nat realized others would be suffering far more than he was. It didn't help.

If only the French had waited until midday, the usual time to announce a devaluation, he would have been at his desk. 'Damn the French,' said Adrian.

'Clever French,' countered Nat, 'to devalue when we're asleep.'

—◦—

The French devaluation meant little to Fletcher as he read the details in the *New York Times* on the train into work the following morning. Several banks had taken a bath, and one or two were even having to report solvency problems to the Securities & Exchange Commission. He turned the page to read a profile about the man who looked certain to be running against Ford for president. Fletcher knew very little about Jimmy Carter, other than that he'd been governor of Georgia and owned a large peanut farm. He paused for a moment, and thought about his own political ambitions, which he'd put on hold while he tried to establish himself at the firm.

Fletcher decided he would sign up to help the 'Back Carter' campaign in New York in whatever spare time he had. Spare time? Harry and Martha complained about never seeing him. Annie had joined yet another non-profit board, and Lucy had chicken pox. When he'd phoned his mother to ask if he'd ever had chicken pox, the first thing she said was, 'Hello, stranger.' However these problems were quickly forgotten only moments after he'd arrived at the office.

The first hint of any trouble came when he said good morning to Meg in reception.

'There's a meeting of all attorneys in the conference room at eight thirty,' she said flatly.

'Any idea what it's about?' asked Fletcher, realizing that it was a silly question the moment he'd asked it. Confidentiality was the firm's hallmark.

Several partners were already in their places, talking in hushed tones, when Fletcher entered the boardroom at eight twenty, and he quickly took a seat directly behind Matt's chair. Could the devaluation of the French franc in Paris affect a law firm in New York? He doubted it. Did the senior partner want to talk about the Higgs & Dunlop deal? No, not Alexander's style. He looked around the boardroom table. If any of them knew what was on the agenda, they weren't giving anything away. But it had to be bad news, because good news was always announced at the six o'clock evening meeting.

At eight twenty-four, the senior partner walked in.

'I must apologize for keeping you away from your desks,' he began, 'but this was not something that I felt could be covered by an internal memo, or slipped into my monthly report.' He paused and cleared his throat. 'The strength of this firm has always been that it has never become involved in scandals of a personal or financial nature; therefore I considered even the hint of such a problem had to be dealt with expeditiously.' Fletcher was now even more puzzled. 'It has been brought to my notice that a member of this firm was seen in a bar frequented by lawyers from rival institutions.' *I do that every day*, thought Fletcher, *it's hardly a crime*. 'And although this in itself is not reprehensible, it can lead to other developments that are unacceptable at Alexander Dupont and Bell. Fortunately, one of our number, with the best interest of the firm at heart, felt it his duty to keep me briefed on what might have become an embarrassing situation. The employee I am referring to was seen in a bar talking to a member of a rival firm. He then left with that person at approximately ten o'clock, took a cab to his home on the West Side, and did not reappear again until six thirty the following morning, when he returned to his own apartment. I immediately confronted the employee concerned, who made no attempt to deny his relationship with the member of a rival firm, and I'm pleased to say that he agreed the wisest course of action was to resign immediately.' He paused. 'I am grateful to the member of staff who reluctantly decided that it was his duty to report this matter to me.'

Fletcher glanced across at Ralph Elliot, who was trying to feign surprise as each new sentence was delivered, but no one had ever told him about over-acting. It was then that Fletcher recalled seeing Elliot on Fifth Avenue after his evening drink. He felt sick the moment he realized it was Logan the senior partner was referring to.

'May I remind everyone,' emphasized Bill Alexander, 'that this matter should not be discussed again in public or in private.' The senior partner rose from his place and left the room without another word.

Fletcher thought it would be diplomatic to be among the last to leave, and when there were no partners left in the room he rose and walked slowly towards the door. On his way back to his office he could hear footsteps behind him, but he didn't look round, until Elliot caught up with him. 'You were in the bar with Logan that night, weren't you?' he paused. 'I didn't tell my uncle.' Fletcher said nothing as Elliot slipped away, but once he was back at his desk he wrote down the exact words Elliot had threatened him with.

The only mistake he made was not to inform Bill Alexander immediately.

—◇—

One of the many things Nat admired about Su Ling was that she never once said, 'I told you so,' although after all her warnings, she had every right to do so.

'So what happens next?' she asked, having already put the incident behind her.

'I have to decide whether to resign or wait to be pushed.'

'But Steven is the head of your department, and even Adrian is senior to you.'

'I know, but they were all my positions, and I signed the buy and sell orders, so no one really believes they made any of the plays.'

'How much did the bank lose?'

'A few dollars short of half a million.'

'But you've made them much more than that in the past couple of years.'

'True, but the other heads of department will now consider me unreliable, and will always be fearful that it just might happen again. Steven and Adrian are already distancing themselves as quickly as they can; they won't want to lose their jobs as well.'

'But you're still capable of making the bank huge profits, so why should they let you go?'

'Because they'll be able to replace me; business schools throw up bright new graduates every year.'

'Not of your calibre, they don't,' said Su Ling.

'But I thought you didn't approve?'

'I didn't say I approve,' replied Su Ling, 'but that doesn't mean I don't recognize and admire your ability.' She hesitated. 'Will anyone else offer you a job?'

'I don't suppose they will be calling me as frequently as they were a month ago, so I'll just have to start calling them.'

Su Ling wrapped her arms round her husband. 'You've faced far worse than this in Vietnam and so did I in Korea, and you didn't flinch.' Nat had almost forgotten what had happened in Korea, although it was obviously still troubling Su Ling.

'What about the Cartwright Fund?' she asked as Nat helped her lay the table.

'Lost around fifty thousand, but it's still showing a small profit over the year. Which reminds me, I must ring Mr Russell and apologize.'

'But you've also made them handsome returns in the past.'

'Which is why they put so much trust in me in the first place,' said Nat, thumping the table. 'Damn it, I should have seen it coming.' He looked across the table at his wife. 'What do you think I should do?'

Su Ling considered his question for some time. 'Resign, and get yourself a proper job.'

◆

Fletcher dialled the number without going through his secretary. 'Are you free for lunch?' He paused. 'No, we need to meet somewhere where no one will recognize us,' – pause – 'is that the one on West 57th?' – pause – 'see you there at twelve thirty.'

Fletcher arrived at Zemarki's a few minutes early. His guest was waiting for him. They both ordered salad, and Fletcher called for a light beer.

'I thought you never drank at lunch?'

'Today is one of those rare exceptions,' said Fletcher. After he'd taken a long draught, he told his friend what had taken place that morning.

'This is 1976 not 1776,' was all Jimmy said.

'I know, but it seems that there are still one or two dinosaurs roaming around, and God knows what other bile Elliot fed to his uncle.'

'Sounds like a nice guy, your Mr Elliot. You'd better

keep your eye on him as you're probably the next one he has in his sights.'

'I can take care of myself,' said Fletcher. 'It's Logan I'm worried about.'

'But surely if he's as good as you say he'll be quickly snapped up?'

'Not after a call to Bill Alexander asking why he left so suddenly.'

'No lawyer would dare to suggest that being gay was a reason for dismissal.'

'He doesn't have to,' said Fletcher. 'Given the circumstances he need only say, "I would prefer not to discuss the matter, it's somewhat delicate", which is far more deadly.' He took another swig. 'I have to tell you, Jimmy, that if your firm were lucky enough to employ Logan, they would never regret it.'

'I'll have a word with the senior partner this afternoon, and let you know how he reacts. Anyway, how's my kid sister?'

'Slowly taking over everything in Ridgewood, including the book club, the neighbourhood swim team and the blood donors' drive. Our next problem is going to be which school to send Lucy to.'

'Hotchkiss is taking girls now,' said Jimmy, 'and we intend . . .'

'I wonder how the senator feels about that,' said Fletcher as he drained his beer. 'How is he, by the way?'

'Exhausted, he never stops preparing for the next election.'

'But no one could oust Harry. I don't know a more popular politician in the state.'

'You tell him that,' said Jimmy. 'When I last saw him he'd put on fifteen pounds, and was looking badly out of shape.'

Fletcher glanced at his watch. 'Send the old warhorse

my best, and tell him Annie and I will try and get up to Hartford for a weekend soon.' He paused. 'This meeting never took place.'

'You're becoming paranoid,' said Jimmy as he picked up the cheque, 'which is exactly what this Elliot guy will be hoping for.'

———◦———

Nat handed in his resignation the following morning, relieved at how calmly Su Ling had taken the whole débâcle. But it was all very well her telling him to get a proper job when there was only one job he felt qualified to do.

When he returned to his office to remove his personal possessions it was as if there was a quarantine notice attached to his desk. Former colleagues walked quickly past, and those occupying desks nearby remained on their phones, their faces turned away.

He took a laden cab back to the apartment, and filled the tiny elevator three times before he had finally deposited everything in his study.

Nat sat alone at his desk. The phone hadn't rung once since he'd arrived home. The apartment felt strangely empty without Su Ling and Luke; he'd got used to them both being there to greet him whenever he came home. Thank God the boy was too young to know what they were going through.

At midday, he went to the kitchen, opened a can of corned beef hash and tipped it into a frying pan, added some butter, cracked two eggs on top and waited until they looked done.

After lunch, he typed out a list of financial institutions that had been in contact with him during the past year, and then settled down to call them one by one. He started with a bank that had phoned him only a few days before.

'Oh hi, Nat, yes sorry, we managed to fill the position last Friday.'

'Good afternoon, Nat, that sounds an interesting proposition, give me a couple of days to think about it, and I'll come back to you.'

'It was good of you to call, Mr Cartwright, but . . .'

When Nat had reached the end of the list, he put the phone down. He'd just been devalued, and there was obviously a sell order out on him. He checked his current account. It was still showing a healthy balance, but for how much longer? He glanced up at the oil painting above his desk. *Reclining Nude* by Camoin. He wondered just how long it would be before he had to return one of his mistresses to the gallery pimp.

The phone rang. Had one of them thought about it and called him back? He picked it up and heard a familiar voice.

'I must apologize, Mr Russell,' Nat said. 'I should have called you earlier.'

—◦—

Once Logan had left the firm, Fletcher felt isolated and hardly a day went by when Elliot didn't try to undermine him, so when Bill Alexander asked to see him on Monday morning, Fletcher sensed it wasn't going to be a friendly encounter.

Over supper with Annie on Sunday evening, he told his wife everything that had taken place during the past few days, trying hard not to exaggerate. Annie listened in silence.

'If you don't tell Mr Alexander the truth about his nephew, both of you will live to regret it.'

'It's not that easy,' said Fletcher.

'The truth is always that easy,' said Annie. 'Logan has been treated disgracefully, and if it hadn't been for you, he might never have been offered another job. Your only mistake was not telling Alexander the moment the meeting was over; that's given Elliot the confidence to go on undermining you.'

'And if he sacks me as well?'

'Then it isn't a firm you should have joined in the first place, Fletcher Davenport, and you would certainly not be the man I chose to marry.'

—◇—

When Fletcher arrived outside Mr Alexander's door a few minutes before nine, Mrs Townsend ushered him straight though to the senior partner's office.

'Have a seat,' said Bill Alexander pointing to the chair on the other side of the desk. No 'nice to see you, Fletcher', just 'have a seat'. No 'how's Annie and Lucy', just have a seat. Those three words resolved Fletcher in the belief that Annie was right, and he must not be fearful of standing up for what he believed in.

'Fletcher, when you first came to Alexander Dupont and Bell nearly two years ago, I had high hopes for you, and indeed during your first year you more than lived up to my expectations. We all recall with some considerable pleasure the Higgs and Dunlop incident. But of late, you have not shown the same resolution.' Fletcher looked puzzled. He had seen Matt Cunliffe's most recent report on him, and the word exemplary had stuck in his mind. 'I think we have the right to assume a standard of loyalty second to none in the legal profession,' continued Alexander. Fletcher remained silent, not yet sure of the crime he was about to be charged with. 'It has been brought to my attention that you were also in the bar with Fitzgerald on the night he was having a drink with his *friend*.'

'Information supplied by your nephew, no doubt,' said Fletcher, 'whose role in this whole affair has been far from impartial.'

'What do you mean by that?'

'Quite simply that Mr Elliot's version of events is based totally on self-interest, as I feel sure a man of your perspicacity has already worked out.'

'Perspicacity?' said Alexander. 'Was it perspicacious of you to be seen in the company of Fitzgerald's *friend*?' He emphasized the word again.

'I did not meet Logan's friend, as I feel sure Mr Elliot told you, unless he only wanted you to know half the story. I left for Ridgewood . . .'

'But Ralph told me that you later returned.'

'Yes I did, and like any good spy, your nephew must also have reported that I only went back to pick up my scarf, which had fallen out of the sleeve of my overcoat.'

'No, he did not report that,' said Alexander.

'Which is what I mean by only telling you half the story,' said Fletcher.

'So you didn't speak to Logan or his friend?'

'No, I didn't,' said Fletcher, 'but that was only because I was in a hurry, and didn't have time.'

'So you would have spoken to him?'

'Yes, I would.'

'Even if you'd known that Logan was a homosexual?'

'I neither knew nor cared.'

'You didn't care?'

'No, I did not consider Logan's private life was any of my business.'

'But it might have been the firm's business, which brings me on to more important matters. Are you aware that Logan Fitzgerald has since joined the firm that employs your brother-in-law?'

'Yes, I am,' said Fletcher, 'I told Mr Gates that Logan would be looking for a job and they'd be lucky to get a man of his calibre.'

'I wonder if that was wise,' said Bill Alexander.

'When it comes to dealing with a friend, I have a tendency to put decency and fairness ahead of my own self-interest.'

'And ahead of the firm's?'

'Yes, if it's morally right. That's what Professor Abrahams taught me.'

'Don't bandy words with me, Mr Davenport.'

'Why not? You've been bandying them with me, Mr Alexander.'

The senior partner turned scarlet. 'You must realize that I could have you thrown out of this firm.'

'Two of us leaving in the same week may take some explaining, Mr Alexander.'

'Are you threatening me?'

'No, I think it's you who is threatening me.'

'It may not be that easy to get rid of you, Mr Davenport, but I can make damn sure you never become a partner while I'm a member of this firm. Now get out.'

As he rose to leave, Fletcher recalled Annie's words. *Then it's not the firm you should have joined in the first place.*

He returned to his office to find the phone ringing. Was Alexander calling him back? He picked it up ready to offer his resignation. It was Jimmy.

'Sorry to bother you at work, Fletcher, but Dad's had a heart attack. He's been taken to St Patrick's. Can you and Annie get over to Hartford as quickly as possible?'

27

'I've got myself a proper job,' said Nat as Su Ling walked through the door.

'You're going to be a New York cab driver?'

'No,' replied Nat. 'I don't have the qualifications for that job.'

'That's never seemed to hinder anyone in the past.'

'But not living in New York might.'

'We're leaving New York? Please tell me that we're going somewhere civilized where skyscrapers will be replaced with trees and exhaust fumes by fresh air.'

'We're going home.'

'Hartford? Then it can only be Russell's.'

'You're right, Mr Russell has offered me a job as vice-president of the bank, working alongside Tom.'

'Serious banking? Not just speculating in the currency market?'

'I'll oversee his currency department, but I can promise you that it concentrates mainly on foreign exchange, not speculation. What Mr Russell most needs is for Tom and me to work on a complete reorganization of the bank. During the past few years Russell's has been falling behind its competitors and . . .' Su Ling placed her bag on the hall table and walked over to the phone. 'Who are you calling?' asked Nat.

'My mother, of course, we must start looking for a house, and then we'll have to consider a school for Luke, and once she's got to work on that, I'll need to be in touch with some former colleagues about a job, and then . . .'

'Hold on, little flower,' said Nat, taking his wife in his arms. 'Am I to assume from this that you approve of the idea?'

'Approve? I can't wait to get out of New York. The idea of Luke starting his education in a school where the kids use machetes to sharpen their pencils horrifies me. I also can't wait . . .' The phone rang and Su Ling picked it up. She cupped her hand over the mouthpiece. 'It's someone named Jason, from Chase Manhattan. Shall I tell him you're no longer available?'

Nat smiled and took the phone.

'Hi, Jason, what can I do for you?'

'I've been thinking about your call, Nat, and we may just have an opening for you at Chase.'

'That's kind of you, Jason, but I've already accepted another offer.'

'Not one of our rivals, I hope?'

'Not yet, but give me a little time,' said Nat, smiling.

—◦►—

When Fletcher reported to Matt Cunliffe that his father-in-law had been taken into the hospital, he was surprised to find that he was not all that sympathetic.

'Domestic crises arise fairly often,' Cunliffe remarked curtly. 'We all have families to worry about. Are you sure this can't wait until the weekend?'

'Yes, I'm sure,' said Fletcher, 'I owe more to this man than anyone other than my parents.'

Fletcher had only left Bill Alexander's room for a few moments, and already there was a less than subtle change in the atmosphere. He assumed that, by the time he returned, that change would have spread like a contagious disease to the rest of the staff.

He phoned Annie from Penn Station. She sounded calm, but relieved to know he was on his way home. When Fletcher stepped on to the train, he suddenly realized that he hadn't brought any work with him for the first time since he joined the firm. He used the journey to consider his next move following his meeting with Bill Alexander, but he'd come to no definite conclusions by the time the train pulled into Ridgewood.

Fletcher took a cab from the station, and was not surprised to find the family car parked outside the front door, two suitcases already in the trunk, and Annie walking down the drive with Lucy in her arms. How different from his mother, he thought, yet how similar. He laughed for the first time that day.

On the journey up to Hartford, Annie reported all the details she'd picked up from her mother. Harry had suffered a heart attack a few minutes after arriving at the Capitol that morning, and was immediately rushed into hospital. Martha was by his side, and Jimmy, Joanna and the children were already on their way down from Vassar.

'What are the doctors saying?'

'That it's too early for anything conclusive, but Dad has been warned that if he doesn't slow down, it could well happen again and next time it might prove fatal.'

'Slow down? Harry doesn't know what the words mean. He's one of life's speeding tickets.'

'He may have been,' said Annie, 'but Mom and I are going to tell him this afternoon that he has to withdraw his name as a senate candidate at the next election.'

—◇—

Bill Russell stared across his desk at Nat and Tom. 'It's what I've always wanted,' he said. 'I'll be sixty in a couple of years' time, and I feel I've earned the right not to be opening up the bank at ten every morning, and locking the front door before I go home at night. The thought of you two working together – to quote the Good Book – fills my heart with joy.'

'I don't know about the Good Book,' said Tom, 'but we feel the same way, Dad. So where do you want us to start?'

'Of course I'm aware that the bank has fallen behind its rivals during the past few years, perhaps because as a family firm we've put greater emphasis on customer relations than on the bottom line. Something your father would approve of, Nat, which is perhaps why he's had an account with us for over thirty years.' Nat nodded his agreement. 'You'll also be aware that there have been one or two approaches from other banks with a view to taking us over, but that isn't how I wanted to end my career with Russell's – just ending up as an anonymous branch of some vast corporation. So I'll tell you what I have in mind. I want both of you to spend your first six months taking the bank apart from top to bottom. I'll give you *carte blanche* to ask any questions, open any doors, read any files, study any accounts. At the end of those six months, you will report back what needs to be done. And don't give a moment's thought to trying to placate my feelings, because I know that if Russell's is to survive into the next century, it will need a complete overhaul. So what's your first question?'

'Can I have the front door keys?' asked Nat.

'Why?' asked Mr Russell.

'Because ten o'clock is a little too late for the staff of a progressive bank to be opening.'

As Tom drove them back to New York, he and Nat set about dividing their responsibilities.

'Dad was touched that you turned down Chase to join us,' said Tom.

'You made exactly the same sacrifice when you left the Bank of America.'

'Yes, but the old man has always assumed that I'd take over from him once he reached his sixty-fifth birthday, and I was just about to warn him that I wasn't willing to do so.'

'Why not?' enquired Nat.

'I don't have the vision or ideas that are required to rescue the bank, but you do.'

'Rescue?' said Nat.

'Yes, don't let's kid ourselves. You've studied the balance sheet, so you know only too well that we're just about clearing enough to allow my parents to maintain their standard of living. But the profits haven't risen for some years; the truth is that the bank needs your particular skills more than it requires an efficient packhorse like me. So it's important to settle one thing before it ever becomes an issue – in banking terms I intend to report to you as chief executive.'

'But it will still be necessary for you to become chairman once your father retires.'

'Why?' asked Tom. 'When you'll obviously be making all the strategic decisions?'

'Because the bank bears your name, and that still matters in a town like Hartford. It's equally important that the customers never find out what the chief executive is up to behind the scenes.'

'I'll go along with that on one condition,' said Tom, 'that all salaries, bonuses and any other financial considerations are allocated on an equal basis.'

'That's very generous of you,' said Nat.

'No, it's not,' said Tom. 'Shrewd perhaps, but not generous, because fifty per cent of you will bring in a far higher return than one hundred per cent of me.'

'Don't forget that I've just lost Morgan's a fortune,' said Nat.

'And no doubt learnt from the experience.'

'Just as we did when we were up against Ralph Elliot.'

'Now there's a name from the past. Any idea what he's up to?' asked Tom as he turned on to Route 95.

'The last thing I heard was that after Stanford he'd become a hot-shot lawyer in New York.'

'I wouldn't want to be one of his clients,' said Tom.

'Or go up against him for that matter,' said Nat.

'Well, at least that's something we don't have to worry about.'

Nat looked out of the grimy window as they travelled through Queens. 'Don't be too sure, Tom, because if anything were to go wrong, he'll want to represent the other side.'

◄○►

They sat in a circle around his bed, chatting about anything and everything except what was on their minds. The one exception was Lucy, who remained firmly in the middle of the bed and treated grandpa as if he was a rocking horse. Joanna's children were more restrained. Fletcher couldn't believe how quickly Harry Junior was growing.

'Now before I get too tired,' said Harry, 'I need to have a private word with Fletcher.'

Martha shepherded the family out of the room, clearly aware of what her husband wanted to discuss with his son-in-law.

'I'll see you back at the house later,' said Annie, as she dragged a reluctant Lucy away.

'And then we should be starting back for Ridgewood,' Fletcher reminded her. 'I can't afford to be late for work tomorrow.' Annie nodded as she closed the door.

Fletcher drew up a chair and sat by the senator's side. He didn't bother with any smalltalk, as his father-in-law was looking tired.

'I've given a great deal of thought to what I'm about to say,' said the senator, 'and the only other person I've discussed it with is Martha, and she is in complete agreement with me. And like so many things over the past thirty years, I can't be sure if it wasn't her idea in the first place.' Fletcher smiled. How like Annie, he thought, as he waited for the senator to continue. 'I've promised Martha that I won't run for re-election.' The senator paused. 'I see you're not putting up any protest, so I must assume that you agree with my wife and daughter on this subject.'

'Annie would prefer you to live to an old age, rather than die making a speech in the Senate Chamber, however important,' said Fletcher, 'and I agree with her.'

'I know they're right, Fletcher, but by God I'll miss it.'

'And they will miss you, sir, as you can see from the flowers and cards already in this room. By this time tomorrow, they'll have filled every other room on this floor and be spilling out on to the pavement.' The senator ignored the compliment, clearly not wishing to be diverted from his course.

'When Jimmy was born, I had the crazy notion that one day he would take my place, perhaps even go on to Washington and represent the state. But it wasn't long before I realized that was never going to be a possibility. I couldn't be more proud of him, but he just isn't cut out for public office.'

'He made a damn fine job of getting me elected as president,' said Fletcher. 'Twice.'

'He did indeed,' said Harry, 'but Jimmy should always be in the engine room, because he isn't destined to be the driver.' He paused again. 'But then some twelve years ago I met a young man at the Hotchkiss–Taft football game, who I knew couldn't wait to be the driver. A meeting incidentally, that I shall never forget.'

'Nor me, sir,' said Fletcher.

'As the years passed, I watched that boy grow into a fine young man, and I'm proud he's now my son-in-law and father of my granddaughter. And before I grow too maudlin, Fletcher, I think I ought to come to the point in case one of us falls asleep.' Fletcher laughed.

'Pretty soon I shall have to let it be known that I will not be running for re-election to the Senate.' He raised his head and looked directly at Fletcher. 'I would, at the same time, like to say how proud I am to announce that my son-in-law, Fletcher Davenport, has agreed to run in my place.'

28

I T DIDN'T TAKE six months for Nat to discover why
Russell's Bank had failed to increase its profits in over a
decade. Almost every modern banking tenet had been
ignored. Russell's still lived in an age of written ledgers,
personalized accounts and a sincerely held belief that the
computer was more likely to make mistakes than a human
being, and was therefore a waste of the bank's time and
money. Nat was in and out of Mr Russell's office three or
four times a day, only to find that something they had
agreed on in the morning had been reversed by the
afternoon. This usually occurred whenever a long-standing member of staff was seen leaving the same office an
hour later with a smile on his or her face. It was often left
for Tom to pick up the pieces; in fact, if he hadn't been
there to explain to his father why the changes were
necessary, there might never have been a six-month
report to present.

Nat would come home most nights exhausted and
sometimes infuriated. He warned Su Ling there was likely
to be a showdown when his report was finally presented.
And he wasn't altogether sure that he would still be the
bank's vice-president if the chairman was unable to stomach
almost all of the changes he was recommending. Su Ling
didn't complain, although she had just about managed to
get the three of them settled in their new house, sell the
apartment in New York, find a nursery school for Luke,
and prepare to take up her new appointment as professor

of statistics at UConn in the fall. The idea of moving back to New York didn't appeal to her.

In between, she had advised Nat on which computers would be most cost-effective for the bank, supervised their installation and also given night classes to those members of the staff who appreciated there was more to learn than how to press the ON button. But Nat's biggest problem was the bank's chronic over-staffing. He had already pointed out to the chairman that Russell's currently employed seventy-one staff and that Bennett's, the only other independent bank in town, offered the same services with only thirty-nine employees. Nat wrote a separate report on the financial implications of over-staffing, suggesting an early retirement programme that, although it would cut into their profits for the next three years, would be highly beneficial in the long term. This was the sticking point on which Nat was unwilling to budge. Because, as he explained to Tom over dinner with Su Ling, if they waited for another couple of years until Mr Russell retired, they would all be joining the ranks of the unemployed.

Once Mr Russell had read Nat's report, he scheduled a Friday evening at six o'clock for the showdown. When Nat and Tom walked into the chairman's office they found him at his desk writing a letter. He looked up as they entered the room.

'I'm sorry to say that I'm unable to go along with your recommendations,' said Mr Russell even before his two vice-presidents had sat down, 'because I do not wish to fire employees, some of whom I have known and worked with for the past thirty years.' Nat tried to smile as he thought about being sacked twice in six months, and wondered if Jason at Chase might still have an opening for him. 'So I have come to the conclusion,' continued the chairman, 'that if this is going to work,' he placed his hands on the report, as if blessing it, 'the one person who will have to go is me.' He scribbled his signature on the bottom of the letter he had been writing, and handed his resignation over to his son.

Bill Russell left the office at 6.12 that evening, and never entered the building again.

⟨◦⟩

'What are your qualifications to run for public office?'

Fletcher looked down from his place on the stage at the small group of journalists seated in front of him. Harry smiled. It was one of the seventeen questions and answers they had prepared the previous evening.

'I don't have a great deal of experience,' admitted Fletcher, he hoped disarmingly, 'but I was born, brought up and educated in Connecticut before going to New York to join one of the most prestigious law firms in the country. I've come home to put those skills to work for the people of Hartford.'

'Don't you feel that twenty-six is a bit young to be telling us how we should be running our lives?' asked a young lady seated in the second row.

'Same age as I was,' said Harry, 'and your father never complained.' One or two of the older hacks smiled, but the young woman wasn't quite so easily put off.

'But you had just returned from a world war, senator, with three year's experience as an officer at the front, so may I ask, Mr Davenport, did you burn your draft card during the height of the Vietnam war?'

'No, I did not,' said Fletcher, 'I was not drafted, but had I been, I would have served willingly.'

'Can you prove that?' the journalist snapped back.

'No,' said Fletcher, 'but if you were to read my speech at the Yale's freshman debate, you would be left in no doubt of my feelings on this subject.'

'If you are elected,' asked another member of the press, 'will your father-in-law be pulling the strings?'

Harry glanced across and saw that the question had annoyed Fletcher. 'Calm down,' he whispered. 'He's only doing his job. Stick to the answer we agreed on.'

'If I am fortunate enough to be elected,' said Fletcher, 'it would be foolish of me not to take advantage of Senator Gates's wealth of experience, and I will stop listening to him only when I consider he has nothing left to teach me.'

'What do you feel about the Kendrick Amendment to the finance bill currently being debated in the house?' The ball came swinging in from left field, and it certainly wasn't one of the seventeen questions they had prepared for.

'That's a bit rough isn't it, Robin?' said the senator, 'after all, Fletcher is . . .'

'In so far as the clause affects senior citizens, I believe it discriminates against those who have already retired and are on fixed incomes. Most of us will have to retire at some time, and the only thing I remember Confucius saying was that a civilized society was one that educated its young and took care of its old. If I am elected, when Senator Kendrick's amendment to the bill comes before the Senate, I will vote against it. Bad laws can be drafted in a legislative session, but then take years to repeal, and I will only ever vote for a bill that I believe can be realistically administered.'

Harry sat back in his chair. 'Next question,' he said.

'In your CV, Mr Davenport, which I must say was most impressive, you claim you resigned from Alexander Dupont and Bell in order to run in this election.'

'That is correct,' said Fletcher.

'Did a colleague of yours, a Mr Logan Fitzgerald, also resign around that time?'

'Yes, he did.'

'Is there any connection between his resignation and yours?'

'None whatsoever,' said Fletcher firmly.

'What are you getting at?' asked Harry.

'Just a call from our New York office which they asked me to follow up,' replied the journalist.

'Anonymous, no doubt,' said Harry.

'I'm not at liberty to reveal my sources,' the journalist replied, trying hard not to smirk.

'Just in case your New York office didn't tell you who that informant was, I'll let you know his name just as soon as this press conference is over,' snapped Fletcher.

'Well, I think that just about wraps it up,' said Harry, before anyone could ask a supplementary question. 'Thank you all for joining us. You'll get a regular shot at the candidate in his weekly campaign press conferences – which is more than I ever gave you.'

'That was awful,' said Fletcher as they walked off the stage. 'I must learn to control my temper.'

'You did just fine, my boy,' said Harry, 'and by the time I've finished with the bastards, the only thing they will remember about this morning was your answer on the Kendrick's amendment to the finance bill. And frankly, the press are the least of our problems.' Harry paused ominously. 'The real battle will begin when we discover who the Republican candidate is.'

29

'WHAT DO YOU know about her?' asked Fletcher as they walked down the street together.

There wasn't a lot Harry didn't know about Barbara Hunter, as she had been his opponent for the past two elections, and a perpetual thorn in his flesh during the intervening years.

'She's forty-eight, born in Hartford, daughter of a farmer, educated in the local school system, and then at the University of Connecticut, married to a successful advertising executive, with three children, all living in the state, and she's currently a member of the State Congress.'

'Any bad news?' asked Fletcher.

'Yes, she doesn't drink and is a vegetarian, so you'll be visiting every bar and butcher in the constituency. And like anyone who has spent a lifetime in local politics, she's made her fair share of enemies on the way, and as she barely won the Republican nomination this time round, you can be sure that several party activists didn't want her in the first place. But more important, she lost the last two elections, so we paint her as a loser.'

Harry and Fletcher entered the Democratic head-quarters on Park Street to find the front window covered in posters and photos of the candidate, something Fletcher still hadn't become used to. *The Right Man for the Job.* He hadn't thought a lot of the slogan until the media experts explained that it was good to have the words 'right' and 'man' in the message when your opponent was a Republican woman. Subliminal, they had explained.

Harry walked up the stairs to the conference room on the first floor, and took his seat at the head of the table. Fletcher yawned as he sat down, although they had only been campaigning for seven days; and there were still twenty-six to go. The mistakes you make today are history tomorrow morning, your triumphs forgotten by the early evening news. Pace yourself, was one of Harry's most repeated maxims.

Fletcher looked around at the assembled group, a combination of pros and seasoned amateurs, with Harry no longer their candidate, but instead pressed into being campaign chairman. It was the only concession Martha had allowed, but she had told Fletcher to send him home the moment he showed the slightest sign of fatigue. As each day passed, it became harder to keep to Martha's instructions, as it was Harry who always set the pace.

'Anything new or devastating?' Harry asked as he looked around the team, one or two of whom had played a role in all seven of his election victories. In the last encounter, he'd beaten Barbara Hunter by over five thousand votes, but with the polls now running neck and neck, they were about to find out just how much of that vote had been personal.

'Yes,' said a voice from the other end of the table. Harry smiled down at Dan Mason who had been with him for six of his seven campaigns. Dan had started by working the copier, and was now in charge of press and public relations.

'The floor's all yours, Dan.'

'Barbara Hunter has just issued a press release challenging Fletcher to a debate. Presumably I tell her to get lost, and add that it's a sign of someone who is desperate and knows they are going to lose. That's what you always did.'

Harry was silent for a moment. 'You're right, Dan, I did,' he eventually said, 'but only because I was the incumbent and treated her as an upstart. In any case, I had nothing to gain from a debate, but that situation has changed now that we're fielding an unknown candidate, so I think we need to discuss the idea more fully before we come to any conclusion. What are the advantages and disadvantages? Opinions?' he said. Voices all started speaking at once.

'Gives our man more exposure.'

'Gives her the centre stage.'

'Proves we have the outstanding debater, which because of his youth will come as a surprise.'

'She knows the local problems – we could look inexperienced and ill-informed.'

'We look young, dynamic, and energetic.'

'She looks experienced, canny and seasoned.'

'We represent the youth of tomorrow.'

'She represents the women of today.'

'Fletcher could wipe the floor with her.'

'She wins the debate, and we lose the election.'

'Well, now we've heard the committee's views, perhaps it's time to consider the candidate's,' said Harry.

'I'm quite happy to debate with Mrs Hunter,' said Fletcher. 'People will assume she's more impressive simply because of her past record and my lack of experience, so I must try and turn that to our advantage.'

'But if she outshines you on local issues, and makes it look as if you're just not ready to do the job,' said Dan, 'then the election will be over in one evening. Don't think of it as a thousand people in a hall. Try to remember that the whole event will be covered by local radio and television, and is certain to be plastered over the front page of the *Hartford Courant* the following morning.'

'But that could work to our advantage as well,' said Harry.

'I agree,' said Dan, 'but it's one hell of a risk to take.'

'How long have I got to think about it?' asked Fletcher.

'Five minutes,' said Harry, 'perhaps ten, because if she's issued a press statement, they'll want to know our immediate response.'

'Can't we say we need a little time to think about it?'

'Certainly not,' said Harry, 'that would look as if we're debating the debate, and in the end you'd have to give in, so she then wins both ways. We either turn it down firmly, or accept it with enthusiasm. Perhaps we should take a vote on it,' he added, looking around the table. 'Those in favour?' Eleven hands shot up. 'Against?' Fourteen hands were raised. 'Well, that's the end of that.'

'No, it isn't,' said Fletcher. Everyone seated round the table stopped talking and looked at the candidate. 'I am grateful for your opinions, but I do not intend to spend my political career being run by a committee, especially when the vote is that close. Dan, you will issue a statement saying I'm delighted to accept Mrs Hunter's challenge, and look forward to debating the real issues with her, rather than the political posturing that the Republicans seem to have specialized in from the start of this campaign.' There was a moment's silence, before the room broke into spontaneous applause.

Harry smiled. 'Those in favour of a debate?' Every hand shot up. 'Those against?' None. 'I declare the motion carried unanimously.'

'Why did we have a second vote?' Fletcher asked Harry as they left the room.

'So that we can tell the press that the decision was unanimous.'

Fletcher smiled as they headed towards the station. Another lesson learnt.

⚊⚬⚊

A team of twelve canvassed the station every morning, most of them handing out leaflets, while the candidate shook hands with the early commuters leaving the city. Harry had told him to concentrate on those going into the station, because they almost certainly lived in Hartford, whereas those coming off the trains probably didn't have a vote in the constituency.

'Hi, I'm Fletcher Davenport . . .'

At eight thirty they crossed the road to Ma's and grabbed an egg and bacon sandwich. Once Ma had given her opinion on how the election was going, they headed off for the city's insurance district to shake hands with 'the suits' as they arrived at their offices. In the car, Fletcher put on a Yale tie, which he knew many of the executives would identify with.

'Hi, I'm Fletcher Davenport . . .'

At nine thirty, they returned to campaign HQ for the early morning press conference. Barbara Hunter had already held hers an hour earlier, so Fletcher knew that there would only be one subject on the agenda that morning. On the way back, he replaced the Yale tie with something more neutral as he listened to the headlines on the morning news update, to make sure he couldn't be surprised by a piece of breaking news. War had broken out in the Middle East. He would leave that to President Ford, because it wasn't going to end up on the front page of the *Hartford Courant*.

'Hi, I'm Fletcher Davenport . . .'

When Harry opened the morning press conference, he told the assembled journalists even before they could ask the question that it had been a unanimous decision to take on Mrs Hunter head to head. Harry never referred to her as Barbara. When questioned about the debate – venue, time, format – Harry said this was yet to be decided, as they had only received the challenge earlier that morning, but he added, 'I don't foresee any problems.' Harry knew only too well that the debate would throw up nothing *but* problems.

Fletcher was surprised by Harry's reply when asked what he thought of the candidate's chances. He had expected the senator to talk about his debating skills, his legal experience and his political acumen, but instead Harry said, 'Well of course, Mrs Hunter starts off with a built-in advantage. We all know that she's a seasoned debater, with a great deal of experience on local issues, but I consider it typical of Fletcher's honest, open approach to this election that he's agreed to take her on.'

'Doesn't that make it a tremendous risk, senator?' asked another journalist.

'Sure does,' admitted Harry, 'but as the candidate has pointed out, if he wasn't man enough to face Mrs Hunter, how could the public expect him to take on the bigger challenge of representing them?' Fletcher couldn't remember saying anything like that, although he didn't disagree with the sentiment.

Once the press conference was over, and the last journalist had departed, Fletcher said, 'I thought you told me Barbara Hunter was a poor debater, and took forever answering questions?'

'Yep, that's exactly what I said,' admitted Harry.

'Then why did you tell the journalists that . . .'

'It's all about expectations, my boy. Now they think

you're not up to it,' Harry replied, 'and that she'll wipe the floor with you, so even if you only manage a draw they'll declare you the winner.'

'*Hi, I'm Fletcher Davenport . . .*' kept repeating itself over and over like some hit song he just couldn't get out of his mind.

30

NAT WAS DELIGHTED when Tom popped his head round the door and asked, 'Can I bring a guest to dinner tonight?'

'Sure, business or pleasure?' Nat asked, looking up from his desk.

Tom hesitated, 'I'm rather hoping that it might be both.'

'Female?' said Nat, now more interested.

'Decidedly female.'

'Name?'

'Julia Kirkbridge.'

'And what . . .'

'That's enough of the third degree, you can ask her all the questions you want to tonight because she's more than capable of taking care of herself.'

'Thanks for the warning,' said Su Ling when Nat sprung an extra guest on her only moments after he'd arrived home.

'I should have called, shouldn't I?' he said.

'It would have made life a little easier, but I expect you were making millions at the time.'

'Something like that,' said Nat.

'What do we know about her?' asked Su Ling.

'Nothing,' said Nat. 'You know Tom; when it comes to his private life, he's even more secretive than a Swiss banker, but as he's willing to let us meet her one can only live in hope.'

'What happened to that gorgeous redhead called Maggie? I'd rather thought that . . .'

'Disappeared like all the others. Can you ever remember him inviting anyone to join us for dinner a second time?'

Su Ling thought about the question for a moment, and then admitted, 'Now you mention it, I can't. I suppose it could just be my cooking.'

'No, it's not your cooking, but I'm afraid that you are to blame.'

'Me?' said Su Ling.

'Yes, you. The poor man has been besotted with you for years, so everyone he goes out with is dragged along to dinner so that Tom can compare . . .'

'Oh no, not that old chestnut again,' said Su Ling.

'It's not an old chestnut, little flower, it's the problem.'

'But he's never done more than kiss me on the cheek.'

'And he never will. I wonder how many people are in love with someone they have never even kissed on the cheek.'

Nat disappeared upstairs to read to Luke as Su Ling set a fourth place at the table. She was polishing an extra glass, when the doorbell rang.

'Can you get it, Nat? I'm a bit tied up.' There was no response, so she took off her apron and went to the front door.

'Hi,' said Tom as he bent down and kissed Su Ling on the cheek, which only brought Nat's words to mind.

'This is Julia,' he said. Su Ling looked up at an elegant woman, who was nearly as tall as Tom, and almost as slim as she was, although her fair hair and blue eyes suggested a heritage nearer Scandinavia than the Far East.

'How nice to meet you,' said Julia. 'I know it's hackneyed, but I really have heard so much about you.'

Su Ling smiled as she took Julia's fur coat. 'My husband,' she said, 'is caught up with . . .'

'Black cats,' said Nat as he appeared by Su Ling's side. 'I've been reading *The Cat in the Hat* to Luke. Hi, I'm Nat, and you must be Julia.'

'Yes, I am,' she said, giving Nat a smile that reminded Su Ling that other women found her husband attractive. 'Let's go into the living room and have a drink,' said Nat, 'I've put some champagne on ice.'

'Do we have something to celebrate?' asked Tom.

'Other than you being able to find someone who is willing to accompany you to dinner, no, I can't think of anything in particular, unless . . .' Julia laughed. 'Unless we include a call from my lawyers to say that the Bennett's takeover has been clinched.'

'When did you hear about that?' asked Tom.

'Late this afternoon; Jimmy called to say that they've signed all the documents. All that we have to do now is hand over the cheque.'

'You didn't mention this when you came in,' said Su Ling.

'The thought of Julia coming to dinner drove it out of my mind,' said Nat, 'but I did discuss the deal with Luke.'

'And what was his considered opinion?' asked Tom.

'He thought that a dollar was far too much to pay for a bank.'

'A dollar?' echoed Julia.

'Yes, Bennett's have been declaring a loss for the past five years and, if you exclude the banking premises, their long-term debt is no longer covered by their assets, so Luke may prove to be right if I can't turn it around in time.'

'How old is Luke?' asked Julia.

'Two, but he already has a proper grasp of financial matters.'

Julia laughed. 'So tell me more about the bank, Nat.'

'It's only the beginning,' he explained as he poured the champagne, 'I still have my eye on Morgan's.'

'And how much is that going to cost you?' asked Su Ling.

'Around three hundred million at today's prices, but by the time I'm ready to make a bid, it could be over a billion.'

'I can't think in those sort of sums,' said Julia, 'it's way out of my league.'

'Now that's not true, Julia,' said Tom. 'Don't forget I've studied your company's accounts, and unlike Bennett's, you've made a profit for the past five years.'

'Yes, but only just over a million,' said Julia, giving him that smile again.

'Excuse me,' said Su Ling, 'while I check on dinner.'

Nat smiled at his wife and then glanced at Tom's guest. He already had the feeling that Julia just might make it to a second date. 'What do you do, Julia?' asked Nat.

'What do you think I do?' was thrown back with the same flirtatious smile.

'I'd say you were a model, possibly an actress.'

'Not bad. I used to be a model when I was younger, but for the past six years I've been involved in real estate.'

Su Ling reappeared. 'If you'd like to come through, dinner is just about ready.'

'Real estate,' said Nat as he accompanied his guest into the dining room, 'I would never have guessed.'

'But it's true,' said Tom. 'And Julia wants us to handle her account. There's a site she's looking at in Hartford, and she will be depositing five hundred thousand dollars with the bank, in case she needs to move quickly.'

'Why did you select us?' asked Nat, as his wife placed a bowl of lobster bisque in front of her.

'Because my late husband dealt with Mr Russell over the Robinson Mall site. Although we were the underbidders on that occasion and failed to secure the deal, Mr Russell didn't charge us,' said Julia. 'Not even a fee.'

'That sounds like my father,' said Tom.

'So my late husband said that if we were ever to look at anything else in this area, we should only bank with Russell's.'

'Things have changed since then,' said Nat, 'Mr Russell has retired and . . .'

'But his son is still there, as chairman.'

'And he has me breathing down his neck to make sure people like you are charged when we give them a professional service. Though you'll be interested to know that the mall has been a great success, showing an excellent return for its investors. So what brings you to Hartford?'

'I read that there are plans to build a second mall on the other side of the city.'

'That's right. The council is putting the land up for sale with a development permit.'

'What sort of figure are they looking for?' asked Julia as she sipped her soup.

'Around three million is the word on the street, but I think it's likely to end up nearer three point three to three point five after the success of the Robinson's site.'

'Three point five is our upper limit,' said Julia. 'My company is by nature cautious, and in any case, there's always another deal around the corner.'

'Perhaps we could interest you in some of the other properties we represent,' said Nat.

'No, thank you,' said Julia. 'My firm specializes in malls, and one of the many things my husband taught me was never to stray away from your field of expertise.'

'Wise man, your late husband.'

'He was,' said Julia. 'But I think that's enough business for one night, so once my money has been deposited, perhaps the bank would be willing to represent me at the auction? However I require complete discretion, I don't want anyone else to know who you're bidding for. Something else my husband taught me.' She turned her attention to the hostess. 'Can I help you with the next course?'

'No, thank you,' said Su Ling, 'Nat's hopeless, but is just about capable of carrying four plates into the kitchen, and when he remembers, pouring the occasional glass of wine.'

'So how did you two meet?' asked Nat while, prompted by Su Ling's comment, he began to refill the glasses.

'You wouldn't believe it,' said Tom, 'but we met on a building site.'

'I'm sure there has to be a more romantic explanation.'

'When I was checking over the council land last Sunday, I came across Julia out jogging.'

'I thought you were insistent about discretion,' said Nat smiling.

'Not many people seeing a woman jogging over a building site on a Sunday morning think she wants to buy it.'

'In fact,' said Tom, 'it wasn't until I'd taken her out for dinner at the Cascade that I discovered what Julia was really up to.'

'Corporate real estate must be a tough world for a woman,' said Nat.

'Yes it is,' said Julia, 'but I didn't choose it, it chose me. You see, when I left college in Minnesota, I did some modelling for a short time, before I met my husband. It was his idea that I should look at sites whenever I went out jogging, and then report back to him. Within a year I knew exactly what he was looking for and within two, I had a place on the board.'

'So you now run the company.'

'No,' said Julia, 'I leave that to my chairman and chief executive officer, but I remain the majority shareholder.'

'So you decided to stay involved after your husband's death?'

'Yes, that was his idea, he knew he only had a couple of years to live, and as we didn't have any children he decided to teach me everything about the business. I think even he was surprised by how willing a pupil I turned out to be.'

Nat began to clear away the plates.

'Anyone for crème brûlée?' asked Su Ling.

'I couldn't eat another mouthful; that lamb was so tender,' said Julia. 'But don't let that stop you,' she added patting Tom's stomach.

Nat glanced across at Tom, and thought he'd never seen him looking so content. He suspected that Julia might even come to dinner a third time.

'Is that really the time?' asked Julia, looking down at her watch. 'It's been a wonderful evening, Su Ling, but please forgive me, I have a board meeting at ten tomorrow morning, so I ought to be leaving.'

'Yes, of course,' said Su Ling, rising from her place.

Tom leapt up from his chair and accompanied Julia out into the hall, before helping her on with her coat. He kissed Su Ling on the cheek, thanking her for a wonderful evening.

'I'm only sorry that Julia has to rush back to New York. Let's make it my place next time.'

Nat glanced across at Su Ling and smiled, but she didn't respond.

Nat found himself chuckling as he closed the front door. 'Some woman that,' he said when he joined his wife in the kitchen and grabbed a drying-up cloth.

'She's a phony,' said Su Ling.

'What do you mean?' asked Nat.

'Exactly what I said, she's a phony – phony accent, phony clothes, and her phony story was altogether too neat and tidy. Don't do any business with her.'

'What can go wrong if she deposits five hundred thousand with the bank?'

'I'd be willing to bet a month's salary that the five hundred thousand never turns up.'

Although Su Ling didn't raise the subject again that night, when Nat arrived at his office the following morning, he asked his secretary to dig up all the financial details she could find on Kirkbridge & Company of New York. She was back an hour later with a copy of their annual report, and latest financial statement. Nat checked carefully through the report and his eye finally settled on the bottom line. They had made a profit of just over a million the previous year, and all the figures tallied with those Julia had talked about over dinner. He then checked the board of directors. Mrs Julia Kirkbridge was listed as a director, below the chairman and chief executive. But because of Su Ling's apprehension, he decided to take the enquiry one step further. He dialled the telephone number of their office in New York, without going through his secretary.

'Kirkbridge and Company, how can I help you?' said a voice.

'Good morning, would it be possible to speak to Mrs Kirkbridge?'

'No, I'm afraid not, sir, she's in a board meeting,' Nat glanced at his watch and smiled, it was ten twenty-five, 'but if you leave your number, I'll ask her to call you back just as soon as she's free.'

'No, that won't be necessary,' said Nat. As he put the phone down it rang again immediately. 'It's Jeb in new accounts, Mr Cartwright, I thought you would want to know that we have just received a wire transfer from Chase for the sum of five hundred thousand, to be credited to the account of a Mrs Julia Kirkbridge.'

Nat couldn't resist calling Su Ling to tell her the news. 'She's still a phony,' his wife repeated.

31

'HEADS OR TAILS?' asked the moderator.

'Tails,' said Barbara Hunter.

'Tails it is,' said the moderator. He looked across at Mrs Hunter and nodded. Fletcher couldn't complain, because he would have called heads – he always did – so only wondered what decision she would make. Would she speak first, because that would determine at the end of the evening that Fletcher spoke last? If, on the other hand . . .

'I'll speak first,' she said.

Fletcher suppressed a smile. The tossing of the coin had proved irrelevant; if he'd won, he would have elected to speak second.

The moderator took his seat behind the desk on the centre of the stage. Mrs Hunter sat on his right, and Fletcher on his left, reflecting the ideology of their two parties. But selecting where they should sit had been the least of their problems. For the past ten days there had been arguments about where the debate should be held, what time it should begin, who the moderator should be, and even the height of the lecterns from which they would speak, because Barbara Hunter was five foot seven, and Fletcher six foot one. In the end, it was agreed there should be two lecterns of different heights, one on either side of the stage.

The moderator acceptable to both was chairman of

the journalism department at UConn's Hartford campus. He rose from his place.

'Good evening, ladies and gentlemen. My name is Frank McKenzie, and I will be moderator for this evening's debate. The format calls on Mrs Hunter to begin with a six-minute opening statement, followed by Mr Davenport. I feel I should warn both candidates that I will ring this bell,' he picked up a small bell by his side and rang it firmly, which caused some laughter in the audience and helped break the tension, 'at five minutes to warn you both that you have sixty seconds left to speak. I will then ring it again after six minutes when you must deliver your final sentence. Following their opening statements, both candidates will then answer questions from a selected panel for forty minutes. Finally, Mrs Hunter followed by Mr Davenport, will each make their closing remarks for three minutes. I now call upon Mrs Hunter to open proceedings.'

Barbara Hunter rose from her place and walked slowly over to her lectern on the right-hand side of the stage. She had calculated that since ninety per cent of the audience would be watching the debate on television, she would address the largest number of potential voters if she spoke first, especially as a world series game was due to be aired at eight thirty, when the majority of viewers would automatically switch channels. Since both of them would have made their opening remarks by that time, Fletcher felt it wasn't that significant. But he also wanted to speak second so that he could pick up on some of the points Mrs Hunter made during her statement, and if at the end of the evening, he had the last word, perhaps it might be the only thing the audience would remember.

Fletcher listened attentively to a predictable and well rehearsed opening from Mrs Hunter. She held the lectern firmly as she spoke. 'I was born in Hartford. I married a

Hartford man, my children were born at St Patrick's Hospital and all of them still live in the state capital, so I feel I am well qualified to represent the people of this great city.' The first burst of applause flooded up from the floor. Fletcher checked the packed audience carefully, and noted that about half of them were joining in, while the other half remained silent.

Among Jimmy's responsibilities for the evening was the allocation of seats. It had been agreed that both parties would be given three hundred tickets each, with four hundred left over for the general public. Jimmy and a small band of helpers had spent hours urging their supporters to apply for the remaining four hundred, but Jimmy realized that the Republicans would be just as assiduous in carrying out the same exercise, so it was always going to end up around fifty–fifty. Fletcher wondered how many genuinely neutral people there were sitting in the auditorium.

'Don't worry about the hall,' Harry had told him, 'the real audience will be watching you on television and they're the ones you need to influence. Stare into the middle of the camera lens, and look sincere,' he added with a grin.

Fletcher made notes as Mrs Hunter outlined her programme, and although the contents were sensible and worthy, she had the sort of delivery that allowed the mind to wander. When the moderator rang the bell at five minutes, Mrs Hunter was only about half-way through her speech and even paused while she turned a couple of pages. Fletcher was surprised that such a seasoned campaigner hadn't calculated that the occasional burst of applause would cut into her time. Fletcher's opening remarks were timed at just over five minutes. 'Better to finish a few seconds early than have to rush towards the end,' Harry had warned him again and again. Mrs

Hunter's peroration closed a few seconds after the second bell had rung, making it sound as if she had been cut short. Nevertheless, she still received rapturous applause from half of the audience, and courteous acknowledgment from the remainder.

'I'll now ask Mr Davenport to make his opening statement.'

Fletcher slowly approached the lectern on his side of the stage, feeling like a man just a few paces away from the gallows. He was somewhat relieved by the warm reception he received. He placed his five-page, double spaced, large-type script on the lectern and checked the opening sentence, though in truth he had been over the speech so many times he virtually knew it by heart. He looked down at the audience and smiled, aware that the moderator wouldn't start the clock until he'd delivered his first word.

'I think I've made one big mistake in my life,' he began. 'I wasn't born in Hartford.' The ripple of laughter helped him, 'But I made up for it. I fell in love with a Hartford girl when I was only fourteen.' Laughter and applause followed. Fletcher relaxed for the first time and delivered the rest of his opening remarks with a confidence that he hoped belied his youth. When the bell for five minutes rang, he was just about to begin his peroration. He completed it with twenty seconds to spare, making the final bell redundant. The applause he received was far greater than he had been greeted with when he first approached the lectern, but then the opening statement was no more than the end of the first round.

He glanced down at Harry and Jimmy, who were seated in the second row. Their smiles suggested he had survived the opening skirmish.

'The time has now come for the question session,' said the moderator, 'which will last for forty minutes. The candidates are to give brief responses. I'll start with Charles Lockhart of the *Hartford Courant*.'

'Does either candidate believe the educational grants system should be reformed?' asked the local editor crisply.

Fletcher was well prepared for this question, as it had come up again and again at local meetings, and was regularly the subject of editorials in Mr Lockhart's paper. He was invited to respond as Hunter had spoken first.

'There should never be any discrimination that makes it harder for someone from a poor background to attend college. It is not enough to believe in equality, we must also insist on equality of opportunity.' This was greeted with a sprinkling of applause and Fletcher smiled down at the audience.

'Fine words,' responded Mrs Hunter cutting into the applause, 'but you out there will also expect fine deeds. I've sat on school boards so you don't have to lecture me on discrimination, Mr Davenport, and if I am fortunate enough to be elected senator, I will back legislation that supports the claims of all men,' she paused, 'and women, to equal opportunities.' She stood back from the lectern while her supporters began cheering. She turned her gaze on Fletcher. 'Perhaps someone who has had the privilege of being educated at Hotchkiss and Yale might not be able to fully grasp that.'

Damn, thought Fletcher, I forgot to tell them that Annie sat on a school board, and they had just enrolled Lucy in Hartford Elementary, a local public school. When there had only been twelve in the audience, he had remembered every time.

Questions on local taxes, hospital staffing, public transportation and crime predictably followed. Fletcher recovered from the opening salvo and began to feel that the session would end in a draw, until the moderator called for the last question.

'Do the candidates consider themselves truly independent, or will their policies be dictated by the party machine, and their vote in the Senate dependent on the views of retired politicians?' The questioner was Jill Bernard, weekend anchor of a local radio talk show, which seemed to have Barbara Hunter on every other day.

Mrs Hunter replied immediately. 'All of you in this hall know that I had to fight every inch of the way to win my party's nomination, and unlike some, it wasn't handed to me on a plate. In fact, I've had to fight for everything in my life, as my parents couldn't afford silver spoons. And may I remind you that I haven't hesitated to stand firm on issues whenever I believed my party was wrong. It didn't always make me popular, but no one has ever doubted my independence. If elected to the senate, I wouldn't be on the phone every day seeking advice on how I should vote. I will be making the decisions and I will stand by them.' She finished to rapturous applause.

The knot in his stomach, the sweat in the palms of his hands, and the weakness in his legs had all returned as Fletcher tried to collect his thoughts. He looked down at the audience to see every eye boring into him.

'I was born in Farmington, just a few miles away from this hall. My parents are long-standing active contributors to the Hartford community through their professional and voluntary work, in particular for St Patrick's hospital.' He looked down at his parents, who were sitting in the fifth row. His father's head was held high, his mother's was bowed. 'My mother sat on so many non-profit boards, I thought I must be an orphan, but they have both come along to support me tonight. Yes, I did go to Hotchkiss, and Mrs Hunter is right. It was a privilege. Yes, I did go to Yale, a great Connecticut university. Yes, I did become president of the college council, and yes I was editor of the *Law Review*, which is why I was invited to join one of the most prestigious legal firms in New York. I make no apology for never being satisfied with second place. And I was equally delighted to give all that up so that I could return to Hartford and put something back into the community where I was raised. By the way, on the salary the state are offering, I won't be able to afford many silver spoons and so far, no one's offered me anything on a plate.' The audience burst into spontaneous applause. He waited for the applause to die down, before he lowered his voice almost to a whisper. 'Don't let's disguise what this questioner was getting at. Will I regularly be on the phone to my father-in-law, Senator Harry Gates? I expect so, I am married to his only daughter.' More laughter followed. 'But let me remind you of something you already know about Harry Gates. He's served this constituency for twenty-eight years with honour and integrity, at a time when those two words seem to have lost their meaning, and frankly,' said Fletcher turning to face his Republican rival, 'neither of us is worthy to take his place. But if I am elected, you bet I'll take advantage of his wisdom, his experience and his foresight; only a blinkered egotist wouldn't. But let me also make one thing clear,' he said, turning back to face the audience, 'I will be the person who represents you in the Senate.'

Fletcher returned to his place with over half of the audience on their feet cheering. Mrs Hunter had made the mistake of attacking him on ground where he needed no preparation. She tried to recover in her closing remarks, but the blow had been landed.

When the moderator said, 'I'd like to thank both candidates,' Fletcher did something Harry had recommended at lunch the previous Sunday. He immediately walked across to his opponent, shook her by the hand, and paused to allow the *Courant*'s photographer to record the moment.

The following day, the picture of the two of them dominated the front page, and achieved exactly what Harry had hoped for – the image of a six-foot-one man, towering over a five-foot-seven woman. 'And don't smile, look serious,' he'd added. 'We need them to forget how young you are.'

Fletcher read the words below the picture – *nothing between them.* The editorial said that he had held his own in the debate, but Barbara Hunter still led the opinion polls by two per cent with only nine days to go.

32

'Do you mind if I smoke?'

'No, it's only Su Ling who doesn't approve of the habit.'

'I don't think she approves of me either,' said Julia Kirkbridge, as she flicked on her lighter.

'You have to remember that she was brought up by a very conservative mother,' said Tom. 'She even disapproved of Nat to begin with, but she'll come round, especially when I tell her . . .'

'Shh,' said Julia, 'for now that must remain our little secret.' She inhaled deeply, and then added, 'I like Nat; you two obviously make a good team.'

'We do, but I'm keen to close this deal while he's on holiday, especially after his triumph in taking over our oldest rival.'

'I can understand that,' said Julia, 'but how do you rate our chances?'

'It's beginning to look as if there are only two or three serious bidders in the field. The restrictions set out in the council's offer document should eliminate any cowboys.'

'Restrictions?'

'The council is demanding not only that the bidding must be by public auction, but that the full amount has to be paid on signature.'

'Why are they insisting on that?' asked Julia, sitting up in bed. 'In the past, I've always put ten per cent down and assumed I would be given at least twenty-eight days before I had to complete.'

'Yes, that would be normal practice, but this site has become a political hot potato. Barbara Hunter is insisting there be no hold-ups, because one or two other deals have fallen through recently when it was discovered that a speculator didn't have the necessary resources to complete the agreement. And don't forget, we're only days away from an election, so they are making sure that there can be no come-backs later.'

'Does that mean I'll have to deposit another three million with you by next Friday?' asked Julia.

'No, if we secure the property, the bank will cover you with a short-term loan.'

'But what if I renege on the deal?' asked Julia.

'It doesn't matter to us,' said Tom. 'We would sell it on to the under-bidder, and still have your five hundred thousand to cover any loss.'

'Banks,' said Julia as she stubbed out her cigarette and slid under the sheets. 'You never lose.'

<hr>

'I want you to do me a favour,' said Su Ling as the plane began its descent into Los Angeles airport.

'Yes, little flower, I'm listening.'

'See if you can go a whole week without phoning the bank. Don't forget this is Luke's first big trip.'

'Mine too,' said Nat, putting his arm round his son, 'I've always wanted to visit Disneyland.'

'Now stop teasing, you made a deal, and I expect you to keep to it.'

'I would like to keep an eye on the deal that Tom's trying to close with Julia's company.'

'Don't you think Tom just might like to have a little triumph of his own, one that hadn't been double-checked by the great Nat Cartwright? It was you, after all, who decided to trust her.'

'I take your point,' said Nat, as Luke clung to him as the plane touched down. 'But do you mind if I phone him on Friday afternoon just to find out if our bid on the Cedar Wood project was successful?'

'No, as long as you do leave it until Friday afternoon.'

'Dad, will we travel in a sputnik?'

'You bet,' said Nat, 'why else would you go to LA?'

−◦−

Tom met Julia off the train from New York and drove her straight to City Hall. They walked in to find the cleaners just leaving after the debate the previous evening. Tom had read in the *Hartford Courant* that over a thousand people attended the event, and the paper's editorial had suggested there wasn't much to pick between the two candidates. He'd always voted Republican in the past, but he thought that Fletcher Davenport sounded like a decent man.

'Why have we arrived so early?' asked Julia, breaking into his thoughts.

'I want to be familiar with the layout of the room,' explained Tom, 'so that when the bidding starts, we can't be taken by surprise. Don't forget, the whole thing could all be over in a few minutes.'

'Where do you think we should sit?'

'Half-way back on the right. I've already told the auctioneer what sign I intend to use when I'm bidding.'

Tom looked up towards the stage and watched as the auctioneer mounted the rostrum, tapped the microphone, and stared down at the tiny audience, checking everything was in place.

'Who are all these people?' asked Julia, looking around the hall.

'A mixture of council officials, including the chief executive, Mr Cooke, representatives from the auctioneer's, and the odd person who's got nothing better to do on a Friday afternoon. But as far as I can see, there are only three serious bidders.' Tom checked his watch. 'Perhaps we should sit down.'

Julia and Tom took their places about half-way back on the end of the row. Tom picked up the sales brochure on the seat beside him, and when Julia touched his hand, he couldn't help wondering how many people would work out that they were lovers. He turned the page and studied an architect's mock-up of what the proposed mall might look like. He was still reading through the small print when the auctioneer indicated he was ready to begin. He cleared his throat.

'Ladies and gentlemen,' he said, 'there is only one item to come under the hammer this afternoon, a prime site on the north side of the city known as Cedar Wood. The city council is offering this property with approval for commercial development. The terms of payment and regulatory requirements are detailed in the brochure to be found on your seats. I must stress that if any of the terms are not adhered to, the council is within its rights to withdraw from the transaction.' He paused to allow his words to sink in. 'I have an opening bid of two million,' he declared, and immediately looked in Tom's direction.

Although Tom said nothing and gave no sign, the auctioneer announced, 'I have a new bidder at two million two hundred and fifty thousand.' The auctioneer made a show of glancing round the room, despite the fact he knew exactly where the three serious bidders were seated. His eyes settled on a well-known local lawyer in the second row, who raised his brochure. 'Two million five hundred thousand, it's with you, sir.' The auctioneer turned his attention back to Tom, who didn't even blink.

'Two million seven hundred and fifty thousand.' His eyes returned to the lawyer, who waited for some time before he once again raised his brochure. 'Three million,' said the auctioneer, and immediately looked in Tom's direction before saying, 'Three million two hundred and fifty thousand.' He returned to the lawyer, who seemed to hesitate. Julia squeezed Tom's hand between the chairs. 'I think we've got it.'

'Three million five hundred thousand?' suggested the auctioneer, his eyes fixed on the lawyer.

'Not yet we haven't,' Tom whispered.

'Three million five hundred thousand,' repeated the auctioneer hopefully. 'Three million five hundred thousand,' he repeated gratefully as the brochure rose for a third time.

'Damn,' said Tom, taking off his glasses, 'I think we must have both settled on the same upper limit.'

'Then let's go to three six,' said Julia. 'That way at least we'll find out.'

Although Tom had removed his glasses – the sign that he was no longer bidding – the auctioneer could see that Mr Russell was in deep conversation with the lady seated next to him. 'Have we finished bidding, sir? Or . . .'

Tom hesitated and then said, 'Three million six hundred thousand.'

The auctioneer swung his attention back to the lawyer, who had placed his brochure on the empty seat beside him. 'Can I say three million seven hundred thousand sir, or are we all finished?'

The brochure remained on the seat. 'Any other bids from the floor?' asked the auctioneer as his eyes swept the dozen or so people who were seated in a hall that had held a thousand the night before. 'One last chance, otherwise I shall let it go at three million six hundred thousand.' He raised his hammer and, receiving no response, brought it down with a thud. 'Sold for three million six hundred thousand dollars to the gentleman at the end of the row.'

'Well done,' said Julia.

'It's going to cost you another hundred thousand,' said Tom, 'but we couldn't have known that two of us would settle on the same upper limit. I'll just go and sort out the paperwork and hand over the cheque, then we can go off and celebrate.'

'What a good idea,' said Julia, as she ran a finger down the inside of his leg.

'Congratulations, Mr Russell,' said Mr Cooke. 'Your client has secured a fine property which I am sure in the long-term will yield an excellent return.'

'I agree,' said Tom, as he wrote out a cheque for three point six million dollars and handed it across to the council's chief executive.

'Is Russell's Bank the principal in this transaction?' enquired Mr Cooke as he studied the signature.

'No, we are representing a New York client who banks with us.'

'I am sorry to appear to be nitpicking about this, Mr Russell, but the terms of the agreement make it clear that the cheque for the full amount must be signed by the principal and not by his or her representative.'

'But we represent the company, and are holding their deposit.'

'Then it shouldn't be too difficult for your client to sign a cheque on behalf of that company,' suggested Mr Cooke.

'But why . . .' began Tom.

'It's not for me to try and fathom the machinations of our elected representatives, Mr Russell, but after the débâcle last year over the Aldwich contract and the questions I have to answer daily from Mrs Hunter,' he let out a sigh. 'I have been left with no choice but to keep to the letter, as well as the spirit, of the agreement.'

'But what can I do about it at this late stage?' asked Tom.

'You still have until five o'clock to produce a cheque signed by the principal. If you fail to do so, the property will be offered to the under-bidder for three point five million, and the council will look to you to make up the difference of one hundred thousand dollars.'

Tom ran to the back of the room. 'Have you got your cheque book with you?'

'No,' said Julia. 'You told me that Russell's would cover the full amount until I transferred the difference on Monday.'

'Yes I did,' said Tom, trying to think on his feet. 'There's nothing else for it,' he added, 'we'll just have to go straight to the bank.' He checked his watch, it was nearly four o'clock. 'Damn,' he added, painfully aware that if Nat hadn't been on holiday, he would have spotted the sub-clause and anticipated its consequences. On the short walk from City Hall to Russell's Bank, Tom explained to Julia what Mr Cooke had insisted on.

'Does that mean I've lost the deal, not to mention a hundred thousand?'

'No, I've already thought of a way round that, but it will need your agreement.'

'If it will secure the property,' said Julia, 'I'll do whatever you advise.'

As soon as they entered the bank, Tom went straight to his office, picked up a phone and asked the chief teller to join him. While he waited for Ray Jackson to arrive, he took out a blank cheque book and began writing out the words three million six hundred thousand dollars. The chief teller knocked on the door and entered the chairman's office.

'Ray, I want you to transfer three million one hundred thousand dollars to Mrs Kirkbridge's account.'

The chief teller hesitated for a moment. 'I'll need a letter of authorization before I can transfer such a large amount,' he said. 'It's way above my limit.'

'Yes, of course,' said the chairman, and removed the standard form from his top drawer and quickly filled in the relevant figures. Tom didn't comment on the fact that it was also the largest sum he had ever authorized. He passed the form across to the chief teller, who studied the details carefully. He looked as if he wanted to query the chairman's decision, and then thought better of it.

'Immediately,' emphasized Tom.

'Yes, sir,' said the chief teller, and departed as quickly as he had arrived.

'Are you sure that was sensible?' asked Julia. 'Aren't you taking an unnecessary risk?'

'We have the property and your five hundred thousand, so we can't lose. As Nat would say, it's a belt and braces job.' He turned the cheque book round and asked Julia to sign it and print beneath her signature the name of her company. Once Tom had checked it he said, 'We'd better get back to City Hall as quickly as possible.'

Tom tried to remain calm as he dodged in and out of the traffic while crossing Main Street before jogging up the steps to City Hall. He kept having to wait for Julia, who explained it wasn't easy to keep up with him in high heels. When they re-entered the building, Tom was relieved to find Mr Cooke was still seated behind his desk at the far end of the hall. The chief executive rose when he saw them heading towards him.

'Hand over the cheque to the thin man with the bald head,' said Tom, 'and smile.'

Julia carried out Tom's instructions to the letter, and received a warm smile in return. Mr Cooke studied the cheque carefully. 'This seems to be in order, Mrs Kirkbridge, if I could just see some form of identification.'

'Certainly,' said Julia, and took a driver's licence out of her handbag.

Mr Cooke studied the photo and the signature. 'It's not a flattering picture of you,' he said. Julia smiled. 'Good, now all that is left for you to do is sign all the necessary documents on behalf of your company.'

Julia signed the council agreement in triplicate and handed a copy over to Tom. 'I think you'd better hold on to this until the money is safely transferred,' she whispered.

Mr Cooke looked at his watch. 'I shall be presenting this cheque first thing on Monday morning, Mr Russell,' he said, 'and I would be obliged if it were cleared as quickly as is convenient. I don't want to give Mrs Hunter any more ammunition than is necessary only days before the election.'

'It will be cleared on the same day it's presented,' Tom assured him.

'Thank you, sir,' said Mr Cooke to a man he regularly had a round of golf with at their local club.

Tom wanted to give Julia a hug, but restrained himself. 'I'll just run back to the bank and let them know that it all went smoothly, then we can go home.'

'Do you really have to?' asked Julia. 'After all, they won't be presenting the cheque until Monday morning.'

'I guess that's right,' said Tom.

'Damn,' said Julia, bending down to take off one of her shoes, 'I've broken the heel running up those steps.'

'Sorry,' said Tom, 'that was my fault, I shouldn't have made you rush back from the bank. As it turned out we had more than enough time.'

'It's not a problem,' said Julia, smiling, 'but if you could fetch the car, I'll join you at the bottom of the steps.'

'Yes, of course,' said Tom. He jogged back down and across to the parking lot.

He was back outside City Hall a few minutes later, but Julia was nowhere to be seen. Perhaps she had slipped back inside? He waited a few moments, but she still didn't appear. He cursed, leapt out of the illegally parked car and ran up the steps and into the building to find Julia in one of the phone booths. The moment she saw him, she hung up.

'I've just been telling New York about your coup, darling, and they've instructed our bank to transfer the three million one hundred thousand before close of business.'

'That's good to hear,' said Tom, as they strolled back to the car together. 'So shall we have supper in town?'

'No, I'd rather go back to your place and have a quiet meal on our own,' said Julia.

When Tom pulled up in his driveway, Julia had already removed her coat, and by the time they reached the bedroom on the second floor, she had left a paper-chase of clothes in her wake. Tom was down to his underwear and Julia was peeling off a stocking when the phone rang.

'Leave it,' Julia said as she fell to her knees and pulled down his boxer shorts.

—◇—

'There's no reply,' said Nat, 'they must have gone out for dinner.'

'Can't it wait until we get back on Monday?' asked Su Ling.

'I suppose so,' admitted Nat reluctantly, 'but I'd like to have known if Tom managed to close the Cedar Wood deal, and if so, at what price.'

33

'TOO CLOSE TO CALL' ran the banner headline in the *Washington Post* on election morning. 'NECK AND NECK' was the opinion of the *Hartford Courant*. The first referred to the national race between Ford and Carter for the White House, the second to the local battle between Hunter and Davenport for the State Senate Chamber. It annoyed Fletcher that they always put her name first, like Harvard before Yale.

'All that matters now,' said Harry as he chaired the final campaign meeting at six that morning, 'is getting our supporters to the polls.' No longer was there any need to discuss tactics, press statements, or policy. Once the first vote had been cast, everyone seated round the table had a new responsibility.

A team of forty would be in charge of the car pool, armed with a list of voters who required a lift to their nearest polling place, the old, the infirm, the downright lazy and even some who took a vicarious pleasure in being taken to the poll just so they could vote for the other side.

The next team, and by far the largest, were those who manned the bank of phones back at headquarters.

'They'll be on two-hour shifts,' said Harry, 'and must spend their time contacting known supporters to remind them that it's election day, and then later to make sure they've cast their vote. Some of this group will need to be called three or four times before the polls close at eight this evening,' Harry reminded them.

The next group, whom Harry described as the beloved amateurs, ran the counting houses all over the borough. They would keep a minute by minute up-date on how the voting was going in their district. They could be responsible for as few as a thousand voters or as many as three thousand, depending on whether theirs was a built-up or a rural area. 'They are,' Harry reminded Fletcher, 'the backbone of the party. From the moment the first vote is cast, they'll have volunteers sitting outside the polling stations ticking off names of the voters as they go to the polls. Every thirty minutes those lists will be handed over to runners, who will take them back to the house where the full register will be laid out on tables or pinned to a wall. That list will then be marked up – a red line through the name for any Republican voter, blue for Democrats, and yellow for unknown. One glance at the boards at any time, and the captain of the precinct will know exactly how the vote is progressing. As many of the captains have done the same job for election after election, they'll be able to give you an immediate comparison with any past poll. The details, once "boarded", are then relayed through to headquarters so that the phoners don't keep bothering a pledge who has already cast their vote.'

'So what's the candidate supposed to do all day?' asked Fletcher, once Harry had come to the end of his briefing.

'Keep out of the way,' said Harry, 'which is why you have a programme of your own. You will visit the forty-four counting houses, because they all expect to see the candidate at some time during the day. Jimmy will act as your driver, known as "the candidate's friend", because we certainly can't afford any spare workers wasting their time on you.'

Once the meeting had broken up, and everyone had dashed off to their new assignments, Jimmy explained just how Fletcher would spend the rest of the day, and he spoke with some experience, because he'd carried out the same exercise for his father during the previous two elections.

'First the no-no's,' said Jimmy when Fletcher joined him in the front of the car. 'As we have to visit all forty-four houses between now and eight o'clock this evening when the polls close, everyone will offer you a coffee, and between 11.45 and 2.15 lunch, and after 5.30 a drink. You must always reply with a polite but firm no to any such offer. You will only drink water in the car, and we'll have lunch at 12.30 for thirty minutes back at headquarters, just so they realize they've got a candidate, and you won't eat again until after the polls close.'

Fletcher thought he might become bored, but each visit produced a new cast of characters and a new set of figures. For the first hour, the sheets showed just a few names crossed out, and the captains were quickly able to tell him how the turnout compared with past elections. Fletcher was encouraged by how many blue lines had appeared before ten o'clock, until Jimmy warned him that the time between seven and nine was always good pickings for the Democrats as the industrial and night-shift workers vote before they start, or after they have finished work. 'Between ten and four, the Republicans should go into the lead,' Jimmy added, 'while after five and up until the close of the polls is always the time when the Democrats have to make their comeback. So just pray for rain between ten and five, followed by a fine warm evening.'

By 11 a.m. all the captains were reporting that the poll was slightly down compared with the last election when it had closed on fifty-five per cent. 'Anything below fifty per cent, we lose, over fifty and we're in with a shout,' said Jimmy, 'above fifty-five and it's yours by a street.'

'Why's that?' asked Fletcher.

'Because the Republicans traditionally are more likely to turn out in any weather, so they always benefit from a low turnout. Making sure our people vote has always been the Democrats' biggest problem.'

Jimmy stuck rigidly to his schedule. Just before arriving he would hand Fletcher a slip of paper with the basic facts on the household running that district. Fletcher would then commit the salient points to memory before he reached the front door.

'Hi, Dick,' he said when the door was opened, 'good of you to allow us to use your house again, because of course this is your fourth election.' Listen to reply. 'How's Ben, is he still at college?' Listen to reply. 'I was sorry to hear about Buster – yes, Senator Gates told me.' Listen to reply. 'But you have another dog now, Buster Jr – is that right?'

Jimmy also had his own routine. After ten minutes he would whisper, 'I think you ought to be leaving.' At twelve, he would begin to sound a little anxious and dispense with think, and at fourteen, he became insistent. After shaking hands and waving, it always took another couple of minutes before they could finally get away. Even with Jimmy keeping to a rigorous schedule, they still arrived back at campaign headquarters twenty minutes late for lunch.

Lunch was a snack rather than a meal, as Fletcher grabbed a sandwich from a table that was heaped with food. He took the occasional bite as he and Annie moved from office to office, shaking hands with as many of the workers as possible.

'Hi, Martha, what's Harry up to?' asked Fletcher as he entered the phone room.

'He's outside the old State House doing what he does best, pressing the flesh, dispensing opinions, and making

341

sure people haven't forgotten to vote. He should be back at any moment.'

Thirty minutes later Fletcher passed Harry in the corridor on his way out, as Jimmy had insisted that, if they were still going to visit every counting house, then they had to leave by 1.10. 'Good morning, senator,' said Fletcher.

'Good afternoon, Fletcher, glad you were able to find time to eat.'

The first house they visited after lunch showed that the Republicans had gone into a slight lead, which continued to increase during the afternoon. By five o'clock there were still fifteen captains left to visit. 'If you miss one of them,' said Jimmy, 'we'll never hear the end of it, and they sure won't be there for you next time around.'

By six o'clock the Republicans had a clear lead, and Fletcher tried not to show that he was feeling a little depressed. 'Relax,' said Jimmy, and promised him it would look better in a couple of hours' time; what he didn't mention was that by this time in the evening, his father always had a small lead and therefore knew he'd won. Fletcher envied those who were running for seats where they weighed the votes.

'How much easier to relax if you knew you were certain to win, or certain to lose.'

'I wouldn't know how that feels,' said Jimmy, 'Dad won his first election by 121 votes before I was born, and during the past thirty years built up his majority to just over 11,000, but he always says if sixty-one people had voted the other way, he would have lost that first election, and might never have been given a second chance.' Jimmy regretted the words the moment he said them.

By seven, Fletcher was relieved to see a few more blue lines appearing on the sheets and although the Republicans were still in the lead, the feeling was that it would go to the line. Jimmy had to cut the last six houses down to eleven minutes each, and even then he didn't reach the final two until after the poll had closed.

'What now?' asked Fletcher as he walked away from the last house.

Jimmy checked his watch. 'Back to HQ and listen to the tallest stories you've ever heard. If you win, they will become folklore, and if you lose, they will be disowned and quickly forgotten.'

'Like me,' commented Fletcher.

Jimmy turned out to be right, because back at HQ everyone was talking at once, but only the foolhardy and naturally optimistic were willing to predict what the result would be. The first exit poll was broadcast minutes after the last vote had been cast and showed that Hunter had won by a whisker. The national polls were predicting that Ford had beaten Carter.

'History repeating itself,' said Harry as he walked into the room. 'Those same guys were telling me that Dewey was going to be our next president. They also said I'd lose by a whisker, and we cut both those whiskers off, so don't worry about straw polls, Fletcher, they're for straw men.'

'What about the turnout?' asked Fletcher, recalling Jimmy's words.

'Too early to be sure, it's certainly over fifty per cent, but not fifty-five.'

Fletcher looked around at his team and realized that it was no longer any use thinking about how to gather in votes, as the time had come to count them.

'There's not much else we can do now,' said Harry, 'except to make sure that our tellers register at City Hall before ten. The rest of you should take a break, and we'll all meet up at the count later. I have a feeling it's going to be a long night.'

In the car on the way to Mario's, Harry told Fletcher

he couldn't see a lot of point in them turning up much before eleven, 'so let's have a quiet meal and follow the party's fortunes in the rest of the country on Mario's television.'

Any chance of a quiet meal evaporated when Fletcher and Harry entered the restaurant, and several of the diners rose to their feet and applauded the two men all the way to their table in the corner. Fletcher was pleased to find his parents had already arrived, and were enjoying a drink.

'So what can I recommend?' asked Mario once everybody had settled down.

'I'm too tired to even think about it,' said Martha. 'Mario, why don't you go ahead and choose for us, as you've never taken any notice of our opinion in the past.'

'Of course, Mrs Gates,' said Mario, 'just leave it to me.'

Annie stood up and waved when Joanna and Jimmy walked in. As Fletcher kissed Joanna on the cheek, he glanced over her shoulder to see Jimmy Carter on Mario's television arriving back at his ranch, and moments later President Ford stepping on to a helicopter. He wondered what sort of a day they'd had.

'Your timing is perfect,' said Harry as Joanna took the seat next to him, 'we've only just arrived. How are the children?'

Within minutes, Mario returned carrying two large plates of antipasti, while a waiter followed with two carafes of white wine. 'The wine is on the house,' declared Mario, 'I think maybe you make it,' he said as he poured a glass for Fletcher to taste. Someone else who wasn't willing to predict the result.

Fletcher put a hand under the table and touched Annie's knee. 'I'm going to say a few words.'

'Must you?' said Jimmy, pouring himself a second

glass of wine. 'I've heard enough speeches from you to last a lifetime.'

'It will be short, I promise you,' Fletcher said as he rose from his place, 'because everyone I want to thank is at this table. Let me start with Harry and Martha. If I hadn't sat next to their dreadful little brat on my first day at school, I would never have met Annie, or indeed Martha and Harry, who have changed my whole life, although in truth it is my mother who is to blame, because it was she who insisted that I went to Hotchkiss rather than Taft. How different my life might have been if my father had had his way.' He smiled at his mother. 'So thank you.' He sat down just as Mario reappeared at their table carrying another bottle of wine.

'I don't remember ordering that,' said Harry.

'You didn't,' said Mario, 'it's a gift from a gentleman sitting on the far side of the room.'

'That's very kind of him,' said Fletcher, 'did he leave his name?'

'No, all he said was that he was sorry not to be able to give you more help during the election, but he's been involved in a takeover. He's one of our regulars,' added Mario, 'I think he's something to do with Russell's Bank.'

Fletcher looked across the restaurant and nodded when Nat Cartwright raised a hand. He had a feeling that he'd seen him somewhere before.

34

'How did she manage it?' asked Tom, his face ashen.

'She chose her victim well and, to be fair, she paid meticulous attention to detail.'

'But that doesn't explain . . .'

'How she knew we would agree to transfer the money? That was the easy part,' said Nat. 'Once all the other pieces had fallen neatly into place, all Julia had to do was call Ray and instruct him to move her account to another bank.'

'But Russell's closes at five, and most of the staff leave before six, especially at a weekend.'

'In Hartford.'

'I don't understand,' said Tom.

'She instructed our chief cashier to transfer the full amount to a bank in San Francisco, where it was still only two in the afternoon.'

'But I only left her alone for a few minutes.'

'Long enough for her to make a phone call to her lawyer.'

'Then why didn't Ray contact me?'

'He tried to, but you weren't in the office and she took the phone off the hook when you got home, and don't forget when I called you from LA, it was three thirty, but it was six thirty in Hartford and Russell's was already closed.'

'If only you hadn't been on vacation.'

'My bet is she took that into consideration as well,' said Nat.

'But how?'

'One call to my secretary asking for an appointment that week, and she would have known I would be in LA, and no doubt you confirmed as much soon after you'd met her.'

Tom hesitated. 'Yes, I did. But it doesn't explain why Ray didn't refuse to action the transfer.'

'Because you'd deposited the full amount in her account, and the law is very clear in a case like this: if she asks for a transfer, we have no choice but to carry out her instructions. As her lawyer pointed out when he called Ray at four fifty, by which time you were on your way back home.'

'But she'd already signed a cheque and handed it over to Mr Cooke.'

'Yes, and if you had returned to the bank and informed our chief teller about that cheque, he might have felt able to hold off any decision until Monday.'

'But how could she be so confident that I would authorize the extra money to be placed in her account?'

'She wasn't, that's why she opened an account with us and deposited $500,000, assuming we would accept that she had more than sufficient funds to cover the purchase of Cedar Wood.'

'But you told me that her company checked out?'

'And it did. Kirkbridge and Co is based in New York and made a profit of just over a million dollars last year, and surprise, surprise, the majority shareholder is a Mrs Julia Kirkbridge. And it was only because Su Ling thought she was a phony that I even called to check and see if the company was having a board meeting that morning. When the switchboard operator informed me that Mrs Kirkbridge couldn't be disturbed as she was in that meeting, the last piece of the jigsaw fell neatly into place. Now that's what I mean by attention to detail.'

'But there's still a missing link,' said Tom.

'Yes, and that's what turns her from an ordinary flim-flam artist into a fraudster of true genius. It was Harry Gates's amendment to the finance bill that presented her with a hoop that she knew we would have to jump through.'

'How does Senator Gates get in on the act?' asked Tom.

'It was he who proposed the amendment to the property bill stipulating that all future transactions enacted with the council should be paid in full on signature of the agreement.'

'But I told her that the bank would cover whatever surplus proved necessary.'

'And she knew that wouldn't be sufficient,' said Nat, 'because the senator's amendment insisted that the principal beneficiary,' Nat opened the brochure at a passage he had underlined, 'had to sign both the cheque and the agreement. The moment you rushed back to enquire if she had a cheque book with her, Julia knew she had you by the balls.'

'But what if I'd said the deal is off unless you can come up with the full amount?'

'She would have returned to New York that night, transferred her half million back to Chase, and you would never have heard from her again.'

'Whereas she pocketed three point one million dollars of our money and held on to her own $500,000,' said Tom.

'Correct,' said Nat, 'and by the time the banks open in San Francisco this morning, that money will have disappeared off to the Cayman Islands via Zurich or possibly even Moscow, and although I'll obviously go through the motions, I don't believe we have a hope in hell of retrieving one cent of it.'

'Oh, God,' said Tom, 'I've just remembered that Mr Cooke will be presenting that cheque this morning, and I gave him my word that it would be cleared the same day.'

'Then we shall have to clear it,' said Nat. 'It's one thing for the bank to lose money, quite another for it to lose its reputation, a reputation which your grandfather and father took a hundred years to establish.'

Tom looked up at Nat. 'The first thing I must do is resign.'

'Despite your naivety, that's the last thing you should do. Unless, of course, you want everyone to find out what a fool you've made of yourself and immediately transfer their accounts to Fairchild's. No, the one commodity I need is time, so I suggest you take a few days off. In fact, don't mention the Cedar Wood project again, and if anyone should raise the subject, you simply refer them to me.'

Tom remained silent for some time, before he said, 'The true irony is that I asked her to marry me.'

'And her true genius is that she accepted,' replied Nat.

'How did you know that?' asked Tom.

'It would have all been part of her plan.'

'Clever girl,' said Tom.

'I'm not so sure,' said Nat, 'because if you two had become engaged, I was ready to offer her a place on the board.'

'So she had you fooled as well,' said Tom.

'Oh yes,' replied Nat, 'with her grasp of finance she wouldn't have been a passenger, and had she married you she would have made a lot more than three point one million, so there must be another man involved.' Nat paused. 'I suspect he was the one on the other end of the

349

phone.' He turned to leave. 'I'll be in my office,' he said, 'and remember, we only ever discuss this matter in private, nothing in writing, never on the phone.'

Tom nodded as Nat closed the door quietly behind him.

'Good morning, Mr Cartwright,' said Nat's secretary as he walked into his office, 'did you have a good vacation?'

'Yes I did thank you, Linda,' he replied cheerily. 'I'm not sure who enjoyed Disneyland more, Luke or myself.' She smiled. 'Any real problems?' he asked innocently.

'No, I don't think so. The final documents for the takeover of Bennett's came through last Friday, so from January 1st, you'll be running two banks.'

Or none, thought Nat. 'I need to speak to a Mrs Julia Kirkbridge, the director of . . .'

'Kirkbridge and Co,' said Linda. Nat froze. 'You asked for the details of her company just before you went on vacation.'

'Of course I did,' said Nat.

Nat was rehearsing what he would say to Mrs Kirkbridge, when his secretary buzzed through to tell him that she was on the line.

'Good morning, Mrs Kirkbridge, my name is Nat Cartwright, I'm the chief executive of Russell's Bank in Hartford, Connecticut. We have a proposition we thought your company might be interested in, and as I'm in New York later today, I hoped you would be able to spare me a few minutes.'

'Can I call you back, Mr Cartwright?' she replied in a crisp English accent.

'Of course,' said Nat, 'I look forward to hearing from you.'

He wondered how long it would take Mrs Kirkbridge to discover that he was the chief executive of Russell's

Bank. She was obviously checking, because she didn't even ask for his telephone number. When the phone rang again his secretary said, 'Mrs Kirkbridge on the line.'

Nat checked his watch; it had taken her seven minutes.

'I could see you at two thirty this afternoon, Mr Cartwright; would that suit you?'

'Suits me just fine,' said Nat.

He put the phone down and buzzed Linda. 'I'll need a ticket on today's eleven-thirty train to New York.'

Nat's next call was to Rigg's Bank in San Francisco, who confirmed his worst fears. They had been instructed to send the money to Banco Mexico only moments after it had been deposited with them. From there, Nat knew it would follow the sun until it finally disappeared over the horizon. He decided it would be pointless to call in the police unless he wanted half the banking community let in on the secret. He suspected that Julia, or whatever her real name was, had also worked that out.

Nat got through a great deal of the backlog caused by his absence before leaving the office to catch the train to New York. He made it to the offices of Kirkbridge & Co on 97th Street with only moments to spare. He hadn't even had time to take a seat in reception before a door opened. He looked up to see an elegant, well-dressed woman standing in the doorway. 'Mr Cartwright?'

'Yes,' he said, rising from his seat.

'I'm Julia Kirkbridge; would you like to come through to my office?' The same crisp English accent. Nat could not recall how long ago it was that a director of any company had come to collect him in the reception area rather than sending a secretary, especially one working out of New York.

'I was intrigued by your call,' said Mrs Kirkbridge as she ushered Nat through to a comfortable seat by the fireplace. 'It's not often a Connecticut banker comes to New York to visit me.'

Nat took some papers out of his case, as he tried to assess the woman sitting opposite him. Her clothes, like those of her impersonator, were smartly tailored, but far more conservative, and although she was slim and in her mid thirties, her dark hair and dark eyes were a total contrast to the blonde from Minnesota.

'Well, it's quite simple really,' began Nat. 'Hartford City Council has put another site on the market that has planning approval for a shopping mall. The bank has purchased the land as an investment and is looking for a partner. We thought you might be interested.'

'Why us?' asked Julia.

'You were among the original companies that bid for the Robinson's site, which, incidentally, has proved to be a great success, so we thought you might want to be involved in this new venture.'

'I'm somewhat surprised that you didn't think of approaching us before you made your bid,' said Mrs Kirkbridge, 'because had you done so, you would have discovered that we had already considered the terms far too restrictive.' Nat was taken by surprise. 'After all,' continued Mrs Kirkbridge, 'that is what we do.'

'Yes, I know,' said Nat, buying time.

'May I ask how much it went for?' asked Mrs Kirkbridge.

'Three point six million.'

'That was way above our estimate,' said Mrs Kirk-bridge, turning a page of the file on the table in front of her.

Nat had always considered himself a good poker player, but he had no way of knowing if Mrs Kirkbridge was bluffing. He only had one card left. 'Well, I'm sorry to have wasted your time,' he said, rising from his place.

'Perhaps you haven't,' said Mrs Kirkbridge, who remained seated, 'because I'm still interested in listening to your proposal.'

'We're looking for a fifty–fifty partner,' said Nat, resuming his seat.

'What does that mean exactly?' asked Mrs Kirkbridge.

'You put up $1.8 million, the bank finances the rest of the project, and once the debt has been recouped, all the profits will be divided fifty–fifty.'

'No bank fees, and the money loaned at prime rate?'

'I think we would consider that,' said Nat.

'Then why don't you leave all the details with me, Mr Cartwright, and I'll come back to you. How long have I got before you need a decision?'

'I'm meeting two other possible investors while I'm in New York,' said Nat. 'They were also bidders for the Robinson's site.'

From the expression on her face, there was no way of telling if she believed him.

Mrs Kirkbridge smiled. 'Half an hour ago,' she said, 'I had a call from the chief executive of the Hartford City Council, a Mr Cooke.' Nat froze. 'I didn't take the call as I thought it would be prudent to see you first. However, I find it hard to believe that this was the type of case study they expected you to analyse at Harvard Business School, Mr Cartwright, so perhaps the time has come for you to tell me why you *really* wanted to see me.'

35

ANNIE DROVE HER husband to City Hall, and it was the first time they had been alone all day. 'Why don't we just go home?' said Fletcher.

'I expect every candidate feels that way just before the count.'

'Do you know, Annie, we haven't once discussed what I'm going to do if I lose.'

'I've always assumed you'd join another law firm. Heaven knows enough have been knocking on your door. Didn't Simpkins and Welland say they needed someone who specializes in criminal law?'

'Yes, and they've even offered me a partnership, but the truth is that politics is what I enjoy doing most. I'm even more obsessed than your father.'

'That's not possible,' said Annie. 'By the way, he said to use his parking space.'

'No way,' said Fletcher, 'only the senator should occupy that spot. No, we'll park down one of the side streets.' Fletcher glanced out of the window to see dozens of people walking up City Hall steps.

'Where are they going?' he asked. 'They can't all be close relations of Mrs Hunter.'

Annie laughed. 'No, they're not, but the public are allowed to watch the count from the gallery. It's an old Hartford tradition,' she added as she finally found a parking space some distance from City Hall.

Fletcher and Annie held hands as they joined the

crowds heading into the hall. Over the years, he had watched countless politicians and their wives holding hands on election day, and often wondered how many performed the ritual simply for the cameras. He squeezed Annie's hand as they strolled up the steps trying to look relaxed.

'Do you feel confident, Mr Davenport?' asked a local newscaster, thrusting a microphone into his face.

'No,' said Fletcher honestly. 'Nervous as hell.'

'Do you think you've beaten Mrs Hunter?' tried the reporter again.

'I'll be happy to answer that question in a couple of hours' time.'

'Do you believe it's been a clean fight?'

'You'd be a better judge of that than me,' said Fletcher as he and Annie reached the top step and walked into the building.

As they entered the hall, there was a ripple of applause from some of those seated in the gallery. Fletcher glanced up, smiled and waved, trying to look confident, even though he didn't feel it. When he glanced back down, the first face he saw was Harry's. He looked pensive.

How different City Hall felt from the day of the debate. All the chairs had been replaced by a horseshoe of long tables. In the centre stood Mr Cooke, who had presided over seven previous elections. This would be his last, as he was due to retire at the end of the year.

One of his officials was checking the black boxes, which were lined up on the floor inside the horseshoe. Mr Cooke had made it clear during the briefing he had given both candidates the previous day that the count would not begin until all forty-eight ballot boxes had arrived from their polling stations and had been authenticated. As the poll closed at 8 p.m. this procedure usually took about an hour.

A second ripple of applause broke out, and Fletcher glanced round to see Barbara Hunter enter the room, also displaying a smile of confidence as she waved to her supporters in the gallery.

Once all forty-eight boxes had been checked, their seals were broken by the officials and the votes emptied on to the tables ready for counting. Seated on either side of the horseshoe were the hundred or so counters. Each group consisted of one representative from the Republican party, one from the Democrats and a neutral observer standing a pace behind them. If an observer was unhappy about anything once the counting had begun, he or she would raise a hand and Mr Cooke or one of his officials would go to that table immediately.

Once the votes had been emptied on to the tables, they were separated into three piles – a Republican pile, a Democratic pile and a third, smaller pile of disputed ballot papers. Most of the constituencies around the nation now carried out this entire process by machine, but not Hartford, although everyone knew that would change the moment Mr Cooke retired.

Fletcher began walking round the room, watching as the different piles grew. Jimmy carried out the same exercise, but strolled in the opposite direction. Harry didn't move as he watched the boxes being unsealed, his eyes rarely straying from what was taking place inside the horseshoe. Once all the boxes had been emptied, Mr Cooke asked his officials to count the votes and place them in piles of one hundred.

'This is where the observer becomes important,' Harry explained as Fletcher came to a halt by his side. 'He has to be sure that no ballot is counted twice, or two aren't stuck together.' Fletcher nodded, and continued his perambulation, occasionally stopping to watch a particular count, one moment feeling confident, the next depressed, until Jimmy pointed out that the boxes came from different districts and he could never be sure which ones had come from a Republican stronghold and which from a Democratic area.

'What happens next?' asked Fletcher, aware that Jimmy was attending his fourth count.

'Arthur Cooke will add up all the ballots and announce how many people have voted, and calculate what percentage that is of the electorate.' Fletcher glanced up at the clock – it was just after eleven, and in the background, he could see Jimmy Carter on the big screen, chatting to his brother Billy. The early polls suggested that the Democrats were returning to the White House for the first time in eight years. Would he be going to the Senate for the first time?

Fletcher turned his attention back to Mr Cooke, who appeared to be in no hurry as he went about his official business. His pace did not reflect the heartbeat of either candidate. Once he had gathered up all the sheets, he went into a huddle with his officials, and transferred his findings on to a calculator, his only concession to the 1970s. This was followed by the pressing of buttons, nods and mutters, before two numbers were written neatly on to a separate piece of paper. He then walked across the floor and up on to the stage at a stately pace. He tapped the microphone, which was enough to bring silence, as the crowd was impatient to hear his words.

'God damn it,' said Harry, 'it's been over an hour already. Why doesn't Arthur get on with it?'

'Calm down,' said Martha, 'and try to remember that you're no longer the candidate.'

'The number of people who cast votes in the election for the Senate is 42,429, which is a turnout of 52.9 per cent.' Mr Cooke left the stage without another word, and returned to the centre of the horseshoe. His team then proceeded to check the piles of one hundreds, but it was another forty-two minutes before the chief executive climbed back on to the stage. This time he didn't need to tap the microphone. 'I have to inform you,' he said, 'that there are seventy-seven disputed ballots, and I will now invite the two candidates to join me in the centre of the room so that they can decide which ones should be considered valid.'

Harry ran for the first time that day and grabbed Fletcher before he joined Mr Cooke in the horseshoe. 'That means that whichever one of you is in the lead, it must be by less than seventy-seven votes, otherwise Cooke wouldn't be bothering to go through this whole rigmarole of seeking your opinions.' Fletcher nodded his agreement. 'So you must select someone to check over those crucial votes for you.'

'That's not a difficult choice,' Fletcher replied. 'I select you.'

'I don't think so,' said Harry, 'because that will put Mrs Hunter on her guard, and for this little exercise you'll need someone who she won't feel threatened by.'

'Then how about Jimmy?'

'Good idea, because she's bound to think that she can get the better of him.'

'Not a hope,' said Jimmy as he appeared by Fletcher's side.

'I may need you to,' said Harry mysteriously.

'Why?' asked Jimmy.

'It's just a hunch,' replied Harry, 'no more, but once it comes to deciding those few precious votes, Mr Cooke will be the man to watch, not Barbara Hunter.'

'But he won't try anything on with four of us standing over him,' said Jimmy, 'not to mention all those staring down from the gallery.'

'And he wouldn't dream of doing so,' said Harry. 'He's

one of the most punctilious officials I've ever dealt with, but he detests Mrs Hunter.'

'For any particular reason?' asked Fletcher.

'She's been on the phone to him every day since this campaign began, demanding statistics on everything from housing to hospitals, even legal opinions on planning permits, so my bet is he'll not relish the idea of her becoming a member of the Senate. He's got quite enough to be worrying about without the likes of Barbara Hunter taking up every spare moment of his time.'

'But, as you said, there's nothing he can do.'

'Nothing that's illegal,' said Harry. 'But should there be any disagreement over a vote, he will be asked to arbitrate, so whatever he recommends, just say "Yes, Mr Cooke", even if you think at the time it favours Mrs Hunter.'

'I think I understand,' said Fletcher.

'I'm damned if I do,' said Jimmy.

—◇—

Su Ling checked the dining-room table. When the front doorbell rang, she didn't bother to call up for Nat, because she knew he was rereading *The Cat in the Hat*. 'Read it again, Dad,' Luke always demanded when they reached the last page. Su Ling opened the door to find Tom clutching a bunch of parrot tulips. She gave him a big hug, as if nothing had happened since they last met.

'Will you marry me?' asked Tom.

'If you can cook, read *The Cat in the Hat*, answer the door and set the table all at the same time I'll give serious consideration to your proposal.' Su Ling took the flowers. 'Thank you, Tom,' she said, giving him a kiss on the cheek. 'They'll look beautiful on the dining table.' Su Ling smiled, 'I'm so sorry about Julia Kirkbridge, or whatever her real name was.'

'Never mention that woman to me again,' said Tom. 'In future, our dinners will just be the three of us, a ménage à trois; sadly without the ménage.'

'Not tonight,' said Su Ling. 'Didn't Nat tell you? He's invited a business colleague to join us. I assumed you knew all about it and I as usual, was the only person he informed at the last minute.'

'He didn't mention anything about it to me,' said Tom as the doorbell rang.

'I'll get it,' said Nat, as he came bounding down the stairs.

'Now, promise me you won't talk shop all evening, because I want to hear all about your trip to London . . .'

'How nice to see you again,' said Nat.

'It was just a short break,' said Tom.

'Let me take your coat,' said Nat.

'Yes, but did you manage to see any theatre?'

'. . . yes, I saw Judi . . .' began Tom as Nat ushered his guest into the living room.

'Let me first introduce you to my wife, Su Ling. Darling, this is Julia Kirkbridge, who, as I'm sure you know, is our partner in the Cedar Wood project.'

'How nice to meet you, Mrs Cartwright.'

Su Ling recovered more quickly than Tom. 'Please call me Su Ling.'

'Thank you, and you must call me Julia.'

'Julia, this is my chairman, Tom Russell, who I know has been looking forward to meeting you.'

'Good evening, Mr Russell. After all Nat has told me about you, I've been looking forward to meeting you too.' Tom shook her hand, but couldn't think of anything to say.

'A glass of champagne I think, to celebrate the signing of the contract.'

'The contract?' mumbled Tom.

'What a nice idea,' said Julia. Nat opened the bottle and poured three glasses, while Su Ling disappeared into the kitchen. Tom continued to stare at the second Mrs Kirkbridge as Nat handed them both a glass of champagne.

'To the Cedar Wood project,' said Nat, raising his glass.

Tom just managed to get out the words, 'The Cedar Wood project.'

Su Ling reappeared, smiled at her husband, and said, 'Perhaps you'd like to bring our guests in for dinner?'

'Now, I think it's only fair, Julia, that I should explain to my wife and Tom that you and I have no secrets.'

Julia smiled. 'None that I can think of, Nat, especially after signing a confidentiality agreement concerning the details of the Cedar Wood transaction.'

'Yes, and I think it should stay that way,' said Nat, smiling across at her, as Su Ling placed the first course on the table.

'Mrs Kirkbridge,' said Tom, not touching his lobster bisque.

'Please call me Julia; after all we have known each other for some time.'

'Have we?' said Tom, 'I don't . . .'

'That's not very flattering, Tom,' said Mrs Kirkbridge, 'after all, it was only a few weeks ago, when I was out jogging that you invited me for a drink and then to dinner at the Cascade the following evening. That's when I first told you about my interest in the Cedar Wood project.'

Tom turned to Nat. 'This is all very clever, but you seem to have forgotten that Mr Cooke, the auctioneer, and our chief teller, have all come into contact with the original Mrs Kirkbridge.'

'The first Mrs Kirkbridge, yes, but not the original,' said Nat. 'And I have already given that problem some considerable thought. There is no reason why Mr Cooke should ever meet Julia, as he retires in a few months' time. As for the auctioneer, it was you who did the bidding, not Julia, and you needn't worry about Ray because I'm going to move him to the Newington branch.'

'But what about the New York end?' said Tom.

'They know nothing,' said Julia, 'other than that I have closed a very advantageous deal.' She paused. 'This is lovely lobster bisque, Su Ling. It's always been my favourite.'

'Thank you,' said Su Ling as she cleared away the soup bowls and returned to the kitchen.

'And, Tom, can I just say while Su Ling is out of the room, that I would prefer to forget any other little indiscretions that are rumoured to have taken place during the past month.'

'You bastard,' said Tom, turning to face Nat.

'No, to be fair,' said Julia, 'I did insist on being told everything before I signed the confidentiality agreement.'

Su Ling returned carrying a serving dish. The smell of roast lamb was tantalizing. 'I've now worked out why Nat asked me to serve exactly the same meal a second time, but I'm bound to ask, how much more do I need to know if I'm to keep up this charade?'

'What would you like to know?' asked Julia.

'Well, I've worked out that you're the real McCoy, and therefore must be the majority shareholder of the Kirkbridge company, but what I'm not sure about is, did you at your husband's request jog over building sites on a Sunday morning and then report back to him?'

Julia laughed. 'No, my husband didn't expect me to do that, as I already have an architecture degree.'

'And may I ask,' continued Su Ling, 'did Mr Kirkbridge die of cancer and then leave the company to you, having taught you everything he knew?'

'No, he's very much alive, but I divorced him two years ago, when I discovered he was siphoning off the company's profits for his personal use.'

'But wasn't it his company?' asked Tom.

'Yes, and I wouldn't have minded so much if he hadn't been lavishing those profits on another woman.'

'Would that woman by any chance be around five foot eight, blonde, like expensive clothes, and claim to hail from Minnesota?'

'You've obviously met her,' said Julia, 'and I expect it was also my ex-husband who called you from a bank in San Francisco claiming to be Mrs Kirkbridge's lawyer.'

'You've no idea where the two of them are at the moment by any chance?' asked Tom. 'Because I'd like to kill them.'

'Absolutely no idea,' said Julia, 'but should you find out, please let me know. Then you can kill her and I can kill him.'

'Anyone for créme brûlée?' asked Su Ling.

'How did the other Mrs Kirkbridge answer that question?' enquired Julia.

---◦---

Members of the public were leaning over the balcony observing every move, and Mr Cooke seemed to want everyone in the hall to witness what was going on. Fletcher and Jimmy left the senator to join Mrs Hunter and her representative inside the horseshoe.

'There are,' said Mr Cooke addressing both candidates, 'seventy-seven disputed ballot papers, of which I believe forty-three are invalid, however there remain difficulties over the other thirty-four.' Both candidates nodded. 'First I am going to show you the forty-three,' said the returning officer, placing his hand on the larger of the two piles, 'which I consider to be invalid. If you agree, I shall then go through the remaining thirty-four that are still in dispute,' his hand transferring across to the smaller pile. Both candidates nodded again. 'Just say no if you disagree,' said Mr Cooke, as he began to turn over the ballot papers in the larger pile, only to reveal that no vote had been registered on any of them. As neither candidate put up any objection, he completed this part of the exercise in under two minutes.

'Excellent,' said Mr Cooke, pushing those ballot papers to one side, 'but now we must consider the crucial thirty-four.' Fletcher noted the word crucial, and realized just how close the final result must be. 'In the past,' continued Mr Cooke, 'if both parties were unable to agree, then the final decision would be left to a third party.' He paused.

'If there is any dispute,' said Fletcher, 'I am quite happy to abide by your decision, Mr Cooke.'

Mrs Hunter didn't immediately respond and began whispering to her aide. Everyone waited patiently for her response. 'I am also happy that Mr Cooke should act as the arbitrator,' she finally conceded.

Mr Cooke gave a slight bow. 'Of the thirty-four votes in the disputed pile,' he said, 'eleven I believe can quickly be dealt with, as they are what I would call, for lack of a better description, the Harry Gates supporters.' He then laid out on the table eleven votes that had 'Harry Gates' written across the ballot paper. Fletcher and Mrs Hunter studied them one by one.

'They are obviously invalid,' said Mrs Hunter.

'However, two of them,' continued Mr Cooke, 'also have a cross against Mr Davenport's name.'

'They must still be invalid,' said Mrs Hunter, 'because as you can see, Mr Gates's name is clearly written across the paper, making them spoilt ballots.'

'But . . .' began Jimmy.

'As there is obviously some disagreement on these two ballots,' said Fletcher, 'I'm happy to allow Mr Cooke to decide.'

Mr Cooke looked towards Mrs Hunter and she nodded reluctantly. 'I concur that the one with "Mr Gates should be president" written across it is indeed invalid." Mrs Hunter smiled. 'However, the one that has a cross by Mr Davenport's name with the added comment, "but I'd prefer Mr Gates", is in my view under election law, a clear indication of the voter's intention, and I therefore deem it to be a vote for Mr Davenport.' Mrs Hunter looked annoyed but, aware of the crowd peering down from the gallery, managed a weak smile. 'Now we can turn to the seven votes where Mrs Hunter's name appears on the ballot.'

'Surely they must all be mine,' said Mrs Hunter as Mr Cooke laid them out neatly in a row so that the two candidates could consider them.

'No, I don't think so,' said Mr Cooke.

The first had written on it, 'Hunter is the winner', with a cross against Hunter.

'That person clearly voted for Mrs Hunter,' said Fletcher.

'I agree,' said Mr Cooke as a ripple of applause emanated from the gallery.

'That boy's honesty will be the death of him,' said Harry.

'Or the making of him,' said Martha.

'Hunter would be a dictator', was written across the next with no cross against either name. 'I believe that to be invalid,' said Mr Cooke. Mrs Hunter reluctantly nodded.

'Despite being accurate,' said Jimmy under his breath.

'Hunter is a bitch', 'Hunter should be shot', 'Hunter is mad', 'Hunter is a loser', 'Hunter for pope' were also declared invalid. Mrs Hunter did not bother to suggest that any of these wanted her to be Hartford's next senator.

'Now we come to the final group of sixteen,' said Mr Cooke. 'Here the voter did not use a cross to indicate his or her preference.' The sixteen votes had been placed in a separate pile, and the top one had a tick in the box opposite the name 'Hunter'.

'That is clearly a vote for me,' insisted the Republican candidate.

'I have a tendency to agree with you,' said Mr Cooke. 'The voter appears to have made his wishes quite clear; however I will need Mr Davenport to accept that judgement before I can proceed.'

Fletcher looked outside the horseshoe and caught Harry's eye. He gave a slight nod. 'I agree that it is clearly a vote for Mrs Hunter,' he said. Applause once again broke out in the gallery from the pro-Hunter supporters. Mr Cooke removed the top ballot paper to reveal that the one underneath also had a tick in the box opposite 'Hunter'.

'Now that we've agreed on the principle,' said Mrs Hunter, 'that must also count as my vote.'

'I have no quarrel with that,' said Fletcher.

'Then those two votes go to Mrs Hunter,' said Mr Cooke, who removed the second voting slip to reveal a tick by Fletcher's name on the one underneath. Both candidates nodded.

'Two–one in favour of Hunter,' said Mr Cooke before he removed that vote, to show the next had a tick in the 'Hunter' box.

'Three–one,' she said, unable to hide a smirk.

Fletcher began to wonder if Harry might have miscalculated. Mr Cooke removed the next ballot paper to reveal a tick by Fletcher's name.

'Three–two,' Jimmy said as the chief executive began

to remove the votes from the pile more quickly. As each one showed a clear tick, neither candidate was able to object. The crowd in the gallery began to chant – three-all, four–three – in Fletcher's favour – five–three, six–three, seven–three, eight–three, eight–four, nine–four, ten–four, eleven–four, ending on twelve–four in Fletcher's favour.

Mrs Hunter couldn't hide her anger as Mr Cooke, looking up at the gallery, proclaimed, 'And that completes the checking of spoilt ballot papers, making an overall position of fourteen for Mr Davenport and six for Mrs Hunter.' He then turned back to the candidates and said, 'May I thank you both for your magnanimous approach to the whole proceedings.'

Harry allowed himself a smile as he joined in the renewed applause that followed Mr Cooke's statement. Fletcher quickly left the horseshoe and rejoined his father-in-law on the outside.

'If you win by fewer than eight votes my boy, we'll know who to thank, because now there's nothing Mrs Hunter can do about it.'

'How long before we find out the result?' asked Fletcher.

'The vote? Only a few minutes,' said Harry, 'but the result, I suspect, won't be sorted out for several hours.'

Mr Cooke studied the figures on his calculator, and then transferred them on to a slip of paper, which all four of his officials dutifully signed. He returned to the stage for a third time. 'Both sides having agreed on the disputed ballots, I can now inform you that the result of the election to the Senate for Hartford County is: Mr Fletcher Davenport 21,218, Mrs Barbara Hunter, 21, 211.' Harry smiled.

Mr Cooke made no attempt to speak during the uproar that followed, but once he had regained the attention of the floor, he announced, 'There will be a recount,' even before Mrs Hunter could demand one.

Harry and Jimmy circled the room, uttering only one word to each of their observers. Concentrate. Fifty minutes later, it was found that three of the piles only had ninety-nine votes, while another four had one hundred and one. Mr Cooke checked all seven offending piles for a third time, before returning to the stage.

'I declare the result of the election to the Senate for Hartford County to be as follows: Mr Davenport 21,217, Mrs Hunter 21,213.'

Mr Cooke had to wait for some time before he could be heard above the noise. 'Mrs Hunter has once again called for a recount.' This time some boos mingled with the cheers, as the gallery settled down to watch the counters begin the entire process again. Mr Cooke was punctilious in making sure that each pile was checked and double-checked, and if there was any doubt he went over it again himself. He didn't walk back on to the stage until a few minutes after one in the morning, when he asked both candidates to join him.

He tapped the microphone to be sure it was still working. 'I declare the result of the election to the Senate for Hartford County, to be Mr Fletcher Davenport 21,216, Mrs Barbara Hunter 21,214.' The cheers and boos were even louder this time, and it was several minutes before order could be restored. Mrs Hunter leant forward and suggested to Mr Cooke in a stage whisper that as it was past one, the council workers should be allowed to go home, and a further recount should take place in the morning.

He listened politely to her protestations, before returning to the microphone. However, he had clearly anticipated every eventuality. 'I have with me,' he said, 'the official election handbook.' He held it up for all to see as a priest might the Bible. 'And I refer to a ruling on page ninety-one. I will read out the relevant passage.' The hall fell silent as they waited for Mr Cooke's deliberations. 'In an election for the Senate, if any one candidate should win the count three times in a row, by however small a majority, he or she will be declared the winner. I therefore declare Mr . . .' But the rest of his words were drowned by Fletcher's cheering supporters.

Harry Gates turned round and shook Fletcher by the hand. He could hardly make out the former senator's words above the uproar.

Fletcher thought he heard Harry say, 'May I be the first to congratulate you, senator.'

BOOK FOUR

ACTS

36

NAT WAS ON the train back from New York when he read the short piece in the *New York Times*. He had attended a board meeting of Kirkbridge & Co, where he was able to report that the first stage of building on the Cedar Wood site had been completed. The next phase was to lease the seventy-three shops, which ranged in size from a thousand to twelve thousand square feet. Many of the successful retailers currently on the Robinson's site had already shown an interest, and Kirkbridge & Co were preparing a brochure and application form for several hundred potential customers. Nat had also booked a full-page ad in the *Hartford Courant* and agreed to be interviewed about the project for the weekly property section.

Mr George Turner, the council's new chief executive, had nothing but praise for the enterprise, and in his annual report, singled out Mrs Kirkbridge's contribution as project coordinator. Earlier in the year, Mr Turner had visited Russell's Bank, but not before Ray Jackson had been promoted to manager of their Newington branch.

Tom's progress was somewhat slower as it had taken him seven months before he plucked up the courage to invite Julia out for dinner. It took her seven seconds to accept.

Within weeks Tom was on the 4.49 p.m. train to New York every Friday afternoon, returning to Hartford on the Monday morning. Su Ling kept asking for progress reports, but Nat seemed unusually ill-informed.

'Perhaps we'll find out more on Friday,' he said, reminding her that Julia was down for the weekend, and they had both accepted an invitation to join them for dinner.

Nat reread the short piece in the *New York Times*, which didn't go into any detail, and left the impression that there was a lot more behind the story. *William Alexander of Alexander Dupont & Bell, has announced his resignation as senior partner of the firm founded by his grandfather. Mr Alexander's only comment was that for some time he had been planning to take early retirement.*

Nat looked out of the window at the Hartford countryside speeding by. He recognized the name, but couldn't place it.

◄◦►

'Mr Logan Fitzgerald is on line one, senator.'

'Thank you, Sally.' Fletcher received over a hundred calls a day, but his secretary only put them through when she knew they were old friends or urgent business.

'Logan, how good to hear from you. How are you?'

'I'm well, Fletcher, and you?'

'Never better,' Fletcher replied.

'And the family?' asked Logan.

'Annie still loves me, heaven knows why, because I rarely leave the building before ten, Lucy is at Hartford Elementary and we've put her down for Hotchkiss. And you?'

'I've just made partner,' said Logan.

'That's no surprise,' said Fletcher, 'but many congratulations'.

'Thanks, but that wasn't why I was calling. I wanted to check if you'd spotted the piece about Bill Alexander's resignation in the *Times*.' Fletcher felt a chill go through his body at the mere mention of the name.

'No,' he said, as he leant across the desk and grabbed his copy of the paper. 'Which page?'

'Seven, bottom right.'

Fletcher quickly flicked through the pages until he saw the headline, *Leading lawyer resigns*. 'Hold on while I just read the piece.' When he'd come to the end, all he said was, 'It doesn't add up. He was married to that firm, and he can't be a day over sixty.'

'Fifty-seven,' said Logan.

'But the partners' mandatory retirement age is sixty-five, and even then they keep you on as an in-house advisor until you're seventy. It doesn't add up.' Fletcher repeated.

'Until you dig a little.'

'And when you dig a little, what do you find?' asked Fletcher.

'A hole.'

'A hole?'

'Yes, it seems that a large sum of money went missing from a client's account when . . .'

'I have no time for Bill Alexander,' Fletcher cut in, 'but I do not believe that he would remove one penny from a client's account. In fact I'd stake my reputation on it.'

'I agree with you, but what will interest you more is that the *New York Times* didn't bother to report the name of the other partner who resigned on the same day.'

'I'm listening.'

'Ralph Elliot, no less.'

'They both went on the same day?'

'They sure did.'

'And what reason did Elliot give for resigning? It certainly can't have been because he was planning to take early retirement.'

'Elliot gave no reason; in fact their PR spokeswoman

is reported to have said that he was unavailable for comment, which must be a first.'

'Did she add anything?' asked Fletcher.

'Only that he was a junior partner, but she failed to point out that he was also Alexander's nephew.'

'So a large sum of money goes missing from a client's account, and Uncle Bill decided to take the rap rather than embarass the firm.'

'That sounds about right,' said Logan.

Fletcher could feel the sweat on the palms of his hands as he put the phone down.

—◦—

Tom burst into Nat's office. 'Did you spot the piece in the *New York Times* about Bill Alexander's resignation?'

'Yes, I recalled the name, but couldn't remember why.'

'It was the law firm Ralph Elliot joined after he left Stanford.'

'Ah yes,' said Nat, putting down his pen, 'so is he the new senior partner?'

'No, but he *is* the other partner who resigned. Joe Stein tells me that half a million has gone missing from a client account, and the partners had to cover the sum out of their own earnings. The name on the street is Ralph Elliot.'

'But why would the senior partner have to resign if Elliot's name is in the frame?'

'Because Elliot's his nephew, and Alexander pushed for him to be the youngest partner in the firm's history.'

'Sit still and revenge will visit thine enemies.'

'No, I don't think so,' said Tom, 'but it might revisit Hartford.'

'What do you mean?' asked Nat.

'He's telling everyone that Rebecca is missing her friends, so he's bringing his wife back home.'

'His wife?'

'Yeah. Joe says they were married in a New York registry office quite recently, but not before she also resembled a big apple.'

'I wonder who the father is,' said Nat almost to himself.

'And he's opened an account at our Newington branch, obviously unaware that you're the bank's chief executive.'

'Elliot knows only too well who the bank's chief executive is. Just let's be sure he doesn't deposit half a million,' Nat added with a smile.

'Joe says there's no proof, and what's more, Alexander's has a reputation for being tight-lipped, so don't expect to hear anything more from that quarter.'

Nat looked up at Tom. 'Elliot wouldn't come home unless he had a job to go to. He's too proud for that. But just who's been foolhardy enough to employ him?'

◄○►

The senator picked up line one. 'Mr Gates,' said his secretary.

'Business or pleasure?' Fletcher asked when Jimmy came on the line.

'Certainly not pleasure,' replied Jimmy. 'Have you heard Ralph Elliot is back in town?'

'No. Logan rang this morning to tell me that he'd resigned from AD and B but he didn't say anything about him returning to Hartford.'

'Yeah, he's joining Belman and Wayland as the partner in charge of corporate business. In fact, part of his agreement is that the firm will in the future be known as

Belman Wayland and Elliot.' Fletcher didn't comment.
'Are you still there?' asked Jimmy.

'Yes, I am,' said Fletcher. 'You do realize they're the
law firm that represents the council?'

'As well as being our biggest rival.'

'And I thought I'd seen the last of him.'

'You could always move to Alaska,' said Jimmy, 'I read
somewhere that they're looking for a new senator.'

'If I did, he'd only follow me.'

'There's no need for us to lose any sleep over it,' said
Jimmy. 'He'll assume we know about the missing five
hundred thousand and realize he'll have to lie low until
the rumours have died down.'

'Ralph Elliot doesn't know the meaning of lying low.
He'll ride into town with both guns blazing, with us lined
up in his sights.'

—◇—

'What else have you found out?' asked Nat, looking up
from behind his desk.

'He and Rebecca already have a son and I'm told
they've put him down for Taft.'

'I hope to God he's younger than Luke, otherwise I'd
send the boy to Hotchkiss.'

Tom laughed. 'I mean it,' said Nat. 'Luke's a sensitive
enough child without having to cope with that.'

'Well, there are also consequences for the bank of his
joining Belman and Wayland.'

'And Elliot,' added Nat.

'Don't forget that they were the lawyers overseeing
the Cedar Wood project on behalf of the council, and if
he ever found out . . .'

'There's no reason he should,' said Nat. 'However,
you'd better warn Julia, even though it's been a couple of
years, and don't forget Ray has also moved on. Only four

people know the full story, and I'm married to one of them.'

'And I'm going to marry the other,' said Tom.

'You're what?' said Nat in disbelief.

'I've been proposing to Julia for the past eighteen months, and last night she finally gave in. So I'll be bringing my fiancée for dinner tonight.'

'That's wonderful news,' said Nat, sounding delighted.

'And Nat, don't leave it until the last moment to tell Su Ling.'

⎯◇⎯

'It's just a shot across our bow,' said Harry in reply to Fletcher's question.

'It's a bloody cannon,' responded Fletcher. 'Ralph Elliot doesn't deal in shots, so we'll need to find out what the hell he's up to.'

'I've no idea,' said Harry. 'All I can tell you is that I had a call from George Turner to alert me that Elliot had asked for all the papers that the bank has ever been involved with, and yesterday morning he called again asking for more details on the Cedar Wood project, and in particular the original terms of agreement that I recommended to the Senate.'

'Why the Cedar Wood project? That's proving to be a huge success story, with a rush of applications to lease space. Just what is he up to?'

'He's also asked to see copies of all my speeches, and any notes I'd made at the time of the Gates Amendment. No one has ever asked me for copies of my old speeches before, let alone my notes,' said Harry. 'It's very flattering.'

'"He only flatters to deceive,"' said Fletcher. 'Remind me of the finer points of the Gates Amendment?'

'I insisted that any purchaser of council land valued at

over one million dollars be named and not be able to hide his or her identity behind the offices of a bank or a law firm so we'd know exactly who we were dealing with. They were also required to pay the full amount on the signing of any contract to prove they were a viable company. That way there would be no hold-ups.'

'But everyone now accepts that as good practice. In fact, several other states have followed your lead.'

'It could just be an innocent enquiry.'

'You've obviously never dealt with Ralph Elliot before,' said Fletcher. 'Innocent is not part of his vocabulary. However, in the past he has always selected his enemies carefully. Once he's driven past the Gates Library a few times, he may decide you're not someone to cross. But be warned, he's up to something.'

'By the way,' said Harry, 'has anyone told you about Jimmy and Joanna?'

'No,' said Fletcher.

'Then I'll keep my mouth shut. I'm sure Jimmy will want to tell you in his own time.'

—◇—

'Congratulations, Tom,' said Su Ling, as she opened the front door. 'I'm so pleased for both of you.'

'That's kind of you,' said Julia, as Tom handed his hostess a bunch of flowers.

'So when are you going to get married?'

'Sometime in August,' said Tom, 'we haven't settled on a date, in case you and Luke were booked for another trip to Disneyland, or Nat was off for a spell of night ops with the reserve.'

'No, Disneyland is a thing of the past,' said Su Ling, 'Can you believe Luke's now talking about Rome, Venice and even Arles – and Nat's not due down at Fort Benning until October.'

'Why Arles?' asked Tom.

'It's where Van Gogh painted at the end of his life,' said Julia as Nat walked into the room.

'Julia, I'm glad you're here, because Luke needs to consult you on a moral dilemma.'

'A moral dilemma? I didn't think you started worrying about those until after puberty.'

'No, this is far more serious than sex, and I don't know the answer.'

'So what's the question?'

'Is it possible to paint a masterpiece of Christ and the Virgin Mary if you are a murderer?'

'It's never seemed to worry the Catholic Church,' said Julia. 'Several of Caravaggio's finest works are hanging in the Vatican, but I'll go up and have a word with him.'

'Caravaggio, of course. And don't stay up there too long,' added Su Ling, 'there are so many questions I want to ask you.'

'I'm sure Tom can answer most of them,' said Julia.

'No, I want to hear your version,' said Su Ling as Julia disappeared upstairs.

'Have you warned Julia what Ralph Elliot is up to?' asked Nat.

'Yes,' Tom replied, 'and she can't foresee any problems. After all, why should it ever occur to Elliot that there were two Julia Kirkbridges. Don't forget, the first one was only with us for a few days and has never been seen or heard of since, whereas Julia has been around for a couple of years now, and everybody knows her.'

'But it's not her signature on the original cheque.'

'Why's that a problem?' asked Tom.

'Because when the bank cleared the $3.6 million, the council asked for the cheque to be returned to them.'

'Then it will be tucked away in a file somewhere, and

even if Elliot did come across it, why should he be suspicious?'

'Because he has the mind of a criminal. Neither of us thinks like him.' Nat paused. 'But to hell with that, let me ask you, before Julia and Su Ling return, am I looking for a new chairman, or has Julia agreed to settle in Hartford and wash dishes?'

'Neither,' said Tom, 'she's decided to accept a take-over bid from that fellow Trump, who's been after her company for some time.'

'Did she get a good price?'

'I thought this was meant to be a relaxed evening to celebrate . . . ?'

'Did she get a good price?' repeated Nat.

'Fifteen million in cash, and a further fifteen million in Trump shares.'

'That's a PE ratio of about sixteen. Not bad,' said Nat, 'although Trump obviously believes in the potential of the Cedar Wood project. So does she plan to open a real estate company in Hartford?'

'No, I think she ought to tell you what she has in mind,' said Tom as Su Ling returned from the kitchen.

'Why don't we invite Julia to join the board?' asked Nat. 'And put her in charge of our property division. That would free me up to spend more time concentrating on the banking side.'

'I think you'll find she considered that scenario at least six months ago,' said Tom.

'Did you by any chance offer her a directorship if she agreed to marry you?' asked Nat.

'Yes, I did originally, and she turned both down. But now I've convinced her to marry me, I'll leave it to you to persuade her to join the board because I have a feeling she has other plans.'

37

FLETCHER WAS ON the floor of the chamber listening to a speech on subsidized housing when the proceedings were interrupted. He'd been checking through his notes, as he was due to speak next. A uniformed officer entered the chamber and passed a slip of paper to the presiding member, who read it, and then read it again, banged his gavel and rose from his place. 'I apologize to my colleague for interrupting proceedings, but a gunman is holding a group of children hostage at Hartford Elementary. I am sure Senator Davenport will need to leave, and, given the circumstances, I believe it would be appropriate to adjourn for the day.'

Fletcher was on his feet immediately and had reached the door of the chamber even before the presiding member had closed the proceedings. He ran all the way to his office, trying to think on the move. The school was in the middle of his district, Lucy was a pupil and Annie was head of the PTA. He prayed that Lucy wasn't among the hostages. The whole of the State House seemed to be on the move. Fletcher was relieved to find Sally standing by the door to his office, notebook in hand. 'Cancel all of today's appointments, call my wife and ask her to join me at the school, and please stay by the phone.'

Fletcher grabbed his car keys and joined the flood of people hurrying out of the building. As he drove out of the members' parking lot, a police car shot in front of him. Fletcher pressed his foot hard down on to the accelerator and swung into the police car's slipstream as they headed towards the school. The line of cars became longer and longer, with parents making their way to pick up their offspring, some looking frantic after hearing the news on their car radios, others still blissfully unaware.

Fletcher kept his foot on the accelerator, staying only a few feet away from the rear bumper in front of him, as the police car shot down the wrong side of the road, lights blinking, sirens blaring. The policeman in the passenger seat used his loudspeaker to warn the pursuing vehicle to drop back, but Fletcher ignored the ultimatum, knowing they wouldn't stop. Seven minutes later both came to a screeching halt at a police barrier outside the school, where a group of hysterical parents was trying to find out what was going on. The policeman in the passenger seat leapt out of his car and ran towards Fletcher as he slammed his door closed. The officer drew his pistol and shouted, 'Put your hands on the roof.' The driver, who was only a yard behind his colleague said, 'Sorry, senator, we didn't realize it was you.'

Fletcher ran to the barrier. 'Where will I find the chief?'

'He's set up headquarters in the principal's office. I'll get someone to take you there, senator.'

'No need,' said Fletcher, 'I know my way.'

'Senator . . .' said the policeman, but it was too late.

Fletcher ran down the path towards the school, unaware that the building was surrounded by military guards, their rifles all aimed in one direction. It surprised him to see how quickly the public stood to one side the moment they saw him. A strange way to be reminded that he was their representative.

'Who the hell's that?' asked the chief of police as a lone figure came running across the yard towards them.

'I think you'll find it's Senator Davenport,' said Alan Shepherd, the school's principal, looking through the window.

'That's all I need,' said Don Culver. A moment later Fletcher came charging into the room. The chief looked up from behind the desk, trying to hide his 'that's all I need' look, as the senator came to a halt in front of him.

'Good afternoon, senator.'

'Good afternoon, chief,' Fletcher replied, slightly out of breath. Despite the wary look, he rather admired the paunchy, cigar-smoking chief of police, who wasn't known for running his force by the book.

Fletcher gave a nod to Alan Shepherd, and then turned his attention back to the chief. 'Can you bring me up to speed?' he asked as he caught his breath.

'We've got a lone gunman out there. It looks as if he strolled up the main path in broad daylight a few minutes before school was due to come out.' The chief turned to a makeshift ground-floor plan taped to the wall, and pointed to a little square with ART ROOM printed across it. 'There appears to be no rhyme or reason why he chose Miss Hudson's class, other than it was the first door he came to.'

'How many children in there?' Fletcher asked, turning his attention back to the principal.

'Thirty-one,' replied Alan Shepherd, 'and Lucy isn't one of them.'

Fletcher tried not to show his relief. 'And the gunman, do we know anything about him?'

'Not a lot,' said the chief, 'but we're finding out more by the minute. His name is Billy Bates. We're told his wife left him about a month ago, soon after he lost his job as the night watchman at Pearl's. Seems he was caught drinking on duty once too often. He's been thrown out of several bars during the past few weeks, and, according to our records, even ended up spending a night in one of our cells.'

'Good afternoon, Mrs Davenport,' said the principal, rising from his place.

Fletcher turned to see his wife, 'Lucy wasn't in Miss Hudson's class,' were his first words.

'I know,' said Annie, 'she was with me. When I got your message, I dropped her off with Martha and came straight over.'

'Do you know Miss Hudson?' asked the chief.

'I'm sure Alan has told you that everyone knows Mary, she's an institution. I think she's the longest-serving member of staff.' The principal nodded. 'I doubt if there's a family in Hartford who doesn't know someone who's been taught by her.'

'Can you give me a profile?' asked the chief, turning to face Alan Shepherd.

'In her fifties, single, calm, firm and well-respected.'

'And something you left out,' added Annie, 'much loved.'

'What do you think she'd be like under pressure?'

'Who knows how anyone would react under this sort of pressure,' said Shepherd, 'but I've no doubt she'd give up her life for those children.'

'That's what I feared you'd say,' said the chief, 'and it's my job to make sure she doesn't have to.' His cigar was no longer glowing. 'I've got over a hundred men surrounding the main block and a sniper on top of the adjacent building who says he occasionally gets a sighting of Bates.'

'Presumably you're trying to negotiate?' said Fletcher.

'Yes, there's a phone in the room which we've been calling every few minutes, but Bates refuses to pick it up. We've set up a loudspeaker system, but he's not responding to that either.'

'Have you thought of sending someone in?' asked Fletcher as the phone on the principal's desk rang. The chief pressed the intercom button.

'Who's this?' Culver barked.

'It's Senator Davenport's secretary, I was hoping . . .'

'Yes, Sally,' said Fletcher, 'what is it?'

'I've just seen a report on the news that says the gunman is called Billy Bates. The name sounded familiar, and it turns out that we have a file on him – he's been to see you twice.'

'Anything helpful in his case notes?'

'He came to lobby you on gun control. He feels very strongly on the subject. In your notes you've written "restrictions not tough enough, locks on triggers, sale of firearms to minors, proof of identification".'

'I remember him,' said Fletcher, 'intelligent, full of ideas but no formal education. Well done, Sally.'

'Are you sure he isn't just crazy?' asked the chief.

'Far from it,' said Fletcher. 'He's thoughtful, shy, even timid, and his biggest complaint was that no one ever listened to him. Sometimes that sort of person feels they have to prove a point when every other approach has failed. And his wife leaving him and taking the children, just when he's lost his job may have tipped the balance.'

'Then I've got to take him out,' said the chief, 'just like they did with that guy in Tennessee who locked up all those officials in the revenue office.'

'No, that's not a parallel case,' insisted Fletcher, 'that man had a record as a psychopath. Billy Bates is a lonely man who's seeking attention, the type that regularly comes to see me.'

'Well, he's sure grabbed my attention, senator,' responded the chief.

'Which could be precisely why he's gone to such

extremes,' said Fletcher. 'Why don't you let me try and speak to him?'

The chief removed his cigar for the first time; junior officers would have warned Fletcher that meant he was thinking.

'OK, but all I want you to do is to get him to pick up the phone, then I'll take over any negotiations. Is that understood?' Fletcher nodded his agreement. The chief turned to his number two and added, 'Dale, tell them that the senator and I are going out there, so to hold their fire.' The chief grabbed the megaphone and said, 'Let's do it, senator.'

As they started walking down the corridor, the chief added firmly, 'You're only to step a couple of paces outside the front door, and don't forget your message needs to be simple, because all I want him to do is pick up the phone.'

Fletcher nodded as the chief opened the door for him. He took a few paces before he came to a halt and held up the megaphone. 'Billy, this is Senator Davenport, you've been to see me a couple of times. We need to speak to you. Could you please pick up the phone on Miss Hudson's desk?'

'Keep repeating the message,' barked the chief.

'Billy, this is Senator Davenport, would you please pick up . . .'

A young officer came running towards the open door, 'He's picked up the phone, chief, but he says he'll only speak to the senator.'

'I'll decide who he talks to,' said Culver. 'No one dictates to me.' He disappeared through the door and almost ran back to the principal's study.

'This is Chief Culver. Now listen, Bates, if you imagine . . .' The phone went dead. 'Damn,' said the chief as

Fletcher walked back into the room. 'He put the phone down on me, we're going to have to try again.'

'Perhaps he meant it when he said he would only speak to me.'

The chief removed his cigar again. 'OK, but the moment you've calmed him down, you pass the phone over.'

Once they'd returned to the playground Fletcher spoke over the megaphone again. 'Sorry, Billy, can you call again, and this time I'll be on the other end of the line?' Fletcher accompanied Don Culver back to the principal's study to find Billy already on the speaker-phone.

'The senator's just walked back into the room,' the principal assured him.

'I'm right here, Billy, it's Fletcher Davenport.'

'Senator, before you say anything, I'm not budging while the chief has all those rifles trained on me. Tell them to back off if he doesn't want a death on his hands.'

Fletcher looked at Culver, who removed his cigar once again before nodding.

'The chief's agreed to that,' said Fletcher.

'I'll call you back when I can't see one of them.'

'Right,' said the chief, 'tell everyone to back off, except for the marksman on the north tower. There's no way Bates could spot him.'

'So what happens next?' asked Fletcher.

'We wait for the bastard to call back.'

—◦—

Nat was answering a question on voluntary redundancies when his secretary came rushing into the boardroom. They all realized that it had to be urgent as Linda had never interrupted a board meeting before. Nat immediately stopped speaking when he saw the anxious look on her face.

'There's a gunman at Hartford Elementary . . .' Nat went cold, '. . . and he's holding Miss Hudson's class hostage.'

'Is Luke . . .'

'Yes he is,' she replied. 'Luke's last lesson on a Friday is always Miss Hudson's art class.'

Nat rose unsteadily from his chair and walked towards the door. The rest of the board remained silent. 'Mrs Cartwright is already on her way to the school,' Linda added as Nat left the room. 'She said to tell you she'll meet you there.'

Nat nodded as he pushed open a door that led into the underground car park. 'Stay by the phone,' was the last thing he said to Linda as he climbed into his car. When he nosed up the ramp and out on to Main Street, he hesitated for a moment before turning left instead of his usual right.

—◦—

The phone rang. The chief touched the speaker and pointed to Fletcher.

'Are you there, senator?'

'Sure am, Billy,'

'Tell the chief to allow the TV crews and press inside the barrier; that way I'll feel safer.'

'Hey, wait a minute,' began the chief.

'No, you wait a minute,' shouted Billy. 'Or you'll have your first body in the playground. Try explaining to the press that it only happened because you didn't let them inside the barrier.' The phone went dead.

'You'd better go along with his request, chief,' said

Fletcher, 'because it looks like he's determined to be heard one way or the other.'

'Let the press through,' said Culver, nodding to one of his deputies. The sergeant quickly left the room, but it was several minutes before the phone rang again. Fletcher touched the console.

'I'm listening, Billy.'

'Thank you, Mr Davenport, you're a man of your word.'

'So what do you want now?' barked the chief.

'Nothing from you, chief, I prefer to go on dealing with the senator. Mr Davenport, I need you to come across and join me; that's the only way I have a chance of getting my case heard.'

'I can't allow that to happen,' said the chief.

'I don't believe it's your call, chief. It's up to the senator to decide, but I guess you'll have to sort that out amongst yourselves. I'll call back in two minutes.' The phone went dead.

'I'm happy to agree to his demand,' said Fletcher. 'Frankly there doesn't seem to be a lot of choice.'

'I don't have the authority to stop you,' said the chief, 'but maybe Mrs Davenport can spell out the consequences.'

'I don't want you to go in there,' said Annie. 'You always think the best of everyone, and bullets aren't that discriminating.'

'I wonder how you'd feel if Lucy was one of the children trapped in there?'

Annie was about to reply when the phone rang again. 'Are you on your way, senator, or do you need a body to help you make up your mind?'

'No, no,' said Fletcher, 'I'm on my way.' The phone went dead.

'Now listen carefully,' said the chief, 'I can cover you while you're in the open, but you're on your own once you're in that classroom.' Fletcher nodded and then took Annie in his arms, holding her for several seconds.

The chief accompanied him along the corridor. 'I'm going to phone the classroom every five minutes. If you get a chance to talk, I'll tell you everything that's happening our end. Whenever I ask a question, just answer yes or no. Don't give Bates any clues as to what I'm trying to find out.' Fletcher nodded. When they reached the door, the chief removed his cigar. 'Let me take your jacket, senator.' Fletcher looked surprised. 'If you're not concealing a gun, why give Bates any reason to believe you might be?' Fletcher smiled as Culver held the door open for him. 'I didn't vote for you last time, senator, but if you get out alive, I just might consider it next time. Sorry,' he added, 'just my warped sense of humour. Good luck.'

Fletcher stepped out on to the playground and began to walk slowly down the path towards the main classroom building. He could no longer spot any of the sharp-shooters, but he sensed that they weren't far away. Although he couldn't see the TV crews, he could hear their tense chatter as he stepped into the light of their massive arc lamps. The path that led to the classrooms couldn't have been more than a hundred yards. To Fletcher it felt like walking a mile-long tightrope in the blazing sun.

Once he'd reached the other side of the playground he climbed the four steps to the entrance. He entered a dark, empty corridor and waited until his eyes became accustomed to the gloom. When he reached a door stencilled with the words Miss Hudson in ten different colours, he knocked quietly. The door was immediately yanked open. Fletcher stepped inside to hear the door slam behind him. When he heard the muffled sobbing,

Fletcher glanced across to see a group of children huddled on the floor in one corner.

'Sit there,' commanded Bates, who looked as nervous as Fletcher felt. Fletcher squeezed into a desk built for a nine-year-old on the end of the front row. He looked up at the dishevelled man, whose ill-fitting jeans were torn and dirty. A paunch hung over his waistline, despite the fact that he couldn't have been more than forty. He watched carefully as Bates crossed the room and stood behind Miss Hudson, who remained seated at her table in the front of the class. Bates held the gun in his right hand, while placing his left arm on her shoulder.

'What's happening out there?' he shouted, 'what's the chief up to?'

'He's waiting to hear from me,' said Fletcher in a quiet voice. 'He's going to phone in every five minutes. He's worried about the children. You've managed to convince everyone out there you're a killer.'

'I'm no killer,' said Bates. 'You know that.'

'Perhaps I do,' said Fletcher, 'but they might be more convinced if you were to release the children.'

'If I do that, then I won't have anything to bargain with.'

'You'll have me,' said Fletcher. 'Kill a child, Billy, and everyone will remember you for the rest of their lives; kill a senator, and they'll have forgotten by tomorrow.'

'Whatever I do, I'm a dead man.'

'Not if we were to face the cameras together.'

'But what would we tell them?'

'That you've already been to see me twice, and you'd put forward some sensible and imaginative ideas on gun control but no one took any notice. Well, now they're going to have to sit up and listen, because you're going to be given the chance to speak to Sandra Mitchell on prime time news.'

'Sandra Mitchell? Is she out there?'

'Sure is,' replied Fletcher, 'and she's desperate to interview you.'

'Do you think she'd be interested in me, Mr Davenport?'

'She hasn't come all this way to talk to anyone else,' said Fletcher.

'Will you stay with me?' asked Bates.

'You bet, Billy. You know exactly where I stand on gun control. When we last met you told me you had read all of my speeches on the subject.'

'Yes I have, but what good did that do?' asked Billy. He took his arm off Mary Hudson's shoulder and began walking slowly towards Fletcher, the gun pointed directly at him. 'The truth is, that you're only repeating exactly what the chief has told you to say.'

Fletcher gripped the sides of the desk, never taking his eyes off Billy. If he was going to risk it, he knew he needed to draw Billy in as close as possible. He leant forward slightly while still holding firmly on to the lid of the desk. The phone by Miss Hudson began ringing. Billy was now only a pace away, but the ringing sound caused him to turn his head for a split second. This gave Fletcher the chance to jerk the lid of the desk up in a sudden movement, crashing it into Billy's right hand. Billy momentarily lost his balance, and as he stumbled, he dropped the gun. They both watched it hurtle across the floor, coming to a halt just a few feet away from Miss Hudson. The children began to scream as she fell on her knees, grabbed the gun and pointed it straight at Billy.

Billy rose slowly and advanced towards her as she remained kneeling on the floor, the gun pointing at his chest. 'You're not going to pull the trigger, are you, Miss Hudson?'

With each step Billy took towards her, Miss Hudson trembled more and more violently. Billy was only a foot away from her when she closed her eyes and pulled the trigger. There was a click. Billy looked up, smiled, and said, 'No bullets, Miss Hudson. I never intended to kill anyone, I just wanted someone to listen for a change.'

Fletcher slid out from behind the desk, ran to the door and yanked it open. 'Out, out,' he yelled, his right hand gesturing in a sweeping movement at the terrified children. A tall girl with long pigtails stood up and ran towards the open door and out into the corridor. Two more followed closely behind her. Fletcher thought he heard a piping voice say 'Go, go,' as he held the door open. All but one of the children came rushing towards him, disappearing out of sight within moments. Fletcher stared towards the corner at the one remaining child. The boy slowly rose from his place and walked to the front of the class. He leant down, took Miss Hudson by the hand, and led her towards the door, never once looking at Billy. When he reached the open door, he said, 'Thank you, senator,' and accompanied his teacher out into the corridor.

—◦—

A loud cheer went up as the tall girl with long black pigtails came charging through the front door. Searchlights beamed down on her and she quickly placed a hand over her eyes, unable to see the welcoming crowd. A mother broke through the cordon and ran across the playground to take the girl in her arms. Two boys followed closely behind, as Nat placed an arm around Su Ling's shoulder, desperately searching for Luke. A few moments later, a larger group came running out of the door, but Su Ling couldn't hold back the tears once she realized Luke was not among them.

'There's still one more to come,' she heard a journalist reporting on the early evening news, 'along with his teacher.'

Su Ling's eyes never left the open door for what she later described as the longest two minutes of her life.

An even bigger cheer went up when Miss Hudson appeared in the doorway clutching on to Luke's hand. Su Ling looked up at her husband, who was vainly attempting to hold back the tears.

'What is it with your Cartwrights,' she said, 'that you always have to be the last out?'

—◦—

Fletcher remained by the door until Miss Hudson was out of sight. He then closed it slowly, and walked across to pick up the insistent phone.

'Is that you, senator?' demanded the chief.

'Yes.'

'Are you OK? We thought we heard a crash, maybe even a shot.'

'No, I'm just fine. Are all the children safe?'

'Yes, we've got all thirty-one of them,' said the chief.

'Including the last one?'

'Yes, he's just joined his parents.'

'And Miss Hudson?'

'She's talking to Sandra Mitchell on *Eyewitness News*. She's telling everyone that you're some kind of hero.'

'I think she's talking about someone else,' said Fletcher.

'Are you and Bates planning to join us sometime?' asked the chief, assuming he was just being modest.

'Give me a few more minutes, chief. By the way, I've agreed that Billy can also talk to Sandra Mitchell.'

'Who's got the gun?'

'I have,' said Fletcher. 'Billy won't be causing you any

more trouble. The gun wasn't even loaded,' he added, before putting the phone down.

'You know they're going to kill me, don't you, senator?'

'No one's going to kill you, Billy, not as long as I'm with you.'

'Do I have your word on that, Mr Davenport?'

'You have my word on it, Billy. So let's go out and face them together.'

Fletcher opened the classroom door. He didn't need to search for a light switch as there were so many megawatts beaming in from the playground that he could clearly see the door at the far end of the passage.

He and Billy walked down the corridor together without a word passing between them. When they reached the main door that led on to the playground, Fletcher opened it tentatively and stepped into a beam of light to be greeted by another huge cheer from the crowd. But he couldn't see their faces.

'It's going to be all right, Billy,' said Fletcher turning back towards him. Billy hesitated for a moment, but finally took a tentative pace forward and stood by Fletcher's side. They walked slowly down the path together. He turned and saw Billy smile. 'It's going to be all right,' Fletcher repeated, just as the bullet ripped through Billy's chest. The sheer impact threw Fletcher to one side.

Fletcher pushed himself up off his knees and leapt on top of Billy, but it was too late. He was already dead.

'No, no, no,' Fletcher screamed. 'Didn't they realize that I gave him my word?'

38

'SOMEONE IS BUYING our shares,' said Nat.

'I do hope so,' said Tom, 'we are, after all, a public company.'

'No, chairman, I mean that someone is *aggressively* buying them.'

'For what purpose?' asked Julia.

Nat put down his pen. 'To try and take us over would be my bet.' Several of the board began to speak at once, until Tom tapped the table. 'Let's hear Nat out.'

'For some years now, our policy has been to buy up small ailing banks and add them to our portfolio, and overall that has proved a worthwhile enterprise. All of you know my long-term strategy is to make Russell's the largest banking presence in the state. What I hadn't planned for was that our success would, in turn, make us attractive to an even larger institution.'

'And you're convinced someone is now trying to take us over?'

'I most certainly am, Julia,' said Nat, 'and you're partly to blame. The most recent phase of the Cedar Wood project has been such a massive success that our overall profits nearly doubled last year.'

'If Nat is right,' said Tom, 'and I suspect he is, there's only one question that needs to be answered. Are we happy to be taken over or do we want to put up a fight?'

'I can only speak for myself, chairman,' said Nat, 'but

I'm not yet forty and I certainly wasn't planning on early retirement. I suggest we have no choice but to fight.'

'I agree,' said Julia, 'I've been taken over once already, and I'm not going to let it happen a second time. In any case, our shareholders will not expect us to roll over.'

'Not to mention one or two of the past chairmen,' said Tom, looking up at the paintings of his father, grandfather and great grandfather staring down at him from the surrounding walls. 'I don't think we need to vote on this,' continued Tom, 'so why don't you take us through the options, Nat.'

The chief executive opened one of the three files on the table in front of him.

'The law in these circumstances couldn't be clearer. Once a company or individual owns six per cent of the target company, they must declare their position to the Securities and Exchange Commission in Washington DC, and state within twenty-eight calendar days if it is their intention to make a takeover bid for the rest of the shares. And if so, what price they are willing to offer.'

'If someone is trying to take us over,' said Tom, 'they won't wait the statutory month. Once they've hit six per cent they'll make a bid the same day.'

'I agree, Mr Chairman,' said Nat, 'but until then, there is nothing to stop us buying our own shares, although they are priced a little on the high side at the moment.'

'But won't that alert the opposition to the fact that we know what they're up to?' asked Julia.

'Possibly, so we must instruct our brokers to buy soft, and that way we'll quickly find out if there's one big purchaser in the market.'

'How much stock do we own between us?' asked Julia.

'Tom and I each hold ten per cent,' said Nat, 'and you are currently holding,' he checked some figures in a second file, 'just over three per cent.'

'And how much cash do I still have on deposit?'

Nat turned the page, 'Just over eight million dollars, not to mention your Trump shares, which you've been liquidating whenever there's a strong demand.'

'Then why don't I pick up any soft shares, which wouldn't be quite so easy for any predators to trace?'

'Especially if you only dealt through Joe Stein in New York,' said Tom, 'and then ask him to let us know if his brokers can identify any particular individual or company who's buying aggressively.' Julia began taking notes.

'The next thing we have to do is select the sharpest takeover lawyer in the business,' said Nat. 'I've talked to Jimmy Gates, who's represented us in all our previous takeover bids, but he says this one is out of his league, and recommends a guy from New York called,' he checked the third file, 'Logan Fitzgerald, who specializes in corporate raids. I thought I'd travel up to New York before the weekend and find out if he'll represent us.'

'Good,' said Tom, 'anything else we ought to be doing in the meantime?'

'Yes, keep your eyes and ears open, chairman. I need to find out as quickly as possible who it is we're up against.'

—◇—

'I'm very sorry to hear that,' said Fletcher.

'It's nobody's fault,' said Jimmy, 'and I can't pretend it's been going well for some time, so when UCLA invited Joanna to head up their history department, it just brought matters to a head.'

'How are the children taking it?'

'Elizabeth's just fine, and now that Harry Junior's at Hotchkiss, they both seem grown up enough to handle the situation. In fact, Harry rather likes the idea of spending his summer vacations in California.'

'I am sorry,' repeated Fletcher.

'I think you'll find it's the norm nowadays,' said Jimmy. 'It won't be long before you and Annie are in the minority. The principal told me that around thirty per cent of the children at Hotchkiss come from broken homes. Do you know when we were there, I can't remember more than one perhaps two of our contemporaries whose parents were divorced.' He paused. 'And the good thing is, if the children are in California during the summer, I'll have more time to spend on your re-election campaign.'

'I'd rather you and Joanna were still together,' said Fletcher.

'Any idea who you'll be up against?' asked Jimmy, obviously wanting to change the subject.

'No,' said Fletcher, 'I hear Barbara Hunter is desperate to run yet again, but the Republicans don't seem to want her as their candidate if they can find a half-decent alternative.'

'There was a rumour circulating,' said Jimmy, 'that Ralph Elliot was considering running, but frankly after your Billy Bates triumph, I don't think the Archangel Gabriel could unseat you.'

'Billy Bates was not a triumph, Jimmy. That man's death haunts me even now. He could still be alive today if I'd only been firmer with Chief Culver.'

'I know that's how you see it, Fletcher, but the public feels otherwise. Your re-election last time proved that. All they remember is that you risked your life to save thirty-one children and their favourite teacher. Dad says if you had run for president that week you'd be living in the White House right now.'

'How is the old buzzard?' asked Fletcher. 'I'm feeling a bit guilty because I haven't had a chance to visit him recently.'

'He's fine, likes to believe he's still running everything and everybody, even if he's only planning your career.'

'What year has he got me running for president?' asked Fletcher with a grin.

'That all depends on whether you're first considering running for governor. By the time you've done four terms as senator, Jim Lewsam will just about have completed his second term.'

'Perhaps I don't want to be governor.'

'Perhaps the pope isn't a Catholic.'

'Good morning,' said Logan Fitzgerald as he looked around the boardroom table. 'Before you ask,' he continued, 'the answer is Fairchild's.'

'Of course,' said Nat. 'Damn it, I should have worked it out for myself. When you think about it, they are the obvious predator. Fairchild's is the largest bank in the state; seventy-one branches with almost no serious rivals.'

'Someone on their board obviously considers we are a serious rival,' said Tom.

'So they've decided to eliminate you before you think of doing the same thing to them,' said Logan.

'I can't blame them,' said Nat, 'it's exactly what I'd do if I were in their position.'

'And I can also tell you that the original idea didn't come from a member of their board,' continued Logan. 'The official notification to the SEC was signed on their behalf by Belman Wayland and Elliot, and there are no prizes for guessing which of the three partners' signature appears on the dotted line.'

'That means we've got one hell of a fight on our hands,' said Tom.

'True,' said Logan, 'so the first thing we have to do is start playing the counting game.' He turned his attention to Julia. 'How many shares have you picked up in the last few days?'

'Less than one per cent,' she replied, 'because someone out there keeps pushing the price up. When I asked my broker yesterday evening, he told me at close of business the shares had touched $5.20.'

'That's way above their realistic value,' said Nat, 'but there's no way back for either of us now. I've asked Logan to join us this morning so he can give us his assessment of our chances of survival, as well as take us through what's likely to happen during the next few weeks.'

'Let me bring you up to date as of nine o'clock this morning, Mr Chairman,' continued Logan. 'In order to avoid a takeover, Russell's must have in their possession, or pledged to them in writing, fifty point one per cent of the bank's shares. The board currently holds just over twenty-four per cent, and we know Fairchild's already has at least six per cent. On the face of it, that looks satisfactory. However, as Fairchild's are now offering $5.10 a share for a period of twenty-one days, I feel it's my duty to point out that should you decide to sell your shares, the cash value alone would net you in the region of twenty million dollars.'

'We've already made our decision on that,' said Tom firmly.

'Fine, then you're left with only two choices. You can either make a higher offer than Fairchild's $5.10 a share, remembering your chief executive's judgement that they are already way above their realistic value, or you can contact all your shareholders, asking them to pledge their stock to you.'

'The latter,' said Nat, without hesitation.

'As I anticipated that would be your response, Mr Cartwright, I've studied the list of stockholders carefully – as of this morning, there were 27,412 in all, mostly holding small amounts, a thousand or less shares. However, five per cent remains in the portfolios of three individuals, two widows residing in Florida who own two per cent each, and Senator Harry Gates, who is in possession of one per cent.'

'How's that possible?' asked Tom. 'Harry Gates is known to have spent his entire public life living on a senator's salary.'

'He has his father to thank for that,' said Logan. 'It seems that he was a friend of the founder of the bank, who offered him one per cent of the company in 1892. He purchased one hundred shares for one hundred dollars, and the Gates family has held on to them ever since.'

'What are they worth now?' asked Tom.

Nat tapped his calculator. 'Close on half a million, and he probably doesn't even realize it.'

'Jimmy Gates, his son, is an old friend of mine,' said Logan. 'In fact I owe my present job to him. And I can tell you that once Jimmy finds out that Ralph Elliot is involved, those shares will immediately be pledged to us. If you can lay your hands on them, and reel in the two old ladies from Florida, you'll be close to controlling thirty per cent, which still means you'll need another twenty point one per cent before anyone can relax.'

'But from my experience of past takeovers, at least five per cent won't get back in touch with either of us,' said Nat, 'when you consider changes of address, trust funds, and even those like Harry Gates who don't bother to check their portfolios from year to year.'

'I agree,' said Logan, 'but I won't rest easy until I know you control over fifty per cent.'

'So how do we go about getting our hands on that extra twenty per cent?' asked Tom.

'Damned hard work, and hours of it,' said Logan. 'To

start with, you will have to send out a personal letter to all your shareholders, just over twenty-seven thousand in all. This is the sort of thing I have in mind.' Logan handed copies of a letter to each of the board members. 'You'll see that I've concentrated on the bank's strengths, long history in the community, highest growth of any financial institution in the state. I've asked if they want one bank to end up with a monopoly.'

'Yes,' said Nat. 'Ours.'

'But not yet,' said Logan. 'Now, before we agree on this letter, I'd welcome your input, as it has to be signed by your chairman or chief executive.'

'But that's over twenty-seven thousand signatures?'

'Yes, but you can split them between you,' said Logan with a smile. 'I wouldn't suggest such a Herculean task if I wasn't fairly sure our rivals will send out a circular headed "Dear Shareholder", with a stylized signature above the name of their chairman. The personal touch might well make the difference between survival and extinction.'

'Can I help in any way?' asked Julia.

'You certainly can, Mrs Russell,' replied Logan. 'I've designed a totally different letter for you to sign that should be sent to every female shareholder. Most of them are either divorced or widowed and probably don't check their portfolios from one year to the next. There are nearly four thousand such investors, so that should take care of your weekend.' He pushed a second letter across the table. 'You'll see I've referred to your particular expertise in having run your own company, as well as being a board member of Russell's for the past seven years.'

'Anything else?' asked Julia.

'Yes,' said Logan, passing her two more sheets of paper. 'I want you to visit the two widows from Florida.'

'I could go early next week,' said Julia, checking her diary.

'No,' said Logan firmly. 'Phone them this morning and fly down to see them tomorrow. You can be sure that Ralph Elliot has already paid them a visit.'

Julia nodded, and began checking through the file to find how much was known of Mrs Bloom and Mrs Hargaten.

'And finally, Nat,' continued Logan, 'you're going to have to get yourself involved in a fairly aggressive media campaign; in other words, let it all hang out.'

'What do you have in mind?' asked Nat.

'Local boy made good, Vietnam hero, Harvard scholar who returned to Hartford to build up the bank with his closest friend. Even throw in your cross-country experience – the nation is going through a bout of jogging mania at the moment – and one or two of them might even be shareholders. And if anyone wants to interview you from *Cycling News* to *Knitting Weekly*, just say yes.'

'And who will I be up against?' asked Nat. 'The chairman of Fairchild's?'

'No, I don't think so,' said Logan, 'Murray Goldblatz is an astute banker, but they won't risk putting him on television.'

'Why not?' asked Tom. 'He's been the chairman of Fairchild's for over twenty years, and he's one of the most respected financiers in the business.'

'I agree, chairman,' said Logan. 'But don't forget that he had a heart attack a couple of years back, and worse, he stutters. It may not worry you because you've become used to it over the years, but the chances are that if he goes on television, the public will only see him once. He may be the most respected banker in the state, but stuttering spells dithering. Unfair, but you can be sure that they'll have thought that through.'

'So I guess it will be Wesley Jackson, my opposite number?' mused Nat. 'He's about the most articulate banker I've come up against. I even offered him a place on our board.'

'You may well have done,' said Logan. 'But he's black.'

'This is 1988,' said Nat angrily.

'I'm aware of that,' said Logan, 'but well over ninety per cent of your shareholders are white, and they will have taken that into consideration as well.'

'So who do you think they'll put up?' asked Nat.

'I don't have any doubt that you'll be up against Ralph Elliot.'

‹•›

'So the Republicans have ended up endorsing Barbara Hunter after all,' said Fletcher.

'Only because no one else wanted to run against you,' Jimmy replied. 'Once they realized you were nine points ahead in the polls.'

'I hear they begged Ralph Elliot to throw his hat in the ring, but he said he couldn't consider it while he was in the middle of a takeover bid for Russell's Bank.'

'A good excuse,' said Jimmy, 'but there was no way that man would have allowed his name to go forward unless he knew he had a reasonable chance of beating you. Did you see him on television last night?'

'Yes,' said Fletcher with a sigh, 'and if I hadn't known better, I might have fallen for that "be assured of your future by joining the largest, safest and most respected bank in the state". He's lost none of his old charisma. I only hope your father didn't fall for it.'

'No, Harry's already pledged his one per cent to Tom Russell, and is telling everyone else to do the same thing, though he was shocked when I told him how much his shares were worth.'

Fletcher laughed. 'I see the financial journalists are speculating that both sides now have around forty per cent, with only another week to go before the offer closes.'

'Yes, it's going to be close. I only hope Tom Russell realizes just how dirty it will become now that Ralph Elliot is involved,' said Fletcher.

'I couldn't have made it clearer,' said Jimmy quietly.

—◇—

'When was this sent out?' Nat asked as the rest of the board studied the latest missive circulated to all shareholders by Fairchild's.

'It's dated yesterday,' said Logan, 'which means we have three days left to respond, but by then I fear the damage will have been done.'

'Even I wouldn't have believed Elliot was capable of sinking this low,' said Tom as he studied the letter signed by Murray Goldblatz:

Things you didn't know about Nathaniel Cartwright, the Chief Executive of Russell's Bank:

— Mr Cartwright was neither born nor raised in Hartford;

— he was rejected by Yale after cheating in the entrance exam;

— he left the University of Connecticut without a degree, after losing the election for student president;

— he was sacked from J P Morgan after losing the bank $500,000;

— he's married to a Korean girl whose family fought against the Americans during the war;

— the only job he could find after being sacked by Morgan's was with an old school friend, who just happened to be chairman of Russell's Bank.

Pledge your shares to Fairchild's: be sure your future is secure.

'This is the response that I propose we send out by express mail today,' said Logan, 'allowing Fairchild's no time to respond to it.' He slid a copy across to each board member.

Things you ought to know about Nat Cartwright, the Chief Executive of Russell's Bank:

— Nat was born and raised in Connecticut;

— he won the Medal of Honour in Vietnam;

— he completed his undergraduate degree at Harvard (summa cum laude), before going on to Harvard business school;

— he resigned from Morgan's, having made a profit for the bank of over a million dollars;

— during his nine years at Russell's as Chief Executive, he has quadrupled the bank's profits;

— his wife is Professor of Statistics at UConn, and her father was a master sergeant in the American Marines.

Stay with Russell's: the bank that cares about you and takes care of your money.

'Can I release it immediately?' asked Logan.

'No,' said Nat, tearing it up. He didn't speak for some time. 'It takes a lot to get me angry, but I am about to kill off Ralph Elliot once and for all, so listen carefully.'

Twenty minutes later, Tom ventured the first comment, 'That would be taking one hell of a risk.'

'Why?' asked Nat, 'if the strategy fails, we'll all end up multi-millionaires, but if it succeeds, we'll take control of the biggest bank in the state.'

—◇—

'Dad's livid with you,' said Jimmy.

'But why?' asked Fletcher, 'when I won.'

'That's the problem, you won by over twelve thousand

409

votes, which was tactless of you,' said Jimmy as he watched Harry Junior running down the wing, the ball at his feet. 'Don't forget that he only managed eleven thousand once in twenty-eight years, and that was when Barry Goldwater was running for president.'

'Thanks for the warning,' said Fletcher. 'I guess I'd better avoid the next couple of Sunday lunches.'

'You'd better not, it's your turn to be told how he made a million overnight.'

'Yes, Annie warned me that he'd sold his shares in Russell's Bank. I thought he'd made a pledge not to release them to Fairchild's at any cost?'

'He did, and he would have kept to it, but the day before the offer was due to close, and the shares had peaked at $7.10, he had a call from Tom Russell, advising him to sell. He even suggested that he got in touch with Ralph Elliot direct so the deal would go through quickly.'

'They're up to something,' said Fletcher. 'There's no way Tom Russell would have told your father to deal with Ralph Elliot unless there's another chapter still to be written in this particular saga.' Jimmy said nothing. 'So can we therefore assume that Fairchild's has secured over fifty per cent?'

'I asked Logan the same question, but he explained that because of client confidentiality, he couldn't say anything until Monday, when the official figures would be released by the SEC.'

'Ouch,' said Jimmy, 'did you see what that Taft kid just did to Harry Junior? He's lucky Joanna's not here, otherwise she would have run on to the field and whacked him.'

◄◦►

'Those in favour?' asked the chairman.

Every hand round the table rose, though Julia seemed to hesitate for a moment. 'Then it's unanimous,' declared Tom and, turning to Nat, added, 'perhaps you should take us through what's likely to happen next.'

'Certainly, chairman,' said Nat. 'At ten o'clock this morning, the SEC will announce that Fairchild's has failed to secure control of Russell's Bank.'

'What percentage do we think they'll end up with?' asked Julia.

'They had 47.89 per cent at midnight on Saturday, and may have picked up a few more shares on Sunday, but I doubt it.'

'And the price?'

'At close of business on Friday they were $7.32,' said Logan, 'but after this morning's announcement, all pledges are automatically released and Fairchild's cannot make another bid for at least twenty-eight days.'

'That's when I plan to put a million of Russell's shares on the market,' said Nat.

'Why would you do that?' asked Julia, 'when our shares would be certain to fall sharply.'

'So will Fairchild's because they own nearly fifty per cent of us,' said Nat, 'and they can do nothing about it for twenty-eight days.'

'Nothing?' repeated Julia.

'Nothing,' confirmed Logan.

'And if we then use the extra cash to buy Fairchild's shares as they begin dropping . . .'

'You would have to inform the SEC the moment you reached six per cent,' said Logan, 'and at the same time let them know that it's your intention to make a full takeover bid for Fairchild's.'

'Good,' said Nat, as he pulled the phone towards him

and dialled ten digits. No one spoke as the chief executive waited for the phone to be answered. 'Hi, Joe, it's Nat, we're going ahead as planned. At one minute past ten, I want you to place a million of the bank's shares on the market.'

'You realize they'll drop like a stone,' said Joe, 'because you're about to turn everyone into a seller.'

'Let's hope you're right, Joe, because that's when I want you to start mopping up Fairchild's shares, but not until you think they've bottomed out. And don't stop until you've got hold of five point nine per cent.'

'Understood,' said Joe.

'And, Joe, just be sure you keep an open line night and day, because you're not going to get much sleep during the next four weeks,' added Nat before replacing the receiver.

'Are you sure we're not breaking the law?' asked Julia.

'Certain,' said Logan, 'but if we pull it off, my bet is that Congress will have to rewrite the legislation on takeovers in the very near future.'

'And do you consider what we're doing is ethical?' asked Julia.

'No,' said Nat, 'and it wouldn't have even crossed my mind to behave this way if we hadn't been dealing with Ralph Elliot.' He paused. 'I did warn you that I was going to kill him. I just didn't tell you how.'

39

'YOU'VE GOT THE chairman of Fairchild's on line one, Joe Stein on line two, and your wife on line three.'

'I'll take the chairman of Fairchild's. Ask Joe Stein to hold and tell Su Ling I'll call back.'

'Your wife said it was urgent.'

'I'll call her back in a few minutes.'

'I'm putting Mr Goldblatz through.'

Nat would have liked a few moments to compose himself before he spoke to the chairman of Fairchild's, perhaps he should have told his secretary that he would call him back. For a start, how should he address him; Mr Goldblatz, Mr Chairman or sir? After all, he had been chairman of Fairchild's when Nat was still at Harvard Business School doing case studies on banking.

'Good morning, Mr Cartwright.'

'Good morning, Mr Goldblatz, how can I help you?'

'I wondered if perhaps we could meet.' Nat hesitated because he wasn't quite sure what to say. 'And I think it would be wise if it were just the two us,' he added. 'Jus . . . jus . . . just the two of us.'

'Yes, I'm sure that would be all right,' said Nat, 'but it will have to be somewhere no one would recognize us.'

'Might I suggest St Joseph's Cathedral?' said Mr Goldblatz, 'I don't think anyone will recognize me there.'

Nat laughed. 'When did you have in mind?' he asked.

'I would have thought sooner rather than later.'

'I agree,' said Nat.

'Shall we say three o'clock this afternoon? I can't imagine there will be that many people in church on a Monday afternoon.'

'St Joseph's, three o'clock, I'll see you there, Mr Goldblatz.' No sooner had Nat put the phone down than it rang again.

'Joe Stein,' said Linda.

'Joe, what's the latest?'

'I've just picked up another hundred thousand of Fairchild's stock, which takes you up to twenty-nine per cent. They're currently around $2.90, which is less than half their high point. But you do have a problem,' said Joe.

'And what's that?'

'If you don't get hold of fifty per cent by Friday week, you'll be facing exactly the same problem Fairchild's had a fortnight ago, so I hope you know what your next move is.'

'It may become clearer after a meeting I'm having at three o'clock this afternoon,' said Nat.

'That sounds interesting,' said Joe.

'It could well be,' said Nat, 'but I can't say anything at the moment because even I'm not sure what it's all about.'

'Curiouser and curiouser,' said Joe. 'I'll look forward to hearing more. But what do you expect me to do in the meantime?'

'I want you to go on buying every Fairchild's share you can lay your hands on until close of business tonight. Then let's talk again just before the market opens tomorrow morning.'

'Understood,' said Joe, 'then I'd better leave you and get back on the floor.'

Nat let out a long sigh, and tried to think what Murray Goldblatz could possibly want to see him about. He picked up the phone again, 'Linda, get me Logan Fitzgerald – he'll be on his New York number.'

'Your wife did stress that it was urgent and she called back again while you were speaking to Mr Stein.'

'Right, I'll phone her while you try and find Logan.'

Nat dialled his home number and then began strumming his fingers on the desk as he continued to think about Murray Goldblatz and what he could possibly want. Su Ling's voice interrupted his thoughts.

'Sorry I didn't call you straight back,' said Nat, 'but Murray . . .'

'Luke's run away from school,' said Su Ling. 'No one's seen him since lights out last night.'

―◇―

'You've got the chairman of the Democratic National Committee on line one, Mr Gates on line two, and your wife on line three.'

'I'll take the party chairman first. Would you ask Jimmy to hold and tell Annie I'll call her right back.'

'She said it was urgent.'

'Tell her I'll only be a couple of minutes.'

Fletcher would have liked a little more time to compose himself. He'd only met the party chairman a couple of times, in a corridor at the national convention, and at a cocktail party in Washington DC. He doubted if Mr Brubaker would remember either occasion. And then there was the problem of how to address him, Mr Brubaker, Alan, or even sir. After all, he'd been appointed chairman before Fletcher had even run for the Senate.

'Good morning, Fletcher, Al Brubaker.'

'Good morning, Mr Chairman, how nice to hear from you. How can I help?'

'I need to have a word with you in private, Fletcher,

415

and wondered if you and your wife could possibly fly down to Washington and join Jenny and me for dinner one evening.'

'We'd be delighted to,' said Fletcher, 'when did you have in mind?'

'How's the evening of the eighteenth looking? That's next Friday.'

Fletcher quickly flicked through the pages of his appointment book. He had a caucus meeting at noon, which he shouldn't miss now that he was deputy leader, but nothing was pencilled in for that evening. 'What time would you like us to be there?'

'Eight suit you?' asked Brubaker.

'Yes, that will be fine, Mr Chairman.'

'Good, then eight o'clock it is, on the eighteenth. My home is in Georgetown, 3038 N Street.'

Fletcher wrote it down in the space below the caucus meeting. 'I look forward to seeing you then, Mr Chairman.'

'Me too,' said Brubaker. 'And Fletcher, I would prefer if you didn't mention this to anyone.'

Fletcher put the phone down. It would be tight, and he might even have to leave the caucus meeting early. The intercom buzzed again.

'Mr Gates,' said Sally.

'Hi, Jimmy, what can I do for you?' asked Fletcher cheerily, wanting to tell him about his invitation to have dinner with the chairman of the party.

'It's not good, I'm afraid,' said Jimmy. 'Dad's had another heart attack and they've rushed him into St Patrick's. I'm just about to leave, but I thought I'd give you a call first.'

'How bad is he?' asked Fletcher quietly.

'Hard to tell until we hear what the doctor has to say. Mom wasn't exactly coherent when she got in touch with me, so I won't know a lot more until I've been to the hospital.'

'Annie and I will be with you as soon as we can,' said Fletcher. He touched the bridge of his telephone and then dialled his home number. It was busy. He replaced the phone and began tapping his fingers. If it was still busy when he tried again he decided he would drive straight home and pick Annie up so they could go over to the hospital together. For a moment, Al Brubaker flashed back into his mind. Why would he want a private meeting that he would prefer not to be mentioned to anyone else? But then his thoughts returned to Harry and he dialled his home number a second time. He heard Annie's voice on the end of the line.

'Have you heard?' she asked.

'Yes,' said Fletcher, 'I've just spoken to Jimmy. I thought I'd go directly to the hospital so we could meet there.'

'No, it's not just Dad,' said Annie. 'It's Lucy, she had a terrible fall when she was out riding this morning. She's concussed and has broken her leg. They've put her in the infirmary. I don't know what to do next.'

—◇—

'I blame myself,' said Nat. 'Because of the takeover battle with Fairchild's I haven't been to see Luke once this term.'

'Me neither,' admitted Su Ling. 'But we were going to the school play next week.'

'I know,' said Nat. 'As he's playing Romeo, do you think the problem might be Juliet?'

'Possibly. After all, you met your first love at the school play, didn't you?' asked Su Ling.

'Yes, and that ended in tears.'

'Don't blame yourself, Nat. I've been just as preoccu-

417

pied with my graduate students these last few weeks, and perhaps I should have questioned Luke more closely about why he was so silent and withdrawn during term break.'

'He's always been a bit of a loner,' said Nat, 'and studious children rarely gather a lot of friends around them.'

'How would you know?' asked Su Ling, glad to see her husband smile. 'And both our mothers have always been quiet and thoughtful,' she added as she drove on to the highway.

'How long do you think it will take us to get there?' asked Nat as he glanced at the clock on the dashboard.

'At this time of day about an hour, so I expect we should arrive around three o'clock,' said Su Ling, as she took her foot off the accelerator, once she'd touched fifty-five.

'Three, oh hell,' said Nat, suddenly remembering, 'I'll have to let Murray Goldblatz know that I won't be able to make his meeting.'

'The chairman of Fairchild's?'

'No less, he requested a private meeting,' said Nat as he picked up the car-phone. He quickly checked Fairchild's number in his phone book.

'To discuss what?' asked Su Ling.

'It has to be something to do with the takeover, but beyond that I haven't a clue.' Nat pressed the eleven digits. 'Mr Goldblatz, please.'

'Who shall I say is calling?' asked the switchboard operator.

Nat hesitated, 'It's a personal call.'

'I will still need to know who it is,' the voice insisted.

'I have an appointment with him at three o'clock.'

'I'll put you though to his secretary.' Nat waited.

'Mr Goldblatz's office,' said a female voice.

'I have a three o'clock appointment with Mr Goldblatz, but I fear I am going . . .'

'I'll put you through, Mr Cartwright.'

'Mr Cartwright.'

'Mr Goldblatz, I must apologize, a family problem has arisen and I won't be able to make our meeting this afternoon.'

'I see,' said Goldblatz, not sounding as though he did.

'Mr Goldblatz,' said Nat, 'I'm not in the habit of playing games, I have neither the time nor the inclination.'

'I wasn't suggesting you did, Mr Cartwright,' said Goldblatz curtly.

Nat hesitated. 'My son has run away from Taft and I'm on my way to see the principal.'

'I'm so . . . so . . . sorry to hear that,' Mr Goldblatz said, his tone immediately changing. 'If it's any consolation, I also ran away from Taft, but once I'd spent all my pocket money I decided to go back the following day.'

Nat laughed. 'Thank you for being so understanding.'

'Not at all, perhaps you'd give me a call and let me know when it's convenient for us to meet.'

'Yes of course, Mr Goldblatz, and I wonder if I might ask a favour.'

'Certainly.'

'That none of this conversation is reported to Ralph Elliot.'

'You have my word on that, but then, Mr Cartwright, he has no idea that I planned to meet you in the first place.'

When Nat put the phone down, Su Ling said, 'Wasn't that a bit of a risk?'

'No, I don't think so,' said Nat. 'I have a feeling that Mr Goldblatz and I have discovered something we have in common.'

As Su Ling drove through the Taft gates, memories

came flooding back to Nat: his mother being late, having to walk down the centre aisle of a packed hall when his knees were knocking, sitting next to Tom, and twenty-five years later, accompanying his son back on his first day. Now he only hoped his boy was safe and well.

Su Ling parked the car outside the principal's house, and before she had turned the engine off, Nat spotted Mrs Henderson coming down the steps. He felt his stomach churn until he saw the smile on her lips. Su Ling jumped out of the car.

'They've found him,' Mrs Henderson said. 'He was with his grandmother, helping her with the laundry.'

—◇—

'Let's both go straight to the hospital and see your father. Then we can decide if one of us should go on to Lakeville and check up on Lucy.'

'Lucy would be so sad if she knew,' said Annie. 'She has always adored Grandpa.'

'I know, and he's already begun planning her life,' said Fletcher. 'Perhaps it would be better not to tell her what has happened, especially as she obviously won't be able to visit him.'

'You may be right. In any case, he did go and see her last week.'

'I didn't know that,' said Fletcher.

'Oh yes, those two are plotting something,' said Annie as she drove into the hospital parking lot, 'but neither of them is letting me in on the secret.'

When the elevator doors opened, the two of them walked quickly down the corridor to Harry's room. Martha stood up the moment they walked in, her face ashen. Annie took her mother in her arms as Fletcher touched Jimmy's shoulder. He looked down at a man whose flesh was drawn and sallow, his nose and mouth covered with a mask. A monitor beeped beside him, the only indication that he was still alive. This was the most energetic man Fletcher had ever known.

The four of them sat around the bed in silence, Martha holding her husband's hand. After a few moments she said, 'Don't you think one of you should go and see how Lucy is getting on? There's not a lot you can do here.'

'I'm not moving,' said Annie, 'but I think Fletcher ought to go.'

Fletcher nodded his agreement. He kissed Martha on the cheek, and looking at Annie said, 'I'll drive straight back just as soon as I've made sure that Lucy is OK.'

Fletcher couldn't recall much of the journey to Lakeville as his mind wondered from Harry to Lucy, and for a moment to Al Brubaker, although he found that he was no longer preoccupied with what the chairman of the party wanted.

When he reached the road sign announcing the intersection for Hotchkiss, Fletcher's thoughts returned to Harry and how they had first met at that football game. 'Please God let him live,' he said out loud as he drove into his old school and brought the car to a halt outside the entrance to the sanatorium. A nurse accompanied the senator to his daughter's bedside. As he walked down the corridor of empty beds, he could see in the distance a plastered leg, hooked high into the air. It reminded him of when he had run for the school presidency and his rival had allowed the voters to sign his cast on the day of the election. Fletcher tried to remember his name.

'You're a fraud,' said Fletcher even before he saw the huge smile on Lucy's face and the bottles of soda and bags of cookies scattered all around her.

'I know, Dad, and I even managed to miss a calculus exam, but I must be back on campus by Monday if I'm to have any chance of becoming class president.'

'So that's why Grandpa came down to see you, the sly old buzzard,' said Fletcher. He kissed his daughter's cheek and was eyeing the cookies when a young man walked in and stood nervously on the other side of the bed.

'This is George,' said Lucy. 'He's in love with me.'

'Nice to meet you, George,' said Fletcher smiling.

'You too, senator,' the young man said as he extended his right hand across the bed.

'George is running my campaign for class president,' said Lucy, 'just like my godfather ran yours. George thinks that the broken leg will help bring in the sympathy vote. I'll have to ask Grandpa for his opinion when he next comes up to visit me – Grandpa's our secret weapon,' she whispered, 'he's already terrified the opposition.'

'I don't know why I bothered to come down to see you at all,' said Fletcher, 'you so obviously don't need me.'

'Yes I do, Dad. Could I get an advance on next month's allowance?'

Fletcher smiled and took out his wallet. 'How much did your grandfather give you?'

'Five dollars,' said Lucy sheepishly. Fletcher extracted another five dollar bill. 'Thanks, Dad. By the way, why isn't Mom with you?'

⟨◦⟩

Nat agreed to drive Luke back to school the following morning. The boy had been very uncommunicative the previous evening, almost as if he wanted to say something, but not while both of them were in the room.

'Perhaps he'll open up on the way back to school, when it's only the two of you,' suggested Su Ling.

Father and son set out on the journey back to Taft soon after breakfast, but Luke still said very little. Despite Nat's trying to raise the subjects of work, the school play and even how Luke's running was going, he received only monosyllabic replies. So Nat changed tactics and also remained silent, hoping that Luke would, in time, initiate a conversation.

His father was in the passing lane, driving just above the speed limit, when Luke asked, 'When did you first fall in love, Dad?' Nat nearly hit the car in front of him, but slowed down in time before drifting back into the middle lane.

'I think the first girl I really took any serious interest in was called Rebecca. She was playing Oliva to my Sebastian in the school play.' He paused. 'Is it Juliet you're having the problem with?'

'Certainly not,' said Luke, 'she's dumb – pretty, but dumb.' This was followed by another long silence. 'And how far did you and Rebecca go?' he finally asked.

'We kissed a little, if I remember,' said Nat, 'and there was a little of what we used to call in those days petting.'

'Did you want to touch her breasts?'

'Sure did, but she wouldn't let me. I didn't get that far until our freshman year at college.'

'But did you love her, Dad?'

'I thought I did, but that bombshell didn't truly hit me until I ran into your mother.'

'So was Mom the first person you made love to?'

'No, there had been a couple of other girls before her, one in Vietnam, and another while I was at college.'

'Did you get either of them pregnant?'

Nat moved across to the inside lane and fell well below the speed limit. He paused. 'Have you got someone pregnant?'

'I don't know,' said Luke, 'and neither does Kathy, but

when we were kissing behind the gym, I made a terrible mess all over her skirt.'

Fletcher spent another hour with his daughter before he drove back to Hartford. He enjoyed George's company. Lucy had described him as the brightest kid in the class. 'That's why I chose him as my campaign manager,' she explained.

Fletcher was back in Hartford an hour later, and when he walked into Harry's hospital room the tableau hadn't changed. He sat down next to Annie and took her hand.

'Any improvement?' he asked.

'No, nothing,' said Annie, 'he hasn't stirred since you left. How about Lucy?'

'A complete fraud, as I told her. She'll be in a plaster cast for around six weeks, which doesn't seem to have cramped her style; in fact she seems convinced it will help her chances of becoming class president.'

'Did you tell her about Grandpa?'

'No, and I had to bluff a little when she asked where you were.'

'Where was I?'

'Chairing a meeting of the school board.'

Annie nodded. 'True, just the wrong day.'

'By the way, did you know she had a boyfriend?' asked Fletcher.

'Do you mean George?'

'You've met George?'

'Yes, but I wouldn't have described him as a boyfriend,' said Annie, 'more a devoted slave.'

'I thought Lincoln abolished slavery in 1863?' said Fletcher.

Annie turned to face her husband, 'Did it worry you?' she asked.

'Certainly not, Lucy's got to have a boyfriend sooner or later.'

'That's not what I meant, and you know it.'

'Annie, she's only sixteen.'

'I was younger when I first met you.'

'Annie, have you forgotten that when we were at college we marched for civil rights, and I'm proud that we've passed that conviction on to our daughter.'

40

WHEN NAT DROPPED his son off at Taft and returned to Hartford, he felt guilty about not having enough time to visit his parents. But he knew he couldn't miss the meeting with Murray Goldblatz two days in a row. When he said goodbye to Luke, at least the boy no longer appeared shrouded in the world's woes. Nat promised his son that he and his mother would be back on Friday evening for the school play. He was still thinking about Luke when the car phone rang – an innovation that had changed his life.

'You were going to call before the market opened,' said Joe. He paused. 'With some possible news?'

'I'm sorry not to have called, Joe; a domestic crisis came up and I simply forgot.'

'Well, are you able to tell me more?'

'Tell you more?'

'Your last words were, "I'll know more in twenty-four hours".'

'Before you burst out laughing, Joe, I'll know more in twenty-four hours.'

'I'll wear that, but what are today's instructions?'

'The same as yesterday, I want you to go on buying Fairchild's aggressively until the close of business.'

'I hope you know what you're doing, Nat, because the bills are going to start coming in next week. Everyone knows Fairchild's can ride out this sort of storm, but are you absolutely certain you can?'

'I can't afford not to,' said Nat, 'so just keep on buying.'

'Whatever you say, boss, I just hope you've got a parachute, because if you haven't secured fifty per cent of Fairchild's by Monday morning at ten o'clock it's going to be a very bumpy landing.'

As Nat continued his journey back to Hartford, he realized that Joe was doing no more than stating the obvious. By this time next week he knew he could well be out of a job, and more important, have allowed Russell's to be taken over by their biggest rival. Was Goldblatz already aware of this? Of course he was.

As Nat drove into the city, he decided not to return to his office, but to park a few blocks from St Joseph's, grab a snack and consider all the alternatives Goldblatz might come up with. He ordered a bacon sandwich in the hope that it would put him in a fighting mood. He then began to write out a list of the pros and cons on the back of the menu.

At ten to three, he left the deli and started to make his way slowly towards the cathedral. Several people nodded or said 'Good afternoon, Mr Cartwright', as they passed, reminding him how well known he'd become recently. Their expressions were of admiration and respect, and he only wished he could advance the reel by one week to see how the faces would react then. He checked his watch – four minutes to three. He decided to circle the block and walk into the cathedral from the quieter south entrance. He climbed the steps in twos and entered the south transept a couple of minutes before the cathedral clock chimed the hour. Nothing would be gained by being late.

It took Nat a few moments to accustom himself to the darkness of the candle-lit cathedral after the strong light of the mid-afternoon sun. He looked down the centre aisle that led to the altar, dominated by a massive gilded cross studded with semi-precious stones. He transferred his attention to the rows and rows of dark oak pews that stretched out in front of him down the nave. They were indeed almost empty as Mr Goldblatz had predicted, save for four or five old ladies shrouded in black, one of them holding a rosary and chanting, 'Hail Mary, full of Grace, the Lord is with you, blessed art thou . . .?'

Nat continued down the centre aisle, but could see no sign of Goldblatz. When he reached the great, carved wooden pulpit, he stopped for a moment to admire the craftsmanship, which reminded him of his trips to Italy. He felt guilty that he'd been unaware of such beauty in his own city. He looked back down the aisle, but the only occupants remained the cluster of old ladies, heads bowed, still mumbling. He decided to make his way to the far side of the cathedral and take a seat near the back. He checked his watch again. It was one minute past three. As he walked, he became aware of the echoing sound his feet made on the marble floor. It was then that he heard a voice say, 'Do you wish to confess, my son?'

Nat swung to his left to see a confessional box with the curtain drawn. A Catholic priest with a Jewish accent? He smiled, took a seat on the small wooden bench and drew the curtain closed.

—◇—

'You're looking very smart,' said the majority leader as Fletcher took his place on Ken's right. 'Anyone else and I'd have said you had a mistress.'

'I do have a mistress,' said Fletcher, 'and her name is Annie. By the way, I may have to leave around two.'

Ken Stratton glanced down the agenda. 'That's fine by me; other than the education bill there doesn't seem to be a lot that involves you except perhaps candidates for the next election. We've all assumed you will be running again for Hartford, unless Harry plans to make a comeback. By the way, how is the old buzzard?'

'He's a little better,' said Fletcher. 'Restless, interfering, irascible and opinionated.'

'Not much change then,' said Ken.

Fletcher considered the agenda. Fund-raising was all he would be missing, and that item had been on every agenda since the day he was elected, and would still be there long after he'd retired.

As twelve struck, the majority leader called for order and asked Fletcher to present his timetable for the education bill. For the next thirty minutes Fletcher outlined his proposals, going into considerable detail about those clauses he anticipated the Republicans would oppose. After five or six questions from his colleagues, Fletcher realized that it would require all his legal and debating skills if he was to get this piece of legislation through the Senate. The last question predictably came from Jack Swales, the longest-serving member of the Senate. He always asked the last question, which was a sign that it was time to move on to the next item on the agenda.

'How much is this all going to cost the taxpayer, senator?'

Other members smiled as Fletcher performed the ritual: 'It's covered in the budget, Jack, and was part of our platform at the last election.'

Jack smiled and the majority leader said, 'Item number two, candidates for the next election.'

Fletcher had intended to slip out as soon as the discussion got under way, but like everyone else in the room, was taken by surprise when Ken went on to say, 'I have to inform my fellow members, with some regret, that I shall not be running at the next election.'

A half-sleepy group meeting suddenly became a

powder-keg, with 'whys?' and 'surely nots' and 'who?' until Ken raised a hand. 'I don't have to explain to you why I feel the time has come to retire.'

Fletcher realized the immediate consequence of Ken's decision was that he was now the favourite to become majority leader. When his name was called, Fletcher made it clear that he would be running for re-election. He slipped out when Jack Swales began a speech on why he felt it was nothing less than his duty to seek re-election at the age of eighty-two.

Fletcher drove the half-mile to the hospital, and ran up the stairs to the second floor rather than wait for the elevator. He walked in to find Harry laying down the law on impeachment to an attentive audience of two. Martha and Annie turned to face him as he entered the room.

'Anything happen at the party caucus that I ought to know about?' Harry asked.

'Ken Stratton won't be running at the next election.'

'That's no surprise. Ellie's been ill for some time, and she's the only thing he loves more than the party. But what it does mean, is that, if we can hold on to the Senate, you could well be the next majority leader.'

'What about Jack Swales? Won't he consider it his by right?'

'In politics, nothing is yours by right,' said Harry. 'In any case, my bet is that the other members wouldn't back him. Now don't waste any more time talking to me, I know you've got to be in Washington for your meeting with Al Brubaker. All I want to know is when you think you'll be back.'

'First thing tomorrow morning,' said Fletcher. 'We're only staying overnight.'

'Then drop in on your way from the airport; I want a blow by blow account of why Al wanted to see you, and make sure you give him my regards, because he's the best chairman the party's had in years. And ask him if he got my letter.'

'Your letter?' said Fletcher.

'Just ask him,' said Harry.

'I thought he looked a lot better,' said Fletcher as he and Annie drove to the airport.

'I agree,' said Annie, 'and they've told Martha that they may even let him go home next week if, and only if, he promises to take things easy.'

'He'll promise,' said Fletcher, 'but just be thankful the election's not for another ten months.'

The shuttle to the capital took off fifteen minutes late, but Fletcher had allowed for that, so when they touched down, he felt confident they would still have enough time to check into the Willard Hotel, shower, and be in Georgetown by eight.

Their cab pulled up outside the hotel at seven ten. The first thing Fletcher asked the porter was how long it would take to get to Georgetown.

'Ten, maybe fifteen minutes,' he replied.

'Then I'd like to book a cab for seven forty-five.'

Annie somehow managed to shower and change into a cocktail dress, while Fletcher paced around the room looking at his watch every few moments. He opened the cab door for his wife at 7.51.

'I need to get to 3038 N Street in,' he checked his watch, 'nine minutes.'

'No, you don't,' said Annie, 'if Jenny Brubaker is anything like me, she'll be grateful if we're a few minutes late.'

The cabbie wove his way in and out of the evening traffic and managed to pull up outside the chairman's house at two minutes past the hour. After all, he knew who would be paying the fare.

'It's nice to see you again, Fletcher,' Al Brubaker said

431

as he opened the front door. 'And it's Annie, isn't it? I don't think we've met, but of course I know about your work for the party.'

'The party?' said Annie.

'Don't you sit on the Hartford school board as well as the hospital committee?'

'Yes, I do,' said Annie, 'but I've always looked on that as working for the community.'

'Just like your father,' said Al. 'By the way, how is the old bruiser?'

'We've just left him,' said Fletcher. 'He was looking a lot better, and sends his best wishes. By the way, he wanted to know if you received his letter.'

'Yes I did. He never gives up, does he?' added Brubaker with a smile. 'Why don't we go through to the library and I'll fix you both a drink. Jenny should be down shortly.'

—◦—

'How's your boy?'

'He's fine, thank you, Mr Goldblatz. His absence turned out to be caused by an affair of the heart.'

'How old is he?'

'Sixteen.'

'A proper age to fall in love. Now, my son, do you have anything to confess?'

'Yes, father, by this time next week I will be the chairman of the largest bank in the state.'

'By this time next week, you might not even be the chief executive of one of the smaller banks in the state.'

'What makes you think that?' asked Nat.

'Because what might have turned out to be a brilliant coup could have backfired, leaving you over-extended. Your brokers must have warned you that there is no chance of you laying your hands on fifty per cent of Fairchild's by Monday morning.'

'It's going to be a close-run thing,' said Nat, 'and I still believe we can make it.'

'Thank heavens neither of us is a Catholic, Mr Cartwright, otherwise you would be blushing, and I would be recommending a penance of three Hail Marys. But fear not, I see redemption for both of us.'

'Do I need redemption, father?'

'We both do, which is wh . . . wh . . . why I asked to see you. This battle has done neither of us any favours and if it continues beyond Sunday, it will harm both the institutions we serve, and possibly even close yours.'

Nat wanted to protest, but he knew that Goldblatz was right. 'So what form does this redemption take?' he asked.

'Well I think I've come up with a better solution than three Hail Marys, which may cleanse us both of our sins and might even show us a little profit.'

'I await your instructions, father.'

'I've watched your career with interest over the years, my son. You're very bright, extremely diligent and ferociously determined, but what I admire most about you is that you're straight – however much one of my legal advisors would have me believe otherwise.'

'I'm flattered, sir, but not overwhelmed.'

'And neither should you be. I am a realist, and I think that if you don't succeed this time, you might well try again in a couple of years, and go on trying until you do succeed. Am I right?'

'You may well be, sir.'

'You have been frank with me, so I shall respond in kind. In eighteen months' time I will be sixty-five, when I wish to retire to the golf course. I would like to hand over to my successor a thriving institution, not an ailing patient

433

continually returning to hospital for more treatment. I believe you may be the solution to my problem.'

'I thought I was the cause.'

'All the more reason for us to try and pull off a coup that is both bold and imaginative.'

'I thought that's exactly what I was doing.'

'And you still may, my son, but for political reasons I need the whole thing to be your idea, which means, Mr Cartwright, that you're going to have to trust me.'

'It's taken you forty years to build your reputation, Mr Goldblatz. I can't believe you'd be willing to trade it in just months before you're due to retire.'

'I too am flattered, young man, but, like you, not overwhelmed. Therefore might I suggest that it was you who requested this meeting to put forward your proposal that, rather than continue to fight each other, we should in fact work together.'

'A partnership?' said Nat.

'Call it what you will, Mr Cartwright, but if our two banks were to merge, no one will have lost out, and more important, all our shareholders will benefit.'

'And what terms are you suggesting that I should recommend to you, not to mention to my board?'

'That the bank be called Fairchild Russell, and that I remain chairman for the next eighteen months, while you are appointed my deputy.'

'But what will happen to Tom and Julia Russell?'

'Obviously they would both be offered a place on the board. If you become chairman in eighteen months' time, it would be up to you to appoint your own deputy, although I think you might be wise to keep Wesley Jackson on as your chief executive. But as you invited him to join your board some years ago, I can't believe you'd find that a setback.'

'No, I wouldn't, but that doesn't solve the problem of stock allocation.'

'You currently hold ten per cent of Russell's, as does your chairman. His wife, who incidentally I think should manage our combined property portfolios, did at one point possess as much as four per cent of the stock. But I suspect that it has been her shares that you have been releasing on to the open market for the past few days.'

'You could be right, Mr Goldblatz.'

'In turnover and profits Fairchild's is rou . . . rou . . . roughly five times the size of Russell's, so I would suggest that when you put forward your proposal, you and Mr Russell ask for four per cent and settle for three. In the case of Mrs Russell, I would have thought one per cent would be appropriate. All three of you will of course retain your present salaries and benefits.'

'And my staff?'

'The status quo should remain for the first eighteen months. After that, the decision will be yours.'

'And you want me to approach you with this offer, Mr Goldblatz?'

'Yes I do.'

'Forgive me for asking, why don't you simply make the proposal yourself, and let my board consider it?'

'Because our legal advisors would recommend against it. It seems that Mr Elliot has only one purpose in this takeover, and that is to destroy you. I also have only one purpose, and that is to maintain the integrity of the bank I have served for over thirty years.'

'Then why not just sack Elliot?'

'I wanted to, the day after he sent out that infamous letter in my name, but I couldn't afford to admit we might have an internal disagreement only days before we were facing a takeover. I can just imagine what the press would make of that, not to men . . . men . . . mention the shareholders, Mr Cartwright.'

'But once Elliot hears the proposal has come from me,' said Nat, 'he'll immediately advise your board against it.'

'I agree,' said Goldblatz, 'which is why I sent him to Washington yesterday so that he can report directly back to me once the Securities and Exchange Commission announces the outcome of your takeover bid on Monday.'

'He'll smell a rat. He knows only too well that he doesn't need to sit around in Washington for four days. He could fly down on Sunday night, and still brief you on the Commission's decision on Monday morning.'

'Funny you should mention that, Mr Cartwright, because it was my secretary who sp . . . sp . . . spotted that the Republicans are having their mid-term get together in Washington ending with a dinner at the White House,' he paused, 'I had to call in more than one favour to ensure that Ralph Elliot received an invitation to that august gathering. So I think you'll find he's fairly preoccupied at the moment. I keep reading in the local press about his political ambitions. He denies them, of course, so I assume it has to be true.'

'So why did you employ him in the first place?'

'We've always used Belman and Wayland in the past, Mr Cartwright, and until this takeover, I hadn't come across Mr Elliot. I blame myself, but I am at least attempting to rectify the mistake. You see, I didn't have your advantage of losing to him twice in the past.'

'Touché,' said Nat, 'so what happens next?'

'I have enjoyed meeting with you, Mr Cartwright, and I shall put your proposal to my board later this afternoon. Sadly one of our members is in Washington, but I would still hope to be able to phone you back with our reaction later this evening.'

'I'll look forward to that call,' said Nat.

'Good, and then we can meet face to face, and I suggest as quickly as possible, as I would like an agreement signed by Friday evening subject to due diligence.' Murray Goldblatz paused. 'Nat,' he said, 'yesterday you asked me to do you a favour; I should now like one in return.'

'Yes, of course,' said Nat.

'The monsignor, a shrewd man, asked for a two-hundred-dollar donation for the use of this box, and I feel now that we are partners you should pay your share. I only mention this because it will amuse my board, and allow me to keep a reputation among my Jewish friends of being ruthless.'

'I shall make sure I'm not the reason you lose that reputation, father,' Nat assured him.

Nat slipped out of the box and quickly made his way to the south entrance, where he saw a priest standing by the door dressed in a long black robe and biretta. Nat removed two fifty-dollar bills from his wallet and handed them over.

'God bless you, my son,' the monsignor said, 'but I have a feeling I could double your contribution if only I knew which of the two banks the church should be investing in.'

—◦—

By the time coffee had been served, Al Brubaker still hadn't given any clue as to why he'd wanted to see Fletcher.

'Jenny, why don't you take Annie through to the drawing room, as there's something I need to discuss with Fletcher. We'll join you in a few minutes.' Once Annie and Jenny had left them Al said, 'Care for a brandy or a cigar, Fletcher?'

'No thank you, Al. I'll stick with the wine.'

'You chose a good weekend to be in Washington. The Republicans are in town preparing for the mid-terms. Bush is throwing a party for them at the White House tonight, so we Democrats have to go into hiding for a few days. But tell me,' said Al, 'how's the party shaping up in Connecticut?'

'The caucus met today to discuss picking our candidates, and inevitably finance.'

'Will you be running again?'

'Yes, I've already made that clear.'

'And I'm told you could be the next majority leader?'

'Unless Jack Swales wants the job; he is, after all, the longest serving member.'

'Jack? Is he still alive? I could have sworn I'd attended his funeral. No, I can't believe the party will get behind him, unless . . .'

'Unless?' said Fletcher.

'You decide to run for governor.' Fletcher put his glass of wine back on the table, so that Al couldn't see that his hand was shaking. 'You must have considered the possibility.'

'Yes, I have,' said Fletcher, 'but I assumed the party would get behind Larry Connick.'

'Our esteemed lieutenant governor,' said Al as he lit his cigar. 'No, Larry's a good man, but he's aware of his limitations, thank God, because not many politicians are. I had a word with him last week at the governor's conference in Pittsburgh. He told me that he would be happy to remain on the ticket but only if we felt it would assist the party.' Al took a puff of his cigar and enjoyed the moment, before adding, 'No, Fletcher, you're our first choice, and if you agree to throw your hat into the ring, you have my word that the party will get behind you. The last thing we need is a bruising election for our candidate.

Let's leave the real scrap for when we have to fight the Republicans, because their candidate will be trying to ride on Bush's coat-tails, so we can expect a tough battle if we hope to hold on to the governor's mansion.'

'Do you have any view on who the Republicans might put up?' asked Fletcher.

'I was rather hoping you'd tell me,' said Al.

'There seem to be two serious contenders who come from different wings of the party. Barbara Hunter, who sits in the House, but her age and record are against her.'

'Record?' said Al.

'She hasn't made a habit of winning,' said Fletcher, 'although she has over the years built up a strong base in the party, and as Nixon showed us after losing in California, you can never count anyone out.'

'Who else?' said Al.

'Does the name Ralph Elliot mean anything to you?'

'No,' said the chairman, 'but I did notice that he's a member of the Connecticut delegation that's having dinner at the White House tonight.'

'Yes, he's on their state central committee, and if he becomes their candidate, it could turn out to be a very dirty campaign. Elliot's a bare-knuckle boxer who scores most of his points between rounds.'

'In which case he may turn out to be as much of a liability as an asset.'

'Well, I can tell you one thing, he's a hell of a street-fighter and doesn't like losing.'

'That's exactly what they say about you,' said Al with a smile. 'Anyone else?'

'Two or three other names are being bandied about, but so far nobody's come forward. Let's face it, few people had even heard of Carter until New Hampshire.'

'And what about this man,' said Al, holding up the cover of the *Banker's Weekly*.

Fletcher stared at the headline *Next Governor of Connecticut?* 'But if you read the article, Al, you'll see he's strongly tipped to become the next chairman of Fairchild's if the two banks can agree terms. I glanced through the piece on the plane.'

Al flicked through the pages. 'You obviously didn't get as far as the last paragraph,' he said, and read aloud, '*Although it's assumed when Murray Goldblatz retires he would be succeeded by Cartwright, this position could just as easily be filled by his close friend Tom Russell, should the CEO of Russell's decide to allow his name to be put forward as the Republican candidate for governor.*'

◄○►

Once he and Annie had returned to their hotel and gone to bed, Fletcher couldn't sleep, and it wasn't just because the bed was more comfortable and the pillows softer than he was used to. Al needed to know his decision by the end of the month, as he was keen to get the party up and running behind their candidate.

Annie woke just after seven. 'Did you have a good night's sleep, darling?' she asked.

'I hardly slept a wink.'

'I slept like a log, but then I didn't have to worry about whether you should run for governor.'

'Why not?' asked Fletcher.

'Because I think you should go for it, and can't imagine why you would have any reservations.'

'First, I need a long session with Harry, because one thing's for sure, he'll already have given the idea a lot of thought.'

'I wouldn't be so sure of that,' said Annie. 'I think you'll find he's more preoccupied with Lucy for class president.'

'Well, perhaps I'll be able to grab a moment of his

undivided attention to discuss the governorship of Connecticut.' Fletcher leapt out of bed. 'Would you mind if we skipped breakfast and caught an early flight? I want to have a word with Harry before going on to the Senate.'

Fletcher barely spoke on the journey back to Hartford, as he read and re-read the article in the *Banker's Weekly* on Nat Cartwright, the possible new deputy-chairman of Fairchild's or the next governor of Connecticut. Once again, he was struck by how much they had in common.

'What are you going to ask Dad?' said Annie as their plane circled Bradley Field.

'For a start, am I too young?'

'But as Al pointed out, there is already one governor younger than you, and two about the same age.'

'Second, how does he rate my chances?'

'He wouldn't be willing to answer that until he knows who your opponent is.'

'And third, am I capable of doing the job?'

'I know what his answer will be to that question, because I've already discussed it with him.'

'Thank God we didn't take this long to land when we flew in to Washington last night,' said Fletcher as they circled the airport for a third time.

'Will you still stop by and see Dad before you go to the Capitol?' asked Annie. 'He's bound to be sitting up in bed waiting to hear your news.'

'I always intended to make Harry my first stop,' said Fletcher as he drove his car out of the airport and on to the highway.

It was a bright autumnal morning when Senator Davenport arrived back in town. He decided to drive up the hill and past the Capitol before cutting across to the hospital.

As they came over the brow of the hill, Annie stared

out of the car window, and began weeping uncontrollably. Fletcher pulled over to the hard shoulder. He took his wife in his arms, as he looked over her shoulder at the Capitol building.

The United States flag was flying at half mast.

41

MR GOLDBLATZ ROSE from his place at the centre of the table and glanced down at his prepared statement. On his right sat Nat Cartwright, and on his left, Tom Russell. The rest of the board was seated in the row behind him.

'Ladies and gentlemen of the press, it is my great pleasure to announce the merger of Fairchild's and Russell's, creating a new bank which will be known as Fairchild Russell. I shall remain as chairman, Mr Nat Cartwright will be my deputy chairman, and Tom and Julia Russell will join the board. Mr Wesley Jackson will continue as the new bank's chief executive. I am able to confirm that Russell's Bank has withdrawn its takeover bid, and a new ownership structure for the company will be announced in the near future. Both Mr Cartwright and I will be happy to answer your questions.'

Hands shot up all over the room. 'Yes,' said the chairman pointing to a woman in the second row, with whom he had prearranged the first question.

'Is it still your intention to resign as chairman in the near future?'

'Yes, it is, and there are no prizes for guessing who I expect to succeed me.'

He turned and looked at Nat as another journalist shouted, 'How does Mr Russell feel about that?'

Mr Goldblatz smiled, as it was a question they had all

anticipated. He turned to his left and said, 'Perhaps Mr Russell should answer that question.'

Tom smiled benevolently at the journalist. 'I'm delighted by the coming together of the two leading banks in the state, and honoured to have been invited to join the board of Fairchild Russell as a non-executive director.' He smiled. 'I'm rather hoping Mr Cartwright will consider reappointing me when he takes over.'

'Word perfect,' whispered the chairman as Tom resumed his place.

Nat quickly rose from the other side to deliver an equally well-scripted response, 'I most certainly will be reappointing Mr Russell, but not as a non-executive director.'

Goldblatz smiled and added, 'I am sure that will not come as a total surprise to anyone who follows these matters closely. Yes?' he said, pointing to another journalist.

'Will there be any lay-offs caused by this merger?'

'No,' said Goldblatz. 'It is our intention to retain all of Russell's staff, but one of Mr Cartwright's immediate responsibilities will be to prepare for a complete restructuring of the bank during the next twelve months. Though I would like to add that Mrs Julia Russell has already been appointed to head up our new combined property division. We at Fairchild's have watched with admiration her handling of the Cedar Wood project.'

'Can I ask why your legal counsel, Ralph Elliot, is not present today?' said a voice from the back of the room.

Another question Goldblatz had anticipated, even though he couldn't quite see where it had come from. 'Mr Elliot has been in Washington DC. Last night he dined with President Bush at the White House, otherwise he would have been with us this morning. Next question?'

Goldblatz made no reference to the 'frank exchange of views' he'd had with Elliot on the phone in the early hours of the morning.

'I spoke to Mr Elliot earlier today,' said the same journalist, 'and I wonder if you would care to comment on the press statement he has just released?'

Nat froze as Goldblatz rose more slowly. 'I'd be happy to comment if I knew what he'd said.'

The journalist looked down at a single sheet of paper and read from it: *'I am delighted that Mr Goldblatz felt able to take my advice and bring the two banks together rather than continue a bruising and damaging battle from which no one would have profited.'* Goldblatz smiled and nodded. *'There will be three members of the board available to replace the current chairman in the near future, but as I consider one of them quite unsuitable to hold a post that requires financial probity, I have been left with no choice but to resign from the board and withdraw as the bank's legal advisor. With that one reservation, I wish the company every success in the future.'*

Mr Goldblatz's smile quickly disappeared, and he was unable to contain his rage. 'I have no comment to make at the present t . . . t . . . time, and that ends this press con . . . con . . . conference.' He rose from his place and marched out of the room with Nat following a pace behind him. 'The bastard broke his agreement,' said Goldblatz furiously, as he strode down the corridor towards the boardroom.

'Which was what precisely?' asked Nat, trying to remain calm.

'I agreed to say that he was a party to the successful negotiations, if in turn he would resign and withdraw as the legal representative of the new company, and make no further comment.'

'Do we have that in writing?'

'No, I agreed to it over the phone last night. He said he would confirm it in writing today.'

'So once again Elliot comes out smelling of roses,' said Nat.

Goldblatz came to a halt outside the boardroom door and turned to face Nat: 'No, he does not. I think the smell is more akin to manure,' he added, 'and this time, he's chosen the wrong man to cro . . . cro . . . cross.'

—◇—

The popularity of an individual in life often only manifests itself in death.

The funeral service for Harry Gates, held at St Joseph's Cathedral, was filled to overflowing, long before the choir had left the vestry. Don Culver, the chief of police, decided to cordon off the block in front of the cathedral, so that mourners could sit on the steps or stand in the street, while they listened to the service being relayed over loudspeakers.

When the cortège came to a halt, an honour guard carried the coffin up the steps and into the cathedral. Martha Gates was accompanied by her son, while her daughter and son-in-law walked a pace behind them. The throng of people on the steps made a passage to allow the family to join the other mourners inside. The congregation rose as an usher accompanied Mrs Gates to the front pew. As they walked down the aisle, Fletcher noted the coming together of Baptists, Jews, Episcopalians, Muslims, Methodists and Mormons, all unified in their respect for this Roman Catholic.

The bishop opened the service with a prayer chosen by Martha, which was followed by hymns and readings that Harry would have enjoyed. Jimmy and Fletcher both read lessons, but it was Al Brubaker, as chairman of the party, who climbed the steps of the wooden pulpit to deliver the address.

He looked down at the packed congregation and remained silent for a moment. 'Few politicians,' he began, 'inspire respect and affection, but if Harry could be with us today, he would see for himself that he was among that select group. I see many in this congregation I have never come across before,' he paused, 'so I have to assume they're Republicans.' Laughter broke out inside the cathedral and a ripple of applause outside in the street. 'Here was a man who, when asked by the president to run for governor of this state, replied simply, "I have not completed my work as the senator for Hartford," and he never did. As chairman of my party, I have attended the funerals of presidents, governors, senators, congressmen and congresswomen, along with the powerful and mighty, but this funeral has a difference, for it is also filled with ordinary members of the public, who have simply come to say thank you.

'Harry Gates was opinionated, verbose, irascible and maddening. He was also passionate in the pursuit of causes he believed in. Loyal to his friends, fair with his opponents, he was a man whose company you sought out simply because it enriched your life. Harry Gates was no saint, but there will be saints standing at the Gates of Heaven waiting to greet him.

'To Martha, we say thank you for indulging Harry and all his dreams, so many achieved; one still to be fulfilled. To Jimmy and Annie, his son and daughter, of whom he was inordinately proud. To Fletcher, his beloved son-in-law, who has been given the unenviable burden of carrying the torch. And to Lucy his grand-daughter, who became class president a few days after he died. America has lost a man who served his country at home and abroad, in war and in peace. Hartford has lost a public servant who will not easily be replaced.

'He wrote to me a few weeks ago,' Brubaker paused, 'begging for money – what a nerve – for his beloved hospital. He said he'd never speak to me again if I didn't send a cheque. I considered the pros and cons of that particular threat.' It was a long time before the laughter and applause died down. 'In the end, my wife sent a cheque. The truth is, that it never crossed Harry's mind that if he asked, you wouldn't give, and why? Because he spent his whole life giving, and now we must make that dream a reality and build a hospital in his memory of which he would have been proud.

'I read in the *Washington Post* last week that Senator Harry Gates had died, and then I travelled to Hartford this morning and drove past the senior citizens' centre, the library and the hospital foundation stone that bears his name. I shall write to the *Washington Post* when I return tomorrow and tell them, "you were wrong. Harry Gates is alive and still kicking".' Mr Brubaker paused as he looked down into the congregation, his eyes settling on Fletcher. '*Here was a man, when comes such another?*'

On the cathedral steps, Martha and Fletcher thanked Al Brubaker for his words.

'Anything less,' said Al, 'and he would have appeared in the pulpit next to me, demanding a recount.' The chairman shook hands with Fletcher. 'I didn't read out the whole of Harry's last letter to me,' he said, 'but I knew you would want to see the final paragraph.' He slipped a hand into an inside pocket, removed the letter, unfolded it and passed it across to Fletcher.

When Fletcher had read Harry's last words, he looked at the chairman and nodded.

—◦—

Tom and Nat walked down the cathedral steps together and joined the crowds as they quietly dispersed.

'I wish I'd known him better,' said Nat. 'You realize that I asked him to join the board when he retired from the Senate?' Tom nodded. 'He wrote – hand wrote – such a charming letter explaining the only board he would ever sit on was the hospital's.'

'I only met him a couple of times,' said Tom, 'he was mad, of course, but you have to be if you choose to spend your life pushing boulders up a hill. Don't ever tell anyone, but he's the only Democrat I've ever voted for.'

Nat laughed. 'You as well?' he admitted.

'How would you feel if I recommended that the board should make a donation of fifty thousand to the hospital fund?' asked Tom.

'I would oppose it,' said Nat. Tom looked surprised. 'Because when the senator sold his Russell's shares, he immediately donated a hundred thousand to the hospital. The least we can do is respond in kind.'

Tom nodded his agreement and turned back to see Mrs Gates standing on the top of the cathedral steps. He would write to her that afternoon enclosing the cheque. He sighed. 'Look who's shaking hands with the widow.'

Nat swung round to see Ralph Elliot holding Martha Gates's hand. 'Are you surprised?' he said. 'I can just hear him telling her how pleased he was that Harry took his advice and sold those shares in Russell's Bank, and made himself a million.'

'Oh, my God,' said Tom, 'you're beginning to think like him.'

'I'm going to have to if I'm to survive during the coming months.'

'That's no longer an issue,' said Tom. 'Everyone at the bank accepts that you'll be the next chairman.'

'It's not the chairmanship I'm talking about,' said Nat. Tom came to a halt in front of the steps of the bank and turned to face his oldest friend.

'If Ralph Elliot puts his name forward as the Republican candidate for governor, then I shall run against him.' He looked back towards the cathedral. 'And this time I will beat him.'

42

'LADIES AND GENTLEMEN, Fletcher Davenport, the next governor of Connecticut.'

It amused Fletcher that within moments of being selected as the Democratic candidate, he was immediately introduced as the next governor; no suggestion of an opponent, no hint that he might lose. But he recalled only too well Walter Mondale continually being introduced as the next president of the United States, and ending up as ambassador to Tokyo while it was Ronald Reagan who moved into the White House.

Once Fletcher had called Al Brubaker to confirm that he was willing to run, the party machine immediately swung behind him. One or two other Democratic heads appeared above the parapet, but like ducks at a shooting range they were quickly flattened.

In the end, Fletcher's only opposition turned out to be a congresswoman who had never done any harm – or enough good – for anyone else to notice. Once Fletcher had defeated her in the September primary, his party machine suddenly turned her into a formidable opponent who had been soundly beaten by the most impressive candidate the party had produced in years. But Fletcher privately acknowledged that she hadn't been much more than a paper opponent, and the real battle would begin once the Republicans had selected their standard bearer.

Although Barbara Hunter was as active and deter-mined as ever, no one really believed she was going to head up the Republican ticket. Ralph Elliot already had the backing of several key party members, and whenever he spoke in public or private, the name of his friend, and even occasionally his close friend, Ronnie, fell easily from his lips. But Fletcher repeatedly heard rumours of just as large a group of Republicans who were searching for a credible alternative; otherwise they were threatening to abstain, even vote Democrat. Fletcher found it nerve-racking waiting to discover who that opponent would be. By late August, he realized that if there was to be a surprise candidate, they were leaving it tantalizingly late to come forward.

Fletcher looked down at the crowd in front of him. It was his fourth speech that day, and it wasn't yet twelve o'clock. He missed Harry's presence at those Sunday lunches, where ideas could be tested and found wanting. Lucy and George were happy to add their contributions, which only reminded him how indulgent Harry had been when he had come up with suggestions the senator must have heard a hundred times before, but never once hinted as much. But the next generation certainly left Fletcher in no doubt what the Hotchkiss student body expected of their governor.

Fletcher's fourth speech that morning didn't differ greatly from the other three: to the Pepperidge Farm plant in Norwalk, the Wiffle Ball headquarters in Shelton and the Stanley tool-workers in New Britain. He just altered the occasional paragraph to acknowledge that the state's economy would not be in such good shape without their particular contribution. On to lunch with the Daughters of the American Revolution, where he failed to mention his Scottish ancestry, followed by three more speeches in the afternoon, before attending a fund-raising dinner, which wouldn't produce much more than ten thousand dollars.

Around midnight he would crawl into bed and put his arms round his sleeping wife and occasionally she would sigh. He'd read somewhere that once, when Reagan was out on the stump, he had been found cuddling a lamppost. Fletcher had laughed at the time, but no longer.

—◇—

'Romeo, Romeo, wherefore art thou Romeo?'

Nat had to agree with his son's assessment. Juliet was beautiful, but not the sort of girl Luke was likely to fall for. With five other females in the cast, he tried to work out which one it could possibly be. When the curtain came down for the interval, he thought that Luke had given a moving performance, and felt a glow of pride as he sat there in the audience listening to the applause. His parents had seen the play the night before, and told him that they'd felt the same pride as when he had performed Sebastian in the same hall.

Whenever Luke left the stage, Nat found his mind wandering back to the phone call he'd taken from Washington that morning. His secretary assumed it was Tom playing one of his practical jokes when he was asked if he was available to speak to the president of the United States.

Nat had found himself standing when George Bush came on the line.

The president congratulated him on Fairchild and Russell's being voted Bank of the Year – his excuse for the call – and then added the simple message, 'Many people in our party hope you will allow your name to go forward as governor. You have a lot of friends and supporters in Connecticut, Nat. Let's hope we can meet soon.'

The whole of Hartford knew within the hour that the president had called, but then switchboard operators also have a network of their own. Nat only told Su Ling and Tom, and they didn't seem all that surprised.

'*The exchange of thy love's faithful vow for mine.*'

The father's mind switched back to the play.

Nat found that people began to stop him in the street and say, 'I hope you'll run for governor, Nat' – Mr Cartwright – even sir. When he and Su Ling had entered the hall that evening, heads had turned and he sensed a buzz all around him. In the car on the way to Taft he didn't ask Su Ling if he should run, simply, 'Do you think I can do the job?'

'The president seemed to think so,' she replied.

When the curtain came down following the death scene, Su Ling remarked, 'Have you noticed that people are staring at us?' She paused. 'I suppose we'll just have to get used to our son being a star.'

How quickly she could bring Nat back down to earth, and what a governor's wife she would make.

The cast and the parents were invited to join the principal for supper, so Nat and Su Ling made their way over to his house.

'It's the nurse.'

'Yes, she gave a very sensitive performance,' said Nat.

'No, you fool, the nurse must have been the one Luke's fallen for,' said Su Ling.

'What makes you so sure of that?' asked Nat.

'Just as the curtain came down, they held hands, and I'm fairly sure that wasn't in Shakespeare's original stage directions,' said Su Ling.

'Well, we're about to find out if you're right,' said Nat as they entered the principal's house.

They found Luke sipping a Coke in the hallway. 'Hi, Dad,' he said turning to face them. 'This is Kathy Marshall; she played the nurse.' Su Ling tried not to smirk.

'And this is my mother. Wasn't Kathy fantastic? But then she plans to major in drama at Sarah Lawrence.'

'Yes she was, but you weren't bad yourself,' said Nat. 'We were both very proud of you.'

'Have you seen the play before, Mr Cartwright?' asked Kathy.

'Yes, when Su Ling and I visited Stratford. The nurse was played by Celia Johnson, but I don't suppose you've even heard of her.'

'*Brief Encounter*,' Kathy responded immediately.

'Noël Coward,' Luke said.

'And Trevor Howard played opposite her,' said Kathy. Nat nodded at his son, who was still dressed as Romeo.

'You must be the first Romeo to have fallen for the nurse,' said Su Ling.

Kathy grinned. 'It's his Oedipus complex,' she said. 'And how did Miss Johnson translate the part? When my drama teacher saw it as an undergraduate with Dame Edith Evans, she said she played the nurse like a school matron – strict and firm, but loving.'

'No,' said Su Ling, 'Celia Johnson portrayed her as slightly dotty, erratic but also loving.'

'What an interesting idea. I must look up the director. Of course I would like to have played Juliet, but I'm just not good looking enough,' she added matter-of-factly.

'But you're beautiful,' said Luke.

'You're hardly a reliable judge on that subject, Luke,' she said, taking his hand. 'After all, you've been wearing glasses since the age of four.'

Nat smiled, and thought how lucky Luke was to have Kathy as a friend.

'Kathy, would you like to come and spend a few days with us during the summer vacation?' asked Nat.

'Yes, if it's not going to cause you too much trouble,

Mr Cartwright,' Kathy replied. 'Because I wouldn't want to be in your way.'

'Be in my way?' queried Nat.

'Yes, Luke tells me that you'll be running for governor.'

◄○►

'LOCAL BANKER RUNS FOR GOVERNOR' ran the banner headline in the *Hartford Courant*. An inside page was given over to a profile of the brilliant young financier who, twenty-five years earlier had been awarded the Medal of Honour, bringing his career up to date with the role he'd played in the merger between the small family bank of Russell's, with its eleven local branches, and Fairchild's with its one hundred and two establishments spread right across the state. Nat smiled when he recalled the confessional at St Joseph's, and the graceful way Murray Goldblatz continued to convey the impression that the original idea had been Nat's. Nat had continued to learn valuable lessons from Murray, who never lowered his guard or his standards.

The *Courant*'s editorial suggested that Nat's decision to run against Ralph Elliot for the Republican nomination had opened up the contest, as both were outstanding candidates at the top of their professions. The editorial did not come out in favour of either man, but promised to report fairly on the duel between the banker and the lawyer, who were known not to like each other. 'Mrs Hunter will also run', they added in the final paragraph almost as an after-thought, which summed up the *Courant*'s view on her chances now that Nat had allowed his name to go forward.

Nat felt well satisfied with the press and television coverage that followed his announcement, and even more pleased by the favourable public reaction on the street.

Tom had taken a two-month leave of absence from the bank to run Nat's campaign, and Murray Goldblatz sent a substantial cheque for the campaign fund.

The first meeting was held at Tom's home that evening, when Nat's chief of staff explained to his carefully selected team what they would be up against during the next six weeks.

Rising before the sun each morning, and collapsing in bed after midnight had few compensations, but an unexpected one for Nat was Luke's fascination with the electoral process. He spent his vacation accompanying his father everywhere, often with Kathy by his side. Nat grew to like her more and more as each day passed.

Nat took a little time getting used to the new routine, and being reminded by Tom that you can't bark out instructions to volunteers, and you must always thank them, however little they've done and however badly they've done it. But even with six speeches and a dozen meetings a day, the learning curve proved steep.

It quickly became clear that Elliot had been out on the stump for several weeks, hoping his early groundwork would give him an unassailable advantage. Nat soon realized that although the first caucus in Ipswich would only yield seventeen electoral votes, its importance was disproportionate to the numbers involved, as in New Hampshire at a presidential election. He visited every one of the caucus voters and never left in any doubt that Elliot had been there before him. Although his rival had already locked up several delegates, there remained a few waverers who were undecided or simply didn't trust the man.

As the days slipped by, Nat discovered that he was always expected to be in two places at once because the primary in Chelsea was only two days after the caucus in Ipswich. Elliot was now spending most of his time in

Chelsea, as he considered he'd already wrapped up the Ipswich caucus.

Nat returned to Ipswich on the night of the caucus vote, to hear the local chairman announce that Elliot had captured ten of the votes while he had secured seven. Elliot's team, while claiming it as a clear-cut victory, were unable to hide their disappointment. As soon as he'd heard the result, Nat ran to his car and Tom had him back in Chelsea by midnight.

To his surprise, the local papers discounted the result in Ipswich, saying that Chelsea, with an electorate of over eleven thousand, would be much more of an indicator as to how the public felt about the two men rather than reading anything into the views of a handful of party *apparatchiks*. And Nat certainly felt more relaxed out on the streets, in the shopping malls, at the factory gates, and in the schools and clubs than he had been in smoke-filled rooms listening to people who believed it was their 'God-given right' to select the candidate.

After a couple of weeks of pressing the flesh, Nat told Tom that he was very encouraged by how many voters were saying they would support him. But was Elliot receiving the same response, he wondered.

'I've no idea,' said Tom as they drove off to yet another meeting, 'but I can tell you that we are fast running out of money. If we're soundly beaten tomorrow, we may have to withdraw from the race, having taken part in one of the shortest campaigns in history. We could of course let the world know that Bush is backing you, because that would be sure to swing a few votes.'

'No,' said Nat firmly. 'That was a private call, not an endorsement.'

'But Elliot never stops talking about his trip to the White House with his old friend, George, as if it was a dinner for two.'

'And how do you feel the rest of the Republican delegation feel about that?'

'That's far too subtle for the average voter,' suggested Tom.

'Never underestimate them,' said Nat.

—◦—

Nat couldn't recall much about the day of the Chelsea primary, except that he never stopped moving. When it was announced just after midnight that Elliot had won by 6,109 votes to 5,302 for Cartwright, Nat's only question was, 'Can we afford to go on now that Elliot has gained a twenty-seven to ten lead among the delegates?'

'The patient is still breathing,' Tom replied, 'but only just, so it's on to Hartford, and if Elliot wins that one as well, we won't be able to stop his bandwagon rolling all over us. Just be thankful you have a day job to go back to,' he added with a smile.

Mrs Hunter, who had only picked up two electoral college votes, conceded defeat and said she was withdrawing from the race and would be announcing in the near future which candidate she would be supporting.

Nat enjoyed returning to his home town, where the people in the streets treated him as a friend. Tom knew how much effort had to be put into Hartford, not only because it was their last chance, but as the state capital it carried the most electoral votes, nineteen in all, with the prehistoric rule of winner takes all, so if Nat topped the poll, he would go into the lead, 29:27. If he lost, he could unpack his bags and stay at home.

During the campaign, the candidates were invited to attend several functions together, but whenever they did, they rarely acknowledged each other's presence, and certainly never stopped for a chat.

With three days to go to the primary, a poll in the

459

Hartford Courant put Nat two points ahead of his rival, and they reported that Mrs Barbara Hunter was throwing her support behind Cartwright. This was exactly the boost Nat's campaign needed. The following morning, he noticed that far more workers were not with him on the street, and many more passers-by came up to shake him by the hand.

He was in Robinson's Mall when the message came through from Murray Goldblatz, 'I need to see you urgently.' Murray was not a man to use the word urgent unless that was exactly what he meant. Nat left his team to go on canvassing, assuring them that he would return shortly. They didn't see him again that day.

When Nat arrived at the bank, the receptionist told him that the chairman was in the boardroom with Mr and Mrs Russell. Nat walked in and took his usual place opposite Murray, but the expressions on the faces of his three colleagues didn't harbour glad tidings. Murray came quickly to the point. 'I understand that you have a town meeting tonight which both you and Elliot will be addressing?'

'Yes,' said Nat, 'it's the last major event before the vote tomorrow.'

'I have a spy in the Elliot camp,' said Murray, 'and she tells me that they have a question planned for tonight that will derail your campaign, but she can't find out what it is, and daren't be too inquisitive, in case they become suspicious. Do you have any idea what it might be?'

'No I don't,' said Nat.

'Perhaps he's found out about Julia,' said Tom quietly.

'Julia?' said Murray sounding puzzled.

'No, not my wife,' said Tom. 'The first Mrs Kirkbridge.'

'I had no idea there was a first Mrs Kirkbridge,' said Murray.

'No reason you should,' said Tom. 'But I've always dreaded the thought that the truth might come out.' Murray listened attentively as Tom recalled how he'd met the woman who passed herself off as Julia Kirkbridge, and how she had signed the bank's cheque and then removed all the money from her account.

'Where is that cheque now?' asked Murray.

'Somewhere in the bowels of City Hall, would be my guess.'

'Then we must assume that Elliot's got his hands on it, but were you technically breaking the law?'

'No, but we didn't keep to our written agreement with the council,' said Tom.

'And the Cedar Wood project went on to be a huge success, making everyone involved a handsome return,' added Nat.

'So,' said Murray, 'we are left with a choice. You either make a clean breast of it and prepare a statement this afternoon, or wait until the bomb drops tonight and hope you have an answer to every question that's thrown at you.'

'What do you recommend?' said Nat.

'I would do nothing. First, my informant could be wrong, and second, the Cedar Wood project may not be the curved ball, in which case you will have opened that can of worms unnecessarily.'

'But what else could it be?' asked Nat.

'Rebecca?' said Tom.

'What do you mean?' asked Nat.

'That you made her pregnant and forced her to have an abortion.'

'That's hardly a crime,' said Murray.

'Unless she tries to claim you raped her.'

Nat laughed. 'Elliot's never going to raise that particular subject, because he might well have been the father himself, and abortion is not part of his holier-than-thou image.'

'Have you considered going on the attack yourself?' asked Murray.

'What do you have in mind?' asked Nat.

'Didn't Elliot have to resign from Alexander Dupont and Bell on the same day as the senior partner because half a million went missing from a client account?'

'No, I will not stoop to his level,' said Nat. 'In any case, Elliot's involvement was never proved.'

'Oh yes it was,' said Murray. Tom and Nat stared across at the chairman. 'A friend of mine was the client in question, and phoned to warn me the moment he heard that Elliot was representing us in the takeover.'

Nat sighed. 'That may well be the case, but the answer is still no.'

'Good,' said Murray, 'then we'll beat him on your terms, which means that we'll have to spend the rest of the afternoon preparing answers to whatever you imagine might be the questions.'

At six o'clock, Nat left the bank feeling wrung out. He phoned Su Ling and told her what had happened. 'Do you want me to come along tonight?' she asked.

'No, little flower, but can you keep Luke well occupied? If it's going to be unpleasant, I'd rather he wasn't around. You know how sensitive he can be, and he always takes it all so personally.'

'I'll take him to a movie – there's a French film playing at the Arcadia that he and Kathy have been pressing me to see all week.'

Nat tried not to appear nervous when he arrived at Goodwin House that night. He walked into the hotel's main dining room to find it was packed with several hundred local businessmen chatting to each other. But who were they supporting, he wondered? He suspected many of them still hadn't made up their minds, as the polls kept reminding them that 10 per cent were still undecided. The head waiter directed him to the top table, where he found Elliot chatting to the local party chairman. Manny Friedman swung round to welcome Nat. Elliot leant across and made a public show of shaking hands. Nat sat down quickly and began to make notes on the back of a menu.

When the chairman called for order he introduced 'the two heavyweights both well qualified to be our next governor', and then invited Elliot to make his opening remarks. Nat had never heard him speak so poorly. The chairman then asked Nat to reply and when he resumed his place, he would have been the first to admit he hadn't done much better. The first round, he thought, had ended in a no-points draw.

When the chairman called for questions, Nat wondered when the missile would be launched and from which direction. His eyes swept the hall as he waited for the first question.

'How do the candidates feel about the education bill that is currently being debated in the Senate?' came from someone sitting at the top table. Nat concentrated on the provisions in the bill that he felt should be amended, while Elliot kept reminding them that he had completed his undergraduate degree at the University of Connecticut.

The second questioner wanted to know about the new state income tax, and whether both candidates would guarantee not to raise it. Yes and yes.

The third questioner was interested in their policy on crime, and with a particular reference to young offenders. Elliot said they should all be locked up and taught a lesson. Nat was less sure that prison was the answer to every problem, and that they should perhaps consider some of the innovations which Utah had recently introduced into their penal system.

When Nat resumed his seat, the chairman rose and looked around the room for another question. As soon as the man stood up without actually looking at him, Nat knew this had to be the plant. He glanced at Elliot, who was scribbling notes, pretending to be oblivious of his presence. 'Yes, sir,' said the chairman, pointing at him.

'Mr Chairman, may I ask if either of the candidates has ever broken the law?'

Elliot was on his feet immediately. 'Several times,' he said. 'I've had three parking tickets in the past week, which is why I'll be easing parking restrictions in town centres the moment I'm elected.' Word perfect, thought Nat; even the timing had been rehearsed. A spattering of applause broke out.

Nat rose slowly and turned to face Elliot. 'I shall not be changing the law to accommodate Mr Elliot, because I believe there should be fewer vehicles in our city centres, not more. It may not be popular, but someone has to stand up and warn people that their future will be bleak if we build bigger and bigger cars that consume more and more gas and then spit out more and more toxic fumes. We owe our children a better heritage than that, and I have no interest in being elected on glib remarks that will be quickly forgotten once I'm in power.' He sat down to loud applause and hoped that the chairman would move on to another questioner, but the man remained standing.

'But, Mr Cartwright, you didn't answer my question as to whether you'd ever broken the law.'

'Not that I'm aware of,' replied Nat.

'But isn't it true that you once cleared a cheque for three million six hundred thousand dollars from Russell's Bank, when you knew that the funds had already been misappropriated and that the signature on the cheque was fraudulent?'

Several of the audience began chattering at once, and Nat had to wait for some time before he could reply.

'Yes, Russell's was swindled out of that money by a very clever fraudster, but as that exact sum was owed to the local council, I felt that the bank had no choice but to honour the debt and pay the council the amount in full.'

'Did you inform the police at the time that the money had been stolen? After all, it belonged to the customers of Russell's Bank and not to you,' continued the questioner.

'No, because we had every reason to believe that the cash had been transferred abroad, so we knew that there would be no possibility of retrieving it.' Nat realized as soon as he had finished speaking that his answer would not placate the questioner or several others in the audience.

'If you were to become governor, Mr Cartwright, would you treat the tax payers' money in the same cavalier fashion?'

Elliot was immediately on his feet. 'Mr Chairman, that was a disgraceful suggestion and nothing more than innuendo and slur; why don't we move on?' He sat down to loud applause while Nat remained standing. He had to admire the sheer nerve of Elliot setting up the question and then being seen to come to his opponent's defence. He waited for complete silence.

'The incident you refer to occurred over ten years ago. It was a mistake on my part that I regret, although it is ironic that it turned out to be a massive financial success for all those involved, because the three point six million the bank invested in the Cedar Wood project has been a boon to the people of Hartford, not to mention the city's economy.'

The questioner still wouldn't sit down. 'Despite Mr Elliot's magnanimous comments, may I ask him if he would have reported such a misappropriation of funds to the police?'

Elliot rose slowly. 'I would prefer not to comment without knowing all the details of this particular case, but I am happy to take Mr Cartwright's word when he says that he did not commit any offence, and bitterly regrets not reporting the matter to the appropriate authorities at the time.' He paused for some time. 'However, if I am elected governor, you can be assured of open government. If I make a mistake, I will admit it at the time and not ten years later.' The questioner sat down, his job completed.

The chairman found it difficult to bring the meeting back to order. There were several more questions, but they were not listened to in silence, as those seated in the body of the hall continued to discuss Nat's revelation.

When the chairman finally brought the meeting to a close, Elliot left the room quickly while Nat remained in his place. He was touched by how many people came up and shook him by the hand, many agreeing that the Cedar Wood project had proved beneficial for the city.

'Well, at least they didn't lynch you,' Tom said as they left the room.

'No they didn't, but there will only be one subject on the voters' minds tomorrow. Am I a suitable person to occupy the governor's mansion?'

43

'THE CEDAR WOOD SCANDAL' was the headline in the *Hartford Courant* the following morning. A photograph of the cheque and Julia's real signature had been placed side by side. It didn't read well, but luckily for Nat half the voters had gone to the polls long before the paper hit the streets. Nat had earlier prepared a short withdrawal statement should he lose, which congratulated his opponent, but fell short of endorsing him for governor. Nat was in his office when the result was announced from Republican headquarters.

Tom took the call and rushed in without knocking. 'You won, you won, 11,792 to 11,673 – it's only by a hundred and nineteen votes, but it still puts you in the lead in the electoral college, 29–27.'

The next day, the leader in the *Hartford Courant* did point out that no one had lost any money by investing in the Cedar Wood project, and perhaps the voters had made their intentions clear.

Nat still had to face three more caucuses and two more primaries before the candidate was finally selected. He was therefore relieved to find that Cedar Wood quickly became yesterday's news. Elliot won the next caucus 19–18, and Nat the primary four days later, 9,702–6,379, which put him even further ahead as they approached the final primary. In the electoral college, Nat now led 116–91 and the polls were showing him seven points ahead in the town of his birth.

On the streets of Cromwell, Nat was joined by his parents, Susan and Michael, who concentrated on the older voters, while Luke and Kathy tried to persuade the young to turn out. As each day passed, Nat became more and more confident that he was going to win. The *Courant* began to suggest that the real battle lay ahead for Nat when he would have to face Fletcher Davenport, the popular senator for Hartford. However, Tom had still insisted that they take the eve-of-poll television debate with Elliot seriously.

'We don't need to trip up at the final hurdle,' he said. 'Clear that, and you'll be the candidate. But I still want you to spend Sunday going over the questions again and again, as well as preparing for anything and everything that might come up during the debate. You can be sure that Fletcher Davenport will be sitting at home watching you on TV and analysing everything you say. If you stumble, he will have issued a press statement within minutes.'

Nat now regretted that some weeks before he'd agreed to appear on a local television programme and debate with Elliot the night before the final primary. He and Elliot had settled on David Anscott to conduct the proceedings. Anscott was an interviewer who was more interested in coming over as popular than incisive. Tom didn't object to him as he felt the occasion would act as a dry run for the inevitably more serious debate with Fletcher Davenport scheduled for some time in the future.

Reports were coming back to Tom each day that volunteers were deserting Ralph Elliot in droves and some were even switching over and joining their team, so by the time he and Nat arrived at the television studio they both felt quietly confident. Su Ling accompanied her

468

husband, but Luke said he wanted to stay at home and watch the debate on television so he could brief his father on how he came over to the larger audience.

'On the sofa with Kathy, no doubt,' suggested Nat.

'No, Kathy went back home this afternoon for her sister's birthday,' said Su Ling, 'and Luke could have joined her, but to be fair he's taking his role as your youth advisor very seriously.'

Tom came rushing into the green room and showed Nat the latest opinion poll figures. They gave him a six per cent lead. 'I think only Fletcher Davenport can now stop you becoming governor.'

'I won't be convinced until the final result has been announced,' said Su Ling. 'Never forget the stunt Elliot pulled with the ballot boxes after we'd all assumed the count was over.'

'He's already tried every stunt he can think of and failed,' said Tom.

'I wish I could be so confident of that,' said Nat quietly.

Both candidates were applauded by the small television audience as they walked out on to the stage for a programme billed as 'The Final Encounter'. The two men met in the centre of the stage and shook hands, but their eyes remained fixed on the camera.

'This will be a live programme,' David Anscott explained to the audience, 'and we'll be going on air in around five minutes. I will open with a few questions, and then turn it over to you. If you have something you want to ask either candidate, make it short and to the point – no speeches, please.'

Nat smiled as he scanned the audience, until his eyes came to rest on the man who had asked the Cedar Wood question. He was sitting in the second row. Nat could feel the sweat on the palm of his hands, but even if he was called, Nat was confident he could handle him. This time he was well prepared.

The television arc lights were switched on, the titles began to roll, and David Anscott, smile in place, opened the show. Once he'd introduced the participants, both candidates made a one-minute opening statement – sixty seconds can be a long time on television. After so many sound-bites, they could have delivered such homilies in their sleep.

Anscott began with a couple of warm-up questions which had been scripted for him. Once the candidates had given their replies, he made no attempt to follow up anything they had said, but simply moved on to the next question as it appeared on the autocue in front of him. Once the interviewer had come to the end of his set piece, he quickly turned it over to the audience.

The first question turned into a speech on choice, which pleased Nat as he watched the seconds ticking away. He knew Elliot would be indecisive on this subject, as he was willing to offend neither the women's movement nor his friends in the Roman Catholic church. Nat made it clear that he supported unequivocally a woman's right to choose. Elliot, as he suspected, was evasive. Anscott called for a second question.

⊸◦⊳

Watching from home, Fletcher made notes on everything Nat Cartwright said. He clearly understood the underlying principle of the education bill and, more important, he obviously thought the changes Fletcher wanted to bring about were quite reasonable.

'He's very bright, isn't he,' said Annie.

'And cute too,' said Lucy.

'Anyone on my side?' asked Fletcher.

470

'Yes, I don't think he's cute,' said Jimmy. 'But he has thought a great deal about your bill and he obviously considers it an election issue.'

'I don't know about cute,' said Annie, 'but have you noticed that at certain angles he looks a little like you, Fletcher?'

'Oh no,' said Lucy, 'he's much better looking than Dad.'

—◇—

The third question was on gun control. Ralph Elliot stated that he backed the gun lobby and the right of every American to defend himself. Nat explained why he would like to see more control of guns, so that incidents like the one his son had experienced while at elementary school could never occur again.

Annie and Lucy started clapping, along with the studio audience.

'Isn't someone going to remind him who it was in that classroom with his son?' asked Jimmy.

'He doesn't need reminding,' said Fletcher.

'One more question,' said Anscott, 'and it will have to be quick, because we're running out of time.'

The plant in the second row rose from his place bang on cue. Elliot pointed at him in case Anscott was considering anyone else.

'How would the two candidates deal with the problem of illegal immigrants?'

'What the hell's that got to do with the governor of Connecticut?' asked Fletcher.

Ralph Elliot looked straight at the questioner and said, 'I'm sure I speak for both of us when I say that America should always welcome anyone who is oppressed and in need of help, as we have always done throughout our history. However, those who wish to enter our country must, of course, abide by the correct procedure and meet all the necessary legal requirements.'

'That sounded to me,' said Fletcher, turning to face Annie, 'over-prepared and over-rehearsed. So what's he up to?'

'Is that also your view on illegal immigrants, Mr Cartwright?' asked David Anscott, a little puzzled as to what the questioner was getting at.

'I confess, David, that I haven't given the matter a great deal of thought, as it has not been high on my priorities when I consider the problems currently facing the state of Connecticut.'

'Wrap it up,' Anscott heard the producer say in his earpiece, just as the questioner added, 'But you must have given it some thought, Mr Cartwright. After all, isn't your wife an illegal immigrant?'

'Hold on, let him answer that,' said the producer. 'If we go off the air now we'll have a quarter million people phoning in to find out his response. Close up on Cartwright.'

Fletcher was among those quarter of a million who waited for Nat's reply as the camera panned across to Elliot, who had a puzzled look on his face.

'You bastard,' said Fletcher, 'you knew that question was coming.'

The camera returned to Nat, but his lips remained pursed.

'Wouldn't I be right in suggesting,' continued the questioner, 'that your wife entered this country illegally?'

'My wife is the Professor of Statistics at the University of Connecticut,' said Nat, trying to disguise a tremble in his voice.

Anscott listened on his earpiece to find out how the producer wanted to play it, as they had already overrun their time slot.

'Say nothing,' said the producer, 'just hang in there. I can always run the credits over them if it gets boring.' Anscott gave a slight nod in the direction of the head-on camera.

'That may well be the case, Mr Cartwright,' continued the questioner, 'but didn't her mother, Su Kai Peng, enter this country with false papers, claiming to be married to an American serviceman, who had in fact died fighting for his country some months before the date on the marriage licence?'

Nat didn't reply.

Fletcher was equally silent as he watched Cartwright being stretched on the rack.

'As you seem unwilling to answer my question, Mr Cartwright, perhaps you can confirm that on the marriage licence your mother-in-law described herself as a seamstress. However, the fact is that before she landed in America, she was a prostitute plying her trade on the streets of Seoul, so heaven knows who your wife's father is.'

'Credits,' said the producer. 'We've run out of time and I daren't break into *Baywatch*, but keep the cameras running. We may pick up some extra footage for the late night news.'

Once the monitor on the stage showed credits rolling, the questioner quickly left the studio. Nat stared down at his wife sitting in the third row. She was pale and shaking.

'It's a wrap,' said the producer.

Elliot turned to the moderator and said, 'That was disgraceful, you should have stopped him a lot earlier,' and looking across at Nat added, 'believe me, I had no idea that . . .'

'You're a liar,' said Nat.

'Stay on him,' said the director to the first cameraman. 'Keep all four cameras rolling, I want every angle on this.'

'What are you suggesting?' asked Elliot.

'That you set the whole thing up. You weren't even subtle about it – you even used the same man that questioned me on the Cedar Wood project a couple of weeks ago. But I'll tell you one thing, Elliot,' he said, jabbing a finger at him, 'I will still kill you.'

Nat stormed off the stage and found Su Ling waiting for him in the wings. 'Come on, little flower, I'm taking you home.' Tom quickly joined them as Nat put an arm around his wife.

'I'm sorry, Nat, but I have to ask,' said Tom. 'Was any of that garbage true?'

'All of it,' said Nat, 'and before you ask another question, I've known since we were first married.'

'Take Su Ling home,' said Tom, 'and whatever you do, don't talk to the press.'

'Don't bother,' said Nat. 'You can issue a statement on my behalf saying that I'm withdrawing from the race. I'm not having my family dragged through any more of this.'

'Don't make a hasty decision that you may well later regret. Let's talk about what needs to be done in the morning,' said Tom.

Nat took Su Ling by the hand, walked out of the studio and through a door leading into the parking lot.

'Good luck,' shouted one supporter as Nat opened the car door for his wife. He didn't acknowledge any of the cheers as they drove quickly away. He looked across at Su Ling, who was thumping the dashboard in anger. Nat took a hand off the steering wheel and placed it gently on Su Ling's leg. 'I love you,' he said, 'and I always will. Nothing and no one will ever change that.'

'How did Elliot find out?'

'He's probably had a team of private detectives delving into my past.'

'And when he couldn't come up with anything about you, he switched his sights on to me and my mother,' whispered Su Ling. There was a long silence before she added, 'I don't want you to withdraw; you must stay in the race. It's the only way we can beat the bastard.' Nat didn't reply as he joined the evening traffic. 'I just feel so sorry for Luke,' Su Ling eventually said. 'He will have taken it so very personally. I only wish Kathy had stayed on for another day.'

'I'll take care of Luke,' said Nat. 'You'd better go and collect your mother and bring her back to our place for the night.'

'I'll call her just as soon as we get in,' said Su Ling. 'I suppose it's just possible that she didn't watch the programme.'

'Not a hope,' said Nat as he pulled into the driveway, 'she's my most loyal fan and never misses any of my TV appearances.'

Nat put his arm around Su Ling as they walked towards the front door. All the lights in the house were off except for one in Luke's bedroom. Nat turned the key in the lock and as he opened the door, said, 'You phone your mother, and I'll pop up and see Luke.'

Su Ling picked up the phone in the hallway as Nat walked slowly up the stairs, trying to compose his thoughts. He knew Luke would expect every question to be answered truthfully. He walked down the corridor and knocked gently on his son's door. There was no reply, so he tried again, saying, 'Luke, can I come in?' Still no reply. He opened the door a little and glanced inside, but Luke wasn't in bed and none of his clothes were laid out neatly over the usual chair. Nat's first reaction was that he must have gone across to the shop to be with his grandmother. He turned out the light and listened to Su Ling talking to her mother. He was about to go down and join her when he noticed that Luke had left a light on in the bathroom. He decided to switch it off.

Nat walked across the room and pushed open the bathroom door. For a moment he remained transfixed as he stared up at his son. He then collapsed on to his knees, unable to get himself to look up a second time, although he knew he would have to remove Luke's hanging body so that it wouldn't be the last memory Su Ling would have of their only child.

Annie picked up the phone and listened. 'It's Charlie from the *Courant* for you,' she said, handing the phone across.

'Did you watch the programme?' the political editor asked, the moment Fletcher came on the line.

'No, I didn't,' said Fletcher, 'Annie and I never miss *Seinfeld*.'

'*Touché*, so do you want to make any statement about your rival's wife being an illegal immigrant and her mother a prostitute?'

'Yes, I think that David Anscott should have cut off the questioner. It was obviously a cheap set-up from the start.'

'Can I quote you?' said Charlie. Jimmy was shaking his head vigorously.

'Yes, you most certainly can, because that made anything Nixon's got up to look like *The Muppet Show*.'

'You'll be glad to hear, senator, that your instincts are in line with public opinion. The station's switchboard has been jammed with calls of sympathy for Nat Cartwright and his wife, and my bet is that Elliot will lose by a landslide tomorrow.'

'Which will make it that much tougher for me,' said Fletcher, 'but at least one good thing comes out of it.'

'And what's that, senator?'

'Everybody has finally found out the truth about that bastard Elliot.'

'I wonder if that was wise?' said Jimmy.

'I'm sure it wasn't,' said Fletcher, 'but it's no more than your father would have said.'

—◦—

When the ambulance arrived Nat decided to accompany his son's body to the hospital, while his mother tried helplessly to comfort Su Ling.

'I'll come straight back,' he promised, before kissing her gently.

When he saw the two paramedics sitting silently on either side of the body, he explained that he would follow in his own car. They just nodded.

The hospital staff tried to be as sympathetic as possible, but there were forms to be filled in, and procedures to be carried out. Once that had been completed, they left him alone. He kissed Luke on the forehead and turned away at the sight of the red and black bruises around his neck, aware that the memory would remain with him for the rest of his life.

Once they had covered Luke's face with a sheet, Nat left his beloved son, passing bowed heads murmuring their sympathy. He must get back to Su Ling, but before that, he knew there was someone else he had to visit first.

Nat drove away from the hospital on automatic pilot, his anger not diminishing as each mile clocked up. Although he had never been to the house before, he knew exactly where it was, and when he eventually turned into the driveway, Nat could see some lights coming from the ground floor. He parked the car and began to walk slowly towards the house. He needed to be calm if he was to see it through. As he approached the front door he could hear raised voices coming from inside. A man and a woman were arguing, unaware of the visitor outside. Nat banged on the knocker and the voices suddenly went silent, as if a television had been switched off. A moment later, the door swung open and Nat came face to face with the man he held responsible for his son's death.

Ralph Elliot looked shocked, but recovered quickly. He tried to slam the door in his face, but Nat had already placed a shoulder firmly against it. The first punch Nat threw landed on Elliot's nose and sent him reeling backwards. Elliot stumbled, but regained his balance quickly, turned and ran down the corridor. Nat strode after him, following Elliot into his study. He looked round for the other raised voice, but there was no sign of Rebecca. He turned his attention back to Elliot, who was pulling open a drawer in his desk. He grabbed a gun and pointed it at Nat.

'Get out of my house,' he shouted, 'or I'll kill you.' Blood was streaming from his nose.

Nat advanced towards him. 'I don't think so,' he said. 'After that stunt you pulled tonight, no one will ever take your word again.'

'Yes, they will, because I have a witness. Don't forget that Rebecca saw you barge into our home making threats and then assaulting me.'

Nat advanced ready to take a second punch, causing Elliot to step back and momentarily lose his balance as he stumbled across the arm of the chair. The gun went off, and Nat leapt on Elliot, knocking him to the ground. As they fell to the floor, Nat jerked his knee into Elliot's groin with such force that his rival bent double, letting go of the gun. Nat grabbed it and pointed the barrel at Elliot, whose face was contorted with fear.

'You planted that bastard in the audience, didn't you?' said Nat.

'Yes, yes, but I didn't know he would go that far, surely you wouldn't kill a man because . . .'

'Because he was responsible for the death of my son?' All the colour drained from Elliot's face.

'Yes, I would,' Nat said, pressing the barrel of the gun against Elliot's forehead. Nat stared down at a man who was now on his knees whimpering and begging for his life. 'I'm not going to kill you,' said Nat, lowering the gun, 'because that would be the easy way out for a coward. No, I want you to suffer a much slower death – year upon year of humiliation. Tomorrow you're going to discover what the people of Hartford really think of you, and then you'll have to live with the final ignominy of watching me take up residence in the governor's mansion.'

Nat rose to his feet, calmly placed the gun on the corner of the desk, turned and left the room to find Rebecca cowering in the hallway. As soon as he had passed her she ran into the study. Nat strode on through the open door and climbed into his car.

He was driving out of the gates when he heard the shot.

—◇—

Fletcher's phone was ringing every few minutes. Annie took all the calls, explaining that her husband had no further comment to make, other than that he had sent his condolences to Mr and Mrs Cartwright.

Just after midnight, Annie unplugged the phone and made her way upstairs. Although the light was on in their bedroom, she was surprised to find that Fletcher wasn't there. She went back downstairs to check the study. The usual papers were piled up on his desk, but he wasn't sitting in his chair. She climbed slowly back up the stairs and noticed a light shining under Lucy's door. Annie turned the handle slowly and quietly pushed the door

479

open in case Lucy had fallen asleep, leaving her light on. She looked inside to see her husband sitting on the bed, clinging on to their sleepy daughter. Tears were streaming down his cheeks. He turned and faced his wife. 'Nothing's worth that,' he said.

–◦–

Nat arrived back home to find his mother sitting on the sofa with Su Ling. Su Ling's face was ashen, her eyes sunken; she had aged ten years in a few hours. 'I'll leave you with her now,' said his mother, 'but I'll come back first thing in the morning. I'll see myself out.'

Nat bent down, kissed his mother goodbye and then sat next to his wife. He held her slight body in his arms, but said nothing. There was nothing to say.

He couldn't remember how long they had been sitting there when he heard the police siren. He assumed that the grating noise would quickly disappear into the distance, but it became louder and louder, and didn't stop until a car came to a screeching halt on the gravel outside their front door. He then heard a door slam, heavy footsteps, followed by a loud banging on the front door.

He removed his arm from around his wife's shoulder and made his way wearily to the front door. He opened it to find Chief Culver with a police officer standing on either side of him.

'What's the problem, chief?'

'I'm sorry about this, remembering what you've already been through,' said Don Culver, 'but I have no choice but to place you under arrest.'

'What for?' asked Nat in disbelief.

'For the murder of Ralph Elliot.'

BOOK FIVE

JUDGES

44

IT WAS NOT the first time in American history that a dead candidate's name was listed on the ballot paper, and it was certainly not the first time an arrested candidate had stood for election, but search as they might, the political historians were unable to find both on the same day.

Nat's one call that the chief permitted was to Tom, who was still wide awake despite it being three in the morning. 'I'll get Jimmy Gates out of bed and join you at the police station as soon as I can.'

They had only just finished taking his fingerprints when Tom arrived, accompanied by his lawyer. 'You remember Jimmy,' said Tom, 'he advised us during the Fairchild's takeover.'

'Yes, I do,' said Nat as he continued to dry his hands after removing the traces of black ink from his fingers.

'I've talked to the chief,' said Jimmy, 'and he's quite happy for you to go home, but you'll have to appear in court at ten o'clock tomorrow morning to be formally charged. I shall apply for bail on your behalf, and there is no reason to believe it won't be granted.'

'Thank you,' said Nat, his voice flat. 'Jimmy, you'll recall that before we began the takeover bid for Fairchild's, I asked you to find me the best corporate lawyer available to represent us?'

'Yes, I do,' said Jimmy, 'and you've always said that Logan Fitzgerald did a first-class job.'

'He certainly did,' said Nat quietly, 'but now I need you to find me the Logan Fitzgerald of criminal law.'

'I'll have two or three names for you to consider by the time we meet up tomorrow. There's a guy in Chicago who's exceptional, but I don't know what his diary's like,' he said as the chief of police walked over to join them.

'Mr Cartwright, can one of my boys drive you home?'

'No, that's good of you, chief,' said Tom, 'but I'll take the candidate home.'

'You say candidate automatically now,' said Nat, 'almost as if it was my Christian name.'

On the journey home, Nat told Tom everything that had taken place while he was at Elliot's house. 'So in the end it will come down to your word against hers,' commented Tom as he pulled up outside Nat's front door.

'Yes, and I'm afraid my story won't be as convincing as hers, even though it's the truth.'

'We can talk about that in the morning,' said Tom. 'But now you need to try and get some sleep.'

'It is the morning,' said Nat as he watched the first rays of sunlight creeping across the lawn.

Su Ling was standing by the open door. 'Did they for a moment believe . . .?'

Nat told her everything that had happened while he was at the police station, and when he finished, all Su Ling said was, 'Such a pity.'

'What do you mean?' asked Nat.

'That *you* didn't kill him.'

Nat climbed the stairs and walked through the bedroom straight on into the bathroom. He stripped off his clothes and threw them in a bag. He would dispose of the bag later so that he would never have to be reminded of this terrible day. He stepped into the shower and allowed the cold jets of water to beat down on him. After putting on a new set of clothes he rejoined his wife in the kitchen.

On the sideboard was his election-day schedule; no mention of a court appearance on arraignment for murder.

Tom turned up at nine. He reported that the voting was going briskly, as if nothing else was happening in Nat's life. 'They took a poll immediately following the television interview,' he told Nat, 'and it gave you a lead of sixty-three to thirty-seven.'

'But that was before I was arrested for killing the other candidate,' said Nat.

'I guess that might push it up to seventy–thirty,' replied Tom. No one laughed.

Tom did his best to focus on the campaign and try to keep their minds off Luke. It didn't work. He looked up at the kitchen clock. 'Time for us to go,' he said to Nat, who turned and took Su Ling in his arms.

'No, I'm coming with you,' she said. 'Nat may not have murdered him, but I would have, given half a chance.'

'Me too,' said Tom gently, 'but let me warn you that when we get to the courthouse it's bound to be a media circus. Look innocent and say nothing, because anything you say will end up on every front page.'

As they left the house, they were greeted by a dozen journalists and three camera crews just to watch them climb into a car. Nat clung on to Su Ling's hand as they were driven through the streets and didn't notice how many people waved the moment they spotted him. When they arrived at the steps of the courthouse fifteen minutes later, Nat faced the largest crowd he'd encountered during the entire election campaign.

The chief had anticipated the problem and detailed twenty uniformed officers to hold back the crowd, and make a gangway so that Nat and his party could enter the building without being hassled. It didn't work, because twenty officers weren't enough to control the scrum of photographers and journalists who shouted and jostled Nat and Su Ling as they tried to make their way up the courtroom steps. Microphones were thrust in Nat's face, and questions came at them from every angle.

'Did you murder Ralph Elliot?' demanded one reporter.

'Will you be withdrawing as candidate?' followed next, as a microphone was thrust forward.

'Was your mother a prostitute, Mrs Cartwright?'

'Do you think you can still win, Nat?'

'Was Rebecca Elliot your mistress?'

'What were Ralph Elliot's last words, Mr Cartwright?'

When they pushed through the swing doors, they found Jimmy Gates standing on the far side, waiting for them. He led Nat to a bench outside the courtroom and briefed his client on the procedure he was about to face.

'Your appearance should only last for about five minutes,' Jimmy explained. 'You will state your name, and having done so, you will be charged, and then asked to enter a plea. Once you've pleaded not guilty, I shall make an application for bail. The state is suggesting fifty thousand dollars at your own recognizance, which I've agreed to. The moment you've signed the necessary papers, you will be released and you won't have to appear again until a trial date has been fixed.'

'When do we anticipate that might be?'

'It would normally take about six months, but I've asked for the whole process to be speeded up on account of the up-coming election.' Nat admired his counsel's professional approach, remembering that Jimmy was also Fletcher Davenport's closest friend. However, like any good lawyer, Nat thought, Jimmy would understand the meaning of Chinese walls.

Jimmy glanced at his watch. 'We ought to go in, the last thing we need is to keep the judge waiting.'

Nat entered a packed courtroom and walked slowly down the aisle with Tom. He was surprised by how many people thrust out their hands and even wished him luck, making it feel more like a party meeting than a criminal arraignment. When they reached the front, Jimmy held open the little wooden gate dividing the court officials from the simply curious. He then guided Nat to a table on the left, and ushered him into the seat next to his. As they waited for the judge to make his entrance, Nat glanced across at the state's attorney, Richard Ebden, a man he'd always admired. He knew that Ebden would be a formidable adversary, and wondered who Jimmy was going to recommend to oppose him.

'All rise, Mr Justice Deakins presiding.'

The procedure Jimmy had described took place exactly as he predicted, and they were back out on the street five minutes later, facing the same journalists repeating the same questions and still failing to get any answers.

As they pushed their way through the scrum to their waiting car, Nat was once again surprised by how many people still wanted to shake him by the hand. Tom slowed them down, aware that this would be the footage seen by the voters on the midday news. Nat spoke to every well-wisher, but wasn't quite sure how to reply to an onlooker who said, 'I'm glad you killed the bastard.'

'Do you want to head straight home?' asked Tom as his car slowly nosed its way through the mêlée.

'No,' said Nat, 'let's go across to the bank and talk things through in the boardroom.'

The only stop they made on the way was to pick up the first edition of the *Courant* after hearing a newsboy's cry of 'Cartwright charged with murder'. All Tom seemed to be interested in was a poll on the second page showing that Nat now led Elliot by over twenty points. 'And,' said

Tom, 'in a separate poll, seventy-two per cent say you shouldn't withdraw from the race.' Tom read on, suddenly looked up but said nothing.

'What is it?' asked Su Ling.

'Seven per cent say they would happily have killed Elliot, if only you'd asked them.'

When they reached the bank, there was another hustle of journalists and cameramen awaiting them; again they were met with the same stony silence. Tom's secretary joined them in the corridor and reported that early polling was at a record high as Republicans obviously wished to make their views known.

Once they were settled in the boardroom, Nat opened the discussion by saying, 'The party will expect me to withdraw, whatever the result, and I feel that might still be my best course of action given the circumstances.'

'Why not let the voters decide?' said Su Ling quietly, 'and if they give you overwhelming support, stay in there fighting, because that will also help convince a jury that you're innocent.'

'I agree,' said Tom. 'And what's the alternative – Barbara Hunter? Let's at least spare the electorate that.'

'And how do you feel, Jimmy? After all you're my legal advisor.'

'On this subject I can't offer an impartial view,' Jimmy admitted. 'As you well know, the Democratic candidate is my closest friend, but were I advising him in the same circumstances, and I knew he was innocent, I would say stick in there and fight the bastards.'

'Well, I suppose it's just possible that the public will elect a dead man; then heaven knows what will happen.'

'His name will remain on the ballot paper,' said Tom, 'and if he goes on to win the election, the party can invite anyone they choose to represent him.'

'Are you serious?' said Nat.

'Couldn't be more serious. Quite often they select the candidate's wife, and my bet is that Rebecca Elliot would happily take his place.'

'And if you're convicted,' said Jimmy, 'she could sure count on the sympathy vote just before an election.'

'More important,' said Nat, 'have you come up with a defence counsel to represent me?'

'Four,' responded Jimmy, removing a thick file from his briefcase. He turned the cover. 'Two from New York, both recommended by Logan Fitzgerald, one from Chicago who worked on Watergate, and the fourth from Dallas. He's only lost one case in the last ten years, and that was when his client had committed the murder on video. I intend to call all four later today to find out if any of them is free. This is going to be such a high profile case, my bet is that they will all make themselves available.'

'Isn't there anyone from Connecticut worthy of the shortlist?' asked Tom. 'It would send out a far better message to the jury.'

'I agree,' said Jimmy, 'but the only man who is of the same calibre as those four simply isn't available.'

'And who's that?' asked Nat.

'The Democratic candidate for governor.'

Nat smiled for the first time. 'Then he's my first choice.'

'But he's in the middle of an election campaign.'

'Just in case you haven't noticed, so is the accused,' said Nat, 'and let's face it, the election isn't for another nine months. If I turn out to be his opponent, at least he'll know where I am the whole time.'

'But . . .' repeated Jimmy.

'You tell Mr Fletcher Davenport that if I become the Republican candidate, he's my first choice, and don't approach anyone else until he's turned me down, because if everything I've heard about that man is true, I feel confident he'll want to represent me.'

'If those are your instructions, Mr Cartwright.'

'Those are my instructions, counsellor.'

—◦—

By the time the polls had closed at eight p.m. Nat had fallen asleep in the car as Tom drove him home. His chief of staff made no attempt to disturb him. The next thing Nat remembered was waking to find Su Ling lying on the bed beside him, and his first thoughts were of Luke. Su Ling stared at him and gripped his hand. 'No,' she whispered.

'What do you mean, no?' asked Nat.

'I can see it in your eyes, my darling, you wonder if I would prefer you to withdraw, so that we can mourn Luke properly, and the answer is no.'

'But we'll have the funeral, and then the preparations for the trial, not to mention the trial itself.'

'Not to mention the endless hours in between, when you'll be brooding and unbearable to live with, so the answer is still no.'

'But it's going to be almost impossible to expect a jury not to accept the word of a grieving widow who also claims to have been an eye witness to her husband's murder.'

'Of course she was an eye witness,' said Su Ling. 'She did it.'

The phone on Su Ling's bedside table began to ring. She picked it up and listened attentively before writing two figures down on the pad by the phone. 'Thank you,' she said. 'I'll let him know.'

'Let him know what?' enquired Nat.

Su Ling tore the piece of paper off the pad and passed it across to her husband. 'It was Tom. He wanted you to know the election result.' Su Ling handed over the piece of paper. All she had written on it were the figures, '69/31'.

'Yes, but who got sixty-nine?' asked Nat.

'The next governor of Connecticut,' she replied.

—◦—

Luke's funeral was, at the principal's request, held in Taft School's chapel. He explained that so many pupils had wanted to be present. It was only after his death that Nat and Su Ling became aware just how popular their son had been. The service was simple, and the choir of which he was so proud to be a member, sang William Blake's 'Jerusalem' and Fats Waller's 'Ain't Misbehavin''. Kathy read one of the lessons, and dear old Thomo another, while the principal delivered the address.

Mr Henderson spoke of a shy, unassuming youth, liked and admired by all. He reminded those present of Luke's remarkable performance as Romeo, and how he had learned only that morning that Luke had been offered a place at Princeton.

The coffin was borne out of the chapel by boys and girls from the ninth grade who had performed with him in the school play. Nat learned so much about Luke that day that he felt guilty he hadn't known what an impact his son had made on his contemporaries.

At the end of the service, Nat and Su Ling attended the tea party given in the principal's house for Luke's closest friends. It was packed to overflowing, but then as Mr Henderson explained to Su Ling, everyone thought they were a close friend of Luke's. 'What a gift,' he remarked simply.

The headboy presented Su Ling with a book of photographs and short essays composed by his fellow pupils. Later, whenever Nat felt low, he would turn a page, read

491

an entry and glance at a photograph, but there was one he kept returning to again and again: *Luke was the only boy ever to speak to me who never once mentioned my turban or my colour. He simply didn't see them. I had looked forward to him being a friend for the rest of my life. Malik Singh (16).*

As they left the principal's house, Nat spotted Kathy sitting alone in the garden, her head bowed. Su Ling walked across and sat down beside her. She put an arm around Kathy and tried to comfort her. 'He loved you very much,' Su Ling said.

Kathy raised her head, the tears streaming down her cheeks. 'I never told him I loved him.'

45

'I CAN'T DO IT,' said Fletcher.

'Why not?' asked Annie.

'I can think of a hundred reasons.'

'Or are they a hundred excuses?'

'Defend the man I'm trying to defeat,' said Fletcher, ignoring her comment.

'Without fear or favour,' quoted Annie.

'Then how would you expect me to conduct the election?'

'That will be the easy part.' She paused. 'Either way.'

'Either way?' repeated Fletcher.

'Yes. Because if he's guilty, he won't even be the Republican candidate.'

'And if he's innocent?'

'Then you'll rightly be praised for setting him free.'

'That's neither practical nor sensible.'

'Two more excuses.'

'Why are you on his side?' asked Fletcher.

'I'm not,' insisted Annie. 'I am, to quote Professor Abrahams, on the side of justice.'

Fletcher was silent for some time. 'I wonder what he would have done faced with the same dilemma?'

'You know very well what he would have done . . . *but some people will forget those standards within moments of leaving this university . . .*'

'*. . . I can only hope that at least one person in every*

493

generation,' said Fletcher, completing the professor's oft-repeated dictum.

'Why don't you meet him,' said Annie, 'and then perhaps that will persuade you . . .'

—◦—

Despite abundant caution from Jimmy and vociferous protests from the local Democrats – in fact from everyone except Annie – it was agreed that the two men should meet the following Sunday.

The chosen venue was Fairchild Russell, as it was felt few citizens would be strolling down Main Street early on a Sunday morning.

Nat and Tom arrived just before ten, and it was the chairman of the bank who unlocked the front door and turned off the alarm for the first time in years. They only had to wait a few minutes before Fletcher and Jimmy appeared on the top step. Tom ushered them quickly through to the boardroom.

When Jimmy introduced his closest friend to his most important client, both men stared at each other, not sure which one of them should make the first move.

'It's good of you . . .'

'I hadn't expected . . .'

Both men laughed and then shook each other warmly by the hand.

Tom suggested that Fletcher and Jimmy sit on one side of the conference table, while he and Nat sat opposite them. Fletcher nodded his agreement, and once seated, he opened his briefcase and removed a yellow notepad, placing it on the table in front of him, along with a fountain pen taken from an inside pocket.

'May I begin by saying how much I appreciate you agreeing to see me,' said Nat. 'I can only imagine the opposition you must have faced from every quarter and

am well aware that you did not settle for the easy option.'
Jimmy lowered his head.

Fletcher raised a hand. 'It's my wife you have to
thank.' He paused. 'Not me. But it's me that you have to
convince.'

'Then please pass on my grateful thanks to Mrs
Davenport, and let me assure you that I will answer any
questions you put to me.'

'I only have one question,' said Fletcher, as he stared
down at the blank sheet of paper, 'and it's the question a
lawyer never asks because it can only compromise his or
her ethical position. But on this occasion I will not
consider discussing this case until that question has been
answered.'

Nat nodded, but didn't respond. Fletcher raised his
head and stared across the table at his would-be rival. Nat
held his gaze.

'Did you murder Ralph Elliot?'

'No, I did not,' replied Nat, without hesitation.

Fletcher looked back down at the blank sheet of paper
in front of him, and flicked over the top page to reveal a
second page covered in row upon row of neatly prepared
questions.

'Then let me next ask you . . .' said Fletcher looking
back up at his client.

—◇—

The trial was set for the second week in July. Nat was
surprised by how little time he needed to spend with his
newly appointed counsel once he had gone over his story
again and again, and that stopped only when Fletcher was
confident he had mastered every detail. Although both
recognized the importance of Nat's evidence, Fletcher
spent just as much time reading and re-reading the two
statements that Rebecca Elliot had made to the police,

495

Don Culver's own report on what had taken place that night, and the notes of Detective Petrowski, who was in charge of the case. He warned Nat, 'Rebecca will have been coached by the state's attorney, and every question you can think of she will have had time to consider and reconsider. By the time she steps onto the witness stand, she'll be as well rehearsed as any actress on opening night. But,' Fletcher paused, 'she still has a problem.'

'And what's that?' asked Nat.

'If Mrs Elliot murdered her husband, she must have lied to the police, so there are bound to be loose ends that they are unaware of. First we have to find them, and then we have to tie them up.'

Interest in the gubernatorial race stretched far beyond the boundaries of Connecticut. Articles on the two men appeared in journals as diverse as the *New Yorker* and the *National Enquirer*, so that by the time the trial opened, there wasn't a hotel room available within twenty miles of Hartford.

With three months still to go before election day, the opinion polls showed Fletcher had a twelve-point lead, but he knew that if he was able to prove Nat's innocence, that could be reversed overnight.

The trial was due to open on 11 July, but the major networks already had their cameras on top of the buildings opposite the courthouse and along the sidewalks, as well as many more hand-helds in the streets. They were there to interview anyone remotely connected with the trial, despite the fact it was days before Nat would hear the words 'All rise'.

Fletcher and Nat tried to conduct their election campaigns as if it was business as usual, although no one pretended it was. They quickly discovered that there wasn't a hall they couldn't fill, a rally they couldn't pack, a clambake they couldn't sell twice over, however remote the district. In fact, when they both attended a charity fund-raiser in support of an orthopaedic wing to be added to the Gates Memorial Hospital in Hartford, tickets were changing hands at five hundred dollars each. This was one of those rare elections when campaign contributions kept pouring in. For several weeks they were a bigger draw than Frank Sinatra.

Neither man slept the night before the trial was due to open, and the chief of police didn't even bother to go to bed. Don Culver had detailed a hundred officers to be on duty outside the courthouse, ruefully remarking how many of Hartford's petty criminals were taking advantage of his overstretched force.

Fletcher was the first member of the defence team to appear on the courthouse steps, and he made it clear to the waiting press that he would not be making a statement or answering any questions until the verdict had been delivered. Nat arrived a few minutes later, accompanied by Tom and Su Ling, and if it hadn't been for police assistance, they might never have got into the building.

Once inside the courthouse, Nat walked straight along the marble corridor that led to court number seven, acknowledging onlookers' kind remarks, but only nodding politely in response as instructed by his counsellor. Once he'd entered the courtroom, Nat felt a thousand eyes boring into him as he continued on down the centre aisle, before taking his place on the left of Fletcher at the defence table.

'Good morning, counsellor,' said Nat.

'Good morning, Nat,' replied Fletcher, looking up from a pile of papers, 'I hope you're prepared for a week of boredom while we select a jury.'

'Have you settled on a profile for the ideal juror?' Nat asked.

'It's not quite that easy,' said Fletcher, 'because I can't

make up my mind if I should select people who support you or me.'

'Are there twelve people in Hartford who support you?' asked Nat.

Fletcher smiled. 'I'm glad you haven't lost your sense of humour, but once the jury's sworn in, I want you looking serious and concerned. A man to whom a great injustice has been done.'

Fletcher turned out to be right, because it wasn't until Friday afternoon that the full complement of twelve jurors and two alternatives were finally seated in their places, following argument, counter argument and several objections being raised by both sides. They finally settled on seven men and five women. Two of the women and one of the men were black, five from a professional background, two working mothers, three blue-collar work-ers, one secretary and one unemployed.

'How about their political persuasions?' asked Nat.

'My bet is, four Republicans, four Democrats, and four I can't be sure of.'

'So what's our next problem, counsellor?'

'How to get you off, and still grab the votes of the four I'm not sure of,' said Fletcher as they parted on the bottom step of the courthouse.

Nat found that, whenever he went home in the eve-ning, he would quickly forget the trial, as his mind continually returned to Luke. However much he tried to discuss other things with Su Ling, there was so often only one thought on her mind. 'If only I'd shared my secret with Luke,' she said again and again, 'perhaps he would still be alive.'

46

ON THE FOLLOWING MONDAY, the jury had been sworn in and Judge Kravats invited the state's attorney to make his opening statement.

Richard Ebden rose slowly from his place. He was a tall, elegant, grey-haired man, who had a reputation for beguiling juries. His dark blue suit was the one he always wore on the opening day of a trial. His white shirt and blue tie instilled a feeling of trust.

The state's attorney was proud of his prosecution record, which was somewhat ironic because he was a mild-mannered, church-going family man, who even sang bass in the local choir. Ebden rose from his place, pushed back his chair, and walked slowly out into the open well of the court, before turning to face the jury.

'Members of the jury,' he began, 'in all my years as an advocate, I have rarely come across a more open-and-shut case of homicide.'

Fletcher leant across to Nat and whispered, 'Don't worry, it's his usual opening – *but despite this*, comes next.'

'But despite this, I must still take you through the events of the late evening and early morning of May 12th and 13th.'

'Mr Cartwright,' he said, turning slowly to face the accused, 'had appeared on a television programme with Ralph Elliot – a popular and much respected figure in our community and, perhaps more importantly, favourite to win the Republican nomination, which might well have taken him on to be governor of the state we all love so much. Here was a man at the pinnacle of his career, about to receive the accolades of a grateful electorate for years of unselfish service to the community, and what was to be his reward? He ended up being murdered by his closest rival.

'And how did this unnecessary tragedy come about? Mr Cartwright is asked a question as to whether his wife was an illegal immigrant – such is the stuff of robust politics – a question I might add that he was unwilling to answer, and why? Because he knew it to be the truth, and he had remained silent on the subject for over twenty years. And having refused to answer that question, what does Mr Cartwright do next? He tries to shift the blame on to Ralph Elliot. The moment the programme is over, he starts to shout obscenities at him, calls him a bastard, accuses him of setting up the question, and the most damning of all, says, "I will still kill you."' Ebden stared at the jury, repeating the five words slowly, 'I will still kill you.'

'Don't rely on my words to convict Mr Cartwright, for you are about to discover that this is not rumour, hearsay or my imagination, because the entire conversation between the two rivals was recorded on television for posterity. I realize this is unusual, your honour, but under the circumstances, I'd like to show this tape to the jury at this juncture.' Ebden nodded towards his table and an assistant pressed a button.

For the next twelve minutes, Nat stared at a screen that had been set up opposite the jury, and was painfully reminded just how angry he had been. Once the tape had been switched off, Ebden continued with his opening statement.

'However, it is still the responsibility of the state to

show what actually took place after this angry and vindictive man had charged out of the studio.' Ebden lowered his voice. 'He returns home to discover that his son – his only child – has committed suicide. Now all of us can well understand the effect that such a tragedy might have on a father. And as it turned out, members of the jury, this tragic death triggered a chain of events that was to end in the cold-blooded murder of Ralph Elliot. Cartwright tells his wife that after he has been to the hospital, he will return home immediately, but he has no intention of doing so, because he has already planned a detour that will take him to Mr and Mrs Elliot's house. And what could possibly have been the reason for this nocturnal visit at two a.m.? There can only have been one purpose, to remove Ralph Elliot from the gubernatorial race. Sadly for his family and our state, Mr Cartwright succeeded in his mission.

'He drives over uninvited to the Elliots' family home at two a.m. The door is answered by Mr Elliot, who has been in his study working on an acceptance speech. Mr Cartwright barges in, punching Mr Elliot so hard on the nose that he staggers back into the corridor, only to see his adversary come charging in after him. Mr Elliot recovers in time to run into his study and retrieve a gun that he kept in a drawer in his desk. He turns just as Cartwright leaps on him, kicking the gun out of his hand, thus ensuring that Mr Elliot has no chance of defending himself. Cartwright then grabs the pistol, stands over his victim and without a moment's hesitation, shoots him through the heart. He then aims a second shot into the ceiling to leave the impression that a struggle had taken place. Cartwright then drops the gun, runs out of the open door and, jumping into his car, drives quickly back to his home. Unbeknown to him, he left behind a witness to the entire episode – the victim's wife, Mrs Rebecca

Elliot. When she heard the first shot, Mrs Elliot ran from her bedroom to the top of the stairs and moments after hearing the second shot, she watched in horror as Cartwright bolted out of the front door. And just as the television camera had recorded every detail earlier in the evening, Mrs Elliot will describe to you with the same accuracy, exactly what took place later that night.'

The state's attorney turned his attention away from the jury for a moment and looked directly at Fletcher. 'In a few moments' time, defence counsel will rise from his place and with all his famed charm and oratory will attempt to bring tears to your eyes as he tries to explain away what really happened. But what he can't explain away is the body of an innocent man murdered in cold blood by his political rival. What he can't explain away is his television message, "I will still kill you". What he can't explain away is a witness to the murder – Mr Elliot's widow, Rebecca.'

The prosecutor transferred his gaze on to Nat. 'I can well understand you feeling some sympathy for this man, but after you have heard all the evidence, I believe you will be left in no doubt of Mr Cartwright's guilt, and with no choice but to carry out your duty to the state and deliver a verdict of guilty.'

There was an eerie silence in the courtroom when Richard Ebden resumed his place. Several heads nodded, even one or two on the jury. Judge Kravats made a note on the pad in front of him, and then looked down towards defence counsel's table.

'Do you wish to respond, counsellor?' asked the judge, making no attempt to hide the irony in his voice.

Fletcher rose from his place and, looking directly at the judge, said, 'No thank you, your honour, it is not my intention to make an opening statement.'

Fletcher and Nat sat in silence looking directly in front of them amidst the pandemonium that broke out in the courtroom. The judge banged his gavel several times, trying to bring the proceedings back to order. Fletcher glanced across at the state attorney's table, to see Richard Ebden, head bowed, in a huddle with his prosecution team. The judge tried to hide a smile once he realized what a shrewd tactical move defence counsel had made; it had thrown the state's team into disarray. He turned his attention back to the prosecution.

'Mr Ebden, that being the case, perhaps you'd like to call your first witness?' he said matter-of-factly.

Ebden rose, not quite as confidently now that he'd worked out what Fletcher was up to. 'Your honour, I would in these unusual circumstances seek an adjournment.'

'Objection, your honour,' cried Fletcher, rising quickly from his place. 'The state has had several months to prepare their case; are we now to understand they cannot even produce a single witness?'

'Is that the case, Mr Ebden?' asked the judge. 'Are you unable to call your first witness?'

'That is correct, your honour. Our first witness would have been Mr Don Culver, the chief of police, and we did not want to take him away from his important duties until it was entirely necessary.'

Fletcher was on his feet again. 'But it is entirely necessary, your honour. He is the chief of police, and this is a murder trial, and I therefore ask that this case be dismissed on the grounds there is no police evidence available to place before the court.'

'Nice try, Mr Davenport,' said the judge, 'but I won't fall for it. Mr Ebden, I shall grant your request for an adjournment. I shall reconvene this court immediately after the lunch break, and if the chief of police is unable to be with us by then, I shall rule his evidence inadmissible.' Ebden nodded, unable to hide his embarrassment.

'All rise,' said the clerk, as Judge Kravats glanced at the clock before leaving the courtroom.

'First round to us, I think,' remarked Tom, as the state's team hurriedly left the courtroom.

'Possibly,' said Fletcher, 'but we'll need more than pyrrhic victories to win the final battle.'

—◦—

Nat hated the hanging around, and was back in his seat long before the lunch break was up. He looked across at the state's table, to see Richard Ebden also in his place, knowing he wouldn't make the same mistake a second time. But had he yet worked out why Fletcher had risked such a bold move? Fletcher had explained to Nat during the adjournment that he believed his only hope of winning the case was to undermine Rebecca Elliot's evidence, and therefore he couldn't afford to let her relax even for a moment. Following the judge's warning, Ebden would now have to keep her waiting in the corridor, perhaps for days on end, before she was finally called.

Fletcher took his seat next to Nat only moments before the judge was due to reconvene. 'The chief's out there in the corridor storming up and down fuming, while Mrs Elliot is sitting alone in a corner biting her nails. I intend to keep that lady hanging around for several days,' he added as the clerk called, 'All rise, Judge Kravats presiding.'

'Good afternoon,' said the judge, and turning to the chief prosecutor added, 'Do you have a witness for us, Mr Ebden?'

'Yes, I do, your honour. The state calls Police Chief Don Culver.'

Nat watched as Don Culver took his place on the stand and repeated the oath. Something was wrong, but he couldn't work out what it was. Then he saw the second and third fingers of Culver's right hand twitching, and realized it was the first time he'd seen him without his trade-mark cigar.

'Mr Culver, would you tell the jury your present rank?'

'I'm the chief of police for the city of Hartford.'

'And how long have you held that position?'

'Just over fourteen years.'

'And how long have you been a law enforcement officer?'

'For the past thirty-six years.'

'So it would be safe to say that you have a great deal of experience when it comes to homicide?'

'I guess that's right,' the chief said.

'And have you ever come into contact with the defendant?'

'Yes, I have, on several occasions.'

'He's stealing some of my questions,' Fletcher whispered to Nat, 'but I haven't yet worked out why.'

'And had you formed an opinion of the man?'

'Yes I had, he's a decent law-abiding citizen, who, until he murdered . . .'

'Objection, your honour,' said Fletcher, rising from his place, 'it is up to the jury to decide who murdered Mr Elliot, not the chief of police. We don't live in a police state yet.'

'Sustained,' said the judge.

'Well, all I can say,' said the chief, 'is that until all this happened, I would have voted for him.' Laughter broke out in the court.

'And after I've finished with the chief,' whispered Fletcher, 'he sure won't be voting for me.'

'Then you must have had some doubt in your mind that such an upstanding citizen was capable of murder?'

'Not at all, Mr Ebden,' said the chief. 'Murderers aren't run-of-the-mill criminals.'

'Would you care to explain what you mean by that, chief?'

'Sure will,' said Culver. 'The average murder is a domestic affair, usually within the family, and is often carried out by someone who not only has never committed a crime before, but probably never will again. Once they're in custody, they are often easier to handle than a petty burglar.'

'Do you feel Mr Cartwright falls into this category?'

'Objection,' said Fletcher from a seated position, 'how can the chief possibly know the answer to that question?'

'Because I've been dealing with murderers for the past thirty-six years,' Don Culver responded.

'Strike that from the record,' said the judge. 'Experience is all very well, but the jury must in the end deal only with the facts in this particular case.'

'Then let's move on to a question that does deal with fact in this particular case,' said the state's attorney. 'How did you become involved in this case, Chief Culver?'

'I took a call at my home from Mrs Elliot in the early hours of May 12th.'

'She called you at home? Is she a personal acquaintance?'

'No, but all candidates for public office are able to get in touch with me directly. They are often the subject of threats, real or imagined, and it was no secret that Mr Elliot had received several death threats since he'd declared for governor.'

'When Mrs Elliot called you, did you record her exact words?'

'You bet I did,' said the chief. 'She sounded hysterical,

and was shouting. I remember I had to hold the phone away from my ear, in fact she woke my wife.' A little laughter broke out in the court for a second time, and Culver waited until it had died down before he added, 'I wrote down her exact words on a pad I keep next to the phone.' He opened a notebook.

Fletcher was on his feet. 'Is this admissible?' he asked.

'It was on the agreed list of prosecutions documents, your honour,' Ebden intervened, 'as I feel sure Mr Davenport is aware. He's had weeks to consider its relevance, not to mention importance.'

The judge nodded to the chief. 'Carry on,' he said as Fletcher resumed his seat.

'"My husband has been shot in his study, please come as quickly as possible",' said the chief, reading from his notebook.

'What did you say?'

'I told her not to touch anything, and I'd be with her just as soon as I could get there.'

'What time was that?'

'Two twenty-six,' the chief replied after rechecking his notebook.

'And when did you arrive at the Elliots' home?'

'Not until three nineteen. First I had to call the station and tell them to send the most senior detective available to the Elliots' residence. I then got dressed, so that when I eventually made it, I found two of my patrolmen had already arrived – but then they didn't have to get dressed.' Once again laughter broke out around the courtroom.

'Please describe to the jury exactly what you saw when you first arrived.'

'The front door was open, and Mrs Elliot was sitting on the floor in the hallway, her knees hunched up under her chin. I let her know I was there, and then joined Detective Petrowski in Mr Elliot's study. Mr Petrowski,' the chief added, 'is one of the most respected detectives on my force, with a great deal of experience of homicide, and as he seemed to have the investigation well under way I left him to get on with his job, while I returned to Mrs Elliot.'

'Did you then question her?'

'Yes, I did,' replied the chief.

'But wouldn't Detective Petrowski already have done that?'

'Yes, but it's often useful to get two statements so that one can compare them later and see if they differ on any essential points.'

'Your honour, these statements are hearsay,' Fletcher interjected.

'And did they?' Ebden hurriedly asked.

'No, they did not.'

'Objection,' Fletcher emphasized.

'Overruled Mr Davenport. As has already been pointed out, you have had access to these documents for several weeks.'

'Thank you, your honour,' said Ebden. 'I would like you to tell the court what you did next, chief.'

'I suggested that we go and sit in the front room, so that Mrs Elliot would be more comfortable. I then asked her to take me slowly through what had happened that evening. I didn't hurry her, as witnesses are quite often resentful of being asked exactly the same questions a second or third time. After she'd finished her cup of coffee, Mrs Elliot eventually told me that she had been asleep in bed when she heard the first shot. She switched on the light, put on her robe and went to the top of the stairs and that was when she heard the second shot. She then watched as Mr Cartwright ran out of the study towards the open door. He turned to look back, but couldn't have seen her in the darkness at the top of the stairs, although she recognized him immediately. She then ran downstairs and into the study where she found her husband lying on the floor in a pool of blood. She immediately called me at home.'

'Did you continue to question her?'

'No, I left a female officer with Mrs Elliot while I checked over her original statement. After a further consultation with Detective Petrowski, I drove to Mr Cartwright's home accompanied by two other officers, arrested the defendant and charged him with the murder of Ralph Elliot.'

'Had he gone to bed?'

'No, he was still in the clothes he had been wearing on the television programme that night.'

'No more questions, your honour.'

'Your witness, Mr Davenport.'

Fletcher walked across to the witness stand with a smile on his face. 'Good afternoon, chief. I won't detain you for long, as I'm only too aware how busy you are, but I do nevertheless have three or four questions that need answering.' The chief didn't return Fletcher's smile. 'To begin with, I would like to know what period of time passed between your receiving the phone call at your home from Mrs Elliot, and when you placed Mr Cartwright under arrest.'

The chief's fingers twitched again while he considered the question. 'Two hours, two and a half at the most,' he eventually said.

'And when you arrived at Mr Cartwright's house, how was he dressed?'

'I've already told the court that – in exactly the same clothes as he was wearing on television that night.'

'So he didn't open the door in his pyjamas and dressing gown looking as if he had just got out of bed?'

'No, he didn't,' said the chief, puzzled.

'Don't you think that a man who had just committed a murder might want to get undressed and into bed at two o'clock in the morning, so that should the police suddenly turn up on his doorstep, he could at least give an impression of having been asleep?'

The chief frowned. 'He was comforting his wife.'

'I see,' said Fletcher. 'The murderer was comforting his wife, so let me ask you, chief, when you arrested Mr Cartwright, did he make a statement?'

'No,' the chief replied, 'he said he wanted to speak to his lawyer first.'

'But did he say anything at all that you might have recorded in your trusty notebook?'

'Yes,' said the chief, and flipped back some pages of the notebook before carefully studying an entry. 'Yes,' he repeated with a smile, 'Cartwright said, "but he was still alive when I left him".'

'But he was still *alive* when I left him,' repeated Fletcher. 'Hardly the words of a man who is trying to hide the fact that he had been there at all. He doesn't get undressed, he doesn't go to bed, and he openly admits he was at Elliot's house earlier that evening.' The chief remained silent. 'When he accompanied you to the police station, did you take his fingerprints?'

'Yes of course.'

'Did you carry out any other tests?' asked Fletcher.

'What did you have in mind?' asked the chief.

'Don't play games with me,' said Fletcher, his voice revealing a slight edge. 'Did you carry out any other tests?'

'Yes,' said the chief. 'We checked under his fingernails to see if there was any sign that he had fired a gun.'

'And was there any indication that Mr Cartwright had fired a gun?' asked Fletcher returning to his more conciliatory tone.

The chief hesitated. 'We could find no powder residue on his hands or under his fingernails.'

'There was no powder residue on his hands or under his fingernails,' said Fletcher, facing the jury.

'Yes, but he'd had a couple of hours to wash his hands and scrub his nails.'

'He certainly did, chief, and he also had a couple of hours to get undressed, go to bed, turn off all the lights in the house, and come up with a far more convincing line than, "but he was still alive when I left him".' Fletcher's eyes never left the jury. Once again, the chief remained silent.

'My final question, Mr Culver, is something that's been nagging at me ever since I took on this case, especially when I think about your thirty-six years of experience, fourteen of them as chief of police.' He turned back to face Culver. 'Did it ever cross your mind that someone else might have committed this crime?'

'There was no sign of anyone else having entered the house other than Mr Cartwright.'

'But there was already someone else in the house.'

'And there was absolutely no evidence of any kind to suggest that Mrs Elliot could possibly have been involved.'

'No evidence of any kind?' repeated Fletcher. 'I do hope, chief, that you will find time in your busy schedule to drop in and hear my cross-examination of Mrs Elliot, when the jury will be able to decide if there was absolutely no evidence of any kind to show she might have been involved in this crime.' Uproar broke out in the courtroom as everyone began talking at once.

The state's attorney leapt to his feet, 'Objection, your honour,' he said sharply. 'It's not Mrs Elliot who is on trial.' But he could not be heard above the noise of the judge banging his gavel as Fletcher walked slowly back to his place.

When the judge had managed to bring some semblance of order back to proceedings, all Fletcher said was, 'No more questions, your honour.'

'Do you have any evidence?' Nat whispered as his counsel sat down.

'Not a lot,' admitted Fletcher, 'but one thing I feel confident about is that if Mrs Elliot did kill her husband, she won't be getting a lot of sleep between now and when she enters that witness stand. And as for Ebden, he'll be spending the next few days wondering what we've come up with that he doesn't yet know about.' Fletcher smiled at the chief as he stepped down from the witness stand, but received a cold, blank stare in response.

The judge looked down from the bench at both attorneys. 'I think that's enough for today, gentlemen,' he said. 'We will convene again at ten o'clock tomorrow morning, when Mr Ebden may call his next witness.'

'All rise.'

47

WHEN THE JUDGE made his entrance the following morning, only a change of tie gave any clue that he had ever left the building. Nat wondered how long it would be before the ties also began to make a second and even a third appearance.

'Good morning,' said Judge Kravats as he took his place on the bench and beamed down at the assembled throng as though he were a benevolent preacher about to address his congregation. 'Mr Ebden,' he said, 'you may call your next witness.'

'Thank you, your honour. I call Detective Petrowski.'

Fletcher studied the senior detective carefully as he made his way to the witness stand. He raised his right hand and began to recite the oath. Petrowski could barely have passed the minimum height the force required of its recruits. His tight-fitting suit implied a wrestler's build, rather than someone who was over-weight. His jaw was square, his eyes narrow and his lips curled slightly down at the edges, leaving an impression that he didn't smile that often. One of Fletcher's researchers had found out that Petrowski was tipped to be the next chief when Don Culver retired. He had a reputation for sticking by the book, but hating paperwork, much preferring to be visiting the scene of the crime than sitting behind a desk back at headquarters.

'Good morning, captain,' said the state's attorney once the witness had sat down. Petrowski nodded, but still didn't smile. 'For the record, would you please state your name and rank.'

'Frank Petrowski, chief of detectives, City of Hartford Police Department.'

'And how long have you been a detective?'

'Fourteen years.'

'And when were you appointed chief of detectives?'

'Three years ago.'

'Having established your record, let us move on to the night of the murder. The police log shows that you were the first officer on the scene of the crime.'

'Yes, I was,' said Petrowski, 'I was the senior officer on duty that night, having taken over from the chief at eight o'clock.'

'And where were you at two thirty that morning when the chief called in?'

'I was in a patrol car, on the way to investigate a break-in at a warehouse on Marsham Street, when the desk sergeant phoned to say the chief wanted me to go immediately to the home of Ralph Elliot in West Hartford, and investigate a possible homicide. As I was only minutes away, I took on the assignment and detailed another patrol car to cover Marsham Street.'

'And you drove straight to the Elliots' home?'

'Yes, but on the way I radioed in to headquarters to let them know that I would be needing the assistance of forensics and the best photographer they could get out of bed at that time in the morning.'

'And what did you find when you arrived at the Elliots' house?'

'I was surprised to discover that the front door was open and Mrs Elliot was crouched on the floor in the hallway. She told me that she had found her husband's body in the study, and pointed to the other end of the corridor. She added that the chief had told her not to touch anything, which was why the front door had been left open. I went straight to the study, and once I had confirmed that Mr Elliot was dead, I returned to the hallway and took a statement from his wife, copies of which are in the court's possession.'

'What did you do next?'

'In her statement, Mrs Elliot said that she had been asleep when she heard two shots coming from downstairs, so I and three other officers returned to the study to search for the bullets.'

'And did you find them?'

'Yes. The first was easy to locate because after it had passed through Mr Elliot's heart it ended up embedded in the wooden panel ehind his desk. The second took a little longer to find, but we eventually spotted it lodged in the ceiling above Mr Elliot's bureau.'

'Could these two bullets have been fired by the same person?'

'It's possible,' said Petrowski, 'if the murderer had wanted to leave the impression of a struggle, or that the victim had turned the gun on himself.'

'Is that common in a homicide case?'

'It's not unknown for a criminal to try and leave conflicting evidence.'

'But can you prove that both bullets came from the same gun?'

'That was confirmed by ballistics the following day.'

'And were any fingerprints found on the firearm?'

'Yes,' said Petrowski, 'a palm mark on the handle of the gun, plus an index finger on the trigger.'

'And were you later able to match up these samples?'

'Yes,' he paused. 'They both matched Mr Cartwright's prints.'

A babble of chatter erupted from the public benches behind Fletcher. He tried not to blink as he observed the jury's reaction to this piece of information. A moment later he scribbled a note on his yellow pad. The judge banged his gavel several times as he called for order, before Ebden was able to resume.

'From the entry of the bullet into the body, and the burn marks on the chest, were you able to ascertain what distance the murderer was from his victim?'

'Yes,' said Petrowski. 'Forensics estimated that the assailant must have been standing four to five feet in front of his victim, and from the angle which the bullet entered the body, they were able to show that both men were standing at the time.'

'Objection, your honour,' said Fletcher, rising from his place. 'We have yet to prove that it was a man who fired either shot.'

'Sustained.'

'And when you had gathered all your evidence,' continued Ebden as if he had not been interrupted, 'was it you who made the decision to arrest Mr Cartwright?'

'No, by then the chief had turned up, and although it was my case, I asked if he would also take a statement from Mrs Elliot, to make sure her story hadn't changed in any way.'

'And had it?'

'No, on all the essential points, it remained consistent.'

Fletcher underlined the word *essential* as both Petrowski and the chief had used it. Well rehearsed or a coincidence, he wondered.

'Was that when you decided to arrest the accused?'

'Yes, it was on my recommendation, but ultimately the chief's decision.'

'Weren't you taking a tremendous risk, arresting a gubernatorial candidate during an election campaign?'

'Yes, we were, and I discussed that problem with the chief. We often find to our cost that the first twenty-four hours are the most important in any investigation, and we had a body, two bullets and a witness to the crime. I considered it would have been an abrogation of my duty not to make an arrest simply because the assailant had powerful friends.'

'Objection, your honour, that was prejudicial,' said Fletcher.

'Sustained,' said the judge, 'and strike it from the record.' He turned to Petrowski and added, 'Please stick to facts detective, I'm not interested in your opinions.'

Petrowski nodded.

Fletcher turned to Nat. 'That last statement sounded to me as if it had been written in the DA's office.' He paused, looked down at his yellow pad and commented that 'abrogation', 'essential points', and 'assailant' were delivered as if they had been learnt by heart. 'Petrowski won't have the opportunity to deliver rehearsed answers when I cross-examine him.'

'Thank you, captain,' said Ebden, 'I have no more questions for Detective Petrowski, your honour.'

'Do you wish to question this witness?' asked the judge, preparing himself for another tactical manoeuvre.

'Yes, I most certainly do, your honour.' Fletcher remained seated while he turned a page of his legal pad. 'Detective Petrowski, you told the court that my client's fingerprints were on the gun?'

'Not just his fingerprints, also a palm print on the butt as confirmed in the forensic report.'

'And didn't you also tell the court that in your experience, criminals often try to leave conflicting evidence in order to fool the police?'

Petrowski nodded, but made no reply.

'Yes or no, captain?'

'Yes,' said Petrowski.

'Would you describe Mr Cartwright as a fool?'

Petrowski hesitated while he tried to work out where Fletcher was attempting to lead him. 'No, I would say he was a highly intelligent man.'

'Would you describe leaving your fingerprints and a palm print on the murder weapon as the act of a highly intelligent man?' asked Fletcher.

'No, but then Mr Cartwright is not a professional criminal, and doesn't think like one. Amateurs often panic and that's when they make simple mistakes.'

'Like dropping the gun on the floor, covered in his prints, and running out of the house leaving the front door wide open?'

'Yes, that doesn't surprise me, given the circumstances.'

'You spent several hours questioning Mr Cartwright, captain; does he strike you as the type of man who panics and then runs away?'

'Objection, your honour,' said Ebden rising from his place, 'how can Detective Petrowski be expected to answer that question?'

'Your honour, Detective Petrowski has been only too willing to give his opinion on the habits of amateur and professional criminals, so I can't see why he wouldn't feel comfortable answering my question.'

'Overruled, counsellor. Move on.'

Fletcher bowed to the judge, stood up, walked over to the witness stand and came to a halt in front of the detective. 'Were there any other fingerprints on the gun?'

'Yes,' said Petrowski, not appearing to be fazed by Fletcher's presence, 'there were partials of Mr Elliot's prints, but they have been accounted for, remembering that he took the gun from his desk to protect himself.'

'But his prints were on the gun?'

'Yes.'

'Did you check to see if there was any powder residue under his fingernails?'

'No,' said Petrowski.

'And why not?' asked Fletcher.

'Because you'd need very long arms to shoot yourself from a distance of four feet.' Laughter broke out in the court.

Fletcher waited for silence before he said, 'But he could well have fired the first bullet that ended up in the ceiling.'

'It could have been the second bullet,' rebutted Petrowski.

Fletcher turned away from the witness stand and walked over to the jury. 'When you took the statement from Mrs Elliot, what was she wearing?'

'A robe – as she explained, she had been asleep at the time when the first shot was fired.'

'Ah yes, I remember,' said Fletcher before he walked back to the table. He picked up a single sheet of paper and read from it. 'It was when Mrs Elliot heard the second shot that she came out of the bedroom and ran to the top of the stairs.' Petrowski nodded.

'Please answer the question, detective, yes or no?'

'I don't recall the question,' said Petrowski, sounding flustered.

'It was when she heard the second shot that Mrs Elliot came out of the bedroom and ran to the top of the stairs.'

'Yes, that's what she told us.'

'And she stood there watching Mr Cartwright as he ran out of the front door. Is that also correct?' Fletcher asked, turning round to look directly at Petrowski.

'Yes it is,' said Petrowski, trying to remain calm.

'Detective, you told the court that among the professionals you called in to assist you was a police photographer.'

'Yes, that's standard practice in a case like this, and all the photographs taken that night have been submitted as evidence.'

'Indeed they have,' said Fletcher as he returned to the table and emptied a large package of photographs on to the surface. He selected one, and walked back to the witness stand. 'Is this one of those photographs?' he asked.

Petrowski studied it carefully, and then looked at the stamp on the back, 'Yes, it is.'

'Would you describe it to the jury?'

'It's a picture of the Elliots' front door, taken from their driveway.'

'Why was this particular photograph submitted as evidence?'

'Because it proved that the door had been left open when the murderer made good his escape. It also shows the long corridor leading through to Mr Elliot's study.'

'Yes of course it does, I should have worked that out for myself,' said Fletcher. He paused. 'And the figure crouched in the corridor, is that Mrs Elliot?'

The detective took a second look, 'Yes it is, she seemed calm at the time, so we decided not to disturb her.'

'How considerate,' said Fletcher. 'So let me ask you finally, detective, you told the district attorney that you did not call for an ambulance until your investigation had been completed?'

'That is correct, paramedics sometimes turn up at the scene of a crime before the police have arrived, and they are notorious for disturbing evidence.'

'Are they?' asked Fletcher. 'But that didn't happen on this occasion, because you were the first person to arrive following Mrs Elliot's call to the chief.'

'Yes, I was.'

'Most commendable,' said Fletcher. 'Do you have any idea how long it took you to reach Mrs Elliot's home in West Hartford?'

'Five, maybe six minutes.'

'You must have had to break the speed limit to achieve that,' said Fletcher, with a smile.

'I put my siren on, but as it was two in the morning, there was very little traffic about.'

'I'm grateful for that explanation,' said Fletcher. 'No more questions, your honour.'

'What was all that about?' muttered Nat when Fletcher had returned to his place.

'Ah, I'm glad you didn't work it out,' said Fletcher. 'Now we must hope that the state's attorney hasn't either.'

48

'I CALL REBECCA ELLIOT to the stand.'

When Rebecca entered the courtroom, every head turned except Nat's. He remained staring resolutely ahead. She walked slowly down the centre aisle, making the sort of entrance that an actress looks for in every script. The court had been packed from the moment the doors were opened at eight o'clock that morning. The front three rows of the public benches had been cordoned off, and only the presence of uniformed police officers kept them from being colonized.

Fletcher had looked around when Don Culver, the chief of police, and Detective Petrowski had taken their seats in the front row, directly behind the state's attorney's table. At one minute to ten, only thirteen seats remained unoccupied.

Nat glanced across at Fletcher, who had a little stack of yellow legal pads in front of him. He could see that the top sheet was blank and prayed that the other three unopened pads had something written on them. A police officer stepped forward to show Mrs Elliot into the well of the court and guide her to the witness stand. Nat looked up at Rebecca for the first time. She was wearing her widow's weeds – fashionable black tailored suit, buttoned to the neck, and a skirt that fell several inches below the knee. Her only jewellery other than her wedding and engagement ring was a simple string of pearls. Fletcher glanced at her left wrist and made the first note on his pad. As she took the stand, Rebecca turned to face the judge, and gave him a shy smile. He nodded courteously. She then haltingly took the oath. She finally sat down and, turning to face the jury, gave them the same shy smile. Fletcher noticed that several of them returned the compliment. Rebecca touched the side of her hair, and Fletcher knew where she must have spent most of the previous afternoon. The state's attorney hadn't missed a trick, and if he could have called for the jury to deliver their verdict before a question had been asked, he suspected that they would have happily sentenced him, as well as his client, to the electric chair.

The judge nodded, and the state's attorney rose from his place. Mr Ebden had also joined in the charade. He was dressed in a dark charcoal suit, white shirt and a sober blue tie – the appropriate attire in which to question the Virgin Mother.

'Mrs Elliot,' he said quietly, as he stepped out into the well of the court. 'Everyone in this courtroom is aware of the ordeal you have been put through, and are now going to have to painfully relive. Let me reassure you that it is my intention to take you through any questions I might have as painlessly as possible, in the hope that you will not have to remain on the witness stand any longer than is necessary.'

'Especially as we have been able to rehearse every question again and again for the past five months,' murmured Fletcher. Nat tried not to smile.

'Let me begin by asking you, Mrs Elliot, how long were you married to your late husband?'

'Tomorrow would have been our seventeenth wedding anniversary.'

'And how did you plan to celebrate that occasion?'

'We were going to stay at the Salisbury Inn, where we had spent the first night of our honeymoon, because I knew Ralph couldn't spare more than a few hours off from his campaign.'

'Typical of Mr Elliot's commitment and conscientious approach to public service,' said the state's attorney as he walked out into the well of the court and across to the jury. 'I must, Mrs Elliot, ask you to bear with me while I return to the night of your husband's tragic and untimely death.' Rebecca bowed her head slightly. 'You didn't attend the debate that Mr Elliot took part in earlier that evening. Was there any particular reason for that?'

'Yes,' said Rebecca, facing the jury, 'Ralph liked me to stay at home and watch him whenever he was on television, where I could make detailed notes that we would discuss later. He felt that if I was part of the studio audience, I might be influenced by those sitting around me, especially once they realized that I was the candidate's wife.'

'That makes a great deal of sense,' said Ebden. Fletcher penned a second note on the pad in front of him.

'Was there anything in particular you recall about that evening's broadcast?'

'Yes,' said Rebecca. She paused and bowed her head. 'I felt sick when Mr Cartwright threatened my husband with the words "I will still kill you".' She slowly raised her head and looked at the jury, as Fletcher made a further note.

'And once the debate was over your husband returned home to West Hartford?'

'Yes, I had prepared a light supper for him, which we had in the kitchen, because he sometimes forgets.' She paused again. 'I'm so sorry, forgot, to take a break from his arduous schedule to eat.'

'Do you recall anything in particular about that supper?'

'Yes, I went over my notes with him, as I felt strongly about some of the issues that had been raised during the debate.' Fletcher turned the page and made another note. 'In fact, it was over supper that I learned Mr Cartwright had accused him of setting up the last question.'

'How did you react to such a suggestion?'

'I was appalled that anyone could think Ralph might have been involved in such underhand tactics. However I remained convinced that the public would not be taken in by Mr Cartwright's false accusations, and that his petulant outburst would only increase my husband's chances of winning the election the following day.'

'And after supper did you both go to bed?'

'No, Ralph always found it difficult to sleep after appearing on television.' She turned to face the jury again. 'He told me that the adrenalin would go on pumping for several hours, and in any case, he wanted to put some finishing touches to his acceptance speech, so I went to bed while he settled down to work in his study.' Fletcher added a further note to his script.

'And what time was that?'

'Just before midnight.'

'And after you had fallen asleep, what was the next thing you remember?'

'Being woken by a shot, and not being certain if it was real or just part of a dream. I turned on the light and checked the time by the clock on my bedside table. It was just after two o'clock, and I remember being surprised that Ralph still hadn't come to bed. Then I thought I heard voices, so I walked over to the door and opened it slightly. That was when I first heard someone shouting at Ralph. I was horrified when I realized it was Nat Cartwright. He was screaming at the top of his voice, and once again threatening to kill my husband. I crept out of the bedroom to the top of the stairs and that was when I heard the second shot. A moment later Mr Cartwright came running out of the study, continued on down the corridor, opened the front door and disappeared into the night.'

'Did you chase after him?'

'No, I was terrified.'

Fletcher scribbled yet another note as Rebecca continued. 'I ran downstairs, and straight into Ralph's study, fearing the worst. The first thing I saw was my husband on the far side of the room slumped in the corner, blood trickling from his mouth, so I immediately picked up the phone on his desk and called Chief Culver at home.'

Fletcher turned yet another page and continued writing furiously. 'I'm afraid I woke him, but the chief said he would come over as quickly as possible and that I was to touch nothing.'

'What did you do next?'

'I suddenly felt cold and sick in my stomach, and I thought I was going to faint. I staggered back out into the corridor and collapsed on the floor. The next thing I remember was a police siren in the distance and a few moments later someone came running through the front door. The policeman knelt down by my side and introduced himself as Detective Petrowski. One of his officers made me a cup of coffee and then he asked me to describe what had happened. I told him all I could remember, but I'm afraid I wasn't very coherent. I recall pointing to Ralph's study.'

'Can you remember what happened next?'

'Yes, a few minutes later I heard another siren, and then the chief walked in. Mr Culver spent a long time with Detective Petrowski in my husband's study, and then returned and asked me to go over my story once again. He didn't stay for very long after that, but I did see him in deep conversation with the detective before he left. It wasn't until the following morning that I discovered that Mr Cartwright had been arrested and charged with the murder of my husband.' Rebecca burst into tears.

'Bang on cue,' said Fletcher as the chief prosecutor removed a handkerchief from his top pocket and handed it over to Mrs Elliot. 'I wonder how long they took rehearsing that?' he added as he turned his attention to the jury and noticed that a woman in the second row was also quietly crying.

'I'm sorry to have put you through such an ordeal, Mrs Elliot.' Ebden paused. 'Perhaps you would like me to ask the court for an adjournment so you have a little time to compose yourself?'

Fletcher would have objected, but he already knew what her answer would be, because they were so obviously sticking to a well-worn script.

'No, I'll be fine,' said Rebecca, 'and in any case I'd rather get it over with.'

'Yes, of course, Mrs Elliot,' Ebden looked up towards the judge, 'I have no more questions for this witness, your honour.'

'Thank you, Mr Ebden,' said the judge. 'Your witness, Mr Davenport.'

'Thank you, your honour.' Fletcher removed a stopwatch from his pocket and placed it on the table in front of him. He then slowly rose from his place. He could feel the eyes of everyone in the courtroom boring into the back of his head. How could he even consider questioning this helpless, saintly woman? He walked over to the stand and didn't speak for some time. 'I will try not to detain you for longer than is necessary, Mrs Elliot, remembering the ordeal you have already been put through.' Fletcher spoke softly. 'But I must ask you one or two questions, as it is my client who is facing the death penalty, based almost solely on your testimony.'

'Yes, of course,' Rebecca replied, trying to sound brave as she wiped away the last tear.

'You told the court, Mrs Elliot, that you had a very fulfilling relationship with your husband.'

'Yes, we were devoted to each other.'

'Were you?' Fletcher paused again. 'And the only reason you did not attend the television debate that evening was because Mr Elliot had asked you to remain at home and make some notes on his performance, so that you could discuss them later that evening?'

'Yes, that is correct,' she said.

'I can appreciate that,' said Fletcher, 'but I'm puzzled as to why you did not accompany your husband to a single public function during the previous month?' He paused. 'Night or day.'

'I did, I feel sure I did,' she said. 'But in any case you must remember that my main task was to run the home, and make life as easy as possible for Ralph, after the long hours he spent on the road campaigning.'

'Did you keep those notes?'

She hesitated, 'No, once I'd gone over them with him, I gave them to Ralph.'

'And on this particular occasion you told the court that you felt very strongly about certain issues?'

'Yes, I did.'

'May I ask which issues in particular, Mrs Elliot?'

Rebecca hesitated again. 'I can't remember exactly.' She paused. 'It was several months ago.'

'But it was the only public function you took an interest in during his entire campaign, Mrs Elliot, so one would have thought you might just have remembered one or two of the issues you felt so strongly about. After all, your husband was running for governor and you, so to speak, for first lady.'

'Yes, no, yes – health care, I think.'

'Then you'll have to think again, Mrs Elliot,' said Fletcher as he returned to the table and picked up one of his yellow notepads. 'I also watched that debate with more than a passing interest, and was somewhat surprised that the subject of health care was not raised. Perhaps you'd like to reconsider your last answer, as I did keep detailed notes on every issue that was debated that night.'

'Objection, your honour. Defence counsel is not here to act as a witness.'

'Sustained. Keep to your brief, counsellor.'

'But there was one thing you felt strongly about, wasn't there, Mrs Elliot?' continued Fletcher. 'The vicious attack on your husband when Mr Cartwright said on television, "I will still kill you".'

'Yes, that was a terrible thing to say with the whole world watching.'

'But the whole world wasn't watching, Mrs Elliot, otherwise I would have seen it. It wasn't said until after the programme had ended.'

'Then my husband must have told me about it over supper.'

'I don't think so, Mrs Elliot. I suspect that you didn't even see that programme, just as you never attended any of his meetings.'

'Yes, I did.'

'Then perhaps you can tell the jury the location of any meeting you attended during your husband's lengthy campaign, Mrs Elliot?'

'How could I be expected to remember every one of them, when Ralph's campaign started over a year ago?'

'I'll settle for just one,' said Fletcher, turning to face the jury.

Rebecca started crying again, but on this occasion the timing was not quite as effective, and there was no one on hand to offer her a handkerchief.

'Now let us consider those words, "I will still kill you", spoken off-air the evening before an election.' Fletcher remained facing the jury. 'Mr Cartwright didn't say "I will kill you", which would have indeed been damning, what he actually said was "I will *still* kill you", and everyone present assumed he was referring to the election that was taking place the following day.'

'He killed my husband,' shouted Mrs Elliot, her voice rising for the first time.

'There are still a few more questions that need to be answered before I come to who killed your husband, Mrs Elliot. But first allow me to return to the events of that evening. Having watched a television programme you can't remember, and had supper with your husband to discuss in detail issues that you don't recall, you went to bed while your husband returned to his study to work on his acceptance speech.'

'Yes, that is exactly what happened,' said Rebecca, staring defiantly at Fletcher.

'But as he was significantly behind in the opinion polls, why waste time working on an acceptance speech he could never hope to deliver?'

'He was still convinced he would win, especially following Mr Cartwright's outburst and . . .'

'And?' repeated Fletcher, but Rebecca remained silent. 'Then perhaps you both knew something the rest of us didn't,' said Fletcher, 'but I'll come to that in a moment. You say you went to bed around midnight?'

'Yes, I did,' said Rebecca, sounding even more defiant.

'And when you were woken by a gunshot, you checked the time by looking at the clock on your side of the bed?'

'Yes, it was just after two o'clock.'

'So you don't wear a wristwatch in bed?'

'No, I lock away all my jewellery in a little safe Ralph

had installed in the bedroom. There have been so many burglaries in the area recently.'

'How wise of him. And you still think it was the first shot that woke you?'

'Yes, I'm sure it was.'

'How long was it between the first and second shot, Mrs Elliot?' Rebecca didn't answer immediately. 'Do take your time, Mrs Elliot, because I wouldn't want you to make a mistake that, like so much of your evidence, needs correcting later.'

'Objection, your honour, my client is not . . .'

'Yes, yes, Mr Ebden, sustained. That last comment will be struck from the record,' and turning to Fletcher, the judge repeated, 'stick to your brief, Mr Davenport.'

'I will try to, your honour,' said Fletcher, but his eyes never left the jury to make sure it wasn't struck from their minds. 'Have you had enough time to consider your reply, Mrs Elliot?' He waited once again before repeating, 'How long was it between the first and second shots?'

'Three, possibly four minutes,' she said.

Fletcher smiled at the chief prosecutor, walked back to his table and picked up the stopwatch, which he placed in his pocket. 'When you heard the first shot, Mrs Elliot, why didn't you phone the police immediately, why wait for three or four minutes until you heard the second shot?'

'Because to begin with I wasn't absolutely sure that I had heard it. Don't forget, I'd been asleep for some time.'

'But you opened your bedroom door and were horrified to hear Mr Cartwright shouting at your husband and threatening to kill him, so you must have believed that Ralph was in some considerable danger, so why not lock your door, and immediately phone the police from the bedroom?' Rebecca looked across at Richard Ebden. 'No,

Mrs Elliot, Mr Ebden can't help you this time, because he didn't anticipate the question, which, to be fair,' said Fletcher, 'wasn't entirely his fault, because you've only told him half the story.'

'Objection' said Ebden, jumping to his feet.

'Sustained,' said the judge. 'Mr Davenport, stick to questioning Mrs Elliot, not giving opinions. This is a court of law, not the Senate Chamber.'

'I apologize, your honour, but on this occasion I do know the answer. You see the reason Mrs Elliot didn't call the police was because she feared that it was her husband who had fired the first shot.'

'Objection,' shouted Ebden, leaping to his feet as several members of the public began talking at once. It was some time before the judge could gavel the court back to order.

'No, no,' said Rebecca, 'from the way Nat was shouting at Ralph I was certain he'd fired the first shot.'

'Then I will ask you again, why not call the police immediately?' Fletcher repeated, turning back to face her. 'Why wait three or four minutes until you heard the second shot?'

'It all happened so quickly, I just didn't have time.'

'What is your favourite work of fiction, Mrs Elliot?' asked Fletcher quietly.

'Objection, your honour. How can this possibly be relevant?'

'Overruled. I have a feeling we're about to find out, Mr Ebden.'

'You are indeed, your honour,' said Fletcher, his eyes never leaving the witness. 'Mrs Elliot, let me assure you that this is not a trick question, I simply want you to tell the court your favourite work of fiction.'

'I'm not sure I have a particular one,' she replied, 'but my favourite author is Hemingway.'

'Mine too,' said Fletcher, taking the stopwatch out of his pocket. Turning to face the judge, he asked, 'Your honour, may I have your permission to briefly leave the courtroom?'

'For what purpose, Mr Davenport?'

'To prove that my client did not fire the first shot.'

The judge nodded. 'Briefly, Mr Davenport.'

Fletcher then pressed the starter button, placed the stopwatch in his pocket, walked down the aisle through the packed courtroom, and out of the door. 'Your honour,' said Ebden jumping up from his place, 'I must object. Mr Davenport is turning this trial into a circus.'

'If that turns out to be the case, Mr Ebden, I shall severely censure Mr Davenport the moment he returns.'

'But, your honour, is this kind of behaviour fair to my client?'

'I believe so, Mr Ebden. As Mr Davenport reminded the court, his client faces the death penalty solely on the evidence of your principal witness.'

The chief prosecutor sat back down, and began to consult his team, while chattering broke out on the public benches behind him. The judge started tapping his fingers, occasionally glancing at the clock on the wall above the public entrance.

Richard Ebden rose again, at which point the judge called for order. 'You honour, I move that Mrs Elliot be released from further questioning on the grounds that the defence counsel is no longer able to carry out his cross-examination as he has left the courtroom without explanation.'

'I shall approve your request, Mr Ebden,' the state's attorney looked delighted, 'should Mr Davenport fail to return in under four minutes.' The judge smiled down at Mr Ebden, assuming they had both worked out the significance of his judgment.

'Your honour, I must . . .' continued the state's attorney, but he was interrupted by the court doors being flung open and Fletcher marching back down the aisle and up to the witness stand. He handed a copy of *For Whom the Bell Tolls* to Mrs Elliot, before turning to the judge.

'Your honour, would the court judicially note the length of time I was absent?' he said, handing over the stopwatch to the judge.

Judge Kravats pressed the stopper and, looking down at the stopwatch, said, 'Three minutes and forty-nine seconds.'

Fletcher turned his attention back to the defence witness. 'Mrs Elliot, I had enough time to leave the courthouse, walk to the public library on the other side of the street, locate the Hemingway shelf, check out a book with my library card, and still be back in the courtroom with eleven seconds to spare. But you didn't have enough time to walk across your bedroom, dial 911 and ask for assistance when you believed your husband might have been in mortal danger. And the reason you didn't is because you knew your husband had fired the first shot, and you were fearful of what he might have done.'

'But even if I did think that,' said Rebecca, losing her composure, 'it's only the second bullet that matters, the one that killed Ralph. Perhaps you've forgotten that the first bullet ended up in the ceiling, or are you now suggesting that my husband killed himself?'

'No I am not,' said Fletcher, 'so why don't you now tell the court exactly what you did when you heard the second shot.'

'I went to the top of the stairs and saw Mr Cartwright running out of the house.'

'But he didn't see you?'

'No, he only glanced back in my direction.'

'I don't think so, Mrs Elliot. I think you saw him very clearly when he calmly walked past you in the corridor.'

'He couldn't have walked passed me in the corridor because I was at the top of the stairs.'

'I agree that he couldn't have seen you if you had been at the top of the stairs,' said Fletcher as he returned to the table and selected a photograph, before walking back across to the witness stand. He passed the photograph over to her. 'As you will see from this picture, Mrs Elliot, anyone who left your husband's study, walked into the corridor and then out of the front door could not have been observed from the top of the stairs.' He paused so that the jury could take in the significance of his statement, before continuing, 'No, the truth is, Mrs Elliot, that you were not standing at the top of the stairs, but in the hallway when Mr Cartwright came out of your husband's study, and if you would like me to ask the judge to adjourn so that the jury can visit your home and check on the veracity of your statement, I would be quite happy to do so.'

'Well, I might have been half-way down the stairs.'

'You weren't even *on* the stairs Mrs Elliot, you were in the hallway, and you were not, as you also claimed, in your robe, but in a blue dress that you had worn to a cocktail party earlier that evening, which is why you didn't see the television debate!'

'I was in a robe and there's a picture of me to prove it.'

'Indeed there is,' said Fletcher, once again returning to the table and extracting another photograph, 'which I am happy to enter as evidence – item 122, your honour.'

The judge, prosecution team and the jury began to rummage through their files as Fletcher handed over his copy to Mrs Elliot.

'There you are,' she said, 'it's just as I told you, I'm sitting in the hallway in my robe.'

'You are indeed, Mrs Elliot, and that photograph was taken by the police photographer, and we've since had it enlarged so we can consider all the details more clearly. Your honour, I would like to submit this enlarged photograph as evidence.'

'Objection, your honour,' said Ebden leaping up from his place. 'We have not been given an opportunity to study this photograph.'

'It's state's evidence, Mr Ebden, and has been in your possession for weeks,' the judge reminded him. 'Your objection is overruled.'

'Please study the photograph carefully,' said Fletcher as he walked away from Mrs Elliot and passed the state's attorney a copy of the enlarged photo. A clerk handed one to each member of the jury. Fletcher then turned back to face Rebecca. 'And do tell the court what you see.'

'It's a photograph of me sitting in the hallway in my robe.'

'It is indeed, but what are your wearing on your left wrist and round your neck?' Fletcher asked, before turning to face the jury, all of whom were now studying the photograph intently.

The blood drained from Rebecca's face.

'I do believe they're your wristwatch and your pearl necklace,' said Fletcher answering his own question. 'Do you remember?' He paused. 'The ones you always locked away in your safe just before going to bed because there had been several burglaries in the area recently?' Fletcher turned to face Chief Culver and Detective Petrowski, who were seated in the front row. 'It is, as Detective Petrowski reminded us, the little mistakes that always reveal the amateur.' Fletcher turned back, and looked directly at

Rebecca, before adding, 'You may have forgotten to take off your watch and necklace, Mrs Elliot, but I can tell you something you didn't forget to take off, your dress.' Fletcher placed his hands on the jury box rail before saying slowly and without expression. 'Because you didn't do that until after you'd killed your husband.'

Several people rose at once, and the judge carried on banging his gavel before it was quiet enough for the state's attorney to say in a loud voice, 'Objection. How can wearing a wristwatch prove that Mrs Elliot murdered her husband?'

'I agree with you, Mr Ebden,' said the judge and turning to Fletcher suggested, 'That's quite a quantum leap, counsellor.'

'Then I will be happy to take the state's attorney through it step by step, your honour.' The judge nodded. 'When Mr Cartwright arrived at the house, he overheard an argument going on between Mr and Mrs Elliot, and after he'd knocked on the door, it was Mr Elliot who answered it, while Mrs Elliot was nowhere to be seen. I'm willing to accept that she did run up to the top of the stairs so that she could overhear what was going on while not being observed, but the moment the first shot was fired, she came back down into the corridor and listened to the quarrel taking place between her husband and my client. Three or four minutes later, Mr Cartwright walked calmly out of the study and passed Mrs Elliot in the corridor, before opening the front door. He looked back at Mrs Elliot, which is why he was able to tell the police questioning him later that night that she was wearing a low-cut blue dress and a string of pearls. If the jury study the photograph of Mrs Elliot, if I'm not mistaken, she is wearing the same string of pearls as the ones she has on today.' Rebecca touched her necklace as Fletcher continued. 'But don't let's rely on my client's word, but on your own statement, Mrs Elliot.' He turned another page of the state's evidence, before he began reading. 'I ran into the study, saw my husband's body slumped on the floor and then called the police.'

'That's right, I did ring Chief Culver at home, he's already confirmed that,' interjected Rebecca.

'But why did you call the chief of police first?'

'Because my husband had been murdered.'

'But in your evidence, Mrs Elliot, given to Detective Petrowski only moments after your husband's death, you stated that you saw Ralph slumped in the corner of his study, blood coming from his mouth, and immediately called the chief of police.'

'Yes, that's exactly what I did,' shouted Rebecca.

Fletcher paused before turning to face the jury. 'If I saw my wife slumped in a corner with blood coming from her mouth, the first thing I would do is to check to see if she was still alive and, if she was, I wouldn't call for the police, I'd call for an ambulance. And at no time did you call for an ambulance, Mrs Elliot. Why? Because you already knew that your husband was dead.'

Once again there was uproar in the body of the court, and the reporters who weren't old-fashioned enough to take shorthand struggled to get down every word.

'Mrs Elliot,' continued Fletcher, once the judge had stopped banging his gavel, 'allow me to repeat the words you said only a few moments ago when questioned by the state's attorney.' Fletcher picked up one of the yellow pads from his desk and began reading. '"I suddenly felt cold and sick in the stomach, and I thought I was going to faint. I staggered back out into the corridor and collapsed on the floor."' Fletcher threw the notepad down on his desk, stared at Mrs Elliot and said, 'You still haven't even bothered to check if your husband is alive, but you

538

didn't need to, did you, because you knew he was dead; after all, it was you who had killed him.'

'Then why didn't they find any traces of gunpowder residue on my robe?' Rebecca shouted above the banging of the judge's gavel.

'Because when you shot your husband, you weren't in your robe, Mrs Elliot, but still in the blue dress you'd been wearing that evening. It was only after you had killed Ralph that you ran upstairs to change into your nightgown and robe. But unfortunately Detective Petrowski switched on his car siren, broke the speed limit, and managed to be with you six minutes later, which is why you had to rush back downstairs, forgetting to take off your watch or pearls. And even more damning, not leaving yourself enough time to close the front door. If, as you have claimed, Mr Cartwright had killed your husband, and then run out of the door, the first thing you would have done would be to make sure that it was closed so he couldn't get back in to harm you. But Detective Petrowski, conscientious man that he is, arrived a little too quickly for you, and even remarked how surprised he was to find the front door open. Amateurs often panic, and that's when they make simple mistakes,' he repeated almost in a whisper. 'Because the truth is that once Mr Cartwright had walked past you in the hallway, you then ran into the study, picked up the gun and realized this was a perfect opportunity to be rid of a husband you'd despised for years. The shot Mr Cartwright heard as he was driving away from the house was indeed the bullet that killed your husband, but it wasn't Mr Cartwright who pulled the trigger, it was you. What Mr Cartwright did do was give you the perfect alibi, and a solution to all your problems.' He paused and, turning away from the jury, added, 'If only you had remembered to remove your wristwatch and pearls before you came downstairs, closed the front door and then phoned for an ambulance, rather than the chief of police, you would have committed the perfect murder, and my client would be facing the death penalty.'

'I didn't kill him.'

'Then who did? Because it can't have been Mr Cartwright, as he left some time *before* the second shot was fired. I feel sure you recall his words when confronted by the chief – "he was still alive when I left him", and by the way, Mr Cartwright didn't find it necessary to change out of the suit he'd been wearing earlier that evening.' Once again Fletcher turned to face the jury, but they were now all staring at Mrs Elliot.

She buried her head in her hands and whispered, 'Ralph's the one who should be on trial. He was responsible for his own death.'

However firmly Judge Kravats called the court to order, it was still some time before he was able to restore calm. Fletcher waited until he had complete silence, before he delivered his next sentence.

'But how is that possible, Mrs Elliot?' he asked. 'After all, it was Detective Petrowski who pointed out that it's quite difficult to shoot yourself from four feet away.'

'He made me do it.'

Ebden leapt to his feet as the public began repeating the sentence to each other.

'Objection, your honour, the witness is being . . .'

'Overruled,' said Judge Kravats firmly. 'Sit down, Mr Ebden, and remain seated.' The judge turned his attention back to the witness. 'What did you mean, Mrs Elliot, by "he made me do it"?'

Rebecca turned to the judge, who looked down at her with concern. 'You honour, Ralph was desperate to win the election at any cost, and after Nat told him that Luke had committed suicide, he knew he no longer had any hope of becoming governor. He kept pacing around the room repeating the words, "I will still kill you", then he snapped his fingers and said, "I've got the solution, you're going to have to do it".'

'What did he mean by that?' asked the judge.

'To begin with I didn't understand myself, your honour, then he started shouting at me. He said, "There's no time to argue, otherwise he'll get away, and then we'll never be able to pin it on him, so I'll tell you exactly what you're going to do. First, you'll shoot me in the shoulder, and then you'll call the chief at home and tell him that you were in the bedroom when you heard the first shot. You came rushing downstairs when you heard the second shot, and that's when you saw Cartwright running out of the front door."'

'But why did you agree to go along with this outrageous suggestion?' asked the judge.

'I didn't,' said Rebecca. 'I told him if there was any shooting to be done, he could do it himself, because I wasn't going to get involved.'

'And what did he say to that?' asked the judge.

'That he couldn't shoot himself because the police would be able to work that out, but if I did it, they would never know.'

'But that still doesn't explain why you agreed to go through with it?'

'I didn't,' repeated Rebecca quietly. 'I told him I would have nothing to do with it, Nat had never done me any harm. But then Ralph grabbed the gun and said, "If you're not willing to go through with it, then there's only one alternative, I'll have to shoot you." I was terrified, but all he said was, "I'll tell everyone that it was Nat Cartwright who killed my wife when she tried to come to my rescue, then they'll be even more sympathetic when I play the part of the grieving widower." He laughed, and added, "Don't think I wouldn't do it." He then took a handkerchief out of his pocket and said, "Wrap this around your hand, so your fingerprints won't be on the gun."' Rebecca was silent for some time before she whispered, 'I remember picking up the gun and pointing it at Ralph's shoulder, but I closed my eyes just as I pulled the trigger. When I opened them, Ralph was slumped in the corner. I didn't need to check to know that he was dead. I panicked, dropped the gun, ran upstairs and called the chief at home just as Ralph had told me to. Then I started to undress. I'd just put on my robe when I heard the siren. I looked through the curtains and saw a police car turning into the driveway. I ran back downstairs as the car was pulling up outside the house, which didn't leave me enough time to close the front door. I slumped down in the hallway just before Detective Petrowski came rushing in.' She bowed her head and this time the weeping was genuine and unrehearsed. Whispering turned to chattering as everyone in the courtroom began to discuss Rebecca's testimony.

Fletcher turned to face the state's attorney, who was in a huddle, consulting his team. He made no attempt to hurry them, and returned to take his seat next to Nat. It was some time before Ebden eventually rose from his place. 'Your honour.'

'Yes, Mr Ebden?' said the judge.

'The state withdraws all charges against the defendant.' He paused for some time. 'On a personal note,' he added as he turned to face Nat and Fletcher, 'having watched you as a team, I can't wait to see what will happen when you're up against each other.'

Spontaneous applause broke out from the public benches, and the noise was such that they did not hear the judge release the prisoner, dismiss the jury, and declare the case closed.

Nat leant across and almost had to shout, 'Thank you,' before adding, 'two inadequate words as I'll spend the rest of my life in your debt without ever being able to properly repay you. But nevertheless, thank you.'

Fletcher smiled. 'Clients,' he said, 'fall into two categories; those you hope never to see again, and just occasionally those who you know will be friends for the rest . . .'

Su Ling suddenly appeared by her husband's side and threw her arms around him.

'Thank God,' she said.

'Governor will do,' said Fletcher, as Nat and Su Ling laughed for the first time in weeks. Before Nat could respond, Lucy came bursting through the barrier and greeted her father with the words, 'Well done, Dad, I'm very proud of you.'

'Praise indeed,' said Fletcher. 'Nat, this is my daughter Lucy, who fortunately isn't yet old enough to vote for you, but if she were . . .' Fletcher looked around, 'so where's the woman who caused all this trouble in the first place?'

'Mom's at home,' replied Lucy. 'After all, you did tell her it would be at least another week before Mr Cartwright would be on the stand.'

'True,' said Fletcher.

'And please pass on my thanks to your wife,' said Su Ling. 'We will always remember that it was Annie who persuaded you to represent my husband. Perhaps we can all get together in the near future, and . . .'

'Not until after the election,' said Fletcher firmly, 'as I'm still hoping that at least one member of my family will be voting for me.' He paused, and turning to Nat said, 'Do you know the real reason I worked so hard on this case?'

'You couldn't face the thought of having to spend the next few weeks with Barbara Hunter,' said Nat.

'Something like that,' he said, with a smile.

Fletcher was about to go across and shake hands with the state's team, but stopped in his tracks when he saw Rebecca Elliot still sitting in the witness stand waiting for the court to clear. Her head was bowed, and she looked forlorn and lonely.

'I know it's hard to believe,' said Fletcher, 'but I actually feel sorry for her.'

'You should,' said Nat, 'because one thing's for certain, Ralph Elliot would have murdered his wife if he had thought it would win him the election.'

BOOK SIX

REVELATION

49

FLETCHER SAT IN his Senate office reading the morning papers the day after the trial.

'What an ungrateful lot,' he said, passing the *Hartford Courant* across to his daughter.

'You should have left him to fry,' said Lucy as she glanced at the latest opinion poll figures.

'Expressed with your usual elegance and charm,' said Fletcher. 'It does make me wonder if all the money I've spent sending you to Hotchkiss has been worthwhile, not to mention what Vassar is going to cost me.'

'I may not be going to Vassar, Dad,' said Lucy in a quieter voice.

'Is that what you wanted to talk to me about?' asked Fletcher, picking up on his daughter's change of tone.

'Yes, Dad, because even though Vassar has offered me a place, I may not be able to take it up.'

Fletcher couldn't always be certain when Lucy was kidding and when she was serious, but as she had asked to see him in his office and not to mention the meeting to Annie, he had to assume she was in earnest. 'What's the problem?' he asked quietly, looking across the desk at her.

Lucy didn't meet his stare. She bowed her head and said, 'I'm pregnant.'

Fletcher didn't reply immediately as he tried to take in his daughter's confession. 'Is George the father?' he eventually asked.

'Yes,' she replied.

'And are you going to marry him?'

Lucy thought about the question for some time before replying. 'No,' she said. 'I adore George, but I don't love him.'

'But you were willing to let him make love to you.'

'That's not fair,' said Lucy. 'It was the Saturday night after the election for president, and I'm afraid we both had a little too much to drink. To be honest, I was sick of being described by everyone in my class as the virgin president. And if I had to lose my virginity, I couldn't think of anyone nicer than George, especially after he admitted that he was also a virgin. In the end I'm not sure who seduced who.'

'How does George feel about all this? After all, it's his child as well as yours and he struck me as rather a serious young man, especially when it came to his feelings for you.'

'He doesn't know yet.'

'You haven't told him?' said Fletcher in disbelief.

'No.'

'How about your mother?'

'No,' she repeated. 'The only person I've shared this with is you.' This time she did look her father in the eye, before adding, 'Let's face it, Dad, Mom was probably still a virgin on the day you married her.'

'And so was I,' said Fletcher, 'but you're going to have to let her know before it becomes obvious to everyone.'

'Not if I were to have an abortion.'

Again Fletcher remained silent for some time, before saying, 'Is that what you really want?'

'Yes, Dad, but please don't tell Mom, because she wouldn't understand.'

'I'm not sure I do myself,' said Fletcher.

'Are you pro-women's choice for everyone except your daughter?' asked Lucy.

–◇–

'It won't last,' said Nat, staring at the headline in the *Hartford Courant*.

'What won't?' said Su Ling as she poured him another coffee.

'My seven-point lead in the polls. In a few weeks' time the electorate won't even remember which one of us was on trial.'

'I guess *she'll* still remember,' said Su Ling quietly as she glanced over her husband's shoulder at a photograph of Rebecca Elliot walking down the courtroom steps, every hair no longer in place. 'Why did she ever marry him?' she said almost to herself.

'I'm just thankful it wasn't me who married Rebecca,' said Nat. 'Let's face it, if Elliot hadn't copied my thesis and prevented me going to Yale we would never have met, to start with,' said Nat, taking his wife's hand.

'I just wish I'd been able to have more children,' said Su Ling, her voice still subdued. 'I miss Luke so much.'

'I know,' said Nat, 'but I'll never regret running up that particular hill, at that particular time, on that particular day.'

'And I'm glad I took the wrong path,' said Su Ling, 'because I couldn't love you any more. But I'd have willingly given up my life if it would have meant saving Luke's.'

'I suspect that would be true of most parents,' said Nat, looking at his wife, 'and you could certainly include your mother, who sacrificed everything for you, and doesn't deserve to have been treated so cruelly.'

'Don't worry about my mother,' said Su Ling, snapping out of her maudlin mood. 'I went round to see her yesterday only to find the shop packed with dirty old men bringing in their even dirtier laundry, secretly hoping that she's running a massage parlour upstairs.'

Nat burst out laughing. 'And to think we kept it secret for all those years. I would certainly never have believed that the day would come when I would be able to laugh about it.'

'She says if you become governor, she's going to open a string of shops right across the state. Her advertising slogan will be "we wash your dirty linen in public".'

'I always knew that there was some overriding reason I still needed to be governor,' said Nat as he rose from the table.

'And who has the privilege of your company today?' asked Su Ling.

'The good folk of New Canaan,' said Nat.

'So when will you be home?'

'Just after midnight would be my guess.'

'Wake me,' she said.

—◦—

'Hi, Lucy,' said Jimmy as he strolled into her father's office. 'Is the great man free?'

'Yes, he is,' said Lucy as she rose from her chair.

Jimmy glanced back as she slipped out of the room. Was it his imagination or had she been crying? Fletcher didn't speak until she'd closed the door. 'Good morning, Jimmy,' he said as he pushed the paper to one side, leaving the photograph of Rebecca staring up at him.

'Do you think they'll arrest her?' asked Jimmy.

Fletcher glanced back down at the photograph of Rebecca. 'I don't think they've been left with much choice, but if I were sitting on a jury I would acquit, because I found her story totally credible.'

'Yes, but then you know what Elliot was capable of. A jury doesn't.'

'But I can hear him saying, *If you won't do it, then I'll have to kill you, and don't think I wouldn't.*'

'I wonder if you would have remained at Alexander Dupont and Bell if Elliot hadn't joined the firm.'

'One of those twists of fate,' said Fletcher, as if his mind was on something else. 'So what have you got lined up for me?'

'We're going to spend the day in Madison.'

'Is Madison worth a whole day?' asked Fletcher, 'when it's such a solid Republican district?'

'Which is precisely why I'm getting it out of the way while there's still a few weeks to go,' said Jimmy, 'though ironically their votes have never influenced the outcome of the election.'

'A vote's a vote,' said Fletcher.

'Not in this particular case,' said Jimmy, 'because while the rest of the state now votes electronically, Madison remains the single exception. They are among the last districts in the country who still prefer to mark their ballots with a pencil.'

'But that doesn't stop their votes being valid, ' insisted Fletcher.

'True, but in the past those votes have proved irrelevant, because they don't begin the count until the morning after the election, when the overall result has already been declared. It's a bit of a farce, but one of those traditions that the good burghers of Madison are unwilling to sacrifice on the altar of modern technology.'

'And you still want me to spend a whole day there?'

'Yes, because if the majority were less than five thousand, suddenly Madison would become the most important town in the state.'

'Do you think it could be that close while Bush still has a record lead in the polls?'

'Still is the operative word, because Clinton's chipping away at that lead every day, so who knows who'll end up in the White House, or in the governor's mansion for that matter?'

Fletcher didn't comment.

'You seem a little preoccupied this morning,' said Jimmy. 'Anything else on your mind that you want to discuss with me?'

—◦—

'It looks as if Nat's going to win by a mile,' said Julia from behind the morning paper.

'A British prime minister once said that "a week's a long time in politics", and we've still got several more of them left before the first vote is cast,' Tom reminded his wife.

'If Nat becomes governor, you'll miss all the excitement. After all you two have been through, returning to Fairchild's may turn out to be something of an anti-climax.'

'The truth is that I lost any interest in banking the day Russell's was taken over.'

'But you're about to become chairman of the biggest bank in the state.'

'Not if Nat wins the election, I won't,' said Tom.

Julia pushed the paper aside. 'I'm not sure I understand.'

'Nat has asked me to be his chief of staff if he becomes governor.'

'Then who will take over as chairman of the bank?'

'You, of course,' said Tom. 'Everyone knows you'd be the best person for the job.'

'But Fairchild's would never appoint a woman as chairman, they're far too traditional.'

552

'We're living in the last decade of the twentieth century Julia, and thanks to you, nearly half our customers are women. And as for the board, not to mention the staff, in my absence most of them think you already *are* the chairman.'

'But if Nat were to lose, he'll quite rightly expect to return to Fairchild's as chairman, with you as his deputy, in which case the question becomes somewhat academic.'

'I wouldn't be so sure of that,' said Tom, 'don't forget that Jimmy Overman, Connecticut's senior senator, has already announced that he'll not be running for re-election next year, in which case Nat would be the obvious choice to replace him. Whichever one of them becomes governor, I feel sure the other will be going to Washington as the state's senator.' He paused. 'I suspect it will only be a matter of time before Nat and Fletcher run against each other for president.'

'Do you believe I can do the job?' asked Julia quietly.

'No,' said Tom, 'you have to be born in America before you can stand for president.'

'I didn't mean president, you idiot, but chairman of Fairchild's.'

'I knew that the day we met,' said Tom. 'My only fear was that you wouldn't consider I was good enough to be your husband.'

'Oh, men are so slow on the uptake,' said Julia. 'I made up my mind that I was going to marry you the night we met at Su Ling and Nat's dinner party.' Tom's mouth opened and then closed.

'How different my life would have been if the other Julia Kirkbridge had come to the same conclusion,' she added.

'Not to mention mine,' said Tom.

50

FLETCHER STARED DOWN at the cheering crowd and waved enthusiastically back at them. He had made seven speeches in Madison that day – on street corners, in market places, outside a library – but even he had been surprised by his reception at the final meeting in the town hall that night.

COME AND HEAR THE WINNER was printed in bold red and blue letters on a massive banner that stretched from one side of the stage to the other. Fletcher had smiled when the local chairman told him that Paul Holbourn, the independent mayor of Madison, had left the banner in place after Nat had spoken at the town hall earlier that week. Holbourn had been the mayor for fourteen years, and didn't keep getting re-elected because he squandered the tax payers' money.

When Fletcher sat down at the end of his speech, he could feel the adrenalin pumping through his body, and the standing ovation that followed was not the usual stage-managed affair, where a bunch of well-placed party hacks leap up the moment the candidate has delivered his last line. On this occasion, the public were on their feet at the same time as the hacks. He only wished Annie could have been there to witness it.

When the chairman held up Fletcher's hand and shouted into the microphone, 'Ladies and gentlemen, I give you the next governor of Connecticut,' Fletcher believed it for the first time. Clinton was neck and neck with Bush in the national polls and Perot's independent candidacy was further chipping away at the Republican's support. It was creating a knock-on effect for Fletcher. He only hoped that four weeks was enough time to make up the four-point deficit in the polls.

It was another half hour before the hall was cleared, and by then Fletcher had shaken every proffered hand. A satisfied chairman accompanied him back to the parking lot.

'You don't have a driver?' he said, sounding a little surprised.

'Lucy took the night off to see *My Cousin Vinny*, Annie's attending some charity meeting, Jimmy's chairing a fund raiser, and as it was less than fifty miles, I felt I could just about manage that by myself,' explained Fletcher as he jumped behind the wheel.

He drove away from the town hall on a high, and began to relax for the first time that day. But he'd only driven a few hundred yards before his thoughts returned to Lucy, as they had done whenever he was alone. He faced a considerable dilemma. Should he should tell Annie that their daughter was pregnant?

—◆—

Nat was having a private dinner with four local industrialists that night. Between them they were in a position to make a significant contribution to the campaign coffers, so he didn't hurry them. During the evening they had left him in no doubt what they expected from a Republican governor, and although they didn't always go along with some of Nat's more liberal ideas, a Democrat wasn't moving into the governor's mansion if they had anything to do with it.

It was well past midnight when Ed Chambers of Chambers Foods suggested that perhaps the candidate should be allowed to go home and get a good night's sleep. Nat couldn't remember when he'd last had one of those.

This was the usual cue for Tom to stand up, agree with whoever had made the suggestion, and then go off in search of Nat's coat. Nat would then look as if he was being dragged away, shaking hands with his hosts before telling them that he couldn't hope to win the election without their support. Flattering though the sentiment might sound, on this occasion it also had the merit of being true.

All four men accompanied Nat back to his car, and as Tom drove down the long winding drive from Ed Chambers's home, Nat tuned into the late news. Fletcher's speech to the citizens of Madison was the fourth item, and the local reporter was highlighting some of the points he'd made about neighbourhood watch schemes, an idea Nat had been promoting for months. Nat began to grumble about such blatant plagiarism until Tom reminded him that he'd also stolen some of Fletcher's innovations on education reform.

Nat switched off the news when the weather forecaster returned to warn them about patchy ice on the roads. Within minutes Nat had fallen asleep, a trick Tom had often wished he could emulate, because the moment Nat woke, he was always back firing on all cylinders. Tom was also looking forward to a decent night's sleep. They didn't have any official function before ten the following morning, when they would attend the first of seven religious services, ending the day with evensong at St Joseph's Cathedral.

He knew that Fletcher Davenport would be covering roughly the same circuit in another part of the state. By the end of the campaign, there wouldn't be a religious gathering where they hadn't knelt down, taken off their shoes, or covered their heads in order to prove that they were both God-fearing citizens. Even if it wasn't necessarily their own particular God being revered, they had at least demonstrated willingness to stand, sit and kneel in His presence.

Tom decided not to switch on the one o'clock news, as he could see no purpose in waking Nat only to hear a regurgitation of what they had listened to thirty minutes before.

They both missed the newsflash.

◄○►

An ambulance was on the scene within minutes, and the first thing the paramedics did was to call in the fire department. The driver was pinned against the steering wheel, they reported, and there was no way of prying open his door without the use of an acetylene torch. They would have to work quickly if they hoped to get the injured man out of the wreck alive.

It wasn't until the police had checked the licence plate on their computer back at headquarters that they realized who it was trapped behind the wheel. As they felt it was unlikely that the senator had been drinking, they assumed he must have fallen asleep. There were no skid marks on the road and no other vehicles involved.

The paramedics radioed ahead to the hospital, and when they learnt the identity of the victim the duty physician decided to page Ben Renwick. Remembering his seniority, Renwick didn't expect to be woken if there was another surgeon available to do the job.

'How many other people in the car?' was Dr Renwick's first question.

'Only the senator,' came back the immediate reply.

'What the hell was he doing driving himself at that time of night?' muttered Renwick rhetorically. 'What's the extent of his injuries?'

'Several broken bones, including at least three ribs and the left ankle,' said the duty physician, 'but I'm more worried about the loss of blood. It took the fire boys nearly an hour to cut him out of the wreck.'

'OK, make sure my team is scrubbed up and ready by the time I arrive. I'll call Mrs Davenport.' He hesitated for a moment. 'Come to think of it,' he said, 'I'll call both Mrs Davenports.'

—◦—

Annie was standing in the biting wind by the hospital emergency entrance when she saw the ambulance speeding towards her. It was the accompanying police outriders that made her think that it had to be her husband. Although Fletcher was still unconscious, they allowed her to clutch on to his limp hand as they wheeled him through to the operating room. When Annie first saw the condition Fletcher was in, she didn't believe anyone could save him.

Why had she attended that charity meeting when she should have been in Madison with her husband? Whenever she was with Fletcher, she always drove him home. Why had she ignored his protestations when he'd insisted that he'd enjoy the drive – it would give him some time to think, and in any case, it was such a short distance, he'd added. He'd only been five miles from home when he'd driven off the road.

Ruth Davenport arrived at the hospital a few moments later, and immediately set about finding out as much as she could. Once she had spoken to the duty administrator, Ruth was able to reassure Annie of one thing. 'Fletcher couldn't be in better hands than Ben Renwick's. He's quite simply the best in the state.' What she didn't tell her daughter-in-law was that they only got him out of bed when the odds of pulling a patient through were low. Ben Renwick wasn't a betting man.

Martha Gates was the next to arrive, and Ruth repeated everything that she'd picked up. She confirmed that Fletcher had three broken ribs, a broken ankle, and a ruptured spleen, but it was the loss of blood that was causing the professionals to be anxious.

'But surely a hospital as large as St Patrick's has a big enough blood bank to cope with that sort of problem?'

'Yes would be the usual answer,' replied Ruth, 'but Fletcher is AB negative, the rarest of all the blood groups, and although we've always maintained a small reserve stock, when that school bus careered off Route 95 in New London last month and the driver and his son turned out to be AB negative, Fletcher was the first to insist that the entire batch should be shipped out to the New London hospital immediately, and we just haven't had enough time to replace it.'

An arc lamp was switched on and lit up the hospital entrance. 'The vultures have arrived,' said Ruth, looking out of the window. She turned and faced her daughter-in-law. 'Annie, I think you should talk to them, it just might be our only chance of locating a blood donor in time.'

◄○►

When she rose on Sunday morning, Su Ling decided not to wake Nat until the last possible moment; after all, she had no idea what time it was when he'd crept into bed.

She sat in the kitchen, made herself some fresh coffee, and began to scan the morning papers. Fletcher's speech seemed to have been well received by the citizens of

Madison, and the latest opinion poll showed the gap between them had narrowed by another point bringing Nat's lead down to three per cent.

Su Ling sipped her coffee and pushed the paper to one side. She always switched on the television just before the hour to catch the weather forecast. The first person to appear on the screen even before the sound came on was Annie Davenport. Why was she standing outside St Patrick's, Su Ling wondered? Was Fletcher announcing some new health care initiative? Sixty seconds later she knew exactly why. She dashed out of the kitchen and up the stairs to wake Nat and tell him the news. A remarkable coincidence. Or was it? As a scientist, Su Ling gave scant credence to coincidence. But she had no time to consider that now.

A sleepy Nat listened as his wife repeated what Annie Davenport had just said. Suddenly he was wide awake, leapt out of bed and quickly threw on yesterday's clothes, not bothering to shave or shower. Once dressed, he ran downstairs, pulling on his shoes only when he was in the car. Su Ling was already behind the wheel with the engine running. She took off the moment Nat slammed the car door.

The radio was still tuned into the 24-hour news station, and Nat listened to the latest bulletin while trying to tie up his laces. The on-the-spot reporter couldn't have been more explicit: Senator Davenport was on a ventilator, and if someone didn't donate four pints of AB negative blood within hours, the hospital feared for his survival.

It took Su Ling twelve minutes to reach St Patrick's by simply ignoring the speed limit – not that there was a lot of traffic on the road at that time on a Sunday morning. Nat ran into the hospital while Su Ling went in search of a parking space.

Nat spotted Annie at the end of the corridor and

immediately called out her name. She turned and looked startled when she saw him charging towards her. *Why was he running?* was her first reaction.

'I came just as soon as I heard,' shouted Nat, still on the move, but all three women just continued to stare at him, like rabbits caught in a headlight. 'I'm the same blood group as Fletcher,' Nat blurted out as he came to a halt by Annie's side.

'You're AB negative?' said Annie in disbelief.

'Sure am,' said Nat.

'Thank God,' said Martha. Ruth quickly disappeared into the intensive care unit, and returned a moment later with Ben Renwick by her side.

'Mr Cartwright,' he said thrusting out his hand, 'My name is Dr Renwick, and I'm . . .'

'The hospital's senior consultant, yes, I know you by reputation,' said Nat, shaking his hand.

The surgeon gave a slight bow. 'We have a technician ready to take your blood . . .'

'Then let's get on with it,' said Nat, pulling off his jacket.

'To begin with we'll need to run some tests and check if your blood is an exact match, and then screen it for HIV and hepatitis B.'

'Not a problem,' said Nat.

'But I'm afraid, Mr Cartwright, I'll also need at least three pints of your blood if Senator Davenport is to have any chance of survival, and that will require several indemnity forms signed in the presence of a lawyer.'

'Why a lawyer?' asked Nat.

'Because there's an outside chance you might suffer severe side effects, and in any case, you'll end up feeling pretty weak yourself, and it may prove necessary to keep you in the hospital for several days just to administer extra fluids.'

'Are there no extremes that Fletcher will not go to to keep me off the campaign trail?'

All three women smiled for the first time that day as Renwick quickly led Nat off to his office. Nat turned round to speak to Annie, to find her being comforted by Su Ling.

'Now I have another problem to consider,' admitted Renwick as he took a seat behind his desk and began sorting through some forms.

'I'll sign anything,' repeated Nat.

'You can't sign the form I have in mind,' said the consultant.

'Why not?' asked Nat.

'Because it's an absentee ballot, and I'm no longer certain which one of you to vote for.'

51

'LOSING THREE PINTS of blood doesn't seem to have slowed down Mr Cartwright,' said the duty nurse as she placed his latest chart in front of Dr Renwick.

'Maybe not,' said Renwick, flicking through the pages, 'but it sure made one hell of a difference to Senator Davenport. It saved his life.'

'True,' said the nurse, 'but I've warned the senator that despite the election, he'll have to stay put for at least another two weeks.'

'I wouldn't bet on that,' said Renwick, 'I anticipate that Fletcher will have discharged himself by the end of the week.'

'You could be right,' said the nurse with a sigh, 'but what can I do to prevent it?'

'Nothing,' said Renwick, turning over the file on his desk so that she couldn't read the names Nathaniel and Peter Cartwright printed in the top right corner. 'But I do need you to make an appointment for me to see both men as soon as possible.'

'Yes, doctor,' replied the nurse making a note on her clipboard before leaving the room.

Once the door was closed, Ben Renwick turned the file back over and read through its contents once again. He'd thought about little else for the past three days.

When he left later that evening, he locked the file away in his private safe. After all, a few more days wouldn't make a great deal of difference, after all what he needed to discuss with the two men had remained a secret for the past forty-three years.

—◦—

Nat was discharged from St Patrick's on Thursday evening, and no one on the hospital staff imagined for a moment that Fletcher would still be around by the weekend, despite his mother trying to convince him that he should take it easy. He reminded her there were now only two weeks to go before election day.

During the longest week in his life, Ben Renwick continued to wrestle with his conscience, just as Dr Greenwood must have done forty-three years before him, but Renwick had come to a different conclusion; he felt he'd been left with no choice but to tell both men the truth.

The two combatants agreed to meet at six a.m. on Tuesday morning in Dr Renwick's office. It was the only time before election day that both candidates had a clear hour in their diaries.

—◦—

Nat was the first to arrive, as he had hoped to be in Waterbury for a nine o'clock meeting, and perhaps even squeeze in a visit to a couple of commuter stations on the way.

Fletcher hobbled into Dr Renwick's office at five fifty-eight, annoyed that Nat had made it before him.

'Just as soon as I get this cast off,' he said, 'I'm going to kick your ass.'

'You shouldn't speak to Dr Renwick like that, after all he's done for you,' said Nat, with a grin.

'Why not?' asked Fletcher. 'He filled me up with your blood, so now I'm half the man I was.'

'Wrong again,' said Nat. 'You're twice the man you were, but still half the man I am.'

'Children, children,' said the doctor, suddenly realizing the significance of his words, 'there is something a little more serious that I need to discuss with you.'

Both men fell silent after hearing the tone in which they had been admonished.

Dr Renwick came from behind his desk to unlock his safe. He removed a file and placed it on the desk. 'I have spent several days trying to work out just how I should go about imparting such confidential information to you both.' He tapped the file with his right index finger. 'Information that would never have come to my attention had it not been for the senator's near-fatal accident and the necessity to check both your files.' Nat and Fletcher glanced at each other, but said nothing. 'Even whether to tell you separately or together became an ethical issue, and at least on that, it will now be obvious what decision I came to.' The two candidates still said nothing. 'I have only one request, that the information I am about to divulge should remain a secret, unless both of you, I repeat, both of you, are willing, even determined, to make it public.'

'I have no problem with that,' said Fletcher, turning to face Nat.

'Neither do I,' said Nat, 'I am after all, in the presence of my lawyer.'

'Even if it were to influence the outcome of the election?' the doctor added, ignoring Nat's levity. Both men hesitated for a moment, but once again nodded. 'Let me make it clear that what I am about to reveal is not a possibility or even a probability; it is quite simply beyond dispute.' The doctor opened the file and glanced down at a birth certificate and a death certificate.

'Senator Davenport and Mr Cartwright,' he said, as if addressing two people he'd never met before, 'I have to inform you that, having checked and double-checked both your DNA samples, there can be no questioning the scientific evidence that you are not only brothers,' he paused, his eyes returning to the birth certificate, 'but dizygotic twins.' Dr Renwick remained silent as he allowed the significance of his statement to sink in.

Nat recalled those days when he still needed to rush to a dictionary to check the meaning of a word. Fletcher was the first to break the silence. 'Which means we're not identical.'

'Correct,' said Dr Renwick, 'the assumption that twins must look alike has always been a myth, mainly perpetrated by romantic novelists.'

'But, that doesn't explain . . .' began Nat.

'Should you wish to know the answer to any other questions you might have,' said Dr Renwick, 'including who are your natural parents, and how you became separated, I am only too happy that you should study this file at your leisure.' Dr Renwick tapped the open file in front of him once again.

Neither man responded immediately. It was some time before Fletcher said. 'I don't need to see the contents of the file.'

It was Dr Renwick's turn to register surprise.

'There's nothing I don't know about Nat Cartwright,' Fletcher explained, 'including the details of the tragic death of his brother.'

Nat nodded. 'My mother still keeps a picture of both of us by her bedside, and often talks of my brother Peter and what he might have grown up to be.' He paused and looked at Fletcher. 'She would have been proud of the man who saved his brother's life. But I do have one question,' he added, turning back to face Dr Renwick, 'I need to ask if Mrs Davenport is aware that Fletcher isn't her son?'

'Not that I know of,' replied Renwick.

'What makes you so sure?' asked Fletcher.

'Because among the many items I came across in this file was a letter from the doctor who delivered you both. He left instructions that it was only to be opened if a dispute should arise concerning your birth that might harm the hospital's reputation. And that letter states that there was only one other person who knew the truth, other than Dr Greenwood.'

'Who was that?' asked Nat and Fletcher simultaneously.

Dr Renwick paused while he turned another page in his file. 'A Miss Heather Nichol, but as she and Dr Greenwood have since died, there's no way of confirming it.'

'She was my nanny,' said Fletcher, 'and from what I can remember of her, she would have done anything to please my mother.' He turned to look at Nat. 'However, I would still prefer that my parents never find out the truth.'

'I have no problem with that,' said Nat. 'What purpose can be served by putting our parents through such an unnecessary ordeal? If Mrs Davenport became aware that Fletcher was not her son, and my mother were to discover that Peter had never died, and she had been deprived of the chance of bringing up both of her children, the distress and turmoil that would quite obviously follow doesn't bear thinking about.'

'I agree,' said Fletcher. 'My parents are now both nearly eighty, so why resurrect such ghosts of the past?' He paused for some time. 'Though I confess I can only wonder how different our lives might have been, had I ended up in your crib, and you in mine,' he said, looking at Nat.

'We'll never know,' Nat replied. 'However, one thing remains certain.'

'What's that?' asked Fletcher.

'I would still be the next governor of Connecticut.'

'What makes you so confident of that?' asked Fletcher.

'I had a head start on you and have remained in the lead ever since. After all, I've been on earth six minutes longer than you.'

'A tiny disadvantage from which I had fully recovered within the hour.'

'Children, children,' admonished Ben Renwick a second time. Both men laughed as the doctor closed the file in front of him. 'Then we are in agreement that any evidence proving your relationship should be destroyed and never referred to again.'

'Agreed,' said Fletcher without hesitation.

'Never referred to again,' repeated Nat.

Both men watched as Dr Renwick opened the file and first extracted a birth certificate which he placed firmly into the shredder. Neither spoke as they watched each piece of evidence disappear. The birth certificate was followed by a three-page letter dated 11 May 1949, signed by Dr Greenwood. After that came several internal hospital documents and memos, all stamped 1949. Dr Renwick continued to place them one by one through the shredder until all he was left with was an empty file. On top were printed the names *Nathaniel and Peter Cartwright*. He tore the file into four pieces before offering the final vestige of proof to the waiting teeth of the shredder.

Fletcher rose unsteadily from his place, and turned to shake hands with his brother. 'See you in the governor's mansion.'

'You sure will,' said Nat, taking him in his arms. 'The first thing I'll do is put in a wheelchair ramp so you can visit me regularly.'

'Well, I have to go,' said Fletcher, turning to shake hands with Ben Renwick. 'I've got an election to win.' He hobbled towards the door, trying to reach it before Nat, but his brother jumped in front and held it open for him.

'I was brought up to open doors for women, senior citizens and invalids,' explained Nat.

'And you can now add future governors to that list,' said Fletcher, hobbling through.

'Have you read my paper on disability benefits?' asked Nat, as he caught up with him.

'No,' Fletcher replied, 'I've never bothered with impractical ideas that could never reach the statute books.'

'You know, I will regret only one thing,' said Nat, once they were alone in the corridor and could no longer be overheard by Dr Renwick.

'Let me guess,' said Fletcher as he waited for the next quip.

'I think you would have been one hell of a brother to grow up with.'

52

DR RENWICK'S PREDICTION turned out to be accurate. Senator Davenport had discharged himself from St Patrick's by the weekend, and a fortnight later no one would have believed he had been within hours of dying only a month before.

With only a few days left before the election, Clinton went further ahead in the national polls as Perot continued to eat into Bush's support. Both Nat and Fletcher went on travelling round the state at a pace that would have impressed an Olympic athlete. Neither waited for the other to challenge them to a debate, and when one of the local television companies suggested they should face each other in three encounters, both accepted without needing any persuasion.

It was universally agreed that Fletcher came off better in the first duel, and the polls confirmed that impression when he went into the lead for the first time. Nat immediately cut down on his travel commitments, and spent several hours in a mocked-up television studio being coached by his staff. It paid off, because even the local Democrats conceded that he had won the second round, when the polls put him back into the lead.

So much rested on the final debate that both men became over anxious not to make a mistake, and it ended up being judged as stalemate or, as Lucy described it, 'dullmate'. Neither candidate was distressed to learn that a rival station had aired a football game that had been watched by ten times as many viewers. The polls the following day put both candidates on forty-six per cent, with eight per cent undecided.

'Where have they been for the past six months?' demanded Fletcher as he stared at the figure of eight per cent.

'Not everyone is as fascinated by politics as you are,' suggested Annie over breakfast that morning. Lucy nodded her agreement.

Fletcher hired a helicopter and Nat chartered the bank's small jet to take them round the state during the final seven days, by which time the don't-knows had fallen to six per cent, shedding one point to each rival. By the end of the week, both men wondered if there was a shopping mall, factory, railway station, town hall, hospital or even street that they hadn't visited, and both accepted that in the end, it was going to be the organization on the ground that mattered. And the winner would be the one who had the best-oiled machine on election day. No one was more aware of this than Tom and Jimmy, but they couldn't think of anything they hadn't already done or prepared for, and could only speculate as to what might go wrong at the last minute.

For Nat, election day was a blur of airports and main streets, as he tried to visit every city that had a runway before the polling booths closed at eight p.m. As soon as his plane touched down, he would run to the second car in the motorcade, and take off at seventy miles an hour, until he reached the city limits, where he would slow down to ten miles an hour, and start waving at anyone who showed the slightest interest. He ended up in the main street at a walking pace, and then reversed the process with a frantic dash back to the airport before taking off for the next city.

Fletcher spent his final morning in Hartford, trying to get out his core vote before taking the helicopter to visit the most densely populated Democratic areas. Later that night, commentators even discussed who had made the better use of the last few hours. Both men landed back at Hartford's Brainard airport a few minutes after the polls had closed.

Normally in these situations, candidates will go to almost any lengths to avoid one another, but when the two teams crossed on the tarmac, like jousters at a fair, they headed straight towards each other.

'Senator,' said Nat, 'I will need to see you first thing in the morning as there are several changes I will require before I feel able to sign your education bill.'

'The bill will be law by this time tomorrow,' replied Fletcher. 'I intend it to be my first executive action as governor.'

Both men became aware that their closest aides had fallen back so that they could have a private conversation, and they realized that the banter served little purpose if there was no audience to play to.

'How's Lucy?' asked Nat. 'I hope her problem's been sorted out.'

'How did you know about that?' asked Fletcher.

'One of my staff was leaked the details a couple of weeks ago. I made it clear that if the subject was raised again he would no longer be part of my team.'

'I'm grateful,' said Fletcher, 'because I still haven't told Annie.' He paused. 'Lucy spent a few days in New York with Logan Fitzgerald, and then returned home to join me on the campaign trail.'

'I wish I'd been able to watch her grow up, like any other uncle. I would have loved to have a daughter.'

'Most days of the week she'd happily swap me for you,' said Fletcher. 'I've even had to raise her allowance in exchange for not continually reminding me how wonderful you are.'

'I've never told you,' said Nat, 'that after your intervention with that gunman who took over Miss Hudson's class at Hartford School, Luke stuck a photograph of you up on his bedroom wall, and never took it down, so please pass on my best wishes to my niece.'

'I will, but be warned that if you win, she's going to postpone college for a year and apply for a job in your office as an intern, and she's already made it clear that she won't be available if her father is the governor.'

'Then I look forward to her joining my team,' said Nat, as one or two aides reappeared and suggested that perhaps it was time for both of them to be moving on.

Fletcher smiled. 'How do you want to play tonight?'

'If either of us gets a clear lead by midnight, the other will call and concede?'

'Suits me,' said Fletcher, 'I think you know my home number.'

'I'll be waiting for your call, senator,' said Nat.

The two candidates shook hands on the concourse outside the airport, and their motorcades whisked off in different directions.

A designated team of state troopers followed both candidates home. Their orders were clear. If your man wins, you are protecting the new governor. If he loses, you take the weekend off.

Neither team took the weekend off.

53

NAT SWITCHED ON the radio the moment he got into the car. The early exit polls were making it clear that Bill Clinton would be taking up residence in the White House next January, and that President Bush would probably have to concede before midnight. A lifetime of public service, a year of campaigning, a day of voting, and your political career becomes a footnote in history. 'That's democracy for you,' President Bush was later heard to remark ruefully.

Other pollsters across the country were suggesting that not only the White House, but both the Senate and Congress, would be controlled by the Democrats. CBS's anchor man, Dan Rather, was reporting a close result in several seats. 'In Connecticut, for example, the gubernatorial race is too close to call, and the exit polls are unable to predict the outcome. But for now it's over to our correspondent in Little Rock, who is outside Governor Clinton's home.'

Nat flicked off the radio, as the little motorcade of three SUVs came to a halt outside his home. He was greeted by two television cameras, a radio reporter and a couple of journalists – how different from Arkansas, where over a hundred television cameras and countless radio and newspaper journalists waited for the first words of the president-elect. Tom was standing by the front door.

'Don't tell me,' said Nat as he walked past the press

and into the house. 'It's too close to call. So when can we hope to hear a result involving some real voters?'

'We're expecting the first indicators to come through within the hour,' said Tom, 'and if it's Bristol, they usually vote Democrat.'

'Yes, but by how much?' asked Nat as they headed towards the kitchen, to find Su Ling glued to the television, a burning smell coming from the stove.

◄○►

Fletcher stood in front of the television, watching Clinton as he waved to the crowds from the balcony of his home in Arkansas. At the same time he tried to listen to a briefing from Jimmy. When he'd first met the Arkansas governor at the Democratic convention in New York City, Fletcher hadn't given him a prayer. To think that only last year, following America's victory in the Gulf War, Bush had enjoyed the highest opinion poll ratings in history.

'Clinton may be declared the winner,' said Fletcher, 'but Bush as sure as hell lost it.' He stared at Bill and Hillary hugging each other, as their bemused twelve-year-old daughter stood by their side. He thought about Lucy and her recent abortion, realizing it would have been front-page news if he had been running for president. He wondered how Chelsea would cope with that sort of pressure.

Lucy came dashing into the room. 'Mom and I have prepared all your favourite dishes, as it will be nothing but public functions for the next four years.' He smiled at her youthful exuberance. 'Corn on the cob, spaghetti bolognese, and if you've won before midnight, crème brûlée.'

'But not all together,' begged Fletcher, and, turning to Jimmy, who had rarely been off the phone since the

575

moment he'd entered the house, he asked, 'When are you expecting the first result in?'

'Any minute now,' Jimmy replied. 'Bristol prides itself on always announcing first, and we have to capture that by three to four per cent if we hope to win overall.'

'And below three per cent?'

'We're in trouble,' Jimmy replied.

—◦—

Nat checked his watch. It was just after nine in Hartford, but the image on the screen showed voters still going to the polls in California. BREAKING NEWS was plastered across the screen. NBC was the first to declare that Clinton would be the new president of the United States. George Bush was already being labelled by the networks with the cruel epitaph, 'one-termer'.

The phones rang constantly in the background, as Tom tried to field all the calls. If he thought Nat ought to speak to the caller personally, the phone was passed across to him, if not, he heard Tom repeating, 'He's tied up at the moment, but thank you for calling, I'll pass your message on.'

'I hope there's a TV wherever I'm "tied up",' said Nat, 'otherwise I'll never know whether to accept or concede,' he added as he tried valiantly to cut into a burnt steak.

'At last a real piece of news,' said Tom, 'but I can't work out who it helps, because the turnout in Connecticut was fifty-one per cent, a couple of points above the national average.' Nat nodded, turning his attention back to the screen. The words 'too close to call' were still being relayed from every corner of the state.

When Nat heard the name Bristol, he pushed aside his steak. 'And now we go over to our eyewitness correspondent for the latest update,' said the newsreader.

'Dan, we're expecting a result here at any moment,

and it should be the first real sign of just how close this gubernatorial race really is. If the Democrats win by . . . hold on, the result is coming over on my earpiece . . . the Democrats have taken Bristol.' Lucy leapt out of her chair, but Fletcher didn't move as he waited for the details to be flashed across the bottom of the screen. 'Fletcher Davenport 8,604 votes, Nat Cartwright 8,379,' said the reporter.

'Three per cent. Who's due up next?'

'Probably Waterbury,' said Tom, 'where we should do well because . . .'

'And Waterbury has gone to the Republicans, by just over five thousand votes, putting Nat Cartwright into the lead.'

Both candidates spent the rest of the evening leaping up, sitting down and then leaping back up again as the lead changed hands sixteen times during the next two hours, by which time even the commentators had run out of hyperboles. But somewhere in between the results flooding in, the local anchor man found time to announce that President Bush had phoned Governor Clinton in Arkansas to concede. He had offered his congratulations and best wishes to the president-elect. Does this herald a new Kennedy era? the politicos were asking . . . 'But now back to the race for governor of Connecticut, and here's one for the statistics buffs, the position at the moment is that the Democrats lead the Republicans by 1,170,141 to 1,168,872, an overall lead for Senator Davenport of 1,269. As that is less than one per cent, an automatic recount would have to take place. And if that isn't enough,' continued the commentator, 'we face an added complication because the district of Madison maintains its age-old tradition of not counting its votes until ten o'clock tomorrow morning.'

Paul Holbourn, the mayor of Madison, was next up on

the screen. The septuagenarian politician invited everyone to visit this picturesque seaside town, which would decide who would be the next governor of the state.

'How do you read it?' asked Nat, as Tom continued to enter numbers into his calculator. 'Fletcher leads at the moment by 1,269 and at the last election, the Republicans took Madison by 1,312.'

'Then we must be favourites?' ventured Nat.

'I wish it was that easy,' said Tom, 'because there's a further complication we have to consider.'

'And what's that?'

'The present governor of the state was born and raised in Madison, so there could be a considerable personal vote somewhere in there.'

'I should have gone to Madison one more time,' said Nat.

'You visited the place twice, which was once more than Fletcher managed.'

'I ought to call him,' said Nat, 'and make it clear that I'm not conceding.'

Tom nodded his agreement as Nat walked over to the phone. He didn't have to look up the senator's private number because he had dialled it every evening during the trial.

'Hi,' said a voice, 'this is the governor's residence.'

'Not yet it isn't,' said Nat firmly.

'Hello, Mr Cartwright,' said Lucy, 'were you hoping to speak to the governor?'

'No, I wanted to speak to your father.'

'Why, are you conceding?'

'No, I'll leave him to do that in person tomorrow, when, if you behave yourself, I'll be offering you a job.'

Fletcher grabbed the telephone, 'I'm sorry about that, Nat,' he said, 'I presume you're calling to say all bets are off until tomorrow when we meet at high noon?'

'Yes, and now you mention it, I'm planning to play Gary Cooper,' said Nat.

'Then I'll see you on Main Street, sheriff.'

'Just be thankful it's not Ralph Elliot you're up against.'

'Why?' asked Fletcher.

'Because right now he would be in Madison filling up ballot boxes with extra votes.'

'It wouldn't have made any difference,' said Fletcher.

'Why not?' asked Nat.

'Because if Elliot had been my opponent, I would have already won by a landslide.'

BOOK SEVEN

NUMBERS

54

IT TOOK NAT about an hour to drive to Madison, and when he reached the outskirts of the town, he could have been forgiven for thinking the little borough had been chosen as the venue for the seventh game in the world series.

The highway was filled with cars festooned with emblems of red, white and blue, with donkeys and elephants staring blankly out of numerous back windows. When he took the turn-off for Madison, population 12,372, half the vehicles left the motorway like steel filings drawn towards a magnet.

'If you take away those who are too young to vote, I presume the turnout should be around five thousand,' said Nat.

'Not necessarily. I suspect it will prove to be a little higher than that,' Tom replied. 'Don't forget Madison is where retired people come to visit their parents, so you won't find it full of youth clubs and discos.'

'Then that should benefit us,' said Nat.

'I've given up predicting,' said Tom with a sigh.

No signpost was needed to guide them to the town hall, as everyone seemed to be heading in the same direction, confident that the person in front of them knew exactly where they were going. By the time Nat's little motorcade arrived in the centre of the town, they were being overtaken by mothers pushing strollers. When they turned into Main Street, they were continually held up by pedestrians spilling on to the road. When Nat's car was overtaken by a man in a wheelchair, he decided the time had come to get out and walk. This slowed his progress down even more, because the moment he was recognized, people rushed up to shake him by the hand, and several asked if he would mind posing for a photograph with his wife.

'I'm glad to see that your re-election campaign has already begun,' teased Tom.

'Let's get elected first,' said Nat as they reached the town hall. He climbed the steps, continuing to shake hands with all the well wishers as if it were the day before the election, rather than the day after. He couldn't help wondering if that would change when he came back down the steps and the same people knew the result. Tom spotted the mayor standing on the top step, looking out for him.

'Paul Holbourn,' whispered Tom. 'He's served three terms and at the age of seventy-seven has just won his fourth election unopposed.'

'Good to see you again, Nat,' said the mayor, as if they were old friends, though in fact they had only met on one previous occasion.

'And it's good to see you too, sir,' said Nat, clutching the mayor's outstretched hand. 'Congratulations on your re-election – unopposed, I'm told.'

'Thank you,' said the mayor. 'Fletcher arrived a few minutes ago, and is waiting in my office, so perhaps we ought to go and join him.' As they walked into the building, Holbourn said, 'I just wanted to spend a few moments taking you both through the way we do things in Madison.'

'That's fine by me,' said Nat, knowing that it wouldn't make a blind bit of difference if it wasn't.

A crowd of officials and journalists followed the little

party down the corridor to the mayor's office, where Nat and Su Ling joined Fletcher and Annie and around thirty other people who felt they had the right to attend the select gathering.

'Can I get you some coffee, Nat, before we proceed?' asked the mayor.

'No thank you, sir,' said Nat.

'And how about your charming little wife?' Su Ling shook her head politely, not fazed by the tactless remark of a past generation. 'Then I'll begin,' the mayor continued, turning his attention to the crowded assembly that had squeezed into his office.

'Ladies and gentlemen,' he paused, 'and future governor,' he tried to look at both men at once. 'The count will commence at ten o'clock this morning, as has been our custom in Madison for over a century, and I can see no reason why this should be delayed simply because there is a little more interest in our proceedings than usual.' Fletcher was amused by the understatement, but wasn't in any doubt that the mayor intended to savour every moment of his fifteen minutes of fame.

'The township,' continued the mayor, 'has 10,942 registered voters, who reside in eleven districts. The twenty-two ballot boxes were, as they always have been in the past, picked up a few minutes after the polls closed, and then transferred into the safe custody of our chief of police, who locked them up for the night.' Several people politely laughed at the mayor's little joke, which caused him to smile and lose his concentration. He seemed to hesitate, until his chief of staff leant forward and whispered in his ear, 'Ballot boxes.'

'Yes, of course, yes. The ballot boxes were collected this morning and brought to the town hall at nine o'clock, when I asked my chief clerk to check that the seals had not been tampered with. He confirmed that they were all intact.' The mayor glanced round to observe his senior officials nodding their agreement. 'At ten o'clock, I shall cut those seals, when the ballots will be removed from the boxes and placed on the counting table in the centre of the main hall. The first count will do no more than verify how many people have cast their votes. Once that has been established, the ballots will then be sorted into three piles. Those who have voted Republican, those who have voted Democrat, and those that might be described as disputed ballots. Though I might add, these are rare in Madison, because for many of us, this might well be our last chance to register a vote.' This was greeted by a little nervous laughter, though Nat wasn't in any doubt he meant it.

'My final task as the election officer will be to declare the result, which in turn will decide who is elected as the next governor of our great state. I hope to have completed the entire exercise by midday.' Not if we continue at this pace, thought Fletcher. 'Now, are there any questions before I accompany you through to the hall?'

Tom and Jimmy both began speaking at the same time, and Tom nodded politely to his opposite number, as he suspected that they would be asking exactly the same questions.

'How many counters do you have?' asked Jimmy.

The official once again whispered in the mayor's ear. 'Twenty, and all of them are employees of the council,' said the mayor, 'with the added qualification of being members of the local bridge club.' Neither Nat nor Fletcher could work out the significance of this remark, but were not inclined to ask for further clarification.

'And how many observers will you be allowing?' asked Tom.

'I shall permit ten representatives from each party,' said the mayor, 'who will be allowed to stand a pace behind each counter and must at no time make any attempt to talk to them. If they have a query, they should refer it to my chief of staff and if it remains unresolved, he will consult me.'

'And who will act as arbitrator should there be any disputed ballots?' asked Tom.

'You will find that they are rare in Madison,' repeated the mayor, forgetting that he had already expressed this sentiment, 'because for many of us this could well be our last chance to register a vote.' This time no one laughed, while at the same time the mayor failed to answer Tom's question. Tom decided not to ask a second time. 'Well, if there are no further questions,' said the mayor, 'I'll escort you all to our historic hall, built in 1867, of which we are inordinately proud.'

The hall had been built to house just under a thousand people, as the population of Madison didn't venture out much at night. But on this occasion, even before the mayor, his executives, Fletcher, Nat and their two respective parties had entered the room, it looked more like a Japanese railway station in the rush hour than a town hall in a sleepy coastal Connecticut resort. Nat only hoped that the senior fire officer was not present, as there couldn't have been a safety regulation that they weren't breaking.

'I shall begin proceedings by letting everyone know how I intend to conduct the count,' said the mayor, before heading off in the direction of the stage, leaving the two candidates wondering if he would ever make it. Eventually the diminutive, grey-haired figure emerged up on to the platform and took his place in front of a lowered microphone. 'Ladies and gentlemen,' he began. 'My name is Paul Holbourn, and only strangers will be unaware that I am the mayor of Madison.' Fletcher suspected that most people in that room were making their first and last visit to the historic town hall. 'But today,' he continued, 'I stand before you in my capacity as elections officer for the district of Madison. I have already explained to both candidates the procedure I intend to adopt, which I will now go over again . . .'

Fletcher began looking around the room and quickly became aware that few people were listening to the mayor as they were busy jostling to secure a place as near to the cordoned-off area as possible where the vote would be taking place.

When the mayor had finished his homily, he made a gallant effort to return to the centre of the room, but would never have completed the course if it hadn't been for the fact that proceedings could not commence without his imprimatur.

When he eventually reached the starting gate, the chief clerk handed the mayor a pair of scissors. He proceeded to cut the seals on the twenty-two boxes as if he were performing an opening ceremony. This task completed, the officials emptied the boxes and began to tip the ballots out on to the elongated centre table. The mayor then checked carefully inside every box – first turning them upside down, and then shaking them, like a conjuror who wishes to prove there's no longer anything inside. Both candidates were invited to double check.

Tom and Jimmy kept their eyes on the centre table as the officials began to distribute the voting slips among the counters, much as a croupier might stack chips at a roulette table. They began by gathering the ballots in tens, and then placing an elastic band around every hundred. This simple exercise took nearly an hour to complete, by which time the mayor had run out of things to say about Madison to anyone who was still willing to listen. The piles were then counted by the chief clerk, who confirmed that there were fifty-nine, with one left over containing fewer than a hundred ballots.

In the past at this point, the mayor had always made his way back up on to the stage, but his chief clerk thought it might be easier if the microphone was brought to him. Paul Holbourn agreed to this innovation and it would have been a shrewd decision had the lead been long enough to reach the cordoned-off area, but at least the mayor now had a considerably shorter journey to complete before having to deliver his ultimatum. He blew into the microphone, producing a sound like a train entering a tunnel, which he hoped would bring some semblance of order to the proceedings.

'Ladies and gentlemen,' he began, checking the piece of paper the chief clerk had placed in his hand, '5,934 good citizens of Madison have taken part in this election, which I am informed is fifty-four per cent of the electorate, being one per cent above the average for the state.'

'That extra percentage point might well turn out to our advantage,' Tom whispered in Nat's ear.

'Extra points usually favour the Democrats,' Nat reminded him.

'Not when the electorate has an average age of sixty-three,' rebutted Tom.

'Our next task,' continued the mayor, 'is to separate the votes of both parties before we can begin the count.' No one was surprised that this exercise took even longer, as the mayor and his officials were regularly called on to settle disputes. Once this task had been completed the counting of the votes began in earnest. Piles of tens in time multiplied into hundreds before being placed in neat little lines like soldiers on a parade ground.

Nat would have liked to circle the room and follow the entire process, but the hall had become so crowded that he had to satisfy himself with the regular reports relayed back to him by his lieutenants in the field. Tom did decide to fight his way round and came to the conclusion that although Nat looked as if he was in the lead, he couldn't be sure if it was sufficient to make up the 118 vote advantage that Fletcher currently enjoyed following the recount of the overnight ballots.

It was another hour before the counting had been completed, and the two piles of slips were lined up facing each other. The mayor then invited both candidates to join him in the cordoned-off area in the centre of the room. He there explained that sixteen ballots had been rejected by his officials, and he therefore wished to consult them before deciding if any should be considered valid.

No one could accuse the mayor of not believing in open government, because all sixteen ballots had been laid out on the centre of the table for everyone to see. Eight appeared to have no mark on them at all, and both candidates agreed that they could be rejected. 'Cartwright should have been sent to the electric chair', and 'no lawyer is fit to hold public office', were also dismissed just as quickly. Of the remaining six, all had marks other than crosses against one of the names, but as they were equally divided, the mayor suggested that they should all be validated. Both Jimmy and Tom checked the six votes and could find no fault with the mayor's logic.

As this little detour had yielded no advantage to either candidate, the mayor gave the green light for the full count to begin. Stacks of hundreds were once again lined up in front of the counters, and Nat and Fletcher tried from a distance to gauge if they had won or lost enough to change the wording on their letterhead for the next four years.

When the counting finally stopped, the chief clerk

passed a piece of paper to the mayor with two figures printed on it. He didn't need to call for silence, because everyone wanted to hear the result. The mayor, having abandoned any thought of returning to the stage, simply announced that the Republicans had won by a margin of 3,019 to 2,905. He then shook hands with both candidates, obviously feeling that his task had been completed, while everyone else tried to work out the significance of the figures.

Within moments, several of Fletcher's supporters were leaping up and down once they realized that, although they had lost Madison by 114, they had won the state by four votes. The mayor was already on his way back to his office, looking forward to a well earned lunch, by the time Tom had caught up with him. He explained the real significance of the local result, and added that on behalf of his candidate, he would be requesting a recount. The mayor made his way slowly back into the hall to be greeted with chants of *recount, recount, recount,* and, without consulting his officials announced that was what he had always intended to do.

Several of the counters who had also begun to pack up and leave, quickly sidled back to their places. Fletcher listened carefully as Jimmy whispered in his ear. He considered the suggestion for a few moments, but replied firmly, 'No.'

Jimmy had pointed out to his candidate that the mayor had no authority to order a recount, as it was Fletcher who had lost the vote in Madison, and only a losing candidate could call for a recount. The *Washington Post* wrote in a leader the following morning that the mayor had also exceeded his authority on another front, namely that Nat had beaten his rival by over one per cent, also rendering a recount unnecessary. However, the columnist did concede that rejecting such a request might well have ended in a riot, not to mention interminable legal wrangles, which would not have been in keeping with the way both candidates had conducted their campaigns.

Once again, the stacks were counted and recounted, before being checked and double checked. This resulted in the discovery that three piles contained 101 votes, while another had only ninety-eight. The chief clerk did not confirm the result until he was sure that the calculators and the hand count were in unison. Then he once again passed a piece of paper to the mayor with two new figures for him to announce.

The mayor read out the revised result of 3,021 for Cartwright to 2,905 for Davenport, which cut the Democrat's overall lead to two votes.

Tom immediately requested a further recount, although he knew he was no longer entitled to do so. He suspected that as Fletcher's majority had fallen, the mayor would find it difficult to turn down his request. He crossed his fingers as the chief clerk briefed the mayor. Whatever it was that the chief clerk had advised, the Mayor simply nodded, and then made his way back to the microphone.

'I shall allow one further recount,' he announced, 'but should the Democrats retain an overall majority for a third time, however small, I shall declare Fletcher Davenport to be the new governor of Connecticut.' This was greeted by cheers from Fletcher's supporters, and a nod of acquiescence from Nat as the counting procedure cranked back into action.

Forty minutes later, the piles were all confirmed as being correct, and the battle looked to be finally over, until someone noticed one of Nat's observers had his hand held high in the air. The mayor walked slowly across to join him, with the chief clerk only a pace behind and enquired what the query was. The observer pointed to a pile of one hundred votes on the Davenport side of the table, and claimed that one of the votes should have been credited to Cartwright.

'Well, there's only one way of finding out,' said the mayor as he began to turn the ballots over, with the crowd chanting in the unison, 'one, two, three . . .'

Nat felt embarrassed and muttered to Su Ling, 'He'd better be right.'

'Twenty-seven, twenty-eight . . .' Fletcher said nothing as Jimmy joined in the counting.

'Thirty-nine, forty, forty-one. . . .' And suddenly there was a hush; the observer had been correct, because the forty-second ballot had a cross against Cartwright's name. The mayor, the chief clerk, Tom and Jimmy all checked the offending ballot and agreed that a mistake had been made, and therefore the overall result was a tie. Tom was surprised by Nat's immediate response.

'I wonder how Dr Renwick voted.'

'I think you'll find he abstained,' whispered Tom.

The mayor was looking exhausted, and agreed with his chief of staff that they should call for a recess, to allow the counters and any other officials to take an hour's break, before the next recount at two o'clock. The mayor invited Fletcher and Nat to join him for lunch, but both candidates politely declined, having no intention of leaving the hall or even straying more than a few feet from the centre table, where the votes were stacked up.

'But what happens if it remains a tie?' Nat heard the mayor ask the chief clerk as they made their way towards the exit. As he didn't hear the reply, he asked Tom the same question. His chief of staff already had his head buried in the *Connecticut State Elections Manual*.

-◄○►-

Su Ling *did* slip out of the hall and walked slowly down the corridor, remaining just a few paces behind the mayor's party. When she spotted LIBRARY printed in gold letters on an oak door, she came to a halt. She was pleased to find the door unlocked and stepped quickly inside. Su Ling took a seat behind one of the large bookcases, leaned back and tried to relax for the first time that day.

'You too,' said a voice.

Su Ling looked up to see Annie sitting in the opposite corner. She smiled. 'The choice was another hour in that hall or . . .'

'. . . or lunch with the mayor, and further epistles of the apostle Paul on the virtues of Madison.' They both laughed.

'I only wish it had all been decided last night,' said Su Ling. 'Now one of them is bound to spend the rest of his life wondering if he should have canvassed another shopping mall . . .'

'I don't think there was another shopping mall,' said Annie.

'Or school, hospital, factory or station come to that.'

'They both should have agreed to govern for six months each year, and then let the electorate decide who they wanted in four years' time.'

'I don't think that would have settled anything.'

'Why not?' asked Annie.

'I have a feeling this will be the first of many contests between them that will prove nothing until the final showdown.'

'Perhaps the problem for the voters is that they are so alike it's impossible to choose between them,' Annie suggested, looking carefully at Su Ling.

'Perhaps it's just that there is nothing between them,' said Su Ling, returning her gaze.

'Yes, my mother often comments on how alike they

594

are whenever they're both on TV, and the coincidence of their shared blood group only emphasizes that feeling.'

'As a mathematician I don't believe in quite so many coincidences,' said Su Ling.

'It's interesting that you should say that,' ventured Annie, 'because whenever I raise the subject with Fletcher, he simply clams up.'

'Snap,' said Su Ling.

'I suspect if we combined our knowledge . . .'

'We would only live to regret it.'

'What do you mean?' asked Annie.

'Only that if those two have decided not to discuss the subject, even with us, they must have a very good reason.'

'So you feel we should remain silent as well.'

Su Ling nodded. 'Especially after what my mother's been put through . . .'

'And my mother-in-law would undoubtedly be put through,' suggested Annie. Su ling smiled and rose from her place. She looked directly at her sister-in-law. 'Let's just hope that they don't both stand for president, other-wise the truth is bound to come out.'

Annie nodded her agreement.

'I'll go back first,' said Su Ling, 'and then no one will ever realize this conversation took place.'

—◦—

'Did you manage to get some lunch?' asked Nat.

Su Ling didn't have to reply as her husband was distracted by the reappearance of the mayor clutching a piece of paper in his right hand. He looked far more relaxed than when last seen disappearing in the direction of his office. On reaching the centre of the room, the mayor gave an immediate order that another recount should commence. The satisfied look on his face was not the result of good food and even better wine; in fact the mayor had forgone lunch to phone the justice department in Washington and seek the advice of the attorney general's office on how they should proceed in the event of a tie.

The tellers were, as ever, thorough and meticulous, and forty-one minutes later came up with exactly the same result. A tie.

The mayor reread the attorney general's fax, and to everyone's disbelief, called for a further recount, which, thirty-four minutes later, confirmed the deadlock.

Once the chief clerk had reported this to his elected representative, the mayor began to make his way towards the stage, having asked both candidates to join him. Fletcher shrugged his shoulders when he caught Nat's eye. So keen were the onlookers to discover what had been decided that they quickly stood aside to allow the three men to pass, as if Moses had placed his staff on the Madison waters.

The mayor stepped up on to the platform with the two candidates in close attendance. When he came to a halt in the centre of the stage, the candidates took their places on each side of him, Fletcher on his left, Nat on his right, as befitted their political persuasion. The mayor had to wait a few more moments for the microphone to be returned to its original position before he could address an audience that had not diminished in size despite the hold-ups.

'Ladies and gentlemen, during the lunch break, I took the opportunity to telephone the justice department in Washington DC, to seek their advice as to what procedure we should follow in the event of a tie.' This statement elicited a silence that until that moment had not been achieved since the doors opened at nine o'clock that morning. 'And to that end,' the mayor continued, 'I have a fax signed by the attorney general confirming the due process of law that must now take place.' Someone coughed, and in the hush that had overcome the assembled gathering it sounded like Vesuvius erupting.

The mayor paused for a moment before returning to the attorney general's fax. 'If in an election for governor, any one candidate wins the count three time in a row, that candidate shall be deemed to be the winner, however small his or her majority. But should the vote end in a tie for a third time, then the result shall be decided,' he paused, and this time no one coughed, 'by the toss of a coin.'

The tension broke and everyone began speaking at once, as they tried to take in the significance of this revelation, and it was some time before the mayor was able to continue.

He once again waited for complete silence before producing a silver dollar from his waistcoat pocket. He placed the coin on his upturned thumb before glancing at the two contestants as if seeking their approval. They both nodded.

One of them called, 'Heads,' but then he always called heads.

The mayor gave a slight bow before spinning the coin high in the air. Every eye followed its ascension, and its even quicker descent, before it finally bounced up and down on the stage, ending up at the mayor's feet. All three men stared down at the thirty-fifth president, who resolutely returned their gaze.

The mayor picked up the coin and turned round to face the two candidates. He smiled at the man now standing on his right, and said, 'May I be the first to congratulate you, governor.'

extracts reading groups
competitions books new
discounts extracts extracts
competitions discounts
books new events
events books reading groups
new titles reading groups
interviews
events extracts extracts
books discounts events
new books events interviews
events new
discounts extracts discounts
www.panmacmillan.com
extracts events reading groups
competitions books extracts new